The yellowbacks... classics of popular fiction

The yellowjackets or yellowbacks were a great series of bestselling adventure and crime thrillers that had its origins in the mid to late 19th century following on from the 'penny dreadfuls'. They virtually began the mass market revolution of the early 20th century with a clear standard format and imprint/series livery (what would today be called branding). Hodder & Stoughton published the yellowjackets in two main series with series run dates of: 1923-1939 and later 1949-1957.

As the tagline ('where thrillers really began') on the back cover implies, the imprint and series focused on thrillers that were the bestsellers of their time. This current reissue or retro revival if you will, brings back many of these masterpieces, now classics in their own way and extends it further by including key titles from that period that were either great crime or thriller or even general commercial fiction (including sub-genres of noir, horror, gothic, romance, westerns, etc.) influences of their time. There are some perennial favourites and many rarities either lost or not easily available being revived in the current series. Writers and characters ranged from adventure heroes like Bulldog Drummond, Allan Quatermain, Richard Hannay or the Saint through thriller grandmasters Edgar Wallace and E. Phillips Oppenheim, crime and mystery maestros like Patricia Wentworth, GK Chesterton, Agatha Christie and the Detection club, to western and swashbucklers like Zane Grey, Max Brand, Captain Blood and even romance or general fiction classics like Hermina Black, Denise Robins, Marie Corelli or Stella Morton. These were books that had storytelling at their heart and always entertained.

The yellowbacks had both hardback (with varying design elements) and paperback (which built the series look) versions with the latter still carrying the imprint 'yellowjacket'. The current reissues pay tribute to both and use an amalgam of elements from both editions while retaining the complete yellow (or 'mustard-plaster') livery with the author's name in blue beveled type with a 'simulated emboss' effect and a white outer 'outline', and the book title in black. These reissues retain the distinctive size of the original mass market paperback and follow the three main category variations—the thrillers (crime, westerns, mystery, adventure) had blue lettering for the author's name, while Romance and softer general fiction had red; and other categories like humour had green.

For more detail and a full list of titles visit https://www.hachetteindia.com/home/yellowbacks

THE COMPLETE FATHER BROWN

VOLUME 2

THE COMPLETE FATHER BROWN

Gilbert Keith Chesterton was an English writer, philosopher, Christian apologist and a literary and art critic. Chesterton was a major literary figure and seen as the successor to intellectuals like Matthew Arnold, Thomas Carlyle, John Henry Newman and John Ruskin. Chesterton created the fictional priest-detective Father Brown a successor and also was a member of the Detection Club.

THE COMPLETE FATHER BROWN

G.K. Chesterton

VOLUME 2

The Incredulity of Father Brown
The Secret of Father Brown
The Scandal of Father Brown
Uncollected Stories

The Complete Father Brown
First published in book form by Cassell & Co, London as *The Secret of Father Brown* in 1927, *The Scandal of Father Brown* in 1935. The Uncollected Stories comprising 'The Donnington Affair' (co-written with Max Pemberton) and The Mask of Midas were first published in magazines in 1914 and 1936 respectively.

1

The texts in these editions in most cases have been reprinted as is, with minimal editorial changes and by and large no bowdlerizing for political correctness; though in some editions, a few words and phrases considered archaic, or those considered offensive now, along with archaic punctuation may have been modified in places to make the text more accessible to today's readers. The narratives, language, beliefs, social mores and/or cultural depictions, in these volumes are a reflection of their times and must be viewed as such. They may also contain certain cultural, racial and gender prejudices and stereotypes that may be outdated or clearly wrong then and wrong today; but their removal would be tantamount to claiming these prejudices never existed. The Publisher does not endorse or support those depictions or stereotypes; and these books have been made available for a discerning audience that will read it for entertainment value and a chronicle/record of popular fiction of past times.

Cover design by Priya Singh adapted from the original classic yellowjacket by Hodder & Stoughton.

Cover illustration by Ishan Trivedi.

Series note: Some of the books in the series (unless otherwise credited) may have cover or inside illustrations from the original yellowbacks or early editions, and while full restoration has been attempted, some images may be grainy or faded due to the condition of the original material. The end notes or bonus material or blurb details may have been sourced from the public domain or free use publications such as Wikipedia and attribution is hereby made also allowing similar free use reproduction from here. Sources requiring further specific attribution may write in and further detailing and/or corrections shall be made in subsequent printings/editions.

Reprint specifications may be subject to change including but not limited to finishes, paper, colour sections.

ISBN: 978-93-5731-016-1

Hachette Book Publishing India Pvt. Ltd.
4th & 5th Floors, Corporate Centre,
Plot No. 94, Sector 44, Gurugram - 122 003, India

Typeset in Electra LT STD 10/12.5 pt by Manipal Technologies Limited, Manipal

Printed and bound in India by Manipal Technologies Limited, Manipal

CONTENTS

The Incredulity of Father Brown

First UK edition: Cassell & Co., London, 1926
First US edition: Dood, Mead & Co., New York, 1926

CONTENTS

The Incredulity of Father Brown
G.K. CHESTERTON

1

THE RESURRECTION OF FATHER BROWN
(No record of prior magazine publication)

There was a brief period during which Father Brown enjoyed, or rather did not enjoy, something like fame. He was a nine days' wonder in the newspapers; he was even a common topic of controversy in the weekly reviews; his exploits were narrated eagerly and inaccurately in any number of clubs and drawing-rooms, especially in America. Incongruous and indeed incredible as it may seem to anyone who knew him, his adventures as a detective were even made the subject of short stories appearing in magazines.

Strangely enough, this wandering limelight struck him in the most obscure, or at least the most remote, of his many places of residence. He had been sent out to officiate, as something between a missionary and a parish priest, in one of those sections of the northern coast of South America, where strips of country still cling insecurely to European powers, or are continually threatening to become independent republics, under the gigantic shadow of President Monroe. The population was red and brown with pink spots; that is, it was Spanish-American, and largely Spanish-American-Indian, but there was a considerable and increasing infiltration of Americans of the northern sort—Englishmen, Germans, and the rest. And the trouble seems to have begun when one of these visitors, very recently landed and very much annoyed at having lost one of his bags, approached the first building of which he came in sight—which happened to be the mission-house and chapel attached to it, in front of which ran a long veranda and a long row of stakes, up which were trained the black twisted vines, their square leaves red with autumn. Behind them, also in a row, a number of human beings sat almost as rigid as the stakes, and coloured in some fashion like the vines. For while their broad-brimmed hats were as black as their unblinking eyes, the complexions of many of them might have been made out of the dark red timber of those transatlantic forests. Many of them were smoking very long, thin black cigars; and in all that group the smoke was almost the only moving thing. The visitor would probably have described them as natives, though some of them were very proud of Spanish blood. But he was not one to draw any fine distinction between Spaniards and Red Indians, being rather disposed to dismiss people from the scene when once he had convicted them of being native to it.

He was a newspaper man from Kansas City, a lean, light-haired man with what Meredith called an adventurous nose; one could almost fancy it found its way by feeling its way and moved like the proboscis of an anteater. His name was Snaith, and his parents, after some obscure meditation, had called him Saul, a fact which he had the good feeling to conceal as far as possible. Indeed, he had ultimately compromised by calling himself Paul, though by no means for the same reason that had affected the Apostle of the Gentiles. On the contrary, so far as he had any views on such things, the name of the persecutor would have been more appropriate; for he regarded organized religion with the conventional contempt which can be learnt more easily from Ingersoll than from Voltaire. And this was, as it happened, the not very important side of his character which he turned towards the mission-station and the groups in front of the veranda. Something in their shameless repose and indifference inflamed his own fury of efficiency; and, as he could get no particular answer to his first questions, he began to do all the talking himself.

Standing out there in the strong sunshine, a spick-and-span figure in his Panama hat and neat clothes, his grip-sack held m a steely grip, he began to shout at the people in the shadow. He began to explain to them very loudly why they were lazy and filthy, and bestially ignorant and lower than the beasts that perish, in case this problem should have previously exercised their minds. In his opinion it was the deleterious influence of priests that had made them so miserably poor and so hopelessly oppressed that they were able to sit in the shade and smoke and do nothing.

'And a mighty soft crowd you must be at that,' he said, 'to be bullied by these stuck-up josses because they walk about in their mitres and their tiaras and their gold copes and other glad rags, looking down on everybody else like dirt—being bamboozled by crowns and canopies and sacred umbrellas like a kid at a pantomime; just because a pompous old High Priest of Mumbo-Jumbo looks as if he was the lord of the earth. What about you? What do you look like, you poor simps? I tell you, that's why you're way-back in barbarism and can't read or write and—'

At this point the High Priest of Mumbo-Jumbo came in an undignified hurry out of the door of the mission-house, not looking very like a lord of the earth, but rather like a bundle of black second-hand clothes buttoned round a short bolster in the semblance of a guy. He was not wearing his tiara, supposing him to possess one, but a shabby broad hat not very dissimilar from those of the Spanish Indians, and it was thrust to the back of his head with a gesture of botheration. He seemed just about to speak to the motionless natives when he caught sight of the stranger and said quickly:

'Oh, can I be of any assistance? Would you like to come inside?'

Mr Paul Snaith came inside; and it was the beginning of a considerable increase of that journalist's information on many things. Presumably his journalistic instinct was stronger than his prejudices, as, indeed, it often is in clever journalists; and he asked a good many questions, the answers to which interested and surprised him. He discovered that the Indians could read and write, for the simple reason that the priest had taught them; but that they did not read or write any more than they could help, from a natural preference for more direct communications. He learned that these strange people, who sat about in heaps on the veranda without stirring a hair, could work quite hard on their own patches of land; especially those of them who were more than half Spanish; and he learned with still more astonishment that they all had patches of land that were really their own. That much was part of a stubborn tradition that seemed quite native to natives. But in that also the priest had played a certain part, and by doing so had taken perhaps what was his first and last part in politics, if it was only local politics.

There had recently swept through that region one of those fevers of atheist and almost anarchist Radicalism which break out periodically in countries of the Latin culture, generally beginning in a secret society and generally ending in a civil war and in very little else. The local leader of the iconoclastic party was a certain Alvarez, a rather picturesque adventurer of Portuguese nationality but, as his enemies said, of partly Black origin, the head of any number of lodges and temples of initiation of the sort that in such places clothe even atheism with something mystical. The leader on the more conservative side was a much more commonplace person, a very wealthy man named Mendoza, the owner of many factories and quite respectable, but not very exciting. It was the general opinion that the cause of law and order would have been entirely lost if it had not adopted a more popular policy of its own, in the form of securing land for the peasants; and this movement had mainly originated from the little mission-station of Father Brown.

While he was talking to the journalist, Mendoza, the Conservative leader, came in. He was a stout, dark man, with a bald head like a pear and a round body also like a pear; he was smoking a very fragrant cigar, but he threw it away, perhaps a little theatrically, when he came into the presence of the priest, as if he had been entering church; and bowed with a curve that in so corpulent a gentleman seemed quite improbable. He was always exceedingly serious in his social gestures, especially towards religious institutions. He was one of those laymen who are much more ecclesiastical than ecclesiastics. It embarrassed Father Brown a good deal, especially when carried thus into private life.

'I think I am an anti-clerical,' Father Brown would say with a faint smile; 'but there wouldn't be half so much clericalism if they would only leave things to the clerics.'

'Why Mr Mendoza,' exclaimed the journalist with a new animation,' I think we have met before. Weren't you at the Trade Congress in Mexico last year?'

The heavy eyelids of Mr Mendoza showed a flutter of recognition, and he smiled in his slow way. 'I remember.'

'Pretty big business done there in an hour or two,' said Snaith with relish.' Made a good deal of difference to you, too, I guess.'

'I have been very fortunate,' said Mendoza modestly.

'Don't you believe it!' cried the enthusiastic Snaith.' Good fortune comes to the people who know when to catch hold; and you caught hold good and sure. But I hope I'm not interrupting your business?'

'Not at all,' said the other. 'I often have the honour of calling on the padre for a little talk. Merely for a little talk.'

It seemed as if this familiarity between Father Brown and a successful and even famous man of business completed the reconciliation between the priest and the practical Mr Snaith. He felt, it might be supposed, a new respectability clothe the station and the mission, and was ready to overlook such occasional reminders of the existence of religion as a chapel and a presbytery can seldom wholly avoid. He became quite enthusiastic about the priest's programme—at least on its secular and social side—and announced himself ready at any moment to act in the capacity of a live wire for its communication to the world at large. And it was at this point that Father Brown began to find the journalist rather more troublesome in his sympathy than in his hostility.

Mr Paul Snaith set out vigorously to feature Father Brown. He sent long and loud eulogies on him across the continent to his newspaper in the Middle West. He took snapshots of the unfortunate cleric in the most commonplace occupations, and exhibited them in gigantic photographs in the gigantic Sunday papers of the United States. He turned his sayings into slogans, and was continually presenting the world with 'A message' from the reverend gentleman in South America. Any stock less strong and strenuously receptive than the American race would have become very much bored with Father Brown. As it was, he received handsome and eager offers to go on a lecturing tour in the States; and when he declined, the terms were raised with expressions of respectful wonder. A series of stories about him, like the stories of Sherlock Holmes, were, by the instrumentality of Mr Snaith, planned out and put before the hero with requests for his assistance and encouragement. As the priest found they had started, he could offer no suggestion except that they should stop. And this in turn was taken by Mr Snaith as the text for a discussion on whether Father Brown should disappear temporarily over a cliff, in the manner of Dr Watson's hero. To all these demands the priest had patiently to reply in writing, saying that he would consent on such terms to the temporary cessation of the stories and begging that a considerable interval might occur before they began again. The notes he wrote grew shorter and shorter; and as he wrote the last of them, he sighed.

Needless to say, this strange boom in the North reacted on the little outpost in the South where he had expected to live in so lonely an exile. The considerable English and American population already on the spot began to be proud of possessing so widely advertised a person. American tourists, of the sort who land with a loud demand for Westminster Abbey, landed on that distant coast with a loud demand for Father Brown. They were within measurable distance of running excursion trains named after him, and bringing crowds to see him as if he were a public monument. He was especially troubled by the active and ambitious new traders and shopkeepers of the place, who were perpetually pestering him to try their wares and to give them testimonials. Even if the testimonials were not forthcoming, they would prolong the correspondence for the purpose of collecting autographs. As he was a good-natured person they got a good deal of what they wanted out of him; and it was in answer to a particular request from a Frankfort wine-merchant named Eckstein that he wrote hastily a few words on a card, which were to prove a terrible turning-point in his life.

Eckstein was a fussy little man with fuzzy hair and pince-nez, who was wildly anxious that the priest should not only try some of his celebrated medicinal port, but should let him know where and when he would drink it, in acknowledging its receipt. The priest was not particularly surprised at the request, for he was long past surprise at the lunacies of advertisement. So he scribbled something down and turned to other business which seemed a little more sensible. He was again interrupted, by a note from no less a person than his political enemy Alvarez, asking him to come to a conference at which it was hoped that a compromise on an outstanding question might be reached; and suggesting an appointment that evening at a cafe just outside the walls of the little town. To this also he sent a message of acceptance by the rather florid and military messenger who was waiting for it; and then, having an hour or two before him, sat down to attempt to get through a little of his own legitimate business. At the end of the time he poured himself out a glass of Mr Eckstein's remarkable wine and, glancing at the clock with a humorous expression, drank it and went out into the night.

Strong moonlight lay on the little Spanish town, so that when he came to the picturesque gateway, with its rather rococo arch and the fantastic fringe of palms beyond it, it looked rather like a scene in a Spanish opera. One long leaf of palm with jagged edges, black against the moon, hung down on the other side of the arch, visible through the archway, and had something of the look of the jaw of a black crocodile. The fancy would not have lingered in his imagination but for something else that caught his naturally alert eye. The air was deathly still, and there was not a stir of wind; but he distinctly saw the pendent palm-leaf move.

He looked around him and realized that he was alone. He had left behind the last houses, which were mostly closed and shuttered, and was walking between two long blank walls built of large and shapeless but flattened stones, tufted here and there with the queer prickly weeds of that region—walls which ran parallel all the way to the gateway. He could not see the lights of the cafe outside the gate; probably it was too far away. Nothing could be seen under the arch but a wider expanse of large-flagged pavement, pale in the moon, with the straggling prickly pear here and there. He had a strong sense of the smell of evil; he felt queer physical oppression; but he did not think of stopping. His courage, which was considerable, was perhaps even less strong a part of him than his curiosity. All his life he had been led by an intellectual hunger for the truth, even of trifles. He often controlled it in the name of proportion; but it was always there. He walked straight through the gateway, and on the other side a man sprang like a monkey out of the tree-top and struck at him with a knife. At the same moment another man came crawling swiftly along the wall and, whirling a cudgel round his head, brought it down. Father Brown turned, staggered, and sank in a heap, but as he sank there dawned on his round face an expression of mild and immense surprise.

There was living in the same little town at this time another young American, particularly different from Mr Paul Snaith. His name was John Adams Race, and he was an electrical engineer, employed by Mendoza to fit out the old town with all the new conveniences. He was a figure far less familiar in satire and international gossip than that of the American journalist. Yet, as a matter of fact, America contains a million men of the moral type of Race to one of the moral type of Snaith. He was exceptional in being exceptionally good at his job, but in every other way he was very simple. He had begun life as a druggist's assistant in a Western village, and risen by sheer work and merit; but he still regarded his hometown as the natural heart of the habitable world. He had been taught a very Puritan, or purely Evangelical, sort of Christianity from the Family Bible at his mother's knee; and in so far as he had time to have any religion, that was still his religion. Amid all the dazzling lights of the latest and even wildest discoveries, when he was at the very edge and extreme of experiment, working miracles of light and sound like a god creating new stars and solar systems, he never for a moment doubted that the things 'back home' were the best things in the world; his mother and the Family Bible and the quiet and quaint morality of his village. He had as serious and noble a sense of the sacredness of his mother as if he had been a frivolous Frenchman. He was quite sure the Bible religion was really the right thing; only he vaguely missed it wherever he went in the modern world. He could hardly be expected to sympathize with the religious externals of Catholic countries; and in a dislike of mitres and croziers he sympathized with Mr Snaith, though not in so cocksure a fashion. He had no liking for the public bowings and scrapings of Mendoza and certainly no temptation to the masonic mysticism of the atheist Alvarez. Perhaps all that semi-tropical life was too coloured for him, shot with Indian red and Spanish gold. Anyhow, when he said there was nothing to touch his home town, he was not boasting. He really meant that there was somewhere something plain and unpretentious and touching, which he really respected more than anything else in the world. Such being the mental attitude of John Adams Race in a South American station, there had been growing on him for some time a curious feeling, which contradicted all his prejudices and for which he could not account. For the truth was this: that the only thing he had ever met in his travels that in the least reminded him of the old wood-pile and the provincial proprieties and the Bible on his mother's knee was (for some inscrutable reason) the round face and black clumsy umbrella of Father Brown.

He found himself insensibly watching that commonplace and even comic black figure as it went bustling about; watching it with an almost morbid fascination, as if it were a walking riddle or contradiction. He had found something he could not help liking in the heart of everything he hated; it was as if he had been horribly tormented by lesser demons and then found that the Devil was quite an ordinary person.

Thus it happened that, looking out of his window on that moonlit night, he saw the Devil go by, the demon of unaccountable blamelessness, in his broad black hat and long black coat, shuffling along the street towards the gateway, and saw it with an interest which he could not himself understand. He wondered where the priest was going, and what he was really up to; and remained gazing out into the moonlit street long after the little black figure had passed. And then he saw something else that intrigued him further. Two other men whom he recognized passed across his window as across a lighted stage. A sort of blue limelight of the moon ran in a spectral halo round the big bush of hair that stood erect on the head of little Eckstein, the wine-seller, and it outlined a taller and darker figure with an eagle profile and a queer old-fashioned and very top-heavy black hat, which seemed to make the whole outline still more bizarre, like a shape in a shadow pantomime. Race rebuked himself for allowing the moon to play such tricks with his fancy; for on a second glance he recognized the black Spanish sidewhiskers and high-featured face of Dr Calderon, a worthy medical man of the town, whom he had once found attending professionally on Mendoza. Still, there was something in the way the men were whispering to each other and peering up the street that struck him as peculiar. On a sudden impulse he leapt over the low window-sill and himself went bareheaded up the road, following their trail. He saw them disappear under the dark archway, and a moment after there came a dreadful cry from beyond; curiously loud and piercing, and all the more blood-curdling to Race because it said something very distinctly in some tongue that he did not know.

The next moment there was a rushing of feet, more cries, and then a confused roar of rage or grief that shook the turrets and tall palm trees of the place; there was a movement in the mob that had gathered, as if they were sweeping backwards through the gateway. And then the dark archway resounded with a new voice, this time intelligible to him and falling with the note of doom, as someone shouted through the gateway:

'Father Brown is dead!'

He never knew what prop gave way in his mind, or why something on which he had been counting suddenly failed him; but he ran towards the gateway and was just in time to meet his countryman, the journalist Snaith, coming out of the dark entrance, deadly pale and snapping his fingers nervously.

'It's quite true,' said Snaith, with something which for him approached to reverence. 'He's a goner. The doctor's been looking at him, and there's no hope. Some of these damned Dagos clubbed him as he came through the gate—God knows why. It'll be a great loss to the place.'

Race did not or perhaps could not reply, but ran on under the arch to the scene beyond. The small black figure lay where it had fallen on the wilderness of wide stones starred here and there with green thorn; and the great crowd was being kept back, chiefly by the mere gestures of one gigantic figure in the foreground. For there were many there who swayed hither and thither at the mere movement of his hand, as if he had been a magician.

Alvarez, the dictator and demagogue, was a tall, swaggering figure, always rather flamboyantly clad, and on this occasion he wore a green uniform with embroideries like silver snakes crawling all over it, with an order round his neck hung on a very vivid maroon ribbon. His close curling hair was already grey, and in contrast his complexion, which his friends called olive and his foes octoroon, looked almost literally golden, as if it were a mask moulded in gold. But his large-featured face, which was powerful and humorous, was at this moment properly grave and grim. He had been waiting, he explained, for Father Brown at the cafe when he had heard a rustle and a fall and, coming out, had found the corpse lying on the flagstones.

'I know what some of you are thinking,' he said, looking round proudly, 'and if you are afraid of me—as you are—I will say it for you. I am an atheist; I have no god to call on for those who will not take my word. But I tell you in the name of every root of honour that may be left to a soldier and a man, that I had no part in this. If I had the men here that did it, I would rejoice to hang them on that tree.'

'Naturally we are glad to hear you say so,' said old Mendoza stiffly and solemnly, standing by the body of his fallen coadjutor.

'This blow has been too appalling for us to say what else we feel at present. I suggest that it will be more decent and proper if we remove my friend's body and break up this irregular meeting. I understand,' he added gravely to the doctor, 'that there is unfortunately no doubt.'

'There is no doubt,' said Dr Calderon.

John Race went back to his lodgings sad and with a singular sense of emptiness. It seemed impossible that he should miss a man whom he never knew. He learned that the funeral was to take place next day; for all felt that the crisis should be past as quickly as possible, for fear of riots that were hourly growing more probable. When Snaith had seen the row of Red Indians sitting on the veranda, they might have been a row of ancient Aztec images carved in red wood. But he had not seen them as they were when they heard that the priest was dead.

Indeed they would certainly have risen in revolution and lynched the republican leader, if they had not been immediately blocked by the direct necessity of behaving respectfully to the coffin of their own religious leader. The actual assassins, whom it would have been most natural to lynch, seemed to have vanished into thin air. Nobody knew their names; and nobody would ever know whether the dying man had even seen their faces. That strange look of surprise that was apparently his last look on earth might have been the recognition of their faces. Alvarez repeated violently that it was no work of his, and attended the funeral, walking behind the coffin in his splendid silver and green uniform with a sort of bravado of reverence.

Behind the veranda a flight of stone steps scaled a very steep green bank, fenced by a cactus-hedge, and up this the coffin was laboriously lifted to the ground above, and placed temporarily at the foot of the great gaunt crucifix that dominated the road and guarded the consecrated ground. Below in the road were great seas of people lamenting and telling their beads—an orphan population that had lost a father. Despite all these symbols that were provocative enough to him, Alvarez behaved with restraint and respect; and all would have gone well—as Race told himself—had the others only let him alone.

Race told himself bitterly that old Mendoza had always looked like an old fool and had now very conspicuously and completely behaved like an old fool. By a custom common in simpler societies, the coffin was left open and the face uncovered, bringing the pathos to the point of agony for all those simple people. This, being consonant to tradition, need have done no harm; but some officious person had added to it the custom of the French freethinkers, of having speeches by the graveside. Mendoza proceeded to make a speech—a rather long speech, and the longer it was, the longer and lower sank John Race's spirits and sympathies with the religious ritual involved. A list of saintly attributes, apparently of the most antiquated sort, was rolled out with the dilatory dullness of an after-dinner speaker who does not know how to sit down. That was bad enough; but Mendoza had also the ineffable stupidity to start reproaching and even taunting his political opponents. In three minutes he had succeeded in making a scene, and a very extraordinary scene it was.

'We may well ask,' he said, looking around him pompously; 'we may well ask where such virtues can be found among those who have madly abandoned the creed of their fathers. It is when we have atheists among us, atheist leaders, nay sometimes even atheist rulers, that we find their infamous philosophy bearing fruit in crimes like this. If we ask who murdered this holy man, we shall assuredly find—'

Africa of the forests looked out of the eyes of Alvarez the hybrid adventurer; and Race fancied he could see suddenly that the man was after all a barbarian, who could not control himself to the end; one might guess that all his 'illuminated' transcendentalism had a touch of Voodoo. Anyhow, Mendoza could not continue, for Alvarez had sprung up and was shouting back at him and shouting him down, with infinitely superior lungs.

'Who murdered him?' he roared. 'Your God murdered him! His own God murdered him! According to you, he murders all his faithful and foolish servants—as he murdered that one,' and he made a violent gesture, not towards the coffin but the crucifix. Seeming to control himself a little, he went on in a tone still angry but more argumentative: 'I don't believe it, but you do. Isn't it better to have no God than one that robs you in this fashion? I, at least, am not afraid to say that there is none. There is no power in all this blind and brainless universe that can hear your prayer or return your friend. Though you beg Heaven to raise him, he will not rise. Though I dare Heaven to raise him, he will not rise. Here and now I will put it to the test—I defy the God who is not there to waken the man who sleeps forever.'

There was a shock of silence, and the demagogue had made his sensation.

'We might have known,' cried Mendoza in a thick gobbling voice, 'when we allowed such men as you—'

A new voice cut into his speech; a high and shrill voice with a Yankee accent.

'Stop! Stop!' cried Snaith the journalist; 'something's up! I swear I saw him move.'

He went racing up the steps and rushed to the coffin, while the mob below swayed with indescribable frenzies. The next moment he had turned a face of amazement over his shoulder and made a signal with his finger to Dr Calderon, who hastened forward to confer with him. When the two men stepped away again from the coffin, all could see that the position of the head had altered. A roar of excitement rose from the crowd and seemed to stop suddenly, as if cut off in mid-air; for the priest in the coffin gave a groan and raised himself on one elbow, looking with bleared and blinking eyes at the crowd.

John Adams Race, who had hitherto known only miracles of science, never found himself able in after-years to describe the topsy-turvydom of the next few days. He seemed to have burst out of the world of time and space, and to be living in the impossible. In half an hour the whole of that town and district had been transformed into something never known for a thousand years; a medieval people turned to a mob of monks by a staggering miracle; a Greek city where the god had descended among men. Thousands prostrated themselves in the road; hundreds took vows on the spot; and even the outsiders, like the two Americans, were able to think and speak of nothing but the prodigy. Alvarez himself was shaken, as well he might be; and sat down, with his head upon his hands.

And in the midst of all this tornado of beatitude was a little man struggling to be heard. His voice was small and faint, and the noise was deafening. He made weak little gestures that seemed more those of irritation than anything else. He came to the edge of the parapet above the crowd, waving it to be quiet, with movements rather like the flap of the short wings of a penguin. There was something a little more like a lull in the noise; and then Father Brown for the first time reached the utmost stretch of the indignation that he could launch against his children.

'Oh, you silly people,' he said in a high and quavering voice; 'Oh, you silly, silly people.'

Then he suddenly seemed to pull himself together, made a bolt for the steps with his more normal gait, and began hurriedly to descend.

'Where are you going, Father?' said Mendoza, with more than his usual veneration.

'To the telegraph office,' said Father Brown hastily. 'What? No; of course it's not a miracle. Why should there be a miracle? Miracles are not so cheap as all that.'

And he came tumbling down the steps, the people flinging themselves before him to implore his blessing.

'Bless you, bless you,' said Father Brown hastily. 'God bless you all and give you more sense.'

And he scuttled away with extraordinary rapidity to the telegraph office, where he wired to his Bishop's secretary: 'There is some mad story about a miracle here; hope his lordship not give authority. Nothing in it.'

As he turned away from his effort, he tottered a little with the reaction, and John Race caught him by the arm.

'Let me see you home,' he said; 'you deserve more than these people are giving you.'

John Race and the priest were seated in the presbytery; the table was still piled up with the papers with which the latter had been wrestling the day before; the bottle of wine and the emptied wine-glass still stood where he had left them.

'And now,' said Father Brown almost grimly, 'I can begin to think.'

'I shouldn't think too hard just yet,' said the American. 'You must be wanting a rest. Besides, what are you going to think about?'

'I have pretty often had the task of investigating murders, as it happens,' said Father Brown. 'Now I have got to investigate my own murder.'

'If I were you,' said Race, 'I should take a little wine first.'

Father Brown stood up and filled himself another glass, lifted it, looked thoughtfully into vacancy, and put it down again. Then he sat down once more and said:

'Do you know what I felt like when I died? You may not believe it, but my feeling was one of overwhelming astonishment.'

'Well,' answered Race, 'I suppose you were astonished at being knocked on the head.'

Father Brown leaned over to him and said in a low voice, 'I was astonished at not being knocked on the head.'

Race looked at him for a moment as if he thought the knock on the head had been only too effective; but he only said: 'What do you mean?'

'I mean that when that man brought his bludgeon down with a great swipe, it stopped at my head and did not even touch it. In the same way, the other fellow made as if to strike me with a knife, but he never gave me a scratch. It was just like play-acting. I think it was. But then followed the extraordinary thing.'

He looked thoughtfully at the papers on the table for a moment and then went on:

'Though I had not even been touched with knife or stick, I began to feel my legs doubling up under me and my very life failing. I knew I was being struck down by something, but it was not by those weapons. Do you know what I think it was?' And he pointed to the wine on the table.

Race picked up the wine-glass and looked at it and smelt it.

'I think you are right,' he said. 'I began as a druggist and studied chemistry. I couldn't say for certain without an analysis; but I think there's something very unusual in this stuff. There are drugs by which the Asiatics produce a temporary sleep that looks like death.'

'Quite so,' said the priest calmly.' The whole of this miracle was faked, for some reason or other. That funeral scene was staged—and timed. I think it is part of that raving madness of publicity that has got hold of Snaith; but I can hardly believe he would go quite so far, merely for that. After all, it's one thing to make copy out of me and run me as a sort of sham Sherlock Holmes, and—'

Even as the priest spoke his face altered. His blinking eyelids shut suddenly and he stood up as if he were choking. Then he put one wavering hand as if groping his way towards the door.

'Where are you going?' asked the other in some wonder.

'If you ask me,' said Father Brown, who was quite white, 'I was going to pray. Or rather, to praise.'

'I'm not sure I understand. What is the matter with you?'

'I was going to praise God for having so strangely and so incredibly saved me—saved me by an inch.'

'Of course,' said Race, 'I am not of your religion; but believe me, I have religion enough to understand that. Of course, you would thank God for saving you from death.'

'No,' said the priest. 'Not from death. From disgrace.'

The other sat staring; and the priest's next words broke out of him with a sort of cry. 'And if it had only been my disgrace! But it was the disgrace of all I stand for; the disgrace of the Faith that they went about to encompass. What it might have been! The most huge and horrible scandal ever launched against us since the last lie was choked in the throat of Titus Oates.'

'What on earth are you talking about?' demanded his companion.

'Well, I had better tell you at once,' said the priest; and sitting down, he went on more composedly: 'It came to me in a flash when I happened to mention Snaith and Sherlock Holmes. Now I happen to remember what I wrote about his absurd scheme; it was the natural thing to write, and yet I think they had ingeniously manoeuvred me into writing just those words. They were something like 'I am ready to die and come to life again like Sherlock Holmes, if that is the best way.' And the moment I thought of that, I realized that I had been made to write all sorts of things of that kind, all pointing to the same idea. I wrote, as if to an accomplice, saying that I would drink the drugged wine at a particular time. Now, don't you see?'

Race sprang to his feet still staring: 'Yes,' he said, 'I think I began to see.'

'They would have boomed the miracle. Then they would have bust up the miracle. And what is the worst, they would have proved that I was in the conspiracy. It would have been our sham miracle. That's all there is to it; and about as near hell as you and I will ever be, I hope.'

Then he said, after a pause, in quite a mild voice: 'They certainly would have got quite a lot of good copy out of me.'

Race looked at the table and said darkly: 'How many of these brutes were in it?'

Father Brown shook his head. 'More than I like to think of,' he said; 'but I hope some of them were only tools. Alvarez might think that all's fair in war, perhaps; he has a queer mind. I'm very much afraid that Mendoza is an old hypocrite; I never trusted him, and he hated my action in an industrial matter. But all that will wait; I have only got to thank God for the escape. And especially that I wired at once to the Bishop.'

John Race appeared to be very thoughtful. 'You've told me a lot I didn't know,' he said at last, 'and I feel inclined to tell you the only thing you don't know. I can imagine how those fellows calculated well enough. They thought any man alive, waking up in a coffin to find himself canonized like a saint, and made into a walking miracle for everyone to admire, would be swept along with his worshippers and accept the crown of glory that fell on him out the sky. And I reckon their calculation was pretty practical psychology, as men go. I've seen all sorts of men in all sorts of places; and I tell you frankly I don't believe there's one man in a thousand who could wake up like that with all his wits about him; and while he was still almost talking in his sleep, would have the sanity and the simplicity and the humility to—' He was much surprised to find himself moved, and his level voice wavering.

Father Brown was gazing abstractedly, and in a rather cockeyed fashion, at the bottle on the table. 'Look here,' he said, ' what about a bottle of real wine?'

2

THE ARROW OF HEAVEN
(No record of prior magazine publication found)

It is to be feared that about a hundred detective stories have begun with the discovery that an American millionaire has been murdered; an event which is, for some reason, treated as a sort of calamity. This story, I am happy to say, has to begin with a murdered millionaire; in one sense, indeed, it has to begin with three murdered millionaires, which some may regard as an embarras de richesse. But it was chiefly this coincidence or continuity of criminal policy that took the whole affair out of the ordinary run of criminal cases and made it the extraordinary problem that it was.

It was very generally said that they had all fallen victims to some vendetta or curse attaching to the possession of a relic of great value both intrinsically and historically: a sort of chalice inlaid with precious stones and commonly called the Coptic Cup. Its origin was obscure, but its use was conjectured to be religious; and some attributed the fate that followed its possessors to the fanaticism of some Oriental Christian horrified at its passing through such materialistic hands. But the mysterious slayer, whether or no he was such a fanatic, was already a figure of lurid and sensational interest in the world of journalism and gossip. The nameless being was provided with a name, or a nickname. But it is only with the story of the third victim that we are now concerned; for it was only in this case that a certain Father Brown, who is the subject of these sketches, had an opportunity of making his presence felt.

When Father Brown first stepped off an Atlantic liner on to American soil, he discovered as many other Englishman has done, that he was a much more important person than he had ever supposed. His short figure, his short-sighted and undistinguished countenance, his rather rusty-black clerical clothes, could pass through any crowd in his own country without being noticed as anything unusual, except perhaps unusually insignificant. But America has a genius for the encouragement of fame; and his appearance in one or two curious criminal problems, together with his long association with Flambeau, the ex-criminal and detective, had consolidated a reputation in America out of what was little more than a rumour in England. His round face was blank with surprise when he found himself held up on the quay by a group of journalists, as by a gang of brigands, who asked him questions about all the subjects on which he was least likely to regard himself as an authority, such as the details of female dress and the criminal statistics of the country that he had only that moment clapped his eyes on. Perhaps it was the contrast with the black embattled solidarity of this group that made more vivid another figure that stood apart from it, equally black against the burning white daylight of that brilliant place and season, but entirely solitary; a tall, rather yellow-faced man in great goggles, who arrested him with a gesture when the journalists had finished and said: 'Excuse me, but maybe you are looking for Captain Wain.'

Some apology may be made for Father Brown; for he himself would have been sincerely apologetic. It must be remembered that he had never seen America before, and more especially that he had never seen that sort of tortoise-shell spectacles before;

for the fashion at this time had not spread to England. His first sensation was that of gazing at some goggling sea-monster with a faint suggestion of a diver's helmet. Otherwise the man was exquisitely dressed; and to Brown, in his innocence, the spectacles seemed the queerest disfigurement for a dandy. It was as if a dandy had adorned himself with a wooden leg as an extra touch of elegance. The question also embarrassed him. An American aviator of the name of Wain, a friend of some friends of his own in France, was indeed one of a long list of people he had some hope of seeing during his American visit; but he had never expected to hear of him so soon.

'I beg your pardon,' he said doubtfully, 'are you Captain Wain? Do you— do you know him?'

'Well, I'm pretty confident I'm not Captain Wain,' said the man in goggles, with a face of wood. 'I was pretty clear about that when I saw him waiting for you over there in the car. But the other question's a bit more problematical. I reckon I know Wain and his uncle, and old man Merton, too. I know old man Merton, but old man Merton don't know me. And he thinks he has the advantage, and I think I have the advantage. See?'

Father Brown did not quite see. He blinked at the glittering seascape and the pinnacles of the city, and then at the man in goggles. It was not only the masking of the man's eyes that produced the impression of something impenetrable. Something in his yellow face was almost Asiatic, even Chinese; and his conversation seemed to consist of stratified layers of irony. He was a type to be found here and there in that hearty and sociable population; he was the inscrutable American.

'My name's Drage,' he said, 'Norman Drage, and I'm an American citizen, which explains everything. At least I imagine your friend Wain would like to explain the rest; so we'll postpone The Fourth of July till another date.'

Father Brown was dragged in a somewhat dazed condition towards a car at some little distance, in which a young man with tufts of untidy yellow hair and a rather harassed and haggard expression, hailed him from afar, and presented himself as Peter Wain. Before he knew where he was he was stowed in the car and travelling with considerable speed through and beyond the city. He was unused to the impetuous practicality of such American action, and felt about as bewildered as if a chariot drawn by dragons had carried him away into fairyland. It was under these disconcerting conditions that he heard for the first time, in long monologues from Wain, and short sentences from Drage, the story of the Coptic Cup and the two crimes already connected with it.

It seemed that Wain had an uncle named Crake who had a partner named Merton, who was number three in the series of rich business men to whom the cup had belonged. The first of them, Titus P. Trant, the Copper King, had received threatening letters from somebody signing himself Daniel Doom. The name was presumably a pseudonym, but it had come to stand for a very public if not a very popular character; for somebody as well known as Robin Hood and Jack the Ripper combined. For it soon became clear that the writer of the threatening letter did not confine himself to threatening. Anyhow, the upshot was that old Trant was found one morning with his head in his own lily-pond, and there was not the shadow of a clue. The cup was, fortunately, safe in the bank; and it passed with the rest of Trant's property to his cousin, Brian Horder, who was also a man of great wealth and who was also threatened by the nameless enemy. Brian Horder was picked up dead at the foot of a cliff outside his seaside residence, at which there was a burglary, this time on a large scale. For though the cup apparently again escaped, enough bonds and securities were stolen to leave Horder's financial affairs in confusion.

'Brian Horder's widow,' explained Wain, 'had to sell most of his valuables, I believe, and Brander Merton must have purchased the cup at that time, for he had it when I first knew him. But you can guess for yourself that it's not a very comfortable thing to have.'

'Has Mr Merton ever had any of the threatening letters?' asked Father Brown, after a pause.

'I imagine he has,' said Mr Drage; and something in his voice made the priest look at him curiously, until he realized that the man in goggles was laughing silently, in a fashion that gave the newcomer something of a chill.

'I'm pretty sure he has,' said Peter Wain, frowning. 'I've not seen the letters, only his secretary sees any of his letters, for he is pretty reticent about business matters, as big businessmen have to be. But I've seen him real upset and annoyed with letters; and letters that he tore up, too, before even his secretary saw them. The secretary himself is getting nervous and says he is sure somebody is laying for the old man; and the long and the short of it is, that we'd be very grateful for a little advice in the matter. Everybody knows your great reputation. Father Brown, and the secretary asked me to see if you'd mind coming straight out to the Merton house at once.'

'Oh, I see,' said Father Brown, on whom the meaning of this apparent kidnapping began to dawn at last. 'But, really, I don't see that I can do anymore than you can. You're on the spot, and must have a hundred times more data for a scientific conclusion than a chance visitor.'

'Yes,' said Mr Drage dryly; 'our conclusions are much too scientific to be true. I reckon if anything hit a man like Titus P. Trant, it just came out of the sky without waiting for any scientific explanation. What they call a bolt from the blue.'

'You can't possibly mean,' cried Wain, 'that it was supernatural!'

But it was by no means easy at any time to discover what Mr Drage could possibly mean; except that if he said somebody was a real smart man, he very probably meant he was a fool. Mr Drage maintained an Oriental immobility until the car stopped, a little while after, at what was obviously their destination. It was rather a singular place. They had been driving through a thinly-wooded country that opened into a wide plain, and just in front of them was a building consisting of a single wall or very high fence, round, like a Roman camp, and having rather the appearance of an aerodrome. The barrier did not look like wood or stone, and closer inspection proved it to be of metal.

They all alighted from the car, and one small door in the wall was slid open with considerable caution, after manipulations resembling the opening of a safe. But, much to Father Brown's surprise, the man called Norman Drage showed no disposition to enter, but took leave of them with sinister gaiety.

'I won't come in,' he said. 'It 'ud be too much pleasurable excitement for old man Merton, I reckon. He loves the sight of me so much that he'd die of joy.'

And he strode away, while Father Brown, with increasing wonder, was admitted through the steel door which instantly clicked behind him. Inside was a large and elaborate garden of gay and varied colours, but entirely without any trees or tall shrubs or flowers. In the centre of it rose a house of handsome and even striking architecture, but so high and narrow as rather to resemble a tower. The burning sunlight gleamed on glass roofing here and there at the top, but there seemed to be no windows at all in the lower part of it. Over everything was that spotless and sparkling cleanliness that seemed so native to the clear American air. When they came inside the portal, they stood amid resplendent marble and metals and enamels of brilliant colours, but there was no staircase. Nothing but a single shaft for a lift went up the centre between the solid walls, and the approach to it was guarded by heavy, powerful men like plainclothes policemen.

'Pretty elaborate protection, I know,' said Wain. 'Maybe it makes you smile a little, Father Brown, to find Merton has to live in a fortress like this without even a tree in the garden for anyone to hide behind. But you don't know what sort of proposition we're up against in this country. And perhaps you don't know just what the name of Brander Merton means. He's a quiet-looking man enough, and anybody might pass him in the street; not that they get much chance nowadays, for he can only go out now and then in a closed car. But if anything happened to Brander Merton there'd be earthquakes from Alaska to the Cannibal Islands. I fancy there was never a king or emperor who had such power over the nations as he has. After all, I suppose if you'd been asked to visit the tsar, or the king of England, you'd have had the curiosity to go. You mayn't care much for tsars or millionaires; but it just means that power like that is always interesting. And I hope it's not against your principles to visit a modern sort of emperor like Merton.'

'Not at all,' said Father Brown, quietly. 'It is my duty to visit prisoners and all miserable men in captivity.'

There was a silence, and the young man frowned with a strange and almost shifty look on his lean face. Then he said, abruptly:

'Well, you've got to remember it isn't only common crooks or the Black Hand that's against him. This Daniel Doom is pretty much like the devil. Look how he dropped Trant in his own gardens and Horder outside his house, and got away with it.'

The top floor of the mansion, inside the enormously thick walls, consisted of two rooms; an outer room which they entered, and an inner room that was the great millionaire's sanctum. They entered the outer room just as two other visitors were coming out of the inner one. One was hailed by Peter Wain as his uncle—a small but very stalwart and active man with a shaven head that looked bald, and a brown face that looked almost too brown to have ever been white. This was old Crake, commonly called Hickory Crake in reminiscence of the more famous Old Hickory, because of his fame in the last Red Indian wars. His companion was a singular contrast—a very dapper gentleman with dark hair like a black varnish and a broad, black ribbon to his monocle: Barnard Blake, who was old Merton's lawyer and had been discussing with the partners the business of the firm. The four men met in the middle of the outer room and paused for a little polite conversation, in the act of respectively going and coming. And through all goings and comings another figure sat at the back of the room near the inner door, massive and motionless in the half-light from the inner window; a black African man with enormous shoulders. This was what the humorous self-criticism of America playfully calls the Bad Man; whom his friends might call a bodyguard and his enemies a bravo.

This man never moved or stirred to greet anybody; but the sight of him in the outer room seemed to move Peter Wain to his first nervous query.

'Is anybody with the chief?' he asked.

'Don't get rattled, Peter,' chuckled his uncle. 'Wilton the secretary is with him, and I hope that's enough for anybody. I don't believe Wilton ever sleeps for watching Merton. He is better than twenty bodyguards. And he's quick and quiet as an Indian.'

'Well, you ought to know,' said his nephew, laughing. 'I remember the Red Indian tricks you used to teach me when I was a boy and liked to read Red Indian stories. But in my Red Indian stories Red Indians seemed always to have the worst of it.'

'They didn't in real life,' said the old frontiersman grimly.

'Indeed?' inquired the bland Mr Blake. 'I should have thought they could do very little against our firearms.'

'I've seen an Indian stand under a hundred guns with nothing but a little scalping-knife and kill a white man standing on the top of a fort,' said Crake.

'Why, what did he do with it?' asked the other.

'Threw it,' replied Crake, 'threw it in a flash before a shot could be fired. I don't know where he learnt the trick.'

'Well, I hope you didn't learn it,' said his nephew, laughing.

'It seems to me,' said Father Brown, thoughtfully, 'that the story might have a moral.'

While they were speaking Mr Wilton, the secretary, had come out of the inner room and stood waiting; a pale, fair-haired man with a square chin and steady eyes with a look like a dog's; it was not difficult to believe that he had the single-eye of a watchdog.

He only said, 'Mr Merton can see you in about ten minutes,' but it served for a signal to break up the gossiping group. Old Crake said he must be off, and his nephew went out with him and his legal companion, leaving Father Brown for the moment alone with his secretary; for the black giant at the other end of the room could hardly be felt as if he were human or alive; he sat so motionless with his broad back to them, staring towards the inner room.

'Arrangements rather elaborate here, I'm afraid,' said the secretary. 'You've probably heard all about this Daniel Doom, and why it isn't safe to leave the boss very much alone.'

'But he is alone just now, isn't he?' said Father Brown.

The secretary looked at him with grave, grey eyes. 'For fifteen minutes,' he said. 'For fifteen minutes out of the twenty-four hours. That is all the real solitude he has; and that he insists on, for a pretty remarkable reason.'

'And what is the reason?' inquired the visitor. Wilton, the secretary, continued his steady gaze, but his mouth, that had been merely grave, became grim.

'The Coptic Cup,' he said. 'Perhaps you've forgotten the Coptic Cup; but he hasn't forgotten that or anything else. He doesn't trust any of us about the Coptic Cup. It's locked up somewhere and somehow in that room so that only he can find it; and he won't take it out till we're all out of the way. So we have to risk that quarter of an hour while he sits and worships it; I reckon it's the only worshipping he does. Not that there's any risk really; for I've turned all this place into a trap I don't believe the devil himself could get into—or at any rate, get out of. If this infernal Daniel Doom pays us a visit, he'll stay to dinner and a good bit later, by God! I sit here on hot bricks for the fifteen minutes, and the instant I heard a shot or a sound of struggle I'd press this button and an electrocuting current would run in a ring round that garden wall, so that it 'ud be death to cross or climb it. Of course, there couldn't be a shot, for this is the only way in; and the only window he sits at is away up on the top of a tower as smooth as a greasy pole. But, anyhow, we're all armed here, of course; and if Doom did get into that room he'd be dead before he got out.'

Father Brown was blinking at the carpet in a brown study. Then he said suddenly, with something like a jerk: 'I hope you won't mind my mentioning it, but a kind of a notion came into my head just this minute. It's about you.'

'Indeed,' remarked Wilton, 'and what about me?'

'I think you are a man of one idea,' said Father Brown, 'and you will forgive me for saying that it seems to be even more the idea of catching Daniel Doom than of defending Brander Merton.'

Wilton started a little and continued to stare at his companion; then very slowly his grim mouth took on a rather curious smile. 'How did you—what makes you think that?' he asked.

'You said that if you heard a shot you could instantly electrocute the escaping enemy,' remarked the priest. 'I suppose it occurred to you that the shot might be fatal to your employer before the shock was fatal to his foe. I don't mean that you wouldn't protect Mr Merton if you could, but it seems to come rather second in your thoughts. The arrangements are very elaborate, as you say, and you seem to have elaborated them. But they seem even more designed to catch a murderer than to save a man.'

'Father Brown,' said the secretary, who had recovered his quiet tone, 'you're very smart, but there's something more to you than smartness. Somehow you're the sort of man to whom one wants to tell the truth; and besides, you'll probably hear it, anyhow, for in one way it's a joke against me already. They all say I'm a monomaniac about running down this big crook, and perhaps I am. But I'll tell you one thing that none of them know. My full name is John Wilton Border.' Father Brown nodded as if he were completely enlightened, but the other went on.

'This fellow who calls himself Doom killed my father and uncle and ruined my mother. When Merton wanted a secretary I took the job, because I thought that where the cup was the criminal might sooner or later be. But I didn't know who the criminal was and could only wait for him; and I meant to serve Merton faithfully.'

'I understand,' said Father Brown gently; 'and, by the way, isn't it time that we attended on him?'

'Why, yes,' answered Wilton, again starting a little out of his brooding so that the priest concluded that his vindictive mania had again absorbed him for a moment.' Go in now by all means.'

Father Brown walked straight into the inner room. No sound of greetings followed, but only a dead silence; and a moment after the priest reappeared in the doorway.

At the same moment the silent bodyguard sitting near the door moved suddenly; and it was as if a huge piece of furniture had come to life. It seemed as though something in the very attitude of the priest had been a signal; for his head was against the light from the inner window and his face was in shadow.

'I suppose you will press that button,' he said with a sort of sigh.

Wilton seemed to awake from his savage brooding with a bound and leapt up with a catch in his voice.

'There was no shot,' he cried.

'Well,' said Father Brown, 'it depends what you mean by a shot.'

Wilton rushed forward, and they plunged into the inner room together. It was a comparatively small room and simply though elegantly furnished. Opposite to them one wide window stood open, overlooking the garden and the wooded plain. Close up against the window stood a chair and a small table, as if the captive desired as much air and light as was allowed him during his brief luxury of loneliness.

On the little table under the window stood the Coptic Cup; its owner had evidently been looking at it in the best light. It was well worth looking at, for that white and brilliant daylight turned its precious stones to many-coloured flames so that it might have been a model of the Holy Grail. It was well worth looking at; but Brander Merton was not looking at it. For his head had fallen back over his chair, his mane of white hair hanging towards the floor, and his spike of grizzled beard thrust up towards the ceiling, and out of his throat stood a long, brown-painted arrow with red leathers at the other end.

'A silent shot,' said Father Brown, in a low voice; 'I was just wondering about those new inventions for silencing firearms. But this is a very old invention, and quite as silent.'

Then, after a moment, he added: 'I'm afraid he is dead. What are you going to do?'

The pale secretary roused himself with abrupt resolution. 'I'm going to press that button, of course,' he said, 'and if that doesn't do for Daniel Doom, I'm going to hunt him through the world till I find him.'

'Take care it doesn't do for any of our friends,' observed Father Brown; 'they can hardly be far off; we'd better call them.'

'That lot know all about the wall,' answered Wilton. 'None of them will try to climb it, unless one of them ... is in a great hurry.'

Father Brown went to the window by which the arrow had evidently entered and looked out. The garden, with its flat flowerbeds, lay far below like a delicately coloured map of the world. The whole vista seemed so vast and empty, the tower seemed set so far up in the sky that as he stared out a strange phrase came back to his memory.

'A bolt from the blue,' he said. 'What was that somebody said about a bolt from the blue and death coming out of the sky? Look how far away everything looks; it seems extraordinary that an arrow could come so far, unless it were an arrow from heaven.'

Wilton had returned, but did not reply, and the priest went on as in soliloquy. 'One thinks of aviation. We must ask young Wain ... about aviation.'

'There's a lot of it round here,' said the secretary.

'Case of very old or very new weapons,' observed Father Brown. 'Some would be quite familiar to his old uncle, I suppose; we must ask him about arrows. This looks rather like a Red Indian arrow. I don't know where the Red Indian shot it from; but you remember the story the old man told. I said it had a moral.'

'If it had a moral,' said Wilton warmly, 'it was only that a real 'Red Indian might shoot a thing farther than you'd fancy. It's nonsense your suggesting a parallel.'

'I don't think you've got the moral quite right,' said Father Brown.

Although the little priest appeared to melt into the millions of New York next day, without any apparent attempt to be anything but a number in a numbered street, he was, in fact, unobtrusively busy for the next fortnight with the commission that had been given him, for he was filled with profound fear about a possible miscarriage of justice. Without having any particular air of singling them out from his other new acquaintances, he found it easy to fall into talk with the two or three men recently involved in the mystery; and with old Hickory Crake especially he had a curious and interesting conversation. It took place on a seat in Central Park, where the veteran sat with his bony hands and hatchet face resting on the oddly-shaped head of a walking-stick of dark red wood, possibly modelled on a tomahawk.

'Well, it may be a long shot,' he said, wagging his head, 'but I wouldn't advise you to be too positive about how far an Indian arrow could go. I've known some bow-shots that seemed to go straighter than any bullets, and hit the mark to amazement, considering how long they had been travelling. Of course, you practically never hear now of a Red Indian with a bow and arrows, still less of a Red Indian hanging about here. But if by any chance there were one of the old Indian marksmen, with one of the old Indian bows, hiding in those trees hundreds of yards beyond the Merton outer wall—why, then I wouldn't put it past the noble savage to be able to send an arrow over the wall and into the top window of Merton's house; no, nor into Merton, either. I've seen things quite as wonderful as that done in the old days.'

'No doubt,' said the priest, 'you have done things quite as wonderful, as well as seen them.'

Old Crake chuckled, and then said gruffly: 'Oh, that's all ancient history.'

'Some people have a way of studying ancient history,' the priest said. 'I suppose we may take it there is nothing in your old record In make people talk unpleasantly about this affair.'

'What do you mean?' demanded Crake, his eyes shifting sharply for the first time, in his red, wooden face, that was rather like the head of a tomahawk.

'Well, since you were so well acquainted with all the arts and crafts of the Redskin—' began Father Brown slowly.

Crake had had a hunched and almost shrunken appearance as he sat with his chin propped on its queer-shaped crutch. But the next instant he stood erect in the path like a fighting bravo with the crutch clutched like a cudgel.

'What?' he cried—in something like a raucous screech—'what the hell! Are you standing up to me to tell me I might happen to have murdered my own brother-in-law?'

From a dozen seats dotted about the path people looked to-wards the disputants, as they stood facing each other in the middle of the path, the bald-headed energetic little man brandishing his outlandish stick like a club, and the black, dumpy figure of the little cleric looking at him without moving a muscle, save for his hinging eyelids. For a moment it looked as if the black, dumpy figure would be knocked on the head, and laid out with true Red Indian promptitude and dispatch; and the large form of an Irish policeman could be seen heaving up in the distance and bearing down on the group. But the priest only said, quite placidly, like one answering an ordinary query:

'I have formed certain conclusions about it, but I do not think I will mention them till I make my report.'

Whether under the influence of the footsteps of the policeman or of the eyes of the priest, old Hickory tucked his stick under his arm and put his hat on again, grunting. The priest bade him a placid good morning, and passed in an unhurried fashion out of the park, making his way to the lounge of the hotel where he knew that young Wain was to be found. The young man sprang up with a greeting, he looked even more haggard and harassed than before, as if some worry were eating him away; and the priest had a suspicion that his young friend had recently been engaged, with only too conspicuous success, in evading the last Amendment to the American Constitution.

But at the first word about his hobby or favourite science he was vigilant and concentrated enough. For Father Brown had asked, in an idle and conversational fashion, whether much flying was done in that district, and had told how he had at first mistaken Mr Merton's circular wall for an aerodrome.

'It's a wonder you didn't see any while we were there,' answered Captain Wain. 'Sometimes they're as thick as flies; that open plain is a great place for them, and I shouldn't wonder if it were the chief breeding-ground, so to speak, for my sort of birds in the future. I've flown a good deal there myself, of course, and I know most of the fellows about here who flew in the war; but there are a whole lot of people taking to it out there now whom I never heard of in my life. I suppose it will be like motoring soon, and every man in the States will have one.'

'Being endowed by his Creator,' said Father Brown with a smile, 'with the right to life, liberty, and the pursuit of motoring—not to mention aviation. So I suppose we may take it that one strange aeroplane passing over that house, at certain times, wouldn't be noticed much.'

'No,' replied the young man; 'I don't suppose it would.'

'Or even if the man were known,' went on the other, 'I suppose he might get hold of a machine that wouldn't be recognized as his. If you, for instance, flew in the ordinary way, Mr Merton and his friends might recognize the rig-out, perhaps; but you might pass pretty near that window on a different pattern of plane, or whatever you call it; near enough for practical purposes.'

'Well, yes,' began the young man, almost automatically, and then ceased, and remained staring at the cleric with an open mouth and eyes standing out of his head.

'My God!' he said, in a low voice; 'my God!'

Then he rose from the lounge seat, pale and shaking from head to foot and still staring at the priest.

'Are you mad?' he said; 'are you raving mad?'

There was a silence and then he spoke again in a swift hissing fashion. 'You positively come here to suggest—'

'No; only to collect suggestions,' said Father Brown, rising. 'I may have formed some conclusions provisionally, but I had better reserve them for the present.'

And then saluting the other with the same stiff civility, he passed out of the hotel to continue his curious peregrinations.

By the dusk of that day they had led him down the dingy streets and steps that straggled and tumbled towards the river in the the oldest and most irregular part of the city. Immediately under the coloured lantern that marked the entrance to a rather low Chinese restaurant he encountered a figure he had seen before, though by no means presenting itself to the eye as he had seen it.

Mr Norman Drage still confronted the world grimly behind his great goggles, which seemed somehow to cover his face like a dark musk of glass. But except for the goggles, his appearance had undergone a strange transformation in the month that had elapsed since the murder. He had then, as Father Brown had noted, been dressed up to the nines—up to that point, indeed, where there begins to be too fine a distinction between the dandy and the dummy outside a tailor's shop. But now all those externals were mysteriously altered for the worse; as if the tailor's dummy had been turned into a scarecrow. His top hat still existed, but it was battered and shabby; his clothes were dilapidated; his watch-chain and minor ornaments were gone. Father Brown, however, addressed him as if they had met yesterday, and made no demur to silting down with him on a bench in the cheap eating-house whither he was bound. It was not he, however, who began the conversation.

'Well?' growled Drage, 'and have you succeeded in avenging your holy and sainted millionaire? We know all millionaires are holy and sainted; you can find it all in the papers next day, about how they lived by the light of the Family Bible they read at their mother's knee. Gee! if they'd only read out some of the things there are in the Family Bible, the mother might have been startled some. And the millionaire, too, I reckon. The old Book's full of a lot of grand fierce old notions they don't grow nowadays; sort of wisdom of the Stone Age and buried under the Pyramids. Suppose somebody had flung old man Merton from the top of that tower of his, and let him be eaten by dogs at the bottom, it would be no worse than what happened to Jezebel. Wasn't Agag hacked into little pieces, for all he went walking delicately? Merton walked delicately all his life, damn him—until he got too delicate to walk at all. But the shaft of the Lord found him out, as it might have done in the old Book, and struck him dead on the top of his tower to be a spectacle to the people.

'The shaft was material, at least,' said his companion.

'The Pyramids are mighty material, and they hold down the dead kings all right,' grinned the man in the goggles. 'I think there's a lot to be said for these old material religions. There's old carvings that have lasted for thousands of years, showing their gods and emperors with bended bows; with hands that look as if they could really bend bows of stone. Material, perhaps—but what materials! Don't you sometimes stand staring at those old Eastern patterns and things, till you have a hunch that old Lord God is still driving like a dark Apollo, and shooting black rays of death?'

'If he is,' replied Father Brown, 'I might call him by another name. But I doubt whether Merton died by a dark ray or even a stone arrow.'

'I guess you think he's St Sebastian,' sneered Drage, 'killed with an arrow. A millionaire must be a martyr. How do you know he didn't deserve it? You don't know much about your millionaire, I fancy. Well, let me tell you he deserved it a hundred times over.'

'Well,' asked Father Brown gently, 'why didn't you murder him?'

'You want to know why I didn't?' said the other, staring. 'Well, you're a nice sort of clergyman.'

'Not at all,' said the other, as if waving away a compliment.

'I suppose it's your way of saying I did,' snarled Drage. 'Well, prove it, that's all. As for him, I reckon he was no loss.'

'Yes, he was,' said Father Brown, sharply. 'He was a loss to you. That's why you didn't kill him.'

And he walked out of the room, leaving the man in goggles gaping after him.

It was nearly a month later that Father Brown revisited the house where the third millionaire had suffered from the vendetta of Daniel Doom. A sort of council was held of the persons most interested. Old Crake sat at the head of the table with his nephew at his right hand, the lawyer on his left; the big man with the African features, whose name appeared to be Harris, was ponderously present, if only as a material witness; a red-haired, sharp-nosed individual addressed as Dixon seemed to be the representative of Pinkerton's or some such private agency; and Father Brown slipped unobtrusively into an empty seat beside him.

Every newspaper in the world was full of the catastrophe of the colossus of finance, of the great organizer of the Big Business that bestrides the modern world; but from the tiny group that had been nearest to him at the very instant of his death very little could be learned. The uncle, nephew, and attendant solicitor declared they were well outside the outer wall before the alarm was raised; and inquiries of the official guardians at both barriers brought answers that were rather confused, but on the whole confirmatory. Only one other complication seemed to call for consideration. It seemed that round about the time of the death, before or after, a stranger had been found hanging mysteriously round the entrance and asking to see Mr Merton. The servants had some difficulty in understanding what he meant, for his language was very obscure; but it was afterwards considered to be also very suspicious, since he had said something about a wicked man being destroyed by a word out of the sky.

Peter Wain leaned forward, the eyes bright in his haggard face, and said:

'I'll bet on that, anyhow. Norman Drage.'

'And who in the world is Norman Drage?' asked his uncle.

'That's what I want to know,' replied the young man. 'I practically asked him, but he has got a wonderful trick of twisting every straight question crooked; it's like lunging at a fencer. He hooked on to me with hints about the flying-ship of the future; but I never trusted him much.'

'But what sort of a man is he?' asked Crake.

'He's a mystagogue,' said Father Brown, with innocent promptitude. 'There are quite a lot of them about; the sort of men about town who hint to you in Paris cafes and cabarets that they've lifted the veil of Isis or know the secret of Stonehenge. In a case like this they're sure to have some sort of mystical explanations.'

The smooth, dark head of Mr Barnard Blake, the lawyer, was inclined politely towards the speaker, but his smile was faintly hostile.

'I should hardly have thought, sir,' he said, 'that you had any quarrel with mystical explanations.'

'On the contrary,' replied Father Brown, blinking amiably at him. 'That's just why I can quarrel with 'em. Any sham lawyer could bamboozle me, but he couldn't bamboozle you; because you're a lawyer yourself. Any fool could dress up as a Red Indian and I'd swallow him whole as the only original Hiawatha; but Mr Crake would see through him at once. A swindler could pretend to me that he knew all about aeroplanes, but not to Captain Wain. And it's just the same with the other, don't you see? It's just because I have picked up a little about mystics that I have no use for mystagogues. Real mystics don't hide mysteries, they reveal them. They set a thing up in broad daylight, and when you've seen it it's still a mystery. But the mystagogues hide a thing in darkness and secrecy, and when you find it, it's a platitude. But in the case of Drage, I admit he had also another and more practical notion in talking about fire from heaven or bolts from the blue.'

'And what was his notion?' asked Wain. 'I think it wants watching whatever it is.'

'Well,' replied the priest, slowly, 'he wanted us to think the murders were miracles because... well, because he knew they weren't.'

'Ah,' said Wain, with a sort of hiss, 'I was waiting for that. In plain words, he is the criminal.'

'In plain words, he is the criminal who didn't commit the crime,' answered Father Brown calmly.

'Is that your conception of plain words?' inquired Blake politely.

'You'll be saying I'm the mystagogue now,' said Father Brown somewhat abashed, but with a broad smile, 'but it was really quite accidental. Drage didn't commit the crime—I mean this crime. His only crime was blackmailing somebody, and he hung about here to do it; but he wasn't likely to want the secret to be public property or the whole business to be cut short by death. We can talk about him afterwards. Just at the moment, I only want him cleared out of the way.'

'Out of the way of what?' asked the other.

'Out of the way of the truth,' replied the priest, looking at him tranquilly, with level eyelids.

'Do you mean,' faltered the other, 'that you know the truth?'

'I rather think so,' said Father Brown modestly.

There was an abrupt silence, after which Crake cried out suddenly and irrelevantly in a rasping voice:

'Why, where is that secretary fellow? Wilton! He ought to be here.'

'I am in communication with Mr Wilton,' said Father Brown gravely; 'in fact, I asked him to ring me up here in a few minutes from now. I may say that we've worked the thing out together, in a manner of speaking.'

'If you're working together, I suppose it's all right,' grumbled Crake. 'I know he was always a sort of bloodhound on the trail of his vanishing crook, so perhaps it was well to hunt in couples with him. But if you know the truth about this, where the devil did you get it from?'

'I got it from you,' answered the priest, quietly, and continued to gaze mildly at the glaring veteran. 'I mean I made the first guess from a hint in a story of yours about an Indian who threw a knife and hit a man on the top of a fortress.'

'You've said that several times,' said Wain, with a puzzled air; 'but I can't see any inference, except that this murderer threw an arrow and hit a man on the top of a house very like a fortress. But of course the arrow wasn't thrown but shot, and would go much further. Certainly it went uncommonly far; but I don't see how it brings us any farther.'

'I'm afraid you missed the point of the story,' said Father Brown. 'It isn't that if one thing cap go far another can go farther. It is that the wrong use of a tool can cut both ways. The men on Crake's fort thought of a knife as a thing for a hand-to-hand fight and forgot that it could be a missile like a javelin. Some other people I know thought of a thing as a missile like a javelin and forgot that, after all, it could be used hand-to-hand as a spear. In short, the moral of the story is that since a dagger can be turned into an arrow, so can an arrow be turned into a dagger.'

They were all looking at him now; but he continued in the same casual and unconscious tone: 'naturally we wondered and worried a good deal about who shot that arrow through the window and whether it came from far away, and so on. But the truth is that nobody shot the arrow at all. It never came in at the window at all.'

'Then how did it come there?' asked the swarthy lawyer, with a rather lowering face.

'Somebody brought it with him, I suppose,' said Father Brown; 'it wouldn't be hard to carry or conceal. Somebody had it in his hand as he stood with Merton in Merton's own room. Somebody thrust it into Merton's throat like a poignard, and then had the highly intelligent idea of placing the whole thing at such a place and angle that we all assumed in a flash that it had flown in at the window like a bird.'

'Somebody,' said old Crake, in a voice as heavy as stone.

The telephone bell rang with a strident and horrible clamour of insistence. It was in the adjoining room, and Father Brown had darted there before anybody else could move.

'What the devil is it all about?' cried Peter Wain, who seemed all shaken and distracted.

'He said he expected to be rung up by Wilton, the secretary,' replied his uncle in the same dead voice.

'I suppose it is Wilton?' observed the lawyer, like one speaking to fill up a silence. But nobody answered the question until Father Brown reappeared suddenly and silently in the room, bringing the answer.

'Gentlemen,' he said, when he had resumed his seat, 'it was you who asked me to look into the truth about this puzzle; and having found the truth, I must tell it, without any pretence of softening the shock. I'm afraid anybody who pokes his nose into things like this can't afford to be a respecter of persons.'

'I suppose,' said Crake, breaking the silence that followed, 'that means that some of us are accused, or suspected.'

'All of us are suspected,' answered Father Brown. 'I may be suspected myself, for I found the body.'

'Of course we're suspected,' snapped Wain. 'Father Brown kindly explained to me how I could have besieged the tower in a flying-machine.'

'No,' replied the priest, with a smile; 'you described to me how you could have done it. That was just the interesting part of it.'

'He seemed to think it likely,' growled Crake, 'that I killed him myself with a Red Indian arrow.'

'I thought it most unlikely,' said Father Brown, making rather a wry face. I'm sorry if I did wrong, but I couldn't think of any other way of testing the matter. I can hardly think of anything more improbable than the notion that Captain Wain went careering in a huge machine past the window, at the very moment of the murder, and nobody noticed it; unless, perhaps, it were the notion that a respectable old gentleman should play at Red Indians with a bow and arrow behind the bushes, to kill somebody he could have killed in twenty much simpler ways. But I had to find out if they had had anything to do with it; and so I had to accuse them in order to prove their innocence.'

'And how have you proved their innocence?' asked Blake the lawyer, leaning forward eagerly.

'Only by the agitation they showed when they were accused,' answered the other.

'What do you mean, exactly?'

'If you will permit me to say so,' remarked Father Brown, composedly enough, 'I did undoubtedly think it my duty to suspect them and everybody else. I did suspect Mr Crake and I did suspect Captain Wain, in the sense that I considered the possibility or probability of their guilt. I told them I had formed conclusions about it; and I will now tell them what those conclusions were. I was sure they were innocent, because of the manner and the moment in which they passed from unconsciousness to indignation. So long as they never thought they were accused, they went on giving me materials to support the accusation. They practically explained to me how they might have committed the crime. Then they suddenly realized with a shock and a shout of rage that they were accused; they realized it long after they might well have expected to be accused, but long before I had accused them. Now no guilty person could possibly do that. He might be snappy and suspicious from the first; or he might simulate unconsciousness and innocence up to the end. But he wouldn't begin by making things worse for himself and then give a great jump and begin furiously denying the notion he had himself helped to suggest. That could only come by his having really failed to realize what he was suggesting. The self-consciousness of a murderer would always be at least morbidly vivid enough to prevent him first forgetting his relation with the thing and then remembering to deny it. So I ruled you both out and others for other reasons I needn't discuss now. For instance, there was the secretary—

'But I'm not talking about that just now. Look here, I've just heard from Wilton on the phone, and he's given me permission to tell you some rather serious news. Now I suppose you all know by this time who Wilton was, and what he was after.'

'I know he was after Daniel Doom and wouldn't be happy till he got him,' answered Peter Wain; 'and I've heard the story that he's the son of old Horder, and that's why he's the avenger of blood. Anyhow, he's certainly looking for the man called Doom.'

'Well,' said Father Brown, 'he has found him.'

Peter Wain sprang to his feet in excitement.

'The murderer!' he cried. 'Is the murderer in the lock-up already?'

'No,' said Father Brown, gravely; 'I said the news was serious, and it's more serious than that. I'm afraid poor Wilton has taken a terrible responsibility. I'm afraid he's going to put a terrible responsibility on us. He hunted the criminal down, and just when he had him cornered at last—well, he has taken the law into his own hands.'

'You mean that Daniel Doom—' began the lawyer.

'I mean that Daniel Doom is dead,' said the priest. 'There was some sort of wild struggle, and Wilton killed him.'

'Serve him right,' growled Mr Hickory Crake.

'Can't blame Wilton for downing a crook like that, especially considering the feud,' assented Wain; 'it was like stepping on a viper.'

'I don't agree with you,' said Father Brown. 'I suppose we all talk romantic stuff at random in defence of lynching and lawlessness; but I have a suspicion that if we lose our laws and liberties we shall regret it. Besides, it seems to me illogical to say there is something to be said for Wilton committing murder, without even inquiring whether there was anything to be said for Doom committing it. I rather doubt whether Doom was merely a vulgar assassin; he may have been a sort of outlaw with a mania about the cup, demanding it with threats and only killing after a struggle; both victims were thrown down just outside their houses. The objection to Wilton's way of doing it is that we shall never hear Doom's side of the case.'

'Oh, I've no patience with all this sentimental whitewashing of worthless, murderous blackguards,' cried Wain, heatedly. 'If Wilton croaked the criminal he did a jolly good day's work, and there's an end of it.'

'Quite so, quite so,' said his uncle, nodding vigorously.

Father Brown's face had a yet heavier gravity as he looked slowly round the semicircle effaces. 'Is that really what you all think?' he asked. even as he did so he realized that he was an englishman and an exile. He realized that he was among foreigners, even if he was among friends. Around that ring of foreigners ran a restless fire that was not native to his own breed; the fiercer spirit of the western nation that can rebel and lynch, and above all, combine. He knew that they had already combined.

'Well,' said Father Brown, with a sigh, 'I am to understand, then, that you do definitely condone this unfortunate man's crime, or act of private justice, or whatever you call it. In that case it will not hurt him if I tell you a little more about it.'

He rose suddenly to his feet; and though they saw no meaning in his movement, it seemed in some way to change or chill the very air in the room.

'Wilton killed Doom in a rather curious way,' he began.

'How did Wilton kill him?' asked Crake, abruptly.

'With an arrow,' said Father Brown.

Twilight was gathering in the long room, and daylight dwindling to a gleam from the great window in the inner room, where the great millionaire had died. Almost automatically the eyes of the group turned slowly towards it, but as yet there was no sound. Then the voice of Crake came cracked and high and senile in a sort of crowing gabble.

'What you mean? What you mean? Brander Merton killed by an arrow. This crook killed by an arrow—'

'By the same arrow,' said the priest, 'and at the same moment.'

Again there was a sort of strangled and yet swollen and bursting silence, and young Wain began: 'You mean—'

'I mean that your friend Merton was Daniel Doom,' said Father Brown firmly;' and the only Daniel Doom you'll ever find. Your friend Merton was always crazy after that Coptic Cup that he used to worship like an idol every day; and in his wild youth he had really killed two men to get it, though I still think the deaths may have been in a sense accidents of the robbery. Anyhow, he had it; and that man Drage knew the story and was blackmailing him. But Wilton was after him for a very different purpose; I fancy he only discovered the truth when he'd got into this house. But anyhow, it was in this house, and in that room, that this hunt ended, and he slew the slayer of his father.'

For a long time nobody answered. Then old Crake could be heard drumming with his fingers on the table and muttering: 'Brander must have been mad. He must have been mad.'

'But, good Lord!' burst out Peter Wain; 'what are we to do? What are we to say? Oh, it's all quite different! What about the papers and the big business people? Brander Merton is a thing like the President or the Pope of Rome.'

'I certainly think it is rather different,' began Barnard Blake, the lawyer, in a low voice. 'The difference involves a whole—'

Father Brown struck the table so that the glasses on it rang; and they could almost fancy a ghostly echo from the mysterious chalice that still stood in the room beyond.

'No!' he cried, in a voice like a pistol-shot. 'There shall be no difference. I gave you your chance of pitying the poor devil when you thought he was a common criminal. You wouldn't listen then; you were all for private vengeance then. You were all for letting him be butchered like a wild beast without a hearing or a public trial, and said he had only got his deserts. Very well then, if Daniel Doom has got his deserts, Brander Merton has got his deserts. If that was good enough for Doom, by all that is holy it is good enough for Merton. Take your wild justice or our dull legality; but in the name of Almighty God, let there be an equal lawlessness or an equal law.'

Nobody answered except the lawyer, and he answered with something like a snarl: 'What will the police say if we tell them we mean to condone a crime?'

'What will they say if I tell them you did condone it?' replied Father Brown. 'Your respect for the law comes rather late, Mr Barnard Blake.'

After a pause he resumed in a milder tone: 'I, for one, am ready to tell the truth if the proper authorities ask me; and the rest of you can do as you like. But as a fact, it will make very little difference. Wilton only rang me up to tell me that I was now free to lay his confession before you; for when you heard it, he would be beyond pursuit.'

He walked slowly into the inner room and stood there by the little table beside which the millionaire had died. The Coptic Cup still stood in the same place, and he remained there for a space staring at its cluster of all the colours of the rainbow, and beyond it into a blue abyss of sky.

3

THE ORACLE OF THE DOG
(First published in *Nash's Magazine*, Dec 1923)

'Yes,' said Father Brown, 'I always like a dog, so long as he isn't spelt backwards.'

Those who are quick in talking are not always quick in listening. Sometimes even their brilliancy produces a sort of stupidity. Father Brown's friend and companion was a young man with a stream of ideas and stories, an enthusiastic young man named Fiennes, with eager blue eyes and blond hair that seemed to be brushed back, not merely with a hairbrush but with the wind of the world as be rushed through it. But he stopped in the torrent of his talk in a momentary bewilderment before he saw the priest's very simple meaning.

'You mean that people make too much of them?' he said. 'Well, I don't know. They're marvellous creatures. Sometimes I think they know a lot more than we do.'

Father Brown said nothing, but continued to stroke the head of the big retriever in a half-abstracted but apparently soothing fashion.

'Why,' said Fiennes, warming again to his monologue, 'there was a dog in the case I've come to see you about: what they call the 'Invisible Murder Case', you know. It's a strange story, but from my point of view the dog is about the strangest thing in it. Of course, there's the mystery of the crime itself, and how old Druce can have been killed by somebody else when he was all alone in the summer-house—'

The hand stroking the dog stopped for a moment in its rhythmic movement, and Father Brown said calmly: 'Oh, it was a summer-house, was it?'

'I thought you'd read all about it in the papers,' answered Fiennes. 'Stop a minute; I believe I've got a cutting that will give you all the particulars.' He produced a strip of newspaper from his pocket and handed it to the priest, who began to read it, holding it close to his blinking eyes with one hand while the other continued its half-conscious caresses of the dog. It looked like the parable of a man not letting his right hand know what his left hand did.

★ ★ ★ ★ ★

Many mystery stories, about men murdered behind locked doors and windows, and murderers escaping without means of entrance and exit, have come true in the course of the extraordinary events at Cranston on the coast of Yorkshire, where Colonel Druce was found stabbed from behind by a dagger that has entirely disappeared from the scene, and apparently even from the neighbourhood.

The summer-house in which he died was indeed accessible at one entrance, the ordinary doorway which looked down the central walk of the garden towards the house. But, by a combination of events almost to be called a coincidence, it appears that both the path and the entrance were watched during the crucial time, and there is a chain of witnesses who confirm each other. The summer-house stands at the extreme end of the garden, where there is no exit or entrance of any kind. The central garden path is a lane between two ranks of tall delphiniums, planted so close that any stray step off the path would leave its traces; and both path and plants run right up to the very mouth of the summer-house, so that no straying from that straight path could fail to be observed, and no other mode of entrance can be imagined.

Patrick Floyd, secretary of the murdered man, testified that he had been in a position to overlook the whole garden from the time when Colonel Druce last appeared alive in the doorway to the time when he was found dead; as he, Floyd, had been on the top of a step-ladder clipping the garden hedge. Janet Druce, the dead man's daughter, confirmed this, saying that she had sat on the terrace of the house throughout that time and had seen Floyd at his work. Touching some part of the time, this is again supported by Donald Druce, her brother—who overlooked the garden—standing at his bedroom window in his dressing-gown, for he had risen late. Lastly, the account is consistent with that given by Dr Valentine, a neighbour, who called for a time to talk with Miss Druce on the terrace, and by the Colonel's solicitor, Mr Aubrey Traill, who was apparently the last to see the murdered man alive—presumably with the exception of the murderer.

All are agreed that the course of events was as follows: About half past three in the afternoon, Miss Druce went down the path to ask her father when he would like tea; but he said he did not want any and was waiting to see Traill, his lawyer, who was to be sent to him in the summer-house. The girl then came away and met Traill coming down the path; she directed him to her father and he went in as directed. About half an hour afterwards he came out again, the Colonel coming with him to the door and showing himself to all appearance in health and even high spirits. He had been somewhat annoyed earlier in the day by his son's irregular hours, but seemed to recover his temper in a perfectly normal fashion, and had been rather markedly genial in receiving other visitors, including two of his nephews, who came over for the day. But as these were out walking during the whole period of the tragedy, they had no evidence to give. It is said, indeed, that the Colonel was not on very good terms with Dr Valentine, but that gentleman only had a brief interview with the daughter of the house, to whom he is supposed to be paying serious attentions.

Trail, the solicitor, says he left the Colonel entirely alone in the summer-house, and this is confirmed by Floyd's bird's-eye view of the garden, which showed nobody else passing the only entrance. Ten minutes later. Miss Druce again went down the garden and had not reached the end of the path when she saw her father, who was conspicuous by his white linen coat, lying in a heap on the floor. She uttered a scream which brought others to the spot, and on entering the place they found the Colonel lying dead beside his basket-chair, which was also upset. Dr Valentine, who was still in the immediate neighbourhood, testified that the wound was made by some sort of stiletto, entering under the shoulder-blade and piercing the heart. The police have searched the neighbourhood for such a weapon, but no trace of it can be found.

'So Colonel Druce wore a white coat, did he?' said Father Brown as he put down the paper.

'Trick he learnt in the tropics,' replied Fiennes, with some wonder. 'He'd had some queer adventures there, by his own account; and I fancy his dislike of Valentine was connected with the doctor coming from the tropics, too. But it's all an infernal puzzle. The account there is pretty accurate. I didn't see the tragedy, in the sense of the discovery; I was out walking with the young nephews and the dog—the dog I wanted to tell you about. But I saw the stage set for it as described; the straight lane between the blue flowers right up to the dark entrance, and the lawyer going down it in his blacks and his silk hat, and the red head of the secretary showing high above the green hedge as he worked on it with his shears. Nobody could have mistaken that red head at any distance; and if people say they saw it there all the time, you may be sure they did.

This red-haired secretary, Floyd, is quite a character; a breathless bounding sort of fellow, always doing everybody's work as he was doing the gardener's. I think he is an American; he's certainly got the American view of life—what they call the viewpoint, bless 'em.'

'What about the lawyer?' asked Father Brown. There was a silence and then Fiennes spoke quite slowly for him. 'Traill struck me as a singular man. In his fine black clothes he was almost foppish, yet you can hardly call him fashionable. For he wore a pair of long, luxuriant black whiskers such as haven't been seen since Victorian times. He had rather a fine grave face and a fine grave manner, but every now and then he seemed to remember to smile. And when he showed his white teeth he seemed to lose a little of his dignity, and there was something faintly fawning about him. It may have been only embarrassment, for he would also fidget with his cravat and his tie-pin, which were at once handsome and unusual, like himself. If I could think of anybody—but what's the good, when the whole thing's impossible? Nobody knows who did it. Nobody knows how it could be done. At least there's only one exception I'd make, and that's why I really mentioned the whole thing. The dog knows.'

Father Brown sighed and then said absently: 'You were there as a friend of young Donald, weren't you? He didn't go on your walk with you?'

'No,' replied Fiennes smiling. 'The young scoundrel had gone to bed that morning and got up that afternoon. I went with his cousins, two young officers from India, and our conversation was trivial enough. I remember the elder, whose name I think is Herbert Druce and who is an authority on horse-breeding, talked about nothing but a mare he had bought and the moral character of the man who sold her; while his brother Harry seemed to be brooding on his bad luck at Monte Carlo. I only mention it to show you, in the light of what happened on our walk, that there was nothing psychic about us. The dog was the only mystic in our company.'

'What sort of a dog was he?' asked the priest.

'Same breed as that one,' answered Fiennes. 'That's what started me off on the story, your saying you didn't believe in believing in a dog. He's a big black retriever, named Nox, and a suggestive name, too; for I think what he did a darker mystery than the murder. You know Druce's house and garden are by the sea; we walked about a mile from it along the sands and then turned back, going the other way. We passed a rather curious rock called the Rock of Fortune, famous in the neighbourhood because it's one of those examples of one stone barely balanced on another, so that a touch would knock it over. It is not really very high but the hanging outline of it makes it look a little wild and sinister; at least it made it look so to me, for I don't imagine my jolly young companions were afflicted with the picturesque. But it may be that I was beginning to feel an atmosphere; for just then the question arose of whether it was time to go back to tea, and even then I think I had a premonition that time counted for a good deal in the business. Neither Herbert Druce nor I had a watch, so we called out to his brother, who was some paces behind, having stopped to light his pipe under the hedge. Hence it happened that he shouted out the hour, which was twenty past four, in his big voice through the growing twilight; and somehow the loudness of it made it sound like the proclamation of something tremendous. His unconsciousness seemed to make it all the more so; but that was always the way with omens; and particular ticks of the clock were really very ominous things that afternoon. According to Dr Valentine's testimony, poor Druce had actually died just about half past four.

'Well, they said we needn't go home for ten minutes, and we walked a little farther along the sands, doing nothing in particular—throwing stones for the dog and throwing sticks into the sea for, him to swim after. But to me the twilight seemed to grow oddly oppressive, and the very shadow of the top-heavy Rock of Fortune lay on me like a load. And then the curious thing happened. Nox had just brought back Herbert's walking-stick out of the sea and his brother had thrown his in also. The dog swam out again, but just about what must have been the stroke of the half-hour, he stopped swimming. He came back again on to the shore and stood in front of us. Then he suddenly threw up his head and sent up a howl or wail of woe—if ever I heard one in the world.

'What the devil's the matter with the dog?' asked Herbert; but none of us could answer. There was a long silence after the brute's wailing and whining died away on the desolate shore; and then the silence was broken. As I live, it was broken by a faint and far-off shriek, like the shriek of a woman from beyond the hedges inland. We didn't know what it was then; but we knew afterwards. It was the cry the girl gave when she first saw the body of her father.'

'You went back, I suppose,' said Father Brown patiently. 'What happened then?'

'I'll tell you what happened then,' said Fiennes with a grim emphasis. 'When we got back into that garden the first thing we saw was Traill, the lawyer; I can see him now with his black hat and black whiskers relieved against the perspective of the blue flowers stretching down to the summer-house, with the sunset and the strange outline of the Rock of Fortune in the distance. His face and figure were in shadow against the sunset; but I swear the white teeth were showing in his head and he was smiling. The moment Nox saw that man the dog dashed forward and stood in the middle of the path barking at him madly, murderously, volleying out curses that were almost verbal in their dreadful distinctness of hatred. And the man doubled up and fled, along the path between the flowers.'

Father Brown sprang to his feet with a startling impatience. 'So the dog denounced him, did he?' he cried. 'The oracle of the dog condemned him. Did you see what birds were flying, and are you sure whether they were on the right hand or the left? Did you consult the augurs about the sacrifices? Surely you didn't omit to cut open the dog and examine his entrails. That is the sort of scientific test you heathen humanitarians seem to trust when you are thinking of taking away the life and honour of a man.'

Fiennes sat gaping for an instant before he found breath to say: 'Why, what's the matter with you? What have I done now?' A sort of anxiety came back into the priest's eyes—the anxiety of a man who has run against a post in the dark and wonders for a moment whether he has hurt it.

'I'm most awfully sorry,' he said with sincere distress. 'I beg your pardon for being so rude; pray forgive me.'

Fiennes looked at him curiously. 'I sometimes think you are more of a mystery than any of the mysteries,' he said. 'But anyhow, if you don't believe in the mystery of the dog, at least you can't get over the mystery of the man. You can't deny that at the very moment when the beast came back from the sea and bellowed, his master's soul was driven out of his body by the blow of some unseen power that no mortal man can trace or even imagine. And as for the lawyer—I don't go only by the dog—there are other curious details, too. He struck me as a smooth, smiling, equivocal sort of person; and one of his tricks seemed like a sort of hint. You know the doctor and the police were on the spot very quickly; Valentine was brought back when walking away from the house, and he telephoned instantly. That, with the secluded house, small numbers, and enclosed space, made it pretty possible to search everybody who could have been near; and everybody was thoroughly searched for a weapon. The whole house, garden, and shore were combed for a weapon. The disappearance of the dagger is almost as crazy as the disappearance of the man.'

'The disappearance of the dagger,' said Father Brown, nodding. He seemed to have become suddenly attentive.

'Well,' continued Fiennes, 'I told you that man Traill had a trick of fidgeting with his tie and tie-pin—especially his tie-pin. His pin, like himself, was at once showy and old-fashioned. It had one of those stones with concentric coloured rings that look like an eye; and his own concentration on it got on my nerves, as if he had been a Cyclops with one eye in the middle of his body. But the pin was not only large but long; and it occurred to me that his anxiety about its adjustment was because it was even longer than it looked; as long as a stiletto in fact.'

Father Brown nodded thoughtfully. 'Was any other instrument ever suggested?' he asked.

'There was another suggestion,' answered Fiennes, 'from one of the young Druces—the cousins, I mean. Neither Herbert nor Harry Druce would have struck one at first as likely to be of assistance in scientific detection; but while Herbert was really the traditional type of heavy Dragoon, caring for nothing but horses and being an ornament to the Horse Guards, his younger brother Harry had been in the Indian Police and knew something about such things. Indeed, in his own way he was quite clever; and I rather fancy he had been too clever; I mean he had left the police through breaking some red-tape regulations and taking some sort of risk and responsibility of his own. Anyhow, he was in some sense a detective out of work, and threw himself into this business with more than the ardour of an amateur. And it was with him that I had an argument about the weapon—an argument that led to something new. It began by his countering my description of the dog barking at Traill; and he said that a dog at his worst didn't bark, but growled.'

'He was quite right there,' observed the priest.

'This young fellow went on to say that, if it came to that, he'd heard Nox growling at other people before then; and among others at Floyd, the secretary. I retorted that his own argument answered itself; for the crime couldn't be brought home to two or three people, and least of all to Floyd, who was as innocent as a harum-scarum schoolboy, and had been seen by everybody all the time perched above the garden hedge with his fan of red hair as conspicuous as a scarlet cockatoo.

'I know there's difficulties anyhow,' said my colleague, 'but I wish you'd come with me down the garden a minute. I want to show you something I don't think anyone else has seen.' This was on the very day of the discovery, and the garden was just as it had been. The step-ladder was still standing by the hedge, and just under the hedge my guide stopped and disentangled something from the deep grass. It was the sheers used for clipping the hedge, and on the point of one of them was a smear of blood.'

There was a short silence, and then Father Brown said suddenly; 'What was the lawyer there for?'

'He told us the Colonel sent for him to alter his will,' answered Fiennes. 'And, by the way, there was another thing about the business of the will that I ought to mention. You see, the will wasn't actually signed in the summer-house that afternoon.'

'I suppose not,' said Father Brown; 'there would have to be two witnesses.'

'The lawyer actually came down the day before and it was signed then; but he was sent for again next day because the old man had a doubt about one of the witnesses and had to be reassured.'

'Who were the witnesses?' asked Father Brown.

'That's just the point,' replied his informant eagerly, 'the witnesses were Floyd, the secretary, and this Dr Valentine, the foreign sort of surgeon or whatever he is; and the two had a quarrel. Now I'm bound to say that the secretary is something of a busybody. He's one of those hot and headlong people whose warmth of temperament has unfortunately turned mostly to pugnacity and bristling suspicion; to distrusting people instead of to trusting them. That sort of red-haired red-hot fellow is always either universally credulous or universally incredulous; and sometimes both. He was not only a Jack-of-all-trades, but he knew better than all tradesmen. He not only knew everything, but he warned everybody against everybody. All that must be taken into account in his suspicions about Valentine; but in that particular case there seems to have been something behind it. He said the name of Valentine was not really Valentine. He said he had seen him elsewhere known by the name of De Villon. He said it would invalidate the will; of course he was kind enough to explain to the lawyer what the law was on that point. They were both in a frightful wax.'

Father Brown laughed. 'People often are when they are to witness a will,' he said; 'for one thing, it means that they can't have any legacy under it. But what did Dr Valentine say? No doubt the universal secretary knew more about the doctor's name than the doctor did. But even the doctor might have some information about his own name.'

Fiennes paused a moment before he replied. 'Dr Valentine took it in a curious way. Dr Valentine is a curious man. His appearance is rather striking but very foreign. He is young but wears a beard cut square; and his face is very pale, dreadfully pale—and dreadfully serious. His eyes have a sort of ache in them, as if he ought to wear glasses, or had given himself a headache with thinking; but he is quite handsome and always very formally dressed, with a top hat and a dark coat and a little red rosette. His manner is rather cold and haughty, and he has a way of staring at you which is very disconcerting. When thus charged with having changed his name, he merely stared like a sphinx and then said with a little laugh that he supposed

Americans had no names to change. At that I think the Colonel also got into a fuss and said all sorts of angry things to the doctor; all the more angry because of the doctor's pretensions to a future place in his family. But I shouldn't have thought much of that but for a few words that I happened to hear later, early in the afternoon of the tragedy. I don't want to make a lot of them, for they weren't the sort of words on which one would like, in the ordinary way, to play the eavesdropper. As I was passing out towards the front gate with my two companions and the dog, I heard voices which told me that Dr Valentine and Miss Druce had withdrawn for a moment in the shadow of the house, in an angle behind a row of flowering plants, and were talking to each other in passionate whisperings—sometimes almost like hissings; for it was something of a lovers' quarrel as well as a lovers' tryst. Nobody repeats the sort of things they said for the most part; but in an unfortunate business like this I'm bound to say that there was repeated more than once a phrase about killing somebody. In fact, the girl seemed to be begging him not to kill somebody, or saying that no provocation could justify killing anybody; which seems an unusual sort of talk to address to a gentleman who has dropped in to tea.'

'Do you know,' asked the priest, 'whether Dr Valentine seemed to be very angry after the scene with the secretary and the Colonel—I mean about witnessing the will?'

'By all accounts,' replied the other, 'he wasn't half so angry as the secretary was. It was the secretary who went away raging after witnessing the will.'

'And now,' said Father Brown,' what about the will itself?'

'The Colonel was a very wealthy man, and his will was important. Traill wouldn't tell us the alteration at that stage, but I have since heard— only this morning in fact—that most of the money was transferred from the son to the daughter. I told you that Druce was wild with my friend Donald over his dissipated hours.'

'The question of motive has been rather overshadowed by the question of method,' observed Father Brown thoughtfully. 'At that moment, apparently, Miss Druce was the immediate gainer by the death.'

'Good God! What a cold-blooded way of talking,' cried Fiennes, staring at him. 'You don't really mean to hint that she—'

'Is she going to marry that Dr Valentine?' asked the other.

'Some people are against it,' answered his friend. 'But he is liked and respected in the place and is a skilled and devoted surgeon.'

'So devoted a surgeon,' said Father Brown, 'that he had surgical instruments with him when he went to call on the young lady at teatime. For he must have used a lancet or something, and he never seems to have gone home.'

Fiennes sprang to his feet and looked at him in a heat of inquiry. 'You suggest he might have used the very same lancet—'

Father Brown shook his head. 'All these suggestions are fancies just now,' he said. 'The problem is not who did it or what did it, but how it was done. We might find many men and even many tools—pins and shears and lancets. But how did a man get into the room? How did even a pin get into it?'

He was staring reflectively at the ceiling as he spoke, but as he said the last words his eye cocked in an alert fashion as if he had suddenly seen a curious fly on the ceiling.

'Well, what would you do about it?' asked the young man. 'You have a lot of experience; what would you advise now?'

'I'm afraid I'm not much use,' said Father Brown with a sigh. 'I can't suggest very much without having ever been near the place or the people. For the moment you can only go on with local inquiries. I gather that your friend from the Indian Police is more or less in charge of your inquiry down there. I should run down and see how he is getting on. See what he's been doing in the way of amateur detection. There may be news already.'

As his guests, the biped and the quadruped, disappeared, Father Brown took up his pen and went back to his interrupted occupation of planning a course of lectures on the Encyclical Rerum Novarum. The subject was a large one and he had to recast it more than once, so that he was somewhat similarly employed some two days later when the big black dog again came bounding into the room and sprawled all over him with enthusiasm and excitement. The master who followed the dog shared the excitement if not the enthusiasm. He had been excited in a less pleasant fashion, for his blue eyes seemed to start from his head and his eager face was even a little pale.

'You told me,' he said abruptly and without preface, 'to find out what Harry Druce was doing. Do you know what he's done?' The priest did not reply, and the young man went on in jerky tones: I'll tell you what he's done. He's killed himself.'

Father Brown's lips moved only faintly, and there was nothing practical about what he was saying—nothing that has anything to do with this story or this world.

'You give me the creeps sometimes,' said Fiennes. 'Did you—did you expect this?'

'I thought it possible,' said Father Brown; 'that was why I asked you to go and see what he was doing. I hoped you might not be too late.'

'It was I who found him,' said Fiennes rather huskily. 'It was the ugliest and most uncanny thing fever knew. I went down that old garden again, and I knew there was something new and unnatural about it besides the murder. The flowers still tossed about in blue masses on each side of the black entrance into the old grey summer-house; but to me the blue flowers looked like blue devils dancing before some dark cavern of the underworld. I looked all round, everything seemed to be in its ordinary place. But the queer notion grew on me that there was something wrong with the very shape of the sky. And then I saw what it was. The Rock of Fortune always rose in the background beyond the garden hedge and against the sea. The Rock of Fortune was gone.'

Father Brown had lifted his head and was listening intently.

'It was as if a mountain had walked away out of a landscape or a moon fallen from the sky; though I knew, of course, that a touch at any time would have tipped the thing over. Something possessed me and I rushed down that garden path like the wind and went crashing through that hedge as if it were a spider's web. It was a thin hedge really, though its undisturbed trimness had made it serve all the purposes of a wall. On the shore I found the loose rock fallen from its pedestal; and poor Harry Druce lay like a wreck underneath it. One arm was thrown round it in a sort of embrace as if he had pulled it down on himself; and on the broad brown sands beside it, in large crazy lettering, he had scrawled the words: 'The Rock of Fortune falls on the Fool'.'

'It was the Colonel's will that did that,' observed Father Brown. 'The young man had staked everything on profiting himself by Donald's disgrace, especially when his uncle sent for him on the same day as the lawyer, and welcomed him with so much warmth. Otherwise he was done; he'd lost his police job; he was beggared at Monte Carlo. And he killed himself when he found he'd killed his kinsman for nothing.'

'Here, stop a minute!' cried the staring Fiennes. 'You're going too fast for me.'

'Talking about the will, by the way,' continued Father Brown calmly,' before I forget it, or we go on to bigger things, there was a simple explanation, I think, of all that business about the doctor's name. I rather fancy I have heard both names before somewhere. The doctor is really a French nobleman with the title of the Marquis de Villon. But he is also an ardent Republican and has abandoned his title and fallen back on the forgotten family surname. 'With your Citizen Riquetti you have puzzled Europe for ten days.'

'What is that?' asked the young man blankly.

'Never mind,' said the priest. 'Nine times out of ten it is a rascally thing to change one's name; but this was a piece of fine fanaticism. That's the point of his sarcasm about Americans having no names—that is, no titles. Now in England the Marquis of Hartington is never called Mr Hartington; but in France the Marquis de Villon is called M. de Villon. So it might well look like a change of name. As for the talk about killing, I fancy that also was a point of French etiquette. The doctor was talking about challenging Floyd to a duel, and the girl was trying to dissuade him.'

'Oh, I see,' cried Fiennes slowly. 'Now I understand what she meant.'

'And what is that about?' asked his companion, smiling.

'Well,' said the young man, 'it was something that happened to me just before I found that poor fellow's body; only the catastrophe drove it out of my head. I suppose it's hard to remember a little romantic idyll when you've just come on top of a tragedy. But as I went down the lanes leading to the Colonel's old place I met his daughter walking with Dr Valentine. She was in mourning, of course, and he always wore black as if he were going to a funeral; but I can't say that their faces were very funereal. Never have I seen two people looking in their own way more respectably radiant and cheerful. They stopped and saluted me, and then she told me they were married and living in a little house on the outskirts of the town, where the doctor was continuing his practice. This rather surprised me, because I knew that her old father's will had left her his property; and I hinted at it delicately by saying I was going along to her father's old place and had half expected to meet her there. But she only laughed and said: 'Oh, we've given up all that. My husband doesn't like heiresses.' And I discovered with some astonishment they really had insisted on restoring the property to poor Donald; so I hope he's had a healthy shock and will treat it sensibly. There was never much really the matter with him; he was very young and his father was not very wise. But it was in connexion with that that she said something I didn't understand at the time; but now I'm sure it must be as you say. She said with a sort of sudden and splendid arrogance that was entirely altruistic:

"I hope it'll stop that red-haired fool from fussing anymore about the will. Does he think my husband, who has given up a crest and a coronet as old as the Crusades for his principles, would kill an old man in a summer-house for a legacy like that?' Then she laughed again and said, 'My husband isn't killing anybody except in the way of business. Why, he didn't even ask his friends to call on the secretary.' Now, of course, I see what she meant.'

'I see part of what she meant, of course,' said Father Brown. 'What did she mean exactly by the secretary fussing about the will?'

Fiennes smiled as he answered, 'I wish you knew the secretary, Father Brown. It would be a joy to you to watch him make things hum, as he calls it. He made the house of mourning hum. He filled the funeral with all the snap and zip of the brightest sporting event. There was no holding him, after something had really happened. I've told you how he used to oversee the gardener as he did the garden, and how he instructed the lawyer in the law. Needless to say, he also instructed the surgeon in the practice of surgery; and as the surgeon was Dr Valentine, you may be sure it ended in accusing him of something worse than bad surgery. The secretary got it fixed in his red head that the doctor had committed the crime, and when the police arrived he was perfectly sublime. Need I say that he became, on the spot, the greatest of all amateur detectives? Sherlock Holmes never towered over Scotland Yard with more Titanic intellectual pride and scorn than Colonel Druce's private secretary over the police investigating Colonel Druce's death. I tell you it was a joy to see him. He strode about with an abstracted air, tossing his scarlet crest of hair and giving curt impatient replies. Of course it was his demeanour during these days that made Druce's daughter so wild with him. Of course he had a theory. It's just the sort of theory a man would have in a book; and Floyd is the sort of man who ought to be in a book. He'd be better fun and less bother in a book.'

'What was his theory?' asked the other.

'Oh, it was full of pep,' replied Fiennes gloomily. 'It would have been glorious copy if it could have held together for ten minutes longer. He said the Colonel was still alive when they found him in the summer-house, and the doctor killed him with the surgical instrument on pretence of cutting the clothes.'

'I see,' said the priest. 'I suppose he was lying flat on his face on the mud floor as a form of siesta.'

'It's wonderful what hustle will do,' continued his informant. 'I believe Floyd would have got his great theory into the papers at any rate, and perhaps had the doctor attested, when all these things were blown sky high as if by dynamite by the discovery of that dead body lying under the Rock of Fortune. And that's what we come back to after all. I suppose the suicide is almost a confession. But nobody will ever know the whole story.'

There was a silence, and then the priest said modestly: 'I rather think I know the whole story.'

Fiennes stared. 'But look here,' he cried; 'how do you come to know the whole story, or to be sure it's the true story? You've been sitting here a hundred miles away writing a sermon; do you mean to tell me you really know what happened already? If you've really come to the end, where in the world do you begin? What started you off with your own story?'

Father Brown jumped up with a very unusual excitement and his first exclamation was like an explosion.

'The dog!' he cried. 'The dog, of course! You had the whole story in your hands in the business of the dog on the beach, if you'd only noticed the dog properly.'

Fiennes stared still more. 'But you told me before that my feelings about the dog were all nonsense, and the dog had nothing to do with it.'

'The dog had everything to do with it,' said Father Brown, 'as you'd have found out if you'd only treated the dog as a dog, and not as God Almighty judging the souls of men.'

He paused in an embarrassed way for a moment, and then said, with a rather pathetic air of apology: 'The truth is, I happen to be awfully fond of dogs. And it seemed to me that in all this lurid halo of dog superstitions nobody was really thinking about the poor dog at all. To begin with a small point, about his barking at the lawyer or growling at the secretary. You asked how I could guess things a hundred miles away; but honestly it's mostly to your credit, for you described people so well that I know the types. A man like Traill, who frowns usually and smiles suddenly, a man who fiddles with things, especially at his throat, is a nervous, easily embarrassed man. I shouldn't wonder if Floyd, the efficient secretary, is nervy and jumpy, too; those Yankee hustlers often are. Otherwise he wouldn't have cut his fingers on the shears and dropped them when he heard Janet Druce scream.

'Now dogs hate nervous people. I don't know whether they make the dog nervous, too; or whether, being after all a brute, he is a bit of a bully; or whether his canine vanity (which is colossal) is simply offended at not being liked. But anyhow there was nothing in poor Nox protesting against those people, except that he disliked them for being afraid of him. Now I know you're awfully clever, and nobody of sense sneers at cleverness. But I sometimes fancy, for instance, that you are too clever to understand animals. Sometimes you are too clever to understand men, especially when they act almost as simply as animals. Animals are very literal; they live in a world of truisms. Take this case: a dog barks at a man and a man runs away from a dog. Now you do not seem to be quite simple enough to see the fact: that the dog barked because he disliked the man and the man fled because he was frightened of the dog. They had no other motives and they needed none; but you must read psychological mysteries into it and suppose the dog had super-normal vision, and was a mysterious mouthpiece of doom. You must suppose the man was running away, not from the dog but from the hangman. And yet, if you come to think if it, all this deeper psychology is exceedingly improbable. If the dog really could completely and consciously realize the murderer of his master he wouldn't stand yapping as he might at a curate at a tea-party; he's much more likely to fly at his throat. And on the other hand, do you really think a man who had hardened his heart to murder an old friend and then walk about smiling at the old friend's family, under the eyes of his old friend's daughter and post-mortem doctor—do you think a man like that would be doubled up by mere remorse because a dog barked? He might feel the tragic irony of it; it might shake his soul, like any other tragic trifle. But he wouldn't rush madly the length of a garden to escape from the only witness whom he knew to be unable to talk. People have a panic like that when they are frightened, not of tragic ironies, but of teeth. The whole thing is simpler than you can understand.

'But when we come to that business by the seashore, things are much more interesting. As you stated them, they were much more puzzling. I didn't understand that tale of the dog going in and out of the water; it didn't seem to me a doggy thing to do. If Nox had been very much upset about something else, he might possibly have refused to go after the stick at all. He'd probably go off nosing in whatever direction he suspected the mischief. But when once a dog is actually chasing a thing, a stone or a stick or a rabbit, my experience is that he won't stop for anything but the most peremptory command, and not always for that. That he should turn round because his mood changed seems to me unthinkable.'

'But he did turn round,' insisted Fiennes; 'and came back without the stick.'

'He came back without the stick for the best reason in the world,' replied the priest. 'He came back because he couldn't find it. He whined because he couldn't find it. That's the sort of thing a dog really does whine about. A dog is a devil of a ritualist. He is as particular about the precise routine of a game as a child about the precise repetition of a fairy-tale. In this case something had gone wrong with the game. He came back to complain seriously of the conduct of the stick. Never had such a thing happened before. Never had an eminent and distinguished dog been so treated by a rotten old walking-stick.'

'Why, what had the walking stick done?' inquired the young man.

'It had sunk,' said Father Brown.

Fiennes said nothing, but continued to stare; and it was the priest who continued: 'It had sunk because it was not really a stick, but a rod of steel with a very thin shell of cane and a sharp point. In other words, it was a sword stick. I suppose a murderer never gets rid of a bloody weapon so oddly and yet so naturally as by throwing it into the sea for a retriever.'

'I begin to see what you mean,' admitted Fiennes; 'but even if a sword-stick was used, I have no guess of how it was used.'

'I had a sort of guess,' said Father Brown, 'right at the beginning when you said the word summer-house. And another when you said that Druce wore a white coat. As long as everybody was looking for a short dagger, nobody thought of it; but if we admit a rather long blade like a rapier, it's not so impossible.'

He was leaning back, looking at the ceiling, and began like one going back to his own first thoughts and fundamentals.

'All that discussion about detective stories like the Yellow Room, about a man found dead in sealed chambers which no one could enter, does not apply to the present case, because it is a summer-house. When we talk of a Yellow Room, or any room, we imply walls that are really homogeneous and impenetrable. But a summer-house is not made like that; it is often made, as it was in this case, of closely interlaced but separate boughs and strips of wood, in which there are chinks here and there. There was one of them just behind Druce's back as he sat in his chair up against the wall. But just as the room was a summer-house, so the chair was a basket-chair. That also was a lattice of loopholes. Lastly, the summer-house was close up under the hedge; and you have just told me that it was really a thin hedge. A man standing outside it could easily see, amid a network of twigs and branches and canes, one white spot of the Colonel's coat as plain as the white of a target.

'Now, you left the geography a little vague; but it was possible to put two and two together. You said the Rock of Fortune was not really high; but you also said it could be seen dominating the garden like a mountain-peak. In other words, it was very near the end of the garden, though your walk had taken you a long way round to it. Also, it isn't likely the young lady really howled so as to be heard half a mile. She gave an ordinary involuntary cry, and yet you heard it on the shore. And among other interesting things that you told me, may I remind you that you said Harry Druce had fallen behind to light his pipe under a hedge.'

Fiennes shuddered slightly. 'You mean he drew his blade there and sent it through the hedge at the white spot. But surely it was a very odd chance and a very sudden choice. Besides, he couldn't be certain the old man's money had passed to him, and as a fact it hadn't.'

Father Brown's face became animated. 'You misunderstand the man's character,' he said, as if he himself had known the man all his life. 'A curious but not unknown type of character. If he had really known the money would come to him, I seriously believe he wouldn't have done it. He would have seen it as the dirty thing it was.'

'Isn't that rather paradoxical?' asked the other.

'This man was a gambler,' said the priest, 'and a man in disgrace for having taken risks and anticipated orders. It was probably for something pretty unscrupulous, for every imperial police is more like a Russian secret police than we like to think. But he had gone beyond the line and failed. Now, the temptation of that type of man is to do a mad thing precisely because the risk will be wonderful in retrospect. He wants to say, 'Nobody but I could have seized that chance or seen that it was then or never. What a wild and wonderful guess it was, when I put all those things together; Donald in disgrace; and the lawyer being sent for; and Herbert and I sent for at the same time—and then nothing more but the way the old man grinned at me and shook hands. Anybody would say I was mad to risk it; but that is how fortunes are made, by the man mad enough to have a little foresight.' In short, it is the vanity of guessing. It is the megalomania of the gambler. The more incongruous the coincidence, the more instantaneous the decision, the more likely he is to snatch the chance. The accident, the very triviality of the white speck and the hole in the hedge intoxicated him like a vision of the world's desire. Nobody clever enough to see such a combination of accidents could be cowardly enough not to use them! That is how the devil talks to the gambler. But the devil himself would hardly have induced that unhappy man to go down in a dull, deliberate way and kill an old uncle from whom he'd always had expectations. It would be too respectable.'

He paused a moment, and then went on with a certain quiet emphasis.

'And now try to call up the scene, even as you saw it yourself. As he stood there, dizzy with his diabolical opportunity, he looked up and saw that strange outline that might have been the image of his own tottering soul; the one great crag poised perilously on the other like a pyramid on its point, and remembered that it was called the Rock of Fortune. Can you guess how such a man at such a moment would read such a signal? I think it strung him up to action and even to vigilance. He who would be a tower must not fear to be a toppling tower. Anyhow, he acted; his next difficulty was to cover his tracks. To be found with a sword-stick, let alone a blood-stained sword-stick, would be fatal in the search that was certain to follow. If he left it anywhere, it would be found and probably traced. Even if he threw it into the sea the action might be noticed, and thought noticeable—unless indeed he could think of some more natural way of covering the action. As you know, he did think of one, and a very good one. Being the only one of you with a watch, he told you it was not yet time to return, strolled a little farther, and started the game of throwing in sticks for the retriever. But how his eyes must have rolled darkly over all that desolate seashore before they alighted on the dog!'

Fiennes nodded, gazing thoughtfully into space. His mind seemed to have drifted back to a less practical part of the narrative.

'It's queer,' he said, 'that the dog really was in the story after all.'

'The dog could almost have told you the story, if he could talk,' said the priest. 'All I complain of is that because he couldn't talk you made up his story for him, and made him talk with the tongues of men and angels. It's part of something I've noticed more and more in the modern world, appearing in all sorts of newspaper rumours and conversational catchwords; something that's arbitrary without being authoritative. People readily swallow the untested claims of this, that, or the other. It's drowning all your old rationalism and scepticism, it's coming in like a sea; and the name of it is superstition.' He stood up abruptly, his face heavy with a sort of frown, and went on talking almost as if he were alone. 'It's the first effect of not believing in God that you lose your common sense and can't see things as they are. Anything that anybody talks about, and says there's a good deal in it, extends itself indefinitely like a vista in a nightmare. And a dog is an omen, and a cat is a mystery, and a pig is a mascot, and a beetle is a scarab, calling up all the menagerie of polytheism from Egypt and old India; Dog Anubis and great green-eyed Pasht and all the holy howling Bulls of Bashan; reeling back to the bestial gods of the beginning, escaping into elephants and snakes and crocodiles; and all because you are frightened of four words:

'He was made Man'.

The young man got up with a little embarrassment, almost as if he had overheard a soliloquy. He called to the dog and left the room with vague but breezy farewells. But he had to call the dog twice, for the dog had remained behind quite motionless for a moment, looking up steadily at Father Brown as the wolf looked at St Francis.

4

THE MIRACLE OF MOON CRESCENT
(First published in *Nash's Magazine*, May 1924)

Moon Crescent was meant in a sense to be as romantic as its name; and the things that happened there were romantic enough in their way. At least it had been an expression of that genuine element of sentiment— historic and almost heroic— which manages to remain side by side with commercialism in the elder cities on the Eastern coast of America. It was originally a curve of classical architecture really recalling that eighteenth-century atmosphere in which men like Washington and Jefferson had seemed to be all the more republicans for being aristocrats. Travellers faced with the recurrent query of what they thought of our city were understood to be specially answerable for what they thought of our Moon Crescent. The very contrasts that confuse its original harmony were characteristic of its survival. At one extremity or horn of the crescent its last windows looked over an enclosure like a strip of a gentleman's park, with trees and hedges as formal as a Queen Anne garden. But immediately round the corner, the other windows, even of the same rooms, or rather 'apartments', looked out on the blank, unsightly wall of a huge warehouse attached to some ugly industry. The apartments of Moon Crescent itself were at that end remodelled on the monotonous pattern of an American hotel, and rose to a height, which, though lower than the colossal warehouse, would have been called a skyscraper in London. But the colonnade that ran round the whole frontage upon the street had a grey and weather-stained stateliness suggesting that the ghosts of the Fathers of the Republic might still be walking to and fro in it. The insides of the rooms, however, were as neat and new as the last New York fittings could make them, especially at the northern end between the neat garden and the blank warehouse wall. They were a system of very small flats, as we should say in England, each consisting of a sitting-room, bedroom, and bathroom, as identical as the hundred cells of a hive. In one of these the celebrated Warren Wynd sat at his desk sorting letters and scattering orders with wonderful rapidity and exactitude. He could only be compared to a tidy whirlwind.

Warren Wynd was a very little man with loose grey hair and a pointed beard, seemingly frail but fierily active. He had very wonderful eyes, brighter than stars and stronger than magnets, which nobody who had ever seen them could easily forget. And indeed in his work as a reformer and regulator of many good works he had shown at least that he had a pair of eyes in his head. All sorts of stories and even legends were told of the miraculous rapidity with which he could form a sound judgement, especially of human character. It was said that he selected the wife who worked with him so long in so charitable a fashion, by picking her out of a whole regiment of women in uniform marching past at some official celebration, some said of the Girl Guides and some of the Women Police. Another story was told of how three tramps, indistinguishable from each other in their community of filth and rags, had presented themselves before him asking for charity. Without a moment's hesitation he had sent one of them to a particular hospital devoted to a certain nervous disorder, had recommended the second to an inebriates' home, and had engaged the third at a handsome salary as his own private servant, a position which he filled successfully for years afterwards. There were, of course, the inevitable anecdotes of his prompt criticisms and curt repartees when brought in contact with Roosevelt, with Henry Ford, and with Mrs Asquith and all other persons with whom an American public man ought to have a historic interview, if only in the newspapers. Certainly he was not likely to be overawed by such personages; and at the moment here in question he continued very calmly his centrifugal whirl of papers, though the man confronting him was a personage of almost equal importance.

Silas T. Vandam, the millionaire and oil magnate, was a lean man with a long, yellow face and blue-black hair, colours which were the less conspicuous yet somehow the more sinister because his face and figure showed dark against the window and the white warehouse wall outside it; he was buttoned up tight in an elegant overcoat with strips of astrakhan. The eager face and brilliant eyes of Wynd, on the other hand, were in the full light from the other window overlooking the little garden, for his chair and desk stood facing it; and though the face was preoccupied, it did not seem unduly preoccupied about the millionaire. Wynd's valet or personal servant, a big, powerful man with flat fair hair, was standing behind his master's desk holding a sheaf of letters; and Wynd's private secretary, a neat, red-haired youth with a sharp face, had his hand already on the door handle, as if guessing some purpose or obeying some gesture of his employer. The room was not only neat, but austere to the point of emptiness; for Wynd, with characteristic thoroughness, had rented the whole floor above, and turned it into a loft or storeroom, where all his other papers and possessions were stacked in boxes and corded bales.

'Give these to the floor-clerk, Wilson,' said Wynd to the servant holding the letters, 'and then get me the pamphlet on the Minneapolis Night Clubs; you'll find it in the bundle marked 'G'. I shall want it in half an hour, but don't disturb me till then. Well, Mr Vandam, I think your proposition sounds very promising; but I can't give a final answer till I've seen the report. It ought to reach me tomorrow afternoon, and I'll phone you at once. I'm sorry I can't say anything more definite just now.'

Mr Vandam seemed to feel that this was something like a polite dismissal; and his sallow, saturnine face suggested that he found a certain irony in the fact.

'Well, I suppose I must be going,' he said.

'Very good of you to call, Mr Vandam,' said Wynd, politely; 'you will excuse my not coming out, as I've something here I must fix at once. Fenner,' he added to the secretary,' show Mr Vandam to his car, and don't come back again for half an hour. I've something here I want to work out by myself; after that I shall want you.'

The three men went out into the hallway together, closing the door behind them. The big servant, Wilson, was turning down the hallway in the direction of the floor-clerk, and the other two moving in the opposite direction towards the lift; for Wynd's apartment was high up on the fourteenth floor. They had hardly gone a yard from the closed door when they became conscious that the corridor was filled with a marching and even magnificent figure. The man was very tall and broad-shouldered, his bulk being the more conspicuous for being clad in white, or a light grey that looked like it, with a very wide white panama hat and an almost equally wide fringe or halo of almost equally white hair. Set in this aureole his face was strong and handsome, like that of a Roman emperor, save that there was something more than boyish, something a little childish, about the brightness of his eyes and the beatitude of his smile. 'Mr Warren Wynd in?' he asked, in hearty tones.

'Mr Warren Wynd is engaged,' said Fenner; 'he must not be disturbed on any account. I may say I am his secretary and can take any message.'

'Mr Warren Wynd is not at home to the Pope or the Crowned Heads,' said Vandam, the oil magnate, with sour satire. 'Mr Warren Wynd is mighty particular. I went in there to hand him over a trifle of twenty thousand dollars on certain conditions, and, he told me to call again like as if I was a call-boy.'

'It's a fine thing to be a boy,' said the stranger, 'and a finer to have a call; and I've got a call he's just got to listen to. It's a call of the great good country out West, where the real American is being made while you're all snoring. Just tell him that Art Alboin of oklahoma City has come to convert him.'

'I tell you nobody can see him,' said the red-haired secretary sharply. 'He has given orders that he is not to be disturbed for half an hour.'

'You folks down East are all against being disturbed,' said the breezy Mr Alboin, 'but I calculate there's a big breeze getting up in the West that will have to disturb you. He's been figuring out how much money must go to this and that stuffy old religion; but I tell you any scheme that leaves out the new Great Spirit movement in Texas and Oklahoma, is leaving out the religion of the future.'

'Oh; I've sized up those religions of the future,' said the millionaire, contemptuously. 'I've been through them with a tooth-comb and they're as mangy as yellow dogs. There was that woman called herself Sophia: ought to have called herself Sapphira, I reckon. Just a plum fraud. Strings tied to all the tables and tambourines. Then there were the Invisible Life bunch; said they could vanish when they liked, and they did vanish, too, and a hundred thousand of my dollars vanished with them. I knew Jupiter Jesus out in Denver; saw him for weeks on end, and he was just a common crook. So was the Patagonian Prophet; you bet he's made a bolt for Patagonia. No, I'm through with all that; from now on I only believe what I see. I believe they call it being an atheist.'

'I guess you got me wrong,' said the man from Oklahoma, almost eagerly. 'I guess I'm as much of an atheist as you are. No supernatural or superstitious stuff in our movement; just plain science. The only real right science is just health, and the only real right health is just breathing. Fill your lungs with the wide air of the prairie and you could blow all your old eastern cities into the sea. You could just puff away their biggest men like thistledown. That's what we do in the new movement out home: we breathe. We don't pray; we breathe.'

'Well, I suppose you do,' said the secretary, wearily. He had a keen, intelligent face which could hardly conceal the weariness; but he had listened to the two monologues with the admirable patience and politeness (so much in contrast with the legends of impatience and insolence) with which such monologues are listened to in America.

'Nothing supernatural,' continued Alboin, 'just the great natural fact behind all the supernatural fancies. What did the Jews want with a God except to breathe into man's nostrils the breath of life? We do the breathing into our own nostrils out in Oklahoma. What's the meaning of the very word Spirit? It's just the Greek for breathing exercises. Life, progress, prophecy; it's all breath.'

'Some would allow it's all wind,' said Vandam; 'but I'm glad you've got rid of the divinity stunt, anyhow.'

The keen face of the secretary, rather pale against his red hair, showed a flicker of some odd feeling suggestive of a secret bitterness.

'I'm not glad,' he said, 'I'm just sure. You seem to like being atheists; so you may be just believing what you like to believe. But. I wish to God there were a God; and there ain't. It's just my luck.'

Without a sound or stir they all became almost creepily conscious at this moment that the group, halted outside Wynd's door, had silently grown from three figures to four. How long the fourth figure had stood there none of the earnest disputants could tell, but he had every appearance of waiting respectfully and even timidly for the opportunity to say something urgent. But to their nervous sensibility he seemed to have sprung up suddenly and silently like a mushroom. And indeed, he looked rather like a big, black mushroom, for he was quite short and his small, stumpy figure was eclipsed by his big, black clerical hat; the resemblance might have been more complete if mushrooms were in the habit of carrying umbrellas, even of a shabby and shapeless sort.

Fenner, the secretary, was conscious of a curious additional surprise at recognizing the figure of a priest; but when the priest turned up a round face under the round hat and innocently asked for Mr Warren Wynd, he gave the regular negative answer rather more curtly than before. But the priest stood his ground.

'I do really want to see Mr Wynd,' he said. 'It seems odd, but that's exactly what I do want to do. I don't want to speak to him. I just want to see him. I just want to see if he's there to be seen.'

'Well, I tell you he's there and can't be seen,' said Fenner, with increasing annoyance. 'What do you mean by saying you want to see if he's there to be seen? Of course he's there. We all left him there five minutes ago, and we've stood outside this door ever since.'

'Well, I want to see if he's all right,' said the priest.

'Why?' demanded the secretary, in exasperation. 'Because I have a serious, I might say solemn, reason,' said the cleric, gravely, 'for doubting whether he is all right.'

'Oh, Lord!' cried Vandam, in a sort of fury; 'not more superstitions.'

'I see I shall have to give my reasons,' observed the little cleric, gravely. 'I suppose I can't expect you even to let me look through the crack of a door till I tell you the whole story.' He was silent a moment as in reflection, and then went on without noticing the wondering faces around him. 'I was walking outside along the front of the colonnade when I saw a very ragged man running hard round the corner at the end of the crescent. He came pounding along the pavement towards me, revealing a great raw-boned figure and a face I knew. It was the face of a wild Irish fellow I once helped a little; I will not tell you his name. When he saw me he staggered, calling me by mine and saying, 'Saints alive, it's Father Brown; you're the only man whose face could frighten me today.'

'I knew he meant he'd been doing some wild thing or other, and I don't think my face frightened him much, for he was soon telling me about it. And a very strange thing it was. He asked me if I knew Warren Wynd, and I said no, though I knew he lived near the top of these flats. He said, 'That's a man who thinks he's a saint of God; but if he knew what I was saying of him he should be ready to hang himself.' And he repeated hysterically more than once, 'Yes, ready to hang himself.' I asked him if he'd done any harm to Wynd, and his answer was rather a queer one. He said: 'I took a pistol and I loaded it with neither shot nor slug, but only with a curse.' As far as I could make out, all he had done was to go down that little alley between this building and the big warehouse, with an old pistol loaded with a blank charge, and merely fire it against the wall, as if that would bring down the building. 'But as I did it,' he said, 'I cursed him with the great curse, that the justice of God should take him by the hair and the vengeance of hell by the heels, and he should be torn asunder like Judas and the world know him no more.'

'Well, it doesn't matter now what else I said to the poor, crazy fellow; he went away quieted down a little, and I went round to the back of the building to inspect. And sure enough, in the little alley at the foot of this wall there lay a rusty antiquated pistol; I know enough about pistols to know it had been loaded only with a little powder, there were the black marks of powder and smoke on the wall, and even the mark of the muzzle, but not even a dent of any bullet. He had left no trace of destruction; he had left no trace of anything, except those black marks and that black curse he had hurled into heaven. So I came back here to ask for this Warren Wynd and find out if he's all right.'

Penner the secretary laughed. 'I can soon settle that difficulty for you. I assure you he's quite all right; we left him writing at his desk only a few minutes ago. He was alone in his flat; it's a hundred feet up from the street, and so placed that no shot could have reached him, even if your friend hadn't fired blank. There's no other entrance to this place but this door, and we've been standing outside it ever since.'

'All the same,' said Father Brown, gravely, 'I should like to look in and see.'

'Well, you can't,' retorted the other. 'Good Lord, you don't tell me you think anything of the curse.'

'You forget,' said the millionaire, with a slight sneer, 'the reverend gentleman's whole business is blessings and cursings. Come, sir, if he's been cursed to hell, why don't you bless him back again? What's the good of your blessings if they can't beat an Irish larrykin's curse?'

'Does anybody believe such things now?' protested the Westerner.

'Father Brown believes a good number of things, I take it,' said Vandam, whose temper was suffering from the past snub and the present bickering. 'Father Brown believes a hermit crossed a river on a crocodile conjured out of nowhere, and then he told the crocodile to die, and it sure did. Father Brown believes that some blessed saint or other died, and had his dead body turned into three dead bodies, to be served out to three parishes that were all I bent on figuring as his hometown. Father Brown believes that a saint hung his cloak on a sunbeam, and another used his for a boat to cross the Atlantic. Father Brown believes the holy donkey had six legs and the house of Loretto flew through the air. He believes in hundreds of stone virgins winking and weeping all day long. It's nothing to him to believe that a man might escape through the keyhole or vanish out of a locked room. I reckon he doesn't take much stock of the laws of nature.'

'Anyhow, I have to take stock in the laws of Warren Wynd,' said the secretary, wearily, 'and it's his rule that he's to be left alone when he says so. Wilson will tell you just the same,' for the large servant who had been sent for the pamphlet, passed placidly down the corridor even as he spoke, carrying the pamphlet, but serenely passing the door. 'He'll go and sit on the bench by the floor-clerk and twiddle his thumbs till he's wanted; but he won't go in before then; and nor will I. I reckon we both know which side our bread is buttered, and it'd take a good many of Father Brown's saint and angels to make us forget it.'

'As for saints and angels—' began the priest.

'It's all nonsense,' repeated Fenner. 'I don't want to say anything offensive, but that sort of thing may be very well for crypts and cloisters and all sorts of moonshiny places. But ghosts can't get through a closed door in an American hotel.'

'But men can open a door, even in an American hotel,' replied Father Brown, patiently. 'And it seems to me the simplest thing would be to open it.'

'It would be simple enough to lose me my job,' answered the secretary, 'and Warren Wynd doesn't like his secretaries so simple as that. Not simple enough to believe in the sort of fairy tales you seem to believe in.'

'Well,' said the priest gravely, 'it is true enough that I believe in a good many things that you probably don't. But it would take a considerable time to explain all the things I believe in, and all the reasons I have for thinking I'm right. It would take about two seconds to open that door and prove I am wrong.'

Something in the phrase seemed to please the more wild and restless spirit of the man from the West.

'I'll allow I'd love to prove you wrong,' said Alboin, striding suddenly past them, 'and I will.'

He threw open the door of the flat and looked in. The first glimpse showed that Warren Wynd's chair was empty. The second glance showed that his room was empty also.

Fenner, electrified with energy in his turn, dashed past the other into the apartment.

'He's in his bedroom,' be said curtly, 'he must be.'

As he disappeared into the inner chamber the other men stood in the empty outer room staring about them. The severity and simplicity of its fittings, which had already been noted, returned on them with a rigid challenge. Certainly in this room there was no question of hiding a mouse, let alone a man. There were no curtains and, what is rare in American arrangements, no cupboards. Even the desk was no more than a plain table with a shallow drawer and a tilted lid. The chairs were hard and high-backed skeletons. A moment after the secretary reappeared at the inner door, having searched the two inner rooms. A staring negation stood in his eyes, and his mouth seemed to move in a mechanical detachment from it as he said sharply: 'He didn't come out through here?'

Somehow the others did not even think it necessary to answer that negation in the negative. Their minds had come up against something like the blank wall of the warehouse that stared in at the opposite window, gradually turning from white to grey as dusk slowly descended with the advancing afternoon. Vandam walked over to the windowsill against which he had leant half an hour before and looked out of the open window. There was no pipe or fire-escape, no shelf or foothold of any kind on the sheer fall to the little by-street below, there was nothing on the similar expanse of wall that rose many stories above. There was even less variation on the other side of the street; there was nothing whatever but the wearisome expanse of whitewashed wall. He peered downwards, as if expecting to see the vanished philanthropist lying in a suicidal wreck on the path. He could see nothing but one small dark object which, though diminished by distance, might well be the pistol that the priest had found lying there. Meanwhile, Fenner had walked to the other window, which looked out from a wall equally blank and inaccessible, but looking out over a small ornamental park instead of a side street. Here a clump of trees interrupted the actual view of the ground; but they reached but a little way up the huge human cliff. Both turned back into the room and faced each other in the gathering twilight where the last silver gleams of daylight on the shiny tops of desks and tables were rapidly turning grey. As if the twilight itself irritated him, Fenner touched the switch and the scene sprang into the startling distinctness of electric light.

'As you said just now,' said Vandam grimly, 'there's no shot from down there could bit him, even if there was a shot in the gun. But even if he was hit with a bullet he wouldn't have just burst like a bubble.'

The secretary, who was paler than ever, glanced irritably at the bilious visage of the millionaire. 'What's got you started on those morbid notions? Who's talking about bullets and bubbles? Why shouldn't he be alive?'

'Why not indeed?' replied Vandam smoothly. 'If you'll tell me where he is, I'll tell you how he got there.'

After a pause the secretary muttered, rather sulkily: 'I suppose you're right. We're right up against the very thing we were talking about. It'd be a queer thing if you or I ever came to think there was anything in cursing. But who could have harmed Wynd shut up in here?'

Mr Alboin, of Oklahoma, had been standing rather astraddle in the middle of the room, his white, hairy halo as well as his round eyes seeming to radiate astonishment. At this point he said, abstractedly, with something of the irrelevant impudence of an enfant terrible: 'You didn't cotton to him much, did you, Mr Vandam?'

Mr Vandam's long yellow face seemed to grow longer as it grew more sinister, while he smiled and answered quietly: 'If it comes to these coincidences, it was you, I think, who said that a wind from the West would blow away out big men like thistledown.'

'I know I said it would,' said the Westerner, with candour; 'but all the same, how the devil could it?'

The silence was broken by Fenner saying with an abruptness amounting to violence: 'There's only one thing to say about this affair. It simply hasn't happened. It can't have happened.'

'Oh, yes,' said Father Brown out of the corner; 'it has happened all right.'

They all jumped; for the truth was they had all forgotten the insignificant little man who had originally induced them to open the door. And the recovery of memory went with a sharp reversal of mood; it came back to them with a rush that they had all dismissed him as a superstitious dreamer for even hinting at the very thing that had since happened before their eyes.

'Snakes!' cried the impetuous Westerner, like one speaking before he could stop himself; 'suppose there were something in it, after all!'

'I must confess,' said Fenner, frowning at the table, 'that his reverence's anticipations were apparently well founded. I don't know whether he has anything else to tell us.'

'He might possibly tell us,' said Vandam, sardonically, 'what the devil we are to do now.'

The little priest seemed to accept the position in a modest, but matter-of-fact manner. 'The only thing I can think of,' he said, 'is first to tell the authorities of this place, and then to see if there were any more traces of my man who let off the pistol. He vanished round the other end of the Crescent where the little garden is. There are seats there, and it's a favourite place for tramps.'

Direct consultations with the headquarters of the hotel, leading to indirect consultations with the authorities of the police, occupied them for a considerable time; and it was already nightfall when they went out under the long, classical curve of the colonnade. The crescent looked as cold and hollow as the moon after which it was named, and the moon itself was rising luminous but spectral behind the black tree-tops when they turned the corner by the little public garden. Night veiled much of what was merely urban and artificial about the place, and as they melted into the shadows of the trees they had a strange feeling of having suddenly travelled many hundred miles from their homes. When they had walked in silence for a little, Alboin, who had something elemental about him, suddenly exploded.

'I give up,' he cried; 'I hand in my checks. I never thought I should come to such things; but what happens when the things come to you? I beg your pardon, Father Brown; I reckon I'll just come across, so far as you and your fairy-tales are concerned. After this, it's me for the fairy-tales. Why, you said yourself, Mr Vandam, that you're an atheist and only believe what you see. Well, what was it you did see? Or rather, what was it you didn't see?'

'I know,' said Vandam and nodded in a gloomy fashion.

'Oh, it's partly all this moon and trees that get on one's nerves,' said Fenner obstinately. 'Trees always look queer by moonlight, with their branches crawling about. Look at that—'

'Yes,' said Father Brown, standing still and peering at the moon through a tangle of trees. 'That's a very queer branch up there.'

When he spoke again he only said: 'I thought it was a broken branch.'

But this time there was a catch in his voice that unaccountably turned his hearers cold. Something that looked rather like a dead branch was certainly dependent in a limp fashion from the tree that showed dark against the moon; but it was not a dead branch. When they came close to it to see what it was Fenner sprang away again with a ringing oath. Then he ran in again and loosened a rope from the neck of the dingy little body dangling with drooping plumes of grey hair. Somehow he knew that the body was a dead body before he managed to take it down from the tree. A very long coil of rope was wrapped round and round the branches, and a comparatively short length of it hung from the fork of the branch to the body. A long garden tub was rolled a yard or so from under the feet, like the stool kicked away from the feet of a suicide.

'Oh, my God!' said Alboin, so that it seemed as much a prayer as an oath. 'What was it that man said about him?—"If he knew, he would be ready to hang himself." Wasn't that what he said, Father Brown?'

'Yes,' said Father Brown.

'Well,' said Vandam in a hollow voice, 'I never thought to see or say such a thing. But what can one say except that the curse has worked?'

Fenner was standing with hands covering his face; and the priest laid a hand on his arm and said, gently, 'Were you very fond of him?'

The secretary dropped his hands and his white face was ghastly under the moon.

'I hated him like hell,' he said; 'and if he died by a curse it might have been mine.'

The pressure of the priest's hand on his arm tightened; and the priest said, with an earnestness he had hardly yet shown: 'It wasn't your curse; pray be comforted.'

The police of the district had considerable difficulty in dealing with the four witnesses who were involved in the case. All of them were reputable, and even reliable people in the ordinary sense; and one of them was a person of considerable power and importance: Silas Vandam of the Oil Trust. The first police-officer who tried to express scepticism about his story struck sparks from the steel of that magnate's mind very rapidly indeed.

'Don't you talk to me about sticking to the facts,' said the millionaire with asperity. 'I've stuck to a good many facts before you were born and a few of the facts have stuck to me. I'll give you the facts all right if you've got the sense to take 'em down correctly.'

The policeman in question was youthful and subordinate, and had a hazy idea that the millionaire was too political to be treated as an ordinary citizen; so he passed him and his companions on to a more stolid superior, one Inspector Collins, a grizzled man with a grimly comfortable way of talking; as one who was genial but would stand no nonsense.

'Well, well,' he said, looking at the three figures before him with twinkling eyes, 'this seems to be a funny sort of a tale.'

Father Brown had already gone about his daily business; but Silas Vandam had suspended even the gigantic business of the markets for an hour or so to testify to his remarkable experience. Fenner's business as secretary had ceased in a sense with his employer's life; and the great Art Alboin, having no business in New York or anywhere else, except the spreading of the Breath of Life religion or the Great Spirit, had nothing to draw him away at the moment from the immediate affair. So they stood in a row in the inspector's office, prepared to corroborate each other.

'Now I'd better tell you to start with,' said the inspector cheerfully, 'that it's no good for anybody to come to me with any miraculous stuff. I'm a practical man and a policeman, and that sort of thing is all very well for priests and parsons. This priest of yours seems to have got you all worked up about some story of a dreadful death and judgement; but I'm going to leave him and his religion out of it altogether. If Wynd came out of that room, somebody let him out. And if Wynd was found hanging on that tree, somebody hung him there.'

'Quite so,' said Fenner; 'but as our evidence is that nobody let him out, the question is how could anybody have hung him there?'

'How could anybody have a nose on his face?' asked the inspector. 'He had a nose on his face, and he had a noose round his neck. Those are facts; and, as I say, I'm a practical man and go by the facts. It can't have been done by a miracle, so it must have been done by a man.'

Alboin had been standing rather in the background; and indeed his broad figure seemed to form a natural background to the leaner and more vivacious men in front of him. His white head was bowed with a certain abstraction; but as the inspector said the last sentence, he lifted it, shaking his hoary mane in a leonine fashion, and looking dazed but awakened. He moved forward into the centre of the group, and they had a vague feeling that he was even vaster than before. They had been only too prone to take him for a fool or a mountebank; but he was not altogether wrong when he said that there was in him a certain depth of lungs and life, like a west wind stored up in its strength, which might some day puff lighter things away.

'So you're a practical man, Mr Collins,' he said, in a voice at once soft and heavy. 'It must be the second or third time you've mentioned in this little conversation that you are a practical man; so I can't be mistaken about that. And a very interesting little fact it is for anybody engaged in writing your life, letters, and table-talk, with portrait at the age of five, daguerreotype of your grandmother and views of the old hometown; and I'm sure your biographer won't forget to mention it along with the fact that you had a pug nose with a pimple on it, and were nearly too fat to walk. And as you're a practical man, perhaps you would just go on practising till you've brought Warren Wynd to life again, and found out exactly how a practical man gets through a deal door. But I think you've got it wrong. You're not a practical man. You're a practical joke; that's what you are.

The Almighty was having a bit of fun with us when he thought of you.'

With a characteristic sense of drama he went sailing towards the door before the astonished inspector could reply; and no after-recriminations could rob him of a certain appearance of triumph.

'I think you were perfectly right,' said Fenner. 'If those are practical men, give me priests.'

Another attempt was made to reach an official version of the event when the authorities fully realized who were the backers of the story, and what were the implications of it. Already it had broken out in the Press in its most sensationally and even shamelessly psychic form. Interviews with Vandam on his marvellous adventure, articles about Father Brown and his mystical intuitions, soon led those who feel responsible for guiding the public, to wish to guide it into a wiser channel. Next time the inconvenient witnesses were approached in a more indirect and tactful manner. They were told, almost in an airy fashion, that Professor Vair was very much interested in such abnormal experiences; was especially interested in their own astonishing case. Professor Vair was a psychologist of great distinction; he had been known to take a detached interest in criminology; it was only some little time afterwards that they discovered that he was in any way connected with the police.

Professor Vair was a courteous gentleman, quietly dressed in pale grey clothes, with an artistic tie and a fair, pointed beard; he looked more like a landscape painter to anyone not acquainted with a certain special type of don. He had an air not only of courtesy, but of frankness.

'Yes, yes, I know,' he said smiling; 'I can guess what you must have gone through. The police do not shine in inquiries of a psychic sort, do they? Of course, dear old Collins said he only wanted the facts. What an absurd blunder! In a case of this kind we emphatically do not only want the facts. It is even more essential to have the fancies.'

'Do you mean,' asked Vandam gravely, 'that all that we thought facts were merely fancies?'

'Not at all,' said the professor; 'I only mean that the police are stupid in thinking they can leave out the psychological element in these things. Well, of course, the psychological element is everything in everything, though it is only just beginning to be understood. To begin with, take the element called personality. Now I have heard of this priest, Father Brown, before; and he is one of the most remarkable men of our time. Men of that sort carry a sort of atmosphere with them; and nobody knows how much his nerves and even his very senses are affected by it for the time being. People are hypnotized—yes, hypnotized; for hypnotism, like everything else, is a matter of degree; it enters slightly into all daily conversation: it is not necessarily conducted by a man in evening-dress on a platform in a public hall. Father Brown's religion has always understood the psychology of atmospheres, and knows bow to appeal to everything simultaneously; even, for instance, to the sense of smell. It understands those curious effects produced by music on animals and human beings; it can—'

'Hang it,' protested Fenner, 'you don't think he walked down the corridor carrying a church organ?'

'He knows better than to do that,' said Professor Vair laughing. 'He knows how to concentrate the essence of all these spiritual sounds and sights, and even smells, in a few restrained gestures; in an art or school of manners. He could contrive so to concentrate your minds on the supernatural by his mere presence, that natural things slipped off your minds to left and right unnoticed. Now you know,' he proceeded with a return to cheerful good sense, 'that the more we study it the more queer the whole question of human evidence becomes. There is not one man in twenty who really observes things at all. There is not one man in a hundred who observes them with real precision; certainly not one in a hundred who can first observe, then remember, and finally describe. Scientific experiments have been made again and again showing that men under strain have thought a door was shut when it was open, or open when it was shut. Men have differed about the number of doors or windows in a wall just in front of them. They have suffered optical illusions in broad daylight. They have done this even without the hypnotic effect of personality; but here we have a very powerful and persuasive personality bent upon fixing only one picture on your minds; the picture of the wild Irish rebel shaking his pistol at the sky and firing that vain volley, whose echoes were the thunders of heaven.'

'Professor,' cried Fenner, 'I'd swear on my deathbed that door never opened.'

'Recent experiments,' went on the professor, quietly, 'have suggested that our consciousness is not continuous, but is a succession of very rapid impressions like a cinema; it is possible that somebody or something may, so to speak, slip in or out between the scenes. It acts only in the instant while the curtain is down. Probably the patter of conjurors and all forms of sleight of hand depend on what we may call these black flashes of blindness between the flashes of sight. Now this priest and preacher of transcendental notions had filled you with a transcendental imagery; the image of the Celt like a Titan shaking the tower with his curse. Probably he accompanied it with some slight but compelling gesture, pointing your eyes and minds in the direction of the unknown destroyer below. Or perhaps something else happened, or somebody else passed by.'

'Wilson, the servant,' grunted Alboin, 'went down the hallway to wait on the bench, but I guess he didn't distract us much.'

'You never know how much,' replied Vair; 'it might have been that or more likely your eyes following some gesture of the priest as he told his tale of magic. It was in one of those black flashes that Mr Warren Wynd slipped out of his door and went to his death. That is the most probable explanation. It is an illustration of the new discovery. The mind is not a continuous line, but rather a dotted line.'

'Very dotted,' said Fenner feebly. 'Not to say dotty.'

'You don't really believe,' asked Vair, 'that your employer was shut up in a room like a box?'

'It's better than believing that I ought to be shut up in a room like a padded cell,' answered Fenner. 'That's what I complain of in your suggestions, professor. I'd as soon believe in a priest who believes in a miracle, as disbelieve in any man having any right to believe in a fact. The priest tells me that a man can appeal to a God I know nothing about to avenge him by the laws of some higher justice that I know nothing about. There's nothing for me to say except that I know nothing about it. But, at least, if the poor Paddy's prayer and pistol could be heard in a higher world, that higher world might act in some way that seems odd to us. But you ask me to disbelieve the facts of this world as they appear to my own five wits. According to you, a whole procession of Irishmen carrying blunderbusses may have walked through this room while we were talking, so long as they took care to tread on the blind spots in our minds. Miracles of the monkish sort, like materializing a crocodile or hanging a cloak on a sunbeam, seem quite sane compared to you.'

'Oh, well,' said Professor Vair, rather curtly, 'if you are resolved to believe in your priest and his miraculous Irishman I can say no more. I'm afraid you have not had an opportunity of studying psychology.'

'No,' said Fenner dryly; 'but I've had an opportunity of studying psychologists.'

And, bowing politely, he led his deputation out of the room and did not speak till he got into the street; then he addressed them rather explosively.

'Raving lunatics!' cried Fenner in a fume. 'What the devil do they think is to happen to the world if nobody knows whether he's seen anything or not? I wish I'd blown his silly head off with a blank charge, and then explained that I did it in a blind flash. Father Brown's miracle may be miraculous or no, but he said it would happen and it did happen. All these blasted cranks can do is to see a thing happen and then say it didn't. Look here, I think we owe it to the padre to testify to his little demonstration. We're all sane, solid men who never believed in anything. We weren't drunk. We weren't devout. It simply happened just as he said it would.'

'I quite agree,' said the millionaire. 'It may be the beginning of mighty big things in the spiritual line; but anyhow, the man who's in the spiritual line himself, Father Brown, has certainly scored over this business.'

A few days afterwards Father Brown received a very polite note signed Silas T. Vandam, and asking him if he would attend at a stated hour at the apartment which was the scene of the disappearance, in order to take steps for the establishment of that marvellous occurrence. The occurrence itself had already begun to break out in the newspapers, and was being taken up everywhere by the enthusiasts of occultism. Father Brown saw the flaring posters inscribed 'Suicide of Vanishing Man', and 'Man's Curse Hangs Philanthropist', as he passed towards Moon Crescent and mounted the steps on the way to the elevator. He found the little group much as he left it, Vandam, Alboin, and the secretary; but there was an entirely new respectfulness and even reverence in their tone towards himself. They were standing by Wynd's desk, on which lay a large paper and writing materials; they turned to greet him.

'Father Brown,' said the spokesman, who was the white-haired Westerner, somewhat sobered with his responsibility, 'we asked you here in the first place to offer our apologies and our thanks. We recognize that it was you that spotted the spiritual manifestation from the first. We were hard-shell sceptics, all of us; but we realize now that a man must break that shell to get at the great things behind the world. You stand for those things; you stand for the supernormal explanation of things; and we have to hand it to you. And in the second place, we feel that this document would not be complete without your signature. We are notifying the exact facts to the Psychical Research Society, because the newspaper accounts are not what you might call exact. We've stated how the curse was spoken out in the street; how the man was sealed up here in a room like a box; how the curse dissolved him straight into thin air, and in some unthinkable way materialized him as a suicide hoisted on a gallows. That's all we can say about it; but all that we know, and have seen with our own eyes. And as you were the first to believe in the miracle, we all feel that you ought to be the first to sign.'

'No, really,' said Father Brown, in embarrassment. 'I don't think I should like to do that.'

'You mean you'd rather not sign first?'

'I mean I'd rather not sign at all,' said Father Brown, modestly. 'You see, it doesn't quite do for a man in my position to joke about miracles.'

'But it was you who said it was a miracle,' said Alboin, staring.

'I'm so sorry,' said Father Brown; 'I'm afraid there's some mistake. I don't think I ever said it was a miracle. All I said was that it might happen. What you said was that it couldn't happen, because it would be a miracle if it did. And then it did. And so you said it was a miracle. But I never said a word about miracles or magic, or anything of the sort from beginning to end.'

'But I thought you believed in miracles,' broke out the secretary.

'Yes,' answered Father Brown, 'I believe in miracles. I believe in man-eating tigers, but I don't see them running about everywhere. If I want any miracles, I know where to get them.'

'I can't understand your taking this line, Father Brown,' said Vandam, earnestly. 'It seems so narrow; and you don't look narrow to me, though you are a parson. Don't you see, a miracle like this will knock all materialism endways? It will just tell the whole world in big print that spiritual powers can work and do work. You'll be serving religion as no parson ever served it yet.'

The priest had stiffened a little and seemed in some strange way clothed with unconscious and impersonal dignity, for all his stumpy figure. 'Well,' he said, 'you wouldn't suggest I should serve religion by what I know to be a lie? I don't know precisely what you mean by the phrase; and, to be quite candid, I'm not sure you do. Lying may be serving religion; I'm sure it's not serving God. And since you are harping so insistently on what I believe, wouldn't it be as well if you had some sort of notion of what it is?'

'I don't think I quite understand,' observed the millionaire, curiously.

'I don't think you do,' said Father Brown, with simplicity. 'You say this thing was done by spiritual powers. What spiritual powers? You don't think the holy angels took him and hung him on a garden tree, do you? And as for the unholy angels—no, no, no. The men who did this did a wicked thing, but they went no further than their own wickedness; they weren't wicked enough to be dealing with spiritual powers. I know something about Satanism, for my sins; I've been forced to know. I know what it is, what it practically always is. It's proud and it's sly. It likes to be superior; it loves to horrify the innocent with things half understood, to make children's flesh creep. That's why it's so fond of mysteries and initiations and secret societies and all the rest of it. Its eyes are turned inwards, and however grand and grave it may look, it's always hiding a small, mad smile.' He shuddered suddenly, as if caught in an icy draught of air. 'Never mind about them; they've got nothing to do with this, believe me. Do you think that poor, wild Irishman of mine, who ran raving down the street, who blurted out half of it when he first saw my face, and ran away for fear he should blurt out more, do you think Satan confides any secrets to him? I admit he joined in a plot, probably in a plot with two other men worse than himself; but for all that, he was just in an everlasting rage when he rushed down the lane and let off his pistol and his curse.'

'But what on earth does all this mean?' demanded Vandam. 'Letting off a toy pistol and a twopenny curse wouldn't do what was done, except by a miracle. It wouldn't make Wynd disappear like a fairy. It wouldn't make him reappear a quarter of a mile away with a rope round his neck.'

'No,' said Father Brown sharply; 'but what would it do?'

'And still I don't follow you,' said the millionaire gravely.

'I say, what would it do?' repeated the priest; showing, for the first time, a sort of animation verging on annoyance. 'You keep on repeating that a blank pistol-shot wouldn't do this and wouldn't do that; that if that was all, the murder wouldn't happen or the miracle wouldn't happen. It doesn't seem to occur to you to ask what would happen. What would happen to you if a lunatic let off a firearm without rhyme or reason right under your window? What's the very first thing that would happen?'

Vandam looked thoughtful. 'I guess I should look out of the window,' he said.

'Yes,' said Father Brown, 'you'd look out of the window. That's the whole story. It's a sad story, but it's finished now; and there were extenuating circumstances.'

'Why should looking out of the window hurt him?' asked Alboin. 'He didn't fall out, or he'd have been found in the lane.'

'No,' said Father Brown, in a low voice. 'He didn't fall. He rose.'

There was something in his voice like the groan of a gong, a note of doom, but otherwise he went on steadily: 'He rose, but not on wings; not on the wings of any holy or unholy angels. He rose at the end of a rope, exactly as you saw him in the garden; a noose dropped over his head the moment it was poked out of the window. Don't you remember Wilson, that big servant of his, a man of huge strength, while Wynd was the lightest of little shrimps? Didn't Wilson go to the floor above to get a pamphlet, to a room full of luggage corded in coils and coils of rope? Has Wilson been seen since that day? I fancy not.'

'Do you mean,' asked the secretary, 'that Wilson whisked him clean out of his own window like a trout on a line?'

'Yes,' said the other, 'and let him down again out of the other window into the park, where the third accomplice hooked him on to a tree. Remember the lane was always empty; remember the wall opposite was quite blank; remember it was all over in five minutes after the Irishman gave the signal with the pistol. There were three of them in it of course; and I wonder whether you can all guess who they were.'

They were all three staring at the plain, square window and the blank, white wall beyond; and nobody answered.

'By the way,' went on Father Brown, 'don't think I blame you for jumping to preternatural conclusions. The reason's very simple, really. You all swore you were hard-shelled materialists; and as a matter of fact you were all balanced on the very edge of belief—of belief in almost anything. There are thousands balanced on it today; but it's a sharp, uncomfortable edge to sit on. You won't rest till you believe something; that's why Mr Vandam went through new religions with a tooth-comb, and Mr Alboin quotes Scripture for his religion of breathing exercises, and Mr Fenner grumbles at the very God he denies. That's where you all split; it's natural to believe in the supernatural. It never feels natural to accept only natural things. But though it wanted only a touch to tip you into preternaturalism about these things, these things really were only natural things. They were not only natural, they were almost unnaturally simple. I suppose there never was quite so simple a story as this.'

Fenner laughed and then looked puzzled. 'I don't understand one thing,' he said. 'If it was Wilson, how did Wynd come to have a man like that on such intimate terms? How did he come to be killed by a man he'd seen every day for years? He was famous as being a judge of men.'

Father Brown thumped his umbrella on the ground with an emphasis he rarely showed.

'Yes,' he said, almost fiercely; 'that was how he came to be killed. He was killed for just that. He was killed for being a judge of men.'

They all stared at him, but he went on, almost as if they were not there.

'What is any man that he should be a judge of men?' he demanded. 'These three were the tramps that once stood before him and were dismissed rapidly right and left to one place or another; as if for them there were no cloak of courtesy, no stages of intimacy, no free-will in friendship. And twenty years has not exhausted the indignation born of that unfathomable insult in that moment when he dared to know them at a glance.'

'Yes,' said the secretary; 'I understand ... and I understand how it is that you understand—all sorts of things.'

'Well, I'm blamed if I understand,' cried the breezy Western gentleman boisterously. 'Your Wilson and your Irishman seem to be just a couple of cutthroat murderers who killed their benefactor. I've no use for a black and bloody assassin of that sort, in my morality, whether it's religion or not.'

'He was a black and bloody assassin, no doubt,' said Fenner quietly. 'I'm not defending him; but I suppose it's Father Brown's business to pray for all men, even for a man like—'

'Yes,' assented Father Brown, 'it's my business to pray for all men, even for a man like Warren Wynd.'

5

THE CURSE OF THE GOLDEN CROSS
(First published in *Nash's Magazine,* May 1925)

Six people sat around a small table, seeming almost as incongruous and accidental as if they had been shipwrecked separately on the same small desert island. At least the sea surrounded them; for in one sense their island was enclosed in another island, a large and flying island like Laputa. For the little table was one of many little tables dotted about in the dining saloon of that monstrous ship the Moravia, speeding through the night and the everlasting emptiness of the Atlantic. The little company had nothing in common except that all were travelling from America to England. Two of them at least might be called celebrities; others might be called obscure, and in one or two cases even dubious.

The first was the famous Professor Smaill, an authority on certain archaeological studies touching the later Byzantine empire. His lectures, delivered in an American University, were accepted as of the first authority even in the most authoritative seats of learning in europe. His literary works were so steeped in a mellow and imaginative sympathy with the european past, that it often gave strangers a start to hear him speak with an American accent. Yet he was, in his way, very American; he had long fair hair brushed back from a big square forehead, long straight features and a curious mixture of preoccupation with a poise of potential swiftness, like a lion pondering absent-mindedly on his next leap.

There was only one lady in the group; and she was (as the journalists often said of her) a host in herself; being quite prepared to play hostess, not to say empress, at that or any other table. She was Lady Diana Wales, the celebrated lady traveller in tropical and other countries; but there was nothing rugged or masculine about her appearance at dinner. She was herself handsome in an almost tropical fashion, with a mass of hot and heavy red hair; she was dressed in what the journalists call a daring fashion, but her face was intelligent and her eyes had that bright and rather prominent appearance which belongs to the eyes of ladies who ask questions at political meetings.

The other four figures seemed at first like shadows in this shining presence; but they showed differences on a close view. One of them was a young man entered on the ship's register as Paul T. Tarrant. He was an American type which might be more truly called an American antitype. Every nation probably has an antitype; a sort of extreme exception that proves the national rule. Americans really respect work, rather as Europeans respect war. There is a halo of heroism about it; and he who shrinks from it is less than a man. The antitype is evident through being exceedingly rare. He is the dandy or dude: the wealthy waster who makes a weak villain for so many American novels. Paul Tarrant seemed to have nothing whatever to do but change his clothes, which he did about six times a day; passing into paler or richer shades of his suit of exquisite light grey, like the delicate silver changes of the twilight. Unlike most Americans, he cultivated very carefully a short, curly beard; and unlike most dandies, even of his own type, he seemed rather sulky than showy. Perhaps there was something almost Byronic about his silence and his gloom.

The next two travellers were naturally classed together; merely because they were both English lecturers returning from an American tour. One of them was described as Leonard Smyth, apparently a minor poet, but something of a major journalist; long-headed, light-haired, perfectly dressed, and perfectly capable of looking after himself. The other was a rather comic contrast, being short and broad, with a black, walrus moustache, and as taciturn as the other was talkative. But as he had been both charged with robbing and praised for rescuing a Roumanian Princess threatened by a jaguar in his travelling menagerie, and had thus figured in a fashionable case, it was naturally felt that his views on God, progress, his own early life, and the future of Anglo-American relations would be of great interest and value to the inhabitants of Minneapolis and Omaha. The sixth and most insignificant figure was that of a little English priest going by the name of Brown. He listened to the conversation with respectful attention, and he was at that moment forming the impression that there was one rather curious thing about it.

'I suppose those Byzantine studies of yours, Professor,' Leonard Smyth was saying, 'would throw some light on this story of a tomb found somewhere on the south coast; near Brighton, isn't it? Brighton's a long way from Byzantium, of course. But I read something about the style of burying or embalming or something being supposed to be Byzantine.'

'Byzantine studies certainly have to reach a long way,' replied the Professor dryly. 'They talk about specialists; but I think the hardest thing on earth is to specialize. In this case, for instance: how can a man know anything about Byzantium till he knows everything about Rome before it and about Islam after it? Most Arab arts were old Byzantine arts. Why, take algebra—'

'But I won't take algebra,' cried the lady decisively. 'I never did, and I never do. But I'm awfully interested in embalming. I was with Gatton, you know, when he opened the Babylonian tombs. Ever since then I found mummies and preserved bodies and all that perfectly thrilling. Do tell us about this one.'

'Gatton was an interesting man,' said the Professor. 'They were an interesting family. That brother of his who went into Parliament was much more than an ordinary politician. I never understood the Fascisti till he made that speech about Italy.'

'Well, we're not going to Italy on this trip,' said Lady Diana persistently, 'and I believe you're going to that little place where they've found the tomb. In Sussex, isn't it?'

'Sussex is pretty large, as these little English sections go,' replied the Professor. 'One might wander about in it for a goodish time; and it's a good place to wander in. It's wonderful how large those low hills seem when you're on them.'

There was an abrupt accidental silence; and then the lady said, 'Oh, I'm going on deck,' and rose, the men rising with her. But the Professor lingered and the little priest was the last to leave the table, carefully folding up his napkin. And as they were thus left alone together the Professor said suddenly to his companion:

'What would you say was the point of that little talk?'

'Well,' said Father Brown, smiling, 'since you ask me, there was something that amused me a little. I may be wrong; but it seemed to me that the company made three attempts to get you to talk about an embalmed body said to be found in Sussex. And you, on your side, very courteously offered to talk—first about algebra, and then about the Fascisti, and then about the landscape of the Downs.'

'In short,' replied the Professor, 'you thought I was ready to talk about any subject but that one. You were quite right.'

The Professor was silent for a little time, looking down at the tablecloth; then he looked up and spoke with that swift impulsiveness that suggested the lion's leap.

'See here, Father Brown,' he said, 'I consider you about wisest and whitest man I ever met.'

Father Brown was very English. He had all the normal nation helplessness about what to do with a serious and sincere compliment suddenly handed to him to his face in the American manner. His reply was a meaningless murmur; and it was the Professor who proceeded, with the same staccato earnestness: 'You see, up to a point it's all simple enough. A Christian tomb of the Dark Ages, apparently that of a bishop, has been found under a little church at Dulham on the Sussex coast. The Vicar happens to be a good bit of an archaeologist himself and has been able to find a good deal more than I know yet. There was a rumour of the corpse being embalmed in a way peculiar to Greeks and Egyptians but unknown in the West, especially at that date. So Mr Walters (that is the Vicar) naturally wonders about Byzantine influences. But he also mentions something else, that is of even more personal interest to me.'

His long grave face seemed to grow even longer and graver as he frowned down at the tablecloth. His long finger seemed to be tracing patterns on it like the plans of dead cities and their temples and tombs.

'So I'm going to tell you, and nobody else, why it is I have to be careful about mentioning that matter in mixed company; and why, the more eager they are to talk about it, the more cautious I have to be. It is also stated that in the coffin is a chain with a cross, common enough to look at, but with a certain secret symbol on the back found on only one other cross in the world. It is from the arcana of the very earliest Church, and is supposed to indicate St Peter setting up his See at Antioch before he came to Rome. Anyhow, I believe there is but one other like it, and it belongs to me. I hear there is some story about a curse on it; but I take no notice of that. But whether or no there is a curse, there really is, in one sense, a conspiracy; though the conspiracy should only consist of one man.'

'Of one man?' repeated Father Brown almost mechanically.

'Of one madman, for all I know,' said Professor Smaill. 'It's a long story and in some ways a silly one.'

He paused again, tracing plans like architectural drawings with his finger on the cloth, and then resumed: 'Perhaps I had better tell you about it from the beginning, in case you see some little point in the story that is meaningless to me. It began years and years ago, when I was conducting some investigations on my own account in the antiquities of Crete and the Greek islands. I did a great deal of it practically single-handed; sometimes with the most rude and temporary help from the inhabitants of the place, and sometimes literally alone. It was under the latter circumstances that I found a maze of subterranean passages which led at last to a heap of rich refuse, broken ornaments and scattered gems which I took to be the ruins of some sunken altar, and in which I found the curious gold cross. I turned it over, and on the back of it I saw the Ichthus or fish, which was an early Christian symbol, but of a shape and pattern rather different from that commonly found; and, as it seemed to me, more realistic—more as if the archaic designer had meant it to be not merely a conventional enclosure or nimbus, but to look a little more like a real fish. It seemed to me that there was a flattening towards one end of it that was not like mere mathematical decoration, but rather like a sort of rude or even savage zoology.

'In order to explain very briefly why I thought this find important, I must tell you the point of the excavation. For one thing, it had something of the nature of an excavation of an excavation. We were on the track not only of antiquities, but of the antiquarians of antiquity. We had reason to believe, or some of us thought we had reason to believe, that these underground passages, mostly of the Minoan period, like that famous one which is actually identified with the labyrinth of the Minotaur, had not really been lost and left undisturbed for all the ages between the Minotaur and the modern explorer. We believed that these underground places, I might almost say these underground towns and villages, had already been penetrated during the intervening period by some persons prompted by some motive. About the motive there were different schools of thought: some holding that the Emperors had ordered an official exploration out of mere scientific curiosity; others that the furious fashion in the later Roman Empire for all sorts of lurid Asiatic superstitions had started some nameless Manichaean sect or other rioting in the caverns in orgies that had to be hidden from the face of the sun. I belong to the group which believed that these caverns had been used in the same way as the catacombs. That is, we believed that, during some of the persecutions which spread like a fire over the whole Empire, the Christians had concealed themselves in these ancient pagan labyrinths of stone. It was therefore with a thrill as sharp I as a thunderclap that I found and picked up the fallen golden cross and saw the design upon it; and it was with still more of a shock of felicity that, on turning to make my way once more outwards and upwards into the light of day, I looked up at the walls of bare rock that extended endlessly along the low passages, and saw scratched in yet ruder outline, but if possible more unmistakable, the shape of the Fish.

'Something about it made it seem as if it might be a fossil fish or some rudimentary organism fixed forever in a frozen sea. I could not analyse this analogy, otherwise unconnected with a mere drawing scratched upon the stone, till I realized that I was saying in my subconscious mind that the first Christians must have seemed something like fish, dumb and dwelling in a fallen world of twilight and silence, dropped far below the feet of men and moving in dark and twilight and a soundless world.

'Everyone walking along stone passages knows what it is to be followed by phantom feet. The echo follows flapping or clapping behind or in front, so that it is almost impossible for the man who is really lonely to believe in his loneliness. I had got used to the effects of this echo and had not noticed it much for some time past, when I caught sight of the symbolical shape scrawled on the wall of rock. I stopped, and at the same instant it seemed as if my heart stopped, too; for my own feet had halted, but the echo went marching on.

'I ran forward, and it seemed as if the ghostly footsteps ran also, but not with that exact imitation which marks the material reverberation of a sound. I stopped again, and the steps stopped also; but I could have sworn they stopped an instant too late; I called out a question; and my cry was answered; but the voice was not my own.

'It came round the corner of a rock just in front of me; and throughout that uncanny chase I noticed that it was always at some such angle of the crooked path that it paused and spoke. The little space in front of me that could be illuminated by my small electric torch was always as empty as an empty room. Under these conditions I had a conversation with I know not whom, which lasted all the way to the first white gleam of daylight, and even there I could not see in what fashion he vanished into the light of day. But the mouth of the labyrinth was full of many openings and cracks and chasms, and it would not have been difficult for him to have somehow darted back and disappeared again into the underworld of the caves. I only know that I came out on the lonely steps of a great mountain like a marble terrace, varied only with a green vegetation that seemed somehow more tropical than the purity of the rock, like the Oriental invasion that has spread sporadically over the fall of classic Hellas. I looked out on a sea of stainless blue, and the sun shone steadily on utter loneliness and silence; and there was not a blade of grass stirred with a whisper of flight nor the shadow of a shadow of man.

'It had been a terrible conversation; so intimate and so individual and in a sense so casual. This being, bodiless, faceless, nameless and yet calling me by my name, had talked to me in those crypts and cracks where we were buried alive with no more passion or melodrama than if we had been sitting in two armchairs at a club. But he had told me also that he would unquestionably kill me or any other man who came into the possession of the cross with the mark of the fish. He told me frankly he was not fool enough to attack me there in the labyrinth, knowing I had a loaded revolver, and that he ran as much risk as I. But he told me, equally calmly, that he would plan my murder with the certainty of success, with every detail developed and every danger warded off, with the sort of artistic perfection that a Chinese craftsman or an Indian embroiderer gives to the artistic work of a lifetime. Yet he was no Oriental; I am certain be was a white man. I suspect that he was a countryman of my own.

'Since then I have received from time to time signs and symbols and queer impersonal messages that have made me certain, at least, that if the man is a maniac he is a monomaniac. He is always telling me, in this airy and detached way, that the preparations for my death and burial are proceeding satisfactorily; and that the only way in which I can prevent their being crowned with a comfortable success is to give up the relic in my possession—the unique cross that I found in the cavern. He does not seem to have any religious sentiment or fanaticism on the point; he seems to have no passion but the passion of a collector of curiosities. That is one of the things that makes me feel sure he is a man of the West and not of the East. But this particular curiosity seems to have driven him quite crazy.

'And then came this report, as yet unsubstantiated, about the duplicate relic found on an embalmed body in a Sussex tomb. If he had been a maniac before, this news turned him into a demoniac possessed of seven devils. That there should be one of them belonging to another man was bad enough, but that there should be two of them and neither belonging to him was a torture not to be borne. His mad messages began to come thick and fast like showers of poisoned arrows, and each cried out more confidently than the last that death would strike me at the moment when I stretched out my unworthy hand towards the cross in the tomb.

"'You will never know me,' he wrote, 'you will never say my name; you will never see my face; you will die, and never know who has killed you. I may be in any form among those about you; but I shall be in that alone at which you have forgotten to look.'

'From those threats I deduce that he is quite likely to shadow me on this expedition; and try to steal the relic or do me some mischief for possessing it. But as I never saw the man in my life, he may be almost any man I meet. Logically speaking, he may be any of the waiters who wait on me at table. He may be any of the passengers who sit with me at table.'

'He may be me,' said Father Brown, with cheerful contempt for grammar.

'He may be anybody else,' answered Smaill seriously. 'That is what I meant by what I said just now. You are the only man I feel sure is not the enemy.'

Father Brown again looked embarrassed; then he smiled and said: 'Well, oddly enough, I'm not. What we have to consider is any chance of finding out if he really is here before he—before he makes himself unpleasant.'

'There is one chance of finding out, I think,' remarked the Professor rather grimly. 'When we get to Southampton I shall take a car at once along the coast; I should be glad if you would come with me, but in the ordinary sense, of course, our little party will break up. If anyone of them turns up again in that little churchyard on the Sussex coast, we shall know who he really is.'

The Professor's programme was duly carried out, at least to the extent of the car and its cargo in the form of Father Brown. They coasted along the road with the sea on one side and the hills of Hampshire and Sussex on the other; nor was there visible to the eye any shadow of pursuit. As they approached the village of Dulham only one man crossed their path who had any connexion with the matter in hand; a journalist who had just visited the church and been courteously escorted by the vicar through the new excavated chapel; but his remarks and notes seemed to be of the ordinary newspaper sort. But Professor Smaill was perhaps a little fanciful, and could not dismiss the sense of something odd and discouraging in the attitude and appearance of the man, who was tall and shabby, hook-nosed and hollow-eyed, with moustaches that drooped with depression. He seemed anything but enlivened by his late experiment as a sightseer; indeed, he seemed to be striding as fast as possible from the sight, when they stopped him with a question.

'It's all about a curse,' he said; 'a curse on the place, according to the guidebook or the parson, or the oldest inhabitant or whoever is the authority; and really, it feels jolly like it. Curse or curse, I'm glad to have got out of it.'

'Do you believe in curses?' asked Smaill curiously.

'I don't believe in anything; I'm a journalist,' answered the melancholy being—'Boon, of the Daily Wire. But there's a something creepy about that crypt; and I'll never deny I felt a chill.' And he strode on towards the railway station with a further accelerated pace.

'Looks like a raven or a crow, that fellow,' observed Smaill as they turned towards the churchyard. 'What is it they say about a bird of ill omen?'

They entered the churchyard slowly, the eyes of the American antiquary lingering luxuriantly over the isolated roof of the lynch-gate and the large unfathomable black growth of the yew looking like night itself defying the broad daylight. The path climbed up amid heaving levels of turf in which the gravestones were tilted at all angles like stone rafts tossed on a green sea, till it came to the ridge beyond which the great sea itself ran like an iron bar, with pale lights in it like steel. Almost at their feet the tough rank grass turned into a tuft of sea-holly and ended in grey and yellow sand; and a foot or two from the holly, and outlined darkly against the steely sea, stood a motionless figure. But for its dark-grey clothing it might almost have been the statue on some sepulchral monument. But Father Brown instantly recognized something in the elegant stoop of the shoulders and the rather sullen outward thrust of the short beard.

'Gee!' exclaimed the professor of archaeology; 'it's that man Tarrant, if you call him a man. Did you think, when I spoke on the boat, that I should ever get so quick an answer to my question?'

'I thought you might get too many answers to it,' answered Father Brown.

'Why, how do you mean?' inquired the Professor, darting a look at him over his shoulder.

'I mean,' answered the other mildly, 'that I thought I heard voices behind the yew-tree. I don't think Mr Tarrant is so solitary as he looks; I might even venture to say, so solitary as he likes to look.'

Even as Tarrant turned slowly round in his moody manner, the confirmation came. Another voice, high and rather hard, but none the less feminine, was saying with experienced raillery: 'And how was I to know he would be here?' It was borne in upon Professor Smaill that this gay observation was not addressed to him; so he was forced to conclude in some bewilderment, that yet a third person was present. As Lady Diana Wales came out, radiant and resolute as ever, from the shadow of the yew, he noted grimly that she had a living shadow of her own. The lean dapper figure of Leonard Smyth, that insinuating man of letters, appeared immediately behind her own flamboyant form, smiling, his head a little on one side like a dog's.

'Snakes!' muttered Smaill; 'why, they're all here! or all except that little showman with the walrus whiskers.'

He heard Father Brown laughing softly beside him; and indeed the situation was becoming something more than laughable. It seemed to be turning topsy-turvy and tumbling about their ears like a pantomime trick; for even while the Professor had been speaking, his words had received the most comical contradiction. The round head with the grotesque black crescent of moustache had appeared suddenly and seemingly out of a hole in the ground. An instant afterwards they realized that the hole was in fact a very large hole, leading to a ladder which descended into the bowels of the earth; that it was in fact the entrance to the subterranean scene they had come to visit. The little man had been the first to find the entrance and had already descended a rung or two of the ladder before he put his head out again to address his fellow-travellers. He looked like some particularly preposterous gravedigger in a burlesque of Hamlet. He only said thickly behind his thick moustaches, 'It is down here.' But it came to the rest of the company with a start of realization that, though they had sat opposite him at mealtimes for a week, they had hardly ever heard him speak before; and that though he was supposed to be an English lecturer, he spoke with a rather occult foreign accent.

'You see, my dear Professor,' cried Lady Diana with trenchant cheerfulness, 'your Byzantine mummy was simply too exciting to be missed. I simply had to come along and see it; and I'm sure the gentlemen felt just the same. Now you must tell us all about it.'

'I do not know all about it,' said the Professor gravely, not to say grimly, 'In some respects I don't even know what it's all about. It certainly seems odd that we should have all met again so soon, but I suppose there are no limits to the modern thirst for information. But if we are all to visit the place it must be done in a responsible way and, if you will forgive me, under responsible leadership. We must notify whoever is in charge of the excavations; we shall probably at least have to put our names in a book.'

Something rather like a wrangle followed on this collision between the impatience of the lady and the suspicions of the archaeologist; but the latter's insistence on the official rights of the Vicar and the local investigation ultimately prevailed; the little man with the moustaches came reluctantly out of his grave again and silently acquiesced in a less impetuous descent. Fortunately, the clergyman himself appeared at this stage—a grey-haired, good-looking gentleman with a droop accentuated by doublet eyeglasses; and while rapidly establishing sympathetic relations with the Professor as a fellow-antiquarian, he did not seem to regard his rather motley group of companions with anything more hostile than amusement.

'I hope you are none of you superstitious,' he said pleasantly. 'I ought to tell you, to start with, that there are supposed to be all sorts of bad omens and curses hanging over our devoted heads in this business. I have just been deciphering a Latin inscription which was found over the entrance to the chapel; and it would seem that there are no less than three curses involved; a curse for entering the sealed chamber, a double curse for opening the coffin, and a triple and most terrible curse for touching the gold relic found inside it. The two first maledictions I have already incurred myself,' he added with a smile; 'but I fear that even you will have to incur the first and mildest of them if you are to see anything at all. According to the story, the curses descend in a rather lingering fashion, at long intervals and on later occasions. I don't know whether that is any comfort to you.' And the Reverend Mr Walters smiled once more in his drooping and benevolent manner.

'Story,' repeated Professor Smaill, 'why, what story is that?'

'It is rather a long story and varies, like other local legends,' answered the Vicar. 'But it is undoubtedly contemporary with the time of the tomb; and the substance of it is embodied in the inscription and is roughly this: Guy de Gisors, a lord of the manor here early in the thirteenth century, had set his heart on a beautiful black horse in the possession of an envoy from Genoa, which that practical merchant prince would not sell except for a huge price. Guy was driven by avarice to the crime of pillaging the shrine and, according to one story, even killing the bishop, who was then resident there. Anyhow, the bishop uttered a curse which was to fall on anybody who should continue to withhold the gold cross from its resting-place in his tomb, or should take steps to disturb it when it had returned there. The feudal lord raised the money for the horse by selling the gold relic to a goldsmith in the town; but on the first day he mounted the horse the animal reared and threw him in front of the church porch, breaking his neck. Meanwhile the goldsmith, hitherto wealthy and prosperous, was ruined by a series of inexplicable accidents, and fell into the power of a Jew moneylender living in the manor. Eventually the unfortunate goldsmith, faced with nothing but starvation, hanged himself on an apple-tree. The gold cross with all his other goods, his house, shop, and tools, had long ago passed into the possession of the moneylender. Meanwhile, the son and heir of the feudal lord, shocked by the judgement on his blasphemous sire, had become a religious devotee in the dark and stern spirit of those times, and conceived it his duty to persecute all heresy and unbelief among his vassals. Thus the Jew, in his turn, who had been cynically tolerated by the father, was ruthlessly burnt by order of the son; so that he, in his turn, suffered for the possession of the relic; and after these three judgements, it was returned to the bishop's tomb; since when no eye has seen and no hand has touched it.'

Lady Diana Wales seemed to be more impressed than might have been expected. 'It really gives one rather a shiver,' she said, 'to think that we are going to be the first, except the vicar.'

The pioneer with the big moustaches and the broken english did not descend after all by his favourite ladder, which indeed had only been used by some of the workmen conducting the excavation; for the clergyman led them round to a larger and more convenient entrance about a hundred yards away, out of which he himself had just emerged from his investigations underground. Here the descent was by a fairly gradual slope with no difficulties save the increasing darkness; for they soon found themselves moving in single file down a tunnel as black as pitch, and it was some little time before they saw a glimmer of light ahead of them. Once during that silent march there was a sound like a catch in somebody's breath, it was impossible to say whose; and once there was an oath like a dull explosion, and it was in an unknown tongue.

They came out in a circular chamber like a basilica in a ring of round arches; for that chapel had been built before the first pointed arch of the Gothic had pierced our civilization like a spear. A glimmer of greenish light between some of the pillars marked the place of the other opening into the world above, and gave a vague sense of being under the sea, which was intensified by one or two other incidental and perhaps fanciful resemblances. For the dog-tooth pattern of the Norman was faintly traceable round all the arches, giving them, above the cavernous darkness, something of the look of the mouths of monstrous sharks. And in the centre the dark bulk of the tomb itself, with its lifted lid of stone, might almost have been the jaws of some such leviathan.

Whether out of the sense of fitness or from the lack of more modern appliances, the clerical antiquary had arranged for the illumination of the chapel only by four tall candles in big wooden candlesticks standing on the floor. Of these only one was alight when they entered, casting a faint glimmer over the mighty architectural forms. When they had all assembled, the clergyman proceeded to light the three others, and the appearance and contents of the great sarcophagus came more clearly into view.

All eyes went first to the face of the dead, preserved across all those ages in the lines of life by some secret Eastern process, it was said, inherited from heathen antiquity and unknown to the simple graveyards of our own island. The Professor could hardly repress an exclamation of wonder; for, though the face was as pale as a mask of wax, it looked otherwise like a sleeping man, who had but that moment closed his eyes. The face was of the ascetic, perhaps even the fanatical type, with a high framework of bones; the figure was clad in a golden cope and gorgeous vestments, and high up on the breast, at the base of the throat, glittered the famous gold cross upon a short gold chain, or rather necklace. The stone coffin had been opened by lifting the lid of it at the head and propping it aloft upon two strong wooden shafts or poles, hitched above under the edge of the upper slab and wedged below into the corners of the coffin behind the head of the corpse. Less could therefore be seen of the feet or the lower part of the figure, but the candlelight shone full on the face; and in contrast with its tones of dead ivory the cross of gold seemed to stir and sparkle like a fire.

Professor Smaill's big forehead had carried a big furrow of reflection, or possibly of worry, ever since the clergyman had told the story of the curse. But feminine intuition, not untouched by feminine hysteria, understood the meaning of his brooding immobility better than did the men around him. In the silence of that candle-lit cavern Lady Diana cried out suddenly: 'Don't touch it, I tell you!'

But the man had already made one of his swift leonine movements, leaning forward over the body. The next instant they all darted, some forward and some backward, but all with a dreadful ducking motion as if the sky were falling.

As the Professor laid a finger on the gold cross, the wooden props, that bent very slightly in supporting the lifted lid of stone, seemed to jump and straighten themselves with a jerk. The lip of the stone slab slipped from its wooden perch; and in all their souls and stomachs came a sickening sense of down-rushing ruin, as if they had all been flung off a precipice. Smaill had withdrawn his head swiftly, but not in time; and he lay senseless beside the coffin, in a red puddle of blood from scalp or skull. And the old stone coffin was once more closed as it had been for centuries; save that one or two sticks or splinters stuck in the crevice, horribly suggestive of bones crunched by an ogre. The leviathan had snapped its jaws of stone.

Lady Diana was looking at the wreck with eyes that had an electric glare as of lunacy; her red hair looked scarlet against the pallor of her face in the greenish twilight. Smyth was looking at her, still with something dog-like in the turn of his head; but it was the expression of a god who looks at a master whose catastrophe he can only partly understand. Tarrant and the foreigner had stiffened in their usual sullen attitudes, but their faces had turned the colour of clay. The Vicar seemed to have fainted. Father Brown was kneeling beside the fallen figure, trying to test its condition.

Rather to the general surprise, the Byronic lounger, Paul Tarrant, came forward to help him.

'He'd better be carried up into the air,' he said. 'I suppose there's just a chance for him.'

'He isn't dead,' said Father Brown in a low voice, 'but I think it's pretty bad; you aren't a doctor by any chance?'

'No; but I've had to pick up a good many things in my time,' said the other. 'But never mind about me just now. My real profession would probably surprise you.'

'I don't think so,' replied Father Brown, with a slight smile. 'I thought of it about halfway through the voyage. You are a detective shadowing somebody. Well, the cross is safe from thieves now, anyhow.'

While they were speaking Tarrant had lifted the frail figure of the fallen man with easy strength and dexterity, and was carefully carrying him towards the exit. He answered over his shoulder:

'Yes, the cross is safe enough.'

'You mean that nobody else is,' replied Brown. 'Are you thinking of the curse, too?'

Father Brown went about for the next hour or two under a burden of frowning perplexity that was something beyond the shock of the tragic accident. He assisted in carrying the victim to the little inn opposite the church, interviewed the doctor, who reported the injury as serious and threatening, though not certainly fatal, and carried the news to the little group of travellers who had gathered round the table in the inn parlour. But wherever he went the cloud of mystification rested on him and seemed to grow darker the more deeply he pondered. For the central mystery was growing more and more mysterious, actually in proportion as many of the minor mysteries began to clear themselves up in his mind. Exactly in proportion as the meaning of individual figures in that motley group began to explain itself, the thing that had happened grew more and more difficult to explain. Leonard Smyth had come merely because Lady Diana had come; and Lady Diana had come merely because she chose. They were engaged in one of those floating Society flirtations that are all the more silly for being semi-intellectual. But the lady's romanticism had a superstitious side to it; and she was pretty well prostrated by the terrible end of her adventure. Paul Tarrant was a private detective, possibly watching the flirtation, for some wife or husband; possibly shadowing the foreign lecturer with the moustaches, who had much the air of an undesirable alien. But if he or anybody else had intended to steal the relic, the intention had been finally frustrated. And to all mortal appearance, what had frustrated it was either an incredible coincidence or the intervention of the ancient curse.

As he stood in unusual perplexity in the middle of the village street, between the inn and the church, he felt a mild shock of surprise at seeing a recently familiar but rather unexpected figure advancing up the street. Mr Boon, the journalist, looking very haggard in the sunshine, which showed up his shabby raiment like that of a scarecrow, had his dark and deep-set eyes (rather close together on either side of the long drooping nose) fixed on the priest. The latter looked twice before he realized that the heavy dark moustache hid something like a grin or at least a grim smile.

'I thought you were going away,' said Father Brown a little sharply. 'I thought you left by that train two hours ago.'

'Well, you see I didn't,' said Boon.

'Why have you come back?' asked the priest almost sternly.

'This is not the sort of little rural paradise for a journalist to leave in a hurry,' replied the other. 'Things happen too fast here to make it worth while to go back to a dull place like London. Besides, they can't keep me out of the affair—I mean this second affair. It was I that found the body, or at any rate the clothes. Quite suspicious conduct on my part, wasn't it? Perhaps you; think I wanted to dress up in his clothes. Shouldn't I make a lovely parson?'

And the lean and long-nosed mountebank suddenly made an extravagant gesture in the middle of the marketplace, stretching out his arms and spreading out his dark-gloved hands in a sort of burlesque benediction and saying: 'Oh, my dear brethren and sisters, for I would embrace you all...'

'What on earth are you talking about?' cried Father Brown, and rapped the stones slightly with his stumpy umbrella, for he was a little less patient than usual.

'Oh, you'll find out all about it if you ask that picnic party of yours at the inn,' replied Boon scornfully. 'That man Tarrant seems to suspect me merely because I found the clothes, though he only came up a minute too late to find them himself. But there are all sorts of mysteries in this business. The little man with the big moustaches may have more in him than meets the eye. For that matter I don't see why you shouldn't have killed the poor fellow yourself.'

Father Brown did not seem in the least annoyed at the suggestion, but he seemed exceedingly bothered and bewildered by the remark. 'Do you mean,' he asked with simplicity, 'that it was I who tried to kill Professor Smaill?'

'Not at all,' said the other, waving his hand with the air of one making a handsome concession. 'Plenty of dead people for you to choose among. Not limited to Professor Smaill. Why, didn't you know somebody else had turned up, a good deal deader than Professor Smaill? And I don't see why you shouldn't have done him in, in a quiet way. Religious differences, you know... lamentable disunion of Christendom... I suppose you've always wanted to get the English parishes back.'

'I'm going back to the inn,' said the priest quietly; 'you say the people there know what you mean, and perhaps they may be able to say it.'

In truth, just afterwards his private perplexities suffered a momentary dispersal at the news of a new calamity. The moment he entered the little parlour where the rest of the company were collected, something in their pale faces told him they were shaken by something yet more recent than the accident at the tomb. Even as he entered, Leonard Smyth was saying: 'Where is all this going to end?'

'It will never end, I tell you,' repeated Lady Diana, gazing into vacancy with glassy eyes; 'it will never end till we all end. One after another the curse will take us; perhaps slowly, as the poor vicar said; but it will take us all as it has taken him.'

'What in the world has happened now?' asked Father Brown.

There was a silence, and then Tarrant said in a voice that sounded a little hollow: 'Mr Walters, the Vicar, has committed suicide. I suppose it was the shock unhinged him. But I fear there can be no doubt about it. We've just found his black hat and clothes on a rock jutting out from the shore. He seems to have jumped into the sea. I thought he looked as if it had knocked him half-witted, and perhaps we ought to have looked after him; but there was so much to look after.'

'You could have done nothing,' said the lady. 'Don't you see the thing is dealing doom in a sort of dreadful order? The Professor touched the cross, and he went first; the Vicar had opened the tomb, and he went second; we only entered the chapel, and we—'

'Hold on,' said Father Brown, in a sharp voice he very seldom used; 'this has got to stop.'

He still wore a heavy though unconscious frown, but in his eyes was no longer the cloud of mystification, but a light of almost terrible understanding. 'What a fool I am!' he muttered. 'I ought to have seen it long ago. The tale of the curse ought to have told me.'

'Do you mean to say,' demanded Tarrant, 'that we can really be killed now by something that happened in the thirteenth century?'

Father Brown shook his head and answered with quiet emphasis: 'I won't discuss whether we can be killed by something that happened in the thirteenth century; but I'm jolly certain that we can't be killed by something that never happened in the thirteenth century, something that never happened at all.'

'Well,' said Tarrant, 'it's refreshing to find a priest so sceptical of the supernatural as all that.'

'Not at all,' replied the priest calmly; 'it's not the supernatural part I doubt. It's the natural part. I'm exactly in the position of the man who said, 'I can believe the impossible, but not the improbable."

'That's what you call a paradox, isn't it?' asked the other.

'It's what I call common sense, properly understood,' replied Father Brown. 'It really is more natural to believe a preternatural story, that deals with things we don't understand, than a natural story that contradicts things we do understand. Tell me that the great Mr Gladstone, in his last hours, was haunted by the ghost of Parnell, and I will be agnostic about it. But tell me that Mr Gladstone, when first presented to Queen Victoria, wore his hat in her drawing-room and slapped her on the back and offered her a cigar, and I am not agnostic at all. That is not impossible; it's only incredible. But I'm much more certain it didn't happen than that Parnell's ghost didn't appear; because it violates the laws of the world I do understand. So it is with that tale of the curse. It isn't the legend that I disbelieve—it's the history.'

Lady Diana had recovered a little from her trance of Cassandra, and her perennial curiosity about new things began to peer once more out of her bright and prominent eyes.

'What a curious man you are!' she said. 'Why should you disbelieve the history?'

'I disbelieve the history because it isn't history,' answered Father Brown. 'To anybody who happens to know a little about the Middle Ages, the whole story was about as probable as Gladstone offering Queen Victoria a cigar. But does anybody know anything about the Middle Ages? Do you know what a Guild was? Have you ever heard of salvo managio suo? Do you know what sort of people were Servi Regis?

'No, of course I don't,' said the lady, rather crossly. 'What a lot of Latin words!'

'No, of course,' said Father Brown. 'If it had been Tutankhamen and a set of dried-up Africans preserved, Heaven knows why, at the other end of the world; if it had been Babylonia or China; if it had been some race as remote and mysterious as the Man in the Moon, your newspapers would have told you all about it, down to the last discovery of a toothbrush or a collar-stud. But the men who built your own parish churches, and gave the names to your own towns and trades, and the very roads you walk on—it has never occurred to you to know anything about them. I don't claim to know a lot myself; but I know enough to see that story is stuff and nonsense from beginning to end. It was illegal for a moneylender to distrain on a man's shop and tools. It's exceedingly unlikely that the Guild would not have saved a man from such utter ruin, especially if he were ruined by a Jew. Those people had vices and tragedies of their own; they sometimes tortured and burned people. But that idea of a man, without God or hope in the world, crawling away to die because nobody cared whether he lived—that isn't a medieval idea. That's a product of our economic science and progress. The Jew wouldn't have been a vassal of the feudal lord. The Jews normally had a special position as servants of the King. Above all, the Jew couldn't possibly have been burned for his religion.'

'The paradoxes are multiplying,' observed Tarrant; 'but surely, you won't deny that Jews were persecuted in the Middle Ages?'

'It would be nearer the truth,' said Father Brown, 'to say they were the only people who weren't persecuted in the Middle Ages. If you want to satirize medievalism, you could make a good case by saying that some poor Christian might be burned alive for 'making a mistake about the Homoousion, while a rich Jew might walk down the street openly sneering at Christ and the Mother of God. Well, that's what the story is like. It was never a story of the Middle Ages; it was never even a legend about the Middle Ages. It was made up by somebody whose notions came from novels and newspapers, and probably made up on the spur of the moment.'

The others seemed a little dazed by the historical digression, and seemed to wonder vaguely why the priest emphasized it and made it so important a part of the puzzle. But Tarrant, whose trade it was to pick the practical detail out of many tangles of digression, had suddenly become alert. His bearded chin was thrust forward farther than ever, out his sullen eyes were wide awake. 'Ah,' he said; 'made up on the spur of the moment!'

'Perhaps that is an exaggeration,' admitted Father Brown calmly. 'I should rather say made up more casually and carelessly than the rest of an uncommonly careful plot. But the plotter did not think the details of medieval history would matter much to anybody. And his calculation in a general way was pretty nearly right, like most of his other calculations.'

'Whose calculations? Who was right?' demanded the lady with a sudden passion of impatience. 'Who is this person you are talking about? Haven't we gone through enough, without your making our flesh creep with your he's and him's?'

'I am talking about the murderer,' said Father Brown.

'What murderer?' she asked sharply. 'Do you mean that the poor Professor was murdered?'

'Well,' said the staring Tarrant gruffly into his beard, 'we can't say 'murdered', for we don't know he's killed.'

'The murderer killed somebody else, who was not Professor Smaill,' said the priest gravely.

'Why, whom else could he kill?' asked the other. 'He killed the Reverend John Walters, the Vicar of Dulham,' replied Father Brown with precision. 'He only wanted to kill those two, because they both had got hold of relics of one rare pattern. The murderer was a sort of monomaniac on the point.'

'It all sounds very strange,' muttered Tarrant. 'Of course we can't swear that the Vicar's really dead either. We haven't seen his body.'

'Oh yes, you have,' said Father Brown.

There was a silence as sudden as the stroke of a gong; a silence in which that subconscious guesswork that was so active and accurate in the woman moved her almost to a shriek.

'That is exactly what you have seen,' went on the priest. 'You have seen his body. You haven't seen him—the real living man; but you have seen his body all right. You have stared at it hard by the light of four great candles; and it was not tossing suicidally in the sea but lying in state like a Prince of the Church in a shrine built before the Crusade.'

'In plain words,' said Tarrant, 'you actually ask us to believe that the embalmed body was really the corpse of a murdered man.'

Father Brown was silent for a moment; then he said almost with an air of irrelevance: 'The first thing I noticed about it was the cross; or rather the string suspending the cross. Naturally, for most of you, it was only a string of beads and nothing else in particular; but, naturally also, it was rather more in my line than yours. You remember it lay close up to the chin, with only a few beads showing, as if the whole necklet were quite short. But the beads that showed were arranged in a special way, first one and then three, and so on; in fact, I knew at a glance that it was a rosary, an ordinary rosary with a cross at the end of it. But a rosary has at least five decades and additional beads as well; and I naturally wondered where all the rest of it was. It would go much more than once round the old man's neck. I couldn't understand it at the time; and it was only afterwards I guessed where the extra length had gone to. It was coiled round and round the foot of the wooden prop that was fixed in the corner of the coffin, holding up the lid. So that when poor Smaill merely plucked at the cross it jerked the prop out of its place and the lid fell on his skull like a club of stone.'

'By George!' said Tarrant; 'I'm beginning to think there's something in what you say. This is a queer story if it's true.'

'When I realized that,' went on Father Brown, 'I could manage more or less to guess the rest. Remember, first of all, that there never was any responsible archaeological authority for anything more than investigation. Poor old Walters was an honest antiquary, who was engaged in opening the tomb to find out if there was any truth in the legend about embalmed bodies. The rest was all rumour, of the sort that often anticipates or exaggerates such finds. As a fact, he found the body had not been embalmed, but had fallen into dust long ago. Only while he was working there by the light of his lonely candle in that sunken chapel, the candlelight threw another shadow that was not his own.'

'Ah!' cried Lady Diana with a catch in her breath; 'and I know what you mean now. You mean to tell us we have met the murderer, talked and joked with the murderer, let him tell us a romantic tale, and let him depart untouched.'

'Leaving his clerical disguise on a rock,' assented Brown. 'It is all dreadfully simple. This man got ahead of the Professor in the race to the churchyard and chapel, possibly while the Professor was talking to that lugubrious journalist. He came on the old clergyman beside the empty coffin and killed him. Then he dressed himself in the black clothes from the corpse, wrapped it in an old cope which had been among the real finds of the exploration, and put it in the coffin, arranging the rosary and the wooden support as I have described. Then, having thus set the trap for his second enemy, he went up into the daylight and greeted us all with the most amiable politeness of a country clergyman.'

'He ran a considerable risk,' objected Tarrant, 'of somebody knowing Walters by sight.'

'I admit he was half-mad,' agreed Father Brown; 'and I think you will admit that the risk was worth taking, for he has got off, after all.'

'I'll admit he was very lucky,' growled Tarrant. 'And who the devil was he?'

'As you say, he was very lucky,' answered Father Brown, 'and not least in that respect. For that is the one thing we may never know.' He frowned at the table for a moment and then went on:

'This fellow has been hovering round and threatening for years, but the one thing he was careful of was to keep the secret of who he was; and he has kept it still. But if poor Smaill recovers, as I think he will, it is pretty safe to say that you will hear more of it.'

'Why, what will Professor Smaill do, do you think?' asked Lady Diana.

'I should think the first thing he would do,' said Tarrant, 'would be to put the detectives on like dogs after this murdering devil. I should like to have a go at him myself.'

'Well,' said Father Brown, smiling suddenly after his long fit of frowning perplexity, 'I think I know the very first thing he ought to do.'

'And what is that?' asked Lady Diana with graceful eagerness.

'He ought to apologize to all of you,' said Father Brown.

It was not upon this point, however, that Father Brown found himself talking to Professor Smaill as he sat by the bedside during the slow convalescence of that eminent archaeologist. Nor, indeed, was it chiefly Father Brown who did the talking; for though the Professor was limited to small doses of the stimulant of conversation, he concentrated most of it upon these interviews with his clerical friend. Father Brown had a talent for being silent in an encouraging way and Smaill was encouraged by it to talk about many strange things not always easy to talk about; such as the morbid phases of recovery and the monstrous dreams that often accompany delirium. It is often rather an unbalancing business to recover slowly from a bad knock on the head; and when the head is as interesting a head as that of Professor Smaill even its disturbances and distortions are apt to be original and curious. His dreams were like bold and big designs rather out of drawing, as they can be seen in the strong but stiff archaic arts that he had studied; they were full of strange saints with square and triangular haloes, of golden outstanding crowns and glories round dark and flattened faces, of eagles out of the east and the high headdresses of bearded men with their hair bound like women. Only, as he told his friend, there was one much simpler and less entangled type, that continually recurred to his imaginative memory. Again and again all these Byzantine patterns would fade away like the fading gold on which they were traced as upon fire; and nothing remained but the dark bare wall of rock on which the shining shape of the fish was traced as with a finger dipped in the phosphorescence of fishes. For that was the sign which he once looked up and saw, in the moment when he first heard round the corner of the dark passage the voice of his enemy.

'And at last,' he said, 'I think I have seen a meaning in the picture and the voice; and one that I never understood before. Why should I worry because one madman among a million of sane men, leagued in a great society against him, chooses to brag of persecuting me or pursuing me to death? The man who drew in the dark catacomb the secret symbol of Christ was persecuted in a very different fashion. He was the solitary madman; the whole sane society was leagued together not to save but to slay him. I have sometimes fussed and fidgeted and wondered whether this or that man was my persecutor; whether it was Tarrant; whether it was Leonard Smyth; whether it was any one of them. Suppose it had been all of them? Suppose it had been all the men on the boat and the men on the train and the men in the village. Suppose, so far as I was concerned, they were all murderers. I thought I had a right to be alarmed because I was creeping through the bowels of the earth in the dark and there was a man who would destroy me. What would it have been like, if the destroyer had been up in the daylight and had owned all the earth and commanded all the armies and the crowds? How if he had been able to stop all the earths or smoke me out of my hole, or kill me the moment I put my nose out in the daylight? What was it like to deal with murder on that scale? The world has forgotten these things, as until a little while ago it had forgotten war.'

'Yes,' said Father Brown, 'but the war came. The fish may be driven underground again, but it will come up into the daylight once more. As St Antony of Padua humorously remarked, 'It is only fishes who survive the Deluge."

6

THE DAGGER WITH WINGS
(First published in *Nash's Magazine,* Feb 1924)

Father Brown, at one period of his life, found it difficult to hang his hat on a hat-peg without repressing a slight shudder. The origin of this idiosyncrasy was indeed a mere detail in much more complicated events; but it was perhaps the only detail that remained to him in his busy life to remind him of the whole business. Its remote origin was to be found in the facts which led Dr Boyne, the medical officer attached to the police force, to send for the priest on a particular frosty morning in December.

Dr Boyne was a big dark Irishman, one of those rather baffling Irishmen to be found all over the world, who will talk scientific scepticism, materialism, and cynicism at length and at large, but who never dream of referring anything touching the ritual of religion to anything except the traditional religion of their native land. It would be hard to say whether their creed is a very superficial varnish or a very fundamental substratum; but most probably it is both, with a mass of materialism in between. Anyhow, when he thought that matters of that sort might be involved, he asked Father Brown to call, though he made no pretence of preference for that aspect of them.

'I'm not sure I want you, you know,' was his greeting. 'I'm not sure about anything yet. I'm hanged if I can make out whether it's a case for a doctor, or a policeman, or a priest.'

'Well,' said Father Brown with a smile, 'as I suppose you're both a policeman and a doctor, I seem to be rather in a minority.'

'I admit you're what politicians call an instructed minority,' replied the doctor. 'I mean, I know you've had to do a little in our line as well as your own. But it's precious hard to say whether this business is in your line or ours, or merely in the line of the Commissioners in Lunacy. We've just had a message from a man living near here, in that white house on the hill, asking for protection against a murderous persecution. We've gone into the facts as far as we could, and perhaps I'd better tell you the story as it is supposed to have happened, from the beginning.

'It seems that a man named Aylmer, who was a wealthy landowner in the West Country, married rather late in life and had three sons, Philip, Stephen, and Arnold. But in his bachelor days, when he thought he would have no heir, he had adopted a boy whom he thought very brilliant and promising, who went by the name of John Strake. His origin seems to be vague; they say he was a foundling; some say he was a gipsy. I think the last notion is mixed up with the fact that Aylmer in his old age dabbled in all sorts of dingy occultism, including palmistry and astrology, and his three sons say that Strake encouraged him in it. But they said a great many other things besides that. They said Strake was an amazing scoundrel, and especially an amazing liar; a genius in inventing lies on the spur of the moment, and telling them so as to deceive a detective. But that might very well be a natural prejudice, in the light of what happened.

Perhaps you can more or less imagine what happened. The old man left practically everything to the adopted son; and when he died the three real sons disputed the will. They said their father had been frightened into surrender and, not to put too fine a point on it, into gibbering idiocy. They said Strake had the strangest and most cunning ways of getting at him, in spite of the nurses and the family, and terrorizing him on his death-bed. Anyhow, they seemed to have proved something about the dead man's mental condition, for the courts set aside the will and the sons inherited. Strake is said to have broken out in the most dreadful fashion, and sworn he would kill all three of them, one after another, and that nothing could hide them from his vengeance. It is the third or last of the brothers, Arnold Aylmer, who is asking for police protection.'

'Third and last,' said the priest, looking at him gravely.

'Yes,' said Boyne. 'The other two are dead.' There was a silence before he continued. 'That is where the doubt comes in. There is no proof they were murdered, but they might possibly have been. The eldest, who took up his position as squire, was supposed to have committed suicide in his garden. The second, who went into trade as a manufacturer, was knocked onthe head by the machinery in his factory; he might very well have taken a false step and fallen. But if Strake did kill them, he is certainly very cunning in his way of getting to work and getting away. On the other hand, it's more than likely that the whole thing is a mania of conspiracy founded on a coincidence. Look here, what I want is this. I want somebody of sense, who isn't an official, to go up and have a talk with this Mr Arnold Aylmer and form an impression of him. You know what a man with a delusion is like, and how a man looks when he is telling the truth. I want you to be the advance guard, before we take the matter up.'

'It seems rather odd,' said Father Brown, 'that you haven't had to take it up before. If there is anything in this business, it seems to have been going on for a good time. Is there any particular reason why he should send for you just now, any more than any other time?'

'That had occurred to me, as you may imagine,' answered Dr Boyne. 'He does give a reason, but I confess it is one of the things that make me wonder whether the whole thing isn't only the whim of some half-witted crank. He declared that all his servants have suddenly gone on strike and left him, so that he is obliged to call on the police to look after his house. And on making inquiries, I certainly do find that there has been a general exodus of servants from that house on the hill; and of course the town is full of tales, very one-sided tales I dare say. Their account of it seems to be that their employer had become quite impossible in his fidgets and fears and exactions; that he wanted them to guard the house like sentries, or sit up like night nurses in a hospital; that they could never be left alone because he must never be left alone. So they all announced in a loud voice that he was a lunatic, and left. Of course that does not prove he is a lunatic; but it seems rather rum nowadays for a man to expect his valet or his parlour-maid to act as an armed guard.'

'And so,' said the priest with a smile, 'he wants a policeman to act as his parlour-maid because his parlour-maid won't act as a policeman.'

'I thought that rather thick, too,' agreed the doctor; 'but I can't take the responsibility of a flat refusal till I've tried a compromise. You are the compromise.'

'Very well,' said Father Brown simply. 'I'll go and call on him now if you like.'

The rolling country round the little town was sealed and bound with frost, and the sky was as clear and cold as steel, except in the north-east where clouds with lurid haloes were beginning to climb up the sky. It was against these darker and more sinister colours that the house on the hill gleamed with a row of pale pillars, forming a short colonnade of the classical sort. A winding road led up to it across the curve of the down, and plunged into a mass of dark bushes. Just before it reached the bushes the air seemed to grow colder and colder, as if he were approaching an ice-house or the north Pole. But he was a highly practical person, never entertaining such fancies except as fancies. And he merely cocked his eye at the great livid cloud crawling up over the house, and remarked cheerfully: 'It's going to snow.'

Through a low ornamental iron gateway of the Italianate pattern he entered a garden having something of that desolation which only belongs to the disorder of orderly things. Deep-green growths were grey with the faint powder of the frost, large weeds had fringed the fading pattern of the flowerbeds as if in a ragged frame; and the house stood as if waist-high in a stunted forest of shrubs and bushes. The vegetation consisted largely of evergreens or very hardy plants; and though it was thus thick and heavy, it was too northern to be called luxuriant. It might be described as an Arctic jungle. So it was in some sense with the house itself, which had a row of columns and a classical facade, which might have looked out on the Mediterranean; but which seemed now to be withering in the wind of the North Sea. Classical ornament here and there accentuated the contrast; caryatides and carved masks of comedy or tragedy looked down from corners of the building upon the grey confusion of the garden paths; but the faces seemed to be frost-bitten. The very volutes of the capitals might have curled up with the cold.

Father Brown went up the grassy steps to a square porch flanked by big pillars and knocked at the door. About four minutes afterwards he knocked again. Then he stood still patiently waiting with his back to the door and looked out on the slowly darkening landscape. It was darkening under the shadow of that one great continent of cloud that had come flying out of the north; and even as he looked out beyond the pillars of the porch, which seemed huge and black above him in the twilight, he saw the opalescent crawling rim of the great cloud as it sailed over the roof and bowed over the porch like a canopy. The great canopy with its faintly coloured fringes seemed to sink lower and lower upon the garden beyond, until what had recently been a clear and pale-hued winter sky was left in a few silver ribbons and rags like a sickly sunset. Father Brown waited, and there was no sound within.

Then he betook himself briskly down the steps and round the house to look for another entrance. He eventually found one, a side door in the flat wall, and on this also he hammered and outside this also he waited. Then he tried the handle and found the door apparently bolted or fastened in some fashion; and then he moved along that side of the house, musing on the possibilities of the position, and wondering whether the eccentric Mr Aylmer had barricaded himself too deep in the house to hear any kind of summons; or whether perhaps he would barricade himself all the more, on the assumption that any summons must be the challenge of the avenging Strake. It might be that the decamping servants had only unlocked one door when they left in the morning, and that their master had locked that; but whatever he might have done it was unlikely that they, in the mood of that moment, had looked so carefully to the defences. He continued his prowl round the place: it was not really a large place, though perhaps a little pretentious; and in a few moments he found he had made the complete circuit. A moment after he found what he suspected and sought. The french window of one room, curtained and shadowed with creeper, stood open by a crack, doubtless accidentally left ajar, and he found himself in a central room, comfortably upholstered in a rather old-fashioned way, with a staircase leading up from it on one side and a door leading out of it on the other. Immediately opposite him was another door with red glass let into it, a little gaudily for later tastes; something that looked like a red-robed figure in cheap stained glass. On a round table to the right stood a sort of aquarium—a great bowl full of greenish water, in which fishes and similar things moved about as in a tank; and just opposite it a plant of the palm variety with very large green leaves. All this looked so very dusty and Early Victorian that the telephone, visible in the curtained alcove, was almost a surprise.

'Who is that?' a voice called out sharply and rather suspiciously from behind the stained-glass door.

'Could I see Mr Aylmer?' asked the priest apologetically.

The door opened and a gentleman in a peacock-green dressing-gown came out with an inquiring look. His hair was rather rough and untidy, as if he had been in bed or lived in a state of slowly getting up, but his eyes were not only awake but alert, and some would have said alarmed. Father Brown knew that the contradiction was likely enough in a man who had rather run to seed under the shadow either of a delusion or a danger. He had a fine aquiline face when seen in profile, but when seen full face the first impression was that of the untidiness and even the wilderness of his loose brown beard.

'I am Mr Aylmer,' he said, 'but I've got out of the way of expecting visitors.'

Something about Mr Aylmer's unrestful eye prompted the priest to go straight to the point. If the man's persecution was only a monomania, he would be the less likely to resent it.

'I was wondering,' said Father Brown softly, 'whether it is quite true that you never expect visitors.'

'You are right,' replied his host steadily. 'I always expect one visitor. And he may be the last.'

'I hope not,' said Father Brown, 'but at least I am relieved to infer that I do not look very like him.'

Mr Aylmer shook himself with a sort of savage laugh. 'You certainly do not,' he said.

'Mr Aylmer,' said Father Brown frankly, 'I apologize for the liberty, but some friends of mine have told me about your trouble, and asked me to see if I could do anything for you. The truth is, I have some little experience in affairs like this.'

'There are no affairs like this,' said Aylmer.

'You mean,' observed Father Brown, 'that the tragedies in your unfortunate family were not normal deaths?'

'I mean they were not even normal murders,' answered the other. 'The man who is hounding us all to death is a hell-hound, and his power is from hell.'

'All evil has one origin,' said the priest gravely. 'But how do you know they were not normal murders?'

Aylmer answered with a gesture which offered his guest a chair; then he seated himself slowly in another, frowning, with his hands on his knees; but when he looked up his expression had grown milder and more thoughtful, and his voice was quite cordial and composed.

'Sir,' he said, 'I don't want you to imagine that I'm in the least an unreasonable person. I have come to these conclusions by reason, because unfortunately reason really leads there. I have read a great deal on these subjects; for I was the only one who inherited my father's scholarship in somewhat obscure matters, and I have since inherited his library. But what I tell you does not rest on what I have read but on what I have seen.'

Father Brown nodded, and the other proceeded, as if picking his words: 'In my elder brother's case I was not certain at first. There were no marks or footprints where he was found shot, and the pistol was left beside him. But he had just received a threatening letter certainly from our enemy, for it was marked with a sign like a winged dagger, which was one of his infernal cabalistic tricks. And a servant said she had seen something moving along the garden wall in the twilight that was much too large to be a cat. I leave it there; all I can say is that if the murderer came, he managed to leave no traces of his coming. But when my brother Stephen died it was different; and since then I have known. A machine was working in an open scaffolding under the factory tower; I scaled the platform a moment after he had fallen under the iron hammer that struck him; I did not see anything else strike him, but I saw what I saw.

'A great drift of factory smoke was rolling between me and the factory tower; but through a rift of it I saw on the top of it a dark human figure wrapped in what looked like a black cloak. Then the sulphurous smoke drove between us again; and when it cleared I looked up at the distant chimney—there was nobody there. I am a rational man, and I will ask all rational men how he had reached that dizzy unapproachable turret, and how he left it.'

He stared across at the priest with a sphinx-like challenge; then after a silence he said abruptly: 'My brother's brains were knocked out, but his body was not much damaged. And in his pocket we found one of those warning messages dated the day before and stamped with the flying dagger.

'I am sure,' he went on gravely, 'that the symbol of the winged dagger is not merely arbitrary or accidental. Nothing about that abominable man is accidental. He is all design; though it is indeed a most dark and intricate design. His mind is woven not only out of elaborate schemes but out of all sorts of secret languages and signs, and dumb signals and wordless pictures which are the names of nameless things. He is the worst sort of man that the world knows: he is the wicked mystic. Now, I don't pretend to penetrate all that is conveyed by this symbol; but it seems surely that it must have a relation to all that was most remarkable, or even incredible, in his movements as he had hovered round my unfortunate family. Is there no connexion between the idea of a winged weapon and the mystery by which Philip was struck dead on his own lawn without the lightest touch of any footprint having disturbed the dust or grass? Is there no connexion between the plumed poignard flying like a feathered arrow and that figure which hung on the far top of the toppling chimney, clad in a cloak for pinions?'

'You mean,' said Father Brown thoughtfully, 'that he is in a perpetual state of levitation.'

'Simon Magus did it,' replied Aylmer, 'and it was one of the commonest predictions of the Dark Ages that Antichrist would be able to fly. Anyhow, there was the flying dagger on the document; and whether or no it could fly, it could certainly strike.'

'Did you notice what sort of paper it was on?' asked Father Brown. 'Common paper?'

The sphinx-like face broke abruptly into a harsh laugh.

'You can see what they're like,' said Aylmer grimly, 'for I got one myself this morning.'

He was leaning back in his chair now, with his long legs thrust out from under the green dressing-gown, which was a little short for him, and his bearded chin pillowed on his chest. Without moving otherwise, he thrust his hand deep in the dressing-gown pocket and held out a fluttering scrap of paper at the end of a rigid arm. His whole attitude was suggestive of a sort of paralysis, that was both rigidity and collapse. But the next remark of the priest had a curious effect of rousing him.

Father Brown was blinking in his short-sighted way at the paper presented to him. It was a singular sort of paper, rough without being common, as from an artist's sketchbook; and on it was drawn boldly in red ink a dagger decorated with wings like the rod of Hermes, with the written words, 'Death comes the day after this, as it came to your brothers.'

Father Brown tossed the paper on the floor and sat bolt upright in his chair.

'You mustn't let that sort of stuff stupefy you,' he said sharply. 'These devils always try to make us helpless by making us hopeless.'

Rather to his surprise, an awakening wave went over the prostrate figure, which sprang from its chair as if startled out of a dream.

'You're right, you're right!' cried Aylmer with a rather uncanny animation; 'and the devils shall find that I'm not so hopeless after all, nor so helpless either. Perhaps I have more hope and better help than you fancy.'

He stood with his hands in his pockets, frowning down at the priest, who had a momentary doubt, during that strained silence, about whether the man's long peril had not touched his brain. But when he spoke it was quite soberly.

'I believe my unfortunate brothers failed because they used the wrong weapons. Philip carried a revolver, and that was how his death came to be called suicide. Stephen had police protection, but he also had a sense of what made him ridiculous; and he could not allow a policeman to climb up a ladder after him to a scaffolding where he stood only a moment. They were both scoffers, reacting into scepticism from the strange mysticism of my father's last days. But I always knew there was more in my father than they understood. It is true that by studying magic he fell at last under the blight of black magic; the black magic of this scoundrel Strake. But my brothers were wrong about the antidote. The antidote to black magic is not brute materialism or worldly wisdom. The antidote to black magic is white magic.'

'It rather depends,' said Father Brown, 'what you mean by white magic.'

'I mean silver magic,' said the other, in a low voice, like one speaking of a secret revelation. Then after a silence he said: 'Do you know what I mean by silver magic? Excuse me a moment.'

He turned and opened the central door with the red glass and went into a passage beyond it. The house had less depth than Brown had supposed; instead of the door opening into interior rooms, the corridor it revealed ended in another door on the garden. The door of one room was on one side of the passage; doubtless, the priest told himself, the proprietor's bedroom whence he had rushed out in his dressing-gown.

There was nothing else on that side but an ordinary hat-stand with the ordinary dingy cluster of old hats and overcoats; but on the other side was something more interesting: a very dark old oak sideboard laid out with some old silver, and overhung by a trophy or ornament of old weapons. It was by that that Arnold Aylmer halted, looking up at a long antiquated pistol with a bell-shaped mouth.

The door at the end of the passage was barely open, and through the crack came a streak of white daylight. The priest had very quick instincts about natural things, and something in the unusual brilliancy of that white line told him what had happened outside. It was indeed what he had prophesied when he was approaching the house. He ran past his rather startled host and opened the door, to face something that was at once a blank and a blaze. What he had seen shining through the crack was not only the most negative whiteness of daylight but the positive whiteness of snow. All round, the sweeping fall of the country was covered with that shining pallor that seems at once hoary and innocent.

'Here is white magic anyhow,' said Father Brown in his cheerful voice. Then, as he turned back into the hall, he murmured, 'And silver magic too, I suppose,' for the white lustre touched the silver with splendour and lit up the old steel here and there in the darkling armoury. The shaggy head of the brooding Aylmer seemed to have a halo of silver fire, as he turned with his face in shadow and the outlandish pistol in his hand.

'Do you know why I chose this sort of old blunderbuss?' he asked. 'Because I can load it with this sort of bullet.'

He had picked up a small apostle spoon from the sideboard and by sheer violence broke off the small figure at the top. 'Let us go back into the other room,' he added.

'Did you ever read about the death of Dundee?' he asked when they had reseated themselves. He had recovered from his momentary annoyance at the priest's restlessness. 'Graham of Claverhouse, you know, who persecuted the Covenanters and had a black horse that could ride straight up a precipice. Don't you know he could only be shot with a silver bullet, because he had sold himself to the Devil? That's one comfort about you; at least you know enough to believe in the Devil.'

'Oh, yes,' replied Father Brown, 'I believe in the Devil. What I don't believe in is the Dundee. I mean the Dundee of Covenanting legends, with his nightmare of a horse. John Graham was simply a seventeenth-century professional soldier, rather better than most. If he dragooned them it was because he was a dragoon, but not a dragon. Now my experience is that it's not that sort of swaggering blade who sells himself to the Devil. The devil-worshippers I've known were quite different. Not to mention names, which might cause a social flutter, I'll take a man in Dundee's own day. Have you ever heard of Dalrymple of Stair?'

'No,' replied the other gruffly.

'You've heard of what he did,' said Father Brown, 'and it was worse than anything Dundee ever did; yet he escapes the infamy by oblivion. He was the man who made the Massacre of Glencoe. He was a very learned man and lucid lawyer, a statesman with very serious and enlarged ideas of statesmanship, a quiet man with a very refined and intellectual face. That's the sort of man who sells himself to the Devil.'

Aylmer half started from his chair with an enthusiasm of eager assent.

'By God! you are right,' he cried. 'A refined intellectual face! That is the face of John Strake.'

Then he raised himself and stood looking at the priest with a curious concentration. 'If you will wait here a little while,' he said, 'I will show you something.'

He went back through the central door, closing it after him; going, the priest presumed, to the old sideboard or possibly to his bedroom. Father Brown remained seated, gazing abstractedly at the carpet, where a faint red glimmer shone from the glass in the doorway. Once it seemed to brighten like a ruby and then darkened again, as if the sun of that stormy day had passed from cloud to cloud. Nothing moved except the aquatic creatures which floated to and fro in the dim green bowl. Father Brown was thinking hard.

A minute or two afterwards he got up and slipped quietly to the alcove of the telephone, where he rang up his friend Dr Boyne, at the official headquarters. 'I wanted to tell you about Aylmer and his affairs,' he said quietly. 'It's a queer story, but I rather think there's something in it. If I were you I'd send some men up here straight away; four or five men, I think, and surround the house. If anything does happen there'll probably be something startling in the way of an escape.'

Then he went back and sat down again, staring at the dark carpet, which again glowed blood-red with the light from the glass door. Something in the filtered light set his mind drifting on certain borderlands of thought, with the first white daybreak before the coming of colour, and all that mystery which is alternately veiled and revealed in the symbol of windows and of doors.

An inhuman howl in a human voice came from beyond the closed doors, almost simultaneously with the noise of firing. Before the echoes of the shot had died away the door was violently flung open and his host staggered into the room, the dressing-gown half torn from his shoulder and the long pistol smoking in his hand. He seemed to be shaking in every limb, yet he was shaken in part with an unnatural laughter.

'Glory be to the White Magic!' he cried. 'Glory be to the silver bullet! The hell-hound had hunted once too often, and my brothers are avenged at last.'

He sank into a chair and the pistol slid from his hand and fell on the floor. Father Brown darted past him, slipped through the glass door and went down the passage. As he did so he put his hand on the handle of the bedroom door, as if half intending to enter; then he stooped a moment, as if examining something—and then he ran to the outer door and opened it.

On the field of snow, which had been so blank a little while before, lay one black object. At the first glance it looked a little like an enormous bat. A second glance showed that it was, after all, a human figure; fallen on its face, the whole head covered by a broad black hat having something of a Latin-American look; while the appearance of black wings came from the two flaps or loose sleeves of a very vast black cloak spread out, perhaps by accident, to their utmost length on either side. Both the hands were hidden, though Father Brown thought he could detect the position of one of them, and saw close to it, under the edge of the cloak, the glimmer of some metallic weapon. The main effect, however, was curiously like that of the simple extravagances of heraldry; like a black eagle displayed on a white ground. But by walking round it and peering under the hat the priest got a glimpse of the face, which was indeed what his host had called refined and intellectual; even sceptical and austere: the face of John Strake.

'Well, I'm jiggered,' muttered Father Brown. 'It really does look like some vast vampire that has swooped down like a bird.'

'How else could he have come?' came a voice from the doorway, and Father Brown looked up to see Aylmer once more standing there.

'Couldn't he have walked?' replied Father Brown evasively.

Aylmer stretched out his arm and swept the white landscape with a gesture.

'Look at the snow,' he said in a deep voice that had a sort of roll and thrill in it. 'Is not the snow unspotted—pure as the white magic you yourself called it? Is there a speck on it for miles, save that one foul black blot that has fallen there? There are no footprints, but a few of yours and mine; there are none approaching the house from anywhere.'

Then he looked at the little priest for a moment with a concentrated and curious expression, and said: 'I will tell you something else. That cloak he flies with is too long to walk with. He was not a very tall man, and it would trail behind him like a royal train. Stretch it out over his body, if you like, and see.'

'What happened to you both?' asked Father Brown abruptly.

'It was too swift to describe,' answered Aylmer. 'I had looked out of the door and was turning back when there came a kind of rushing of wind all around me, as if I were being buffeted by a wheel revolving in mid-air. I spun round somehow and fired blindly; and then I saw nothing but what you see now. But I am morally certain that you wouldn't see it if I had not had a silver shot in my gun. It would have been a different body lying there in the snow.'

'By the way,' remarked Father Brown, 'shall we leave it lying there in the snow? Or would you like it taken into your room—I suppose that's your bedroom in the passage?'

'No, no,' replied Aylmer hastily, 'we must leave it here till the police have seen it. Besides, I've had as much of such things as I can stand for the moment. Whatever else happens, I'm going to have a drink. After that, they can hang me if they like.'

Inside the central apartment, between the palm plant and the bowl of fishes, Aylmer tumbled into a chair. He had nearly knocked the bowl over as he lurched into the room, but he had managed to find the decanter of brandy after plunging his hand rather blindly into several cupboards and corners. He did not at any time look like a methodical person, but at this moment his distraction must have been extreme. He drank with a long gulp and began to talk rather feverishly, as if to fill up a silence.

'I see you are still doubtful,' he said, 'though you have seen the thing with your own eyes. Believe me, there was something more behind the quarrel between the spirit of Strake and the spirit of the house of Aylmer. Besides, you have no business to be an unbeliever. You ought to stand for all the things these stupid people call superstitions. Come now, don't you think there's a lot in those old wives' tales about luck and charms and so on, silver bullets included? What do you say about them as a Catholic?'

'I say I'm an agnostic,' replied Father Brown, smiling.

'Nonsense,' said Aylmer impatiently. 'It's your business to believe things.'

'Well, I do believe some things, of course,' conceded Father Brown; 'and therefore, of course, I don't believe other things.'

Aylmer was leaning forward, and looking at him with a strange intensity that was almost like that of a mesmerist.

'You do believe it,' he said. 'You do believe everything. We all believe everything, even when we deny everything. The denyers believe. The unbelievers believe. Don't you feel in your heart that these contradictions do not really contradict: that there is a cosmos that contains them all? The soul goes round upon a wheel of stars and all things return; perhaps Strake and I have striven in many shapes, beast against beast and bird against bird, and perhaps we shall strive forever. But since we seek and need each other, even that eternal hatred is an eternal love. Good and evil go round in a wheel that is one thing and not many. Do you not realize in your heart, do you not believe behind all your beliefs, that there is but one reality and we are its shadows; and that all things are but aspects of one thing: a centre where men melt into Man and Man into God?'

'No,' said Father Brown.

Outside, twilight had begun to fall, in that phase of such a snow-laden evening when the land looks brighter than the sky. In the porch of the main entrance, visible through a half-curtained window. Father Brown could dimly see a bulky figure standing. He glanced casually at the french windows through which he had originally entered, and saw they were darkened with two equally motionless figures. The inner door with the coloured glass stood slightly ajar; and he could see in the short corridor beyond, the ends of two long shadows, exaggerated and distorted by the level light of evening, but still like grey caricatures of the figures of men. Dr Boyne had already obeyed the telephone message. The house was surrounded.

'What is the good of saying no?' insisted his host, still with the same hypnotic stare. 'You have seen part of that eternal drama with your own eyes. You have seen the threat of John Strake to slay Arnold Aylmer by black magic. You have seen Arnold Aylmer slay John Strake by white magic. You see Arnold Aylmer alive and talking to you now. And yet you don't believe it.'

'No, I do not believe it,' said Father Brown, and rose from his chair like one terminating a visit.

'Why not?' asked the other.

The priest only lifted his voice a little, but it sounded in every corner of the room like a bell. 'Because you are not Arnold Aylmer,' he said. 'I know who you are. Your name is John Strake; and you have murdered the last of the brothers, who is lying outside in the snow.'

A ring of white showed round the iris of the other man's eyes; he seemed to be making, with bursting eyeballs, a last effort to mesmerize and master his companion. Then he made a sudden movement sideways; and even as he did so the door behind him opened and a big detective in plain clothes put one hand quietly on his shoulder. The other hand hung down, but it held a revolver. The man looked wildly round, and saw plain-clothes men in all corners of the quiet room.

That evening Father Brown had another and longer conversation with Dr Boyne about the tragedy of the Aylmer family. By that time there was no longer any doubt of the central fact of the case, for John Strake had confessed his identity and even confessed his crimes; only it would be truer to say that he boasted of his victories. Compared to the fact that he had rounded off his life's work with the last Aylmer lying dead, everything else, including existence itself, seemed to be indifferent to him.

'The man is a sort of monomaniac,' said Father Brown. 'He is not interested in any other matter; not even in any other murder. I owe him something for that; for I had to comfort myself with the reflection a good many times this afternoon. As has doubtless occurred to you, instead of weaving all that wild but ingenious romance about winged vampires and silver bullets, he might have put an ordinary leaden bullet into me, and walked out of the house. I assure you it occurred quite frequently to me.'

'I wonder why he didn't,' observed Boyne. 'I don't understand it; but I don't understand anything yet. How on earth did you discover it, and what in the world did you discover?'

'Oh, you provided me with very valuable information,' replied Father Brown modestly, 'especially the one piece of information that really counted. I mean the statement that Strake was a very inventive and imaginative liar, with great presence of mind in producing his lies. This afternoon he needed it; but he rose to the occasion. Perhaps his only mistake was in choosing a preternatural story; he had the notion that because I am a clergyman I should believe anything. Many people have little notions of that kind.'

'But I can't make head or tail of it,' said the doctor. 'You must really begin at the beginning.'

'The beginning of it was a dressing-gown,' said Father Brown simply. 'It was the one really good disguise I've ever known. When you meet a man in a house with a dressing-gown on, you assume quite automatically that he's in his own house. I assumed it myself; but afterwards queer little things began to happen. When he took the pistol down he clicked it at arm's length, as a man does to make sure a strange weapon isn't loaded; of course he would know whether the pistols in his own hall were loaded or not. I didn't like the way he looked for the brandy, or the way he nearly barged into the bowl of fishes. For a man who has a fragile thing of that sort as a fixture in his rooms gets a quite mechanical habit of avoiding it. But these things might possibly have been fancies; the first real point was this. He came out from the little passage between the two doors; and in that passage there's only one other door leading to a room; so I assumed it was the bedroom he had just come from. I tried the handle; but it was locked. I thought this odd; and looked through the keyhole. It was an utterly bare room, obviously deserted; no bed, no anything. Therefore he had not come from inside any room, but from outside the house. And when I saw that, I think I saw the whole picture.

'Poor Arnold Aylmer doubtless slept and perhaps lived upstairs, and came down in his dressing-gown and passed through the red glass door. At the end of the passage, black against the winter daylight, he saw the enemy of his house. He saw a tall bearded man in a broad-brimmed black hat and a large flapping black cloak. He did not see much more in this world. Strake sprang at him, throttling or stabbing him; we cannot be sure till the inquest. Then Strake, standing in the narrow passage between the hat-stand and the old sideboard, and looking down in triumph on the last of his foes heard something he had not expected. He heard footsteps in the parlour beyond. It was myself entering by the french windows.

'His masquerade was a miracle of promptitude. It involved not only a disguise but a romance—an impromptu romance. He took off his big black hat and cloak and put on the dead man's dressing-gown. Then he did a rather grisly thing; at least a thing that affects my fancy as more grisly than the rest. He hung the corpse like a coat on one of the hat pegs. He draped it in his own long cloak, and found it hung well below the heels;

he covered the head entirely with his own wide hat. It was the only possible way of hiding it in that little passage with the locked door; but it was really a very clever one. I myself walked past the hat-stand once without knowing it was anything but a hat-stand. I think that unconsciousness of mine will always give me a shiver.

'He might perhaps have left it at that; but I might have discovered the corpse at any minute; and, hung where it was, it was a corpse calling for what you might call an explanation. He adopted the bolder stroke of discovering it himself and explaining it himself.

'Then there dawned on this strange and frightfully fertile mind the conception of a story of substitution; the reversal of the parts. He had already assumed the part of Arnold Aylmer. Why should not his dead enemy assume the part of John Strake? There must have been something in that topsy-turyydom to take the fancy of that darkly fanciful man. It was like some frightful fancy-dress ball to which the two mortal enemies were to go dressed up as each other. Only, the fancy-dress ball was to be a dance of death: and one of the dancers would be dead. That is why I can imagine that man putting it in his own mind, and I can imagine him smiling.'

Father Brown was gazing into vacancy with his large grey eyes, which, when not blurred by his trick of blinking, were the one notable thing in his face. He went on speaking simply and seriously: 'All things are from God; and above all, reason and imagination and the great gifts of the mind. They are good in themselves; and we must not altogether forget their origin even in their perversion. Now this man had in him a very noble power to be perverted; the power of telling stories. He was a great novelist; only he had twisted his fictive power to practical and to evil ends; to deceiving men with false fact instead of with true fiction. It began with his deceiving old Aylmer with elaborate excuses and ingeniously detailed lies; but even that may have been, at the beginning, little more than the tall stories and tarradiddles of the child who may say equally he has seen the King of England or the King of the Fairies. It grew strong in him through the vice that perpetuates all vices, pride; he grew more and more vain of his promptitude in producing stories of his originality, and subtlety in developing them. That is what the young Aylmers meant by saying that he could always cast a spell over their father; and it was true. It was the sort of spell that the storyteller cast over the tyrant in the Arabian Nights. And to the last he walked the world with the pride of a poet, and with the false yet unfathomable courage of a great liar. He could always produce more Arabian Nights if ever his neck was in danger. And today his neck was in danger.

'But I am sure, as I say, that he enjoyed it as a fantasy as well as a conspiracy. He set about the task of telling the true story the wrong way round: of treating the dead man as living and the live man as dead. He had already got into Aylmer's dressing-gown; he proceeded to get into Aylmer's body and soul. He looked at the corpse as if it were his own corpse lying cold in the snow. Then he spread-eagled it in that strange fashion to suggest the sweeping descent of a bird of prey, and decked it out not only in his own dark and flying garments but in a whole dark fairy-tale about the black bird that could only fall by the silver bullet. I do not know whether it was the silver glittering on the sideboard or the snow shining beyond the door that suggested to his intensely artistic temperament the theme of white magic and the white metal used against magicians. But whatever its origin, he made it his own like a poet; and did it very promptly, like a practical man. He completed the exchange and reversal of parts by flinging the corpse out on to the snow as the corpse of Strake. He did his best to work up a creepy conception of Strake as something hovering in the air everywhere, a harpy with wings of speed and claws of death; to explain the absence of footprints and other things. For one piece of artistic impudence I hugely admire him. He actually turned one of the contradictions in his case into an argument for it; and said that the man's cloak being too long for him proved that he never walked on the ground like an ordinary mortal. But he looked at me very hard while he said that; and something told me that he was at that moment trying a very big bluff.'

Dr Boyne looked thoughtful. 'Had you discovered the truth by then?' he asked. 'There is something very queer and close to the nerves, I think, about notions affecting identity. I don't know whether it would be more weird to get a guess like that swiftly or slowly. I wonder when you suspected and when you were sure.'

'I think I really suspected when I telephoned to you,' replied his friend. 'And it was nothing more than the red light from the closed door brightening and darkening on the carpet. It looked like a splash of blood that grew vivid as it cried for vengeance. Why should it change like that? I knew the sun had not come out; it could only be because the second door behind it had been opened and shut on the garden. But if he had gone out and seen his enemy then, he would have raised the alarm then; and it was some time afterwards that the fracas occurred. I began to feel he had gone out to do something ... to prepare something ... but as to when I was certain, that is a different matter. I knew that right at the end he was trying to hypnotize me, to master me by the black art of eyes like talismans and a voice like an incantation. That's what he used to do with old Aylmer, no doubt. But it wasn't only the way he said it, it was what he said. It was the religion and philosophy of it.'

'I'm afraid I'm a practical man,' said the doctor with gruff humour, 'and I don't bother much about religion and philosophy.'

'You'll never be a practical man till you do,' said Father Brown. 'Look here, doctor; you know me pretty well; I think you know I'm not a bigot. You know I know there are all sorts in all religions; good men in bad ones and bad men in good ones. But there's just one little fact I've learned simply as a practical man, an entirely practical point, that I've picked up by experience, like the tricks of an animal or the trademark of a good wine. I've scarcely ever met a criminal who philosophized at all, who didn't philosophize along those lines of orientalism and recurrence and reincarnation, and the wheel of destiny and the serpent biting its own tail. I have found merely in practice that there is a curse on the servants of that serpent; on their belly shall they go and the dust shall they eat; and there was never a blackguard or a profligate born who could not talk that sort of spirituality. It may not be like that in its real religious origins; but here in our working world it is the religion of rascals; and I knew it was a rascal who was speaking.'

'Why,' said Boyne, 'I should have thought that a rascal could pretty well profess any religion he chose.'

'Yes,' assented the other; 'he could profess any religion; that is he could pretend to any religion, if it was all a pretence. If it was mere mechanical hypocrisy and nothing else, no doubt it could be done by a mere mechanical hypocrite. Any sort of mask can be put on any sort of face. Anybody can learn certain phrases or state verbally that he holds certain views. I can go out into the street and state that I am a Wesleyan Methodist or a Sandemanian, though I fear in no very convincing accent. But we are talking about an artist; and for the enjoyment of the artist the mask must be to some extent moulded on the face. What he makes outside him must correspond to something inside him, he can only make his effects out of some of the materials of his soul. I suppose he could have said he was a Wesleyan Methodist; but he could never be an eloquent Methodist as he can be an eloquent mystic and fatalist. I am talking of the sort of ideal such a man thinks of if he really tries to be idealistic. It was his whole game with me to be as idealistic as possible;

and whenever that is attempted by that sort of man, you will generally find it is that sort of ideal. That sort of man may be dripping with gore; but he will always be able to tell you quite sincerely that Buddhism is better than Christianity. Nay, he will tell you quite sincerely that Buddhism is more Christian than Christianity. That alone is enough to throw a hideous and ghastly ray of light on his notion of Christianity.'

'Upon my soul,' said the doctor, laughing, 'I can't make out whether you're denouncing or defending him.'

'It isn't defending a man to say he is a genius,' said Father Brown. 'Far from it. And it is simply a psychological fact that an artist will betray himself by some sort of sincerity. Leonardo da Vinci cannot draw as if he couldn't draw. Even if he tried, it will always be a strong parody of a weak thing. This man would have made something much too fearful and wonderful out of the Wesleyan Methodist.'

When the priest went forth again and set his face homeward, the cold had grown more intense and yet was somehow intoxicating. The trees stood up like silver candelabra of some incredible cold candlemas of purification. It was a piercing cold, like that silver sword of pure pain that once pierced the very he of purity. But it was not a killing cold, save in the sense of seeming to kill all the mortal obstructions to our immortal and immeasurable vitality. The pale green sky of twilight, with one star like the star of Bethlehem, seemed by some strange contradiction to be a cavern of clarity. It was as if there could be a green furnace of cold which wakened all things to life like warmth, and that the deeper they went into those cold crystalline colours the more were they light like winged creatures and clear like coloured glass! It tingled with truth and it divided truth from error with a blade like ice; but all that was left had never felt so much alive. It was as if all joy were a jewel in the heart of an iceberg. The priest hardly understood his own mood as he advanced deeper and, deeper into the green gloaming, drinking deeper and deeper draughts of that virginal vivacity of the air. Some forgotten muddle and morbidity seemed to be left behind, or wiped out as the snow had painted out the footprints of the man of blood. As he shuffled homewards through the snow, he muttered to himself: 'And yet he is right enough about there being a white magic, if he only knows where to look for it.'

7

THE DOOM OF THE DARNAWAYS (No record of prior magazine publication found)

Two landscape-painters stood looking at one landscape, which was also a seascape, and both were curiously impressed by it, though their impressions were not exactly the same. To one of them, who was a rising artist from London, it was new as well as strange. To the other, who was a local artist but with something more than a local celebrity, it was better known; but perhaps all the more strange for what he knew of it.

In terms of tone and form, as these men saw it, it was a stretch of sands against a stretch of sunset, the whole scene lying in strips of sombre colour, dead green and bronze and brown and a drab that was not merely dull but in that gloaming in some way more mysterious than gold. All that broke these level lines was a long building which ran out from the fields into the sands of the sea, so that its fringe of dreary weeds and rushes seemed almost to meet the seaweed. But its most singular feature was that the upper part of it had the ragged outlines of a ruin, pierced by so many wide windows and large rents as to be a mere dark skeleton against the dying light; while the lower bulk of the building had hardly any windows at all, most of them being blind and bricked up and their outlines only faintly traceable in the twilight. But one window at least was still a window; and it seemed strangest of all that it showed a light.

'Who on earth can live in that old shell?' exclaimed the Londoner, who was a big, bohemian-looking man, young but with a shaggy red beard that made him look older; Chelsea knew him familiarly as Harry Payne.

'Ghosts, you might suppose,' replied his friend Martin Wood. 'Well, the people who live there really are rather like ghosts.'

It was perhaps rather a paradox that the London artist seemed almost bucolic in his boisterous freshness and wonder, while the local artist seemed a more shrewd and experienced person, regarding him with mature and amiable amusement; indeed, the latter was altogether a quieter and more conventional figure, wearing darker clothes and with his square and stolid face clean shaven.

'It is only a sign of the times, of course,' he went on, 'or of the passing of old times and old families with them. The last of the great Darnaways live in that house, and not many of the new poor are as poor as they are. They can't even afford to make their own top-storey habitable; but have to live in the lower rooms of a ruin, like bats and owls. Yet they have family portraits that go back to the Wars of the Roses and the first portrait-painting in England, and very fine some of them are; I happen to know, because they asked for my professional advice in overhauling them. There's one of them especially, and one of the earliest, but it's so good that it gives you the creeps.'

'The whole place gives you the creeps, I should think by the look of it,' replied Payne.

'Well,' said his friend, 'to tell you the truth, it does.'

The silence that followed was stirred by a faint rustle among the rushes by the moat; and it gave them, rationally enough, a slight nervous start when a dark figure brushed along the bank, moving rapidly and almost like a startled bird. But it was only a man walking briskly with a black bag in his hand: a man with a long sallow face and sharp eyes that glanced at the London stranger in a slightly darkling and suspicious manner.

'It's only Dr Barnet,' said Wood with a sort of relief. 'Good evening, Doctor. Are you going up to the house? I hope nobody's ill.'

'Everybody's always ill in a place like that,' growled the doctor; 'only sometimes they're too ill to know it. The very air of the place is a blight and a pestilence. I don't envy the young man from Australia.'

'And who,' asked Payne abruptly and rather absently, 'may the young man from Australia be?'

'Ah!' snorted the doctor; 'hasn't your friend told you about him? As a matter of fact I believe he is arriving today. Quite a romance in the old style of melodrama: the heir back from the colonies to his ruined castle, all complete even down to an old family compact for his marrying the lady watching in the ivied tower. Queer old stuff, isn't it? but it really happens sometimes. He's even got a little money, which is the only bright spot there ever was in this business.'

'What does Miss Darnaway herself, in her ivied tower, think of the business?' asked Martin Wood dryly.

'What she thinks of everything else by this time,' replied the doctor. 'They don't think in this weedy old den of superstitions, they only dream and drift. I think she accepts the family contract and the colonial husband as part of the Doom of the Darnaways, don't you know. I really think that if he turned out to be a humpbacked black with one eye and a homicidal mania, she would only think it added a finishing touch and fitted in with the twilight scenery.'

'You're not giving my friend from London a very lively picture of my friends in the country,' said Wood, laughing. 'I had intended taking him there to call; no artist ought to miss those Darnaway portraits if he gets the chance. But perhaps

I'd better postpone it if they're in the middle of the Australian invasion.'

'Oh, do go in and see them, for the Lord's sake,' said Dr Barnet warmly. 'Anything that will brighten their blighted lives will make my task easier. It will need a good many colonial cousins to cheer things up, I should think; and the more the merrier. Come, I'll take you in myself.'

As they drew nearer to the house it was seen to be isolated like an island in a moat of brackish water which they crossed by a bridge. On the other side spread a fairly wide stony floor or embankment with great cracks across it, in which little tufts of weed and thorn sprouted here and there. This rock platform looked large and bare in the grey twilight, and Payne could hardly have believed that such a corner of space could have contained so much of the soul of a wilderness. This platform only jutted out on one side, like a giant doorstep and beyond it was the door; a very low-browed Tudor archway standing open, but dark like a cave.

When the brisk doctor led them inside without ceremony, Payne had, as it were, another shock of depression. He could have expected to find himself mounting to a very ruinous tower, by very narrow winding staircases; but in this case the first steps into the house were actually steps downwards. They went down several short and broken stairways into large twilit rooms which but for their lines of dark pictures and dusty bookshelves, might have been the traditional dungeons beneath the castle moat. Here and there a candle in an old candlestick lit up some dusty accidental detail of a dead elegance; but the visitor was not so much impressed or depressed by this artificial light as by the one pale gleam of natural light. As he passed down the long room he saw the only window in that wall—a curious low oval window of a late-seventeenth-century fashion. But the strange thing about it was that it did not look out directly on any space of sky but only on a reflection of sky; a pale strip of daylight merely mirrored in the moat, under the hanging shadow of the bank. Payne had a memory of the Lady of Shallot who never saw the world outside except in a mirror. The lady of this Shallot not only in some sense saw the world in a mirror, but even saw the world upside-down.

'It's as if the house of Darnaway were falling literally as well as metaphorically,' said Wood in a low voice; 'as if it were sinking slowly into a swamp or a quicksand, until the sea goes over it like a green roof.'

Even the sturdy Dr Barnet started a little at the silent approach of the figure that came to receive them. Indeed, the room was so silent that they were all startled to realize that it was not empty. There were three people in it when they entered: three dim figures motionless in the dim room; all three dressed in black and looking like dark shadows. As the foremost figure drew nearer the grey light from the window, he showed a face that looked almost as grey as its frame of hair. This was old Vine, the steward, long left in loco parentis since the death of that eccentric parent, the last Lord Darnaway. He would have been a handsome old man if he had had no teeth. As it was, he had one which showed every now and then and gave him a rather sinister appearance. He received the doctor and his friends with a fine courtesy and escorted them to where the other two figures in black were seated. One of them seemed to Payne to give another appropriate touch of gloomy antiquity to the castle by the mere fact of being a Roman Catholic priest, who might have come out of a priest's hole in the dark old days. Payne could imagine him muttering prayers or telling beads, or tolling bells or doing a number of indistinct and melancholy things in that melancholy place. Just then he might be supposed to have been giving religious consolation to the lady; but it could hardly be supposed that the consolation was very consoling, or at any rate that it was very cheering. For the rest, the priest was personally insignificant enough, with plain and rather expressionless features; but the lady was a very different matter. Her face was very far from being plain or insignificant; it stood out from the darkness of her dress and hair and background with a pallor that was almost awful, but a beauty that was almost awfully alive. Payne looked at it as long as he dared; and he was to look at it a good deal longer before he died.

Wood merely exchanged with his friends such pleasant and polite phrases as would lead up to his purpose of revisiting the portraits. He apologized for calling on the day which he heard was to be one of family welcome; but he was soon convinced that the family was rather mildly relieved to have visitors to distract them or break the shock. He did not hesitate, therefore, to lead Payne through the central reception-room into the library beyond, where hung the portrait, for there was one which he was especially bent on showing, not only as a picture but almost as a puzzle. The little priest trudged along with them; he seemed to know something about old pictures as well as about old prayers.

'I'm rather proud of having spotted this,' said Wood.' I believe it's a Holbein. If it isn't, there was somebody living in Holbein's time who was as great as Holbein.'

It was a portrait in the hard but sincere and living fashion of the period, representing a man clad in black trimmed with gold and fur, with a heavy, full, rather pale face but watchful eyes.

'What a pity art couldn't have stopped forever at just that transition stage,' cried Wood, 'and never transitioned anymore. Don't you see it's just realistic enough to be real? Don't you see the face speaks all the more because it stands out from a rather stiffer framework of less essential things? And the eyes are even more real than the face. On my soul, I think the eyes are too real for the face! It's just as if those sly, quick eyeballs were protruding out of a great pale mask.'

'The stiffness extends to the figure a little, I think,' said Payne. 'They hadn't quite mastered anatomy when medievalism ended, at least in the north. That left leg looks to me a good deal out of drawing.'

'I'm not so sure,' replied Wood quietly. "Those fellows who painted just when realism began to be done, and before it began to be overdone, were often more realistic than we think. They put real details of portraiture into things that are thought merely conventional. You might say this fellow's eyebrows or eye-sockets are a little lopsided; but I bet if you knew him you'd find that one of his eyebrows did really stick up more than the other. And I shouldn't wonder if he was lame or something, and that black leg was meant to be crooked.'

'What an old devil he looks!' burst out Payne suddenly. 'I trust his reverence will excuse my language.'

'I believe in the devil, thank you,' said the priest with an inscrutable face. 'Curiously enough there was a legend that the devil was lame.'

'I say,' protested Payne, 'you can't really mean that he was the devil; but who the devil was he?'

'He was the Lord Darnaway under Henry VII and Henry VIII,' replied his companion. 'But there are curious legends about him, too; one of them is referred to in that inscription round the frame, and further developed in some notes left by somebody in a book I found here. They are both rather curious reading.'

Payne leaned forward, craning his head so as to follow the archaic inscription round the frame. Leaving out the antiquated lettering and spelling, it seemed to be a sort of rhyme running somewhat thus:

In the seventh heir I shall return:
In the seventh hour I shall depart:
None in that hour shall hold my hand:
And woe to her that holds my heart.

'It sounds creepy somehow,' said Payne, 'but that may be partly because I don't understand a word of it.'

'It's pretty creepy even when you do,' said Wood in a low voice. 'The record made at a later date, in the old book I found, is all about how this beauty deliberately killed himself in such a way that his wife was executed for his murder. Another note commemorates a later tragedy, seven successions later—under the Georges—in which another Darnaway committed suicide, having first thoughtfully left poison in his wife's wine. It's said that both suicides took place at seven in the evening. I suppose the inference is that he does really return with every seventh inheritor and makes things unpleasant, as the rhyme suggests, for any lady unwise enough to marry him.'

'On that argument,' replied Payne, 'it would be a trifle uncomfortable for the next seventh gentleman.'

Wood's voice was lower still as he said: 'The new heir will be the seventh.'

Harry Payne suddenly heaved up his great chest and shoulders like a man flinging off a burden.

'What crazy stuff are we all talking?' he cried. 'We're all educated men in an enlightened age, I suppose. Before I came into this damned dank atmosphere I'd never have believed I should be talking of such things, except to laugh at them.'

'You are right,' said Wood. 'If you lived long enough in this underground palace you'd begin to feel differently about things. I've begun to feel very curiously about that picture, having had so much to do with handling and hanging it. It sometimes seems to me that the painted face is more alive than the dead faces of the people living here; that it is a sort of talisman or magnet: that it commands the elements and draws out the destinies of men and things. I suppose you would call it very fanciful.'

'What is that noise?' cried Payne suddenly.

They all listened, and there seemed to be no noise except the dull boom of the distant sea; then they began to have the sense of something mingling with it; something like a voice calling through the sound of the surf, dulled by it at first, but coming nearer and nearer. The next moment they were certain: someone was shouting outside in the dusk.

Payne turned to the low window behind him and bent to look out. It was the window from which nothing could be seen except the moat with its reflection of bank and sky. But that inverted vision was not the same that he had seen before. From the hanging shadow of the bank in the water depended two dark shadows reflected from the feet and legs of a figure standing above upon the bank. Through that limited aperture they could see nothing but the two legs black against the reflection of a pale and livid sunset. But somehow that very fact of the head being invisible, as if in the clouds, gave something dreadful to the sound that followed; the voice of a man crying aloud what they could not properly hear or understand. Payne especially was peering out of the little window with an altered face, and he spoke with an altered voice:

'How queerly he's standing!'

'No, no,' said Wood, in a sort of soothing whisper. 'Things often look like that in reflection. It's the wavering of the water that makes you think that.'

'Think what?' asked the priest shortly.

'That his left leg is crooked,' said Wood.

Payne had thought of the oval window as a sort of mystical mirror; and it seemed to him that there were in it other inscrutable images of doom. There was something else beside the figure that he did not understand; three thinner legs showing in dark lines against the light, as if some monstrous three-legged spider or bird were standing beside the stranger. Then he had the less crazy thought of a tripod like that of the heathen oracles; and the next moment the thing had vanished and the legs of the human figure passed out of the picture.

He turned to meet the pale face of old Vine, the steward, with his mouth open, eager to speak, and his single tooth showing. 'He has come,' he said. 'The boat arrived from Australia this morning.'

Even as they went back out of the library into the central salon they heard the footsteps of the newcomer clattering down the entrance steps, with various items of light luggage trailed behind him. When Payne saw one of them, he laughed with a reaction of relief. His tripod was nothing but the telescopic legs of a portable camera, easily packed and unpacked; and the man who was carrying it seemed so far to take on equally solid and normal qualities. He was dressed in dark clothes, but of a careless and holiday sort; his shirt was of grey flannel, and his boots echoed uncompromisingly enough in those still chambers. As he strode forward to greet his new circle his stride had scarcely more than the suggestion of a limp. But Payne and his companions were looking at his face, and could scarcely take their eyes from it.

He evidently felt there was something curious and uncomfortable about his reception; but they could have sworn that he did not himself know the cause of it. The lady, supposed to be in some sense already betrothed to him, was certainly beautiful enough to attract him; but she evidently also frightened him. The old steward brought him a sort of feudal homage, yet treated him as if he were the family ghost. The priest still looked at him with a face which was quite indecipherable, and therefore perhaps all the more unnerving. A new sort of irony, more like the Greek irony, began to pass over Payne's mind. He had dreamed of the stranger as a devil, but it seemed almost worse that he was an unconscious destiny. He seemed to march towards crime with the monstrous innocence of Oedipus. He had approached the family mansion in so blindly buoyant a spirit as to have set up his camera to photograph his first sight of it; and even the camera had taken on the semblance of the tripod of a tragic pythoness.

Payne was surprised, when taking his leave a little while after, at something which showed that the Australian was already less unconscious of his surroundings. He said in a low voice:

'Don't go ... or come again soon. You look like a human being. This place fairly gives me the jumps.'

When Payne emerged out of those almost subterranean halls and came into the night air and the smell of the sea, he felt as if he had come out of that underworld of dreams in which events jumble on top of each other in a way at once unrestful and unreal.

The arrival of the strange relative had been somehow unsatisfying and, as it were, unconvincing. The doubling of the same face in the old portrait and the new arrival troubled him like a two headed monster. And yet it was not altogether a nightmare; nor was it that face, perhaps, that he saw most vividly.

'Did you say?' he asked of the doctor, as they strode together across the striped dark sands by the darkening sea; 'did you say that young man was betrothed to Miss Darnaway by a family compact or something? Sounds rather like a novel.'

'But an historical novel,' answered Dr Barnet. 'The Darnaways all went to sleep a few centuries ago, when things were really done that we only read of in romances. Yes; I believe there's some family tradition by which second or third cousins always marry when they stand in a certain relation of age, in order to unite the property. A damned silly tradition, I should say; and if they often married in and in, in that fashion, it may account on principles of heredity for their having gone so rotten.'

'I should hardly say,' answered Payne a little stuffily, 'that they had all gone rotten.'

'Well,' replied the doctor, 'the young man doesn't look rotten, of course, though he's certainly lame.'

'The young man!' cried Payne, who was suddenly and unreasonably angry. 'Well, if you think the young lady looks rotten, I think it's you who have rotten taste.'

The doctor's face grew dark and bitter. 'I fancy I know more about it than you do,' he snapped.

They completed the walk in silence, each feeling that he had been irrationally rude and had suffered equally irrational rudeness; and Payne was left to brood alone on the matter, for his friend Wood had remained behind to attend to some of his business in connexion with the pictures.

Payne took very full advantage of the invitation extended by the colonial cousin, who wanted somebody to cheer him up. During the next few weeks he saw a good deal of the dark interior of the Darnaway home; though it might be said that he did not confine himself entirely to cheering up the colonial cousin. The lady's melancholy was of longer standing and perhaps needed more lifting; anyhow, he showed a laborious readiness to lift it. He was not without a conscience, however, and the situation made him doubtful and uncomfortable. Weeks went by and nobody could discover from the demeanour of the new Darnaway whether he considered himself engaged according to the old compact or no. He went mooning about the dark galleries and stood staring vacantly at the dark and sinister picture. The shades of that prison-house were certainly beginning to close on him, and there was little of his Australian assurance left. But Payne could discover nothing upon the point that concerned him most. Once he attempted to confide in his friend Martin Wood, as he was pottering about in his capacity of picture-hanger; but even out of him he got very little satisfaction.

'It seems to me you can't butt in,' said Wood shortly, 'because of the engagement.'

'Of course I shan't butt in if there is an engagement,' retorted his friend; 'but is there? I haven't said a word to her of course;

but I've seen enough of her to be pretty certain she doesn't think there is, even if she thinks there may be. He doesn't say there is, or even hint that there ought to be. It seems to me this shillyshallying is rather unfair on everybody.'

'Especially on you, I suppose,' said Wood a little harshly. 'But if you ask me, I'll tell you what I think—I think he's afraid.'

'Afraid of being refused?' asked Payne.

'No; afraid of being accepted,' answered the other. 'Don't bite my head off—I don't mean afraid of the lady. I mean afraid of the picture.'

'Afraid of the picture!' repeated Payne.

'I mean afraid of the curse,' said Wood. 'Don't you remember the rhyme about the Darnaway doom falling on him and her.'

'Yes, but look here,' cried Payne; 'even the Darnaway doom can't have it both ways. You tell me first that I mustn't have my own way because of the compact, and then that the compact mustn't have its own way because of the curse. But if the curse can destroy the compact, why should she be tied to the compact? If they're frightened of marrying each other, they're free to marry anybody else, and there's an end of it. Why should I suffer for the observance of something they don't propose to observe? It seems to me your position is very unreasonable.'

'Of course it's all a tangle,' said Wood rather crossly, and went on hammering at the frame of a canvas.

Suddenly, one morning, the new heir broke his long and baffling silence. He did it in a curious fashion, a little crude, as was his way, but with an obvious anxiety to do the right thing. He asked frankly for advice, not of this or that individual as Payne had done, but collectively as of a crowd. When he did speak he threw himself on the whole company like a statesman going to the country. He called it 'a showdown'. Fortunately the lady was not included in this large gesture; and Payne shuddered when he thought of her feelings. But the Australian was quite honest; he thought the natural thing was to ask for help and for information, calling a sort of family council at which he put his cards on the table. It might be said that he flung down his cards on the table, for he did it with a rather desperate air, like one who had been harassed for days and nights by the increasing pressure of a problem. In that short time the shadows of that place of low windows and sinking pavements had curiously changed him, and increased a certain resemblance that crept through all their memories.

The five men, including the doctor, were sitting round a table; and Payne was idly reflecting that his own light tweeds and red hair must be the only colours in the room, for the priest and the steward were in black, and Wood and Darnaway habitually wore dark grey suits that looked almost like black. Perhaps this incongruity had been what the young man had meant by calling him a human being. At that moment the young man himself turned abruptly in his chair and began to talk. A moment after the dazed artist knew that he was talking about the most tremendous thing in the world.

'Is there anything in it?' he was saying. 'That is what I've come to asking myself till I'm nearly crazy. I'd never have believed I should come to thinking of such things; but I think of the portrait and the rhyme and the coincidences or whatever you call them, and I go cold. Is there anything in it? Is there any Doom of the Darnaways, or only a damned queer accident? Have I got a right to marry, or shall I bring something big and black out of the sky, that I know nothing about, on myself and somebody else?'

His rolling eye had roamed round the table and rested on the plain face of the priest, to whom he now seemed to be speaking. Payne's submerged practicality rose in protest against the problem of superstition being brought before that supremely superstitious tribunal. He was sitting next to Darnaway and struck in before the priest could answer.

'Well, the coincidences are curious, I admit,' he said, rather forcing a note of cheerfulness; 'but surely we—' and then he stopped as if he had been struck by lightning. For Darnaway had turned his head sharply over his shoulder at the interruption, and with the movement, his left eyebrow jerked up far above its fellow and for an instant the face of the portrait glared at him with a ghastly exaggeration of exactitude. The rest saw it; and all had the air of having been dazzled by an instant of light. The old steward gave a hollow groan.

'It is no good,' he said hoarsely, 'we are dealing with something too terrible.'

'Yes,' assented the priest in a low voice, 'we are dealing with something terrible; with the most terrible thing I know, and the name of it is nonsense.'

'What did you say?' said Darnaway, still looking towards him.

'I said nonsense,' repeated the priest. 'I have not said anything in particular up to now, for it was none of my business; I was only taking temporary duty in the neighbourhood and Miss Darnaway wanted to see me. But since you're asking me personally and point-blank, why, it's easy enough to answer. Of course there's no Doom of the Darnaways to prevent your marrying anybody you have any decent reason for marrying. A man isn't fated to fall into the smallest venial sin, let alone into crimes like suicide and murder. You can't be made to do wicked things against your will because your name is Darnaway, any more than I can because my name is Brown. The Doom of the Browns,' he added with relish—'the Weird of the Browns would sound even better.'

'And you of all people,' repeated the Australian, staring, 'tell me to think like that about it.'

'I tell you to think about something else,' replied the priest cheerfully. 'What has become of the rising art of photography? How is the camera getting on? I know it's rather dark downstairs, but those hollow arches on the floor above could easily be turned into a first-rate photographic studio. A few workmen could fit it out with a glass roof in no time.'

'Really,' protested Martin Wood, 'I do think you should be the last man in the world to tinker about with those beautiful Gothic arches, which are about the best work your own religion has ever done in the world. I should have thought you'd have had some feeling for that sort of art; but I can't see why you should be so uncommonly keen on photography.'

'I'm uncommonly keen on daylight,' answered Father Brown, 'especially in this dingy business; and photography has the virtue of depending on daylight. And if you don't know that I would grind all the Gothic arches in the world to powder to save the sanity of a single human soul, you don't know so much about my religion as you think you do.'

The young Australian had sprung to his feet like a man rejuvenated. 'By George! that's the talk,' he cried; 'though I never thought to hear it from that quarter. I'll tell you what, reverend sir, I'll do something that will show I haven't lost my courage after all.'

The old steward was still looking at him with quaking watchfulness, as if he felt something fey about the young man's defiance. 'Oh,' he cried, 'what are you going to do now?'

'I am going to photograph the portrait,' replied Darnaway.

Yet it was barely a week afterwards that the storm of the catastrophe seemed to stoop out of the sky, darkening that sun of sanity to which the priest had appealed in vain, and plunging the mansion once more in the darkness of the Darnaway doom. It had been easy enough to fit up the new studio; and seen from inside it looked very like any other such studio, empty except for the fullness of the white light. A man coming from the gloomy rooms below had more than normally the sense of stepping into a more than modern brilliancy, as blank as the future. At the suggestion of Wood, who knew the castle well and had got over his first aesthetic grumblings, a small room remaining intact in the upper ruins was easily turned into a dark room, into which Darnaway went out of the white daylight to grope by the crimson gleams of a red lamp. Wood said, laughing, that the red lamp had reconciled him to the vandalism; as that bloodshot darkness was as romantic as an alchemist's cave.

Darnaway had risen at daybreak on the day that he meant to photograph the mysterious portrait, and had it carried up from the library by the single corkscrew staircase that connected the two floors. There he had set it up in the wide white daylight on a sort of easel and planted his photographic tripod in front of it. He said he was anxious to send a reproduction of it to a great antiquary who had written on the antiquities of the house; but the others knew that this was an excuse covering much deeper things. It was, if not exactly a spiritual duel between Darnaway and the demoniac picture, at least a duel between Darnaway and his own doubts. He wanted to bring the daylight of photography face to face with that dark masterpiece of painting; and to see whether the sunshine of the new art would not drive out the shadows of the old.

Perhaps this was why he preferred to do it by himself, even if some of the details seemed to take longer and involve more than normal delay. Anyhow, he rather discouraged the few who visited his studio during the day of the experiment, and who found him focusing and fussing about in a very isolated and impenetrable fashion. The steward had left a meal for him, as he refused to come down; the old gentleman also returned some hours afterwards and found the meal more or less normally disposed of; but when he brought it he got no more gratitude than a grunt. Payne went up once to see how he was getting on, but finding the photographer disinclined for conversation came down again. Father Brown had wandered that way in an unobtrusive style to lake Darnaway a letter from the expert to whom the photograph was to be sent. But he left the letter on a tray, and whatever he thought of that great glasshouse full of daylight and devotion to a hobby, a world he had himself in some sense created, he kept it to himself and came down. He had reason to remember very soon that he was the last to come down the solitary staircase connecting the floors, leaving a lonely man and an empty room behind him. The others were standing in the salon that led into the library, just under the great black ebony clock that looked like a titanic coffin.

'How was Darnaway getting on,' asked Payne, a little later, 'when you last went up?'

The priest passed a hand over his forehead. 'Don't tell me I'm getting psychic,' he said with a sad smile. 'I believe I'm quite dazzled with daylight up in that room and couldn't see things straight. Honestly, I felt for a flash as if there were something uncanny about Darnaway's figure standing before that portrait.'

'Oh, that's the lame leg,' said Barnet promptly. 'We know all about that.'

'Do you know,' said Payne abruptly, but lowering his voice, 'I don't think we do know all about it or anything about it. What's the matter with his leg? What was the matter with his ancestor's leg?'

'Oh, there's something about that in the book I was reading in there, in the family archives,' said Wood; 'I'll fetch it for you.' And he stepped into the library just beyond.

'I think,' said Father Brown quietly, 'Mr Payne must have some particular reason for asking that.'

'I may as well blurt it out once and for all,' said Payne, but in a yet lower voice. 'After all, there is a rational explanation. A man from anywhere might have made up to look like the portrait. What do we know about Darnaway? He is behaving rather oddly—'

The others were staring at him in a rather startled fashion; but the priest seemed to take it very calmly.

'I don't think the old portrait's ever been photographed,' he said. 'That's why he wants to do it. I don't think there's anything odd about that.'

'Quite an ordinary state of things, in fact,' said Wood with a smile; he had just returned with the book in his hand. And even as he spoke there was a stir in the clockwork of the great dark clock behind him and successive strokes thrilled through the room up to the number of seven. With the last stroke there came a crash from the floor above that shook the house like a thunderbolt; and Father Brown was already two steps up the winding staircase before the sound had ceased.

'My God!' cried Payne involuntarily; 'he is alone up there.'

'Yes,' said Father Brown without turning, as he vanished up the stairway. 'We shall find him alone.'

When the rest recovered from their first paralysis and ran helter-skelter up the stone steps and found their way to the new studio, it was true in that sense that they found him alone. They found him lying in a wreck of his tall camera, with its long splintered legs standing out grotesquely at three different angles; and Darnaway had fallen on top of it with one black crooked leg lying at a fourth angle along the floor. For the moment the dark heap looked as if he were entangled with some huge and horrible spider. Little more than a glance and a touch were needed to tell them that he was dead. Only the portrait stood untouched upon the easel, and one could fancy the smiling eyes shone.

An hour afterwards Father Brown in helping to calm the confusion of the stricken household, came upon the old steward muttering almost as mechanically as the clock had ticked and struck the terrible hour. Almost without hearing them, he knew what the muttered words must be.

In the seventh heir I shall return; In the seventh hour I shall depart.

As he was about to say something soothing, the old man seemed suddenly to start awake and stiffen into anger; his mutterings changed to a fierce cry.

'You!' he cried; 'you and your daylight! even you won't say now there is no Doom for the Darnaways.'

'My opinion about that is unchanged,' said Father Brown mildly. Then after a pause he added: 'I hope you will observe poor Darnaway's last wish, and see the photograph is sent off.'

'The photograph!' cried the doctor sharply. 'What's the good of that? As a matter of fact, it's rather curious; but there isn't any photograph. It seems he never took it after all, after pottering about all day.'

Father Brown swung round sharply. 'Then take it yourselves,' he said. 'Poor Darnaway was perfectly right. It's most important that the photograph should be taken.'

As all the visitors, the doctor, the priest, and the two artists trailed away in a black and dismal procession across the brown and yellow sands, they were at first more or less silent, rather as if they had been stunned. And certainly there had been something like a crack of thunder in a clear sky about the fulfilment of that forgotten superstition at the very time when they had most forgotten it; when the doctor and the priest had both filled their minds with rationalism as the photographer had filled his rooms with daylight. They might be as rationalistic as they liked; but in broad daylight the seventh heir had returned, and in broad daylight at the seventh hour he had perished.

'I'm afraid everybody will always believe in the Darnaway superstition now,' said Martin Wood.

'I know one who won't,' said the doctor sharply. 'Why should I indulge in superstition because somebody else indulges in suicide?'

'You think poor Mr Darnaway committed suicide?' asked the priest.

'I'm sure he committed suicide,' replied the doctor.

'It is possible,' agreed the other.

'He was quite alone up there, and he had a whole drugstore of poisons in the dark room. Besides, it's just the sort of thing that Darnaways do.'

'You don't think there's anything in the fulfilment of the family curse?'

'Yes,' said the doctor; 'I believe in one family curse, and that is the family constitution. I told you it was heredity, and they are all half mad. If you stagnate and breed in and brood in your own swamp like that, you're bound to degenerate whether you like it or not. The laws of heredity can't be dodged; the truths of science can't be denied. The minds of the Darnaways are falling to pieces, as their blighted old sticks and stones are falling to pieces, eaten away by the sea and the salt air. Suicide—of course he committed suicide; I dare say all the rest will commit suicide. Perhaps the best thing they could do.'

As the man of science spoke there sprang suddenly and with startling clearness into Payne's memory the face of the daughter of the Darnaways, a tragic mask pale against an unfathomable blackness, but itself of a blinding and more than mortal beauty. He opened his mouth to speak and found himself speechless.

'I see,' said Father Brown to the doctor; 'so you do believe in the superstition after all?'

'What do you mean—believe in the superstition? I believe in the suicide as a matter of scientific necessity.'

'Well,' replied the priest, 'I don't see a pin to choose between your scientific superstition and the other magical superstition. They both seem to end in turning people into paralytics, who can't move their own legs or arms or save their own lives or souls. The rhyme said it was the Doom of the Darnaways to be killed, and the scientific textbook says it is the Doom of the Darnaways to kill themselves. Both ways they seem to be slaves.'

'But I thought you said you believed in rational views of these things,' said Dr Barnet. 'Don't you believe in heredity?'

'I said I believed in daylight,' replied the priest in a loud and clear voice, 'and I won't choose between two tunnels of subterranean superstition that both end in the dark. And the proof of it is this: that you are all entirely in the dark about what really happened in that house.'

'Do you mean about the suicide?' asked Payne.

'I mean about the murder,' said Father Brown; and his voice, though only slightly lifted to a louder note, seemed somehow to resound over the whole shore. 'It was murder; but murder is of the will, which God made free.'

What the other said at the moment in answer to it Payne never knew. For the word had a rather curious effect on him; stirring him like the blast of a trumpet and yet bringing him to a halt. He stood still in the middle of the sandy waste and let the others go on in front of him; he felt the blood crawling through all his veins and the sensation that is called the hair standing on end; and yet he felt a new and unnatural happiness. A psychological process too quick and too complicated for himself to follow had already reached a conclusion that he could not analyse; but the conclusion was one of relief. After standing still for a moment he turned and went back slowly across the sands to the house of the Darnaways.

He crossed the moat with a stride that shook the bridge, descended the stairs and traversed the long rooms with a resounding tread, till he came to the place where Adelaide Darnaway sat haloed with the low light of the oval window, almost like some forgotten saint left behind in the land of death. She looked up, and an expression of wonder made her face yet more wonderful.

'What is it?' she said. 'Why have you come back?'

'I have come for the Sleeping Beauty,' he said in a tone that had the resonance of a laugh. 'This old house went to sleep long ago, as the doctor said; but it is silly for you to pretend to be old. Come up into the daylight and hear the truth. I have brought you a word; it is a terrible word, but it breaks the spell of your captivity.'

She did not understand a word he said, but something made her rise and let him lead her down the long hall and up the stairs and out under the evening sky. The ruins of a dead garden stretched towards the sea, and an old fountain with the figure of a triton, green with rust, remained poised there, pouring nothing out of a dried horn into an empty basin. He had often seen that desolate outline against the evening sky as he passed, and it had seemed to him a type of fallen fortunes in more ways than one. Before long, doubtless, those hollow fonts would be filled, but it would be with the pale green bitter waters of the sea and the flowers would be drowned and strangled in seaweed. So, he had told himself, the daughter of the Darnaways might indeed be wedded; but she would be wedded to death and a doom as deaf and ruthless as the sea. But now he laid a hand on the bronze triton that was like the hand of a giant, and shook it as if he meant to hurl it over like an idol or an evil god of the garden.

'What do you mean?' she asked steadily. 'What is this word that will set us free?'

'The word is murder,' he said, 'and the freedom it brings is as fresh as the flowers of spring. No; I do not mean I have murdered anybody. But the fact that anybody can be murdered is itself good news, after the evil dreams you have been living in. Don't you understand? In that dream of yours everything that happened to you came from inside you; the Doom of the Darnaways was stored up in the Darnaways; it unfolded itself like a horrible flower. There was no escape even by happy accident; it was all inevitable; whether it was Vine and his old-wives' tales, or Barnet and his new-fangled heredity. But this man who died was not the victim of a magic curse or an inherited madness. He was murdered; and for us that murder is simply an accident; yes, requiescat in pace: but a happy accident. It is a ray of daylight, because it comes from outside.'

She suddenly smiled. 'Yes, I believe I understand. I suppose you are talking like a lunatic, but I understand. But who murdered him?'

'I do not know,' he answered calmly, 'but Father Brown knows. And as Father Brown says, murder is at least done by the will, free as that wind from the sea.'

'Father Brown is a wonderful person,' she said after a pause; 'he was the only person who ever brightened my existence in any way at all until—'

'Until what?' asked Payne, and made a movement almost impetuous, leaning towards her and thrusting away the bronze monster so that it seemed to rock on its pedestal.

'Well, until you did,' she said and smiled again.

So was the sleeping palace awakened, and it is no part of this story to describe the stages of its awakening, though much of it had come to pass before the dark of that evening had fallen upon the shore. As Harry Payne strode homewards once more, across those dark sands that he had crossed in so many moods, he was at the highest turn of happiness that is given in this mortal life—and the whole red sea within him was at the top of its tide. He would have had no difficulty in picturing all that place again in flower, and the bronze triton bright as a golden god and the fountain flowing with water or with wine. But all this brightness and blossoming had been unfolded for him by the one word 'murder', and it was still a word that he did not understand. He had taken it on trust, and he was not unwise; for he was one of those who have a sense of the sound of truth.

It was more than a month later that Payne returned to his London house to keep an appointment with Father Brown, taking the required photograph with him. His personal romance had prospered as well as was fitting under the shadow of such a tragedy, and the shadow itself therefore lay rather more lightly on him; but it was hard to view it as anything but the shadow of a family fatality. In many ways he had been much occupied; and it was not until the Darnaway household had resumed its somewhat stern routine, and the portrait had long been restored to its place in the library, that he had managed to photograph it with a magnesium flare. Before sending it to the antiquary, as originally arranged, he brought it to the priest who had so pressingly demanded it.

'I can't understand your attitude about all this. Father Brown,' he said. 'You act as if you had already solved the problem in some way of your own.'

The priest shook his head mournfully. 'Not a bit of it,' he answered. 'I must be very stupid, but I'm quite stuck; stuck about the most practical point of all. It's a queer business; so simple up to a point and then—Let me have a look at that photograph, will you?'

He held it close to his screwed, short-sighted eyes for a moment, and then said: 'Have you got a magnifying glass?'

Payne produced one, and the priest looked through it intently for some time and then said: 'Look at the title of that book at the edge of the bookshelf beside the frame; it's 'The History of Pope Joan'. Now, I wonder ... yes, by George; and the one above is something or other of Iceland. Lord! what a queer way to find it out! What a dolt and donkey I was not to notice it when I was there!'

'But what have you found out?' asked Payne impatiently.

'The last link,' said Father Brown, 'and I'm not stuck any longer. Yes; I think I know how that unhappy story went from first to last now.'

'But why?' insisted the other.

'Why, because,' said the priest with a smile, 'the Darnaway library contained books about Pope Joan and Iceland, not to mention another I see with the title beginning 'The Religion of Frederick', which is not so very hard to fill up.'

Then, seeing the other's annoyance, his smile faded and he said more earnestly: 'As a matter of fact, this last point, though it is the last link, is not the main business. There were much more curious things in the case than that. One of them is rather a curiosity of evidence. Let me begin by saying something that may surprise you. Darnaway did not die at seven o'clock that evening. He had been already dead for a whole day.'

'Surprise is rather a mild word,' said Payne grimly, 'since you and I both saw him walking about afterwards.'

'No, we did not,' replied Father Brown quietly. 'I think we both saw him, or thought we saw him, fussing about with the focusing of his camera. Wasn't his head under that black cloak when you passed through the room? It was when I did. And that's why I felt there was something queer about the room and the figure. It wasn't that the leg was crooked, but rather that it wasn't crooked. It was dressed in the same sort of dark clothes; but if you see what you believe to be one man standing in the way that another man stands, you will think he's in a strange and strained attitude.'

'Do you really mean,' cried Payne with something like a shudder, 'that it was some unknown man?'

'It was the murderer,' said Father Brown. 'He had already killed Darnaway at daybreak and hid the corpse and himself in the dark room—an excellent hiding-place, because nobody normally goes into it or can see much if he does. But he let it fall out on the floor at seven o'clock, of course, that the whole thing might be explained by the curse.'

'But I don't understand' observed Payne. 'Why didn't he kill him at seven o'clock then, instead of loading himself with a corpse for fourteen hours?'

'Let me ask you another question,' said the priest. 'Why was there no photograph taken? Because the murderer made sure of killing him when he first got up, and before he could take it. It was essential to the murderer to prevent that photograph reaching the expert on the Darnaway antiquities.'

There was a sudden silence for a moment, and then the priest went on in a lower tone: 'Don't you see how simple it is? Why, you yourself saw one side of the possibility; but it's simpler even than you thought. You said a man might be faked to resemble an old picture. Surely it's simpler that a picture should be faked to resemble a man. In plain words, it's true in a rather special way that there was no Doom of the Darnaways. There was no old picture; there was no old rhyme; there was no legend of a man who caused his wife's death. But there was a very wicked and a very clever man who was willing to cause another man's death in order to rob him of his promised wife.'

The priest suddenly gave Payne a sad smile, as if in reassurance. 'For the moment I believe you thought I meant you,' he said,' but you were not the only person who haunted that house for sentimental reasons. You know the man, or rather you think you do. But there were depths in the man called Martin Wood, artist and antiquary, which none of his mere artistic acquaintances were likely to guess. Remember, that he was called in to criticize and catalogue the pictures; in an aristocratic dustbin of that sort that practically means simply to tell the Darnaways what art treasures they had got. They would not be surprised at things turning up they had never noticed before. It had to be done well, and it was; perhaps he was right when he said that if it wasn't Holbein it was somebody of the same genius.'

'I feel rather stunned,' said Payne; 'and there are twenty things I don't see yet. How did he know what Darnaway looked like? How did he actually kill him? The doctors seem rather puzzled at present.'

'I saw a photograph the lady had which the Australian sent on before him,' said the priest, 'and there are several ways in which he could have learned things when the new heir was once recognized. We may not know these details; but they are not difficulties. You remember he used to help in the dark room; it seems to me an ideal place, say, to prick a man with a poisoned pin, with the poison's all handy. No; I say these were not difficulties. The difficulty that stumped me was how Wood could be in two places at once. How could he take the corpse from the dark-room and prop it against the camera so that it would fall in a few seconds, without coming downstairs, when he was in the library looking out a book? And I was such a fool that I never looked at the books in the library; and it was only in this photograph, by very undeserved good luck, that I saw the simple fact of a book about Pope Joan.'

'You've kept your best riddle for the end,' said Payne grimly. 'What on earth can Pope Joan have to do with it?'

'Don't forget the book about the Something of Iceland,' advised the priest, 'or the religion of somebody called Frederick. It only remains to ask what sort of man was the late Lord Darnaway.'

'Oh, does it?' observed Payne heavily.

'He was a cultivated, humorous sort of eccentric, I believe,' went on Father Brown. 'Being cultivated, he knew there was no such person as Pope Joan. Being humorous, he was very likely to have thought of the title of 'The Snakes of Iceland' or something else that didn't exist. I venture to reconstruct the third title as 'The Religion of Frederick the Great'—which also doesn't exist. Now, doesn't it strike you that those would be just the titles to put on the backs of books that didn't exist; or in other words on a bookcase that wasn't a bookcase?'

'Ah!' cried Payne; 'I see what you mean now. There was some hidden staircase—'

'Up to the room Wood himself selected as a dark room,' said the priest nodding. 'I'm sorry. It couldn't be helped. It's dreadfully banal and stupid, as stupid as I have been on this pretty banal case. But we were mixed up in a real musty old romance of decayed gentility and a fallen family mansion; and it was too much to hope that we could escape having a secret passage. It was a priest's hole; and I deserve to be put in it.'

8

THE GHOST OF GIDEON WISE
(No record of prior magazine publication found)

Father Brown always regarded the case as the queerest example of the theory of an alibi: the theory by which it is maintained, in defiance of the mythological Irish bird, that it is impossible for anybody to be in two places at once. To begin with, James Byrne, being an Irish journalist, was perhaps the nearest approximation to the Irish bird. He came as near as anybody could to being in two places at once: for he was in two places at the opposite extremes of the social and political world within the space of twenty minutes. The first was in the Babylonian halls of the big hotel, which was the meeting place of the three commercial magnates concerned with arranging for a coal lockout and denouncing it as a coal-strike, the second was in a curious tavern, having the facade of a grocery store, where met the more subterranean triumvirate of those who would have been very glad to turn the lockout into a strike—and the strike into a revolution. The reporter passed to and fro between the three millionaires and the three Bolshevist leaders with the immunity of the modern herald or the new ambassador.

He found the three mining magnates hidden in a jungle of flowering plants and a forest of fluted and florid columns of gilded plaster; gilded birdcages hung high under the painted domes amid the highest leaves of the palms; and in them were birds of motley colours and varied cries. No bird in the wilderness ever sang more unheeded, and no flower ever wasted its sweetness on the desert air more completely than the blossoms of those tall plants wasted theirs upon the brisk and breathless business men, mostly American, who talked and ran to and fro in that place. And there, amid a riot of rococo ornament that nobody ever looked at, and a chatter of expensive foreign birds that nobody ever heard, and a mass of gorgeous upholstery and a labyrinth of luxurious architecture, the three men sat and talked of how success was founded on thought and thrift and a vigilance of economy and self-control.

One of them indeed did not talk so much as the others; but he watched with very bright and motionless eyes, which seemed to be pinched together by his pince-nez, and the permanent smile under his small black moustache was rather like a permanent sneer. This was the famous Jacob P. Stein, and he did not speak till he had something to say. But his companion, old Gallup the Pennsylvanian, a huge fat fellow with reverend grey hair but a face like a pugilist, talked a great deal. He was in a jovial mood and was half rallying, half bullying the third millionaire, Gideon Wise—a hard, dried, angular old bird of the type that his countrymen compare to hickory, with a stiff grey chin-beard and the manners and clothes of any old farmer from the central plains. There was an old argument between Wise and Gallup about combination and competition. For old Wise still retained, with the manners of the old backwoodsman, something of his opinions of the old individualist; he belonged, as we should say in England, to the Manchester School; and Gallup was always trying to persuade him to cut out competition and pool the resources of the world.

'You'll have to come in, old fellow, sooner or later,' Gallup was saying genially as Byrne entered. 'It's the way the world is going, and we can't go back to the one-man-business now. We've all got to stand together.'

'If I might say a word,' said Stein, in his tranquil way, 'I would say there is something a little more urgent even than standing together commercially. Anyhow, we must stand together politically; and that's why I've asked Mr Byrne to meet us here today. On the political issue we must combine; for the simple reason that all our most dangerous enemies are already combined.'

'Oh, I quite agree about political combination,' grumbled Gideon Wise.

'See here,' said Stein to the journalist; 'I know you have the run of these queer places, Mr Byrne, and I want you to do something for us unofficially. You know where these men meet; there are only two or three of them that count, John Elias and Jake Halket, who does all the spouting, and perhaps that poet fellow Home.'

'Why Home used to be a friend of Gideon,' said the jeering Mr Gallup; 'used to be in his Sunday School class or something.'

'He was a Christian, then,' said old Gideon solemnly; 'but when a man takes up with atheists you never know. I still meet him now and then. I was quite ready to back him against war and conscription and all that, of course, but when it comes to all the goddam bolshies in creation—'

'Excuse me,' interposed Stein, 'the matter is rather urgent, so I hope you will excuse me putting it before Mr Byrne at once. Mr Byrne, I may tell you in confidence that I hold information, or rather evidence that would land at least two of those men in prison for long terms, in connexion with conspiracies during the late war. I don't want to use that evidence. But I want you to go to them quietly and tell them that I shall use it, and use it tomorrow, unless they alter their attitude.'

'Well,' replied Byrne, 'what you propose would certainly be called compounding a felony and might be called blackmail, Don't you think it is rather dangerous?'

'I think it is rather dangerous for them,' said Stein with a snap; 'and I want you to go and tell them so.'

'Oh, very well,' said Byrne standing up, with a half humorous sigh. 'It's all in the day's work; but if I get into trouble, I warn you I shall try to drag you into it.'

'You will try, boy,' said old Gallup with a hearty laugh.

For so much still lingers of that great dream of Jefferson and, the thing that men have called Democracy that in his country, while the rich rule like tyrants, the poor do not talk like slaves; but there is candour between the oppressor and the oppressed.

The meeting-place of the revolutionists was a queer, bare, whitewashed place, on the walls of which were one or two distorted uncouth sketches in black and white, in the style of something that was supposed to be Proletarian Art, of which not one proletarian in a million could have made head or tail. Perhaps the one point in common to the two council chambers was that both violated the American Constitution by the display of strong drink. Cocktails of various colours had stood before the three millionaires. Halket, the most violent of the Bolshevists, thought it only appropriate to drink vodka. He was a long, hulking fellow with a menacing stoop, and his very profile was aggressive like a dog's, the nose and lips thrust out together, the latter carrying a ragged red moustache and the whole curling outwards with perpetual scorn. John Elias was a dark watchful man in spectacles, with a black pointed beard; and he had learnt in many European cafes a taste for absinthe. The journalist's first and last feeling was how very like each other, after all, were John Elias and Jacob P. Stein. They were so like in face and mind and manner, that the millionaire might have disappeared down a trapdoor in the Babylon Hotel and come up again in the stronghold of the Bolshevists.

The third man also had a curious taste in drinks, and his drink was symbolic of him. For what stood in front of the poet Home was a glass of milk, and its very mildness seemed in that setting to have something sinister about it, as if its opaque and colourless colour were of some leprous paste more poisonous than the dead sick green of absinthe. Yet in truth the mildness was so far genuine enough; for Henry Home came to the camp of revolution along a very different road and from very different origins from those of Jake, the common tub-thumper, and Elias, the cosmopolitan wire-puller. He had had what is called a careful upbringing, had gone to chapel in his childhood, and carried through life a teetotalism which he could not shake off when he cast away such trifles as Christianity and marriage. He had fair hair and a fine face that might have looked like Shelley, if he had not weakened the chin with a little foreign fringe of beard. Somehow the beard made him look more like a woman; it was as if those few golden hairs were all he could do.

When the journalist entered, the notorious Jake was talking, as he generally was. Home had uttered some casual and conventional phrase about 'Heaven forbid' something or other, and this was quite enough to set Jake off with a torrent of profanity.

'Heaven forbid! and that's about all it bally well does do,' he said. 'Heaven never does anything but forbid this, that and the other; forbids us to strike, and forbids us to fight, and forbids us to shoot the damned usurers and bloodsuckers where they sit. Why doesn't Heaven forbid them something for a bit? Why don't the damned priests and parsons stand up and tell the truth about those brutes for a change? Why doesn't their precious God –'

Elias allowed a gentle sigh, as of faint fatigue, to escape him.

'Priests,' he said, 'belonged, as Marx has shown, to the feudal stage of economic development and are therefore no longer really any part of the problem. The part once played by the priest is now played by the capitalist expert and—'

'Yes,' interrupted the journalist, with his grim and ironic implacability, 'and it's about time you knew that some of them are jolly expert in playing it.' And without moving his own eyes from the bright but dead eyes of Elias, he told him of the threat of Stein.

'I was prepared for something of that sort,' said the smiling Elias without moving; 'I may say quite prepared.'

'Dirty dogs!' exploded Jake. 'If a poor man said a thing like that he'd go to penal servitude. But I reckon they'll go somewhere worse before they guess. If they don't go to hell, I don't know where the hell they'll go to—'

Home made a movement of protest, perhaps not so much at what the man was saying as at what he was going to say, and Elias cut the speech short with cold exactitude.

'It is quite unnecessary for us,' he said, looking at Byrne steadily through his spectacles, 'to bandy threats with the other side. It is quite sufficient that their threats are quite ineffective so far as we are concerned. We also have made all our own arrangements, and some of them will not appear until they appear in motion. So far as we are concerned, an immediate rupture and an extreme trial of strength will be quite according to plan.'

As he spoke in a quite quiet and dignified fashion, something in his motionless yellow face and his great goggles started a faint fear creeping up the journalist's spine. Halket's savage face might seem to have a snarl in its very silhouette when seen sideways; but when seen face to face, the smouldering rage in his eyes had also something of anxiety, as if the ethical and economic riddle were after all a little too much for him; and Home seemed even more hanging on wires of worry and self-criticism. But about this third man with the goggles, who spoke so sensibly and simply, there was something uncanny; it was like a dead man talking at the table.

As Byrne went out with his message of defiance, and passed along the very narrow passage beside the grocery store, he found the end of it blocked by a strange though strangely familiar figure: short and sturdy, and looking rather quaint when seen in dark outline with its round head and wide hat.

'Father Brown!' cried the astonished journalist. 'I think you must have come into the wrong door. You're not likely to be in this little conspiracy.'

'Mine is a rather older conspiracy,' replied Father Brown smiling, 'but it is quite a widespread conspiracy.'

'Well,' replied Byrne, 'you can't imagine any of the people here being within a thousand miles of your concern.'

'It is not always easy to tell,' replied the priest equably; 'but as a matter of fact, there is one person here who's within an inch of it.'

He disappeared into the dark entrance and the journalist went on his way very much puzzled. He was still more puzzled by a small incident that happened to him as he turned into the hotel to make his report to his capitalist clients. The bower of blossoms and bird-cages in which those crabbed old gentlemen were embosomed was approached by a flight of marble steps, flanked by gilded nymphs and tritons. Down these steps ran an active young man with black hair, a snub nose, and a flower in his buttonhole, who seized him and drew him aside before he could ascend the stair.

'I say,' whispered the young man, 'I'm Potter—old Gid's secretary, you know: now, between ourselves, there is a sort of a thunderbolt being forged, isn't there, now?'

'I came to the conclusion,' replied Byrne cautiously, 'that the Cyclops had something on the anvil. But always remember that the Cyclops is a giant, but he has only one eye. I think Bolshevism is—'

While he was speaking the secretary listened with a face that had a certain almost Mongolian immobility, despite the liveliness of his legs and his attire. But when Byrne said the word 'Bolshevism', the young man's sharp eyes shifted and he said quickly:

'What has that—oh yes, that sort of thunderbolt; so sorry, my mistake. So easy to say anvil when you mean ice-box.'

With which the extraordinary young man disappeared down the steps and Byrne continued to mount them, more and more mystification clouding his mind.

He found the group of three augmented to four by the presence of a hatchet-faced person with very thin straw-coloured hair and a monocle, who appeared to be a sort of adviser to old Gallup, possibly his solicitor, though he was not definitely so called. His name was Nares, and the questions which he directed towards Byrne referred chiefly, for some reason or other, to the number of those probably enrolled in the revolutionary organization. Of this, as Byrne knew little, he said less; and the four men eventually rose from their seats, the last word being with the man who had been most silent.

'Thank you, Mr Byrne,' said Stein, folding up his eyeglasses. 'It only remains to say that everything is ready; on that point I quite agree with Mr Elias. Tomorrow, before noon, the police will have arrested Mr Elias, on evidence I shall by then have put before them, and those three at least will be in jail before night. As you know, I attempted to avoid this course. I think that is all, gentlemen.'

But Mr Jacob P. Stein did not lay his formal information next day, for a reason that has often interrupted the activities of such industrious characters. He did not do it because he happened to be dead; and none of the rest of the programme was carried out, for a reason which Byrne found displayed in gigantic letters when he opened his morning paper: 'Terrific Triple Murder: Three Millionaires Slain in One Night.' Other exclamatory phrases followed in smaller letters, only about four times the size of normal type, which insisted on the special feature of the mystery: the fact that the three men had been killed not only simultaneously but in three widely separated places—Stein in his artistic and luxurious country seat a hundred miles inland, Wise outside the little bungalow on the coast where he lived on sea breezes and the simple life, and old Gallup in a thicket just outside the lodge-gates of his great house at the other end of the county. In all three cases there could be no doubt about the scenes of violence that had preceded death, though the actual body of Gallup was not found till the second day, where it hung, huge and horrible, amid the broken forks and branches of the little wood into which its weight had crashed, like a bison rushing on the spears: while Wise had clearly been flung over the cliff into the sea, not without a struggle, for his scraping and slipping footprints could still be traced upon the very brink. But the first signal of the tragedy had been the sight of his large limp straw hat, floating far out upon the waves and conspicuous from the cliffs above. Stein's body also had at first eluded search, till a faint trail of blood led the investigators to a bath on the ancient Roman model he had been constructing in his garden; for he had been a man of an experimental turn of mind with a taste for antiquities.

Whatever he might think, Byrne was bound to admit that there was no legal evidence against anybody as things stood. A motive for murder was not enough. Even a moral aptitude for murder was not enough. And he could not conceive that pale young pacifist, Henry Home, butchering another man by brutal violence, though he might imagine the blaspheming Jake and even the sneering Jew as capable of anything. The police, and the man who appeared to be assisting them (who was no other than the rather mysterious man with the monocle, who had been introduced as Mr Nares), realized the position quite as clearly as the journalist.

They knew that at the moment the Bolshevist conspirators could not be prosecuted and convicted, and that it would be a highly sensational failure if they were prosecuted and acquitted. Nares started with an artful candour by calling them in some sense to the council, inviting them to a private conclave and asking them to give their opinions freely in the interests of humanity. He had started his investigations at the nearest scene of tragedy, the bungalow by the sea; and Byrne was permitted to be present at a curious scene, which was at once a peaceful parley of diplomatists and a veiled inquisition or putting of suspects to the question. Rather to Byrne's surprise the incongruous company, seated round the table in the seaside bungalow, included the dumpy figure and owlish head of Father Brown, though his connexion with the affair did not appear until some time afterwards. The presence of young Potter, the dead man's secretary, was more natural; yet somehow his demeanour was not quite so natural. He alone was quite familiar with their meeting-place, and was even in some grim sense their host; yet he offered little assistance or information. His round snub-nosed face wore an expression more like sulks than sorrow.

Jake Halket as usual talked most; and a man of his type could not be expected to keep up the polite fiction that he and his friends were not accused. Young Home, in his more refined way, tried to restrain him when he began to abuse the men who had been murdered; but Jake was always quite as ready to roar down his friends as his foes. In a spout of blasphemies he relieved his soul of a very unofficial obituary notice of the late Gideon Wise. elias sat quite still and apparently indifferent behind those spectacles that masked his eyes.

'It would be useless, I suppose,' said nares coldly, 'to tell you that your remarks are indecent. It may affect you more if I tell you they are imprudent. You practically admit that you hated the dead man.'

'Going to put me in quod for that, are you?' jeered the demagogue. 'All right. Only you'll have to build a prison for a million men if you're going to jail all the poor people who had reason to hate Gid Wise. And you know it's God truth as well as I do.'

Nares was silent; and nobody spoke until Elias interposed with his clear though faintly lisping drawl.

'This appears to me to be a highly unprofitable discussion on both sides,' he said. 'You have summoned us here either to ask us for information or to subject us to cross-examination. If you trust us, we tell you we have no information. If you distrust us, you must tell us of what we are accused, or have the politeness to keep the fact to yourselves. Nobody has been able to suggest the faintest trace of evidence connecting any one of us with these tragedies any more than with the murder of Julius Caesar. You dare not arrest us, and you will not believe us. What is the good of our remaining here?'

And he rose, calmly buttoning his coat, his friends following his example. As they went towards the door, young Home turned back and faced the investigators for a moment with his pale fanatical face.

'I wish to say,' he said, 'that I went to a filthy jail during the whole war because I would not consent to kill a man.'

With that they passed out, and the members of the group remaining looked grimly at each other.

'I hardly think,' said Father Brown, 'that we remain entirely victorious, in spite of the retreat.'

'I don't mind anything,' said Nares, 'except being bullyragged by that blasphemous blackguard Halket. Home is a gentleman, anyhow. But whatever they say, I am dead certain they know; they are in it, or most of them are. They almost admitted it. They taunted us with not being able to prove we're right, much more than with being wrong. What do you think, Father Brown?'

The person addressed looked across at Nares with a gaze almost disconcertingly mild and meditative.

'It is quite true,' he said, 'that I have formed an idea that one particular person knows more than he has told us. But I think it would be well if I did not mention his name just yet.'

Nares' eyeglass dropped from his eye, and he looked up sharply. 'This is unofficial so far,' he said. 'I suppose you know that at a later stage if you withhold information, your position may be serious.'

'My position is simple,' replied the priest. 'I am here to look after the legitimate interests of my friend Halket. I think it will be in his interest, under the circumstances, if I tell you I think he will before long sever his connexion with this organization, and cease to be a Socialist in that sense. I have every reason to believe he will probably end as a Catholic.'

'Halket!' exploded the other incredulously. 'Why he curses priests from morning till night!'

'I don't think you quite understand that kind of man,' said Father Brown mildly. 'He curses priests for failing (in his opinion) to defy the whole world for justice. Why should he expect them to defy the whole world for justice, unless he had already begun to assume they were—what they are? But we haven't met here to discuss the psychology of conversion. I only mention this because it may simplify your task—perhaps narrow your search.'

'If it is true, it would jolly well narrow it to that narrow-faced rascal Elias—and I shouldn't wonder, for a more creepy, coldblooded, sneering devil I never saw.'

Father Brown sighed. 'He always reminded me of poor Stein,' he said, 'in fact I think he was some relation.'

'Oh, I say,' began Nares, when his protest was cut short by the door being flung open, revealing once more the long loose figure and pale face of young Home; but it seemed as if he had not merely his natural, but a new and unnatural pallor.

'Hullo,' cried Nares, putting up his single eyeglass, 'why have you come back again?'

Home crossed the room rather shakily without a word and sat down heavily in a chair. Then he said, as in a sort of daze: 'I missed the others ... I lost my way. I thought I'd better come back.'

The remains of evening refreshments were on the table, and Henry Home, that lifelong Prohibitionist, poured himself out a wine-glassful of liqueur brandy and drank it at a gulp. 'You seem upset,' said Father Brown.

Home had put his hands to his forehead and spoke as from under the shadow of it: he seemed to be speaking to the priest only, in a low voice.

'I may as well tell you. I have seen a ghost.'

'A ghost!' repeated Nares in astonishment. 'Whose ghost?'

'The ghost of Gideon Wise, the master of this house,' answered Home more firmly, 'standing over the abyss into which he fell.'

'Oh, nonsense!' said Nares; 'no sensible person believes in ghosts.'

'That is hardly exact,' said Father Brown, smiling a little. 'There is really quite as good evidence for many ghosts as there is for most crimes.'

'Well, it's my business to run after the criminals,' said Nares rather roughly, 'and I will leave other people to run away from the ghosts. If anybody at this time of day chooses to be frightened of ghosts it's his affair.'

'I didn't say I was frightened of them, though I dare say I might be,' said Father Brown. 'Nobody knows till he tries. I said I believed in them, at any rate, enough to want to hear more about this one. What, exactly, did you see, Mr Home?'

'It was over there on the brink of those crumbling cliffs; you know there is a sort of gap or crevice just about the spot where he was thrown over. The others had gone on ahead, and I was crossing the moor towards the path along the cliff. I often went that way, for I liked seeing the high seas dash up against the crags. I thought little of it tonight, beyond wondering that the sea should be so rough on this sort of clear moonlight night. I could see the pale crests of spray appear and disappear as the great waves leapt up at the headland. Thrice I saw the momentary flash of foam in the moonlight and then I saw something inscrutable. The fourth flash of the silver foam seemed to be fixed in the sky. It did not fall; I waited with insane intensity for it to fall. I fancied I was mad, and that time had been for me mysteriously arrested or prolonged. Then I drew nearer, and then I think I screamed aloud. For that suspended spray, like unfallen snowflakes, had fitted together into a face and a figure, white as the shining leper in a legend, and terrible as the fixed lightning.'

'And it was Gideon Wise, you say?'

Home nodded without speech. There was a silence broken abruptly by Nares rising to his feet; so abruptly indeed that he knocked a chair over.

'Oh, this is all nonsense,' he said, 'but we'd better go out and see.'

'I won't go,' said Home with sudden violence. 'I'll never walk by that path again.'

'I think we must all walk by that path tonight,' said the priest gravely; 'though I will never deny it has been a perilous path ... to more people than one.'

'I will not... God, how you all goad me,' cried Home, and his eyes began to roll in a strange fashion. He had risen with the rest, hut he made no motion towards the door.

'Mr Home,' said Nares firmly, 'I am a police-officer, and this house, though you may not know it, is surrounded by the police. I have tried to investigate in a friendly fashion, but I must investigate everything, even anything so silly as a ghost. I must ask you to take me to the spot you speak of.'

There was another silence while Home stood heaving and panting as with indescribable fears. Then he suddenly sat down on his chair again and said with an entirely new and much more composed voice:

'I can't do it. You may just as well know why. You will know it sooner or later. I killed him.'

For an instant there was the stillness of a house struck by a thunderbolt and full of corpses. Then the voice of Father Brown sounded in that enormous silence strangely small like the squeak of a mouse.

'Did you kill him deliberately?' he asked.

'How can one answer such a question?' answered the man in the chair, moodily gnawing his finger. 'I was mad, I suppose. He was intolerable and insolent, I know. I was on his land and I believe he struck me; anyhow, we came to a grapple and he went over the cliff. When I was well away from the scene it burst upon me that I had done a crime that cut me off from men; the brand of Cain throbbed on my brow and my very brain; I realized for the first time that I had indeed killed a man. I knew I should have to confess it sooner or later.' He sat suddenly erect in his chair. 'But I will say nothing against anybody else. It is no use asking me about plots or accomplices—I will say nothing.'

'In the light of the other murders,' said nares, 'it is difficult to believe that the quarrel was quite so unpremeditated. Surely somebody sent you there?'

'I will say nothing against anybody I worked with,' said Home proudly. 'I am a murderer, but I will not be a traitor.'

Nares stepped between the man and the door and called out in an official fashion to someone outside.

'We will all go to the place, anyhow,' he said in a low voice to the secretary; 'but this man must go in custody.'

The company generally felt that to go spook-hunting on a seacliff was a very silly anti-climax after the confession of the murderer. But Nares, though the most sceptical and scornful of all, thought it his duty to leave no stone unturned; as one might say, no gravestone unturned. For, after all, that crumbling cliff was the only gravestone over the watery grave of poor Gideon

Wise. Nares locked the door, being the last out of the house, and followed the rest across the moor to the cliff, when he was astonished to see young Potter, the secretary, coming back quickly towards them, his face in the moonlight looking white as a moon.

'By God, sir,' he said, speaking for the first time that night, 'there really is something there. It—it's just like him.'

'Why, you're raving,' gasped the detective. 'Everybody's raving.'

'Do you think I don't know him when I see him?' cried the secretary with singular bitterness. 'I have reason to.'

'Perhaps,' said the detective sharply, 'you are one of those who had reason to hate him, as Halket said.'

'Perhaps,' said the secretary; 'anyhow, I know him, and I tell you I can see him standing there stark and staring under this hellish moon.'

And he pointed towards the crack in the cliffs, where they could already see something that might have been a moonbeam or a streak of foam, but which was already beginning to look a little more solid. They had crept a hundred yards nearer, and it was still motionless; but it looked like a statue in silver.

Nares himself looked a little pale and seemed to stand debating what to do. Potter was frankly as much frightened as Home himself; and even Byrne, who was a hardened reporter, was rather reluctant to go any nearer if he could help it. He could not help considering it a little quaint, therefore, that the only man who did not seem to be frightened of a ghost was the man who had said openly that he might be. For Father Brown was advancing as steadily, at his stumping pace, as if he were going to consult a noticeboard.

'It don't seem to bother you much,' said Byrne to the priest; 'and yet I thought you were the only one who believed in spooks.'

'If it comes to that,' replied Father Brown, 'I thought you were one who didn't believe in them. But believing in ghosts is one thing, and believing in a ghost is quite another.'

Byrne looked rather ashamed of himself, and glanced almost covertly at the crumbling headlands in the cold moonlight which were the haunts of the vision or delusion. 'I didn't believe in it till I saw it,' he said.

'And I did believe in it till I saw it,' said Father Brown. The journalist stared after him as he went stumping across the great waste ground that rose towards the cloven headland like the sloping side of a hill cut in two. Under the discolouring moon the grass looked like long grey hair all combed one way by the wind, and seeming to point towards the place where the breaking cliff showed pale gleams of chalk in the grey-green turf, and where stood the pale figure or shining shade that none could yet understand. As yet that pale figure dominated a desolate landscape that was empty except for the black square back and business-like figure of the priest advancing alone towards it. Then the prisoner Home broke suddenly from his captors with a piercing cry and ran ahead of the priest, falling on his knees before the spectre.

'I have confessed,' they heard him crying. 'Why have you come to tell them I killed you?'

'I have come to tell them you did not,' said the ghost, and stretched forth a hand to him. Then the kneeling man sprang up with quite a new kind of scream; and they knew it was the hand of flesh.

It was the most remarkable escape from death in recent records, said the experienced detective and the no less experienced journalist. Yet, in a sense, it had been very simple after all. Flakes and shards of the cliff were continually falling away, and some had caught in the gigantic crevice, so as to form what was really a ledge or pocket in what was supposed to be a sheer drop through darkness to the sea. The old man, who was a very tough and wiry old man, had fallen on this lower shoulder of rock and had passed a pretty terrible twenty-four hours in trying to climb back by crags that constantly collapsed under him, but at length formed by their very ruins a sort of stairway of escape. This might be the explanation of Home's optical illusion about a white wave that appeared and disappeared, and finally came to stay. But anyhow there was Gideon Wise, solid in bone and sinew, with his white hair and white dusty country clothes and harsh country features, which were, however, a great deal less harsh than usual. Perhaps it is good for millionaires to spend twenty-four hours on a ledge of rock within a foot of eternity. Anyhow, he not only disclaimed all malice against the criminal, but gave an account of the matter which considerably modified the crime. He declared that Home had not thrown him over at all; that the continually breaking ground had given way under him, and that Home had even made some movement as of attempted rescue.

'On that providential bit of rock down there,' he said solemnly, 'I promised the Lord to forgive my enemies; and the Lord would think it mighty mean if I didn't forgive a little accident like that.'

Home had to depart under police supervision, of course, but the detective did not disguise from himself that the prisoner's detention would probably be short, and his punishment, if any, trifling. It is not every murderer who can put the murdered man in the witness-box to give him a testimonial.

'It's a strange case,' said Byrne, as the detective and the others hastened along the cliff path towards the town.

'It is,' said Father Brown. 'It's no business of ours; but I wish you'd stop with me and talk it over.'

There was a silence and then Byrne complied by saying suddenly: 'I suppose you were thinking of Home already, when you said somebody wasn't telling all he knew.'

'When I said that,' replied his friend, 'I was thinking of the exceedingly silent Mr Potter, the secretary of the no longer late or (shall we say) lamented Mr Gideon Wise.'

'Well, the only time Potter ever spoke to me I thought he was a lunatic,' said Byrne, staring, 'but I never thought of his being a criminal. He said something about it all having to do with an icebox.'

'Yes, I thought he knew something about it,' said Father Brown reflectively. 'I never said he had anything to do with it ... I suppose old Wise really is strong enough to have climbed out of that chasm.'

'What do you mean?' asked the astonished reporter. 'Why, of course he got out of that chasm; for there he is.'

The priest did not answer the question but asked abruptly: 'What do you think of Home?'

'Well, one can't call him a criminal exactly,' answered Byrne. 'He never was at all like any criminal I ever knew, and I've had some experience; and, of course, Nares has had much more. I don't think we ever quite believed him a criminal.'

'And I never believed in him in another capacity,' said the priest quietly. 'You may know more about criminals. But there's one class of people I probably do know more about than you do, or even Nares for that matter. I've known quite a lot of them, and I know their little ways.'

'Another class of people,' repeated Byrne, mystified.' Why, what class do you know about?'

'Penitents,' said Father Brown.

'I don't quite understand,' objected Byrne. 'Do you mean you don't believe in his crime?'

'I don't believe in his confession,' said Father Brown. 'I've heard a good many confessions, and there was never a genuine one like that. It was romantic; it was all out of books. Look how he talked about having the brand of Cain. That's out of books. It's not what anyone would feel who had in his own person done a thing hitherto horrible to him. Suppose you were an honest clerk or shop-boy shocked to feel that for the first time you'd stolen money. Would you immediately reflect that your action was the same as that of Barabbas? Suppose you'd killed a child in some ghastly anger. Would you go back through history, till you could identify your action with that of an Idumean potentate named Herod? Believe me, our own crimes are far too hideously private and prosaic to make our first thoughts turn towards historical parallels, however apt. And why did he go out of his way to say he would not give his colleagues away? Even in saying so, he was giving them away. Nobody had asked him so far to give away anything or anybody. No; I don't think he was genuine, and I wouldn't give him absolution. A nice state of things, if people started getting absolved for what they hadn't done.' And Father Brown, his head turned away, looked steadily out to sea.

'But I don't understand what you're driving at,' cried Byrne. 'What's the good of buzzing round him with suspicions when he's pardoned? He's out of it anyhow. He's quite safe.'

Father Brown spun round like a teetotum and caught his friend by the coat with unexpected and inexplicable excitement.

'That's it,' he cried emphatically. 'Freeze on to that! He's quite safe. He's out of it. That's why he's the key of the whole puzzle.'

'Oh, help,' said Byrne feebly.

'I mean,' persisted the little priest, 'he's in it because he's out of it. That's the whole explanation.'

'And a very lucid explanation too,' said the journalist with feeling.

They stood looking out to sea for a time in silence, and then Father Brown said cheerfully: 'And so we come back to the ice-box. Where you have all gone wrong from the first in this business is where a good many of the papers and the public men do go wrong. It's because you assumed that there is nothing whatever in the modern world to fight about except Bolshevism. This story has nothing whatever to do with Bolshevism; except perhaps as a blind.'

'I don't see how that can be,' remonstrated Byrne. 'Here you have the three millionaires in that one business murdered—'

'No!' said the priest in a sharp ringing voice. 'You do not. That is just the point. You do not have three millionaires murdered. You have two millionaires murdered; and you have the third millionaire very much alive and kicking and quite ready to kick. And you have that third millionaire freed forever from the threat that was thrown at his head before your very face, in playfully polite terms, and in that conversation you described as taking place in the hotel. Gallup and Stein threatened the more old-fashioned and independent old huckster that if he would not come into their combine they would freeze him out. Hence the ice-box, of course.'

After a pause he went on. 'There is undoubtedly a Bolshevist movement in the modern world, and it must undoubtedly be resisted, though I do not believe very much in your way of resisting it. But what nobody notices is that there is another movement equally modern and equally moving: the great movement towards monopoly or the turning of all trades into trusts. That also is a revolution. That also produces what all revolutions produce. Men will kill for that and against that, as they do for and against Bolshevism. It has its ultimatums and its invasions and its executions. These trust magnates have their courts like kings; they have their bodyguard and bravos; they have their spies in the enemy camp. Horne was one of old Gideon's spies in one of the enemy camps, but he was used here against another enemy: the rivals who were ruining him for standing out.'

'I still don't quite see how he was used,' said Byrne, 'or what was the good of it.'

'Don't you see,' cried Father Brown sharply, 'that they gave each other an alibi?'

Byrne still looked at him a little doubtfully, though understanding was dawning on his face.

'That's what I mean,' continued the other, 'when I say they were in it because they were out of it. Most people would say they must be out of the other two crimes, because they were in this one. As a fact, they were in the other two because they were out of this one; because this one never happened at all. A very queer, improbable sort of alibi, of course; improbable and therefore impenetrable. Most people would say a man who confesses a murder must be sincere; a man who forgives his murderer must be sincere. Nobody would think of the notion that the thing never happened, so that one man had nothing to forgive and the other nothing to fear. They were fixed here for that night by a story against themselves. But they were not here that night; for Home was murdering old Gallup in the Wood, while Wise was strangling that little Jew in his Roman bath. That's why I ask whether Wise was really strong enough for the climbing adventure.'

'It was quite a good adventure,' said Byrne regretfully. 'It fitted into the landscape, and was really very convincing.'

'Too convincing to convince,' said Father Brown, shaking his head. 'How very vivid was that moonlit foam flung up and turning to a ghost. And how very literary! Home is a sneak and a skunk, but do not forget that, like many other sneaks and skunks in history, he is also a poet.'

THE END

The Secret of Father Brown

First UK edition: Cassell & Co., London, 1927
First US edition: Harper & Brothers,
New York, 1927

To Father John O'connor, of St. Cuthbert's Bradford,
Whose truth is stranger than fiction,
With a gratitude greater than the world.

CONTENTS

1

THE SECRET OF FATHER BROWN
(No record of prior magazine publication found)

Flambeau, once the most famous criminal in France and later a very private detective in England, had long retired from both professions. Some say a career of crime had left him with too many scruples for a career of detection. Anyhow, after a life of romantic escapes and tricks of evasion, he had ended at what some might consider an appropriate address: in a castle in Spain. The castle, however, was solid though relatively small; and the black vineyard and green stripes of kitchen garden covered a respectable square on the brown hillside. For Flambeau, after all his violent adventures, still possessed what is possessed by so many Latins, what is absent (for instance) in so many Americans, the energy to retire. It can be seen in many a large hotel-proprietor whose one ambition is to be a small peasant. It can be seen in many a French provincial shopkeeper, who pauses at the moment when he might develop into a detestable millionaire and buy a street of shops, to fall back quietly and comfortably on domesticity and dominoes. Flambeau had casually and almost abruptly fallen in love with a Spanish Lady, married and brought up a large family on a Spanish estate, without displaying any apparent desire to stray again beyond its borders. But on one particular morning he was observed by his family to be unusually restless and excited; and he outran the little boys and descended the greater part of the long mountain slope to meet the visitor who was coming across the valley; even when the visitor was still a black dot in the distance.

The black dot gradually increased in size without very much altering in the shape; for it continued, roughly speaking, to be both round and black. The black clothes of clerics were not unknown upon those hills; but these clothes, however clerical, had about them something at once commonplace and yet almost jaunty in comparison with the cassock or soutane, and marked the wearer as a man from the northwestern islands, as clearly as if he had been labelled Clapham Junction. He carried a short thick umbrella with a knob like a club, at the sight of which his Latin friend almost shed tears of sentiment; for it had figured in many adventures that they shared long ago. For this was the Frenchman's English friend. Father Brown, paying a long-desired but long-delayed visit. They had corresponded constantly, but they had not met for years.

Father Brown was soon established in the family circle, which was quite large enough to give the general sense of company or a community. He was introduced to the big wooden images of the Three Kings, of painted and gilded wood, who bring the gifts to the children at Christmas; for Spain is a country where the affairs of the children bulk large in the life of the home. He was introduced to the dog and the cat and the livestock on the farm. But he was also, as it happened, introduced to one neighbour who, like himself, had brought into that valley the garb and manners of distant lands.

It was on the third night of the priest's stay at the little chateau that he beheld a stately stranger who paid his respects to the Spanish household with bows that no Spanish grandee could emulate. He was a tall, thin grey-haired and very handsome gentleman, and his hands, cuffs and cuff-links had something overpowering in their polish. But his long face had nothing of that languor which is associated with long cuffs and manicuring in the caricatures of our own country. It was rather arrestingly alert and keen; and the eyes had an innocent intensity of inquiry that does not go often with grey hairs. That alone might have marked the man's nationality, as well the nasal note in his refined voice and his rather too ready assumption of the vast antiquity of all the European things around him. This was, indeed, no less a person than Mr Grandison Chace, of Boston, an American traveller who had halted for a time in his American travels by taking a lease of the adjoining estate; a somewhat similar castle on a somewhat similar hill. He delighted in his old castle, and he regarded his friendly neighbour as a local antiquity of the same type. For Flambeau managed, as we have said, really to look retired in the sense of rooted. He might have grown there with his own vine and fig-tree for ages. He had resumed his real family name of Duroc; for the other title of "The Torch" had only been a title de guerre, like that under which such a man will often wage war on society. He was fond of his wife and family; he never went farther afield than was needed for a little shooting; and he seemed, to the American globetrotter, the embodiment of that cult of a sunny respectability and a temperate luxury, which the American was wise enough to see and admire in the Mediterranean peoples. The rolling stone from the West was glad to rest for a moment on this rock in the South that had gathered so very much moss. But Mr Chace had heard of Father Brown, and his tone faintly changed, as towards a celebrity. The interviewing instinct awoke, tactful but tense. If he did try to draw Father Brown, as if he were a tooth, it was done with the most dexterous and painless American dentistry.

They were sitting in a sort of partly unroofed outer court of the house, such as often forms the entrance to Spanish houses. It was dusk turning to dark; and as all that mountain air sharpens suddenly after sunset, a small stove stood on the flagstones, glowing with red eyes like a goblin, and painting a red pattern on the pavement; but scarcely a ray of it reached the lower bricks of the great bare, brown brick wall that went soaring up above them into the deep blue night. Flambeau's big broad-shouldered figure and great moustaches, like sabres, could be traced dimly in the twilight, as he moved about, drawing dark wine from a great cask and handing it round. In his shadow, the priest looked very shrunken and small, as if huddled over the stove; but the American visitor leaned forward elegantly with his elbow on his knee and his fine pointed features in the full light; his eyes shone with inquisitive intelligence.

"I can assure you, sir," he was saying, "we consider your achievement in the matter of the Moonshine Murder the most remarkable triumph in the history of detective science."

Father Brown murmured something; some might have imagined that the murmur was a little like a moan.

"We are well acquainted," went on the stranger firmly, "with the alleged achievements of Dupin and others; and with those of Lecocq, Sherlock Holmes, Nicholas Carter, and other imaginative incarnations of the craft. But we observe there is in many ways, a marked difference between your own method, of approach and that of these other thinkers, whether fictitious or actual. Some have spec'lated, sir, as to whether the difference of method may perhaps involve rather the absence of method."

Father Brown was silent; then he started a little, almost as if he had been nodding over the stove, and said: "I beg your pardon. Yes... Absence of method... Absence of mind, too, I'm afraid."

"I should say of strictly tabulated scientific method," went on the inquirer. "Edgar Poe throws off several little essays in a conversational form, explaining Dupin's method, with its fine links of logic. Dr Watson had to listen to some pretty exact expositions of Holmes's method with its observation of material details. But nobody seems to have got on to any full account of your method. Father Brown, and I was informed you declined the offer to give a series of lectures in the States on the matter."

"Yes," said the priest, frowning at the stove; "I declined."

"Your refusal gave rise to a remarkable lot of interesting talk," remarked Chace. "I may say that some of our people are saying your science can't be expounded, because it's something more than just natural science. They say your secret's not to be divulged, as being occult in its character."

"Being what?" asked Father Brown, rather sharply.

"Why, kind of esoteric," replied the other. "I can tell you, people got considerably worked up about Gallup's murder, and Stein's murder, and then old man Merton's murder, and now Judge Gwynne's murder, and a double murder by Dalmon, who was well known in the States. And there were you, on the spot every time, slap in the middle of it; telling everybody how it was done and never telling anybody how you knew. So some people got to think you knew without looking, so to speak. And Carlotta Brownson gave a lecture on Thought-Forms with illustrations from these cases of yours. The Second Sight Sisterhood of Indianapolis—"

Father Brown, was still staring at the stove; then he said quite loud yet as if hardly aware that anyone heard him: "Oh, I say. This will never do."

"I don't exactly know how it's to be helped," said Mr Chace humorously. "The Second Sight Sisterhood want a lot of holding down. The only way I can think of stopping it is for you to tell us the secret after all."

Father Brown groaned. He put his head on his hands and remained a moment, as if full of a silent convulsion of thought. Then he lifted his head and said in a dull voice:

"Very well. I must tell the secret."

His eyes rolled darkly over the whole darkling scene, from the red eyes of the little stove to the stark expanse of the ancient wall, over which were standing out, more and more brightly, the strong stars of the south.

"The secret is," he said; and then stopped as if unable to go on. Then he began again and said:

"You see, it was I who killed all those people."

"What?" repeated the other, in a small voice out of a vast silence.

"You see, I had murdered them all myself," explained Father Brown patiently. "So, of course, I knew how it was done."

Grandison Chace had risen to his great height like a man lifted to the ceiling by a sort of slow explosion. Staring down at the other he repeated his incredulous question.

"I had planned out each of the crimes very carefully," went on Father Brown, "I had thought out exactly how a thing like that could be done, and in what style or state of mind a man could really do it. And when I was quite sure that I felt exactly like the murderer myself, of course I knew who he was."

Chace gradually released a sort of broken sigh.

"You frightened me all right," he said. "For the minute I really did think you meant you were the murderer. Just for the minute I kind of saw it splashed over all the papers in the States: 'Saintly Sleuth Exposed as Killer: Hundred Crimes of Father Brown.' Why, of course, if it's just a figure of speech and means you tried to reconstruct the psychogy—"

Father Brown rapped sharply on the stove with the short pipe he was about to fill; one or his very rare spasms of annoyance contracted his face.

"No, no, no," he said, almost angrily; "I don't mean just a figure of speech. This is what comes of trying to talk about deep things... What's the good of words...? If you try to talk about a truth that's merely moral, people always think it's merely metaphorical. A real live man with two legs once said to me: 'I only believe in the Holy Ghost in a spiritual sense.' Naturally, I said: 'In what other sense could you believe it?' And then he thought I meant he needn't believe in anything except evolution, or ethical fellowship, or some bilge... I mean that I really did see myself, and my real self, committing the murders. I didn't actually kill the men by material means; but that's not the point. Any brick or bit of machinery might have killed them by material means. I mean that I thought and thought about how a man might come to be like that, until I realized that I really was like that, in everything except actual final consent to the action. It was once suggested to me by a friend of mine, as a sort of religious exercise. I believe he got it from Pope Leo XIII, who was always rather a hero of mine."

"I'm afraid," said the American, in tones that were still doubtful, and keeping his eye on the priest rather as if he were a wild animal, "that you'd have to explain a lot to me before I knew what you were talking about. The science of detection—"

Father Brown snapped his fingers with the same animated annoyance. "That's it," he cried; "that's just where we part company. Science is a grand thing when you can get it; in its real sense one of the grandest words in the world. But what do these men mean, nine times out often, when they use it nowadays? When they say detection is a science? When they say criminology is a science? They mean getting outside a man and studying him as if he were a gigantic insect: in what they would call a dry impartial light, in what I should call a dead and dehumanized light. They mean getting a long way off him, as if he were a distant prehistoric monster; staring at the shape of his 'criminal skull' as if it were a sort of eerie growth, like the horn on a rhinoceros' nose. When the scientist talks about a type, he never means himself, but always his neighbour; probably his poorer neighbour. I don't deny the dry light may sometimes do good; though in one sense it's the very reverse of science. So far from being knowledge, it's actually suppression of what we know. It's treating a friend as a stranger, and pretending that something familiar is really remote and mysterious. It's like saying that a man has a proboscis between the eyes, or that he falls down in a fit of insensibility once every twenty-four hours. Well, what you call 'the secret' is exactly the opposite. I don't try to get outside the man. I try to get inside the murderer... Indeed it's much more than that, don't you see? I am inside a man. I am always inside a man, moving his arms and legs; but I wait till I know I am inside a murderer, thinking his thoughts, wrestling with his passions; till I have bent myself into the posture of his hunched and peering hatred; till I see the world with his bloodshot and squinting eyes, looking between the blinkers of his half-witted concentration; looking up the short and sharp perspective of a straight road to a pool of blood. Till I am really a murderer."

"Oh," said Mr Chace, regarding him with a long, grim face, and added: "And that is what you call a religious exercise."

"Yes," said Father Brown; "that is what I call a religious exercise."

After an instant's silence he resumed: "It's so real a religious exercise that I'd rather not have said anything about it. But I simply couldn't have you going off and telling all your countrymen that I had a secret magic connected with Thought-Forms, could I? I've put it badly, but it's true. No man's really any good till he knows how bad he is, or might be; till he's realized exactly how much right he has to all this snobbery, and sneering, and talking about 'criminals,' as if they were apes in a forest ten thousand miles away; till he's got rid of all the dirty self-deception of talking about low types and deficient skulls; till he's squeezed out of his soul the last drop of the oil of the Pharisees; till his only hope is somehow or other to have captured one criminal, and kept him safe and sane under his own hat."

Flambeau came forward and filled a great goblet with Spanish wine and set it before his friend, as he had already set one before his fellow guest. Then he himself spoke for the first time:

"I believe Father Brown has had a new batch of mysteries. We were talking about them the other day, I fancy. He has been dealing with some queer people since we last met."

"Yes; I know the stories more or less—but not the application," said Chace, lifting his glass thoughtfully. "Can you give me any examples, I wonder... I mean, did you deal with this last batch in that introspective style?"

Father Brown also lifted his glass, and the glow of the fire turned the red wine transparent, like the glorious blood-red glass of a martyr's window. The red flame seemed to hold his eyes and absorb his gaze that sank deeper and deeper into it, as if that single cup held a red sea of the blood of all men, and his soul were a diver, ever plunging in dark humility and inverted imagination, lower than its lowest monsters and its most ancient slime. In that cup, as in a red mirror, he saw many things; the doings of his last days moved in crimson shadows; the examples that his companions demanded danced in symbolic shapes; and there passed before him all the stories that are told here. Now, the luminous wine was like a vast red sunset upon dark red sands, where stood dark figures of men; one was fallen and another running towards him. Then the sunset seemed to break up into patches: red lanterns swinging from garden trees and a pond gleaming red with reflection; and then all the colour seemed to cluster again into a great rose of red crystal, a jewel that irradiated the world like a red sun, save for the shadow of a tall figure with a high head-dress as of some prehistoric priest; and then faded again till nothing was left but a flame of wild red beard blowing in the wind upon a wild grey moor. All these things, which may be seen later from other angles and in other moods than his own, rose up in his memory at the challenge and began to form themselves into anecdotes and arguments.

"Yes," he said, as he raised the wine cup slowly to his lips, "I can remember pretty well—"

2

THE MIRROR OF THE MAGISTRATE
(No record of prior magazine publication found)

James Bagshaw and Wilfred Underhill were old friends, and were fond of rambling through the streets at night, talking interminably as they turned corner after corner in the silent and seemingly lifeless labyrinth of the large suburb in which they lived. The former, a big, dark, good-humoured man with a strip of black moustache, was a professional police detective; the latter, a sharp-faced, sensitive- looking gentleman with light hair, was an amateur interested in detection. It will come as a shock to the readers of the best scientific romance to learn that it was the policeman who was talking and the amateur who was listening, even with a certain respect.

"Ours is the only trade," said Bagshaw, "in which the professional is always supposed to be wrong. After all, people don't write stories in which hairdressers can't cut hair and have to be helped by a customer; or in which a cabman can't drive a cab until his fare explains to him the philosophy of cab-driving. For all that, I'd never deny that we often tend to get into a rut: or, in other words, have the disadvantages of going by a rule. Where the romancers are wrong is, that they don't allow us even the advantages of going by a rule."

"Surely," said Underhill, "Sherlock Holmes would say that he went by a logical rule."

"He may be right," answered the other; "but I mean a collective rule. It's like the staff work of an army. We pool our information."

"And you don't think detective stories allow for that?" asked his friend.

"Well, let's take any imaginary case of Sherlock Holmes, and Lestrade, the official detective. Sherlock Holmes, let us say, can guess that a total stranger crossing the street is a foreigner, merely because he seems to look for the traffic to go to the right instead of the left. I'm quite ready to admit Holmes might guess that. I'm quite sure Lestrade wouldn't guess anything of the kind. But what they leave out is the fact that the policeman, who couldn't guess, might very probably know. Lestrade might know the man was a foreigner merely because his department has to keep an eye on all foreigners; some would say on all natives, too. As a policeman I'm glad the police know so much; for every man wants to do his own job well. But as a citizen, I sometimes wonder whether they don't know too much."

"You don't seriously mean to say," cried Underhill incredulously, "that you know anything about strange people in a strange street. That if a man walked out of that house over there, you would know anything about him?"

"I should if he was the householder," answered Bagshaw. "That house is rented by a literary man of Anglo-Roumanian extraction, who generally lives in Paris, but is over here in connexion with some poetical play of his. His name's Osric Orm, one of the new poets, and pretty steep to read, I believe."

"But I mean all the people down the road," said his companion. "I was thinking how strange and new and nameless everything looks, with these high blank walls and these houses lost in large gardens. You can't know all of them."

"I know a few," answered Bagshaw. "This garden wall we're walking under is at the end of the grounds of Sir Humphrey Gwynne, better known as Mr Justice Gwynne, the old judge who made such a row about spying during the war. The house next door to it belongs to a wealthy cigar merchant. He comes from Spanish-America and looks very swarthy and Spanish himself; but he bears the very English name of Buller. The house beyond that—did you hear that noise?"

"I heard something," said Underhill, "but I really don't know what it was."

"I know what it was," replied the detective, "it was a rather heavy revolver, fired twice, followed by a cry for help. And it came straight out of the back garden of Mr Justice Gwynne, that paradise of peace and legality."

He looked up and down the street sharply and then added:

"And the only gate of the back garden is half a mile round on the other side. I wish this wall were a little lower, or I were a little lighter; but it's got to be tried."

"It is lower a little farther on," said Underhill, "and there seems to be a tree that looks helpful."

They moved hastily along and found a place where the wall seemed to stoop abruptly, almost as if it had half-sunk into the earth; and a garden tree, flamboyant with the gayest garden blossom, straggled out of the dark enclosure and was gilded by the gleam of a solitary street-lamp. Bagshaw caught the crooked branch and threw one leg over the low wall; and the next moment they stood knee-deep amid the snapping plants of a garden border.

The garden of Mr Justice Gwynne by night was rather a singular spectacle. It was large and lay on the empty edge of the suburb, in the shadow of a tall, dark house that was the last in its line of houses. The house was literally dark, being shuttered and unlighted, at least on the side overlooking the garden. But the garden itself, which lay in its shadow: and should have been a tract of absolute darkness, showed a random glitter, like that of fading fireworks; as if a giant rocket had fallen in fire among the trees. As they advanced they were able to locate it as the light of several coloured lamps, entangled in the trees like the jewel fruits of Aladdin, and especially as the light from a small, round lake or pond, which gleamed, with pale colours as if a lamp were kindled under it.

"Is he having a party?" asked Underhill. "The garden seems to be illuminated."

"No," answered Bagshaw. "It's a hobby of his, and I believe he prefers to do it when he's alone. He likes playing with a little plant of electricity that he works from that bungalow or hut over there, where he does his work and keeps his papers. Buller, who knows him very well, says the coloured lamps are rather more often a sign he's not to be disturbed."

"Sort of red danger signals," suggested the other.

"Good Lord! I'm afraid they are danger signals!" and he began suddenly to run.

A moment after Underhill saw what he had seen. The opalescent ring of light, like the halo of the moon, round the sloping sides of the pond, was broken by two black stripes or streaks which soon proved themselves to be the long, black legs of a figure fallen head downwards into the hollow, with the head in the pond.

"Come on," cried the detective sharply, "that looks to me like—"

His voice was lost, as he ran on across the wide lawn, faintly luminous in the artificial light, making a beeline across the big garden for the pool and the fallen figure. Underhill was trotting steadily in that straight track, when something happened that startled him for the moment. Bagshaw, who was travelling as steadily as a bullet towards the black figure by the luminous pool, suddenly turned at a sharp angle and began to run even more rapidly towards the shadow of the house. Underhill could not imagine what he meant by the altered direction. The next moment, when the detective had vanished into the shadow of the house, there came out of that obscurity the sound of a scuffle and a curse; and Bagshaw returned lugging with him a little struggling man with red hair. The captive had evidently been escaping under the shelter of the building, when the quicker ears of the detective had heard him rustling like a bird among the bushes.

"Underhill," said the detective, "I wish you'd run on and see what's up by the pool. And now, who are you?" he asked, coming to a halt. "What's your name?"

"Michael Flood," said the stranger in a snappy fashion. He was an unnaturally lean little man, with a hooked nose too large for his face, which was colourless, like parchment, in contrast with the ginger colour of his hair. "I've got nothing to do with this. I found him lying dead and I was scared; but I only came to interview him for a paper."

"When you interview celebrities for the Press," said Bagshaw, "do you generally climb over the garden wall?"

And he pointed grimly to a trail of footprints coming and going along the path towards the flower bed.

The man calling himself Flood wore an expression equally grim.

"An interviewer might very well get over the wall," he said, "for I couldn't make anybody hear at the front door. The servant had gone out."

"How do you know he'd gone out?" asked the detective suspiciously.

"Because," said Flood, with an almost unnatural calm, "I'm not the only person who gets over garden walls. It seems just possible that you did it yourself. But, anyhow, the servant did; for I've just this moment seen him drop over the wall, away on the other side of the garden, just by the garden door."

"Then why didn't he use the garden door?" demanded the cross-examiner.

"How should I know?" retorted Flood. "Because it was shut, I suppose. But you'd better ask him, not me; he's coming towards the house at this minute."

There was, indeed, another shadowy figure beginning to be visible through the fire-shot gloaming, a squat, square-headed figure, wearing a red waistcoat as the most conspicuous part of a rather shabby livery. He appeared to be making with unobtrusive haste towards a side- door in the house, until Bagshaw halloed to him to halt. He drew nearer to them very reluctantly, revealing a heavy, yellow face, with a touch of something Asiatic which was consonant with his flat, blue-black hair.

Bagshaw turned abruptly to the man called Flood. "Is there anybody in this place," he said, "who can testify to your identity?"

"Not many, even in this country," growled Flood. "I've only just come from Ireland; the only man I know round here is the priest at St. Dominic's Church—Father Brown."

"Neither of you must leave this place," said Bagshaw, and then added to the servant: "But you can go into the house and ring up St. Dominic's Presbytery and ask Father Brown if he would mind coming round here at once. No tricks, mind."

While the energetic detective was securing the potential fugitives, his companion, at his direction, had hastened on to the actual scene of the tragedy. It was a strange enough scene; and, indeed, if the tragedy had not been tragic it would have been highly fantastic. The dead man (for the briefest examination proved him to be dead) lay with his head in the pond, where the glow of the artificial illumination encircled the head with something of the appearance of an unholy halo. The face was gaunt and rather sinister, the brow bald, and the scanty curls dark grey, like iron rings; and, despite the damage done by the bullet wound in the temple, Underhill had no difficulty in recognizing the features he had seen in the many portraits of Sir Humphrey Gwynne. The dead man was in evening-dress, and his long, black legs, so thin as to be almost spidery, were sprawling at different angles up the steep bank from which he had fallen. As by some weird whim of diabolical arabesque, blood was eddying out, very slowly, into the luminous water in snaky rings, like the transparent crimson of sunset clouds.

Underhill did not know how long he stood staring down at this macabre figure, when he looked up and saw a group of four figures standing above him on the bank. He was prepared for Bagshaw and his Irish captive, and he had no difficulty in guessing the status of the servant in the red waistcoat. But the fourth figure had a sort of grotesque solemnity that seemed strangely congruous to that incongruity. It was a stumpy figure with a round face and a hat like a black halo. He realized that it was, in fact, a priest; but there was something about it that reminded him of some quaint old black woodcut at the end of a Dance of Death.

Then he heard Bagshaw saying to the priest:

"I'm glad you can identify this man; but you must realize that he's to some extent under suspicion. Of course, he may be innocent; but he did enter the garden in an irregular fashion."

"Well, I think he's innocent myself," said the little priest in a colourless voice. "But, of course, I may be wrong."

"Why do you think he is innocent?"

"Because he entered the garden in an irregular fashion," answered the cleric. "You see, I entered it in a regular fashion myself. But I seem to be almost the only person who did. All the best people seem to get over garden walls nowadays."

"What do you mean by a regular fashion?" asked the detective.

"Well," said Father Brown, looking at him with limpid gravity, "I came in by the front door. I often come into houses that way."

"Excuse me," said Bagshaw, "but does it matter very much how you came in, unless you propose to confess to the murder?"

"Yes, I think it does," said the priest mildly. "The truth is, that when I came in at the front door I saw something I don't think any of the rest of you have seen. It seems to me it might have something to do with it."

"What did you see?"

"I saw a sort of general smash-up," said Father Brown in his mild voice. "A big looking-glass broken, and a small palm tree knocked over, and the pot smashed all over the floor. Somehow, it looked to me as if something had happened."

"You are right," said Bagshaw after a pause. "If you saw that, it certainly looks as if it had something to do with it."

"And if it had anything to do with it," said the priest very gently, "it looks as if there was one person who had nothing to do with it; and that is Mr Michael Flood, who entered the garden over the wall in an irregular fashion, and then tried to leave it in the same irregular fashion. It is his irregularity that makes me believe in his innocence."

"Let us go into the house," said Bagshaw abruptly.

As they passed in at the side-door, the servant leading the way, Bagshaw fell back a pace or two and spoke to his friend.

"Something odd about that servant," he said. "Says his name is Green, though he doesn't look it; but there seems no doubt he's really Gwynne's servant, apparently the only regular servant he had. But the queer thing is, that he flatly denied that his master was in the garden at all, dead or alive. Said the old judge had gone out to a grand legal dinner and couldn't be home for hours, and gave that as his excuse for slipping out."

"Did he," asked Underhill, "give any excuse for his curious way of slipping in?"

'No, none that I can make sense of," answered the detective. "I can't make him out. He seems to be scared of something."

Entering by the side-door, they found themselves at the inner end of the entrance hall, which ran along the side of the house and ended with the front door, surmounted by a dreary fanlight of the old-fashioned pattern. A faint, grey light was beginning to outline its radiation upon the darkness, like some dismal and discoloured sunrise; but what light there was in the hall came from a single, shaded lamp, also of an antiquated sort, that stood on a bracket in a corner. By the light of this Bagshaw could distinguish the debris of which Brown had spoken. A tall palm, with long sweeping leaves, had fallen full length, and its dark red pot was shattered into shards. They lay littered on the carpet, along with pale and gleaming fragments of a broken mirror, of which the almost empty frame hung behind them on the wall at the end of the vestibule. At right angles to this entrance, and directly opposite the side-door as they entered, was another and similar passage leading into the rest of the house. At the other end of it could be seen the telephone which the servant had used to summon the priest; and a half-open door, showing, even through the crack, the serried ranks of great leather-bound books, marked the entrance to the judge's study.

Bagshaw stood looking down at the fallen pot and the mingled fragments at his feet.

"You're quite right," he said to the priest; "there's been a struggle here. And it must have been a struggle between Gwynne and his murderer."

"It seemed to me," said Father Brown modestly, "that something had happened here."

"Yes; it's pretty clear what happened," assented the detective. "The murderer entered by the front door and found Gwynne; probably Gwynne let him in. There was a death grapple, possibly a chance shot, that hit the glass, though they might have broken it with a stray kick or anything. Gwynne managed to free himself and fled into the garden, where he was pursued and shot finally by the pond. I fancy that's the whole story of the crime itself; but, of course, I must look round the other rooms."

The other rooms, however, revealed very little, though Bagshaw pointed significantly to the loaded automatic pistol that he found in a drawer of the library desk.

"Looks as if he was expecting this," he said; "yet it seems queer he didn't take it with him when he went out into the hall."

Eventually they returned to the hall, making their way towards the front door. Father Brown letting his eye rove around in a rather absent-minded fashion. The two corridors, monotonously papered in the same grey and faded pattern, seemed to emphasize the dust and dingy floridity of the few early Victorian ornaments, the green rust that devoured the bronze of the lamp, the dull gold that glimmered in the frame of the broken mirror.

"They say it's bad luck to break a looking-glass," he said. "This looks like the very house of ill-luck. There's something about the very furniture ? "

"That's rather odd," said Bagshaw sharply. "I thought the front door would be shut, but it's left on the latch."

There was no reply; and they passed out of the front door into the front garden, a narrower and more formal plot of flowers, having at one end a curiously clipped hedge with a hole in it, like a green cave, under the shadow of which some broken steps peeped out.

Father Brown strolled up to the hole and ducked his head under it. A few moments after he had disappeared they were astonished to hear his quiet voice in conversation above their heads, as if he were talking to somebody at the top of a tree. The detective followed, and found that the curious covered stairway led to what looked like a broken bridge, overhanging the darker and emptier spaces of the garden. It just curled round the corner of the house, bringing in sight the field of coloured lights beyond and beneath. Probably it was the relic of some abandoned architectural fancy of building a sort of terrace on arches across the lawn. Bagshaw thought it a curious cul-de-sac in which to find anybody in the small hours between night and morning; but he was not looking at the details of it just then. He was looking at the man who was found.

As the man stood with his back turned—a small man in light grey clothes—the one outstanding feature about him was a wonderful head of hair, as yellow and radiant as the head of a huge dandelion. It was literally outstanding like a halo, and something in that association made the face, when it was slowly and sulkily turned on them, rather a shock of contrast. That halo should have enclosed an oval face of the mildly angelic sort; but the face was crabbed and elderly with a powerful jowl and a short nose that somehow suggested the broken nose of a pugilist.

"This is Mr Orm, the celebrated poet, I understand," said Father Brown, as calmly as if he were introducing two people in a drawing-room.

"Whoever he is," said Bagshaw, "I must trouble him to come with me and answer a few questions."

Mr Osric Orm, the poet, was not a model of self-expression when it came to the answering of questions. There, in that corner of the old garden, as the grey twilight before dawn began to creep over the heavy hedges and the broken bridge, and afterwards in a succession of circumstances and stages of legal inquiry that grew more and more ominous, he refused to say anything except that he had intended to call on Sir Humphrey Gwynne, but had not done so because he could not get anyone to answer the bell. When it was pointed out that the door was practically open, he snorted. When it was hinted that the hour was somewhat late, he snarled. The little that he said was obscure, either because he really knew hardly any English, or because he knew better than to know any. His opinions seemed to be of a nihilistic and destructive sort, as was indeed the tendency of his poetry for those who could follow it; and it seemed possible that his business with the judge, and perhaps his quarrel with the judge, had been something in the anarchist line. Gwynne was known to have had something of a mania about Bolshevist spies, as he had about German spies. Anyhow, one coincidence, only a few moments after his capture, confirmed Bagshaw in the impression that the case must be taken seriously. As they went out of the front gate into the street, they so happened to encounter yet another neighbour, Duller, the cigar merchant from next door, conspicuous by his brown, shrewd face and the unique orchid in his buttonhole; for he had a name in that branch of horticulture. Rather to the surprise of the rest, he hailed his neighbour, the poet, in a matter-of-fact manner, almost as if he had expected to see him.

"Hallo, here we are again," he said. "Had a long talk with old Gwynne, I suppose?"

"Sir Humphrey Gwynne is dead," said Bagshaw. "I am investigating the case and I must ask you to explain."

Buller stood as still as the lamp-post beside him, possibly stiffened with surprise. The red end of his cigar brightened and darkened rhythmically, but his brown face was in shadow; when he spoke it was with quite a new voice.

"I only mean," he said, "that when I passed two hours ago Mr Orm was going in at this gate to see Sir Humphrey."

"He says he hasn't seen him yet," observed Bagshaw, "or even been into the house."

"It's a long time to stand on the door-step," observed Buller.

"Yes," said Father Brown; "it's rather a long time to stand in the street."

"I've been home since then," said the cigar merchant. "Been writing letters and came out again to post them."

"You'll have to tell all that later," said Bagshaw. "Good night—or good morning."

The trial of Osric Orm for the murder of Sir Humphrey Gwynne, which filled the newspapers for so many weeks, really turned entirely on the same crux as that little talk under the lamp-post, when the grey-green dawn was breaking about the dark streets and gardens. Everything came back to the enigma of those two empty hours between the time when Buller saw Orm going in at the garden gate, and the time when Father Brown found him apparently still lingering in the garden. He had certainly had the time to commit six murders, and might almost have committed them for want of something to do; for he could give no coherent account of what he was doing. It was argued by the prosecution that he had also the opportunity, as the front door was unlatched, and the side-door into the larger garden left standing open. The court followed, with considerable interest, Bagshaw's clear reconstruction of the struggle in the passage, of which the traces were so evident; indeed, the police had since found the shot that had shattered the glass. Finally, the hole in the hedge to which he had been tracked, had very much the appearance of a hiding-place. On the other hand. Sir Matthew Blake, the very able counsel for the defence, turned this last argument the other way: asking why any man should entrap himself in a place without possible exit, when it would obviously be much more sensible to slip out into the street. Sir Matthew Blake also made effective use of the mystery that still rested upon the motive for the murder. Indeed, upon this point, the passages between Sir Matthew Blake and Sir Arthur Travers, the equally brilliant advocate for the prosecution, turned rather to the advantage of the prisoner. Sir Arthur could only throw out suggestions about a Bolshevist conspiracy which sounded a little thin. But when it came to investigating the facts of Orm's mysterious behaviour that night he was considerably more effective.

The prisoner went into the witness-box, chiefly because his astute counsel calculated that it would create a bad impression if he did not. But he was almost as uncommunicative to his own counsel as to the prosecuting counsel. Sir Arthur Travers made all possible capital out of his stubborn silence, but did not succeed in breaking it. Sir Arthur was a long, gaunt man, with a long, cadaverous face, in striking contrast to the sturdy figure and bright, bird-like eye of Sir Matthew Blake. But if Sir Matthew suggested a very cocksure sort of cock, sparrow, Sir Arthur might more truly have been compared to a crane or stork; as he leaned forward, prodding the poet with questions, his long nose might have been a long beak.

"Do you mean to tell the jury," he asked, in tones of grating incredulity, "that you never went in to see the deceased gentleman at all?"

"No!" replied Orm shortly.

"You wanted to see him, I suppose. You must have been very anxious to see him. Didn't you wait two whole hours in front of his front door?"

"Yes," replied the other.

"And yet you never even noticed the door was open?"

"No," said Orm.

"What in the world were you doing for two hours in somebody's else's front garden?" insisted the barrister; "You were doing something, I suppose?"

"Yes."

"Is it a secret?" asked Sir Arthur, with adamantine jocularity.

"It's a secret from you," answered the poet.

It was upon this suggestion of a secret that Sir Arthur seized in developing his line of accusation. With a boldness which some thought unscrupulous, he turned the very mystery of the motive, which was the strongest part of his opponent's case, into an argument for his own. He gave it as the first fragmentary hint of some far-flung and elaborate conspiracy, in which a patriot had perished like one caught in the coils of an octopus.

"Yes," he cried in a vibrating voice, "my learned friend is perfectly right! We do not know the exact reason why this honourable public servant was murdered. We shall not know the reason why the next public servant is murdered. If my learned friend himself falls a victim to his eminence, and the hatred which the hellish powers of destruction feel for the guardians of law, he will be murdered, and he will not know the reason. Half the decent people in this court will be butchered in their beds, and we shall not know the reason. And we shall never know the reason and never arrest the massacre, until it has depopulated our country, so long as the defence is permitted to stop all proceedings with this stale tag about 'motive,' when every other fact in the case, every glaring incongruity, every gaping silence, tells us that we stand in the presence of Cain."

"I never knew Sir Arthur so excited," said Bagshaw to his group of companions afterwards. "Some people are saying he went beyond the usual limit and that the prosecutor in a murder case oughtn't to be so vindictive. But I must say there was something downright creepy about that little goblin with the yellow hair, that seemed to play up to the impression. I was vaguely recalling, all the time, something that De Quincey says about Mr Williams, that ghastly criminal who slaughtered two whole families almost in silence. I think he says that Williams had hair of a vivid unnatural yellow; and that he thought it had been dyed by a trick learned in India, where they dye horses green or blue. Then there was his queer, stony silence, like a troglodyte's; I'll never deny that it all worked me up until I felt there was a sort of monster in the dock. If that was only Sir Arthur's eloquence, then he certainly took a heavy responsibility in putting so much passion into it."

"He was a friend of poor Gwynne's, as a matter of fact," said Underhill, more gently; "a man I know saw them hobnobbing together after a great legal dinner lately. I dare say that's why he feels so strongly in this case. I suppose it's doubtful whether a man ought to act in such a case on mere personal feeling."

"He wouldn't," said Bagshaw. "I bet Sir Arthur Travers wouldn't act only on feeling, however strongly he felt. He's got a very stiff sense of his own professional position. He's one of those men who are ambitious even when they've satisfied their ambition. I know nobody who'd take more trouble to keep his position in the world. No; you've got hold of the wrong moral to his rather thundering sermon. If he lets himself go like that, it's because he thinks he can get a conviction, anyhow, and wants to put himself at the head of some political movement against the conspiracy he talks about. He must have some very good reason for wanting to convict Orm and some very good reason for thinking he can do it. That means that the facts will support him. His confidence doesn't look well for the prisoner." He became conscious of an insignificant figure in the group.

"Well, Father Brown," he said with a smile; "what do you think of our judicial procedure?"

"Well," replied the priest rather absently, "I think the thing that struck me most was how different men look in their wigs. You talk about the prosecuting barrister being so tremendous. But I happened to see him take his wig off for a minute, and he really looks quite a different man. He's quite bald, for one thing."

"I'm afraid that won't prevent his being tremendous," answered Bagshaw. "You don't propose to found the defence on the fact that the prosecuting counsel is bald, do you?"

"Not exactly," said Father Brown good-humouredly. "To tell the truth, I was thinking how little some kinds of people know about other kinds of people. Suppose I went among some remote people who had never even heard of England. Suppose I told them that there is a man in my country who won't ask a question of life and death, until he has put an erection made of horse-hair on the top of his head, with little tails behind, and grey corkscrew curls at the side, like an Early Victorian old woman. They would think he must be rather eccentric; but he isn't at all eccentric, he's only conventional. They would think so, because they don't know anything about English barristers; because they don't know what a barrister is. Well, that barrister doesn't know what a poet is. He doesn't understand that a poet's eccentricities wouldn't seem eccentric to other poets. He thinks it odd that Orm should walk about in a beautiful garden for two hours, with nothing to do. God bless my soul! a poet would think nothing of walking about in the same backyard for ten hours if he had a poem to do. Orm's own counsel was quite as stupid. It never occurred to him to ask Orm the obvious question."

"What question do you mean?" asked the other.

"Why, what poem he was making up, of course," said Father Brown rather impatiently. "What line he was stuck at, what epithet he was looking for, what climax he was trying to work up to. If there were any educated people in court, who know what literature is, they would have known well enough whether he had had anything genuine to do. You'd have asked a manufacturer about the conditions of his factory; but nobody seems to consider the conditions under which poetry is manufactured. It's done by doing nothing."

"That's all very well," replied the detective; "but why did he hide? Why did he climb up that crooked little stairway and stop there; it led nowhere."

"Why, because it led nowhere, of course," cried Father Brown explosively. "Anybody who clapped eyes on that blind alley ending in mid-air might have known an artist would want to go there, just as a child would."

He stood blinking for a moment, and then said apologetically: "I beg your pardon; but it seems odd that none of them understand these things. And then there was another thing. Don't you know that everything has, for an artist, one aspect or angle that is exactly right? A tree, a cow, and a cloud, in a certain relation only, mean something; as three letters, in one order only, mean a word. Well, the view of that illuminated garden from that unfinished bridge was the right view of it. It was as unique as the fourth dimension. It was a sort of fairy foreshortening; it was like looking down at heaven and seeing all the stars growing on trees and that luminous pond like a moon fallen flat on the fields in some happy nursery talc. He could have looked at it forever. If you told him the path led nowhere, he would tell you it had led him to the country at the end of the world. But do you expect him to tell you that in the witness is box? What would you say to him if he did? You talk about a man having a jury of his peers. Why don't you have a jury of poets?"

"You talk as if you were a poet yourself," said Bagshaw.

"Thank your stars I'm not," said Father Brown. "Thank your lucky stars a priest has to be more charitable than a poet. Lord have mercy on us, if you knew what a crushing, what a cruel contempt he feels for the lot of you, you'd feel as if you were under Niagara."

"You may know more about the artistic temperament than I do," said Bagshaw after a pause; "but, after all, the answer is simple. You can only show that he might have done what he did, without committing the crime. But it's equally true that he might have committed the crime. And who else could have committed it?"

"Have you thought about the servant, Green?" asked Father Brown, reflectively. "He told a rather queer story."

"Ah," cried Bagshaw quickly, "you think Green did it, after all."

"I'm quite sure he didn't," replied the other. "I only asked if you'd thought about his queer story. He only went out for some trifle, a drink or an assignation or what not. But he went out by the garden door and came back over the garden wall. In other words, he left the door open, but he came back to find it shut. Why? Because Somebody Else had already passed out that way."

"The murderer," muttered the detective doubtfully. "Do you know who he was?"

"I know what he looked like," answered Father Brown quietly. "That's the only thing I do know. I can almost see him as he came in at the front door, in the gleam of the hall lamp; his figure, his clothes, even his face!"

"What's all this?"

"He looked like Sir Humphrey Gwynne," said the priest.

"What the devil do you mean?" demanded Bagshaw. "Gwynne was lying dead with his head in the pond."

"Oh, yes," said Father Brown.

After a moment he went on: "Let's go back to that theory of yours, which was a very good one, though I don't quite agree with it. You suppose the murderer came in at the front door, met the Judge in the front hall, struggling with him and breaking the mirror; that the judge then retreated into the garden, where he was finally shot. Somehow, it doesn't sound natural to me. Granted he retreated down the hall, there are two exits at the end, one into the garden and one into the house. Surely, he would be more likely to retreat into the house? His gun was there; his telephone was there; his servant, so far as he knew, was there. Even the nearest neighbours were in that direction. Why should he stop to open the garden door and go out alone on the deserted side of the house?"

"But we know he did go out of the house," replied his companion, puzzled. "We know he went out of the house, because he was found in the garden."

"He never went out of the house, because he never was in the house," said Father Brown. "Not that evening, I mean. He was sitting in that bungalow. I read that lesson in the dark, at the beginning, in red and golden stars across the garden. They were worked from the hut; they wouldn't have been burning at all if he hadn't been in the hut. He was trying to run across to the house and the telephone, when the murderer shot him beside the pond."

"But what about the pot and the palm and the broken mirror?" cried Bagshaw. "Why, it was you who found them! It was you yourself who said there must have been a struggle in the hall."

The priest blinked rather painfully. "Did I?" he muttered. "Surely, I didn't say that. I never thought that. What I think I said, was that something had happened in the hall. And something did happen; but it wasn't a struggle."

"Then what broke the mirror?" asked Bagshaw shortly.

"A bullet broke the mirror," answered Father Brown gravely; "a bullet fired by the criminal. The big fragments of falling glass were quite enough to knock over the pot and the palm."

"Well, what else could he have been firing at except Gwynne?" asked the detective.

"It's rather a fine metaphysical point," answered his clerical companion almost dreamily. "In one sense, of course, he was firing at Gwynne. But Gwynne wasn't there to be fired at. The criminal was alone in the hall."

He was silent for a moment, and then went on quietly. "Imagine the looking-glass at the end of the passage, before it was broken, and the tall palm arching over it. In the half-light, reflecting these monochrome walls, it would, look like the end of the passage. A man reflected in it would look like a man coming from inside the house. It would look like the master of the house—if only the reflection were a little like him."

"Stop a minute," cried Bagshaw. "I believe I begin—"

"You begin to see," said Father Brown. "You begin to see why all the suspects in this case must be innocent. Not one of them could possibly have mistaken his own reflection for old Gwynne. Orm would have known at once that his bush of yellow hair was not a bald head. Flood would have seen his own red head, and Green his own red waistcoat. Besides, they're all short and shabby; none of them could have thought his own image was a tall, thin, old gentleman in evening-dress. We want another, equally tall and thin, to match him. That's what I meant by saying that I knew what the murderer looked like."

"And what do you argue from that?" asked Bagshaw, looking at him steadily.

The priest uttered a sort of sharp, crisp laugh, oddly different from his ordinary mild manner of speech.

"I am going to argue," he said, "the very thing that you said was so ludicrous and impossible."

"What do you mean?"

"I'm going to base the defence," said Father Brown, "on the fact that the prosecuting counsel has a bald head."

"Oh, my God!" said the detective quietly, and got to his feet, staring.

Father Brown had resumed his monologue in an unruffled manner.

"You've been following the movements of a good many people in this business; you policemen were prodigiously interested in the movements of the poet, and the servant, and the Irishman. The man whose movements seem to have been rather forgotten is the dead man himself. His servant was quite honestly astonished at finding his master had returned. His master had gone to a great dinner of all the leaders of the legal profession, but had left it abruptly and come home. He was not ill, for he summoned no assistance; he had almost certainly quarrelled with some leader of the legal profession. It's among the leaders of that profession that we should have looked first for his enemy. He returned, and shut himself up in the bungalow, where he kept all his private documents about treasonable practices. But the leader of the legal profession, who knew there was something against him in those documents, was thoughtful enough to follow his accuser home; he also being in evening-dress, but with a pistol in his pocket. That is all; and nobody could ever have guessed it except for the mirror."

He seemed to be gazing into vacancy for a moment, and then added:

"A queer thing is a mirror; a picture frame that holds hundreds of different pictures, all vivid and all vanished forever. Yet, there was something specially strange about the glass that hung at the end of that grey corridor under that green palm. It is as if it was a magic glass and had a different fate from others, as if its picture could somehow survive it, hanging in the air of that twilight house like a spectre; or at least like an abstract diagram, the skeleton of an argument. We could, at least, conjure out of the void the thing that Sir Arthur Travers saw. And by the way, there was one very true thing that you said about him."

"I'm glad to hear it," said Bagshaw with grim good nature. "What was it?"

"You said," observed the priest, "that Sir Arthur must have some good reason for wanting to get Orm hanged."

A week later the priest met the police detective once more, and learned that the authorities had already been moving on the new lines of inquiry when they were interrupted by a sensational event.

"Sir Arthur Travers," began Father Brown.

"Sir Arthur Travers is dead," said Bagshaw, briefly.

"Ah!" said the other, with a little catch in his voice; "you mean that he—"

"Yes," said Bagshaw, "he shot at the same man again, but not in a mirror."

3

THE MAN WITH TWO BEARDS (No record of prior magazine publication found)

This tale was told by Father Brown to Professor Crake, the celebrated criminologist, after dinner at a club, where the two were introduced to each other as sharing a harmless hobby of murder and robbery. But, as Father Brown's version rather minimized his own part in the matter, it is here re-told in a more impartial style. It arose out of a playful passage of arms, in which the professor was very scientific and the priest rather sceptical.

"My good sir," said the professor in remonstrance, "don't you believe that criminology is a science?"

"I'm not sure," replied Father Brown. "Do you believe that hagiology is a science?"

"What's that?" asked the specialist sharply.

"No; it's not the study of hags, and has nothing to do with burning witches," said the priest, smiling. "It's the study of holy things, saints and so on. You see, the Dark Ages tried to make a science about good people. But our own humane and enlightened age is only interested in a science about bad ones. Yet I think our general experience is that every conceivable sort of man has been a saint. And I suspect you will find, too, that every conceivable sort of man has been a murderer."

"Well, we believe murderers can be pretty well classified," observed Crake. "The list sounds rather long and dull; but I think it's exhaustive. First, all killing can be divided into rational and irrational, and we'll take the last first, because they are much fewer. There is such a thing as homicidal mania, or love of butchery in the abstract. There is such a thing as irrational antipathy, though it's very seldom homicidal. Then we come to the true motives: of these, some are less rational in the sense of being merely romantic and retrospective. Acts of pure revenge are acts of hopeless revenge. Thus a lover will sometimes kill a rival he could never supplant, or a rebel assassinate a tyrant after the conquest is complete. But, more often, even these acts have a rational explanation. They are hopeful murders. They fall into the larger section of the second division, of what we may call prudential crimes. These, again, fall chiefly under two descriptions. A man kills either in order to obtain what the other man possesses, either by theft or inheritance, or to stop the other man from acting in some way: as in the case of killing a blackmailer or a political opponent; or, in the case of a rather more passive obstacle, a husband or wife whose continued functioning, as such, interferes with other things. We believe that classification is pretty thoroughly thought out and, properly applied, covers the whole ground. But I'm afraid that it perhaps sounds rather dull; I hope I'm not boring you."

"Not at all," said Father Brown. "If I seemed a little absent-minded I must apologize; the truth is, I was thinking of a man I once knew. He was a murderer; but I can't see where he fits into your museum of murderers. He was not mad, nor did he like killing. He did not hate the man he killed; he hardly knew him, and certainly had nothing to avenge on him. The other man did not possess anything that he could possibly want. The other man was not behaving in any way which the murderer wanted to stop. The murdered man was not in a position to hurt, or hinder, or even affect the murderer in any way. There was no woman in the case. There were no politics in the case. This man killed a fellow-creature who was practically a stranger, and that for a very strange reason; which is possibly unique in human history."

And so, in his own more conversational fashion, he told the story. The story may well begin in a sufficiently respectable setting, at the breakfast table of a worthy though wealthy suburban family named Bankes, where the normal discussion of the newspaper had, for once, been silenced by the discussion about a mystery nearer home. Such people are sometimes accused of gossip about their neighbours, but they are in that matter almost inhumanly innocent. Rustic villagers tell tales about their neighbours, true and false; but the curious culture of the modern suburb will believe anything it is told in the papers about the wickedness of the Pope, or the martyrdom of the King of the Cannibal Islands, and, in the excitement of these topics, never knows what is happening next door. In this case, however, the two forms of interest actually coincided in a coincidence of thrilling intensity. Their own suburb had actually been mentioned in their favourite newspaper. It seemed to them like a new proof of their own existence when they saw the name in print. It was almost as if they had been unconscious and invisible before; and now they were as real as the King of the Cannibal Islands.

It was stated in the paper that a once famous criminal, known as Michael Moonshine, and many other names that were presumably not his own, had recently been released after a long term of imprisonment for his numerous burglaries; that his whereabouts was being kept quiet, but that he was believed to have settled down in the suburb in question, which we will call for convenience Chisham. A resume of some of his famous and daring exploits and escapes was given in the same issue. For it is a character of that kind of press, intended for that kind of public, that it assumes that its reader have no memories.

While the peasant will remember an outlaw like Robin Hood or Rob Roy for centuries, the clerk will hardly remember the name of the criminal about whom he argued in trams and tubes two years before. Yet, Michael Moonshine had really shown some of the heroic rascality of Rob Roy or Robin Hood. He was worthy to be turned into legend and not merely into news. He was far too capable a burglar to be a murderer. But his terrific strength and the ease with which he knocked policemen over like ninepins, stunned people, and bound and gagged them, gave something almost like a final touch of fear or mystery to the fact that he never killed them. People almost felt that he would have been more human if he had.

Mr Simon Bankes, the father of the family, was at once better read and more old-fashioned than the rest. He was a sturdy man, with a short grey beard and a brow barred with wrinkles. He had a turn for anecdotes and reminiscence, and he distinctly remembered the days when Londoners had lain awake listening for Mike Moonshine as they did for Spring-heeled Jack. Then there was his wife, a thin, dark lady. There was a sort of acid elegance about her, for her family had much more money than her husband's, if rather less education; and she even possessed a very valuable emerald necklace upstairs, that gave her a right to prominence in a discussion about thieves. There was his daughter. Opal, who was also thin and dark and supposed to be psychic—at any rate, by herself; for she had little domestic encouragement. Spirits of an ardently astral turn will be well advised not to materialize as members of a large family. There was her brother John, a burly youth, particularly boisterous in his indifference to her spiritual development; and otherwise distinguishable only by his interest in motor-cars. He seemed to be always in the act of selling one car and buying another; and by some process, hard for the economic theorist to follow, it was always possible to buy a much better article by selling the one that was damaged or discredited. There was his brother Philip, a young man with dark curly hair, distinguished by his attention to dress; which is doubtless part of the duty of a stockbroker's clerk, but, as the stockbroker was prone to hint, hardly the whole of it. Finally, there was present at this family scene his friend, Daniel Devine, who was also dark and exquisitely dressed, but bearded in a fashion that was somewhat foreign, and therefore, for many, slightly menacing.

It was Devine who had introduced the topic of the newspaper paragraph, tactfully insinuating so effective an instrument of distraction at what looked like the beginning of a small family quarrel; for the psychic lady had begun the description of a vision she had had of pale faces floating in empty night outside her window, and John Bankes was trying to roar down this revelation of a higher state with more than his usual heartiness.

But the newspaper reference to their new and possibly alarming neighbour soon put both controversialists out of court.

"How frightful," cried Mrs Bankes. "He must be quite a newcomer; but who can he possibly be?"

"I don't know any particularly newcomers," said her husband, "except Sir Leopold Pulman, at Beechwood House."

"My dear," said the lady, "how absurd you are—Sir Leopold!" Then, after a pause, she added: "If anybody suggested his secretary now—that man with the whiskers; I've always said, ever since he got the place Philip ought to have had—"

"Nothing doing," said Philip languidly, making his sole contribution to the conversation. "Not good enough."

"The only one I know," observed Devine, "is that man called Carver, who is stopping at Smith's Farm. He lives a very quiet life, but he's quite interesting to talk to. I think John has had some business with him."

"Knows a bit about cars," conceded the monomaniac John. "He'll know a bit more when he's been in my new car."

Devine smiled slightly; everybody had been threatened with the hospitality of John's new car. Then he added reflectively:

"That's a little what I feel about him. He knows a lot about motoring and travelling, and the active ways of the world, and yet he always stays at home pottering about round old Smith's beehives. Says he's only interested in bee culture, and that's why he's staying with Smith. It seems a very quiet hobby for a man of his sort. However, I've no doubt John's car will shake him up a bit."

As Devine walked away from the house that evening his dark face wore an expression of concentrated thought. His thoughts would, perhaps, have been worthy of our attention, even at this stage; but it is enough to say that their practical upshot was a resolution to pay an immediate visit to Mr Carver at the house of Mr Smith. As he was making his way thither he encountered Barnard, the secretary at Beechwood House, conspicuous by his lanky figure and the large side whiskers which Mrs Bankes counted among her private wrongs. Their acquaintance was slight, and their conversation brief and casual; but Devine seemed to find in it food for further cogitation.

"Look here," he said abruptly, "excuse my asking, but is it true that Lady Pulman has some very famous jewellery up at the House? I'm not a professional thief, but I've just heard there's one hanging about."

"I'll get her to give an eye to them," answered the secretary. "To tell the truth, I've ventured to warn her about them already myself. I hope she has attended to it."

As they spoke, there came the hideous cry of a motor-horn just behind, and John Bankes came to a stop beside them, radiant at his own steering-wheel. When he heard of Devine's destination he claimed it as his own, though his tone suggested rather an abstract relish for offering people a ride. The ride was consumed in continuous praises of the car, now mostly in the matter of its adaptability to weather.

"Shuts up as tight as a box," he said, "and opens as easy—as easy as opening your mouth."

Devine's mouth, at the moment, did not seem so easy to open, and they arrived at Smith's farm to the sound of a soliloquy. Passing the outer gate, Devine found the man he was looking for without going into the house. The man was walking about in the garden, with his hands in his pockets, wearing a large, limp straw hat; a man with a long face and a large chin. The wide brim cut off the upper part of his face with a shadow that looked a little like a mask. In the background was a row of sunny beehives, along which an elderly man, presumably Mr Smith, was moving accompanied by a short, commonplace-looking companion in black clerical costume.

"I say," burst in the irrepressible John, before Devine could offer any polite greeting, "I've brought her round to give you a little run. You see if she isn't better than a 'Thunderbolt.'"

Mr Carver's mouth set into a smile that may have been meant to be gracious, but looked rather grim. "I'm afraid I shall be too busy for pleasure this evening," he said.

"How doth the little busy bee," observed Devine, equally enigmatically. "Your bees must be very busy if they keep you at it all night. I was wondering if—"

"Well," demanded Carver, with a certain cool defiance.

"Well, they say we should make hay while the sun shines," said Devine. "Perhaps you make honey while the moon shines."

There came a flash from the shadow of the broad-brimmed hat, as the whites of the man's eyes shifted and shone.

"Perhaps there is a good deal of moonshine in the business," he said; "but I warn you my bees do not only make honey. They sting."

"Are you coming along in the car?" insisted the staring John. But Carver, though he threw off the momentary air of sinister significance with which he had been answering Devine, was still positive in his polite refusal.

"I can't possibly go," he said. "Got a lot of writing to do. Perhaps you'd be kind enough to give some of my friends a run, if you want a companion. This is my friend, Mr Smith, Father Brown."

"Of course," cried Bankes; "let 'em all come."

"Thank you very much," said Father Brown. "I'm afraid I shall have to decline; I've got to go on to Benediction in a few minutes."

"Mr Smith is your man, then," said Carver, with something almost like impatience. "I'm sure Smith is longing for a motor ride."

Smith, who wore a broad grin, bore no appearance of longing for anything. He was an active little old man with a very honest wig; one of those wigs that look no more natural than a hat. Its tinge of yellow was out of keeping with his colourless complexion. He shook his head and answered with amiable obstinacy:

"I remember I went over this road ten years ago—in one of those contraptions. Came over in it from my sister's place at Holmgate, and never been over that road in a car since. It was rough going I can tell you,"

"Ten years ago!" scoffed John Bankes. "Two thousand years ago you went in an ox wagon. Do you think cars haven't changed in ten years—and roads, too, for that matter? In my little bus you don't know the wheels are going round. You think you're just flying."

"I'm sure Smith wants to go flying," urged Carver. "It's the dream of his life. Come, Smith, go over to Holmgate and see your sister. You know you ought to go and see your sister. Go over and stay the night if you like."

"Well, I generally walk over, so I generally do stay the night," said old Smith. "No need to trouble the gentleman today, particularly."

"But think what fun it will be for your sister to see you arrive in a car!" cried Carver. "You really ought to go. Don't be so selfish."

"That's it," assented Bankes, with buoyant benevolence. "Don't you be selfish. It won't hurt you. You aren't afraid of it, are you?"

"Well," said Mr Smith, blinking thoughtfully, "I don't want to be selfish, and I don't think I'm afraid I'll come with you if you put it that way."

The pair drove off, amid waving salutations that seemed somehow to give the little group the appearance of a cheering crowd. Yet Devine and the priest only joined in out of courtesy, and they both felt it was the dominating gesture of their host that gave it its final air of farewell. The detail gave them a curious sense of the pervasive force of his personality.

The moment the car was out of sight he turned to them with a sort of boisterous apology and said: "Well!"

He said it with that curious heartiness which is the reverse of hospitality. That extreme geniality is the same as a dismissal.

"I must be going," said Devine. "We must not interrupt the busy bee. I'm afraid I know very little about bees; sometimes I can hardly tell a bee from a wasp."

"I've kept wasps, too," answered the mysterious Mr Carver. When his guests were a few yards down the street, Devine said rather impulsively to his companion: "Rather an odd scene that, don't you think?"

"Yes," replied Father Brown. "And what do you think about it?"

Devine looked at the little man in black, and something in the gaze of his great, grey eyes seemed to renew his impulse.

"I think," he said, "that Carver was very anxious to have the house to himself tonight. I don't know whether you had any such suspicions?"

"I may have my suspicions," replied the priest, "but I'm not sure whether they're the same as yours."

That evening, when the last dusk was turning into dark in the gardens round the family mansion, Opal Bankes was moving through some of the dim and empty rooms with even more than her usual abstraction; and anyone who had looked at her closely would have noted that her pale face had more than its usual pallor. Despite its bourgeois luxury, the house as a whole had a rather unique shade of melancholy. It was the sort of immediate sadness that belongs to things that are old rather than ancient. It was full of faded fashions, rather than historic customs; of the order and ornament that is just recent enough to be recognized as dead. Here and there, Early Victorian coloured glass tinted the twilight; the high ceilings made the long rooms look narrow; and at the end of the long room down which she was walking was one of those round windows, to be found in the buildings of its period. As she came to about the middle of the room, she stopped, and then suddenly swayed a little, as if some invisible hand had struck her on the face.

An instant after there was the noise or knocking on the front door, dulled by the closed doors between. She knew that the rest of the household were in the upper parts of the house, but she could not have analysed the motive that made her go to the front door herself. On the doorstep stood a dumpy and dingy figure in black, which she recognized as the Roman Catholic priest, whose name was Brown. She knew him only slightly; but she liked him. He did not encourage her psychic views; quite the contrary; but he discouraged them as if they mattered and not as if they did not matter. It was not so much that he did not sympathize with her opinions, as that he did sympathize but did not agree. All this was in some sort of chaos in her mind as she found herself saying, without greeting, or waiting to hear his business:

"I'm so glad you've come. I've seen a ghost."

"There's no need to be distressed about that," he said. "It often happens. Most of the ghosts aren't ghosts, and the few that may be won't do you any harm. Was it any ghost in particular?"

"No," she admitted, with a vague feeling of relief, "it wasn't so much the thing itself as an atmosphere of awful decay, a sort of luminous ruin. It was a face. A face at the window. But it was pale and goggling, and looked like the picture of Judas."

"Well, some people do look like that," reflected the priest, "and I dare say they look in at windows, sometimes. May I come in and see where it happened?"

When she returned to the room with the visitor, however, other members of the family had assembled, and those of a less psychic habit had thought it convenient to light the lamps. In the presence of Mrs Bankes, Father Brown assumed a more conventional civility, and apologized for his intrusion.

"I'm afraid it is taking a liberty with your house, Mrs Bankes," he said. "But I think I can explain how the business happens to concern you. I was up at the Pulmans' place just now, when I was rung up and asked to come round here to meet a man who is coming to communicate something that may be of some moment to you. I should not have added myself to the party, only I am wanted, apparently, because I am a witness to what has happened up at Beechwood. In fact, it was I who had to give the alarm."

"What has happened?" repeated the lady.

"There has been a robbery up, at Beechwood House," said Father Brown, gravely; "a robbery, and what I fear is worse, Lady Pulman's jewels have gone; and her unfortunate secretary, Mr Barnard, was picked up in the garden, having evidently been shot by the escaping burglar."

"That man," ejaculated the lady of the house. "I believe he was—"

She encountered the grave gaze of the priest, and her words suddenly went from her; she never knew why.

"I communicated with the police," he went on, "and with another authority interested in this case; and they say that even a superficial examination has revealed foot-prints and fingerprints and other indications of a well-known criminal."

At this point, the conference was for a moment disturbed, by the return of John Bankes, from what appeared to be an abortive expedition in the car. Old Smith seemed to have been a disappointing passenger, after all.

"Funked it, after all, at the last minute," he announced with noisy disgust. "Bolted off while I was looking at what I thought was a puncture. Last time I'll take one of these yokels—"

But his complaints received small attention in the general excitement that gathered round Father Brown and his news.

"Somebody will arrive in a moment," went on the priest, with the same air of weighty reserve, "who will relieve me of this responsibility. When I have confronted, you with him I shall have done my duty as a witness in a serious business. It only remains for me to say that a servant up at Beechwood House told me that she had seen a face at one of the windows—"

"I saw a face," said Opal, "at one of our windows."

"Oh, you are always seeing faces," said her brother John roughly.

"It is as well to see facts even if they are faces," said Father Brown equably, "and I think the face you saw—"

Another knock at the front door sounded through the house, and a minute afterwards the door of the room opened and another figure appeared. Devine half-rose from his chair at the sight of it.

It was a tall, erect figure, with a long, rather cadaverous face, ending in a formidable chin. The brow was rather bald, and the eyes bright and blue, which Devine had last seen obscured with a broad straw hat.

"Pray don't let anybody move," said the man called Carver, in clear and courteous tones. But to Devine's disturbed mind the courtesy had an ominous resemblance to that of a brigand who holds a company motionless with a pistol.

"Please sit down, Mr Devine," said Carver; "and, with Mrs Bankes's permission, I will follow your example. My presence here necessitates an explanation. I rather fancy you suspected me of being an eminent and distinguished burglar."

"I did," said Devine grimly.

"As you remarked," said Carver, "it is not always easy to know a wasp from a bee."

After a pause, he continued: "I can claim to be one of the more useful, though equally annoying, insects. I am a detective, and I have come down to investigate an alleged renewal of the activities of the criminal calling himself Michael Moonshine. Jewel robberies were his speciality; and there has just been one of them at Beechwood House, which, by all the technical tests, is obviously his work. Not only do the prints correspond, but you may possibly know that when he was last arrested, and it is believed on other occasions also, he wore a simple but effective disguise of a red beard and a pair of large horn-rimmed spectacles."

Opal Bankes leaned forward fiercely.

"That was it," she cried in excitement, "that was the face I saw, with great goggles and a red, ragged beard like Judas. I thought it was a ghost."

"That was also the ghost the servant at Beechwood saw," said Carver dryly.

He laid some papers and packages on the table, and began carefully to unfold them. "As I say," he continued, "I was sent down here to make inquiries about the criminal plans of this man, Moonshine. That is why I interested myself in bee-keeping and went to stay with Mr Smith."

There was a silence, and then Devine started and spoke: "You don't seriously mean to say that nice old man—"

"Come, Mr Devine," said Carver, with a smile, "you believed a beehive was only a hiding-place for me. Why shouldn't it be a hiding-place for him?"

Devine nodded gloomily, and the detective turned back to his papers. "Suspecting Smith, I wanted to get him out of the way and go through his belongings; so I took advantage of Mr Bankes's kindness in giving him a joyride. Searching his house, I found some curious things to be owned by an innocent old rustic interested only in bees. This is one of them."

From the unfolded paper he lifted a long, hairy object almost scarlet in colour—the sort of sham beard that is worn in theatricals.

Beside it lay an old pair of heavy horn-rimmed spectacles.

"But I also found something," continued Carver, "that more directly concerns this house, and must be my excuse for intruding to-night. I found a memorandum, with notes of the names and conjectural value of various pieces of jewellery in the neighbourhood. Immediately after the note of Lady Pulman's tiara was the mention of an emerald necklace belonging to Mrs Bankes."

Mrs Bankes, who had hitherto regarded the invasion of her house with an air of supercilious bewilderment, suddenly grew attentive. Her face suddenly looked ten years older and much more intelligent. But before she could speak the impetuous John had risen to his full height like a trumpeting elephant.

"And the tiara's gone already," he roared; "and the necklace—I'm going to see about that necklace!"

"Not a bad idea," said Carver, as the young man rushed from the room; "though, of course, we've been keeping our eyes open since we've been here. Well, it took me a little time to make out the memorandum, which was in cipher, and Father Brown's telephone message from the House came as I was near the end. I asked him to run round here first with the news, and I would follow; and so—"

His speech was sundered by a scream. Opal was standing up and pointing rigidly at the round window.

"There it is again!" she cried.

For a moment they all saw something—something that cleared the lady of the charges of lying and hysteria not uncommonly brought against her. Thrust out of the slate-blue darkness without, the face was pale, or, perhaps, blanched by pressure against the glass; and the great, glaring eyes, encircled as with rings, gave it rather the look of a great fish out of the dark-blue sea nosing at the port-hole of a ship. But the gills or fins of the fish were a coppery red; they were, in truth, fierce red whiskers and the upper part of a red beard. The next moment it had vanished.

Devine had taken a single stride towards the window when a shout resounded through the house, a shout that seemed to shake it. It seemed almost too deafening to be distinguishable as words; yet it was enough to stop Devine in his stride, and he knew what had happened.

"Necklace gone!" shouted John Bankes, appearing huge and heaving in the doorway, and almost instantly vanishing again with the plunge of a pursuing hound.

"Thief was at the window just now!" cried the detective, who had already darted to the door, following the headlong John, who was already in the garden.

"Be careful," wailed the lady, "they have pistols and things."

"So have I," boomed the distant voice of the dauntless John out of the dark garden.

Devine had, indeed, noticed as the young man plunged past him that he was defiantly brandishing a revolver, and hoped there would be no need for him to so defend himself. But even as he had the thought, came the shock of two shots, as if one answered the other, and awakened a wild flock of echoes in that still suburban garden. They flapped into silence.

"Is John dead?" asked Opal in a low, shuddering voice.

Father Brown had already advanced deeper into the darkness, and stood with his back to them, looking down at something. It was he who answered her.

"No," he said; "it is the other."

Carver had joined him, and for a moment the two figures, the tall and the short, blocked out what view the fitful and stormy moonlight would allow. Then they moved to one side and, the others saw the small, wiry figure lying slightly twisted, as if with its last struggle. The false red beard was thrust upwards, as if scornfully at the sky, and the moon shone on the great sham spectacles of the man who had been called Moonshine.

"What an end," muttered the detective, Carver. "After all his adventures, to be shot almost by accident by a stockbroker in a suburban garden."

The stockbroker himself naturally regarded his own triumph with more solemnity, though not without nervousness.

"I had to do it," he gasped, still panting with exertion. "I'm sorry, he fired at me."

"There will have to be an inquest, of course," said Carver, gravely. "But I think there will be nothing for you to worry about. There's a revolver fallen from his hand with one shot discharged; and he certainly didn't fire after he'd got yours."

By this time they had assembled again in the room, and the detective was getting his papers together for departure. Father Brown was standing opposite to him, looking down at the table, as if in a brown study. Then he spoke abruptly:

"Mr Carver, you have certainly worked out a very complete case in a very masterly way. I rather suspected your professional business; but I never guessed you would link everything up together so quickly—the bees and the beard and the spectacles and the cipher and the necklace and everything."

"Always satisfactory to get a case really rounded off." said Carver.

"Yes," said Father Brown, still looking at the table. "I admire it very much." Then he added with a modesty verging on nervousness: "It's only fair to you to say that I don't believe a word of it."

Devine leaned forward with sudden interest. "Do you mean you don't believe he is Moonshine, the burglar?"

"I know he is the burglar, but he didn't burgle," answered Father Brown. "I know he didn't come here, or to the great house, to steal jewels, or get shot getting away with them. Where are the jewels?"

"Where they generally are in such cases," said Carver. "He's either hidden them or passed them on to a confederate. This was not a one-man job. Of course, my people are searching the garden and warning the district."

"Perhaps," suggested Mrs Bankes, "the confederate stole the necklace while Moonshine was looking in at the window."

"Why was Moonshine looking in at the window?" asked Father Brown quietly. "Why should he want to look in at the window?"

"Well, what do you think?" cried the cheery John.

"I think," said Father Brown, "that he never did want to look in at the window."

"Then why did he do it?" demanded Carver. "What's the good of talking in the air like that? We've seen the whole thing acted before our very eyes."

"I've seen a good many things acted before my eyes that I didn't believe in," replied the priest. "So have you, on the stage and off."

"Father Brown," said Devine, with a certain respect in his tones, "will you tell us why you can't believe your eyes?"

"Yes, I will try to tell you," answered the priest. Then he said gently:

"You know what I am and what we are. We don't bother you much. We try to be friends with all our neighbours. But you can't think we do nothing. You can't think we know nothing. We mind our own business; but we know our own people. I knew this dead man very well indeed; I was his confessor, and his friend. So far as a man can, I knew his mind when he left that garden today; and his mind was like a glass hive full of golden bees. It's an understatement to say his reformation was sincere. He was one of those great penitents who manage to make more out of penitence than others can make out of virtue. I say I was his confessor; but, indeed, it was I who went to him for comfort. It did me good to be near so good a man. And when I saw him lying there dead in the garden, it seemed to me as if certain strange words that were said of old were spoken over him aloud in my ear. They might well be; for if ever a man went straight to heaven, it might be he."

"Hang it all," said John Bankes restlessly, "after all, he was a convicted thief."

"Yes," said Father Brown; "and only a convicted thief has ever in this world heard that assurance: 'This night shalt thou be with Me in Paradise.'"

Nobody seemed to know what to do with the silence that followed, until Devine said, abruptly, at last:

"Then how in the world would you explain it all?"

The priest shook his head. "I can't explain it at all, just yet," he said, simply. "I can see one or two odd things, but I don't understand them. As yet I've nothing to go on to prove the man's innocence, except the man. But I'm quite sure I'm right."

He sighed, and put out his hand for his big, black hat. As he removed it he remained gazing at the table with rather a new expression, his round, straight-haired head cocked at a new angle. It was rather as if some curious animal had come out of his hat, as out of the hat of a conjurer. But the others, looking at the table, could see nothing there but the detective's documents and the tawdry old property beard and spectacles.

"Lord bless us," muttered Father Brown, "and he's lying outside dead, in a beard and spectacles." He swung round suddenly upon Devine. "Here's something to follow up, if you want to know. Why did he have two beards?"

With that he bustled in his undignified way out of the room; but Devine was now devoured with curiosity, and pursued him into the front garden.

"I can't tell you now,"-said Father Brown. "I'm not sure, and I'm bothered about what to do. Come round and see me tomorrow, and I may be able to tell you the whole tiling. It may already be settled for me, and—did you hear that noise?"

"A motorcar starting," remarked Devine.

"Mr John Bankes's motorcar," said the priest. "I believe it goes very fast."

"He certainly is of that opinion." said Devine, with a smile.

"It will go far, as well as fast, tonight," said Father Brown.

"And what do you mean by that?" demanded the other.

"I mean it will not return," replied the priest. "John Bankes suspected something of what I knew from what I said. John Bankes has gone and the emeralds and all the other jewels with him."

Next day, Devine found. Father Brown moving to and fro in front of the row of beehives, sadly, but with a certain serenity.

"I've been telling the bees," he said. "You know one has to tell the bees! Those singing masons building roofs of gold. What a line!" Then more abruptly. "He would like the bees looked after."

"I hope he doesn't want the human beings neglected, when the whole swarm is buzzing with curiosity," observed the young man. "You were quite right when you said that Bankes was gone with the jewels; but I don't know how you knew, or even what there was to be known."

Father Brown blinked benevolently at the beehives and said:

"One sort of stumbles on things, and there was one stumbling-block at the start. I was puzzled by poor Barnard being shot up at Beechwood House. Now, even when Michael was a master criminal, he made it a point of honour, even a point of vanity, to succeed without any killing. It seemed extraordinary that when he had become a sort of saint he should go out of his way to commit the sin he had despised when he was a sinner. The rest of the business puzzled me to the last; I could make nothing out of it, except that it wasn't true. Then I had a belated gleam of sense when I saw the beard and goggles and remembered the thief had come in another beard with other goggles. Now, of course, it was just possible that he had duplicates; but it was at least a coincidence that he used neither the old glasses nor the old beard, both in good repair. Again, it was just possible that he went out without them and had to procure new ones; but it was unlikely. There was nothing to make him go motoring with Bankes at all; if he was really going burgling, he could have taken his outfit easily in his pocket. Besides, beards don't grow on bushes. He would have found it hard to get such things anywhere in the time.

"No, the more I thought of it the more I felt there was something funny about his having a completely new outfit. And then the truth began to dawn on me by reason, which I knew already by instinct. He never did go out with Bankes with any intention of putting on the disguise. He never did put on the disguise. Somebody else manufactured the disguise at leisure, and then put it on him."

"Put it on him!" repeated Devine. "How the devil could they?"

"Let us go back," said Father Brown, "and look at the thing through another window—the window through which the young lady saw the ghost."

"The ghost!" repeated the other, with a slight start.

"She called it the ghost," said the little man, with composure, "and perhaps she was not so far wrong. It's quite true that she is what they call psychic. Her only mistake is in thinking that being psychic is being spiritual. Some animals are psychic; anyhow, she is a sensitive, and she was right when she felt that the face at the window had a son of horrible halo of deathly things."

"You mean—" began Devine.

"I mean it was a dead man who looked in at the window," said Father Brown. "It was a dead man who crawled round more than one house, looking in at more than one window. Creepy, wasn't it? But in one way it was the reverse of a ghost; for it was not the antic of the soul freed from the body. It was the antic of the body freed from the soul."

He blinked again at the beehive and continued: "But, I suppose, the shortest explanation is to take it from the standpoint of the man who did it. You know the man who did it. John Bankes."

"The very last man I should have thought of," said Devine.

"The very first man I thought of," said Father Brown; "in so far as I had any right to think of anybody. My friend, there are no good or bad social types or trades. Any man can be a murderer like poor John; any man, even the same man, can be a saint like poor Michael. But if there is one type that tends at times to be more utterly godless than another, it is that rather brutal sort of business man. He has no social ideal, let alone religion; he has neither the gentleman's traditions nor the trade unionist's class loyalty. All his boasts about getting good bargains were practically boasts of having cheated people. His snubbing of his sister's poor little attempts at mysticism was detestable. Her mysticism was all nonsense; but he only hated spiritualism because it was spirituality. Anyhow, there's no doubt he was the villain of the piece; the only interest is in a rather original piece of villainy. It was really a new and unique motive for murder. It was the motive of using the corpse as a stage property—a sort of hideous doll or dummy. At the start he conceived a plan of killing Michael in the motor, merely to take him home and pretend to have killed him in the garden. But ail sorts of fantastic finishing touches followed quite naturally from the primary fact; that he had at his disposal in a closed car at night the dead body of a recognized and recognizable burglar. He could leave his fingerprints and footprints; he could lean the familiar face against windows and take it away. You will notice that Moonshine ostensibly appeared and vanished while Bankes was ostensibly out of the room looking for the emerald necklace.

"Finally, he had only to tumble the corpse on to the lawn, fire a shot from each pistol, and there he was. It might never have been found out but for a guess about the two beards."

"Why had your friend Michael kept the old beard?" Devine said thoughtfully. "That seems to me questionable."

"To me, who knew him, it seems quite inevitable," replied Father Brown. "His whole attitude was like that wig that he wore. There was no disguise about his disguises. He didn't want the old disguise anyone, but he wasn't frightened of it; he would have felt it false to destroy the false beard. It would have been like hiding; and he was not hiding. He was not hiding from God; he was not hiding from himself. He was in the broad daylight. If they'd taken him back to prison, he'd still have been quite happy. He was not whitewashed, but washed white. There was something very strange about him; almost as strange as the grotesque dance of death through which he was dragged after he was dead. When he moved to and fro smiling among these beehives, even then, in a most radiant and shining sense, he was dead. He was out of the judgment of this world."

There was a short pause, and then Devine shrugged his shoulders and said: "It all comes back to bees and wasps looking very much alike in this world, doesn't it?"

4

THE SONG OF THE FLYING FISH
(No record of prior magazine publication found)

The soul of Mr Peregrine Smart hovered like a fly round one possession and one joke. It might be considered a mild joke, for it consisted merely of asking people if they had seen his goldfish. It might also be considered an expensive joke; but it is doubtful whether he was not secretly more attached to the joke than to the evidence of expenditure. In talking to his neighbours in the little group of new houses that had grown up round the old village green, he lost no time in turning the conversation in the direction of his hobby. To Dr Burdock, a rising biologist with a resolute chin and hair brushed back like a German's, Mr Smart made the easy transition. "You are interested in natural history; have you seen my goldfish?" To so orthodox an evolutionist as Dr Burdock doubtless all nature was one; but at first sight the link was not close, as he was a specialist who had concentrated entirely upon the primitive ancestry of the giraffe. To Father Brown, from a church in the neighbouring provincial town, he traced a rapid train of thought which touched on the topics of "Rome—St. Peter—fisherman—fish—goldfish." In talking to Mr Imlack Smith, the bank manager, a slim and sallow gentleman of dressy appearance but quiet demeanour, he violently wrenched the conversation to the subject of the gold standard, from which it was merely a step to goldfish. In talking to that brilliant Oriental traveller and scholar. Count Yvon de Lara (whose title was French and his face rather Russian, not to say Tartar), the versatile conversationalist showed an intense and intelligent interest in the Ganges and the Indian Ocean, leading naturally to the possible presence of goldfish in those waters.

From Mr Harry Hartopp, the very rich but very shy and silent young gentleman who had recently come down from London, he had at last extorted the information that the embarrassed youth in question was not interested in fishing, and had then added: "Talking about fishing, have you seen my goldfish?"

The peculiar thing about the goldfish was that they were made of gold. They were part of an eccentric but expensive toy, said to have been made by the freak of some rich Eastern prince, and Mr Smart had picked it up at some sale or in some curiosity shop, such as he frequented for the purpose of lumbering up his house with unique and useless things. From the other end of the room it looked like a rather unusually large bowl containing rather unusually large living fish; a closer inspection showed it to be a huge bubble of beautifully blown Venetian glass, very thin and delicately clouded with faintly iridescent colour, in the tinted twilight of which hung grotesque golden fishes with great rubies for eyes. The whole thing was undoubtedly worth a great deal in solid material; how much more would depend upon the waves of lunacy passing over the world of collectors. Mr Smart's new secretary, a young man named Francis Boyle, though an Irishman and not credited with caution, was mildly surprised at his talking so freely of the gems of his collection to the group of comparative strangers who happened to have alighted in a rather nomadic fashion in the neighbourhood; for collectors are commonly vigilant and sometimes secretive. In the course of settling down to his new duties, Mr Boyle found he was not alone in this sentiment, and that in others, it passed from a mild wonder to a grave disapproval.

"It's a wonder his throat isn't cut," said Mr Smart's valet, Harris, not without a hypothetical relish, almost as if he had said, in a purely artistic sense: "It's a pity."

"It's extraordinary how he leaves things about," said Mr Smart's head clerk, Jameson, who had come up from the office to assist the new secretary, "and he won't even put up those ramshackle old bars across his ramshackle old door."

"It's all very well with Father Brown and the doctor," said Mr Smart's housekeeper, with a certain vigorous vagueness that marked her opinions, "but when it comes to foreigners, I call it tempting providence. It isn't only the Count, either; that man at the bank looks to me much too yellow to be English."

"Well, that young Hartopp is English enough," said Boyle good- humouredly, "to the extent of not having a word to say for himself."

"He thinks the more," said the housekeeper. "He may not be exactly a foreigner, but he is not such a fool as he looks. Foreign is as foreign does, I say," she added darkly.

Her disapproval would probably have deepened if she had heard the conversation, in her master's drawing-room that afternoon, a conversation of which the goldfish were the text, though the offensive foreigner tended more and more to be the central figure. It was not that he spoke so very much; but even his silences had something positive about them. He looked the more massive for sitting in a sort of heap on a heap of cushions, and in the deepening twilight his wide Mongolian face seemed faintly luminous, like a moon. Perhaps his background brought out something atmospherically Asiatic about his face and figure, for the room was a chaos of more or less costly curiosities, amid which could be seen the crooked curves and burning colours of countless Eastern weapons, Eastern pipes and vessels, Eastern musical instruments and illuminated manuscripts. Anyhow, as the conversation proceeded, Boyle felt more and more that the figure seated on the cushions and dark against the twilight had the exact outline of a huge image of Buddha.

The conversation was general enough, for all the little local group were present. They were, indeed, often in the habit of dropping in at each other's houses, and by this time constituted a sort of club, of people coming from the four or five houses standing round the green. Of these houses Peregrine Smart's was the oldest, largest, and most picturesque; it straggled down almost the whole of one side of the square, leaving only room for a small villa, inhabited by a retired colonel named Varney, who was reported to be an invalid, and certainly was never seen to go abroad. At right angles to these stood two or three shops that served the simpler needs of the hamlet, and at the corner the inn of the Blue Dragon, at which Mr Hartopp, the stranger from London, was staying. On the opposite side were three houses, one rented by the Count de Lara, one by Dr Burdock, and the third still standing empty. On the fourth side was the bank, with an adjoining house for the bank manager, and a line offence enclosing some land that was let for building. It was thus a very self-contained group, and the comparative emptiness of the open ground for miles round it threw the members more and more on each other's society. That afternoon, one stranger had indeed broken into the magic circle: a hatchet-faced fellow with fierce tufts of eyebrows and moustache, and so shabbily dressed that he must have been a millionaire or a duke if he had really (as was alleged) come down to do business with the old collector. But he was known, at the Blue Dragon at least, as Mr Harmer.

To him had been recounted anew the glories of the gilded fish and the criticisms regarding their custody.

"People are always telling me I ought to lock them up more carefully," observed Mr Smart, cocking an eyebrow over his shoulder at the dependant who stood there holding some papers from the office. Smart was a round-faced, round-bodied little old man rather like a bald parrot. "Jameson and Harris and the rest are always at me to bar the doors as if it were a mediaeval fortress, though really these rotten old rusty bars are too mediaeval to keep anybody out, I should think. I prefer to trust to luck and the local police."

"It is not always the best bars that keep people out," said the Count. "It all depends on who's trying to get in. There was an ancient Hindu hermit who lived naked in a cave and passed through the three armies that encircled the Mogul and took the great ruby out of the tyrant's turban, and went back unscathed like a shadow. For he wished to teach the great how small are the laws of space and time."

"When we really study the small laws of space and time," said Dr Burdock dryly, "we generally find out how those tricks are done. Western science has let in daylight on a good deal of Eastern magic. Doubtless a great deal can be done with hypnotism and suggestion, to say nothing of sleight-of-hand."

"The ruby was not in the royal tent," observed the Count in his dream fashion; "but he found it among a hundred tents."

"Can't all that be explained by telepathy?" asked the doctor sharply. The question sounded the sharper because it was followed by a heavy silence, almost as if the distinguished Oriental traveller had, with imperfect politeness, gone to sleep.

"I beg your pardon," he said rousing himself with a sudden smile. "I had forgotten we were talking with words. In the east we talk with thoughts, and so we never misunderstand each other. It is strange how you people worship words and are satisfied with words. What difference does it make to a thing that you now call it telepathy, as you once called it tomfoolery? If a man climbs into the sky on a mango-tree, how is it altered by saying it is only levitation, instead of saying it is only lies.

If a medieval witch waved a wand and turned me into a blue baboon, you would say it was only atavism."

The doctor looked for a moment as if he might say that it would not be so great a change after all. But before his irritation could find that or any other vent, the man called Harmer interrupted gruffly:

"It's true enough those Indian conjurers can do queer tilings, but I notice they generally do them in India. Confederates, perhaps, or merely mass psychology. I don't think those tricks have ever been played in an English village, and I should say our friend's goldfish were quite safe."

"I will tell you a story," said de Lara, in his motionless way, "which happened not in India, but outside an English barrack in the most modernized part of Cairo. A sentinel was standing inside the grating of an iron gateway looking out between the bars on to the street. There appeared outside the gate a beggar, barefoot and in native rags, who asked him, in English that was startlingly distinct and refined, for a certain official document kept in the building for safety. The soldier told the man, of that he could not come inside; and the man answered, smiling: course, 'What is inside and what is outside?' The soldier was still staring scornfully through the iron grating when he gradually realized that, though neither he nor the gate had moved, he was actually standing in the street and looking in at the barrack yard, where the beggar stood still and smiling and equally motionless. Then, when the beggar turned towards the building, the sentry awoke to such sense as he had left, and shouted a warning to all the soldiers within the gated enclosure to hold the prisoner fast. 'You won't get out of there anyhow,' he said vindictively. Then the beggar said in his silvery voice: 'What is outside and what is inside?' And the soldier, still glaring through the same bars, saw that they were once more between him and the street, where the beggar stood free and smiling with a paper in his hand."

Mr Imlack Smith, the bank manager, was looking at the carpet with his dark sleek head bowed, and he spoke for the first time.

"Did anything happen about the paper?" he asked.

"Your professional instincts are correct, sir," said the Count with grim affability. "It was a paper of considerable financial importance. Its consequences were international."

"I hope they don't occur often," said young Hartopp gloomily.

"I do not touch the political side," said the Count serenely, "but only the philosophical. It illustrates how the wise man can get behind time and space and turn the levers of them, so to speak, so that the whole world turns round before our eyes. But is it so hard for you people to believe that spiritual powers are really more powerful than material ones."

"Well," said old Smart cheerfully, "I don't profess to be an authority on spiritual powers. What do you say, Father Brown?"

"The only thing that strikes me," answered the little priest, "is that all the supernatural acts we have yet heard of seem to be thefts. And stealing by spiritual methods seem to me much the same as stealing by material ones."

"Father Brown is a Philistine," said the smiling Smith.

"I have a sympathy with the tribe," said Father Brown. "A Philistine is only a man who is right without knowing why."

"All this is too clever for me," said Hartopp heartily.

"Perhaps," said Father Brown with a smile, "you would like to speak without words, as the Count suggests. He would begin by saying nothing in a pointed fashion, and you would retort with a burst of taciturnity."

"Something might be done with music," murmured the Count dreamily. "It would be better than all these words."

"Yes, I might understand that better," said the young man in a low voice.

Boyle had followed the conversation with curious attention, for there was something in the demeanour of more than one of the talkers that seemed to him significant or even odd. As the talk drifted to music, with an appeal to the dapper bank manager (who was an amateur musician of some merit), the young secretary awoke with a start to his secretarial duties, and reminded his employer that the head clerk was still standing patiently with the papers in his hand.

"Oh, never mind about those just now, Jameson," said Smart rather hurriedly. "Only something about my account; I'll see Mr Smith about it later. You were saying that the cello, Mr Smith—"

But the cold breath of business had sufficed to disperse the fumes of transcendental talk, and the guests began one after another to say farewell. Only Mr Imlack Smith, bank manager and musician, remained to the last; and when the rest were gone he and his host went into the inner room, where the goldfish were kept, and closed the door.

The house was long and narrow, with a covered balcony running along the first floor, which consisted mostly of a sort of suite of rooms used by the householder himself, his bedroom and dressing-room, and an inner room in which his very valuable treasures were sometimes stored for the night instead of being left in the rooms below. This balcony, like the insufficiently barred door below it, was a matter of concern to the housekeeper and the head clerk and the others who lamented the carelessness of the collector; but, in truth, that cunning old gentleman was more careful than he seemed. He professed no great belief in the antiquated fastenings of the old house, which the housekeeper lamented to see rusting in idleness, but he had an eye to the more important point of strategy. He always put his favourite goldfish in the room at the back of his bedroom for the night, and slept in front of it, as it were, with a pistol under his pillow. And when Boyle and Jameson, awaiting his return from the tete-a-tete, at length saw the door open and their employer reappear, he was carrying the great glass bowl as reverently as it if had been the relic of a saint.

Outside, the last edges of the sunset still clung to the corners of the green square; but inside, a lamp had already been kindled; and in the mingling of the two lights the coloured globe glowed like some monstrous jewel, and the fantastic outlines of the fiery fishes seemed to give it, indeed, something of the mystery of a talisman, like strange shapes seen by a seer in the crystal of doom. Over the old man's shoulder the olive face of Imlack Smith stared like a sphinx.

"I am going up to London tonight, Mr Boyle," said old Smart, with more gravity than he commonly showed. "Mr Smith and I are catching the six-forty-five. I should prefer you, Jameson, to sleep upstairs in my room tonight; if you put the bowl in the back room as usual, it will be quite safe then. Not that I suppose anything could possibly happen."

"Anything may happen anywhere," said the smiling Mr Smith. "I think you generally take a gun to bed with you. Perhaps you had better leave it behind in this case."

Peregrine Smart did not reply, and they passed out of the house on to the road round the village green.

The secretary and the head clerk slept that night as directed in their employer's bedroom. To speak more strictly, Jameson, the head clerk, slept in a bed in the dressing-room, but the door stood open between, and the two rooms running along the front were practically one. Only the bedroom had a long French window giving on the balcony, and an entrance at the back into the inner apartment where the goldfish bowl had been placed for safety. Boyle dragged his bed right across so as to bar this entrance, put the revolver under his pillow, and then undressed and went to bed, feeling that he had taken all possible precautions against an impossible or improbable event. He did not see why there should be any particular danger of normal burglary; and as for the spiritual burglary that figured in the traveller's tales of the Count de Lara, if his thoughts ran on them so near to sleep it was because they were such stuff as dreams are made of. They soon turned into dreams with intervals of dreamless slumber. The old clerk was a little more restless as usual; but after fussing about a little longer and repeating some of his favourite regrets and warnings, he also retired to his bed in the same manner and slept. The moon brightened and grew dim again above the green square and the grey blocks of houses in a solitude and silence that seemed to have no human witness; and it was when the white cracks of daybreak had already appeared in the corners of the grey sky that the thing happened.

Boyle, being young, was naturally both the healthier and the heavier sleeper of the two. Though active enough when he was once awake, he always had a load to lift in waking. Moreover, he had dreams of the sort that cling to the emerging minds like the dim tentacles of an octopus. They were a medley of many things, including his last look from the balcony across the four grey roads and the green square. But the pattern of them changed and shifted and turned dizzily, to the accompaniment of a low grinding noise, which sounded somehow like a subterranean river, and may have been no more than old Mr Jameson snoring in the dressing-room. But in the dreamer's mind all that murmur and motion was vaguely connected with the words of the Count de Lara, about a wisdom that could hold the levers of time and space and turn the world. In the dream it seemed as if a vast murmuring machinery under the world were really moving whole landscapes hither and thither, so that the ends of the earth might appear in a man's front-garden, or his own front-garden be exiled beyond the sea.

The first complete impressions he had were the words of a song, with a rather thin metallic accompaniment; they were sung in a foreign accent and a voice that was still strange and yet faintly familiar. And yet he could hardly feel sure that he was not making up poetry in his sleep.

Over the land and over the sea
My flying fishes will come to me,
For the note is not of the world that wakes them,
But in—

He struggled to his feet and saw that his fellow-guardian was already out of bed; Jameson was peering out of the long window on to the balcony and calling out sharply to someone in the street below.

"Who's that?" he called out sharply. "What do you want?"

He turned to Boyle in agitation, saying: "There's somebody prowling about just outside. I knew it wasn't safe. I'm going down to bar that front door, whatever they say."

He ran downstairs in a flutter and Boyle could hear the clattering of the bars upon the front door; but Boyle himself stepped out upon the balcony and looked out on the long grey road that led up to the house, and he thought he was still dreaming.

Upon that grey road leading across that empty moor and through that little English hamlet, there had appeared a figure that might have stepped straight out of the jungle or the bazaar—a figure out of one of the Count's fantastic stories; a figure out of the "Arabian nights." The rather ghostly grey twilight which begins to define and yet to discolour everything when the light in the east has ceased to be localized, lifted slowly like a veil of grey gauze and showed him a figure wrapped in outlandish raiment. A scarf of a strange sea-blue, vast and voluminous, went round the head like a turban, and then again round the chin, giving rather the general character of a hood; so far as the face was concerned it had a the effects of a mask. For the raiment round the head was drawn close as a veil; and the head itself was bowed over a queer-looking musical instrument made of silver or steel, and shaped like a deformed or crooked violin. It was played with something like a silver comb, and the notes were curiously thin and keen. Before Boyle could open his mouth, the same haunting alien accent came from under the shadow of the burnous, singing-words of the same sort:

As the golden birds go back to the tree
My golden fishes return to me.
Return—

"You've no right here," called out Boyle in exasperation, hardly knowing what he said.

"I have a right to the goldfish," said the stranger, speaking more like King Solomon than an unsandalled Bedouin in a ragged blue cloak. "And they will come to me. Come!"

He struck his strange fiddle as his voice rose sharply on the word. There was a pang of sound that seemed to pierce the mind, and then there came a fainter sound, like an answer: a vibrant whisper. It came from the dark room behind where the bowl of goldfish was standing.

Boyle turned towards it; and even as he turned the echo in the inner room changed to a long tingling sound like an electric bell, and then to a faint crash. It was still a matter of seconds since he had challenged the man from the balcony; but the old clerk had already regained the top of the stairs, panting a little, for he was an elderly gentleman.

"I've locked up the door, anyhow," he said.

"The stable door," said Boyle out of the darkness of the inner room.

Jameson followed him into that apartment and found him staring down at the floor, which was covered with a litter of coloured glass like the curved bits of a broken rainbow.

"What do you mean by the stable door?" began Jameson.

"I mean that the steed is stolen," answered Boyle. "The flying steeds. The flying fishes our Arab friend outside has just whistled to like so many performing puppies."

"But how could he?" exploded the old clerk, as if such events were hardly respectable.

"Well, they're gone," said Boyle shortly. "The broken bowl is here, which would have taken a long time to open properly, but only a second to smash. But the fish are gone, God knows how, though I think our friend ought to be asked."

"We are wasting time," said the distracted Jameson. "We ought to be after him at once."

"Much better be telephoning the police at once," answered Boyle. "They ought to outstrip him in a flash with motors and telephones that go a good deal farther than we should ever get, running through the village in our nightgowns. But it may be there are things even the police cars and wires won't outstrip."

While Jameson was talking to the police-station through the telephone in an agitated voice, Boyle went out again on to the balcony and hastily scanned that grey landscape of daybreak. There was no trace of the man in the turban, and no other sign of life, except some faint stirrings an expert might have recognized in the hotel of the Blue Dragon. Only Boyle, for the first time, noted consciously something that he had all along been noting unconsciously. It was like a fact struggling in the submerged mind and demanding its own meaning. It was simply the fact that the grey landscape had never been entirely grey; there was one gold spot amid its stripes of colourless colour, a lamp lighted in one of the houses on the other side of the green. Something, perhaps irrational, told him that it had been burning through all the hours of the darkness and was only fading with the dawn. He counted the houses, and his calculation brought out a result which seemed to fit in with something, he knew not what. Anyhow, it was apparently the house of the Count Yvon de Lara.

Inspector Pinner had arrived with several policemen, and done several things of a rapid and resolute sort, being conscious that the very absurdity of the costly trinkets might give the case considerable prominence in the newspapers. He had examined everything, measured, everything, taken down everybody's deposition, taken everybody's finger -prints, put everybody's back up, and found himself at the end left facing a fact which he could not believe. An Arab from the desert had walked up the public road and stopped in front of the house of Mr Peregrine Smart, where a bowl of artificial goldfish was kept in an inner room; he had then sung or recited a little poem, and the bowl had exploded like a bomb and the fishes vanished into thin air. Nor did it soothe the inspector to be told by a foreign Count—in a soft, purring voice—that the bounds of experience were being enlarged.

Indeed, the attitude of each member of the little group was characteristic enough. Peregrine Smart himself had come back from London the next morning to hear the news of his loss. Naturally he admitted a shock; but it was typical of something sporting and spirited in the little old gentleman, something that always made his small strutting figure look like a cock-sparrow's, that he showed more vivacity in the search than depression at the loss. The man named Harmer, who had come to the village on purpose to buy the goldfish, might be excused for being a little testy on learning they were not there to be bought. But, in truth, his rather aggressive moustache and eyebrows seemed to bristle with something more definite than disappointment, and the eyes that darted over the company were bright with a vigilance that might well be suspicion. The sallow face of the bank manager, who had also returned from London though by a later train, seemed again and again to attract those shining and shifting eyes like a magnet. Of the two remaining figures of the original circle. Father Brown was generally silent when he was not spoken to, and the dazed Hartopp was often silent even when he was.

But the Count was not a man to let anything pass that gave an apparent advantage to his views. He smiled at his rationalistic rival, the doctor, in the manner of one who knows how it is possible to be irritating by being ingratiating.

"You will admit, doctor," he said, "that at least some of the stories you thought so improbable look a little more realistic today than they did yesterday. When a man as ragged as those I described is able, by speaking a word, to dissolve a solid vessel inside the four walls of the house he stands outside, it might perhaps be called an example of what I said about spiritual powers and material barriers."

"And it might be called an example of what I said," said the doctor sharply, "about a little scientific knowledge being enough to show how the tricks are done."

"Do you really mean, doctor," asked Smart in some excitement, "that you can throw any scientific light on this mystery?"

"I can throw light on what the Count calls a mystery," said the doctor, "because it is not a mystery at all. That part of it is plain enough. A sound is only a wave of vibration, and certain vibrations can break glass, if the sound is of a certain kind and the glass of a certain kind. The man did not stand in the road and think, which the Count tells us is the ideal method when Orientals want a little chat. He sang out what he wanted, quite loud, and struck a shrill note on an instrument. It is similar to many experiments by which glass of special composition has been cracked."

"Such as the experiment," said the Count lightly, "by which several lumps of solid gold have suddenly ceased to exist."

"Here comes Inspector Pinner," said Boyle. "Between ourselves, I think he would regard the doctor's natural explanation as quite as much of a fairy tale as the Count's preternatural one. A very sceptical intellect, Mr Pinner's, especially about me. I rather think I am under suspicion."

"I think we are all under suspicion," said the Count.

It was the presence of this suspicion in his own case that led Boyle to seek the personal advice of Father Brown. They were walking round the village green together, some hours later in the day, when the priest, who was frowning thoughtfully at the ground as he listened, suddenly stopped.

"Do you see that?" he asked. "Somebody's been washing the pavement here—just this little strip of pavement outside Colonel Varney's house. I wonder whether that was done yesterday."

Father Brown looked rather earnestly at the house, which was high and narrow, and carried rows of striped sun-blinds of gay but already faded colours. The chinks or crannies that gave glimpses of the interior looked all the darker; indeed, they looked almost black in contrast with the facade thus golden in the morning light.

"That is Colonel Varney's house, isn't it?" he asked. "He comes from the East, too, I fancy. What sort of man is he?"

"I've never even seen him," answered Boyle. "I don't think anybody's seen him, except Dr Burdock, and I rather fancy the doctor doesn't see him more than he need."

"Well, I'm going to see him for a minute," said Father Brown.

The big front door opened and swallowed the small priest, and his friend stood staring at it in a dazed and irrational manner, as if wondering whether it would ever open again. It opened in a few minutes, and Father Brown emerged, still smiling, and continued his slow and pottering progress round the square of roads. Sometimes he seemed to have forgotten the matter in hand altogether, for he would make passing remarks on historical and social questions, or on the prospects of development in the district. He remarked on the soil used for the beginning of a new road by the bank; he looked across the old village green with a vague expression.

"Common land. I suppose people ought to feed their pigs and geese on it, if they had any pigs or geese; as it is, it seems to feed nothing but nettles and thistles. What a pity that what was supposed to be a sort of large meadow has been turned into a small and petty wilderness. That's Dr Burdock's house opposite, isn't it?"

"Yes," answered Boyle, almost jumping at this abrupt postscript.

"Very well," answered Father Brown, "then I think we'll go indoors again."

As they opened the front door of Smart's house and mounted the stairs, Boyle repeated to his companion many details of the drama enacted there at daybreak.

"I suppose you didn't doze off again?" asked Father Brown, "giving time for somebody to scale the balcony while Jameson ran down to secure the door."

"No," answered Boyle; "I am sure of that. I woke up to hear Jameson challenging the stranger from the balcony; then I heard him running downstairs and putting up the bars, and then in two strides I was on the balcony myself."

"Or could he have slipped in between you from another angle? Are there any other entrances besides the front entrance?"

"Apparently there are not," said Boyle gravely.

"I had better make sure, don't you think?" asked Father Brown apologetically, and scuttled softly downstairs again. Boyle remained in the front bedroom gazing rather doubtfully after him. After a comparatively brief interval the round and rather rustic visage appeared again at the head of the stairs, looking rather like a turnip ghost with a broad grin.

"No; I think that settles the matter of entrances," said the turnip ghost, cheerfully. "And now, I think, having got everything in a tight box, so to speak, we can take stock of what we've got. It's rather a curious business."

"Do you think," asked Boyle, 'that the Count or the colonel, or any of these Eastern travellers have anything to do with it? Do you think it is—preternatural?"

"I will grant you this," said the priest gravely, "if the Count, or the colonel, or any of your neighbours did dress up in Arab masquerade and creep up to this house in the dark—then it was preternatural."

"What do you mean? Why?"

"Because the Arab left no footprints," answered Father Brown. "The colonel on the one side and the banker on the other are the nearest of your neighbours. That loose red soil is between you and the bank, it would print off bare feet like a plaster cast and probably leave red marks everywhere. I braved the colonel's curry-seasoned temper to verify the fact that the front pavement was washed yesterday and not today; it was wet enough to make wet footprints all along the road. Now, if the visitor were the Count or the doctor in the houses opposite, he might possibly, of course, have come across the common. But he must have found it exceedingly uncomfortable with bare feet, for it is, as I remarked, one mass of thorns and thistles and stinging nettles. He would surely have pricked himself and probably left traces of it. Unless, as you say, he was a preternatural being."

Boyle looked steadily at the grave and indecipherable face of his clerical friend.

"Do you mean that he was?" he asked, at length.

"There is one general truth to remember," said Father Brown, after a pause. "A thing can sometimes be too close to be seen, as, for instance, a man cannot see himself. There was a man who had a fly in his eye when he looked through the telescope, and he discovered that there was a most incredible dragon in the moon. And I am told that if a man hears the exact reproduction of his own voice it sounds like the voice of a stranger. In the same way, if anything is right in the foreground of our life we hardly see it, and if we did we might think it quite odd. If the thing in the foreground got into the middle distance, we should probably think it had come from the remote distance. Just come outside the house again for a moment. I want to show you how it looks from another standpoint."

He had already risen, and as they descended the stairs he continued his remarks in a rather groping fashion as if he were thinking aloud.

"The Count and the Asiatic atmosphere all come in, because, in a case like this, everything depends on the preparation of the mind. A man can reach a condition in which a brick, falling on his head, will seem to be a Babylonian brick carved with cuneiform, and dropped from the Hanging Gardens of Babylon, so that he will never even look at the brick and see it is of one pattern with the bricks or his own house. So in your case—"

"What does this mean?" interrupted Boyle, staring and pointing at the entrance. "What in the name of wonder does it mean? The door is barred again."

He was staring at the front door by which they had entered but a little while before, and across which stood, once more, the great dark bands of rusty iron which had once, as he had said, locked the stable door too late. There was something darkly and dumbly ironic in those old fastenings closing behind them and imprisoning them as if of their own motion.

"Oh those!" said Father Brown casually. "I put up those bars myself, just now. Didn't you hear me?"

"No," answered Boyle, staring. "I heard nothing."

"Well, I rather thought you wouldn't," said the other equably. "There's really no reason why anybody upstairs should hear those bars being put up. A sort of hook fits easily into a sort of hole. When you're quite close you hear a dull click; but that's all. The only thing that makes any noise a man could hear upstairs, is this."

And he lifted the bar out of its socket and let it fall with a clang at the side of the door,

"It does make a noise if you unbar the door," said Father Brown gravely, "even if you do it pretty carefully."

"You mean—"

"I mean," said Father Brown, "that what you heard upstairs was Jameson opening the door and not shutting it. And now let's open the door ourselves and go outside."

When they stood outside in the street, under the balcony, the little priest resumed his previous explanation as coolly as if it had been a chemical lecture.

"I was saying that a man may be in the mood to look for something very distant, and not realize that it is something very close, something very close to himself, perhaps something very like himself. It was a strange and outlandish thing that you saw when you looked down at this road. I suppose it never occurred to you to consider what he saw when he looked up at that balcony?"

Boyle was staring at the balcony and did not answer, and the other added:

"You thought it very wild and wonderful that an Arab should come through civilized England with bare feet. You did not remember that at the same moment you had bare feet yourself."

Boyle at last found words, and it was to repeat words already spoken.

"Jameson opened the door," he said mechanically.

"Yes," assented, his friend. "Jameson opened the door and came out into the road in his nightclothes, just as you came out on the balcony. He caught up two things that you had seen a hundred times: the length of old blue curtain that he wrapped round his head, and the Oriental musical instrument you must have often seen in that heap of Oriental curiosities. The rest was atmosphere and acting, very fine acting, for he is a very fine artist in crime."

"Jameson!" exclaimed Boyle incredulously. "He was such a dull old stick that I never even noticed him."

"Precisely," said the priest, "he was an artist. If he could act a wizard or a troubadour for six minutes, do you think he could not act a clerk for six weeks?"

"I am still not quite sure of his object," said Boyle.

"His object has been achieved," replied Father Brown, "or very nearly achieved. He had taken the goldfish already, of course, as he had twenty chances of doing. But if he had simply taken, them, everybody would have realized that he had twenty chances of doing it. By creating a mysterious magician from the end of the earth, he set everybody's thoughts wandering far afield to Arabia and India, so that you yourself can hardly believe that the whole thing was so near home. It was too close to you to be seen."

"If this is true," said Boyle, "it was an extraordinary risk to run, and he had to cut it very fine. It's true I never heard the man in the street say anything while Jameson was talking from the balcony, so I suppose that was all a fake. And I suppose it's true that there was time for him to get outside before I had fully woken up and got out on to the balcony."

"Every crime depends on somebody not waking up too soon," replied Father Brown; "and in every sense most of us wake up too late. I, for one, have woken up much too late. For I imagine he's bolted long ago, just before or just after they took his finger-prints."

"You woke up before anybody else, anyhow," said Boyle, "and I should never have woken up in that sense. Jameson was so correct and colourless that I forgot all about him."

"Beware of the man you forget," replied his friend; "he is the one man who has you entirely at a disadvantage. But I did not suspect him, either, until you told me how you had heard him barring the door."

"Anyhow, we owe it all to you," said Boyle warmly.

"You owe it all to Mrs Robinson," said Father Brown with a smile.

"Mrs Robinson?" questioned the wondering secretary. "You don't mean the housekeeper?"

"Beware of the woman you forget, and even more," answered the other. "This man was a very high-class criminal; he had been an excellent actor, and therefore he was a good psychologist. A man like the Count never hears any voice but his own; but this man could listen, when you had all forgotten he was there, and gather exactly the right materials for his romance and know exactly the right note to strike to lead you all astray. But he made one bad mistake in the psychology of Mrs Robinson, the housekeeper."

"I don't understand," answered Boyle, "what she can have to do with it."

"Jameson did not expect the doors to be barred," said Father Brown. "He knew that a lot of men, especially careless men like you and your employer, could go on saying for days that something ought to be done, or might as well be done. But if you convey to a woman that something ought to be done, there is always a dreadful danger that she will suddenly do it."

5

THE ACTOR AND THE ALIBI (No record of prior magazine publication found)

Mr Mundon Mandeville, the theatrical manager, walked briskly through the passages behind the scenes, or rather below the scenes. His attire was smart and festive, perhaps a little too festive; the flower in his buttonhole was festive; the very varnish on his boots was festive; but his face was not at all festive. He was a big, bull-necked, black-browed man, and at the moment his brow was blacker than usual. He had in any case, of course, the hundred botherations that besiege a man in such a position; and they ranged from large to small and from new to old. It annoyed him to pass through the passages where the old pantomime scenery was stacked; because he had successfully begun, his career at that theatre with very popular pantomimes, and had since been induced to gamble in more serious and classical drama over which he had dropped a good deal of money. Hence, to see the sapphire Gates of Bluebeard's Blue Palace, or portions of the enchanted Grove of Golden orange Trees, leaning up against the wall to be festooned with cobwebs or nibbled by mice, did not give him that soothing sense of a return to simplicity which we all ought to have when given a glimpse of that wonderland of our childhood. Nor had he any time to drop a tear where he had dropped the money, or to dream of this Paradise of Peter Pan; for he had been summoned hurriedly to settle a practical problem, not of the past but of the moment. It was the sort of thing that does sometimes happen in that strange world behind the scenes; but it was big enough to be serious. Miss Maroni, the talented young actress of Italian parentage, who had undertaken to act an important part in the play that was to be rehearsed that afternoon and performed that evening, had abruptly and even violently refused at the last moment to do anything of the kind. He had not even seen the exasperating lady yet; and as she had locked herself up in her dressing-room and defied the world through the door, it seemed unlikely, for the present, that he would. Mr Mundon Mandeville was sufficiently British to explain it by murmuring that all foreigners were mad; but the thought of his good fortune in inhabiting the only sane island of the planet did not suffice to soothe him any more than the memory of the Enchanted Grove. All these things, and many more, were annoying; and yet a very intimate observer might have suspected that something was wrong with Mr Mandeville that went beyond annoyance.

If it be possible for a heavy and healthy man to look haggard, he looked haggard. His face was full, but his eye-sockets were hollow; his mouth twitched as if it were always trying to bite the black strip of moustache that was just too short to be bitten. He might have been a man who had begun to take drugs; but even on that assumption there was something that suggested that he had a reason for doing it; that the drug was not the cause of the tragedy, but the tragedy the cause of the drug. Whatever was his deeper secret, it seemed to inhabit that dark end of the long passage where was the entrance to his own little study; and as he went along the empty corridor, he threw back a nervous glance now and then.

However, business is business; and he made his way to the opposite end of the passage where the blank green door of Miss Maroni defied the world. A group of actors and other people involved were already standing in front of it, conferring and considering, one might almost fancy, the advisability of a battering-ram. The group contained one figure, at least, who was already well enough known; whose photograph was on many mantelpieces and his autograph in many albums. For though Norman Knight was playing the hero in a theatre that was still a little provincial and old-fashioned and capable of calling him the first walking gentleman, he, at least, was certainly on the way to wider triumphs. He was a good-looking man with a long cleft chin and fair hair low on his forehead, giving him a rather Neronian look that did not altogether correspond to his impulsive and plunging movements. The group also contained Ralph Randall, who generally acted elderly character parts, and had a humorous hatchet face, blue with shaving, and discoloured with grease paint. It contained Mandeville's second walking gentleman, carrying on the not yet wholly vanished tradition of Charles's Friend, a dark, curly-haired youth of somewhat Semitic profile bearing the name of Aubrey Vernon.

It included Mr Mundon Mandeville's wife's maid or dresser, a very powerful-looking person with tight red hair and a hard wooden face. It also, incidentally, included Mandeville's wife, a quiet woman in the background, with a pale, patient face, the lines of whch had not lost a classical symmetry and severity, but which looked all the paler because her very eyes were pale, and her pale yellow hair lay in two plain bands like some very archaic Madonna. Not everybody knew that she had once been a serious and successful actress in Ibsen and the intellectual drama. But her husband did not think much of problem plays; and certainly at the moment was more interested in the problem of getting a foreign actress out of a locked room; a new version of the conjuring trick of the Vanishing Lady.

"Hasn't she come out yet?" he demanded, speaking to his wife's business-like attendant rather than to his wife.

"No, sir," answered the woman—who was known as Mrs Sands—in a sombre manner.

"We are beginning to get a little alarmed," said old Randall. "She seemed quite unbalanced, and we're afraid she might even do herself some mischief."

"Hell!" said Mandeville in his simple and artless way. "Advertisement's very good, but we don't want that sort of advertisement. Hasn't she any friends here? Has nobody any influence with her?"

"Jarvis thinks the only man who might manage her is her own priest round the corner," said Randall; "and in case she does start hanging herself on a hat peg, I really thought perhaps he'd better be here. Jarvis has gone to fetch him and, as a matter of fact, here he comes."

Two more figures appeared in that subterranean passage under the stage: the first was Ashton Jarvis, a jolly fellow who generally acted villains, but who had surrendered that high vocation for the moment to the curly-headed youth with the nose. The other figure was short and square and clad all in black; it was Father Brown from the church round the corner.

Father Brown seemed to take it quite naturally and even casually, that he should be called in to consider the queer conduct of one of his flock, whether she was to be regarded as a black sheep or only as a lost lamb. But he did not seem to think much of the suggestion of suicide.

"I suppose there was some reason for her flying off the handle like that," he said. "Does anybody know what it was?"

"Dissatisfied with her part, I believe," said the older actor.

"They always are," growled Mr Mundon Mandeville. "And I thought my wife would look after those arrangements."

"I can only say," said Mrs Mundon Mandeville rather wearily, "that I gave her what ought to be the best part. It's supposed to be what stage-struck young women want, isn't it—to act the beautiful young heroine and marry the beautiful young hero in a shower of bouquets and cheers from the gallery? Women of my age naturally have to fall back on acting respectable matrons, and I was careful to confine myself to that."

"It would be devilish awkward to alter the parts now, anyhow," said Randall.

"It's not to be thought of," declared Norman Knight firmly. "Why, I could hardly act—but anyhow it's much too late."

Father Brown had slipped forward and was standing outside the locked door listening.

"Is there no sound?" asked the manager anxiously; and then added in a lower voice: "Do you think she can have done herself in?"

"There is a certain sound," replied Father Brown calmly. "I should be inclined to deduce from the sound that she is engaged in breaking windows or looking-glasses, probably with her feet. No; I do not think there is much danger of her going on to destroy herself. Breaking looking-glasses with your feet is a very unusual prelude to suicide. If she had been a German, gone away to think quietly about metaphysics and weltschmerz, I should be all for breaking the door down. These Italians don't really die so easily; and are not liable to kill themselves in a rage. Somebody else, perhaps—yes, possibly—it might be well to take ordinary precautions if she comes out with a leap."

"So you're not in favour of forcing the door?" asked Mandeville.

"Not if you want her to act in your play," replied Father Brown. "If you do that, she'll raise the roof and refuse to stay in the place; if you leave her alone, she'll probably come out from mere curiosity. If I were you, I should just leave somebody to guard the door, more or less, and trust to time for an hour or two."

"In that case," said Mandeville, "we can only get on with rehearsing the scenes where she doesn't appear. My wife will arrange all that is necessary for scenery just now. After all, the fourth act is the main business. You had better get on with that."

"Not a dress rehearsal," said Mandeville's wife to the others.

"Very well," said Knight, "not a dress rehearsal, of course. I wish the dresses of the infernal period weren't so elaborate."

"What is the play?" asked the priest with a touch of curiosity.

"The School for Scandal," said Mandeville. "It may be literature, but I want plays. My wife likes what she calls classical comedies. A long sight more classic than comic."

At this moment, the old doorkeeper known as Sam, and the solitary inhabitant of the theatre during off-hours, came waddling up to the manager with a card, to say that Lady Miriam Marden wished to see him. He turned away, but Father Brown continued to blink steadily for a few seconds in the direction of the manager's wife, and saw that her wan face wore a faint smile; not altogether a cheerful smile.

Father Brown moved off in company with the man who had brought him in, who happened, indeed, to be a friend and person of a similar persuasion, which is not uncommon among actors. As he moved off, however, he heard Mrs Mandeville give quiet directions to Mrs Sands that she should take up the post of watcher beside the closed door.

"Mrs Mandeville seems to be an intelligent woman," said the priest to his companion, "though she keeps so much in the background."

"She was once a highly intellectual woman," said Jarvis sadly; "rather washed-out and wasted, some would say, by marrying a bounder like Mandeville. She has the very highest ideals of the drama, you know; but, of course, it isn't often she can get her lord and master to look at anything in that light. Do you know, he actually wanted a woman like that to act as a pantomime boy?

Admitted that she was a fine actress, but said pantomimes paid better. That will give you about a measure of his psychological insight and sensibility. But she never complained. As she said to me once: 'Complaint always comes back in an echo from the ends of the world; but silence strengthens us.' If only she were married to somebody who understood her ideas she might have been one of the great actresses of the age; indeed, the highbrow critics still think a lot of her. As it is, she is married to that."

And he pointed to where the big black bulk of Mandeville stood with his back to them, talking to the ladies who had summoned him forth into the vestibule. Lady Miriam was a very long and languid and elegant lady, handsome in a recent fashion largely modelled on Egyptian mummies; her dark hair cut low and square, like a sort of helmet, and her lips very painted and prominent and giving her a permanent expression of contempt. Her companion was a very vivacious lady with an ugly attractive face and hair powdered with grey. She was a Miss Theresa Talbot and she talked a great deal, while her companion seemed too tired to talk at all. Only, just as the two men passed. Lady Miriam summoned up the energy to say:

"Plays are a bore; but I've never seen a rehearsal in ordinary clothes. Might be a bit funny. Somehow, nowadays, one can never find a thing one's never seen."

"Now, Mr Mandeville," said Miss Talbot, tapping him on the arm with animated persistence, "you simply must let us see that rehearsal. We can't come tonight, and we don't want to. We want to see all the funny people in the wrong clothes."

"Of course I can give you a box if you wish it," said Mandeville hastily. "Perhaps your ladyship would come this way." And he led them off down another corridor.

"I wonder," said Jarvis in a meditative manner, "whether even Mandeville prefers that sort of woman."

"Well," asked his clerical companion, "have you any reason to suppose that Mandeville does prefer her?"

Jarvis looked at him steadily for an instant before answering.

"Mandeville is a mystery," he said gravely. "Oh, yes, I know that he looks about as commonplace a cad as ever walked down Piccadilly. But he really is a mystery for all that. There's something on his conscience. There's a shadow in his life. And I doubt whether it has anything more to do with a few fashionable flirtations than it has with his poor neglected wife. If it has, there's something more in them than meets the eye. As a matter of fact, I happen to know rather more about it than anyone else does, merely by accident. But even I can't make anything of what I know, except a mystery."

He looked around him in the vestibule to see that they were alone and then added, lowering his voice:

"I don't mind telling you, because I know you are a tower of silence where secrets are concerned. But I had a curious shock the other day; and it has been repeated several times since. You know that Mandeville always works in that little room at the end of the passage, just under the stage. Well, twice over I happened to pass by there when everyone thought he was alone; and what's more, when I myself happened to be able to account for all the women in the company, and all the women likely to have to do with him, being absent or at their usual posts."

"All the women?" remarked Father Brown inquiringly.

"There was a woman with him," said Jarvis almost in a whisper. "There is some woman who is always visiting him; somebody that none of us knows. I don't even know how she comes there, since it isn't down the passage to the door; but I think I once saw a veiled or cloaked figure passing out into the twilight at the back of the theatre, like a ghost. But she can't be a ghost. And I don't believe she's even an ordinary 'affair'. I don't think it's love-making. I think it's blackmail."

"What makes you think that?" asked the other.

"Because," said Jarvis, his face turning from grave to grim, "I once heard sounds like a quarrel; and then the strange woman said in a metallic, menacing voice, four words: 'I am your wife.'"

"You think he's a bigamist," said Father Brown reflectively. "Well, bigamy and blackmail often go together, of course. But she may be bluffing as well as blackmailing. She may be mad. These theatrical people often have monomaniacs running after them. You may be right, but I shouldn't jump to conclusions... And talking about theatrical people, isn't the rehearsal going to begin, and aren't you a theatrical person?"

"I'm not on in this scene," said Jarvis with a smile. "They're only doing one act, you know, until your Italian friend comes to her senses."

"Talking about my Italian friend," observed the priest, "I should rather like to know whether she has come to her senses."

"We can go back and see, if you like," said Jarvis; and they descended again to the basement and the long passage, at one end of which was Mandeville's study and at the other the closed door of Signora Maroni. The door seemed to be still closed; and. Mrs Sands sat grimly outside it, as motionless as a wooden idol.

Near the other end of the passage they caught a glimpse of some of the other actors in the scene mounting the stairs to the stage just above. Vernon and old Randall went ahead, running rapidly up the stairs; but Mrs Mandeville went more slowly, in her quietly dignified fashion, and norman Knight seemed to linger a little to speak to her. A few words fell on the ears of the unintentional eavesdroppers as they passed.

"I tell you a woman visits him," Knight was saying violently.

"Hush!" said the lady in her voice of silver that still had in it something of steel. "You must not talk like this. Remember, he is my husband."

"I wish to God I could forget it," said Knight, and rushed up the stairs to the stage.

The lady followed him, still pale and calm, to take up her own position there.

"Somebody else knows it," said the priest quietly; "but I doubt whether it is any business of ours."

"Yes," muttered Jarvis; "it seems as if everybody knows it and nobody knows anything about it."

They proceeded along the passage to the other end, where the rigid attendant sat outside the Italian's door.

"No; she ain't come out yet," said the woman in her sullen way; "and she ain't dead, for I heard her moving about now and then. I dunno what tricks she's up to."

"Do you happen to know, ma'am," said Father Brown with abrupt politeness, "where Mr Mandeville is just now?"

"Yes," she replied promptly. "Saw him go into his little room at the end of the passage a minute or two ago; just before the prompter called and the curtain went up. Must be there still, for I ain't seen him come out."

"There's no other door to his office, you mean," said Father Brown in an off-hand way. "Well, I suppose the rehearsal's going in full swing now, for all the Signora's sulking."

"Yrs," said Jarvis after a moment's silence; "I can just hear the voices on the stage from here. Old Randall has a splendid carrying voice."

They both remained for an instant in a listening attitude, so that the booming voice of the actor on the stage could indeed be heard rolling faintly down the stairs and along the passage. Before they had spoken again or resumed their normal poise, their ears were filled with another sound. It was a dull but heavy crash and it came from behind the closed door of Mundon Mandeville's private room.

Father Brown went racing along the passage like an arrow from the bow and was struggling with the door-handle before Jarvis had wakened with a start and begun to follow him.

"The door is locked," said the priest, turning a face that was a little pale. "And I am all in favour of breaking down this door."

"Do you mean," asked Jarvis with a rather ghastly look, "that the unknown visitor has got in here again? Do you think it's anything serious?" After a moment he added: "I may be able to push back the bolt; I know the fastening on these doors."

He knelt down and pulled out a pocketknife with a long steel implement, manipulated it for a moment, and the door swung open on the manager's study. Almost the first thing they noticed was that there was no other door and even no window, but a great electric lamp stood on the table. But it was not quite the first thing that they noticed; for even before that they had seen that Mandeville was lying flat on his face in the middle of the room and the blood was crawling out from under his fallen face like a pattern of scarlet snakes that glittered evilly in that unnatural subterranean light.

They did not know how long they had been staring at each other when Jarvis said, like one letting loose something that he had held back with his breath:

"If the stranger got in somehow, she has gone somehow."

"Perhaps we think too much about the stranger," said Father Brown. "There are so many strange things in this strange theatre that you rather tend to forget some of them."

"Why, which things do you mean?" asked his friend quickly.

"There are many," said the priest. "There is the other locked door, for instance."

"But the other door is locked," cried Jarvis staring.

"But you forgot it all the same," said Father Brown. A few moments afterwards he said thoughtfully: "That Mrs Sands is a grumpy and gloomy sort of card."

"Do you mean," asked the other in a lowered voice, "that she's lying and the Italian did come out?"

"No," said the priest calmly; "I think I meant it more or less as a detached study of character."

"You can't mean," cried the actor, "that Mrs Sands did it herself?"

"I didn't mean a study of her character," said Father Brown.

While they had been exchanging these abrupt reflections, Father Brown had knelt down by the body and ascertained that it was beyond any hope or question a dead body. Lying beside it, though not immediately visible from the doorway, was a dagger of the theatrical sort; lying as if it had fallen from the wound or from the hand of the assassin. According to Jarvis, who recognized the instrument, there was not very much to be learned from it, unless the experts could find some finger-prints. It was a property dagger; that is, it was nobody's property; it had been kicking about the theatre for a long time, and anybody might have picked it up. Then the priest rose and looked gravely round the room.

"We must send for the police," he said; "and for a doctor, though the doctor comes too late. Looking at this room, by the way, I don't see how our Italian friend could manage it."

"The Italian!" cried his friend; "I should think not. I should have thought she had an alibi, if anybody had. Two separate rooms, both locked, at opposite ends of a long passage, with a fixed witness watching it."

"No," said Father Brown. "Not quite. The difficulty is how she could have got in this end. I think she might have got out the other end."

"And why?" asked the other.

"I told you," said Father Brown, "that it sounded as if she was breaking glass—mirrors or windows. Stupidly enough I forgot something I knew quite well; that she is pretty superstitious. She wouldn't be likely to break a mirror; so I suspect she broke a window. It's true that all this is under the ground floor; but it might be a skylight or a window opening on an area. But there don't seem to be any skylights or areas here." And he stared at the ceiling very intently for a considerable time.

Suddenly he came back to conscious life again with a start. "We must go upstairs and telephone and tell everybody, It is pretty painful... My God, can you hear those actors still shouting and ranting upstairs? The play is still going on. I suppose that's what they mean by tragic irony."

When it was fated that the theatre should be turned into a house of mourning, an opportunity was given to the actors to show many of the real virtues of their type and trade. They did, as the phrase goes, behave like gentlemen; and not only like first walking gentlemen. They had not all of them liked or trusted Mandeville, but they knew exactly the right things to say about him; they showed not only sympathy but delicacy in their attitude to his widow. She had become, in a new and very different sense, a tragedy queen—her lightest word was law and while she moved about slowly and sadly, they ran her many errands.

"She was always a strong character," said old Randall rather huskily; "and had the best brains of any of us. Of course poor Mandeville was never on her level in education and so on; but she always did her duty splendidly. It was quite pathetic the way she would sometimes say she wished she had more intellectual life; but Mandeville—well, nil nisi bonum, as they say." And the old gentleman went away wagging his head sadly.

"Nil nisi bonum indeed," said Jarvis grimly. "I don't think Randall at any rate has heard of the story of the strange lady visitor. By the way, don't you think it probably was the strange woman?"

"It depends," said the priest, "whom you mean by the strange woman."

"Oh! I don't mean the Italian woman," said Jarvis hastily. "Though, as a matter of fact, you were quite right about her, too. When they went in the skylight was smashed and the room was empty; but so far as the police can discover, she simply went home in the most harmless fashion. No, I mean the woman who was heard threatening him at that secret meeting; the woman who said she was his wife. Do you think she really was his wife?"

"It is possible," said Father Brown, staring blankly into the void, "that she really was his wife."

"That would give us the motive of jealousy over his bigamous remarriage," reflected Jarvis, "for the body was not robbed in any way. No need to poke about for thieving servants or even impecunious actors. But as for that, of course, you've noticed the outstanding and peculiar thing about the case?"

"I have noticed several peculiar things," said Father Brown. "Which one do you mean?"

"I mean the corporate alibi," said Jarvis gravely. "It's not often that practically a whole company has a public alibi like that; an alibi on a lighted stage and all witnessing to each other. As it turns out it is jolly lucky for our friends here that poor Mandeville did put those two silly society women in the box to watch the rehearsal. They can bear witness that the whole act was performed without a hitch, with the characters on the stage all the time. They began long before Mandeville was last seen going into his room. They went on at least five or ten minutes after you and I found his dead body. And, by a lucky coincidence, the moment we actually heard him fall was during the time when all the characters were on the stage together."

"Yes, that is certainly very important and simplifies everything," agreed Father Brown. "Let us count the people covered by the alibi. There was Randall: I rather fancy Randall practically hated the manager, though he is very properly covering his feelings just now. But he is ruled out; it was his voice we heard thundering over our heads from the stage. There is our jeune premier, Mr Knight: I have rather good reason to suppose he was in love with Mandeville's wife and not concealing that sentiment so much as he might; but he is out of it, for he was on the stage at the same time, being thundered at. There was that amiable Jew who calls himself Aubrey Vernon, he's out of it; and there's Mrs Mandeville, she's out of it. Their corporate alibi, as you say, depends chiefly on Lady Miriam and her friend in the box; though there is the general common-sense corroboration that the act had to be gone through and the routine of the theatre seems to have suffered no interruption. The legal witnesses, however, are Lady Miriam and her friend, Miss Talbot. I suppose you feel sure they are all right?"

"Lady Miriam?" said Jarvis in surprise. "Oh, yes... I suppose you mean that she looks a queer sort of vamp. But you've no notion what even the ladies of the best families are looking like nowadays. Besides, is there any particular reason for doubting their evidence?"

"Only that it brings us up against a blank wall," said Father Brown. "Don't you see that this collective alibi practically covers everybody? Those four were the only performers in the theatre at the time; and there were scarcely any servants in the theatre; none indeed, except old Sam, who guards the only regular entrance, and the woman who guarded Miss Maroni's door. There is nobody else left available but you and me. We certainly might be accused of the crime, especially as we found the body. There seems nobody else who can be accused. You didn't happen to kill him when I wasn't looking, I suppose?"

Jarvis looked up with a slight start and stared a moment, then the broad grin returned to his swarthy face. He shook his head.

"You didn't do it," said Father Brown; "and we will assume for the moment, merely for the sake of argument, that I didn't do it. The people on the stage being out of it, it really leaves the Signora behind her locked door, the sentinel in front other door, and old Sam. Or are you thinking of the two ladies in the box? Of course they might have slipped out of the box."

"No," said Jarvis; "I am thinking of the unknown woman who came and told Mandeville she was his wife."

"Perhaps she was," said the priest; and this time there was a note in his steady voice that made his companion start to his feet once more and lean across the table.

"We said," he observed in a low, eager voice, "that this first wife might have been jealous of the other wife."

"No," said Father Brown; "she might have been jealous of the Italian girl, perhaps, or of Lady Miriam Marden. But she was not jealous of the other wife."

"And why not?"

"Because there was no other wife," said Father Brown. "So far from being a bigamist, Mr Mandeville seems to me to have been a highly monogamous person. His wife was almost too much with him; so much with him that you all charitably suppose that she must be somebody else. But I don't see how she could have been with him when he was killed, for we agree that she was acting all the time in front of the footlights. Acting an important part, too..."

"Do you really mean," cried Jarvis, "that the strange woman who haunted him like a ghost was only the Mrs Mandeville we know?" But he received no answer; for Father Brown was staring into vacancy with a blank expression almost like an idiot's. He always did look most idiotic at the instant when he was most intelligent.

The next moment he scrambled to his feet, looking very harassed and distressed. "This is awful," he said. "I'm not sure it isn't the worst business I ever had; but I've got to go through with it. Would you go and ask Mrs Mandeville if I may speak to her in private?"

"Oh, certainly," said Jarvis, as he turned towards the door. "But what's the matter with you?"

"Only being a born fool," said Father Brown; "a very common complaint in this vale of tears. I was fool enough to forget altogether that the play was The School For Scandal."

He walked restlessly up and down the room until Jarvis reappeared at the door with an altered and even alarmed face.

"I can't find her anywhere," he said. "Nobody seems to have seen her."

"They haven't seen Norman Knight either, have they?" asked Father Brown dryly. "Well, it saves me the most painful interview of my life. Saving the grace of God, I was very nearly frightened of that woman. But she was frightened of me, too; frightened of something I'd seen or said. Knight was always begging her to bolt with him. Now she's done it; and I'm devilish sorry for him."

"For him?" inquired Jarvis.

"Well, it can't be very nice to elope with a murderess," said the other dispassionately. "But as a matter of fact she was something very much worse than a murderess."

"And what is that?"

"An egoist," said Father Brown. "She was the sort of person who had looked in the mirror before looking out of the window, and it is the worst calamity of mortal life. The looking-glass was unlucky for her, all right; but rather because it wasn't broken."

"I can't understand what all this means," said Jarvis. "Everybody regarded her as a person of the most exalted ideals, almost moving on a higher spiritual plane than the rest of us..."

"She regarded herself in that light," said the other; "and she knew how to hypnotize everybody else into it. Perhaps I hadn't known her long enough to be wrong about her. But I knew the sort of person she was five minutes after I clapped eyes on her."

"Oh, come." cried Jarvis; "I'm sure her behaviour about the Italian was beautiful."

"Her behaviour always was beautiful," said the other. "I've heard from everybody here all about her refinements and subtleties and spiritual soarings above poor Mandeville's head. But all these spiritualities and subtleties seem to me to boil themselves clown to the simple fact that she certainly was a lady and he most certainly was not a gentleman. But, do you know, I have never felt quite sure that St. Peter will make that the only test at the gate of heaven.

"As for the rest," he went on with increasing animation, "I knew from the very first words she said that she was not really being fair to the poor Italian, with all her fine airs of frigid magnanimity. And again, I realized it when I knew that the play was The School for Scandal.'

"You are going rather too fast for me," said Jarvis in some bewilderment. "What does it matter what the play was?"

"Well," said the priest, "she said she had given the girl the part of the beautiful heroine and had retired into the background herself with the older part of a matron. Now that might have applied to almost any play; but it falsifies the facts about that particular play. She can only have meant that she gave the other actress the part of Maria, which is hardly a part at all. And the part of the obscure and self-effacing married woman, if you please, must have been the part of Lady Teazle, which is the only part any actress wants to act. If the Italian was a first-rate actress who had been promised a first-rate part, there was really some excuse, or at least some cause, for her mad Italian rage. There generally is for mad Italian rages: Latins are logical and have a reason for going mad. But that one little thing let in daylight for me on the meaning of her magnanimity. And there was another thing, even then. You laughed when I said that the sulky look of Mrs Sands was a study in character; but not in the character of Mrs Sands. But it was true. If you want to know what a lady is really like, don't look at her; for she may be too clever for you. Don't look at the men round her, for they may be too silly about her. But look at some other woman who is always near to her, and especially one who is under her. You will see in that mirror her real face, and the face mirrored in Mrs Sands was very ugly.

"And as for all the other impressions, what were they? I heard a lot about the unworthiness of poor old Mandeville; but it was all about his being unworthy other, and I am pretty certain it came indirectly from her. And, even so, it betrayed itself. Obviously, from what every man said, she had confided in every man about her confounded intellectual loneliness. You yourself said she never complained; and then quoted her about how her uncomplaining silence strengthened her soul. And that is just the note; that's the unmistakable style. People who complain are just jolly, human Christian nuisances; I don't mind them. But people who complain that they never complain are the devil. They are really the devil; isn't that swagger of stoicism the whole point of the Byronic cult of Satan? I heard all this; but for the life of me I couldn't hear of anything tangible she had to complain of. Nobody pretended that her husband drank, or beat her, or left her without money, or even was unfaithful, until the rumour about the secret meetings, which were simply her own melodramatic habit of pestering him with curtain-lectures in his own business office. And when one looked at the facts, apart from the atmospheric impression of martyrdom she contrived to spread, the facts were really quite the other way. Mandeville left off making money on pantomimes to please her; he started losing money on classical drama to please her. She arranged the scenery and furniture as she liked. She wanted Sheridan's play and she had it; she wanted the part of Lady Teazle and she had it; she wanted a rehearsal without costume at that particular hour and she had it. It may be worth remarking on the curious fact that she wanted that."

"But what is the use of all this tirade?" asked the actor, who had hardly ever heard his clerical friend, make so long a speech before. "We seem to have got a long way from the murder in all this psychological business. She may have eloped with Knight;

she may have bamboozled Randall; she may have bamboozled me. But she can't have murdered her husband—for everyone agrees she was on the stage through the whole scene. She may be wicked; but she isn't a witch."

"Well, I wouldn't be so sure," said Father Brown, with a smile. "But she didn't need to use any witchcraft in this case. I know now that she did it, and very simply indeed."

"Why are you so sure of that?" asked Jarvis, looking at him in a puzzled way.

"Because the play was The School for Scandal," replied Father Brown, "and that particular act of The School for Scandal. I should like to remind you, as I said just now, that she always arranged the furniture how she liked. I should also like to remind you that this stage was built and used for pantomimes; it would naturally have trapdoors and trick exits of that sort. And when you say that witnesses could attest to having seen all the performers on the stage, I should like to remind you that in the principal scene of The School for Scandal one of the principal performers remains for a considerable time on the stage, but is not seen. She is technically 'on,' but she might practically be very much 'off.' That is the Screen of Lady Teazle and the Alibi of Mrs Mandeville."

There was a silence and then the actor said: "You think she slipped through a trapdoor behind a screen down to the floor below, where the manager's room was?"

"She certainly slipped away in some fashion; and that is the most probable fashion," said the other. "I think it all the more probable because she took the opportunity of an undress rehearsal, and even indeed arranged for one. It is a guess; but I fancy if it had been a dress rehearsal it might have been more difficult to get through a trapdoor in the hoops of the eighteenth century. There are many little difficulties, of course, but I think they could all be met in time and in turn."

"What I can't meet is the big difficulty," said Jarvis, putting his head on his hand with a sort of groan. "I simply can't bring myself to believe that a radiant and serene creature like that could so lose, so to speak, her bodily balance, to say nothing of her moral balance. Was any motive strong enough? Was she very much in love with Knight?"

"I hope so," replied his companion; "for really it would be the most human excuse. But I'm sorry to say that I have my doubts. She wanted to get rid of her husband, who was an old-fashioned, provincial hack, not even making much money. She wanted to have a career as the brilliant wife of a brilliant and rapidly-rising actor. But she didn't want in that sense to act in The School for Scandal. She wouldn't have run away with a man except in the last resort. It wasn't a human passion with her, but a sort of hellish respectability. She was always dogging her husband in secret and badgering him to divorce himself or otherwise get out of the way; and as he refused he paid at last for his refusal. There's another thing you've got to remember. You talk about these highbrows having a higher art and a more philosophical drama. But remember what a lot of the philosophy is! Remember what sort of conduct those highbrows often present to the highest! All about the Will to Power and the Right to Live and the Right to Experience—damned nonsense and more than damned nonsense—nonsense that can damn."

Father Brown frowned, which he did very rarely; and there was still a cloud on his brow as he put on his hat and went out into the night.

6

THE VANISHING OF VAUDREY
(No record of prior magazine publication found)

Sir Arthur Vaudrey, in his light-grey summer suit, and wearing on his grey head the white hat which he so boldly affected, went walking briskly up the road by the river from his own house to the little group of houses that were almost like outhouses to his own, entered that little hamlet, and then vanished completely as if he had been carried away by the fairies.

The disappearance seemed the more absolute and abrupt because of the familiarity of the scene and the extreme simplicity of the conditions of the problem. The hamlet could not be called a village; indeed, it was little more than a small and strangely-isolated street. It stood in the middle of wide and open fields and plains, a mere string of the four or five shops absolutely needed by the neighbours; that is, by a few farmers and the family at the great house. There was a butcher's at the corner, at which, it appeared, Sir Arthur had last been seen. He was seen by two young men staying at his house—Evan Smith, who was acting as his secretary, and John Dalmon, who was generally supposed to be engaged to his ward. There was next to the butcher's a small shop combining a large number of functions, such as is found in villages, in which a little old woman sold sweets, walking-sticks, golf-balls, gum, balls of string and a very faded sort of stationery. Beyond this was the tobacconist, to which the two young men were betaking themselves when they last caught a glimpse of their host standing in front of the butcher's shop; and beyond that was a dingy little dressmaker's, kept by two ladies. A pale and shiny shop, offering to the passerby great goblets of very wan, green lemonade, completed the block of buildings; for the only real and Christian inn in the neighbourhood stood by itself some way, down the main road. Between the inn and the hamlet was a crossroads, at which stood a policeman and a uniformed official of a motoring club; and both agreed that Sir Arthur had never passed that point on the road.

It had been at an early hour of a very brilliant summer day that the old gentleman had gone gaily striding up the road, swinging his walking-stick and flapping his yellow gloves. He was a good deal of a dandy, but one of a vigorous and virile sort, especially for his age. His bodily strength and activity were still very remarkable, and his curly hair might have been a yellow so pale as to look white instead of a white that was a faded yellow. His clean-shaven face was handsome, with a high-bridged nose like the Duke of Wellington's; but the most outstanding features were his eyes. They were not merely metaphorically outstanding; something prominent and almost bulging about them was perhaps the only disproportion in his features; but his lips were sensitive and set a little tightly, as if by an act of will. He was the squire of all that country and the owner of the little hamlet. In that sort of place everybody not only knows everybody else, but generally knows where anybody is at any given moment. The normal course would have been for Sir Arthur to walk to the village, to say whatever he wanted to say to the butcher or anybody else, and then walk back to his house again, all in the course of about half an hour: as the two young men did when they had bought their cigarettes. But they saw nobody on the road returning; indeed, there was nobody in sight except the one other guest at the house, a certain Dr Abbott, who was sitting with his broad back to them on the river bank, very patiently fishing.

When all the three guests returned to breakfast, they seemed to think little or nothing of the continued absence of the squire; but when the day wore on and he missed one meal after another, they naturally began to be puzzled, and Sybil Rye, the lady of the household, began to be seriously alarmed. Expeditions of discovery were dispatched to the village again and again without finding any trace; and eventually, when darkness fell, the house was full of a definite fear. Sybil had sent for Father Brown, who was a friend of hers and had helped her out of a difficulty in the past; and under the pressure of the apparent peril he had consented to remain at the house and see it through.

Thus it happened that when the new day's dawn broke without news, Father Brown was early afoot and on the lookout for anything; his black, stumpy figure could be seen pacing the garden path where the garden was embanked along the river, as he scanned the landscape up and down with his short-sighted and rather misty gaze.

He realized that another figure was moving even more restlessly along the embankment, and saluted Evan Smith, the secretary, by name.

Evan Smith was a tall, fair-haired young man, looking rather harassed, as was perhaps natural in that hour of distraction. But something of the sort hung about him at all times. Perhaps it was more marked because he had the sort of athletic reach and poise and the sort of leonine yellow hair and moustache which accompany (always in fiction and sometimes in fact) a frank and cheerful demeanour of "English youth." As in his case they accompanied deep and cavernous eyes and a rather haggard look, the contrast with the conventional tall figure and fair hair of romance may have had a touch of something sinister. But Father Brown smiled at him amiably enough and then said more seriously:

"This is a trying business."

"It's a very trying business for Miss Rye," answered the young man gloomily; "and I don't see why I should disguise what's the worst part of it for me, even if she is engaged to Dalmon. Shocked, I suppose?"

Father Brown did not look very much shocked, but his face was often rather expressionless; he merely said, mildly:

"Naturally, we all sympathize with her anxiety. I suppose you haven't any news or views in the matter?"

"I haven't any news exactly," answered Smith; "no news from outside at least. As for views..." And he relapsed into moody silence.

"I should be very glad to hear your views," said the little priest pleasantly. "I hope you don't mind my saying that you seem to have something on your mind."

The young man stirred rather than started and looked at the priest steadily, with a frown that threw his hollow eyes into dense shadow.

"Well, you're right enough," he said at last. "I suppose I shall have to tell somebody. And you seem a safe sort of person to tell."

"Do you know what has happened to Sir Arthur?" asked Father Brown calmly, as if it were the most casual matter in the world.

"Yes," said the secretary harshly, "I think I know what has happened to Sir Arthur."

"A beautiful morning," said a bland voice in his ear; "a beautiful morning for a rather melancholy meeting."

This time the secretary jumped as if he had been shot, as the large shadow of Dr Abbott fell across his path in the already strong sunshine. Dr Abbott was still in his dressing-gown—a sumptuous oriental dressing-gown covered with coloured flowers and dragons, looking rather like one of the most brilliant flowerbeds that were growing under the glowing sun. He also wore large, flat slippers, which was doubtless why he had come so close to the others without being heard. He would normally have seemed the last person for such a light and airy approach, for he was a very big, broad and heavy man, with a powerful benevolent face very much sunburnt, in a frame of old- fashioned grey whiskers and chin beard, which hung about him luxuriantly, like the long, grey curls of his venerable head. His long slits of eyes were rather sleepy and, indeed, he was an elderly gentleman to be up so early; but he had a look at once robust and weatherbeaten, as of an old farmer or sea captain who had once been out in all weathers. He was the only old comrade and contemporary of the squire in the company that met at the house.

"It seems truly extraordinary," he said, shaking his head. "Those little houses are like dolls' houses, always open front and back, and there's hardly room to hide anybody, even if they wanted to hide him. And I'm sure they don't. Dalmon and I cross-examined them all yesterday; they're mostly little old women that couldn't hurt a fly. The men are nearly all away harvesting, except the butcher; and Arthur was seen coining out of the butcher's. And nothing could have happened along that stretch by the river, for I was fishing there all day."

Then he looked at Smith and the look in his long eyes seemed for the moment not only sleepy, but a little sly.

"I think you and Dalmon can testify," he said, "that you saw me sitting there through your whole journey there and back."

"Yes," said Evan Smith shortly, and seemed rather impatient at the long interruption.

"The only thing I can think of," went on Dr Abbott slowly; and then the interruption was itself interrupted. A figure at once light and sturdy strode very rapidly across the green lawn between the gay flowerbeds, and John Dalmon appeared among them, holding a paper in his hand. He was neatly dressed and rather swarthy, with a very fine square Napoleonic face and very sad eyes—eyes so sad that they looked almost dead. He seemed to be still young, but his black hair had gone prematurely grey about the temples.

"I've just had this telegram from the police," he said "I wired to them last night and they say they're sending down a man at once. Do you know, Dr Abbott, of anybody else we ought to send for? Relations, I mean, and that sort of thing."

"There is his nephew, Vernon Vaudrey, of course," said the old man. "If you will come with me, I think I can give you his address and—and tell you something rather special about him."

Dr Abbott and Dalmon moved away in the direction of the house and, when they had gone a certain distance, Father Brown said simply, as if there had been no interruption:

"You were saying?"

"You're a cool hand," said the secretary. "I suppose it comes of hearing confessions. I feel rather as if I were going to make a confession. Some people would feel a bit jolted out of the mood of confidence by that queer old elephant creeping up like a snake. But I suppose I'd better stick to it, though it really isn't my confession, but somebody else's." He stopped a moment, frowning and pulling his moustache; then he said, abruptly:

"I believe Sir Arthur has bolted, and I believe I know why."

There was a silence and then he exploded again.

"I'm in a damnable position, and most people would say I was doing a damnable thing. I am now going to appear in the character of a sneak and a skunk and I believe I am doing my duty."

"You must be the judge," said Father Brown gravely. "What is the matter with your duty?"

"I'm in the perfectly foul position of telling tales against a rival, and a successful rival, too," said the young man bitterly; "and I don't know what else in the world I can do. You were asking what was the explanation of Vaudrey's disappearance. I am absolutely convinced that Dalmon is the explanation."

"You mean," said the priest, with composure, "that Dalmon has killed Sir Arthur?"

"No!" exploded Smith, with startling violence. "No, a hundred times! He hasn't done that, whatever else he's done. He isn't a murderer, whatever else he is. He has the best of all alibis; the evidence of a man who hates him. I'm not likely to perjure myself for love of Dalmon; and I could swear in any court he did nothing to the old man yesterday. Dalmon and I were together all day, or all that part of the day, and he did nothing in the village except buy cigarettes, and nothing here except smoke them and read in the library. No; I believe he is a criminal, but he did not kill Vaudrey. I might even say more; because he is a criminal he did not kill Vaudrey."

"Yes," said the other patiently, "and what does that mean?"

"It means," replied the secretary, "that he is a criminal committing another crime: and his crime depends on keeping Vaudrey alive."

"Oh, I see," said Father Brown.

"I know Sybil Rye pretty well, and her character is a great part of this story. It is a very fine character in both senses: that is, it is of a noble quality and only too delicate a texture. She is one of those people who are terribly conscientious, without any of that armour of habit and hard common sense that many conscientious people get. She is almost insanely sensitive and at the same time quite unselfish. Her history is curious: she was left literally penniless like a foundling and Sir Arthur took her into his house and treated her with consideration, which puzzled many; for, without being hard on the old man, it was not much in his line. But, when she was about seventeen, the explanation came to her with a shock; for her guardian asked her to marry him. Now I come to the curious part of the story. Somehow or other, Sybil had heard from somebody (I rather suspect from old Abbott) that Sir Arthur Vaudrey, in his wilder youth, had committed some crime or, at least, done some great wrong to somebody, which had got him into serious trouble. I don't know what it was. But it was a sort of nightmare to the girl at her crude sentimental age, and made him seem like a monster, at least too much so for the close relation of marriage. What she did was incredibly typical of her. With helpless terror and with heroic courage she told him the truth with her own trembling lips. She admitted that her repulsion might be morbid; she confessed it like a secret madness. To her relief and surprise he took it quietly and courteously, and apparently said no more on the subject; and her sense of his generosity was greatly increased by the next stage of the story. There came into her lonely life the influence of an equally lonely man. He was camping-out like a sort of hermit on one of the islands in the river; and I suppose the mystery made him attractive, though I admit he is attractive enough; a gentleman, and quite witty, though very melancholy—which, I suppose, increased the romance. It was this man, Dalmon, of course; and to this day I'm not sure how far she really accepted him; but it got as far as his getting permission to see her guardian. I can fancy her awaiting that interview in an agony of terror and wondering how the old beau would take the appearance of a rival. But here, again, she found she had apparently done him an injustice. He received the younger man with hearty hospitality and seemed to be delighted with the prospects of the young couple. He and Dalmon went shooting and fishing together and were the best of friends, when one day she had another shock. Dalmon let slip in conversation some chance phrase that the old man 'had not changed much in thirty years,' and the truth about the odd intimacy burst upon her. All that introduction and hospitality had been a masquerade; the men had obviously known each other before. That was why the younger man had come down rather covertly to that district. That was why the elder man was lending himself so readily to promote the match. I wonder what you are thinking?"

"I know what you are thinking," said Father Brown, with a smile, "and it seems entirely logical. Here we have Vaudrey, with some ugly story in his past—a mysterious stranger come to haunt him, and getting whatever he wants out of him. In plain words, you think Dalmon is a blackmailer."

"I do," said the other; "and a rotten thing to think, too."

Father Brown reflected for a moment and then said: "I think I should like to go up to the house now and have a talk to Dr Abbott."

When he came out of the house again an hour or two afterwards, he may have been talking to Dr Abbott, but he emerged in company with Sybil Rye, a pale girl with reddish hair and a profile delicate and almost tremulous; at the sight other, one could instantly understand all the secretary's story of her shuddering candour. It recalled Godiva and certain tales of virgin martyrs; only the shy can be so shameless for conscience's sake. Smith came forward to meet them, and for a moment they stood talking on the lawn. The day which had been brilliant from daybreak was now glowing and even glaring; but Father Brown carried his black bundle of an umbrella as well as wearing his black umbrella of a hat; and seemed, in a general way, buttoned up to breast the storm. But perhaps it was only an unconscious effect of attitude; and perhaps the storm was not a material storm.

"What I hate about it all," Sybil was saying in a low voice, "is the talk that's beginning already; suspicions against everybody. John and Evan can answer for each other, I suppose; but Dr Abbott has had an awful scene with the butcher, who thinks he is accused and is throwing accusations about in consequence."

Evan Smith looked very uncomfortable; then blurted out: “Look here, Sybil, I can’t say much, but we don’t believe there’s any need for all that. It’s all very beastly, but we don’t think there’s been— any violence.”

‘Have you got a theory, then?” said the girl, looking instantly at the priest.

“I have heard a theory,” he replied, “which seems to me very convincing.”

He stood looking rather dreamily towards the river; and Smith and Sybil began to talk to each other swiftly, in lowered tones. The priest drifted along the river bank, ruminating, and plunged into a plantation of thin trees on an almost overhanging bank. The strong sun beat on the thin veil of little dancing leaves like small green flames, and all the birds were singing as if the tree had a hundred tongues. A minute or two later, Evan Smith heard his own name called cautiously and yet clearly from the green depths of the thicket. He stepped rapidly in that direction and met Father Brown returning. The priest said to him, in a very low voice:

“Don’t let the lady come down here. Can’t you get rid of her? Ask her to telephone or something; and then come back here again.”

Evan Smith turned with a rather desperate appearance of carelessness and approached the girl; but she was not the sort of person whom it is hard to make busy with small jobs for others. In a very short time she had vanished into the house and Smith turned to find that Father Brown had once more vanished into the thicket. Just beyond the clump of trees was a sort of small chasm where the turf had subsided to the level of the sand by the river. Father Brown was standing on the brink of this cleft, looking down; but, either by accident or design, he was holding his hat in his hand, in spite of the strong sun pouring on his head.

“You had better see this yourself,” he said, heavily, “as a matter of evidence. But I warn you to be prepared.”

"Prepared for what?" asked the other

"Only for the most horrible thing I ever saw in my life," said Father Brown.

Even Smith stepped to the brink of the bank of turf and with difficulty repressed a cry rather like a scream.

Sir Arthur Vaudrey was glaring and grinning up at him; the face was turned up so that he could have put his foot on it; the head was thrown back, with its wig of whitish yellow hair towards him, so that he saw the face upside down. This made it seem all the more like a part of a nightmare; as if a man were walking about with his head stuck on the wrong way. What was he doing? Was it possible that Vaudrey was really creeping about, hiding in the cracks of field and bank, and peering out at them in this unnatural posture? The rest of the figure seemed hunched and almost crooked, as if it had been crippled or deformed but on looking more closely, this seemed only the foreshortening of limbs fallen in a heap. Was he mad? Was he? The more Smith looked at him the stiffer the posture seemed.

"You can't see it from here properly," said Father Brown, "but his throat is cut."

Smith shuddered suddenly. "I can well believe it's the most horrible thing you've seen," he said. "I think it's seeing the face upside down. I've seen that face at breakfast, or dinner, every day for ten years; and it always looked quite pleasant and polite. You turn it upside down and it looks like the face of a fiend."

"The face really is smiling," said Father Brown, soberly; "which is perhaps not the least part of the riddle. Not many men smile while their throats are being cut, even if they do it themselves. That smile, combined with those gooseberry eyes of his that always seemed standing out of his head, is enough, no doubt, to explain the expression. But it's true, things look different upside down. Artists often turn their drawings upside down to test their correctness. Sometimes, when it's difficult to turn the object itself upside down (as in the case of the

Matterhorn, let us say), they have been known to stand on their heads, or at least look between their legs."

The priest, who was talking thus flippantly to steady the other man's nerves, concluded by saying, in a more serious tone: "I quite understand how it must have upset you. Unfortunately, it also upset something else."

"What do you mean?"

"It has upset the whole of our very complete theory," replied the other; and he began clambering down the bank on to the little strip of sand by the river.

"Perhaps he did it himself," said Smith abruptly. "After all, that's the most obvious sort of escape, and fits in with our theory very well. He wanted a quiet place and he came here and cut his throat."

"He didn't come here at all," said Father Brown. "At least, not alive, and not by land. He wasn't killed here; there's not enough blood. This sun has dried his hair and clothes pretty well by now; but there are the traces of two trickles of water in the sand. Just about here the tide comes up from the sea and makes an eddy that washed the body into the creek and left it when the tide retired. But the body must first have been washed down the river, presumably from the village, for the river runs just behind the row of little houses and shops. Poor Vaudrey died up in the hamlet, somehow; after all, I don't think he committed suicide; but the trouble is who would, or could, have killed him up in that potty little place?"

He began to draw rough designs with the point of his stumpy umbrella on the strip of sand.

"Let's see; how does the row of shops run? First, the butcher's; well, of course, a butcher would be an ideal performer with a large carving- knife. But you saw Vaudrey come out, and it isn't very probable that he stood in the outer shop while the butcher said: 'Good morning. Allow me to cut your throat! Thank you. And the next article, please?' Sir

Arthur doesn't strike me as the sort of man who'd have stood there with a pleasant smile while this happened. He was a very strong and vigorous man, with rather a violent temper. And who else, except the butcher, could have stood up to him? The next shop is kept by an old woman. Then comes the tobacconist, who is certainly a man, but I am told quite a small and timid one. Then there is the dressmaker's, run by two maiden ladies, and then a refreshment shop run by a man who happens to be in hospital and who has left his wife in charge. There are two or three village lads, assistants and errand boys, but they were away on a special job. The refreshment shop ends the street; there is nothing beyond that but the inn, with the policeman between."

He made a punch with the ferrule of his umbrella to represent the policeman, and remained moodily staring up the river. Then he made a slight movement with his hand and, stepping quickly across, stooped over the corpse.

"Ah," he said, straightening himself and letting out a great breath. "The tobacconist! Why in the world didn't I remember that about the tobacconist?"

"What is the matter with you?" demanded Smith in some exasperation; for Father Brown was rolling his eyes and muttering, and he had uttered the word "tobacconist" as if it were a terrible word of doom.

"Did you notice," said the priest, after a pause, "something rather curious about his face?"

"Curious, my God!" said Evan, with a retrospective shudder. "Anyhow, his throat was cut..."

"I said his face," said the cleric quietly. "Besides, don't you notice he has hurt his hand and there's a small bandage round it?"

"Oh, that has nothing to do with it," said Evan hastily. "That happened before and was quite an accident. He cut his hand with a broken ink-bottle while we were working together."

"It has something to do with it, for all that," replied Father Brown.

There was a long silence, and the priest walked moodily along the sand, trailing his umbrella and sometimes muttering the word "tobacconist," till the very word chilled his friend with fear. Then he suddenly lifted the umbrella and pointed to a boat-house among the rushes.

"Is that the family boat?" he asked. "I wish you'd just scull me up the river; I want to look at those houses from the back. There's no time to lose. They may find the body; but we must risk that."

Smith was already pulling the little boat upstream towards the hamlet before Father Brown spoke again. Then he said:

"By the way, I found out from old Abbott what was the real story about poor Vaudrey's misdemeanour. It was a rather curious story about an Egyptian official who had insulted him by saying that a good Moslem would avoid swine and Englishmen, but preferred swine; or some such tactful remark. Whatever happened at the time, the quarrel was apparently renewed some years after, when the official visited England; and Vaudrey, in his violent passion, dragged the man to a pig-sty on the farm attached to the country house and threw him in, breaking his arm and leg and leaving him there till next morning. There was rather a row about it, of course, but many people thought Vaudrey had acted in a pardonable passion of patriotism. Anyhow, it seems not quite the thing that would have kept a man silent under deadly blackmail for decades."

"Then you don't think it had anything to do with the story we are considering?" asked the secretary, thoughtfully.

"I think it had a thundering lot to do with the story I am considering now," said Father Brown.

They were now floating past the low wall and the steep strips of back garden running down from the back doors to the river. Father Brown counted them carefully, pointing with his umbrella, and when he came to the third he said again:

"Tobacconist! Is the tobacconist by any chance...? But I think I'll act on my guess till I know. Only, I'll tell you what it was I thought odd about Sir Arthur's face."

"And what was that?" asked his companion, pausing and resting on his oars for an instant.

"He was a great dandy," said Father Brown, "and the face was only half-shaved... Could you stop here a moment? We could tie up the boat to that post."

A minute or two afterwards they had clambered over the little wall and were mounting the steep cobbled paths of the little garden, with its rectangular beds of vegetables and flowers.

"You see, the tobacconist does grow potatoes," said Father Brown. "Associations with Sir Walter Raleigh, no doubt. Plenty of potatoes and plenty of potato sacks. These little country people have not lost all the habits of peasants; they still run two or three jobs at once. But country tobacconists very often do one odd job extra, that I never thought of till I saw Vaudrey's chin. Nine times out of ten you call the shop the tobacconist's, but it is also the barber's. He'd cut his hand and couldn't shave himself; so he came up here. Does that suggest anything else to you?"

"It suggests a good deal," replied Smith; "but I expect it will suggest a good deal more to you."

"Docs it suggest, for instance," observed Father Brown, "the only conditions in which a vigorous and rather violent gentleman might be smiling pleasantly when his throat was cut?"

The next moment they had passed through a dark passage or two at the back of the house, and came into the back room of the shop, dimly lit by filtered light from beyond and a dingy and cracked looking-glass. It seemed, somehow, like the green twilight of a tank; but there was light enough to see the rough apparatus of a barber's shop and the pale and even panic-sticken face of a barber.

Father Brown's eye roamed round the room, which seemed to have been just recently cleaned and tidied, till his gaze found something in a dusty corner just behind the door. It was a hat hanging on a hat-peg. It was a white hat, and one very well known to all that village. And yet, conspicuous as it had always seemed in the street, it seemed only an example of the sort of little thing a certain sort of man often entirely forgets, when he has most carefully washed floors or destroyed stained rags.

"Sir Arthur Vaudrey was shaved here yesterday morning, I think," said Father Brown in a level voice.

To the barber, a small, bald-headed, spectacled man whose name was Wicks, the sudden appearance of these two figures out of his own back premises was like the appearance of two ghosts risen out of a grave under the floor. But it was at once apparent that he had more to frighten him than any fancy of superstition. He shrank, we might almost say that he shrivelled, into a corner of the dark room; and everything about him seemed to dwindle, except his great goblin spectacles.

"Tell me one thing," continued the priest, quietly. "You had a reason for hating the squire?"

The man in the corner babbled something that Smith could not hear; but the priest nodded.

"I know you had," be said. "You hated him; and that's how I know you didn't kill him. Will you tell us what happened, or shall I?"

There was a silence filled with the faint ticking of a clock in the back kitchen, and then Father Brown went on.

"What happened was this. When Mr Dalmon stepped inside your outer shop, he asked for some cigarettes that were in the window. You stepped outside for a moment, as shopmen often do, to make sure of what he meant; and in that moment of time he perceived in the inner room the razor you had just laid down, and the yellow-white head of Sir Arthur in the barber's chair; probably both glimmering in the light of that little window beyond. It took but an instant for him to pick up the razor and cut the throat and come back to the counter. The victim would not even be alarmed at the razor and the hand. He died smiling at his own thoughts. And what thoughts! Nor, I think, was Dalmon alarmed. He had done it so quickly and quietly that Mr Smith here could have sworn in court that the two were together all the time. But there was somebody who was alarmed, very legitimately, and that was you. You had quarrelled with your landlord about arrears of rent and so on; you came back into your own shop and found your enemy murdered in your own chair, with your own razor. It was not altogether unnatural that you despaired of clearing yourself, and preferred to clear up the mess; to clean the floor and throw the corpse into the river at night, in a potato sack rather loosely tied. It was rather lucky that there were fixed hours after which your barber's shop was shut; so you had plenty of time. You seem to have remembered everything but the hat... Oh, don't be frightened; I shall forget everything, including the hat."

And he passed placidly through the outer shop into the street beyond, followed by the wondering Smith, and leaving behind the barber stunned and staring.

"You see," said Father Brown to his companion, "it was one of those cases where a motive really is too weak to convict a man and yet strong enough to acquit him. A little nervous fellow like that would be the last man really to kill a big strong man for a tiff about money. But he would be the first man to fear that he would be accused of having done it... Ah, there was a thundering difference in the motive of the man who did do it." And he relapsed into reflection, staring and almost glaring at vacancy.

"It is simply awful," groaned Evan Smith. "I was abusing Dalmon as a blackmailer and a blackguard an hour or two ago, and yet it breaks me all up to hear he really did this, after all."

The priest still seemed to be in a sort of trance, like a man staring down into an abyss. At last his lips moved and he murmured, more as if it were a prayer than an oath: "Merciful God, what a horrible revenge!"

His friend questioned him, but he continued as if talking to himself.

"What a horrible tale of hatred! What a vengeance for one mortal worm to take on another! Shall we ever get to the bottom of this bottomless human heart, where such abominable imaginations can abide? God save us all from pride; but I cannot yet make any picture in my mind of hate and vengeance like that."

"Yes," said Smith; "and I can't quite picture why he should kill Vaudrey at all. If Dalmon was a blackmailer, it would seem more natural for Vaudrey to kill him. As you say, the throat-cutting was a horrid business, but—"

Father Brown started, and blinked like a man awakened from sleep.

"Oh, that!" he corrected hastily. "I wasn't thinking about that. I didn't mean the murder in the barber's shop, when—when I said a horrible tale of vengeance. I was thinking of a much more horrible tale than that; though, of course, that was horrible enough, in its way. But that was much more comprehensible; almost anybody might have done it. In fact, it was very nearly an act of self-defence."

"What?" exclaimed the secretary incredulously. "A man creeps up behind another man and cuts his throat, while he is smiling pleasantly at the ceiling in a barber's chair, and you say it was self-defence!"

"I do not say it was justifiable self-defence," replied the other. "I only say that many a man would have been driven to it, to defend himself against an appalling calamity—which was also an appalling crime. It was that other crime that I was thinking about. To begin with, about that question you asked just now—why should the blackmailer be the murderer? Well, there are a good many conventional confusions and errors on a point like that." He paused, as if collecting his thoughts after his recent trance of horror, and went on in ordinary tones.

"You observe that two men, an older and a younger, go about together and agree on a matrimonial project; but the origin of their intimacy is old and concealed. One is rich and the other poor; and you guess at blackmail. You are quite right, at least to that extent. Where you are quite wrong is in guessing which is which. You assume that the poor man was blackmailing the rich man. As a matter offset, the rich man was blackmailing the poor man."

"But that seems nonsense," objected the secretary.

"It is much worse than nonsense; but it is not at all uncommon," replied the other. "Half modern politics consists of rich men blackmailing people. Your notion that it's nonsense rests on two illusions which are both nonsensical. One is, that rich men never want to be richer; the other is, that a man can only be blackmailed for money. It's the last that is in question here. Sir Arthur Vaudrey was acting not for avarice, but for vengeance. And he planned the most hideous vengeance I ever heard of."

"But why should he plan vengeance on John Dalmon?" inquired Smith.

"It wasn't on John Dalmon that he planned vengeance," replied the priest, gravely.

There was a silence; and he resumed, almost as if changing the subject. "When we found the body, you remember, we saw the face upside down; and you said it looked like the face of a fiend. Has it occurred to you that the murderer also saw the face upside down, coming behind the barber's chair?"

"But that's all morbid extravagance," remonstrated his companion. "I was quite used to the face when it was the right way up."

"Perhaps you have never seen it the right way up," said Father Brown. "I told you that artists turn a picture the wrong way up when they want to see it the right way up. Perhaps, over all those breakfasts and tea-tables, you had got used to the face of a fiend."

"What on earth are you driving at?" demanded Smith, impatiently.

"I speak in parables," replied the other in a rather sombre tone "Of course. Sir Arthur was not actually a fiend; he was a man with a character which he had made out of a temperament that might also have been turned to good. But those goggling, suspicious eyes; that tight, yet quivering mouth, might have told you something if you had not been so used to them. You know, there are physical bodies on which a wound will not heal. Sir Arthur had a mind of that sort. It was as if it lacked a skin; he had a feverish vigilance of vanity; those strained eyes were open with an insomnia of egoism. Sensibility need not be selfishness. Sybil Rye, for instance, has the same thin skin and manages to be a sort of saint. But Vaudrey had turned it all to poisonous pride; a pride that was not even secure and self-satisfied. Every scratch on the surface of his soul festered. And that is the meaning of that old story about throwing the man into the pig-sty. If he'd thrown him then and there, after being called a pig, it might have been a pardonable burst of passion. But there was no pig-sty; and that is just the point. Vaudrey remembered the silly insult for years and years, till he could get the oriental into the improbable neighbourhood of a pig-sty; and then he took, what he considered the only appropriate and artistic revenge... Oh, my God! he liked his revenges to be appropriate and artistic."

Smith looked at him curiously. "You are not thinking of the pig-sty story," he said.

"No," said Father Brown; "of the other story." He controlled the shudder in his voice, and went on:

"Remembering that story of a fantastic and yet patient plot to make the vengeance fit the crime, consider the other story before us. Had anybody else, to your knowledge, ever insulted Vaudrey, or offered him what he thought a mortal insult? Yes; a woman insulted him."

A sort of vague horror began to dawn in Evan's eyes; he was listening intently.

"A girl, little more than a child, refused to marry him, because he had once been a sort of criminal; had, indeed, been in prison for a short time for the outrage on the Egyptian. And that madman said, in the hell of his heart: 'She shall marry a murderer.'"

They took the road towards the great house and went along by the river for some time in silence, before he resumed: "Vaudrey was in a position to blackmail Dalmon, who had committed a murder long ago; probably he knew of several crimes among the wild comrades of his youth. Probably it was a wild crime with some redeeming features; for the wildest murders are never the worst. And Dalmon looks to me like a man who knows remorse, even for killing Vaudrey. But he was in Vaudrey's power and, between them, they entrapped the girl very cleverly into an engagement; letting the lover try his luck first, for instance, and the other only encouraging magnificently. But Dalmon himself did not know, nobody but the Devil himself did know, what was really in that old man's mind.

"Then, a few days ago, Dalmon made a dreadful discovery. He had obeyed, not altogether unwillingly; he had been a tool; and he suddenly found how the tool was to be broken and thrown away. He came upon certain notes of Vaudrey's in the library which, disguised as they were, told of preparations for giving information to the police. He understood the whole plot and stood stunned as I did when I first understood it. The moment the bride and bridegroom were married, the bridegroom would be arrested and hanged. The fastidious lady, who objected to a husband who had been in prison, should have no husband except a husband on the gallows. That is what Sir Arthur Vaudrey considered an artistic rounding off of the story."

Evan Smith, deadly pale, was silent; and, far away, down the perspective of the road, they saw the large figure and wide hat of Dr Abbott advancing towards them; even in the outline there was a certain agitation. But they were still shaken with their own private apocalypse.

"As you say, hate is a hateful thing," said Evan at last; "and, do you know, one thing gives me a sort of relief. All my hatred of poor Dalmon is gone out of me—now I know how he was twice a murderer."

It was in silence that they covered the rest of the distance and met the big doctor coming towards them, with his large gloved hands thrown out in a sort of despairing gesture and his grey beard tossing in the wind.

"There is dreadful news," he said. "Arthur's body has been found. He seems to have died in his garden."

"Dear me," said Father Brown, rather mechanically. "How dreadful!"

"And there is more," cried the doctor breathlessly. "John Dalmon went off to see Vernon Vaudrey, the nephew; but Vernon Vaudrey hasn't heard of him and Dalmon seems to have disappeared entirely."

"Dear me," said Father Brown. "How strange!"

7

THE WORST CRIME IN THE WORLD (First published in Harper's Magazine, Oct 1925)

Father Brown was wandering through a picture gallery with an expression that suggested that he had not come there to look at the pictures. Indeed, he did not want to look at the pictures, though he liked pictures well enough. Not that there was anything immoral or improper about those highly modern pictorial designs. He would indeed be of an inflammable temperament who was stirred to any of the more pagan passions by the display of interrupted spirals, inverted cones and broken cylinders with which the art of the future inspired or menaced mankind. The truth is that Father Brown was looking for a young friend who had appointed that somewhat incongruous meeting-place, being herself of a more futuristic turn. The young friend was also a young relative; one of the few relatives that he had. Her name was elizabeth Fane, simplified into Betty, and she was the child of a sister who had married into a race of refined but impoverished squires. As the squire was dead as well as impoverished. Father Brown stood in the relation of a protector as well as a priest, and in some sense a guardian as well is an uncle. At the moment, however, he was blinking about at the groups in the gallery without catching sight of the familiar brown hair and bright face of his niece. Nevertheless, he saw some people he knew and a number of people he did not know, including some that, as a mere matter of taste, he did not much want to know.

Among the people the priest did not know and who yet aroused his interest was a lithe and alert young man, very beautifully dressed and looking rather like a foreigner, because, while his beard was cut in a spade shape like an old Spaniard's, his dark hair was cropped so close as to look like a tight black skull-cap. Among the people the priest did not particularly want to know was a very dominant-looking lady, sensationally clad in scarlet, with a mane of yellow hair too long to be called bobbed, but too loose to be called anything else. She had a powerful and rather heavy face of a pale and rather unwholesome complexion, and when she looked at anybody she cultivated the fascinations of a basilisk. She towed in attendance behind her a short man with a big beard and a very broad face, with long sleepy slits of eyes. The expression of his face was beaming and benevolent, if only partially awake; but his bull neck, when seen from behind, looked a little brutal.

Father Brown gazed at the lady, feeling that the appearance and approach of his niece would be an agreeable contrast. Yet he continued to gaze, for some reason, until he reached the point of feeling that the appearance of anybody would be an agreeable contrast It was therefore with a certain relief, though with a slight start as of awakening, that he turned at the sound of his name and saw another face that he knew.

It was the sharp but not unfriendly face of a lawyer named Granby, whose patches of grey hair might almost have been the powder from a wig, so incongruous were they with his youthful energy of movement. He was one of those men in the City who run about like schoolboys in and out of their offices. He could not run round the fashionable picture gallery quite in that fashion; but he looked as if he wanted to, and fretted as he glanced to left and right, seeking somebody he knew.

"I didn't know," said Father Brown, smiling, "that you were a patron of the New Art."

"I didn't know that you were," retorted the other. "I came here to catch a man."

"I hope you will have good sport," answered the priest. "I'm doing much the same."

"Said he was passing through to the Continent," snorted the solicitor, "and could I meet him in this cranky place." He ruminated a moment, and said abruptly: "Look here, I know you can keep a secret. Do you know Sir John Musgrave?"

"No," answered the priest; "but I should hardly have thought he was a secret, though they say be does hide himself in a castle. Isn't he the old man they tell all those tales about—how he lives in a tower with a real portcullis and drawbridge, and generally refuses to emerge from the Dark Ages? Is he one of your clients?"

"No," replied Granby shortly: "it's his son, Captain Musgrave, who has come to us. But the old man counts for a good deal in the affair, and I don't know him; that's the point. Look here, this is confidential, as I say, but I can confide in you." He dropped his voice and drew his friend apart into a side gallery containing representations of various real objects, which was comparatively empty.

"This young Musgrave," he said, "wants to raise a big sum from us on a post obit on his old father in Northumberland. The old man's long past seventy and presumably will obit some time or other; but what about the post, so to speak? What will happen afterwards to his cash and castles and portcullises and all the rest? It's a very fine old estate, and still worth a lot, but strangely enough it isn't entailed. So you see how we stand. The question is, as the man said in Dickens, is the old man friendly?"

"If he's friendly to his son you'll feel all the friendlier," observed Father Brown. "No, I'm afraid I can't help you. I never met Sir John Musgrave, and I understand very few people do meet him nowadays. But it seems obvious you have a right to an answer on that point before you lend the young gentleman your firm's money. Is he the sort that people cut off with a shilling?"

"Well, I'm doubtful," answered the other. "He's very popular and brilliant and a great figure in society; but he's a great deal abroad, and he's been a journalist."

"Well," said Father Brown, "that's not a crime. At least not always."

"Nonsense!" said Granby curtly. "You know what I mean—he's rather a rolling stone, who's been a journalist and a lecturer and an actor, and all sorts of things. I've got to know where I stand... Why, there he is."

And the solicitor, who had been stamping impatiently about the emptier gallery, turned suddenly and darted into the more crowded room at a run. He was running towards the tall and well-dressed young man with the short hair and the foreign-looking beard.

The two walked away together talking, and for some moments afterwards Father Brown followed them with his screwed, short-sighted eyes. His gaze was shifted and recalled, however, by the breathless and even boisterous arrival of his niece, Betty. Rather to the surprise of her uncle, she led him back into the emptier room and planted him on a seat that was like an island in that sea of floor.

"I've got something I must tell you," she said. "It's so silly that nobody else will understand it."

"You overwhelm me," said Father Brown. "Is it about this business your mother started telling me about? Engagements and all that; not what the military historians call a general engagement."

"You know," she said, "that she wants me to be engaged to Captain Musgrave."

"I didn't," said Father Brown with resignation; "but Captain Musgrave seems to be quite a fashionable topic."

"Of course we're very poor," she said, "and it's no good saying it makes no difference."

"Do you want to marry him?" asked Father Brown, looking at her through his half-closed eyes.

She frowned at the floor, and answered in a lower tone:

"I thought I did. At least I think I thought I did. But I've just had rather a shock."

"Then tell us all about it."

"I heard him laugh," she said.

"It is an excellent social accomplishment," he replied.

"You don't understand," said the girl. "It wasn't social at all. That was just the point of it—that it wasn't social."

She paused a moment, and then went on firmly: "I came here quite early, and saw him sitting quite alone in the middle of that gallery with the new pictures, that was quite empty then. He had no idea I or anybody was near; he was sitting quite alone, and he laughed."

"Well, no wonder,' said Father Brown. "I'm not an art critic myself, but as a general view of the pictures taken as a whole—"

"Oh, you won't understand," she said almost angrily. "It wasn't a bit like that. He wasn't looking at the pictures. He was staring right up at the ceiling; but his eyes seemed to be turned inwards, and he laughed so that my blood ran cold."

The priest had risen and was pacing the room with his hands behind him. "You mustn't be hasty in a case of this sort," he began. "There are two kinds of men—but we can hardly discuss him just now, for here he is."

Captain Musgrave entered the room swiftly and swept it with a smile. Granby, the lawyer, was just behind him, and his legal face bore a new expression of relief and satisfaction.

'I must apologize for everything I said about the Captain," he said to the priest as they drifted together towards the door. "He's a thoroughly sensible fellow and quite sees my point. He asked me himself why I didn't go north amd see his old father; I could hear from the old man's own lips how it stood about the inheritance. Well, he couldn't say fairer than that, could he? But he's so anxious to get the thing settled that he offered to take me up in his own car to Musgrave Moss. That's the name of the estate. I suggested that, if he was so kind, we might go together; and we're starting to-morrow morning."

As they spoke Betty and the Captain came through the doorway together, making in that framework at least a sort of picture that some would be sentimental enough to prefer to cones and cylinders. Whatever their other affinities, they were both very good-looking; and the lawyer was moved to a remark on the fact, when the picture abruptly altered.

Captain James Musgrave looked out into the main gallery, and his laughing and triumphant eyes were riveted on something that seemed to change him from head to foot. Father Brown looked round as under an advancing shadow of premonition; and he saw the lowering, almost livid face of the large woman in scarlet under its leonine yellow hair. She always stood with a slight stoop, like a bull lowering its horns, and the expression of her pale pasty face was so oppressive and hypnotic that they hardly saw the little man with the large beard standing beside her.

Musgrave advanced into the centre of the room towards her, almost like a beautifully dressed wax-work wound up to walk. He said a few words to her that could not be heard. She did not answer; but they turned away together, walking down the long gallery as if in debate, the short, bull-necked man with the beard bringing up the rear like some grotesque goblin page.

"Heaven help us!" muttered Father Brown, frowning after them. "Who in the world is that woman?"

"No pal of mine, I'm happy to say," replied Granby with grim flippancy. "Looks as if a little flirtation with her might end fatally, doesn't it?"

"I don't think he's flirting with her," said Father Brown.

Even as he spoke the group in question turned at the end of the gallery and broke up, and Captain Musgrave came back to them in hasty strides.

"Look here," he cried, speaking naturally enough, though they fancied his colour was changed. "I'm awfully sorry, Mr Granby, but I find I can't come north with you tomorrow. Of course, you will take the car all the same. Please do; I shan't want it. I—I have to be in London for some days. Take a friend with you if you like."

"My friend, Father Brown—" began the lawyer.

"If Captain Musgrave is really so kind," said Father Brown gravely. "I may explain that I have some status in Mr Granby's inquiry, and it would be a great relief to my mind if I could go."

Which was how it came about that a very elegant car, with an equally elegant chauffeur, shot north the next day over the Yorkshire moors, bearing the incongruous burden of a priest who looked rather like a black bundle, and a lawyer who had the habit of running about on his feet instead of racing on somebody else's wheels.

They broke their journey very agreeably in one of the great dales of the West Riding, dining and sleeping at a comfortable inn, and starting early next day, began to run along the Northumbrian coast till they reached a country that was a maze of sand dunes and rank sea meadows, somewhere in the heart of which lay the old Border castle which had remained so unique and yet so secretive a monument of the old Border wars. They found it at last, by following a path running beside a long arm of the sea that ran inland, and turned eventually into a sort of rude canal ending in the moat of the castle. The castle really was a castle, of the square, embattled plan that the

Normans built everywhere from Galilee to the Grampians. It did really and truly have a portcullis and a drawbridge, and they were very realistically reminded of the fact by an accident that delayed their entrance.

They waded amid long coarse grass and thistle to the bank of the moat which ran in a ribbon of black with dead leaves and scum upon it, like ebony inlaid with a pattern of gold. Barely a yard or two beyond the black ribbon was the other green bank and the big stone pillars of the gateway. But so little, it would seem, had this lonely fastness been approached from outside that when the impatient Granby halloed across to the dim figures behind the portcullis, they seemed, to have considerable difficulty even in lowering the great rusty drawbridge. It started on its way, turning over like a great falling tower above them, and then stuck, sticking out in mid-air at a threatening angle.

The impatient Granby, dancing upon the bank, called out to his companion:

"Oh, I can't stand these stick-in-the-mud ways! Why, it'd be less trouble to jump."

And with characteristic impetuosity he did jump, landing with a slight stagger in safety on the inner shore. Father Brown's short legs were not adapted to jumping. But his temper was more adapted than most people's to falling with a splash into very muddy water. By the promptitude of his companion he escaped falling in very far. But as he was being hauled up the green, slimy bank, he stopped with bent head, peering at a particular point upon the grassy slope.

"Are you botanizing?" asked Granby irritably. "We've got no time for you to collect rare plants after your last attempt as a diver among the wonders of the deep. Come on, muddy or no, we've got to present ourselves before the baronet."

When they had penetrated into the castle, they were received courteously enough by an old servant, the only one in sight, and after indicating their business were shown into a long-oak-panelled room with latticed windows of antiquated pattern. Weapons of many different centuries hung in balanced patterns on the dark walls, and a complete suit of fourteenth-century armour stood like a sentinel beside the large fireplace. In another long room beyond could be seen, through the half-open door, the dark colours of the rows of family portraits.

"I feel as if I'd got into a novel instead of a house," said the lawyer. "I'd no idea anybody did really keep up the 'Mysteries of Udolpho' in this fashion."

"Yes; the old gentleman certainly carries out his historical craze consistently," answered the priest; "and these things are not fakes, either. It's not done by somebody who thinks all mediaeval people lived at the same time. Sometimes they make up suits of armour out of different bits; but that suit all covered one man, and covered him very completely. You, see it's the late sort of tilting-armour."

"I think he's a late sort of host, if it comes to chat," grumbled Granby. "He's keeping us waiting the devil of a time."

"You must expect everything to go slowly in a place like this," said Father Brown. "I think it's very decent of him to see us at all: two total strangers come to ask him highly personal questions."

And, indeed, when the master of the house appeared they had no reason to complain of their reception; but rather became conscious of something genuine in the traditions of breeding and behaviour that could retain their native dignity without difficulty in that barbarous solitude, and after those long years of rustication and moping. The baronet did not seem either surprised or embarrassed at the rare visitation; though they suspected that he had not had a stranger in his house for a quarter of a life-time, he behaved as if he had been bowing out duchesses a moment before. He showed neither shyness nor impatience when they touched on the very private matter of their errand; after a little leisurely reflection he seemed to recognize their curiosity as justified under the circumstances. He was a thin, keen-looking old gentleman, with black eyebrows and a long chin, and though the carefully-curled hair he wore was undoubtedly a wig, he had the wisdom to wear the grey wig of an elderly man.

"As regards the question that immediately concerns you," he said, "the answer is very simple indeed. I do most certainly propose to hand on the whole of my property to my son, as my father handed it on to me; and nothing—I say advisedly, nothing—would induce me to take any other course."

"I am most profoundly grateful for the information," answered the lawyer. "But your kindness encourages me to say that you are putting it very strongly. I would not suggest that it is in the least likely that your son would do anything to make you doubt his fitness for the charge. Still, he might—"

"Exactly," said Sir John Musgrave dryly, "he might. It is rather an understatement to say that he might. Will you be good enough to step into the next room with me for a moment."

He led them into the further gallery, of which they had already caught a glimpse, and gravely paused before a row of the blackened and lowering portraits.

"This is Sir Roger Musgrave," he said, pointing to a long-faced person in a black periwig. "He was one of the lowest liars and rascals in the rascally time of William of Orange, a traitor to two kings and something like the murderer of two wives. That is his father, Sir Robert, a perfectly honest old cavalier. That is his son, Sir James, one of the noblest of the Jacobite martyrs and one of the first men to attempt some reparation to the Church and the poor. Does it matter that the House of Musgrave, the power, the honour, the authority, descended from one good man to another good man through the interval of a bad one? Edward I governed England well. Edward III covered England with glory. And yet the second glory came from the first glory through the infamy and imbecility of Edward II, who fawned upon Gaveston and ran away from Bruce. Believe me, Mr Granby, the greatness of a great house and history is something more than these accidental individuals who carry it on, even though they do not grace it. From father to son our heritage has come down, and from father to son it shall continue. You may assure yourselves, gentlemen, and you may assure my son, that I shall not leave my money to a home for lost cats. Musgrave shall leave it to Musgrave till the heavens fall."

"Yes," said Father Brown thoughtfully; "I see what you mean."

"And we shall be only too glad," said the solicitor, "to convey such a happy assurance to your son."

"You may convey the assurance," said their host gravely, "He is secure in any event of having the castle, the title, the land and the money. There is only a small and merely private addition to that arrangement. Under no circumstances whatever will I ever speak to him as long as I live."

The lawyer remained in the same respectful attitude, but he was now respectfully staring.

"Why, what on earth has he—"

"I am a private gentleman," said Musgrave, "as well as the custodian of a great inheritance. And my son did something so horrible that he has ceased to be—I will not say a gentleman—but even a human being. It is the worst crime in the world. Do you remember what Douglas said when Marmion, his guest, offered to shake hands with him?"

"Yes," said Father Brown.

"'My castles are my king's alone, from turret to foundation stone,'" said Musgrave. "'The hand of Douglas is his own.'"

He turned towards the other room and showed his rather dazed visitors back into it.

"I hope you will take some refreshment," he said, in the same equable fashion. "If you have any doubt about your movements, I should be delighted to offer you the hospitality of the castle for the night."

"Thank you, Sir John," said the priest in a dull voice, "but I think we had better go."

"I will have the bridge lowered at once," said their host; and in a few moments the creaking of that huge and absurdly antiquated apparatus filled the castle like the grinding of a mill. Rusty as it was, however, it worked successfully this time, and they found themselves standing once more on the grassy bank beyond the moat.

Granby was suddenly shaken by a shudder.

"What in hell was it that his son did?" he cried.

Father Brown made no answer. But when they had driven off again in their car and pursued their journey to a village not far off, called Graystones, where they alighted at the inn of the Seven Stars, the lawyer learned with a little mild surprise that the priest did not propose to travel much farther; in other words, that he had apparently every intention of remaining in the neighbourhood.

"I cannot bring myself to leave it like this," he said gravely. "I will send back the car, and you, of course, may very naturally want to go with it. Your question is answered; it is simply whether your firm can afford to lend money on young Musgrave's prospects. But my question isn't answered; it is whether he is a fit husband for Betty. I must try to discover whether he's really done something dreadful, or whether it's the delusion of an old lunatic."

"But," objected the lawyer, "if you want to find out about him, why don't you go after him? Why should you hang about in this desolate hole where he hardly ever comes?"

"What would be the use of my going after him?" asked the other. There's no sense in going up to a fashionable young man in Bond Street and saying: 'Excuse me, but have you committed a crime too horrible for a human being?' If he's bad enough to do it, he's certainly bad enough to deny it. And we don't even know what it is. No, there's only one man that knows, and may tell, in some further outburst of dignified eccentricity. I'm going to keep near him for the present."

And in truth Father Brown did keep near the eccentric baronet, and did actually meet him on more than one occasion, with the utmost politeness on both sides. For the baronet, in spite of his years, was very vigorous and a great walker, and could often be seen stumping through the village, and along the country lanes. Only the day after their arrival, Father Brown, coming out of the inn on to the cobbled marketplace, saw the dark and distinguished figure stride past in the direction of the post office. He was very quietly dressed in black, but his strong face was even more arresting in the strong sunlight; with his silvery hair, swarthy eyebrows and long chin, he had something of a reminiscence of Henry Irving, or some other famous actor. In spite of his hoary hair, his figure as well as his face suggested strength, and he carried his stick more like a cudgel than a crutch. He saluted the priest, and spoke with the same air of coming fearlessly to the point which had marked his revelations of yesterday.

"If you are still interested in my son," he said, using the term with an icy indifference, "you will not see very much of him. He has just left the country. Between ourselves, I might say fled the country."

"Indeed," said Father Brown with a grave stare.

"Some people I never heard of, called Grunov, have been pestering me, of all people, about his whereabouts," said Sir John; "and I've just come in to send off a wire to tell them that, so far as I know, he's living in the Poste Restante, Riga. Even that has been a nuisance. I came in yesterday to do it, but was five minutes too late for the post office. Are you staying long? I hope you will pay me another visit."

When the priest recounted to the lawyer his little interview with old Musgrave in the village, the lawyer was both puzzled and interested. "Why has the Captain bolted?" he asked. "Who are the other people who want him? Who on earth are the Grunovs?"

"For the first, I don't know," replied Father Brown. "Possibly his mysterious sin has come to light. I should rather guess that the other people are blackmailing him about it. For the third, I think I do know. That horrible fat woman with yellow hair is called Madame Grunov, and that little man passes as her husband."

The next day Father Brown came in rather wearily, and threw down his black bundle of an umbrella with the air of a pilgrim laying down his staff. He had an air of some depression. But it was as it was so often in his criminal investigations. It was not the depression of failure, but the depression of success.

"It's rather a shock," he said in a dull voice; "but I ought to have guessed it. I ought to have guessed it when I first went in and saw the thing standing there."

"When you saw what?" asked Granby impatiently.

"When I saw there was only one suit of armour," answered Father Brown. There was a silence during which the lawyer only stared at his friend, and then the friend resumed.

"Only the other day I was just going to tell my niece that there are two types of men who can laugh when they are alone. One might almost say the man who does it is either very good or very bad. You see, he is either confiding the joke to God or confiding it to the Devil. But anyhow he has an inner life. Well, there really is a kind of man who confides the joke to the Devil. He does not mind if nobody sees the joke; if nobody can safely be allowed even to know the joke. The joke is enough in itself, if it is sufficiently sinister and malignant."

"But what are you talking about?" demanded Granby. "Whom are you talking about? Which of them, I mean? Who is this person who is having a sinister joke with his Satanic Majesty?"

Father Brown looked across at him with a ghastly smile.

"Ah," he said, "that's the joke."

There was another silence, but this time the silence seemed to be rather full and oppressive than merely empty; it seemed to settle down on them like the twilight that was gradually turning from dusk to dark. Father Brown went on speaking in a level voice, sitting stolidly with his elbows on the table.

"I've been locking up the Musgrave family," he said. "They are vigorous and long-lived stock, and even in the ordinary way I should think you would wait a good time for your money."

"We're quite prepared for that," answered the solicitor; "but anyhow it can't last indefinitely. The old man is nearly eighty, though he still walks about, and the people at the inn here laugh and say they don't believe he will ever die."

Father Brown jumped up with one of his rare but rapid movements, but remained with his hands on the table, leaning forward and looking his friend in the face.

"That's it," he cried in a low but excited voice. "That's the only problem. That's the only real difficulty. How will he die? How on earth is he to die?"

"What on earth do you mean?" asked Granby.

"I mean," came the voice of the priest out of the darkening room, "that I know the crime that James Musgrave committed."

His tones had such a chill in them that Granby could hardly repress a shiver; he murmured a further question.

"It was really the worst crime in the world," said Father Brown. "At least, many communities and civilizations have accounted it so. It was always from the earliest times marked out in tribe and village for tremendous punishment. But anyhow, I know now what young Musgrave really did and why he did it."

"And what did he do?" asked the lawyer.

"He killed his father," answered the priest.

The lawyer in his turn rose from his seat and gazed across the table with wrinkled brows.

"But his father is at the castle," he cried in sharp tones.

"His father is in the moat," said the priest, "and I was a fool not to have known it from the first when something bothered me about that suit of armour. Don't you remember the look of that room? How very carefully it was arranged and decorated? There were two crossed battle-axes hung on one side of the fire-place, two crossed battle-axes on the other. There was a round Scottish shield on one wall, a round Scottish shield on the other. And there was a stand of armour guarding one side of the hearth, and an empty space on the other. Nothing will make me believe that a man who arranged all the rest of that room with that exaggerated symmetry left that one feature of it lopsided. There was almost certainly another man in armour. And what has become of him?"

He paused a moment, and then went on in a more matter-of-fact tone; "When you come to think of it, it's a very good plan for a murder, and meets the permanent problem of the disposal of the body. The body could stand inside that complete tilting-armour for hours, or even days, while servants came and went, until the murderer could simply drag it out in the dead of night and lower it into the moat, without even crossing the bridge. And then what a good chance he ran! As soon as the body was at all decayed in the stagnant water there would sooner or later be nothing but a skeleton in fourteenth-century armour, a thing very likely to be found in the moat of an old Border castle. It was unlikely that anybody would look for anything there, but if they did, that would soon be all they would find. And I got some confirmation of that. That was when you said I was looking for a rare plant; it was a plant in a good many senses, if you'll excuse the jest. I saw the marks of two feet sunk so deep into the solid bank I was sure that the man was either very heavy or was carrying something very heavy. Also, by the way, there's another moral from that little incident when I made my celebrated graceful and cat-like leap."

"My brain is rather reeling," said Granby, "but I begin to have some notion of what all this nightmare is about. What about you and your cat-like leap?"

"At the post office today," said Father Brown, "I casually confirmed the statement the baronet made to me yesterday, that he had been there just after closing-time on the day previous—that is, not only on the very day we arrived, but at the very time we arrived. Don't you see what that means? It means that he was actually out when we called, and came back while we were waiting; and that was why we had to wait so long. And when I saw that, I suddenly saw a picture that told the whole story.'

"Well," asked the other impatiently, "and what about it?"

"An old man of eighty can walk," said Father Brown. "An old man can even walk a good deal, pottering about in country lanes. But an old man can't jump. He would be an even less graceful jumper than I was. Yet, if the baronet came back while we were waiting, he must have come in as we came in—by jumping the moat—for the bridge wasn't lowered till later. I rather guess he had hampered it himself to delay inconvenient visitors, to judge by the rapidity with which it was repaired. But that doesn't matter. When I saw that fancy picture of the black figure with the grey hair taking a flying leap across the moat I knew instantly that it was a young man dressed up as an old man. And there you have the whole story."

"You mean," said Granby slowly, "that this pleasing youth killed his father, hid the corpse first in the armour and then in the moat, disguised himself and so on?"

"They happened to be almost exactly alike," said the priest. "You could sec from the family portraits how strong the likeness ran. And then you talk of his disguising himself. But in a sense everybody's dress is a disguise. The old man disguised himself in a wig, and the young man in a foreign beard. When he shaved and put the wig on his cropped head he was exactly like his father, with a little make-up. Of course, you understand now why he was so very polite about getting you to come up next day here by car. It was because he himself was coming up that night by train. He got in front of you, committed his crime, assumed his disguise, and was ready for the legal negotiations."

"Ah," said Granby thoughtfully, "the legal negotiations! You mean, of course, that the real old baronet would have negotiated very differently.

"He would have told you plainly that the Captain would never get a penny," said Father Brown. "The plot, queer as it sounds, was really the only way of preventing his telling you so. But I want you to appreciate the cunning of what the fellow did tell you. His plan answered several purposes at once. He was being blackmailed by these Russians for some villainy; I suspect for treason during the war. He escaped from them at a stroke, and probably sent them chasing off to Riga after him. But the most beautiful refinement of all was that theory he enunciated about recognizing his son as an heir, but not as a human being. Don't you see that while it secured the *post-obit*, it also provided some sort of answer to what would soon be the greatest difficulty of all?"

"I see several difficulties," said Granby; "which one do you mean?"

"I mean that if the son was not even disinherited, it would look rather odd that the father and son never met. The theory of a private repudiation answered that. So there only remained one difficulty, as I say, which is probably perplexing the gentleman now. How on earth is the old man to die?"

"I know how he ought to die," said Granby.

Father Brown seemed to be a little bemused, and went on in a more abstracted fashion.

"And yet there is something more in it than that," he said. "There was something about that theory that he liked in a way that is more—well, more theoretical. It gave him an insane intellectual pleasure to tell you in one character that he had committed a crime in another character— when he really had. That is what I mean by the infernal irony; by the joke shared with the Devil. Shall I tell you something that sounds like what they call a paradox? Sometimes it is a joy in the very heart of hell to tell the truth. And above all, to tell it so that everybody misunderstands it. That is why he liked that antic of pretending to be somebody else, and then painting himself as black—as he was. And that was why my niece heard him laughing to himself all alone in the picture gallery."

Granby gave a slight start, like a person brought back to common things with a bump.

"Your niece," he cried. "Didn't her mother want her to marry Musgrave? A question of wealth and position, I suppose."

"Yes," said Father Brown dryly; "her mother was all in favour of a prudent marriage."

8

THE RED MOON OF MERU
(No record of prior magazine publication found)

Everyone agreed that the bazaar at Mallowood Abbey (by kind permission of Lady Mounteagle) was a great success; there were roundabouts and swings and side-shows, which the people greatly enjoyed; I would also mention the Charity, which was the excellent object of the proceedings, if any of them could tell me what it was. However, it is only with a few of them that we are here concerned; and especially with three of them, a lady and two gentlemen, who passed between two of the principal tents or pavilions, their voices high in argument. On their right was the tent of the Master of the Mountain, that world-famous fortune-teller by crystals and chiromancy; a rich purple tent, all over which were traced, in black and gold, the sprawling outlines of Asiatic gods waving any number of arms like octopods. Perhaps they symbolized the readiness of divine help to be had within; perhaps they merely implied that the ideal being of a pious palmist would have as many hands as possible. On the other side stood the plainer tent of Phroso the Phrenologist; more austerely decorated with diagrams of the heads of Socrates and Shakespeare, which were apparently of a lumpy sort. But these were presented merely in black and white, with numbers and notes, as became the rigid dignity of a purely rationalistic science. The purple tent had an opening like a black cavern, and all was fittingly silent within. But Phroso the Phrenologist, a lean, shabby, sunburnt person, with an almost improbably fierce black moustache and whiskers, was standing outside his own temple, and talking, at the top of his voice, to nobody in particular, explaining that the head of any passerby would doubtless prove, on examination, to be every bit as knobbly as Shakespeare's. Indeed, the moment the lady appeared between the tents, the vigilant Phroso leapt on her and offered, with a pantomime of old-world courtesy, to feel her bumps.

She refused with civility that was rather like rudeness; but she must be excused, because she was in the middle of an argument. She also had to be excused, or at any rate was excused, because she was Lady Mounteagle. She was not a nonentity, however, in any sense; she was at once handsome and haggard, with a hungry look in her deep, dark eyes and something eager and almost fierce about her smile. Her dress was bizarre for the period; for it was before the Great War had left us in our present mood of gravity and recollection. Indeed, the dress was rather like the purple tent; being of a semi-oriental sort, covered with exotic and esoteric emblems. But everyone knew that the Mounteagles were mad; which was the popular way of saying that she and her husband were interested in the creeds and culture of the East.

The eccentricity of the lady was a great contrast to the conventionality of the two gentlemen, who were braced and buttoned up in all the stiffer fashion of that far-off day, from the tips of their gloves to their bright top hats. Yet even here there was a difference; for James Hardcastle managed at once to look correct and distinguished, while Tommy Hunter only looked correct and commonplace. Hardcastle was a promising politician; who seemed in society to be interested in everything except politics. It may be answered gloomily that every politician is emphatically a promising politician. But to do him justice, he had often exhibited himself as a performing politician. No purple tent in the bazaar, however, had been provided for him to perform in.

"For my part," he said, screwing in the monocle that was the only gleam in his hard, legal face, "I think we must exhaust the possibilities of mesmerism before we talk about magic. Remarkable psychological powers undoubtedly exist, even in apparently backward peoples. Marvellous things have been done by fakirs."

"Did you say done by fakers?" asked the other young man, with doubtful innocence.

"Tommy, you are simply silly," said the lady. "Why will you keep barging in on things you don't understand? You're like a schoolboy screaming out that he knows how a conjuring trick is done. It's all so Early Victorian—that schoolboy scepticism. As for mesmerism, I doubt whether you can stretch it to—"

At this point Lady Mounteagle seemed to catch sight of somebody she wanted; a black stumpy figure standing at a booth where children were throwing hoops at hideous table ornaments. She darted across and cried:

"Father Brown, I've been looking for you. I want to ask you something, Do you believe in fortune-telling?"

The person addressed looked rather helplessly at the little hoop in his hand and said at last:

"I wonder in which sense you're using the word 'believe.' Of course, if it's all a fraud—"

"Oh, but the Master of the Mountain isn't a bit of a fraud," she cried. "He isn't a common conjurer or a fortune-teller at all. It's really a great honour for him to condescend to tell fortunes at my parties; he's a great religious leader in his own country; a Prophet and a Seer. And even his fortune-telling isn't vulgar stuff about coming into a fortune. He tells you great spiritual truths about yourself, about your ideals."

"Quite so," said Father Brown. "That's what I object to. I was just going to say that if it's all a fraud, I don't mind it so much. It can't be much more of a fraud than most things at fancy bazaars; and there, in a way, it's a sort of practical joke. But if it's a religion and reveals spiritual truths—then it's all as false as hell and I wouldn't touch it with a bargepole."

"That is something of a paradox," said Hardcastle, with a smile.

"I wonder what a paradox is," remarked the priest in a ruminant manner. "It seems to me obvious enough. I suppose it wouldn't do very much harm if somebody dressed up as a German spy and pretended to have told all sorts of lies to the Germans. But if a man is trading in the truth with the Germans—well! So I think if a fortune-teller is trading in truth like that—"

"You really think," began Hardcastle grimly.

"Yes," said the other; "I think he is trading with the enemy."

Tommy Hunter broke into a chuckle. "Well," he said, "if Father Brown thinks they're good so long as they're frauds, I should think he'd consider this copper-coloured prophet a sort of saint."

"My cousin Tom is incorrigible," said Lady Mounteagle. "He's always going about showing up adepts, as he calls it. He only came down here in a hurry when he heard the Master was to be here, I believe. He'd have tried to show up Buddha or Moses."

"Thought you wanted looking after a bit," said the young man, with a grin on his round face. "So I toddled down. Don't like this brown monkey crawling about."

"There you go again!" said Lady Mounteagle. "Years ago, when I was in India, I suppose we all had that sort of prejudice against brown people. But now I know something about their wonderful spiritual powers, I'm glad to say I know better."

"Our prejudices seem to cut opposite ways," said Father Brown. "You excuse his being brown because he is brahminical;

and I excuse his being brahminical because he is brown. Frankly, I don't care for spiritual powers much myself. I've got much more sympathy with spiritual weaknesses. But I can't see why anybody should dislike him merely because he is the same beautiful colour as copper, or coffee, or nut-brown ale, or those jolly peat-streams in the North. But then," he added, looking across at the lady and screwing up his eyes, "I suppose I'm prejudiced in favour of anything that's called brown."

"There now!" cried Lady Mounteagle with a sort of triumph. "I knew you were only talking nonsense!"

"Well," grumbled the aggrieved youth with the round face. "When anybody talks sense you call it schoolboy scepticism. When's the crystal-gazing going to begin?"

"Any time you like, I believe," replied the lady. "It isn't crystal-gazing, as a matter of fact, but palmistry; I suppose you would say it was all the same sort of nonsense."

"I think there is a via media between sense and nonsense," said Hardcastle, smiling. "There are explanations that are natural and not at all nonsensical; and yet the results are very amazing. Are you coming in to be operated on? I confess I am full of curiosity."

"Oh, I've no patience with such nonsense," spluttered the sceptic, whose round face had become rather a red face with the heat of his contempt and incredulity. "I'll let you waste your time on your mahogany mountebank; I'd rather go and throw at coconuts."

The Phrenologist, still hovering near, darted at the opening.

"Heads, my dear sir," he said, "human skulls are of a contour far more subtle than that of coconuts. No coconut can compare with your own most—"

Hardcastle had already dived into the dark entry of the purple tent; and they heard a low murmur of voices within. As Tom Hunter turned on the Phrenologist with an impatient answer, in which he showed a regrettable indifference to the line between natural and preternatural sciences, the lady was just about to continue her little argument with the little priest, when she stopped in some surprise. James Hardcastle had come out of the tent again, and in his grim face and glaring monocle, surprise was even more vividly depicted. "He's not there," remarked the politician abruptly. '"He's gone. Some aged nigger, who seems to constitute his suite, jabbered something I to me to the effect that the Master had gone forth rather than sell sacred secrets for gold."

Lady Mounteagle turned radiantly to the rest. "There now," she cried. "I told you he was a cut above anything you fancied! He hates being here in a crowd; he's gone back to his solitude."

"I am sorry," said Father Brown gravely. "I may have done him an injustice. Do you know where he has gone?"

"I think so," said his hostess equally gravely. "When he wants to be alone, he always goes to the cloisters, just at the end of the left wing, beyond my husband's study and private museum, you know. Perhaps you know this house was once an abbey."

"I have heard something about it," answered the priest, with a faint smile.

"We'll go there, if you like," said the lady, briskly. "You really ought to see my husband's collection; or the Red Moon at any rate. Haven't you ever heard of the Red Moon of Meru? Yes, it's a ruby."

"I should be delighted to see the collection," said Hardcastle quietly, "including the Master of the Mountain, if that prophet is one exhibit in the museum." And they all turned towards the path leading to the house.

"All the same," muttered the sceptical Thomas, as he brought up the rear, "I should very much like to know what the brown beast did come here for, if he didn't come to tell fortunes."

As he disappeared, the indomitable Phroso made one more dart after him, almost snatching at his coat-tails. "The bump—" he began.

"No bump," said the youth, "only a hump. Hump I always have when I come down to see Mounteagle." And he took to his heels to escape the embrace of the man of science.

On their way to the cloisters the visitors had to pass through the long room that was devoted by Lord Mounteagle to his remarkable private museum of Asiatic charms and mascots. Through one open door, in the length of the wall opposite, they could see the Gothic arches and the glimmer of daylight between them, marking the square open space, round the roofed border of which the monks had walked in older days. But they had to pass something that seemed at first sight rather more extraordinary than the ghost of a monk.

It was an elderly gentleman, robed from head to foot in white, with a pale green turban, but a very pink and white English complexion and the smooth white moustaches of some amiable Anglo-Indian colonel. This was Lord Mounteagle, who had taken his Oriental pleasures more sadly, or at least more seriously than his wife. He could talk of nothing whatever, except Oriental religion and philosophy; and had thought it necessary even to dress in the manner of an Oriental hermit. While he was delighted to show his treasures, he seemed to treasure them much more for the truths supposed to be symbolized in them than for their value in collections, let alone cash. Even when he brought out the great ruby, perhaps the only thing of great value in the museum, in a merely monetary sense, he seemed to be much more interested in its name than in its size, let alone its price.

The others were all staring at what seemed a stupendously large red stone, burning like a bonfire seen through a rain of blood. But Lord Mounteagle rolled it loosely in his palm without looking at it; and staring at the ceiling, told them a long tale about the legendary character of Mount Meru, and how, in the Gnostic mythology, it had been the place of the wrestling of nameless primeval powers.

Towards the end of the lecture on the Demiurge of the Gnostics (not forgetting its connexion with the parallel concept of Manichaeus), even the tactful Mr Hardcastle thought it time to create a diversion. He asked to be allowed to look at the stone; and as evening was closing in, and the long room with its single door was steadily darkening, he stepped out in the cloister beyond, to examine the jewel by a better light. It was then that they first became conscious, slowly and almost creepily conscious, of the living presence of the Master of the Mountain.

The cloister was on the usual plan, as regards its original structure; but the line of Gothic pillars and pointed arches that formed the inner square was linked together all along by a low wall, about waist high, turning the Gothic doors into Gothic windows and giving each a sort of flat windowsill of stone. This alteration was probably of ancient date; but there were other alterations of a quainter sort, which witnessed to the rather unusual individual ideas of Lord and Lady Mounteagle. Between the pillars hung thin curtains, or rather veils, made of beads or light canes, in a continental or southern manner; and on these again could be traced the lines and colours of Asiatic dragons or idols, that contrasted with the grey Gothic framework in which they were suspended. But this, while it further troubled the dying light of the place, was the least of the incongruities of which the company, with very varying feelings, became aware.

In the open space surrounded by the cloisters, there ran, like a circle in a square, a circular path paved with pale stones and edged with some sort of green enamel like an imitation lawn. Inside that, in the very centre, rose the basin of a dark-green fountain, or raised pond, in which water-lilies floated and goldfish flashed to and fro; and high above these, its outline dark against the dying light, was a great green image. Its back was turned to them and its face so completely invisible in the hunched posture that the statue might almost have been headless. But in that mere dark outline, in the dim twilight, some of them could see instantly that it was the shape of no Christian thing.

A few yards away, on the circular path, and looking towards the great green god, stood the man called the Master of the Mountain. His pointed and finely-finished features seemed moulded by some skilful craftsman as a mask of copper. In contrast with this, his dark-grey beard looked almost blue like indigo; it began in a narrow tuft on his chin, and then spread outwards like a great fan or the tail of a bird. He was robed in peacock green and wore on his bald head a high cap of uncommon outline: a head-dress none of them had ever seen before; but it looked rather Egyptian than Indian. The man was standing with staring eyes; wide open, fish-shaped eyes, so motionless that they looked like the eyes painted on a mummy-case. But though the figure of the Master of the Mountain was singular enough, some of the company, including Father Brown, did not look at him; they still looked at the dark-green idol at which he himself was looking.

"This seems a queer thing," said Hardcastle, frowning a little, "to set up in the middle of an old abbey cloister."

"Now, don't tell me you're going to be silly," said Lady Mounteagle. "That's just what we meant; to link up the great religions of East and West; Buddha and Christ. Surely you must understand that all religions are really the same."

"If they are," said Father Brown mildly, "it seems rather unnecessary to go into the middle of Asia to get one."

"Lady Mounteagle means that they are different aspects or facets, as there are of this stone," began Hardcastle; and becoming interested in the new topic, laid the great ruby down on the stone sill or ledge under the Gothic arch. "But it does not follow that we can mix the aspects in one artistic style. You may mix Christianity and Islam, but you can't mix Gothic and Saracenic, let alone real Indian."

As he spoke, the Master of the Mountain seemed to come to life like a cataleptic, and moved gravely round another quarter segment of the circle, and took up his position outside their own row of arches, standing with his back to them and looking now towards the idol's back. It was obvious that he was moving by stages round the whole circle, like a hand round a clock; but pausing for prayer or contemplation.

"What is his religion?" asked Hardcastle, with a faint touch of impatience.

"He says," replied Lord Mounteagle, reverently, "that it is older than Brahminism and purer than Buddhism."

"Oh," said Hardcastle, and continued to stare through his single eyeglass, standing with both his hands in his pockets.

"They say," observed the nobleman in his gentle but didactic voice, "that the deity called the God of Gods is carved in a colossal form in the cavern of Mount Meru—"

Even his lordship's lecturing serenity was broken abruptly by the voice that came over his shoulder. It came out of the darkness of the museum they had just left, when they stepped out into the cloister. At the sound of it the two younger men looked first incredulous, then furious, and then almost collapsed into laughter.

"I hope I do not intrude," said the urbane and seductive voice of Professor Phroso, that unconquerable wrestler of the truth, "but it occurred to me that some of you might spare a little time for that much despised science of Bumps, which—"

"Look here," cried the impetuous Tommy Hunter, "I haven't got any bumps; but you'll jolly well have some soon, you—"

Hardcastle mildly restrained him as he plunged back through the door; and for the moment all the group had turned again and were looking back into the inner room.

It was at that moment that the thing happened. It was the impetuous Tommy, once more, who was the first to move, and this time to better effect. Before anyone else had seen anything, when Hardcastle had barely remembered with a jump that he had left the gem on the stone sill, Tommy was across the cloister with the leap of a cat and, leaning with his head and shoulders out of the aperture between two columns, had cried out in a voice that rang down all the arches: "I've got him!"

In that instant of time, just after they turned, and just before they heard his triumphant cry, they had all seen it happen. Round the corner of one of the two columns, there had darted in and out again a brown or rather bronze-coloured hand, the colour of dead gold; such as they had seen elsewhere. The hand had struck as straight as a striking snake; as instantaneous as the flick of the long tongue of an anteater. But it had licked up the jewel. The stone slab of the windowsill shone bare in the pale and fading light.

"I've got him," gasped Tommy Hunter; "but he's wriggling pretty hard. You fellows run round him in front—he can't have got rid of it, anyhow."

The others obeyed, some racing down the corridor and some leaping over the low wall, with the result that a little crowd, consisting of Hardcastle, Lord Mounteagle, Father Brown, and even the undetachable Mr Phroso of the bumps, had soon surrounded the captive Master of the Mountain, whom Hunter was hanging on to desperately by the collar with one hand, and shaking every now and then in a manner highly insensible to the dignity of Prophets as a class.

"Now we've got him, anyhow," said Hunter, letting go with a sigh. "We've only got to search him. The thing must be here."

Three quarters of an hour later. Hunter and Hardcastle, their top hats, ties, gloves, slips and spats somewhat the worse for their recent activities, came face to face in the cloister and gazed at each other.

"Well," asked Hardcastle with restraint, "have you any views on the mystery?"

"Hang it all," replied Hunter; "you can't call it a mystery. Why, we all saw him take it ourselves."

"Yes," replied the other, "but we didn't all see him lose it ourselves. And the mystery is, where has he lost it so that we can't find it?"

"It must be somewhere," said Hunter. "Have you searched the fountain and all round that rotten old god there?"

"I haven't dissected the little fishes," said Hardcastle, lifting his eyeglass and surveying the other. "Are you thinking of the ring of Polycrates?"

Apparently the survey, through the eyeglass, of the round face before him, convinced him that it covered no such meditation on Greek legend.

"It's not on him, I admit," repeated Hunter, suddenly, "unless he's swallowed it."

"Are we to dissect the Prophet, too?" asked the other smiling. "But here comes our host."

"This is a most distressing matter," said Lord Mounteagle, twisting his white moustache with a nervous and even tremulous hand. "Horrible thing to have a theft in one's house, let alone connecting it with a man like the Master. But, I confess, I can't quite make head or tail of the way in which he is talking about it. I wish you'd come inside and see what you think."

They went in together, Hunter falling behind and dropping into conversation with Father Brown, who was kicking his heels round the cloister.

"You must be very strong," said the priest pleasantly. "You held him with one hand; and he seemed pretty vigorous, even when we had eight hands to hold him, like one of those Indian gods."

They took a turn or two round the cloister, talking; and then they also went into the inner room, where the Master of the Mountain was seated on a bench, in the capacity of a captive, but with more of the air of a king.

It was true, as Lord Mounteagle said, that his air and tone were not very easy to understand. He spoke with a serene, and yet secretive sense of power. He seemed rather amused at their suggestions about trivial hiding-places for the gem; and certainly he showed no resentment whatever. He seemed to be laughing, in a still unfathomable fashion at their efforts to trace what they had all seen him take.

"You are learning a little," he said, with insolent benevolence, "of the laws of time and space; about which your latest science is a thousand years behind our oldest religion. You do not even know what is really meant by hiding a thing. Nay, my poor little friends, you do not even know what is meant by seeing a thing; or perhaps you would see this as plainly as I do."

"Do you mean it is here?" demanded Hardcastle harshly.

"Here is a word of many meanings, also," replied the mystic. "But I did not say it was here. I only said I could see it."

There was an irritated silence, and he went on sleepily.

"If you were to be utterly, unfathomably, silent, do you think you might hear a cry from the other end of the world? The cry of a worshipper alone in those mountains, where the original image sits, itself like a mountain. Some say that even Jews and Moslems might worship that image; because it was never made by man. Hark! Do you hear the cry with which he lifts his head and sees in that socket of stone, that has been hollow for ages, the one red and angry moon that is the eye of the mountain?"

"Do you really mean," cried Lord Mounteagle, a little shaken, "that you could make it pass from here to Mount Meru? I used to believe you had great spiritual powers, but—"

"Perhaps," said the Master, "I have more than you will ever believe."

Hardcastle rose impatiently and began to pace the room with his hands in his pockets.

"I never believed so much as you did; but I admit that powers of a certain type may... Good God!"

His high, hard voice had been cut off in mid-air, and he stopped staring; the eyeglass fell out of his eye. They all turned their faces in the same direction; and on every face there seemed to be the same suspended animation.

The Red Moon of Meru lay on the stone windowsill, exactly as they had last seen it. It might have been a red spark blown there from a bonfire, or a red rose-petal tossed from a broken rose; but it had fallen in precisely the same spot where Hardcastle had thoughtlessly laid it down.

This time Hardcastle did not attempt to pick it up again; but his demeanour was somewhat notable. He turned slowly and began to stride about the room again; but there was in his movements something masterful, where before it had been only restless. Finally, he brought himself to a standstill in front of the seated Master, and bowed with a somewhat sardonic smile.

"Master," he said, "we all owe you an apology and, what is more important, you have taught us all a lesson. Believe me, it will serve as a lesson as well as a joke. I shall always remember the very remarkable powers you really possess, and how harmlessly you use them. Lady Mounteagle," he went on, turning towards her, "you will forgive me for having addressed the Master first; but it was to you I had the honour of offering this explanation some time ago. I may say that I explained it before it had happened. I told you that most of these things could be interpreted by some kind of hypnotism. Many believe that this is the explanation of all those Indian stories about the mango plant and the boy who climbs a rope thrown into the air. It does not really happen; but the spectators are mesmerized into imagining that it happened. So we were all mesmerized into imagining this theft had happened. That brown hand coming in at the window, and whisking away the gem, was a momentary delusion; a hand in a dream. Only, having seen the stone vanish, we never looked for it where it was before. We plunged into the pond and turned every leaf of the water lilies; we were almost giving emetics to the goldfish. But the ruby has been here all the time."

And he glanced across at the opalescent eyes and smiling bearded mouth of the Master, and saw that the smile was just a shade broader. There was something in it that made the others jump to their feet with an air of sudden relaxation and general, gasping relief.

"This is a very fortunate escape for us all," said Lord Mounteagle, smiling rather nervously. "There cannot be the least doubt it is as you say. It has been a most painful episode and I really don't know what apologies—"

"I have no complaints," said the Master or the Mountain, still smiling. "You have never touched me at all."

While the rest went off rejoicing, with Hardcastle for the hero of the hour, the little Phrenologist with the whiskers sauntered back towards his preposterous tent. Looking over his shoulder he was surprised to find Father Brown following him.

"Can I feel your bumps?" asked the expert, in his mildly sarcastic tone.

"I don't think you want to feel anyone, do you?" said the priest good-humouredly. "You're a detective, aren't you?"

"Yep," replied the other. "Lady Mounteagle asked me to keep an eye on the Master, being no fool, for all her mysticism; and when he left his tent, I could only follow by behaving like a nuisance and a monomaniac. If anybody had come into my tent, I'd have had to look up Bumps in an encyclopaedia."

"Bumps, What Ho She; see Folk-Lore," observed Father Brown, dreamily. "Well, you were quite in the part in pestering people—at a bazaar."

"Rum case, wasn't it?" remarked the fallacious Phrenologist. "Queer to think the thing was there all the time."

"Very queer," said the priest.

Something in his voice made the other man stop and stare.

"Look here!" he cried; "what's the matter with you? What are you looking like that for! Don't you believe that it was there all the time?"

Father Brown blinked rather as if he had received a buffet; then he said slowly and with hesitation: "No, the fact is ... I can't—I can't quite bring myself to believe it."

"You're not the sort of chap," said the other shrewdly, "who'd say that without reason. Why don't you think the ruby had been there all the time?"

"Only because I put it back myself," said Father Brown.

The other man stood rooted to the spot, like one whose hair was standing on end. He opened his mouth without speech.

"Or rather," went on the priest, "I persuaded the thief to let me put it back. I told him what I'd guessed and showed him there was still time for repentance. I don't mind telling you in professional confidence; besides, I don't think the Mounteagles would prosecute, now they've got the thing back, especially considering who stole it."

"Do you mean the Master?" asked the late Phroso.

"No," said Father Brown, "the Master didn't steal it."

"But I don't understand," objected the other. "Nobody was outside the window except the Master; and a hand certainly came from outside."

"The hand came from outside, but the thief came from the inside," said Father Brown.

"We seem to be back among the mystics again. Look here, I'm a practical man; I only wanted to know if it is all right with the ruby—"

"I knew it was all wrong," said Father Brown, "before I even knew there was a ruby."

After a pause he went on thoughtfully. "Right away back in that argument of theirs, by the tents, I knew things were going wrong. People will tell you that theories don't matter and that logic and philosophy aren't practical. Don't you believe them.

Reason is from God, and when things are unreasonable there is something the matter. Now, that quite abstract argument ended with something funny. Consider what the theories were. Hardcastle was a trifle superior and said that all things were perfectly possible; but they were mostly done merely by mesmerism, or clairvoyance; scientific names for philosophical puzzles, in the usual style. But Hunter thought it all sheer fraud and wanted to show it up. By Lady Mounteagle's testimony, he not only went about showing up fortune-tellers and such like, but he had actually come down specially to confront this one. He didn't often come; he didn't get on with Mounteagle, from whom, being a spendthrift, he always tried to borrow; but when he heard the Master was coming, he came hurrying down. Very well. In spite of that, it was Hardcastle who went to consult the wizard and Hunter who refused. He said he'd waste no time on such nonsense; having apparently wasted a lot of his life on proving it to be nonsense. That seems inconsistent. He thought in this case it was crystal-gazing; but he found it was palmistry."

"Do you mean he made that an excuse?" asked his companion, puzzled.

"I thought so at first," replied the priest; "but I know now it was not an excuse, but a reason. He really was put off by finding it was a palmist, because—"

"Well," demanded the other impatiently.

"Because he didn't want to take his glove off," said Father Brown.

"Take his glove off?" repeated the inquirer.

"If he had," said Father Brown mildly, "we should all have seen that his hand was painted pale brown already... Oh, yes, he did come down specially because the Master was here. He came down very fully prepared."

"You mean," cried Phroso, "that it was Hunter's hand, painted brown, that came in at the window? Why, he was with us all the time!"

"Go and try it on the spot and you'll find it's quite possible," said the priest. "Hunter leapt forward and leaned out of the window; in a flash he could tear off his glove, tuck up his sleeve, and thrust his hand back round the other side of the pillar, while he gripped the Indian with the other hand and halloed out that he'd caught the thief. I remarked at the time that he held the thief with one hand, where any sane man would have used two. But the other hand was slipping the jewel into his trouser pocket."

There was a long pause and then the ex-Phrenologist said slowly. "Well, that's a staggerer. But the thing stumps me still. For one thing, it doesn't explain the queer behaviour of the old magician himself. If he was entirely innocent, why the devil didn't he say so? Why wasn't he indignant at being accused and searched? Why did he only sit smiling and hinting in a sly way what wild and wonderful things he could do?"

"Ah!" cried Father Brown, with a sharp note in his voice: "there you come up against it! Against everything these people don't and won't understand. All religions are the same, says Lady Mounteagle. Are they, by George! I tell you some of them are so different that the best man of one creed will be callous, where the worst man of another will be sensitive. I told you I didn't like spiritual power, because the accent is on the word; power. I don't say the Master would steal a ruby, very likely he wouldn't; very likely he wouldn't think it worth stealing. It wouldn't be specially his temptation to take jewels; but it would be his temptation to take credit for miracles that didn't belong to him any more than the jewels. It was to that sort of temptation, to that sort of stealing that he yielded today. He liked us to think that he had marvellous mental powers that could make a material object fly through space; and even when he hadn't done it, he allowed us to think he had. The point about private property wouldn't occur primarily to him at all. The question wouldn't present itself in the form: 'Shall I steal this pebble?' but only in the form: 'Could I make a pebble vanish and reappear on a distant mountain?' The question of whose pebble would strike him as irrelevant. That is what I mean by religious being different. He is very proud of having what he calls spiritual powers. But what he calls spiritual doesn't mean what we call moral. It means rather mental; the power of the mind over matter; the magician controlling the elements. Now we are not like that, even when we are no better; even when we are worse. We, whose fathers at least were Christians, who have grown up under those mediaeval arches even if we bedizen them with all the demons in Asia—we have the very opposite ambition and the very opposite shame. We should all be anxious that nobody should think we had done it. He was actually anxious that everybody should think he had—even when he hadn't. He actually stole the credit of stealing. While we were all casting the crime from us like a snake, he was actually luring it to him like a snake-charmer. But snakes are not pets in this country! Here the traditions of Christendom tell at once under a test like this. Look at old Mounteagle himself, for instance! Ah, you may be as Eastern and esoteric as you like, and weal a turban and a long robe and live on messages from Mahatmas; but if a bit of stone is stolen in your house, and your friends are suspected, you will jolly soon find out that you're an ordinary English gentleman in a fuss. The man who really did it would never want us to think he did it, for he also was an English gentleman. He was also something very much better; he was a Christian thief. I hope and believe he was a penitent thief."

"By your account," said his companion laughing, "the Christian thief and the heathen fraud went by contraries. one was sorry he'd done it and the other was sorry he hadn't."

"We mustn't be too hard on either of them," said Father Brown. "Other English gentlemen have stolen before now, and been covered by legal and political protection; and the West also has its own way of covering theft with sophistry. After all, the ruby is not the only kind of valuable stone in the world that has changed owners; it is true of other precious stones; often carved like cameos and coloured like flowers." The other looked at him inquiringly; and the priest's finger was pointed to the Gothic outline of the great Abbey. "A great graven stone," he said, "and that was also stolen."

9

THE CHIEF MOURNER OF MARNE (First published in *Harper's Magazine,* May 1925)

A Blaze of lightning blanched the grey woods tracing all the wrinkled foliage down to the last curled leaf, as if every detail were drawn in silverpoint or graven in silver. The same strange trick of lightning by which it seems to record millions of minute things in an instant of time, picked out everything, from the elegant litter of the picnic spread under the spreading tree to the pale lengths of winding road, at the end of which a white car was waiting. In the distance a melancholy mansion with four towers like a castle, which in the grey evening had been but a dim and distant huddle of walls like a crumbling cloud, seemed to spring into the foreground, and stood up with all its embattled, roofs and blank and staring windows. And in this, at least, the light had something in it of revelation. For to some of those grouped under the tree that castle was, indeed, a thing faded and almost forgotten, which was to prove its power to spring up again in the foreground of their lives.

The light also clothed for an instant, in the same silver splendour, at least one human figure that stood up as motionless as one of the towers. It was that of a tall man standing on a rise of ground above the rest, who were mostly sitting on the grass or stooping to gather up the hamper and crockery. He wore a picturesque short cloak or cape clasped with a silver clasp and chain, which blazed like a star when the flash touched it; and something metallic in his motionless figure was emphasized by the fact that his closely-curled hair was of the burnished yellow that can be really called gold; and had the look of being younger than his face, which was handsome in a hard aquiline fashion, but looked, under the strong light, a little wrinkled and withered. Possibly it had suffered from wearing a mask of make-up, for Hugo Romaine was the greatest actor of his day. For that instant of illumination the golden curls and ivory mask and silver ornament made his figure gleam like that of a man in armour; the next instant his figure was a dark and even black silhouette against the sickly grey of the rainy evening sky.

But there was something about its stillness, like that of a statue, that distinguished it from the group at his feet. All the other figures around him had made the ordinary involuntary movement at the unexpected shock of light; for though the skies were rainy it was the first flash of the storm. The only lady present, whose air of carrying grey hair gracefully, as if she were really proud of it, marked her a matron of the United States, unaffectedly shut her eyes and uttered a sharp cry. Her English husband, General Outram, a very stolid Anglo-Indian, with a bald head and black moustache and whiskers of antiquated pattern, looked up with one stiff movement and then resumed his occupation of tidying up. A young man of the name of Mallow, very big and shy, with brown eyes like a dog's, dropped a cup and apologized awkwardly. A third man, much more dressy, with a resolute head, like an inquisitive terrier's, and grey hair brushed stiffly back, was no other than the great newspaper proprietor, Sir John Cockspur; he cursed freely, but not in an English idiom or accent, for he came from Toronto. But the tall man in the short cloak stood up literally like a statue in the twilight; his eagle face under the full glare had been like the bust of a Roman Emperor, and the carved eyelids had not moved.

A moment after, the dark dome cracked across with thunder, and the statue seemed to come to life. He turned his head over his shoulder and said casually;

"About a minute and half between the flash and the bang, but I think the storm's coming nearer. A tree is not supposed to be a good umbrella for the lightning, but we shall want it soon for the rain. I think it will be a deluge."

The young man glanced at the lady a little anxiously and said: "Can't we get shelter anywhere? There seems to be a house over there."

"There is a house over there," remarked the general, rather grimly; "but not quite what you'd call a hospitable hotel."

"It's curious," said his wife sadly, "that we should be caught in a storm with no house near but that one, of all others."

Something in her tone seemed to check the younger man, who was both sensitive and comprehending; but nothing of that sort daunted the man from Toronto.

"What's the matter with it?" he asked. "Looks rather like a ruin."

"That place," said the general dryly, "belongs to the Marquis of Marne."

"Gee!" said Sir John Cockspur. "I've heard all about that bird, anyhow; and a queer bird, too. Ran him as a front-page mystery in the Comet last year. 'The nobleman nobody knows.'"

"Yes, I've heard of him, too," said young Mallow in a low voice. "There seem to be all sorts of weird stories about why he hides himself like that. I've heard that he wears a mask because he's a leper. But somebody else told me quite seriously that there's a curse on the family; a child born with some frightful deformity that's kept in a dark room."

"The Marquis of Marne has three heads," remarked Romaine quite gravely. "Once in every three hundred years a three-headed nobleman adorns the family tree. No human being dares approach the accursed house except a silent procession of hatters, sent to provide an abnormal number of hats. But," —and his voice took one of those deep and terrible turns, that could cause such a thrill in the theatre—"my friends, those hats are of no human shape."

The American lady looked at him with a frown and a slight air of distrust, as if that trick of voice had moved her in spite of herself.

"I don't like your ghoulish jokes," she said; "and I'd rather you didn't joke about this, anyhow."

"I hear and obey," replied the actor; "but am I, like the Light Brigade, forbidden even to reason why?"

"The reason," she replied, "is that he isn't the Nobleman Nobody Knows. I know him myself, or, at least, I knew him very well when he was an attache at Washington thirty years ago, when we were all young. And he didn't wear a mask, at least, he didn't wear it with me. He wasn't a leper, though he may he almost as lonely. And he had only one head and only one heart, and that was broken.'

"Unfortunate love affair, of course," said Cockspur. "I should like that for the Comet."

"I suppose it's a compliment to us," she replied thoughtfully, "that you always assume a man's heart is broken by a woman. But there are other kinds of love and bereavement. Have you never read 'In Memoriam'? Have you never heard of David and Jonathan? What broke poor Marne up was the death of his brother; at least, he was really a first cousin, but had been brought up with him like a brother, and was much nearer than most brothers. James Mair, as the marquis was called when I knew him, was the elder of the two, but he always played the part of worshipper, with Maurice Mair as a god. And, by his account, Maurice Mair was certainly a wonder. James was no fool, and very good at his own political job; but it seems that Maurice could do that and everything else; that he was a brilliant artist and amateur actor and musician, and all the rest of it. James was very good-looking himself, long and strong and strenuous, with a high-bridged nose; though I suppose the young people would think he looked very quaint with his beard divided into two bushy whiskers in the fashion of those Victorian times. But Maurice was clean-shaven, and, by the portraits shown to me, certainly quite beautiful; though he looked a little more like a tenor than a gentleman ought to look. James was always asking me again and again whether his friend was not a marvel, whether any woman wouldn't fall in love with him, and so on, until it became rather a bore, except that it turned so suddenly into a tragedy. His whole life seemed to be in that idolatry, and one day the idol tumbled down, and was broken like any china doll. A chill caught at the seaside, and it was all over."

"And after that," asked the young man, "did he shut himself up like this?"

"He went abroad at first," she answered; "away to Asia and the cannibal Islands and Lord knows where. These deadly strokes take different people in different ways. It took him in the way of an utter sundering or severance from everything, even from tradition and as far as possible from memory. He could not bear a reference to the old tie; a portrait or an anecdote or even an association. He couldn't bear the business of a great public funeral. He longed to get away. He stayed away for ten years. I heard some rumour that he had begun to revive a little at the end of the exile; but when he came back to his own home he relapsed completely. He settled down into religious melancholia, and that's practically madness."

"The priests got hold of him, they say," grumbled the old general. "I know he gave thousands to found a monastery, and lives himself rather like a monk—or, at any rate, a hermit. Can't understand what good they think that will do."

"Goddarned superstition," snorted Cockspur; "that sort of thing ought to be shown up. Here's a man that might have been useful to the Empire and the world, and these vampires get hold of him and suck him dry. I bet with their unnatural notions they haven't even let him marry."

"No, he has never married," said the lady. "He was engaged when I knew him, as a matter of fact, but I don't think it ever came first with him, and I think it went with the rest when everything else went. Like Hamlet and Ophelia—he lost hold of love because he lost hold of life. But I knew the girl; indeed, I know her still. Between ourselves, it was Viola Grayson, daughter of the old admiral. She's never married either."

"It's infamous! It's infernal!" cried Sir John, bounding up. "It's not only a tragedy, but a crime. I've got a duty to the public, and I mean to see all this nonsensical nightmare. In the twentieth century—"

He was almost choked with his own protest, and then, after a silence, the old soldier said:

"Well, I don't profess to know much about those things, but I think these religious people need to study a text which says: 'Let the dead bury their dead.'"

"Only, unfortunately, that's just what it looks like," said his wife with a sigh. "It's just like some creepy story of a dead man burying another dead man, over and over again forever."

"The storm has passed over us," said Romaine, with a rather inscrutable smile. "You will not have to visit the inhospitable house after all."

She suddenly shuddered.

"Oh, I'll never do that again!" she exclaimed.

Mallow was staring at her.

"Again! Have you tried it before?" he cried.

"Well, I did once," she said, with a lightness not without a touch of pride; "but we needn't go back on all that. It's not raining now, but I think we'd better be moving back to the car."

As they moved off in procession, Mallow and the general brought up the rear; and the latter said abruptly, lowering his voice:

"I don't want that little cad Cockspur to hear but as you've asked you'd better know. It's the one thing I can't forgive Marne; but I suppose these monks have drilled him that way. My wife, who had been the best friend he ever had in America, actually came to that house when he was walking in the garden. He was looking at the ground like a monk, and hidden in a black hood that was really as ridiculous as any mask. She had sent her card in, and stood there in his very path. And lie walked past her without a word or a glance, as if she had been a stone. He wasn't human; he was like some horrible automaton. She may well call him a dead man."

"It's all very strange," said the young man rather vaguely. "It isn't like—like what I should have expected."

Young Mr Mallow, when he left that rather dismal picnic, took himself thoughtfully in search of a friend. He did not know any monks, but he knew one priest, whom he was very much concerned to confront with the curious revelations he had heard that afternoon. He felt he would very much like to know the truth about the cruel superstition that hung over the house of Marne, like the black thundercloud he had seen hovering over it.

After being referred from one place to another, he finally ran his friend Father Brown to earth in the house of another friend, a Roman Catholic friend, with a large family. He entered somewhat abruptly to find Father Brown sitting on the floor with a serious expression, and attempting to pin the somewhat florid hat belonging to a wax doll on to the head of a teddy bear.

Mallow felt a faint sense of incongruity; but he was far too full of his problem to put off the conversation if he could, help it. He was staggering from a sort of setback in a subconscious process that had been going on for some time. He poured out the whole tragedy of the house of Marne as he had heard it from the general's wife, along with most of the comments of the general and the newspaper proprietor. A new atmosphere of attention seemed to be created with the mention of the newspaper proprietor.

Father Brown neither knew nor cared that his attitudes were comic or commonplace. He continued to sit on the floor, where his large head and short legs made him look very like a baby playing with toys. But there came into his great grey eyes a certain expression that has been seen in the eyes of many men in many centuries through the story of nineteen hundred years; only the men were not generally sitting on floors, but at council tables, or on the seats of chapters, or the thrones of bishops and cardinals; a far-off, watchful look, heavy with the humility of a charge too great for men. Something of that anxious and far-reaching look is found in the eyes of sailors and of those who have steered through so many storms the ship of St. Peter.

"It's very good of you to tell me this," he said. "I'm really awfully grateful, for we may have to do something about it. If it were only people like you and the general, it might be only a private matter; but if Sir John Cockspur is going to spread some sort or scare in his papers—well, he's a Toronto Orangeman, and we can hardly keep out of it."

"But what will you say about it?" asked Mallow anxiously.

"The first thing I should say about it," said Father Brown, "is that, as you tell it, it doesn't sound like life. Suppose, for the sake of argument, that we are all pessimistic vampires blighting all human happiness. Suppose I'm a pessimistic vampire." He scratched his nose with the teddy bear, became faintly conscious of the incongruity, and put it down.

"Suppose we do destroy all human and family ties. Why should we entangle a man again in an old family tie just when he showed signs of getting loose from it? Surely it's a little unfair to charge us both with crushing such affection and encouraging such infatuation. I don't see why even a religious maniac should be that particular sort of monomaniac, or how religion could increase that mania, except by brightening it with a little hope."

Then he said, after a pause: "I should like to talk to that general of yours."

"It was his wife who told me," said Mallow.

"Yes," replied the other; "but I'm more interested in what he didn't tell you than in what she did."

"You think he knows more than she does?"

"I think he knows more than she says," answered Father Brown. "You tell me he used a phrase about forgiving everything except the rudeness to his wife. After all, what else was there to forgive?"

Father Brown had risen and shaken his shapeless clothes, and stood looking at the young man with screwed up eyes and slightly quizzical expression. The next moment he had turned, and picking up his equally shapeless umbrella and large shabby hat, went stumping down the street.

He plodded through a variety of wide streets and squares till he came to a handsome old-fashioned house in the West End, where he asked the servant if he could see General Outram. After some little palaver he was shown into a study, fitted out less with books than with maps and globes, where the bald-headed, black-whiskered Anglo-Indian sat smoking a long, thin, black cigar and playing with pins on a chart.

"I am sorry to intrude," said the priest, "and all the more because I can't help the intrusion looking like interference. I want to speak to you about a private matter, but only in the hope of keeping it private. Unfortunately, some people are likely to make it public. I think, general, that you know Sir John Cockspur."

The mass of black moustache and whisker served as a sort of mask for the lower half of the old general's face; it was always hard to see whether he smiled, but his brown eyes often had a certain twinkle.

"Everybody knows him, I suppose," he said. "I don't know him very well."

"Well, you know everybody knows whatever he knows," said Father Brown, smiling, "when he thinks it convenient to print it. And I understand from my friend Mr Mallow, whom, I think, you know, that Sir John is going to print some scorching anti-clerical articles founded on what he would call the Marne Mystery. 'Monks Drive Marquis Mad,' etc."

"If he is," replied the general, "I don't see why you should come to me about it. I ought to tell you I'm a strong Protestant."

"I'm very fond of strong Protestants," said Father Brown. "I came to you because I was sure you would tell the truth. I hope it is not uncharitable to feel less sure of Sir John Cockspur."

The brown eyes twinkled again, but the general said nothing.

"General," said Father Brown, "suppose Cockspur or his sort were going to make the world ring with tales against your country and your flag. Suppose he said your regiment ran away in battle, or your staff were in the pay of the enemy. Would you let anything stand between you and the facts that would refute him? Wouldn't you get on the track of the truth at all costs to anybody? Well, I have a regiment, and I belong to an army. It is being discredited by what I am certain is a fictitious story; but I don't know the true story. Can you blame me for trying to find it out?"

The soldier was silent, and the priest continued:

"I have heard the story Mallow was told yesterday, about Marne retiring with a broken heart through the death of his more than brother. I am sure there was more in it than that. I came to ask you if you know anyone."

"No," said the general shortly; "I cannot tell you anymore."

"General," said Father Brown with a broad grin, "you would have called me a Jesuit if I had used that equivocation."

The soldier laughed gruffly, and then growled with much greater hostility.

"Well, I won't tell you, then," he said. "What do you say to that?"

"I only say," said the priest mildly, "that in that case I shall have to tell you."

The brown eyes stared at him; but there was no twinkle in them now. He went on:

"You compel me to state, less sympathetically perhaps than you could, why it is obvious that there is more behind. I am quite sure the marquis has better cause for his brooding and secretiveness than merely having lost an old friend. I doubt whether priests have anything to do with it; I don't even know if he's a convert or merely a man comforting his conscience with charities; but I'm sure he's something more than a chief mourner. Since you insist, I will tell you one or two of the things that made me think so.

"First, it was stated that James Mair was engaged to be married, but somehow became unattached again after the death of Maurice Mair. Why should an honourable man break off his engagement merely because he was depressed by the death of a third party? He's much more likely to have turned for consolation to it; but, anyhow, he was bound in decency to go through with it."

The general was biting his black moustache, and his brown eyes had become very watchful and even anxious, but he did not answer.

"A second point," said Father Brown, frowning at the table. "James Mair was always asking his lady friend whether his cousin Maurice was not very fascinating, and whether women would not admire him. I don't know if it occurred to the lady that there might be another meaning to that inquiry."

The general got to his feet and began to walk or stamp about the room.

"Oh, damn it all," he said, but without any air of animosity.

"The third point," went on Father Brown, "is James Mair's curious manner of mourning—destroying all relics, veiling all portraits, and so on. It does sometimes happen, I admit; it might mean mere affectionate bereavement. But it might mean something else."

"Confound you," said the other. "How long are you going on piling this up?"

"The fourth and fifth points are pretty conclusive," said the priest calmly, "especially if you take them together. The first is that Maurice Mair seems to have had no funeral in particular, considering he was a cadet of a great family. He must have been buried hurriedly; perhaps secretly. And the last point is, that James Mair instantly disappeared to foreign parts; fled, in fact, to the ends of the earth.

"And so," he went on, still in the same soft voice, "when you would blacken my religion to brighten the story of the pure and perfect affection of two brothers, it seems—"

"Stop!" cried Outram in a tone like a pistol shot. "I must tell you more, or you will fancy worse. Let me tell you one thing to start with. It was a fair fight."

"Ah," said Father Brown, and seemed to exhale a huge breath.

"It was a duel," said the other. "It was probably the last duel fought in England, and it is long ago now."

"That's better," said Father Brown. "Thank God; that's a great deal better."

"Better than the ugly things you thought of, I suppose?" said the general gruffly. "Well, it's all very well for you to sneer at the pure and perfect affection; but it was true for all that. James Mair really was devoted to his cousin, who'd grown up with him like a younger brother. Elder brothers and sisters do sometimes devote themselves to a child like that, especially when he's a sort of infant phenomenon. But James Mair was the sort of simple character in whom even hate is in a sense unselfish. I mean that even when his tenderness turns to rage it is still objective, directed outwards to its object; he isn't conscious of himself. Now poor Maurice Mair was just the opposite. He was far more friendly and popular; but his success had made him live in a house of mirrors. He was first in every sort of sport and art and accomplishment; he nearly always won and took his winning amiably. But if ever, by any chance, he lost, there was just a glimpse of something not so amiable; he was a little jealous. I needn't tell you the whole miserable story of how he was a little jealous of his cousin's engagement; how he couldn't keep his restless vanity from interfering. It's enough to say that one of the few things in which James Mair was admittedly ahead of him was marksmanship with a pistol; and with that the tragedy ended."

"You mean the tragedy began," replied the priest. "The tragedy of the survivor. I thought he did not need any monkish vampires to make him miserable."

"To my mind he's more miserable than he need be," said the general. "After all, as I say, it was a ghastly tragedy, but it was a fair fight. And Jim had great provocation."

"How do you know all this?" asked the priest.

"I know it because I saw it," answered Outram stolidly. "I was James Mair's second, and I saw Maurice Mair shot dead on the sands before my very eyes."

"I wish you would tell me more about it," said Father Brown reflectively. "Who was Maurice Mair's second?"

"He had a more distinguished backing," replied the general grimly. "Hugo Romaine was his second; the great actor, you know. Maurice was mad on acting and had taken up Romaine (who was then a rising but still a struggling man), and financed the fellow and his ventures in return for taking lessons from the professional in his own hobby of amateur acting. But Romaine was then, I suppose, practically dependent on his rich friend; though he's richer now than any aristocrat. So his serving as second proves very little about what he thought of the quarrel. They fought in the English fashion, with only one second apiece; I wanted at least to have a surgeon, but Maurice boisterously refused it, saying the fewer people who knew, the better; and at the worst we could immediately get help. 'There's a doctor in the village not half a mile away,' he said; 'I know him and he's got the fastest horse in the country. He could be brought here in no time; but there's no need to bring him here till we know.' Well, we all knew that Maurice ran most risk, as the pistol was not his weapon; so when he refused aid nobody liked to ask for it. The duel was fought on a flat stretch of sand on the east coast of Scotland; and both the sight and sound of it were masked from the hamlets inland by a long rampart of sandhills patched with rank grass; probably part of the links, though in those days no Englishman had heard of golf. There was one deep, crooked cranny in the sandhills through which we came out on the sands. I can see them now; first a wide strip of dead yellow, and beyond, a narrower strip of dark red; a dark red that seemed already like the long shadow of a deed of blood.

"The thing itself seemed to happen with horrible speed; as if a whirlwind had struck the sand. With the very crack of sound Maurice Mair seemed to spin like a teetotum and pitch upon his face like a ninepin. And queerly enough, while I'd been worrying about him up to that moment, the instant he was dead all my pity was for the man who killed him; as it is to this day and hour. I knew that with that, the whole huge terrible pendulum of my friend's life-long love would swing back; and that whatever cause others might find to pardon him, he would never pardon himself forever and ever. And so, somehow, the really vivid thing, the picture that burns in my memory so that I can't forget it, is not that of the catastrophe, the smoke and the flash and the falling figure. That seemed to be all over, like the noise that wakes a man up. What I saw, what I shall always see, is poor Jim hurrying across towards his fallen friend and foe; his brown beard looking black against the ghastly pallor of his face, with its high features cut out against the sea; and the frantic gestures with which he waved me to run for the surgeon in the hamlet behind the sandhills. He had dropped his pistol as he ran; he had a glove in one hand and the loose and fluttering fingers of it seemed to elongate and emphasize his wild pantomime of pointing or hailing for help. That is the picture that really remains with me; and there is nothing else in that picture, except the striped background of sands and sea and the dark, dead body lying still as a stone, and the dark figure of the dead man's second standing grim and motionless against the horizon."

"Did Romaine stand motionless?" asked the priest. "I should have thought he would have run even quicker towards the corpse."

"Perhaps he did when I had left," replied the general. "I took in that undying picture in an instant and the next instant I had dived among the sandhills, and was far out of sight of the others. Well, poor Maurice had made a good choice in the matter of doctors; though the doctor came too late, he came quicker than I should have thought possible. This village surgeon was a very remarkable man, redhaired, irascible, but extraordinarily strong in promptitude and presence of mind. I saw him but for a flash as he leapt on his horse and went thundering away to the scene of death, leaving me far behind. But in that flash I had so strong a sense of his personality that I wished to God he had really been called in before the duel began; for I believe on my soul he would have prevented it somehow. As it was, he cleaned up the mess with marvellous swiftness; long before I could trail back to the seashore on my two feet his impetuous practicality had managed everything; the corpse wis temporarily buried in the sandhills and the unhappy homicide had been persuaded to do the only thing he could do—to flee for his life. He slipped along the coast till he came to a port and managed to get out of the country. You know the rest; poor Jim remained abroad for many years; later, when the whole thing had been hushed up or forgotten, he returned to his dismal castle and automatically inherited the title. I have never seen him from that day to this, and yet I know what is written in red letters in the inmost darkness of his brain."

"I understand," said Father Brown, "that some of you have made efforts to see him?"

"My wife never relaxed her efforts," said the general. "She refuses to admit that such a crime ought to cut a man off forever; and I confess I am inclined to agree with her. Eighty years before it would have been thought quite normal; and really it was manslaughter rather than murder. My wife is a great friend of the unfortunate lady who was the occasion of the quarrel and she has an idea that if Jim would consent to see Viola Grayson once again, and receive her assurance that old quarrels are buried, it might restore his sanity. My wife is calling a sort of council of old friends tomorrow, I believe. She is very energetic."

Father Brown was playing with the pins that lay beside the general's map; he seemed to listen rather absent-mindedly. He had the sort of mind that sees things in pictures; and the picture which had coloured even the prosaic mind of the practical soldier took on tints yet more significant and sinister in the more mystical mind of the priest. He saw the dark-red desolation of sand, the very hue of Aceldama, and the dead man lying in a dark heap, and the slayer, stooping as he ran, gesticulating with a glove in demented remorse, and always his imagination came back to the third thing that he could not yet fit into any human picture: the second of the slain man standing motionless and mysterious, like a dark statue on the edge of the sea. It might seem to some a detail; but for him it was that stiff figure that stood up like a standing note of interrogation.

Why had not Romaine moved instantly? It was the natural thing for a second to do, in common humanity, let alone friendship. Even if there were some double-dealing or darker motive not yet understood, one would think it would be done for the sake of appearances. Anyhow, when the thing was all over, it would be natural for the second to stir long before the other second had vanished beyond the sandhills.

"Docs this man Romanic move very slowly?" he askcd.

"It's queer you should ask that," answered. Outram, with a sharp glance. "No, as a matter of fact he moves very quickly when he moves at all. But, curiously enough, I was just thinking that only this afternoon I saw him stand exactly like that, during the thunderstorm. He stood in that silver-clasped cape of his, and with one hand on his hip, exactly and in every line as he stood on those bloody sands long ago. The lightning blinded us all, but he did not blink. When it was dark again he was standing there still."

"I suppose he isn't standing there now?" inquired Father Brown. "I mean, I suppose he moved sometime?"

"No, he moved quite sharply when the thunder came," replied the other. "He seemed to have been waiting for it, for he told us the exact time of the interval. Is anything the matter?"

"I've pricked myself with one of your pins," said Father Brown. "I hope I haven't damaged it." But his eyes had snapped and his mouth abruptly shut.

"Are you ill?" inquired the general, staring at him.

"No," answered the priest; "I'm only not quite so stoical as your friend Romaine. I can't help blinking when I see light."

He turned to gather up his hat and umbrella; but when he had got to the door he seemed to remember something and turned back. Coming up close to Outram, he gazed up into his face with a rather helpless expression, as of a dying fish, and made a motion as if to hold him by the waistcoat.

"General," he almost whispered, "for God's sake don't let your wife and that other woman insist on seeing Marne again. Let sleeping dogs lie, or you'll unleash all the hounds of hell."

The general was left alone with a look of bewilderment in his brown eyes, as he sat down again to play with his pins.

Even greater, however, was the bewilderment which attended the successive stages of the benevolent conspiracy of the general's wife, who had assembled her little group of sympathizers to storm the castle of the misanthrope. The first surprise she encountered was the unexplained absence of one of the actors in the ancient tragedy. When they assembled by agreement at a quiet hotel quite near the castle, there was no sign of Hugo Romaine, until a belated telegram from a lawyer told them that the great actor had suddenly left the country. The second surprise, when they began the bombardment by sending up word to the castle with an urgent request for an interview, was the figure which came forth from those gloomy gates to receive the deputation in the name of the noble owner. It was no such figure as they would have conceived suitable to those sombre avenues or those almost feudal formalities. It was not some stately steward or major-domo, nor even a dignified butler or tall and ornamental footman. The only figure that came out of the cavernous castle doorway was the short and shabby figure of Father Brown.

"Look here," he said, in his simple, bothered fashion. "I told you you'd much better leave him alone. He knows what he's doing and it'll only make everybody unhappy."

Lady Outram, who was accompanied by a tall and quietly-dressed lady, still very handsome, presumably the original Miss Grayson, looked at the little priest with cold contempt.

"Really, sir," she said; "this is a very private occasion, and I don't understand what you have to do with it.'

"Trust a priest to have to do with a private occasion," snarled Sir John Cockspur. "Don't you know they live behind the scenes like rats behind a wainscot burrowing their way into everybody's private rooms. See how he's already in possession of poor Marne." Sir John was slightly sulky, as his aristocratic friends had persuaded him to give up the great scoop of publicity in return for the privilege of being really inside a Society secret. It never occurred to him to ask himself whether he was at all like a rat in a wainscot.

"Oh, that's all right," said Father Brown, with the impatience of anxiety. "I've talked it over with the marquis and the only priest he's ever had anything to do with; his clerical tastes have been much exaggerated. I tell you he knows what he's about; and I do implore you all to leave him alone."

"You mean to leave him to this living death of moping and going mad in a ruin!" cried Lady Outram, in a voice that shook a little. "And all because he had the bad luck to shoot a man in a duel more than a quarter of a century ago. Is that what you call Christian charity?"

"Yes," answered the priest stolidly; "that is what I call Christian charity."

"It's about all the Christian charity you'll ever get out of these priests," cried Cockspur bitterly. "That's their only idea of pardoning a poor fellow for a piece of folly; to wall him up alive and starve him to death with fasts and penances and pictures of hell-fire. And all because a bullet went wrong."

"Really, Father Brown," said General Outram, "do you honestly think he deserves this? Is that your Christianity?"

"Surely the true Christianity," pleaded his wife more gently, "is that which knows all and pardons all; the love that can remember—and forget."

"Father Brown," said young Mallow, very earnestly, "I generally agree with what you say; but I'm hanged if I can follow you here. A shot in a duel, followed instantly by remorse, is not such an awful offence."

"I admit." said Father Brown dully, "that I take a more serious view of his offence."

"God soften your hard heart," said the strange lady speaking for the first time. "I am going to speak to my old friend."

Almost as if her voice had raised a ghost in that great grey house, something stirred within and a figure stood in the dark doorway at the top of the great stone flight of steps. It was clad in dead black, but there was something wild about the blanched hair and something in the pale features that was like the wreck of a marble statue.

Viola Grayson began calmly to move up the great flight of steps; and Outram muttered in his thick black moustache: "He won't cut her dead as he did my wife, I fancy."

Father Brown, who seemed in a collapse of resignation, looked up at him for a moment.

"Poor Marne has enough on his conscience," he said. "Let us acquit him of what we can. At least he never cut your wife."

"What do you mean by that?"

"He never knew her," said Father Brown.

As they spoke, the tall lady proudly mounted the last step and came face to face with the Marquis of Marne. His lips moved, but something happened before he could speak.

A scream rang across the open space and went wailing away in echoes along those hollow walls. By the abruptness and agony with which it broke from the woman's lips it might have been a mere inarticulate cry. But it was an articulated word; and they all heard it with a horrible distinctness.

"Maurice!"

"What is it, dear?" cried Lady Outram, and began to run up the steps; for the other woman was swaying as if she might fall down the whole stone flight. Then she faced about and began to descend, all bowed and shrunken and shuddering. "Oh, my God," she was saying. "Oh, my God, it isn't Jim at all. it's Maurice!"

"I think, Lady Outram," said the priest gravely, "you had better go with your friend."

As they turned, a voice fell on them like a stone from the top of the stone stair, a voice that might have come out of an open grave. It was hoarse and unnatural, like the voices of men who are left alone with wild birds on desert islands. It was the voice of the Marquis of Marne, and it said: "Stop!"

"Father Brown," he said, "before your friends disperse I authorize you to tell them all I have told you. Whatever follows, I will hide from it no longer."

"You are right," said the priest, "and it shall be counted to you."

"Yes," said Father Brown quietly to the questioning company afterwards. "He has given me the right to speak; but I will not tell it as he told me, but as I found it out for myself. Well, I knew from the first that the blighting monkish influence was all nonsense out of novels. Our people might possibly, in certain cases, encourage a man to go regularly into a monastery, but certainly not to hang about in a mediaeval castle. In the same way, they certainly wouldn't want him to dress up as a monk when he wasn't a monk. But it struck me that he might himself want to wear a monk's hood or even a mask. I had heard of him as a mourner, and then as a murderer; but already I had hazy suspicions that his reason for hiding might not only be concerned with what lie was, but with who he was.

"Then came the general's vivid description of the duel; and the most vivid thing in it to me was the figure of

Mr Romaine in the background; it was vivid because it was in the background. Why did the general leave behind him on the sand a dead man, whose friend stood yards away from him like a stock or a stone? Then I heard something, a mere trifle, about a trick habit that Romaine has of standing quite still when he is waiting for something to happen; as he waited for the thunder to follow the lightning. Well, that automatic trick in this case betrayed everything. Hugo Romaine on that old occasion, also, was waiting for something."

"But it was all over," said the general. "What could he have been waiting for?"

"He was waiting for the duel," said Father Brown.

"But I tell you I saw the duel!" cried the general.

"And I tell you you didn't see the duel," said the priest.

"Are you mad?" demanded the other. "Or why should you think I am blind?"

"Because you were blinded—that you might not see," said the priest. "Because you are a good man and God had mercy on your innocence, and he turned your face away from that unnatural strife. He set a wall of sand and silence between you and what really happened on that horrible red shore, abandoned to the raging spirits of Judas and of Cain."

"Tell us what happened!" gasped the lady impatiently.

"I will tell it as I found it," proceeded the priest. "The next thing I found was that Romaine the actor had been training Maurice Mair in all the tricks of the trade of acting. I once had a friend who went in for acting. He gave me a very amusing account of how his first week's training consisted entirely of falling down; of learning how to fall flat without a stagger, as if he were stone dead."

"God have mercy on us!" cried the general, and gripped the arms of his chair as if to rise.

"Amen," said Father Brown. "You told me how quickly it seemed to come; in fact, Maurice fell before the bullet flew, and lay perfectly still, waiting. And his wicked friend and teacher stood also in the background, waiting."

"We are waiting," said Cockspur, "and I feel as if I couldn't wait."

"James Mair, already broken with remorse, rushed across to the fallen man and bent over to lift him up. He had thrown away his pistol like an unclean thing; but Maurice's pistol still lay under his hand and it was undischarged. Then as the elder man bent over the younger, the younger lifted himself on his left arm and shot the elder through the body. He knew he was not so good a shot, but there was no question of missing the heart at that distance."

The rest of the company had risen and stood staring down at the narrator with pale faces. "Are you sure of this?" asked Sir John at last, in a thick voice.

"I am sure of it," said Father Brown, "and now I leave Maurice Mair, the present Marquis of Marne, to your Christian charity. You have told me something today about Christian charity. You seemed to me to give it almost too large a place; but how fortunate it is for poor sinners like this man that you err so much on the side of mercy, and are ready to be reconciled to all mankind."

"Hang it all," exploded the general; "if you think I'm going to be reconciled to a filthy viper like that, I tell you I wouldn't say a word to save him from hell. I said I could pardon a regular decent duel, but of all the treacherous assassins—"

"He ought to be lynched," cried Cockspur excitedly. "He ought to burn alive like a nigger in the States. And if there is such a thing as burning forever, he jolly well—"

"I wouldn't touch him with a bargepole myself," said Mallow.

"There is a limit to human charity," said Lady Outram, trembling all over.

"There is," said Father Brown dryly; "and that is the real difference between human charity and Christian charity.

You must forgive me if I was not altogether crushed by your contempt for my uncharitableness today; or by the lectures you read me about pardon for every sinner. For it seems to me that you only pardon the sins that you don't really think sinful. You only forgive criminals when they commit what you don't regard as crimes, but rather as conventions. So you tolerate a conventional duel, just as you tolerate a conventional divorce. You forgive because there isn't anything to be forgiven."

"But, hang it all," cried Mallow, "you don't expect us to be able to pardon a vile thing like this?"

"No," said the priest; "but we have to be able to pardon it."

He stood up abruptly and looked round at them.

"'We have to touch such men, not with a bargepole, but with a benediction," he said. "We have to say the word that will save them from hell. We alone are left to deliver them from despair when your human charity deserts them. Go on your own primrose path pardoning all your favourite vices and being generous to your fashionable crimes; and leave us in the darkness, vampires of the night, to console those who really need consolation; who do things really indefensible, things that neither the world nor they themselves can defend; and none but a priest will pardon. Leave us with the men who commit the mean and revolting and real crimes; mean as St. Peter when the cock crew, and yet the dawn came."

"The dawn," repeated Mallow doubtfully. "You mean hope—for him?"

"Yes," replied the other. "Let me ask you one question. You are great ladies and men of honour and secure of yourselves; you would never, you can tell yourselves, stoop to such squalid reason as that. But tell me this. If any of you had so stooped, which of you, years afterwards, when you were old and rich and safe, would have been driven by conscience or confessor to tell such a story of yourself? You say you could not commit so base a crime. Could you confess so base a crime?" The others gathered their possessions together and drifted by twos and threes out of the room in silence. And Father Brown, also in silence, went back to the melancholy castle of Marne.

10

THE SECRET OF FLAMBEAU
(No record of prior magazine publication found)

"—the sort of murders in which I played the part of the murderer," said Father Brown, putting down the wineglass. The row of red pictures of crime had passed before him in that moment.

"It is true," he resumed, after a momentary pause, "that somebody else had played the part of the murderer before me and done me out of the actual experience. I was a sort of understudy; always in a state of being ready to act the assassin. I always made it my business, at least, to know the part thoroughly. What I mean is that, when I tried to imagine the state of mind in which such a thing would be done, I always realized that I might have done it myself under certain mental conditions, but not under others; and not generally under the obvious ones. And then, of course, I knew who really had done it; and he was not generally the obvious person.

"For instance, it seemed obvious to say that the revolutionary poet had killed the old judge who saw red about red revolutionaries. But that isn't really a reason for the revolutionary poet killing him. It isn't, if you think what it would really be like to be a revolutionary poet. Now I set myself conscientiously down to be a revolutionary poet. I mean that particular sort of pessimistic anarchial lover of revolt, not as reform, but rather as destruction. I tried to clear my mind of such elements of sanity and constructive common sense as I have had the luck to learn or inherit. I shut down and darkened all the skylights through which comes the good daylight out of heaven; I imagined a mind lit only by a red light from below; a fire rending rocks and cleaving abysses upwards. And even with the vision at its wildest and worst, I could not see why such a visionary should cut short his own career by colliding with a common policeman, for killing one out of a million conventional old fools, as he would have called them. He wouldn't do it; however much he wrote songs of violence. He wouldn't do it, because he wrote songs of violence. A man who can express himself in song need not express himself in suicide. A poem was an event to him; and he would want to have more of them. Then I thought of another sort of heathen; the sort that is not destroying the world but entirely depending on the world. I thought that, save for the grace of God, I might have been a man for whom the world was a blaze of electric lights, with nothing but utter darkness beyond and around it. The worldly man, who really lives only for this world and believes in no other, whose worldly success and pleasure are all he can ever snatch out of nothingness—that is the man who will really do anything, when he is in danger of losing the whole world and saving nothing. It is not the revolutionary man but the respectable man who would commit any crime—to save his respectability. Think what exposure would mean to a man like that fashionable barrister; and exposure of the one crime still really hated by his fashionable world—treason against patriotism. If I had been in his position, and had nothing better than his philosophy, heaven alone knows what I might have done. That is just where this little religious exercise is so wholesome."

"Some people would think it was rather morbid," said Grandison Chace dubiously.

"Some people," said Father Brown gravely, "undoubtedly do think that charity and humility are morbid. Our friend the poet probably would. But I'm not arguing those questions; I'm only trying to answer your question about how I generally go to work. Some of your countrymen have apparently done me the honour to ask how I managed to frustrate a few miscarriages of justice. Well, you can go back and tell them that I do it by morbidity. But I most certainly don't want them to think I do it by magic."

Chace continued to look at him with a reflective frown; he was too intelligent not to understand the idea; he would also have said that he was too healthy-minded to like it. He felt as if he were talking to one man and yet to a hundred murderers. There was something uncanny about that very small figure, perched like a goblin beside the goblin stove; and the sense that its round head had held such a universe of wild unreason and imaginative injustice. It was as if the vast void of dark behind it were a throng of dark gigantic figures, the ghosts of great criminals held at bay by the magic circle of the red stove, but ready to tear their master in pieces.

"Well, I'm afraid I do think it's morbid," he said frankly. "And I'm not sure it isn't almost as morbid as magic. But morbidity or no, there's one thing to be said; it must be an interesting experience." Then he added, after reflection: "I don't know whether you would make a really good criminal. But you ought to make a rattling good novelist."

"I only have to deal with real events," said Father Brown. "But it's sometimes harder to imagine real things than unreal ones."

"Especially," said the other, "when they are the great crimes of the world."

"It's not the great crimes but the small crimes that are really hard to imagine," replied the priest.

"I don't quite know what you mean by that," said Chace.

"I mean commonplace crimes like stealing jewels," said Father Brown; "like that affair of the emerald necklace or the Ruby of Meru or the artificial goldfish. The difficulty in those cases is that you've got to make your mind small. High and mighty humbugs, who deal in big ideas, don't do those obvious things. I was sure the Prophet hadn't taken the ruby; or the Count the goldfish; though a man like Bankes might easily take the emeralds. For them, a jewel is a piece of glass: and they can see through the glass. But the little, literal people take it at its market value.

"For that you've got to have a small mind. It's awfully hard to get; like focusing smaller and sharper in a wobbling camera. But some things helped; and they threw a lot of light on the mystery, too. For instance, the sort of man who brags about having 'shown up' sham magicians or poor quacks of any sort—he's always got a small mind. He is the sort of man who 'sees through' tramps and trips them up in telling lies. I dare say it might sometimes be a painful duty. It's an uncommonly base pleasure. The moment I realized what a small mind meant, I knew where to look for it—in the man who wanted to expose the Prophet—and it was he that sneaked the ruby; in the man who jeered at his sister's psychic fancies—and it was he who nabbed the emeralds. Men like that always have their eye on jewels; they never could rise, with the higher humbugs, to despising jewels. Those criminals with small minds are always quite conventional. They become criminals out of sheer conventionality.

"It takes you quite a long time to feel so crudely as that, though. It's quite a wild effort of imagination to be so conventional. To want one potty little object as seriously as all that. But you can do it... You can get nearer to it. Begin by thinking of being a greedy child; of how you might have stolen a sweet in a shop; of how there was one particular sweet you wanted; then you must subtract the childish poetry; shut off the fairy light that shone on the sweet-stuff shop; imagine you really think you know the world and the market value of sweets; you contract your mind like the camera focus; the thing shapes and then sharpens... and then, suddenly, it comes!"

He spoke like a man who had once captured a divine vision. Grandison Chace was still looking at him with a frown of mingled mystification and interest. It must be confessed that there did flash once beneath his heavy frown a look of something almost like alarm. It was as if the shock of the first strange confession of the priest still thrilled faintly through him like the last vibration of a thunderclap in the room. Under the surface he was saying to himself that the mistake had only been a temporary madness; that, of course. Father Brown could not really be the monster and murderer he had beheld for that blinding and bewildering instant. But was there not something wrong with the man who talked in that calm way about being a murderer? Was it possible that the priest was a little mad?

"Don't you think," he said, abruptly; "that this notion of yours, of a man trying to feel like a criminal, might make him a little too tolerant of crime?"

Father Brown sat up and spoke in a more staccato style.

"I know it does just the opposite. It solves the whole problem of time and sin. It gives a man his remorse beforehand."

There was a silence; the American looked at the high and steep roof that stretched half across the enclosure; his host gazed into the fire without moving; and then the priest's voice came on a different note, as if from lower down.

"There are two ways of renouncing the devil," he said; "and the difference is perhaps the deepest chasm in modem religion. One is to have a horror of him because he is so far off; and the other to have it because he is so near. And no virtue and vice are so much divided as those two virtues."

They did not answer and he went on in the same heavy tone, as if he were dropping words like molten lead.

"You may think a crime horrible because you could never commit it. I think it horrible because I could commit it. You think of it as something like an eruption of Vesuvius; but that would not really be so terrible as this house catching fire. If a criminal suddenly appeared in this room—"

"If a criminal appeared in this room," said Chace, smiling, "I think you would be a good deal too favourable to him. Apparently you would start by telling him that you were a criminal yourself and explaining how perfectly natural it was that he should have picked his father's pocket or cut his mother's throat. Frankly, I don't think it's practical. I think that the practical effect would be that no criminal would ever reform. It's easy enough to theorize and take hypothetical cases; but we all know we're only talking in the air. Sitting here in M. Duroc's nice, comfortable house, conscious of our respectability and all the rest of it, it just gives us a theatrical thrill to talk about thieves and murderers and the mysteries of their souls. But the people who really have to deal with thieves and murderers have to deal with them differently. We are safe by the fireside; and we know the house is not on fire. We know there is not a criminal in the room."

The M. Duroc to whom allusion had been made rose slowly from what had been called his fireside, and his huge shadow flung from the fire seemed to cover everything and darken even the very night above him.

"There is a criminal in this room," he said. "I am one. I am Flambeau, and the police of two hemispheres are still hunting for me."

The American remained gazing at him with eyes of a stony brightness; he seemed unable to speak or move.

"There is nothing mystical, or metaphorical, or vicarious about my confession," said Flambeau. "I stole for twenty years with these two hands; I fled from the police on these two feet. I hope you will admit that my activities were practical. I hope you will admit that my judges and pursuers really had to deal with crime. Do you think I do not know all about their way of reprehending it? Have I not heard the sermons of the righteous and seen the cold stare of the respectable; have I not been lectured in the lofty and distant style, asked how it was possible for anyone to fall so low, told that no decent person could ever have dreamed of such depravity? Do you think all that ever did anything but make me laugh? Only my friend told me that he knew exactly why I stole; and I have never stolen since."

Father Brown made a gesture as of deprecation; and Grandison Chace at last let out a long breath like a whistle.

"I have told you the exact truth," said Flambeau; "and it is open to you to hand me over to the police."

There was an instant of profound stillness, in which could be faintly heard the belated laughter of Flambeau's children in the high, dark house above them, and the crunching and snorting of the great, grey pigs in the twilight. And then it was cloven by a high voice, vibrant and with a touch of offence, almost surprising for those who do not understand the sensitive American spirit, and how near, in spite of commonplace contrasts, it can sometimes come to the chivalry of Spain.

"Monsieur Duroc," he said rather stiffly. "We have been friends, I hope, for some considerable period; and I should be pretty much pained to suppose you thought me capable of playing you such a trick while I was enjoying your hospitality and the society of your family, merely because you chose to tell me a little of your own autobiography of your own free will. And when you spoke merely in defence of your friend—no, sir, I can't imagine any gentleman double-crossing another under such circumstances; it would be a damned sight better to be a dirty informer and sell men's blood for money. But in a case like this—! Could you conceive any man being such a Judas?"

"I could try," said Father Brown.

THE END

The Scandal of Father Brown

First UK edition: Cassel & Co., London, 1935
First US edition: Dodd, Mead & Co., New York, 1935

CONTENTS

LIST OF ILLUSTRATIONS

"Father Brown has always been one of my favorite sleuths."—AGATHA CHRISTIE

The SCANDAL of FATHER BROWN

8 MYSTERY STORIES BY

G. K. CHESTERTON

"Father Brown is one of the few characters in all fiction who is likely to survive the fickle years."—ELLERY QUEEN

1

THE SCANDAL OF FATHER BROWN
(No record of prior magazine publication found)

It would not be fair to record the adventures of Father Brown, without admitting that he was once involved in a grave scandal. There still are persons, perhaps even of his own community, who would say that there was a sort of blot upon his name. It happened in a picturesque Mexican road-house of rather loose repute, as appeared later; and to some it seemed that for once the priest had allowed a romantic streak in him, and his sympathy for human weakness, to lead him into loose and unorthodox action. The story in itself was a simple one; and perhaps the whole surprise of it consisted in its simplicity.

Burning Troy began with Helen; this disgraceful story began with the beauty of Hypatia Potter. Americans have a great power, which Europeans do not always appreciate, of creating institutions from below; that is by popular initiative. Like every other good thing, it has its lighter aspects; one of which, as has been remarked by Mr Wells and others, is that a person may become a public institution without becoming an official institution. A girl of great beauty or brilliancy will be a sort of uncrowned queen, even if she is not a Film Star or the original of a Gibson Girl. Among those who had the fortune, or misfortune, to exist beautifully in public in this manner, was a certain Hypatia Hard, who had passed through the preliminary stage of receiving florid compliments in society paragraphs of the local press, to the position of one who is actually interviewed by real pressmen. On War and Peace and Patriotism and Prohibition and evolution and the Bible she had made her pronouncements with a charming smile; and if none of them seemed very near to the real grounds of her own reputation, it was almost equally hard to say what the grounds of her reputation really were. Beauty, and being the daughter of a rich man, are things not rare in her country; but to these she added whatever it is that attracts the wandering eye of journalism. Next to none of her admirers had even seen her, or even hoped to do so; and none of them could possibly derive any sordid benefit from her father's wealth. It was simply a sort of popular romance, the modern substitute for mythology; and it laid the first foundations of the more turgid and tempestuous sort of romance in which she was to figure later on; and in which many held that the reputation of Father Brown, as well as of others, had been blown to rags.

It was accepted, sometimes romantically, sometimes resignedly, by those whom American satire has named the Sob Sisters, that she had already married a very worthy and respectable businessman of the name of Potter. It was even possible to regard her for a moment as Mrs Potter, on the universal understanding that her husband was only the husband of Mrs Potter.

Then came the Great Scandal, by which her friends and enemies were horrified beyond their wildest hopes. Her name was coupled (as the queer phrase goes) with a literary man living in Mexico; in status an American, but in spirit a very Spanish American. Unfortunately his vices resembled her virtues, in being good copy. He was no less a person than the famous or infamous Rudel Romanes; the poet whose works had been so universally popularized by being vetoed by libraries or prosecuted by the police. Anyhow, her pure and placid star was seen in conjunction with this comet. He was of the sort to be compared to a comet, being hairy and hot; the first in his portraits, the second in his poetry. He was also destructive; the comet's tail was a trail of divorces, which some called his success as a lover and some his prolonged failure as a husband. It was hard on Hypatia; there are disadvantages in conducting the perfect private life in public; like a domestic interior in a shop-window. Interviewers reported doubtful utterances about Love's Larger Law of Supreme Self-Realization. The Pagans applauded. The Sob Sisterhood permitted themselves a note of romantic regret; some having even the hardened audacity to quote from the poem of Maud Mueller, to the effect that of all the words of tongue or pen, the saddest are 'It might have been.' And Mr Agar P. Rock, who hated the Sob Sisterhood with a holy and righteous hatred, said that in this case he thoroughly agreed with Bret Harte's emendation of the poem:

'More sad are those we daily see; it is, but it hadn't ought to be.'

For Mr Rock was very firmly and rightly convinced that a very large number of things hadn't ought to be. He was a slashing and savage critic of national degeneration, on the Minneapolis Meteor, and a bold and honest man. He had perhaps come to specialize too much in the spirit of indignation, but it had had a healthy enough origin in his reaction against sloppy attempts to confuse right and wrong in modern journalism and gossip. He expressed it first in the form of a protest against an unholy halo of romance being thrown round the gunman and the gangster. Perhaps he was rather too much inclined to assume, in robust impatience, that all gangsters were Dagos and that all

Dagos were gangsters. But his prejudices, even when they were a little provincial, were rather refreshing after a certain sort of maudlin and unmanly hero-worship, which was ready to regard a professional murderer as a leader of fashion, so long as the pressmen reported that his smile was irresistible or his tuxedo was all right. Anyhow, the prejudices did not boil the less in the bosom of Mr Rock, because he was actually in the land of the Dagos when this story opens; striding furiously up a hill beyond the Mexican border, to the white hotel, fringed with ornamental palms, in which it was supposed that the Potters were staying and that the mysterious Hypatia now held her court. Agar Rock was a good specimen of a Puritan, even to look at; he might even have been a virile Puritan of the seventeenth century, rather than the softer and more sophisticated Puritan of the twentieth. If you had told him that his antiquated black hat and habitual black frown, and fine flinty features, cast a gloom over the sunny land of palms and vines, he would have been very much gratified. He looked to right and left with eyes bright with universal suspicions. And, as he did so, he saw two figures on the ridge above him, outlined against the clear sub-tropical sunset; figures in a momentary posture which might have made even a less suspicious man suspect something.

One of the figures was rather remarkable in itself. It was poised at the exact angle of the turning road above the valley, as if by an instinct for the site as well as the attitude of statuary. It was wrapt in a great black cloak, in the Byronic manner, and the head that rose above it in swarthy beauty was remarkably like Byron's. This man had the same curling hair and curling nostrils; and he seemed to be snorting something of the same scorn and indignation against the world. He grasped in his hand a rather long cane or walking-stick, which having a spike of the sort used for mountaineering, carried at the moment a fanciful suggestion of a spear. It was rendered all the more fanciful by something comically contradictory in the figure of the other man, who carried an umbrella. It was indeed a new and neatly-rolled umbrella, very different, for instance, from Father Brown's umbrella: and he was neatly clad like a clerk in light holiday clothes; a stumpy stoutish bearded man; but the prosaic umbrella was raised and even brandished at an acute angle of attack. The taller man thrust back at him, but in a hasty defensive manner; and then the scene rather collapsed into comedy; for the umbrella opened of itself and its owner almost seemed to sink behind it, while the other man had the air of pushing his spear through a great grotesque shield. But the other man did not push it, or the quarrel, very far; he plucked out the point, turned away impatiently and strode down the road; while the other, rising and carefully refolding his umbrella, turned in the opposite direction towards the hotel. Rock had not heard any of the words of the quarrel, which must have immediately preceded this brief and rather absurd bodily conflict; but as he went up the road in the track of the short man with the beard, he revolved many things. And the romantic cloak and rather operatic good looks of the one man, combined with the sturdy self-assertion of the other, fitted in with the whole story which he had come to seek; and he knew that he could have fixed those two strange figures with their names: Romanes and Potter.

His view was in every way confirmed when he entered the pillared porch; and heard the voice of the bearded man raised high in altercation or command. He was evidently speaking to the manager or staff of the hotel, and Rock heard enough to know that he was warning them of a wild and dangerous character in the neighbourhood.

'If he's really been to the hotel already,' the little man was saying, in answer to some murmur, 'all I can say is that you'd better not let him in again. Your police ought to be looking after a fellow of that sort, but anyhow, I won't have the lady pestered with him.'

Rock listened in grim silence and growing conviction; then he slid across the vestibule to an alcove where he saw the hotel register and turning to the last page, saw 'the fellow' had indeed been to the hotel already. There appeared the name of 'Rudel Romanes,' that romantic public character, in very large and florid foreign lettering; and after a space under it, rather close together, the names of Hypatia Potter and Ellis T. Potter, in a correct and quite American handwriting.

Agar Rock looked moodily about him, and saw in the surroundings and even the small decorations of the hotel everything that he hated most. It is perhaps unreasonable to complain of oranges growing on orange-trees, even in small tubs; still more of their only growing on threadbare curtains or faded wallpapers as a formal scheme of ornament. But to him those red and golden moons, decoratively alternated with silver moons, were in a queer way the quintessence of all moonshine. He saw in them all that sentimental deterioration which his principles deplored in modern manners, and which his prejudices vaguely connected with the warmth and softness of the South. It annoyed him even to catch sight of a patch of dark canvas, half-showing a Watteau shepherd with a guitar, or a blue tile with a commonplace design of a Cupid on a dolphin. His common sense would have told him that he might have seen these things in a shop-window on Fifth Avenue; but where they were, they seemed like a taunting siren voice of the Paganism of the Mediterranean. And then suddenly, the look of all these things seemed to alter, as a still mirror will flicker when a figure has flashed past it for a moment; and he knew the whole room was full of a challenging presence. He turned almost stiffly, and with a sort of resistance, and knew that he was facing the famous Hypatia, of whom he had read and heard for so many years.

Hypatia Potter, nee Hard, was one of those people to whom the word 'radiant' really does apply definitely and derivatively.

That is, she allowed what the papers called her Personality to go out from her in rays. She would have been equally beautiful, and to some tastes more attractive, if she had been self-contained; but she had always been taught to believe that self-containment was only selfishness. She would have said that she had lost Self in Service; it would perhaps be truer to say that she had asserted Self in Service; but she was quite in good faith about the service. Therefore her outstanding starry blue eyes really struck outwards, as in the old metaphor that made eyes like Cupid's darts, killing at a distance; but with an abstract conception of conquest beyond any mere coquetry. Her pale fair hair, though arranged in a saintly halo, had a look of almost electric radiation. And when she understood that the stranger before her was Mr Agar Rock, of the Minneapolis Meteor, her eyes took on themselves the range of long searchlights, sweeping the horizon of the States.

But in this the lady was mistaken; as she sometimes was. For Agar Rock was not Agar Rock of the Minneapolis Meteor. He was at that moment merely Agar Rock; there had surged up in him a great and sincere moral impulsion, beyond the coarse courage of the interviewer. A feeling profoundly mixed of a chivalrous and national sensibility to beauty, with an instant itch for moral action of some definite sort, which was also national, nerved him to face a great scene; and to deliver a noble insult. He remembered the original Hypatia, the beautiful Neo-Platonist, and how he had been thrilled as a boy by Kingsley's romance in which the young monk denounces her for harlotries and idolatries. He confronted her with an iron gravity and said:

'If you'll pardon me. Madam, I should like to have a word with you in private.'

'Well,' she said, sweeping the room with her splendid gaze, 'I don't know whether you consider this place private.'

Rock also gazed round the room and could see no sign of life less vegetable than the orange trees, except what looked like a large black mushroom, which he recognized as the hat of some native priest or other, stolidly smoking a black local cigar, and otherwise as stagnant as any vegetable. He looked for a moment at the heavy, expressionless features, noting the rudeness of that peasant type from which priests so often come, in Latin and especially Latin-American countries; and lowered his voice a little as he laughed.

'I don't imagine that Mexican padre knows our language,' he said. 'Catch those lumps of laziness learning any language but their own. Oh, I can't swear he's a Mexican; he might be anything; mongrel Indian or nigger, I suppose. But I'll answer for it he's not an American. Our ministries don't produce that debased type.'

'As a matter of fact,' said the debased type, removing his black cigar, 'I'm english and my name is Brown. But pray let me leave you if you wish to be private.'

'If you're English,' said Rock warmly, 'you ought to have some normal Nordic instinct for protesting against all this nonsense. Well, it's enough to say now that I'm in a position to testify that there's a pretty dangerous fellow hanging round this place; a tall fellow in a cloak, like those pictures of crazy poets.'

'Well, you can't go much by that,' said the priest mildly; 'a lot of people round here use those cloaks, because the chill strikes very suddenly after sunset.'

Rock darted a dark and doubtful glance at him; as if suspecting some evasion in the interests of all that was symbolized to him by mushroom hats and moonshine. 'It wasn't only the cloak,' he growled, 'though it was partly the way he wore it. The whole look of the fellow was theatrical, down to his damned theatrical good looks. And if you'll forgive me, Madam, I strongly advise you to have nothing to do with him, if he comes bothering here. Your husband has already told the hotel people to keep him out—'

Hypatia sprang to her feet and, with a very unusual gesture, covered her face, thrusting her fingers into her hair. She seemed to be shaken, possibly with sobs, but by the time she had recovered they had turned into a sort of wild laughter.

'Oh, you are all too funny,' she said, and, in a way very unusual with her, ducked and darted to the door and disappeared.

'Bit hysterical when they laugh like that,' said Rock uncomfortably; then, rather at a loss, and turning to the little priest: 'as I say, if you're English, you ought really to be on my side against these Dagos, anyhow. Oh, I'm not one of those who talk tosh about Anglo-Saxons; but there is such a thing as history. You can always claim that America got her civilization from England.'

'Also, to temper our pride,' said Father Brown, 'we must always admit that England got her civilization from Dagos.'

Again there glowed in the other's mind the exasperated sense that his interlocutor was fencing with him, and fencing on the wrong side, in some secret and evasive way; and he curtly professed a failure to comprehend.

'Well, there was a Dago, or possibly a Wop, called Julius Caesar,' said Father Brown; 'he was afterwards killed in a stabbing match; you know these Dagos always use knives. And there was another one called Augustine, who brought Christianity to our little island; and really, I don't think we should have had much civilization without those two.'

'Anyhow, that's all ancient history,' said the somewhat irritated journalist, 'and I'm very much interested in modern history. What I see is that these scoundrels are bringing Paganism to our country, and destroying all the Christianity there is. Also destroying all the common sense there is. All settled habits, all solid social order, all the way in which the farmers who were our fathers and grandfathers did manage to live in the world, melted into a hot mush by sensations and sensualities about filmstars who divorced every month or so, and make every silly girl think that marriage is only a way of getting divorced.'

'You are quite right,' said Father Brown. 'Of course I quite agree with you there. But you must make some allowances. Perhaps these Southern people are a little prone to that sort of fault. You must remember that Northern people have other kinds of faults. Perhaps these surroundings do encourage people to give too rich an importance to mere romance.'

The whole integral indignation of Agar Rock's life rose up within him at the word.

'I hate Romance,' he said, hitting the little table before him. 'I've fought the papers I worked for for forty years about the infernal trash. Every blackguard bolting with a barmaid is called a romantic elopement or something; and now our own Hypatia Hard, a daughter of a decent people, may get dragged into some rotten romantic divorce case, that will be trumpeted to the whole world as happily as a royal wedding. This mad poet Romanes is hanging round her; and you bet the spotlight will follow him, as if he were any rotten little Dago who is called the Great Lover on the films. I saw him outside; and he's got the regular spotlight face. Now my sympathies are with decency and common sense. My sympathies are with poor Potter, a plain straightforward broker from Pittsburgh, who thinks he has a right to his own home. And he's making a fight for it, too. I heard him hollering at the management, telling them to keep that rascal out; and quite right too. The people here seem a sly and slinky lot; but I rather fancy he's put the fear of God into them already.'

'As a matter of fact,' said Father Brown, 'I rather agree with you about the manager and the men in this hotel; but you mustn't judge all Mexicans by them. Also I fancy the gentleman you speak of has not only hollered, but handed round dollars enough to get the whole staff on his side. I saw them locking doors and whispering most excitedly. By the way, your plain straightforward friend seems to have a lot of money.'

'I've no doubt his business does well,' said Rock. 'He's quite the best type of sound businessman. What do you mean?'

'I fancied it might suggest another thought to you,' said Father Brown; and, rising with rather heavy civility, he left the room.

Rock watched the Potters very carefully that evening at dinner; and gained some new impressions, though none that disturbed his deep sense of the wrong that probably threatened the peace of the Potter home. Potter himself proved worthy of somewhat closer study; though the journalist had at first accepted him as prosaic and unpretentious, there was a pleasure in recognizing finer lines in what he considered the hero or victim of a tragedy. Potter had really rather a thoughtful and distinguished face, though worried and occasionally petulant. Rock got an impression that the man was recovering from an illness; his faded hair was thin but rather long, as if it had been lately neglected, and his rather unusual beard gave the onlooker the same notion. Certainly he spoke once or twice to his wife in a rather sharp and acid manner, fussing about tablets or some detail of digestive science; but his real worry was doubtless concerned with the danger from without. His wife played up to him in the splendid if somewhat condescending manner of a Patient Griselda; but her eyes also roamed continually to the doors and shutters, as if in half-hearted fear of an invasion. Rock had only too good reason to dread, after her curious outbreak, the fact that her fear might turn out to be only half-hearted.

It was in the middle of the night that the extraordinary event occurred. Rock, imagining himself to be the last to go up to bed, was surprised to find Father Brown still tucked obscurely under an orange-tree in the hall, and placidly reading a book. He returned the other's farewell without further words, and the journalist had his foot on the lowest step of the stair, when suddenly the outer door sprang on its hinges and shook and rattled under the shock of blows planted from without; and a great voice louder than the blows was heard violently demanding admission. Somehow the journalist was certain that the blows had been struck with a pointed stick like an alpenstock. He looked back at the darkened lower floor, and saw the servants of the hotel sliding here and there to see that the doors were locked; and not unlocking them. Then he slowly mounted to his room, and sat down furiously to write his report.

He described the siege of the hotel; the evil atmosphere; the shabby luxury of the place; the shifty evasions of the priest; above all, that terrible voice crying without, like a wolf prowling round the house. Then, as he wrote, he heard a new sound and sat up suddenly. It was a long repeated whistle, and in his mood he hated it doubly, because it was like the signal of a conspirator and like the love-call of a bird. There followed an utter silence, in which he sat rigid; then he rose abruptly; for he had heard yet another noise. It was a faint swish followed by a sharp rap or rattle; and he was almost certain that somebody was throwing something at the window. He walked stiffly downstairs, to the floor which was now dark and deserted; or nearly deserted. For the little priest was still sitting under the orange shrub, lit by a low lamp; and still reading his book.

'You seem to be sitting up late,' he said harshly.

'Quite a dissipated character,' said Father Brown, looking up with a broad smile, 'reading Economics of Usury at all wild hours of the night.'

'The place is locked up,' said Rock.

'Very thoroughly locked up,' replied the other. 'Your friend with the beard seems to have taken every precaution. By the way, your friend with the beard is a little rattled; I thought he was rather cross at dinner.'

'Natural enough,' growled the other, 'if he thinks savages in this savage place are out to wreck his home life.'

'Wouldn't it be better,' said Father Brown, 'if a man tried to make his home life nice inside, while he was protecting it from the things outside.'

'Oh, I know you will work up all the casuistical excuses,' said the other; 'perhaps he was rather snappy with his wife; but he's got the right on his side. Look here, you seem to me to be rather a deep dog. I believe you know more about this than you say. What the devil is going on in this infernal place? Why are you sitting up all night to see it through?'

'Well,' said Father Brown patiently, 'I rather thought my bedroom might be wanted.'

'Wanted by whom?'

'As a matter of fact, Mrs Potter wanted another room,' explained Father Brown with limpid clearness. 'I gave her mine, because I could open the window. Go and see, if you like.'

'I'll see to something else first,' said Rock grinding his teeth. 'You can play your monkey tricks in this Spanish monkey-house, but I'm still in touch with civilization.' He strode into the telephone-booth and rang up his paper; pouring out the whole tale of the wicked priest who helped the wicked poet. Then he ran upstairs into the priest's room, in which the priest had just lit a short candle, showing the windows beyond wide open.

He was just in time to see a sort of rude ladder unhooked from the windowsill and rolled up by a laughing gentleman on the lawn below. The laughing gentleman was a tall and swarthy gentleman, and was accompanied by a blonde but equally laughing lady. This time, Mr Rock could not even comfort himself by calling her laughter hysterical. It was too horribly genuine; and rang down the rambling garden-paths as she and her troubadour disappeared into the dark thickets.

Agar Rock turned on his companion a face of final and awful justice; like the Day of Judgement.

'Well, all America is going to hear of this,' he said. 'In plain words, you helped her to bolt with that curly-haired lover.'

'Yes,' said Father Brown, 'I helped her to bolt with that curly-haired lover.'

'You call yourself a minister of Jesus Christ,' cried Rock, 'and you boast of a crime.'

'I have been mixed up with several crimes,' said the priest gently. 'Happily for once this is a story without a crime. This is a simple fireside idyll; that ends with a glow of domesticity.'

'And ends with a rope-ladder instead of a rope,' said Rock. 'Isn't she a married woman?'

'Oh, yes,' said Father Brown.

'Well, oughtn't she to be with her husband?' demanded Rock.

'She is with her husband,' said Father Brown.

The other was startled into anger. 'You lie,' he said. 'The poor little man is still snoring in bed.'

'You seem to know a lot about his private affairs,' said Father Brown plaintively. 'You could almost write a life of the Man with a Beard. The only thing you don't seem ever to have found out about him is his name.'

'Nonsense,' said Rock. 'His name is in the hotel book.'

'I know it is,' answered the priest, nodding gravely, 'in very large letters; the name of Rudel Romanes. Hypatia Potter, who met him here, put her name boldly under his, when she meant to elope with him; and her husband put his name under that, when he pursued them to this place. He put it very close under hers, by way of protest. The Romanes (who has pots of money, as a popular misanthrope despising men) bribed the brutes in this hotel to bar and bolt it and keep the lawful husband out. And I, as you truly say, helped him to get in.'

When a man is told something that turns things upside-down; that the tail wags the dog; that the fish has caught the fisherman; that the earth goes round the moon; he takes some little time before he even asks seriously if it is true. He is still content with the consciousness that it is the opposite of the obvious truth. Rock said at last: 'You don't mean that little fellow is the romantic Rudel we're always reading about; and that curly haired fellow is Mr Potter of Pittsburgh.'

'Yes,' said Father Brown. 'I knew it the moment I clapped eyes on both of them. But I verified it afterwards.'

Rock ruminated for a time and said at last: 'I suppose it's barely possible you're right. But how did you come to have such a notion, in the face of the facts?'

Father Brown looked rather abashed; subsided into a chair, and stared into vacancy, until a faint smile began to dawn on his round and rather foolish face.

'Well,' he said, 'you see—the truth is, I'm not romantic.'

'I don't know what the devil you are,' said Rock roughly.

'Now you are romantic,' said Father Brown helpfully. 'For instance, you see somebody looking poetical, and you assume he is a poet. Do you know what the majority of poets look like? What a wild confusion was created by that coincidence of three good-looking aristocrats at the beginning of the nineteenth century: Byron and Goethe and Shelley! Believe me, in the common way, a man may write: "Beauty has laid her flaming lips on mine," or whatever that chap wrote, without being himself particularly beautiful. Besides, do you realize how old a man generally is by the time his fame has filled the world? Watts painted Swinburne with a halo of hair; but Swinburne was bald before most of his last American or Australian admirers had heard of his hyacinthine locks. So was D'Annunzio. As a fact, Romanes still has rather a fine head, as you will see if you look at it closely; he looks like an intellectual man; and he is. Unfortunately, like a good many other intellectual men, he's a fool. He's let himself go to seed with selfishness and fussing about his digestion. So that the ambitious American lady, who thought it would be like soaring to olympus with the Nine

Muses to elope with a poet, found that a day or so of it was about enough for her. So that when her husband came after her, and stormed the place, she was delighted to go back to him.'

'But her husband?' queried Rock. 'I am still rather puzzled about her husband.'

'Ah, you've been reading too many of your erotic modern novels,' said Father Brown; and partly closed his eyes in answer to the protesting glare of the other. 'I know a lot of stories start with a wildly beautiful woman wedded to some elderly swine in the stock market. But why? In that, as in most things, modern novels are the very reverse of modern. I don't say it never happens; but it hardly ever happens now except by her own fault. Girls nowadays marry whom they like; especially spoilt girls like Hypatia. And whom do they marry? A beautiful wealthy girl like that would have a ring of admirers; and whom would she choose? The chances are a hundred to one that she'd marry very young and choose the handsomest man she met at a dance or a tennis-party. Well, ordinary business men are sometimes handsome. A young god appeared (called Potter) and she wouldn't care if he was a broker or a burglar. But, given the environment, you will admit it's more likely he would be a broker; also, it's quite likely that he'd be called Potter. You see, you are so incurably romantic that your whole case was founded on the idea that a man looking like a young god couldn't be called Potter. Believe me, names are not so appropriately distributed.'

'Well,' said the other, after a short pause, 'and what do you suppose happened after that?'

Father Brown got up rather abruptly from the seat in which he had collapsed; the candlelight threw the shadow of his short figure across the wall and ceiling, giving an odd impression that the balance of the room had been altered.

'Ah,' he muttered, 'that's the devil of it. That's the real devil. Much worse than the old Indian demons in this jungle. You thought I was only making out a case for the loose ways of these Latin Americans—well, the queer thing about you'—and he blinked owlishly at the other through his spectacles—'the queerest thing about you is that in a way you're right.

'You say down with romance. I say I'd take my chance in fighting the genuine romances—all the more because they are precious few, outside the first fiery days of youth. I say—take away the Intellectual Friendships; take away the Platonic Unions; take away the Higher Laws of Self-Fulfilment and the rest, and I'll risk the normal dangers of the job. Take away the love that isn't love, but only pride and vainglory and publicity and making a splash; and we'll take our chance of fighting the love that is love, when it has to be fought, as well as the love that is lust and lechery. Priests know young people will have passions, as doctors know they will have measles. But Hypatia Potter is forty if she is a day, and she cares no more for that little poet than if he were her publisher or her publicity man. That's just the point—he was her publicity man. It's your newspapers that have ruined her; it's living in the limelight; it's wanting to see herself in the headlines, even in a scandal if it were only sufficiently psychic and superior. It's wanting to be George Sand, her name immortally linked with Alfred de Musset. When her real romance of youth was over, it was the sin of middle age that got hold of her; the sin of intellectual ambition. She hasn't got any intellect to speak of; but you don't need any intellect to be an intellectual.'

'I should say she was pretty brainy in one sense,' observed Rock reflectively.

'Yes, in one sense,' said Father Brown. 'In only one sense. In a business sense. Not in any sense that has anything to do with these poor lounging Dagos down here. You curse the film stars and tell me you hate romance. Do you suppose the film star, who is married for the fifth time, is misled by any romance? Such people are very practical; more practical than you are. You say you admire the simple solid businessman. Do you suppose that Rudel Romanes isn't a businessman? Can't you see he knew, quite as well as she did, the advertising advantages of this grand affair with a famous beauty. He also knew very well that his hold on it was pretty insecure; hence his fussing about and bribing servants to lock doors. But what I mean to say, first and last, is that there'd be a lot less scandal if people didn't idealize sin and pose as sinners. These poor Mexicans may seem sometimes to live like beasts, or rather sin like men; but they don't go in for Ideals. You must at least give them credit for that.'

He sat down again, as abruptly as he had risen, and laughed apologetically. 'Well, Mr Rock,' he said, 'that is my complete confession; the whole horrible story of how I helped a romantic elopement. You can do what you like with it.'

'In that case,' said Rock, rising, 'I will go to my room and make a few alterations in my report. But, first of all, I must ring up my paper and tell them I've been telling them a pack of lies.'

Not much more than half an hour had passed, between the time when Rock had telephoned to say the priest was helping the poet to run away with the lady, and the time when he telephoned to say that the priest had prevented the poet from doing precisely the same thing. But in that short interval of time was born and enlarged and scattered upon the winds the Scandal of Father Brown. The truth is still half an hour behind the slander; and nobody can be certain when or where it will catch up with it. The garrulity of pressmen and the eagerness of enemies had spread the first story through the city, even before it appeared in the first printed version. It was instantly corrected and contradicted by Rock himself, in a second message stating how the story had really ended; but it was by no means certain that the first story was killed. A positively incredible number of people seemed to have read the first issue of the paper and not the second. Again and again, in every corner of the world, like a flame bursting from blackened ashes, there would appear the old tale of the Brown Scandal, or Priest Ruins Potter Home. Tireless apologists of the priest's party watched for it, and patiently tagged after it with contradictions and exposures and letters of protest. Sometimes the letters were published in the papers; and sometimes they were not. But still nobody knew how many people had heard the story without hearing the contradiction. It was possible to find whole blocks of blameless and innocent people who thought the Mexican Scandal was an ordinary recorded historical incident like the Gunpowder Plot. Then somebody would enlighten these simple people, only to discover that the old story had started afresh among a few quite educated people, who would seem the last people on earth to be duped by it. And so the two Father Browns chase each other round the world forever; the first a shameless criminal fleeing from justice; the second a martyr broken by slander, in a halo of rehabilitation. But neither of them is very like the real Father Brown, who is not broken at all; but goes stumping with his stout umbrella through life, liking most of the people in it; accepting the world as his companion, but never as his judge.

2

THE QUICK ONE

(First published in *The Saturday Evening Post*, Nov 25, 1933)

The strange story of the incongruous strangers is still remembered along that strip of the Sussex coast, where the large and quiet hotel called the Maypole and Garland looks across its own gardens to the sea. Two quaintly assorted figures did, indeed, enter that quiet hotel on that sunny afternoon; one being conspicuous in the sunlight, and visible over the whole shore, by the fact of wearing a lustrous green turban, surrounding a brown face and a black beard; the other would have seemed to some even more wild and weird, by reason of his wearing a soft black clergyman's hat with a yellow moustache and yellow hair of leonine length. He at least had often been seen preaching on the sands or conducting Band of Hope services with a little wooden spade; only he had certainly never been seen going into the bar of an hotel. The arrival of these quaint companions was the climax of the story, but not the beginning of it; and, in order to make a rather mysterious story as clear as possible, it is better to begin at the beginning.

Half an hour before those two conspicuous figures entered the hotel, and were noticed by everybody, two other very inconspicuous figures had also entered it, and been noticed by nobody. One was a large man, and handsome in a heavy style, but he had a knack of taking up very little room, like a background; only an almost morbidly suspicious examination of his boots would have told anybody that he was an Inspector of Police in plain clothes; in very plain clothes. The other was a drab and insignificant little man, also in plain clothes, only that they happened to be clerical clothes; but nobody had ever seen him preaching on the sands.

These travellers also found themselves in a sort of large smoking-room with a bar, for a reason which determined all the events of that tragic afternoon. The truth is that the respectable hotel called the Maypole and Garland was being 'done-up'. Those who had liked it in the past were moved to say that it was being done down; or possibly done in. This was the opinion of the local grumbler, Mr Raggley, the eccentric old gentleman who drank cherry brandy in a corner and cursed. Anyhow, it was being carefully stripped of all the stray indications that it had once been an English inn; and being busily turned, yard by yard and room by room, into something resembling the sham palace of a Levantine usurer in an American film. It was, in short, being 'decorated'; but the only part where the decoration was complete, and where customers could yet be made comfortable, was this large room leading out of the hall. It had once been honourably known as a Bar Parlour and was now mysteriously known as a Saloon Lounge, and was newly 'decorated', in the manner of an Asiatic Divan. For Oriental ornament pervaded the new scheme; and where there had once been a gun hung on hooks, and sporting prints and a stuffed fish in a glass case, there were now festoons of Eastern drapery and trophies of scimitars, tulwards and yataghans, as if in unconscious preparation for the coming of the gentleman with the turban. The practical point was, however, that the few guests who did arrive had to be shepherded into this lounge, now swept and garnished, because all the more regular and refined parts of the hotel were still in a state of transition. Perhaps that was also the reason why even those few guests were somewhat neglected, the manager and others being occupied with explanations or exhortations elsewhere. Anyhow, the first two travellers who arrived had to kick their heels for some time unattended. The bar was at the moment entirely empty, and the Inspector rang and rapped impatiently on the counter; but the little clergyman had already dropped into a lounge seat and seemed in no hurry for anything. Indeed his friend the policeman, turning his head, saw that the round face of the little cleric had gone quite blank, as it had a way of doing sometimes; he seemed to be staring through his moonlike spectacles at the newly decorated wall.

'I may as well offer you a penny for your thoughts,' said Inspector Greenwood, turning from the counter with a sigh, 'as nobody seems to want my pennies for anything else. This seems to be the only room in the house that isn't full of ladders and whitewash; and this is so empty that there isn't even a potboy to give me a pot of beer.'

'Oh... my thoughts are not worth a penny, let alone a pot of beer,' answered the cleric, wiping his spectacles, 'I don't know why... but I was thinking how easy it would be to commit a murder here.'

'It's all very well for you. Father Brown,' said the Inspector good-humouredly. 'You've had a lot more murders than your fair share; and we poor policemen sit starving all our lives, even for a little one. But why should you say... Oh I see, you're looking at all those Turkish daggers on the wall. There are plenty of things to commit a murder with, if that's what you mean. But not more than there are in any ordinary kitchen: carving knives or pokers or what not. That isn't where the snag of a murder comes in.'

Father Brown seemed to recall his rambling thoughts in some bewilderment; and said that he supposed so.

'Murder is always easy,' said Inspector Greenwood. 'There can't possibly be anything more easy than murder. I could murder you at this minute—more easily than I can get a drink in this damned bar. The only difficulty is committing a murder without committing oneself as a murderer. It's this shyness about owning up to a murder; it's this silly modesty of murderers about their own masterpieces, that makes the trouble. They will stick to this extraordinary fixed idea of killing people without being found out; and that's what restrains them, even in a room full of daggers. Otherwise every cutler's shop would be piled with corpses. And that, by the way, explains the one kind of murder that really can't be prevented. Which is why, of course, we poor bobbies are always blamed for not preventing it. When a madman murders a King or a President, it can't be prevented. You can't make a King live in a coal-cellar, or carry about a President in a steel box. Anybody can murder him who does not mind being a murderer. That is where the madman is like the martyr—sort of beyond this world. A real fanatic can always kill anybody he likes.'

Before the priest could reply, a joyous band of bagmen rolled into the room like a shoal of porpoises; and the magnificent bellow of a big, beaming man, with an equally big and beaming tie-pin, brought the eager and obsequious manager running like a dog to the whistle, with a rapidity which the police in plain clothes had failed to inspire.

'I'm sure I'm very sorry, Mr Jukes,' said the manager, who wore a rather agitated smile and a wave or curl of very varnished hair across his forehead. 'We're rather understaffed at present; and I had to attend to something in the hotel, Mr Jukes.'

Mr Jukes was magnanimous, but in a noisy way; and ordered drinks all round, conceding one even to the almost cringing manager. Mr Jukes was a traveller for a very famous and fashionable wine and spirits firm; and may have conceived himself as lawfully the leader in such a place. Anyhow, he began a boisterous monologue, rather tending to tell the manager how to manage his hotel; and the others seemed to accept him as an authority. The policeman and the priest had retired to a low bench and small table in the background, from which they watched events, up to that rather remarkable moment when the policeman had very decisively to intervene.

For the next thing that happened, as already narrated, was the astonishing apparition of a brown Asiatic in a green turban, accompanied by the (if possible) more astonishing apparition of a noncomformist minister; omens such as appear before a doom. In this case there was no doubt about evidence for the portent. A taciturn but observant boy cleaning the steps for the last hour (being a leisurely worker), the dark, fat, bulky bar-attendant, even the diplomatic but distracted manager, all bore witness to the miracle.

The apparitions, as the sceptics say, were due to perfectly natural causes. The man with the mane of yellow hair and the semi-clerical clothes was not only familiar as a preacher on the sands, but as a propagandist throughout the modern world. He was no less a person than the Rev. David Pryce-Jones, whose far-resounding slogan was Prohibition and Purification for Our Land and the Britains Overseas. He as an excellent public speaker and organizer; and an idea had occurred to him that ought to have occurred to Prohibitionists long ago. It was the simple idea that, if Prohibition is right, some honour is due to the Prophet who was perhaps the first Prohibitionist. He had corresponded with the leaders of Mahommedan religious thought, and had finally induced a distinguished Moslem (one of whose names was Akbar and the rest an untranslatable ululation of Allah with attributes) to come and lecture in England on the ancient Moslem veto on wine. Neither of them certainly had been in a public-house bar before; but they had come there by the process already described; driven from the genteel tea-rooms, shepherded into the newly-decorated saloon. Probably all would have been well, if the great Prohibitionist, in his innocence, had not advanced to the counter and asked for a glass of milk.

The commercial travellers, though a kindly race, emitted involuntary noises of pain; a murmur of suppressed jests was heard, as 'Shun the bowl,' or 'Better bring out the cow'. But the magnificent Mr Jukes, feeling it due to his wealth and tie-pin to produce more refined humour, fanned himself as one about to faint, and said pathetically: 'They know they can knock me down with a feather. They know a breath will blow me away. They know my doctor says I'm not to have these shocks. And they come and drink cold milk in cold blood, before my very eyes.'

The Rev. David Pryce-Jones, accustomed to deal with hecklers at public meetings, was so unwise as to venture on remonstrance and recrimination, in this very different and much more popular atmosphere. The Oriental total abstainer abstained from speech as well as spirits; and certainly gained in dignity by doing so. In fact, so far as he was concerned, the Moslem culture certainly scored a silent victory; he was obviously so much more of a gentleman than the commercial gentlemen, that a faint irritation began to arise against his aristocratic aloofness; and when Mr Pryce-Jones began to refer in argument to something of the kind, the tension became very acute indeed.

'I ask you, friends,' said Mr Pryce-Jones, with expansive platform gestures, 'why does our friend here set an example to us Christians in truly Christian self-control and brotherhood? Why does he stand here as a model of true Christianity, of real refinement, of genuine gentlemanly behaviour, amid all the quarrels and riots of such places as these? Because, whatever the doctrinal differences between us, at least in his soil the evil plant, the accursed hop or vine, has never—'

At this crucial moment of the controversy it was that John Raggley, the stormy petrel of a hundred storms of controversy, red-faced, white-haired, his antiquated top hat on the back of his head, his stick swinging like a club, entered the house like an invading army.

John Raggley was generally regarded as a crank. He was the sort of man who writes letters to the newspaper, which generally do not appear in the newspaper; but which do appear afterwards as pamphlets, printed (or misprinted) at his own expense; and circulated to a hundred waste-paper baskets. He had quarrelled alike with the Tory squires and the Radical County Councils; he hated Jews; and he distrusted nearly everything that is sold in shops, or even in hotels. But there was a backing of facts behind his fads; he knew the county in every corner and curious detail; and he was a sharp observer. Even the manager, a Mr Wills, had a shadowy respect for Mr Raggley, having a nose for the sort of lunacy allowed in the gentry; not indeed the prostrate reverence which he had for the jovial magnificence of Mr Jukes, who was really good for trade, but a least a disposition to avoid quarrelling with the old grumbler, partly perhaps out of fear of the old grumbler's tongue.

'And you will have your usual, Sir,' said Mr Wills, leaning and leering across the counter.

'It's the only decent stuff you've still got,' snorted Mr Raggley, slapping down his queer and antiquated hat. 'Damn it, I sometimes think the only English thing left in England is cherry brandy. Cherry brandy does taste of cherries. Can you find me any beer that tastes of hops, or any cider that tastes of apples, or any wine that has the remotest indication of being made out of grapes? There's an infernal swindle going on now in every inn in the country, that would have raised a revolution in any other country. I've found out a thing or two about it, I can tell you. You wait till I can get it printed, and people will sit up. If I could stop our people being poisoned with all this bad drink—'

Here again the Rev. David Pryce-Jones showed a certain failure in tact; though it was a virtue he almost worshipped. He was so unwise as to attempt to establish an alliance with Mr Raggley, by a fine confusion between the idea of bad drink and the idea that drink is bad. Once more he endeavoured to drag his stiff and stately Eastern friend into the argument, as a refined foreigner superior to our rough English ways. He was even so foolish as to talk of a broad theological outlook; and ultimately to mention the name of Mahomet, which was echoed in a sort of explosion.

'God damn your soul!' roared Mr Raggley, with a less broad theological outlook. 'Do you mean that Englishmen mustn't drink English beer, because wine was forbidden in a damned desert by that dirty old humbug Mahomet?'

In an instant the Inspector of Police had reached the middle of the room with a stride. For, the instant before that, a remarkable change had taken place in the demeanour of the Oriental gentleman, who had hitherto stood perfectly still, with steady and shining eyes. He now proceeded, as his friend had said, to set an example in truly Christian self-control and brotherhood by reaching the wall with the bound of a tiger, tearing down one of the heavy knives hanging there and sending it smack like a stone from a sling, so that it stuck quivering in the wall exactly half an inch above Mr Raggley's ear. It would undoubtedly have stuck quivering in Mr Raggley, if Inspector Greenwood had not been just in time to jerk the arm and deflect the aim. Father Brown continued in his seat, watching the scene with screwed-up eyes and a screw of something almost like a smile at the corners of his mouth, as if he saw something beyond the mere momentary violence of the quarrel.

And then the quarrel took a curious turn; which may not be understood by everybody, until men like Mr John Raggley are better understood than they are. For the red-faced old fanatic was standing up and laughing uproariously as if it were the best joke he had ever heard. All his snapping vituperation and bitterness seemed to have gone out of him; and he regarded the other fanatic, who had just tried to murder him, with a sort of boisterous benevolence.

'Blast your eyes,' he said, 'you're the first man I've met in twenty years!'

'Do you charge this man, Sir?' said the Inspector, looking doubtful.

'Charge him, of course not,' said Raggley. 'I'd stand him a drink if he were allowed any drinks. I hadn't any business to insult his religion; and I wish to God all you skunks had the guts to kill a man, I won't say for insulting your religion, because you haven't got any, but for insulting anything—even your beer.'

'Now he's called us all skunks,' said Father Brown to Greenwood, 'peace and harmony seem to be restored. I wish that teetotal lecturer could get himself impaled on his friend's knife; it was he who made all the mischief.'

As he spoke, the odd groups in the room were already beginning to break up; it had been found possible to clear the commercial room for the commercial travellers, and they adjourned to it, the potboy carrying a new round of drinks after them on a tray. Father Brown stood for a moment gazing at the glasses left on the counter; recognizing at once the ill-omened glass of milk, and another which smelt of whisky; and then turned just in time to see the parting between those two quaint figures, fanatics of the East and West. Raggley was still ferociously genial; there was still something a little darkling and sinister about the Moslem, which was perhaps natural; but he bowed himself out with grave gestures of dignified reconciliation; and there was every indication that the trouble was really over.

Some importance, however, continued attached, in the mind of Father Brown at least, to the memory and interpretation of those last courteous salutes between the combatants. Because curiously enough, when Father Brown came down very early next morning, to perform his religious duties in the neighbourhood, he found the long saloon bar, with its fantastic Asiatic decoration, filled with a dead white light of daybreak in which every detail was distinct; and one of the details was the dead body of John Raggley bent and crushed into a corner of the room, with the heavy-hilted crooked dagger rammed through his heart.

Father Brown went very softly upstairs again and summoned his friend the Inspector; and the two stood beside the corpse, in a house in which no one else was as yet stirring. 'We mustn't either assume or avoid the obvious,' said Greenwood after a silence, 'but it is well to remember, I think, what I was saying to you yesterday afternoon. It's rather odd, by the way, that I should have said it—yesterday afternoon.'

'I know,' said the priest, nodding with an owlish stare.

'I said,' observed Greenwood, 'that the one sort of murder we can't stop is murder by somebody like a religious fanatic. That brown fellow probably thinks that if he's hanged, he'll go straight to Paradise for defending the honour of the Prophet.'

'There is that, of course,' said Father Brown. 'It would be very reasonable, so to speak, of our Moslem friend to have stabbed him. And you may say we don't know of anybody else yet, who could at all reasonably have stabbed him. But... but I was thinking...' And his round face suddenly went blank again and all speech died on his lips.

'What's the matter now?' asked the other.

'Well, I know it sounds funny,' said Father Brown in a forlorn voice. 'But I was thinking ... I was thinking, in a way, it doesn't much matter who stabbed him.'

'Is this the new Morality?' asked his friend. 'Or the old Casuistry, perhaps. Are the Jesuits really going in for murder?'

'I didn't say it didn't matter who murdered him,' said Father Brown. 'Of course the man who stabbed him might possibly be the man who murdered him. But it might be quite a different man. Anyhow, it was done at quite a different time. I suppose you'll want to work on the hilt for fingerprints; but don't take too much notice of them. I can imagine other reasons for other people sticking this knife in the poor old boy. Not very edifying reasons, of course, but quite distinct from the murder. You'll have to put some more knives into him, before you find out about that.'

'You mean—' began the other, watching him keenly.

'I mean the autopsy,' said the priest, 'to find the real cause of death.'

'You're quite right, I believe,' said the Inspector, 'about the stabbing, anyhow. We must wait for the doctor; but I'm pretty sure he'll say you're right. There isn't blood enough. This knife was stuck in the corpse when it had been cold for hours. But why?'

'Possibly to put the blame on the Mahommedan,' answered Father Brown. 'Pretty mean, I admit, but not necessarily murder. I fancy there are people in this place trying to keep secrets, who are not necessarily murderers.'

'I haven't speculated on that line yet,' said Greenwood. 'What makes you think so?'

'What I said yesterday, when we first came into this horrible room. I said it would be easy to commit a murder here. But I wasn't thinking about all those stupid weapons, though you thought I was. About something quite different.'

For the next few hours the Inspector and his friend conducted a close and thorough investigation into the goings and comings of everybody for the last twenty-four hours, the way the drinks had been distributed, the glasses that were washed or unwashed, and every detail about every individual involved, or apparently not involved. One might have supposed they thought that thirty people had been poisoned, as well as one.

It seemed certain that nobody had entered the building except by the big entrance that adjoined the bar; all the others were blocked in one way or another by the repairs. A boy had been cleaning the steps outside this entrance; but he had nothing very clear to report. Until the amazing entry of the Turk in the Turban, with his teetotal lecturer, there did not seem to have been much custom of any kind, except for the commercial travellers who came in to take what they called 'quick ones'; and they seemed to have moved together, like Wordsworth's Cloud; there was a slight difference of opinion between the boy outside and the men inside about whether one of them had not been abnormally quick in obtaining a quick one, and come out on the doorstep by himself; but the manager and the barman had no memory of any such independent individual. The manager and the barman knew all the travellers quite well, and there was no doubt about their movements as a whole. They had stood at the bar chaffing and drinking; they had been involved, through their lordly leader, Mr Jukes, in a not very serious altercation with Mr Pryce-Jones; and they had witnessed the sudden and very serious altercation between Mr Akbar and Mr Raggley. Then they were told they could adjourn to the Commercial Room and did so, their drinks being borne after them like a trophy.

'There's precious little to go on,' said Inspector Greenwood. 'Of course a lot of officious servants must do their duty as usual, and was out all the glasses; including old Raggley's glass. If it weren't for everybody else's efficiency, we detectives might be quite efficient.'

'I know,' said Father Brown, and his mouth took on again the twisted smile. 'I sometimes think criminals invented hygiene. Or perhaps hygienic reformers invented crime; they look like it, some of them. Everybody talks about foul dens and filthy slums in which crime can run riot; but it's just the other way. They are called foul, not because crimes are committed, but because crimes are discovered. It's in the neat, spotless, clean and tidy places that crime can run riot; no mud to make footprints; no dregs to contain poison; kind servants washing out all traces of the murder; and the murderer killing and cremating six wives and all for want of a little Christian dirt. Perhaps I express myself with too much warmth—but look here. As it happens, I do remember one glass, which has doubtless been cleaned since, but I should like to know more about it."

'Do you mean Raggley's glass?' asked Greenwood.

'No; I mean Nobody's glass,' replied the priest. 'It stood near that glass of milk and it still held an inch or two of whisky. Well, you and I had no whisky. I happen to remember that the manager, when treated by the jovial Jukes, had "a drop of gin". I hope you don't suggest that our Moslem was a whisky-drinker disguised in a green turban; or that the Rev. David Pryce-Jones managed to drink whisky and milk together, without noticing it.'

'Most of the commercial travellers took whisky,' said the Inspector. 'They generally do.'

'Yes; and they generally see they get it too,' answered Father Brown. 'In this case, they had it all carefully carted after them to their own room. But this glass was left behind.'

'An accident, I suppose,' said Greenwood doubtfully. 'The man could easily get another in the Commercial Room afterwards.'

Father Brown shook his head. 'You've got to see people as they are. Now these sort of men—well, some call them vulgar and some common; but that's all likes and dislikes. I'd be content to say that they are mostly simple men. Lots of them very good men, very glad to go back to the missus and the kids; some of them might be blackguards; might have had several missuses; or even murdered several missuses. But most of them are simple men; and, mark you, just the least tiny bit drunk. Not much; there's many a duke or don at Oxford drunker; but when that sort of man is at that stage of conviviality, he simply can't help noticing things, and noticing them very loud. Don't you observe that the least little incident jerks them into speech; if the beer froths over, they froth over with it, and have to say, "Whoa, emma," or "Doing me proud, aren't you?" Now I should say it's flatly impossible for five of these festive beings to sit round a table in the Commercial Room, and have only four glasses set before them, the fifth man being left out, without making a shout about it. Probably they would make a shout about it. Certainly he would make a shout about it. He wouldn't wait, like an Englishman of another class, till he could get a drink quietly later. The air would resound with things like, "And what about little me?" or, "Here, George, have I joined the Band of Hope?" or, "Do you see any green in my turban, George?" But the barman heard no such complaints. I take it as certain that the glass of whisky left behind had been nearly emptied by somebody else; somebody we haven't thought about yet.'

'But can you think of any such person?' ask the other.

'It's because the manager and the barman won't hear of any such person, that you dismiss the one really independent piece of evidence; the evidence of that boy outside cleaning the steps. He says that a man, who well may have been a bagman, but who did not, in fact, stick to the other bagmen, went in and came out again almost immediately. The manager and the barman never saw him; or say they never saw him. But he got a glass of whisky from the bar somehow. Let us call him, for the sake of argument, The Quick One. Now you know I don't often interfere with your business, which I know you do better than I should do it, or should want to do it. I've never had anything to do with setting police machinery at work, or running down criminals, or anything like that. But, for the first time in my life, I want to do it now. I want you to find The Quick One; to follow The Quick One to the ends of the earth; to set the whole infernal official machinery at work like a dragnet across the nations, and jolly well recapture The Quick One. Because he is the man we want.'

Greenwood made a despairing gesture. 'Has he face or form or any visible quality except quickness?' he inquired.

'He was wearing a sort of Inverness cape,' said Father Brown, 'and he told the boy outside he must reach Edinburgh by next morning. That's all the boy outside remembers. But I know your organization has got on to people with less clue than that.'

'You seem very keen on this,' said the Inspector, a little puzzled.

The priest looked puzzled also, as if at his own thoughts; he sat with knotted brow and then said abruptly: 'You see, it's so easy to be misunderstood. All men matter. You matter. I matter. It's the hardest thing in theology to believe.'

The Inspector stared at him without comprehension; but he proceeded.

'We matter to God—God only knows why. But that's the only possible justification of the existence of policemen.' The policeman did not seem enlightened as to his own cosmic justification. 'Don't you see, the law really is right in a way, after all. If all men matter, all murders matter. That which He has so mysteriously created, we must not suffer to be mysteriously destroyed. But—'

He said the last word sharply, like one taking a new step in decision.

'But, when once I step off that mystical level of equality, I don't see that most of your important murders are particularly important. You are always telling me that this case and that is important. As a plain, practical man of the world, I must realize that it is the Prime Minister who has been murdered. As a plain, practical man of the world, I don't think that the Prime Minister matters at all. As a mere matter of human importance, I should say he hardly exists at all. Do you suppose if he and the other public men were shot dead tomorrow, there wouldn't be other people to stand up and say that every avenue was being explored, or that the Government had the matter under the gravest consideration? The masters of the modern world don't matter. Even the real masters don't matter much. Hardly anybody you ever read about in a newspaper matters at all.'

He stood up, giving the table a small rap: one of his rare gestures; and his voice changed again. 'But Raggley did matter. He was one of a great line of some half a dozen men who might have saved England. They stand up stark and dark like disregarded signposts, down all that smooth descending road which has ended in this swamp of merely commercial collapse. Dean Swift and Dr Johnson and old William Cobbett; they had all without exception the name of being surly or savage, and they were all loved by their friends, and they all deserved to be. Didn't you see how that old man, with the heart of a lion, stood up and forgave his enemy as only fighters can forgive? He jolly well did do what that temperance lecturer talked about; he set an example to us Christians and was a model of Christianity. And when there is foul and secret murder of a man like that—then I do think it matters, matters so much that even the modern machinery of police will be a thing that any respectable person may make use of ... Oh, don't mention it. And so, for once in a way, I really do want to make use of you.'

And so, for some stretch of those strange days and nights, we might almost say that the little figure of Father Brown drove before him into action all the armies and engines of the police forces of the Crown, as the little figure of Napoleon drove the batteries and the battle-lines of the vast strategy that covered Europe. Police stations and post offices worked all night; traffic was stopped, correspondence was intercepted, inquiries were made in a hundred places, in order to track the flying trail of that ghostly figure, without face or name, with an Inverness cape and an Edinburgh ticket.

Meanwhile, of course, the other lines of investigation were not neglected. The full report of the post-mortem had not yet come in; but everybody seemed certain that it was a case of poisoning. This naturally threw the primary suspicion upon the cherry brandy; and this again naturally threw the primary suspicion on the hotel.

'Most probably on the manager of the hotel,' said Greenwood gruffly. 'He looks a nasty little worm to me. Of course it might be something to do with some servant, like the barman; he seems rather a sulky specimen, and Raggley might have cursed him a bit, having a flaming temper, though he was generally generous enough afterwards. But, after all, as I say, the primary responsibility, and therefore the primary suspicion, rests on the manager.'

'Oh, I knew the primary suspicion would rest on the manager,' said Father Brown. 'That was why I didn't suspect him. You see, I rather fancied somebody else must have known that the primary suspicion would rest on the manager; or the servants of the hotel. That is why I said it would be easy to kill anybody in the hotel... But you'd better go and have it out with him, I suppose.'

The Inspector went; but came back again after a surprisingly short interview, and found his clerical friend turning over some papers that seemed to be a sort of dossier of the stormy career of John Raggley.

'This is a rum go,' said the Inspector. 'I thought I should spend hours cross-examining that slippery little toad there, for we haven't legally got a thing against him. And instead of that, he went to pieces all at once, and I really think he's told me all he knows in sheer funk.'

'I know,' said Father Brown. 'That's the way he went to pieces when he found Raggley's corpse apparently poisoned in his hotel. That's why he lost his head enough to do such a clumsy thing as decorate the corpse with a Turkish knife, to put the blame on the nigger, as he would say. There never is anything the matter with him but funk; he's the very last man that ever would really stick a knife into a live person. I bet he had to nerve himself to stick it into a dead one. But he's the very first person to be frightened of being charged with what he didn't do; and to make a fool of himself, as he did.'

'I suppose I must see the barman too,' observed Greenwood.

'I suppose so,' answered the other. 'I don't believe myself it was any of the hotel people—well, because it was made to look as if it must be the hotel people... But look here, have you seen any of this stuff they've got together about Raggley? He had a jolly interesting life; I wonder whether anyone will write his biography.'

'I took a note of everything likely to affect an affair like this,' answered the official. 'He was a widower; but he did once have a row with a man about his wife; a Scotch land-agent then in these parts; and Raggley seems to have been pretty violent. They say he hated Scotchmen; perhaps that's the reason... Oh, I know what you are smiling grimly about. A Scotchman... Perhaps an Edinburgh man.'

'Perhaps,' said Father Brown. 'It's quite likely, though, that he did dislike Scotchmen, apart from private reasons. It's an odd thing, but all that tribe of Tory Radicals, or whatever you call them, who resisted the Whig mercantile movement, all of them did dislike Scotchmen. Cobbett did; Dr Johnson did; Swift described their accent in one of his deadliest passages; even Shakespeare has been accused of the prejudice. But the prejudices of great men generally have something to do with principles. And there was a reason, I fancy. The Scot came from a poor agricultural land, that became a rich industrial land. He was able and active; he thought he was bringing industrial civilization from the north; he simply didn't know that there had been for centuries a rural civilization in the south. His own grandfather's land was highly rural but not civilized... Well, well, I suppose we can only wait for more news.'

'I hardly think you'll get the latest news out of Shakespeare and Dr Johnson,' grinned the police officer. 'What Shakespeare thought of Scotchmen isn't exactly evidence.'

Father Brown cocked an eyebrow, as if a new thought had surprised him. 'Why, now I come to think of it,' he said, 'there might be better evidence, even out of Shakespeare. He doesn't often mention Scotchmen. But he was rather fond of making fun of Welshmen.'

The Inspector was searching his friend's face; for he fancied he recognized an alertness behind its demure expression. 'By Jove,' he said. 'Nobody thought of turning the suspicions that way, anyhow.'

'Well,' said Father Brown, with broad-minded calm, 'you started by talking about fanatics; and how a fanatic could do anything. Well, I suppose we had the honour of entertaining in this bar-parlour yesterday, about the biggest and loudest and most fat-headed fanatic in the modern world. If being a pig-headed idiot with one idea is the way to murder, I put in a claim for my reverend brother Pryce-Jones, the Prohibitionist, in preference to all the fakirs in Asia, and it's perfectly true, as I told you, that his horrible glass of milk was standing side by side on the counter with the mysterious glass of whisky.'

'Which you think was mixed up with the murder,' said Greenwood, staring. 'Look here, I don't know whether you're really serious or not.'

Even as he was looking steadily in his friend's face, finding something still inscrutable in its expression, the telephone rang stridently behind the bar. Lifting the flap in the counter Inspector Greenwood passed rapidly inside, unhooked the receiver, listened for an instant, and then uttered a shout; not addressed to his interlocutor, but to the universe in general.

Then he listened still more attentively and said explosively at intervals, 'Yes, yes... Come round at once; bring him round if possible... Good piece of work... Congratulate you.'

Then Inspector Greenwood came back into the outer lounge, like a man who has renewed his youth, sat down squarely on his seat, with his hands planted on his knees, stared at his friend, and said:

'Father Brown, I don't know how you do it. You seem to have known he was a murderer before anybody else knew he was a man. He was nobody; he was nothing; he was a slight confusion in the evidence; nobody in the hotel saw him; the boy on the steps could hardly swear to him; he was just a fine shade of doubt founded on an extra dirty glass. But we've got him, and he's the man we want.'

Father Brown had risen with the sense of the crisis, mechanically clutching the papers destined to be so valuable to the biographer of Mr Raggley; and stood staring at his friend. Perhaps this gesture jerked his friend's mind to fresh confirmations.

'Yes, we've got The Quick One. And very quick he was, like quicksilver, in making his getaway; we only just stopped him—off on a fishing trip to Orkney, he said. But he's the man, all right; he's the Scotch land-agent who made love to Raggley's wife; he's the man who drank Scotch whisky in this bar and then took a train to Edinburgh. And nobody would have known it but for you.'

'Well, what I meant,' began Father Brown, in a rather dazed tone; and at that instant there was a rattle and rumble of heavy vehicles outside the hotel; and two or three other and subordinate policemen blocked the bar with their presence. One of them, invited by his superior to sit down, did so in an expansive manner, like one at once happy and fatigued; and he also regarded Father Brown with admiring eyes.

'Got the murderer. Sir, oh yes,' he said: 'I know he's a murderer, 'cause he bally nearly murdered me. I've captured some tough characters before now; but never one like this—hit me in the stomach like the kick of a horse and nearly got away from five men. Oh, you've got a real killer this time. Inspector.'

'Where is he?' asked Father Brown, staring.

'Outside in the van, in handcuffs,' replied the policeman, 'and, if you're wise, you'll leave him there—for the present.'

Father Brown sank into a chair in a sort of soft collapse; and the papers he had been nervously clutching were shed around him, shooting and sliding about the floor like sheets of breaking snow. Not only his face, but his whole body, conveyed the impression of a punctured balloon.

'Oh... Oh,' he repeated, as if any further oath would be inadequate. 'Oh... I've done it again.'

'If you mean you've caught the criminal again,' began Greenwood. But his friend stopped him with a feeble explosion, like that of expiring soda-water.

'I mean,' said Father Brown, 'that it's always happening; and really, I don't know why. I always try to say what I mean. But everybody else means such a lot by what I say.'

'What in the world is the matter now?' cried Greenwood, suddenly exasperated.

'Well, I say things,' said Father Brown in a weak voice, which could alone convey the weakness of the words. 'I say things, but everybody seems to know they mean more than they say. Once I saw a broken mirror and said "Something has happened" and they all answered, "Yes, yes, as you truly say, two men wrestled and one ran into the garden," and so on. I don't understand it, "Something happened," and "Two men wrestled," don't seem to me at all the same; but I dare say I read old books of logic. Well, it's like that here. You seem to be all certain this man is a murderer. But I never said he was a murderer. I said he was the man we wanted. He is. I want him very much. I want him frightfully. I want him as the one thing we haven't got in the whole of this horrible case—a witness!'

They all stared at him, but in a frowning fashion, like men trying to follow a sharp new turn of the argument; and it was he who resumed the argument.

'From the first minute I entered that big empty bar or saloon, I knew what was the matter with all this business was emptiness; solitude; too many chances for anybody to be alone. In a word, the absence of witnesses. All we knew was that when we came in, the manager and the barman were not in the bar. But when were they in the bar? What chance was there of making any sort of timetable of when anybody was anywhere? The whole thing was blank for want of witnesses. I rather fancy the barman or somebody was in the bar just before we came; and that's how the Scotchman got his Scotch whisky. He certainly didn't get it after we came. But we can't begin to inquire whether anybody in the hotel poisoned poor Raggley's cherry brandy, till we really know who was in the bar and when. Now I want you to do me another favour, in spite of this stupid muddle, which is probably all my fault. I want you to collect all the people involved in this room—I think they're all still available, unless the Asiatic has gone back to Asia—and then take the poor Scotchman out of his handcuffs, and bring him in here, and let him tell us who did serve him with whisky, and who was in the bar, and who else was in the room, and all the rest. He's the only man whose evidence can cover just that period when the crime was done. I don't see the slightest reason for doubting his word.'

'But look here,' said Greenwood. 'This brings it all back to the hotel authorities; and I thought you agreed that the manager isn't the murderer. Is it the barman, or what?'

'I don't know,' said the priest blankly. 'I don't know for certain even about the manager. I don't know anything about the barman. I fancy the manager might be a bit of a conspirator, even if he wasn't a murderer. But I do know there's one solitary witness on earth who may have seem something; and that's why I set all your police dogs on his trail to the ends of the earth.'

The mysterious Scotchman, when he finally appeared before the company thus assembled, was certainly a formidable figure; tall, with a hulking stride and a long sardonic hatchet face, with tufts of red hair; and wearing not only an Inverness cape but a Glengarry bonnet, he might well be excused for a somewhat acrid attitude; but anybody could see he was of the sort to resist arrest, even with violence. It was not surprising that he had come to blows with a fighting fellow like Raggley. It was not even surprising that the police had been convinced, by the mere details of capture, that he was a tough and a, typical killer. But he claimed to be a perfectly respectable farmer, in Aberdeenshire, his name being James Grant; and somehow not only Father Brown, but Inspector Greenwood, a shrewd man with a great deal of experience, was pretty soon convinced that the Scot's ferocity was the fury of innocence rather than guilt.

'Now what we want from you, Mr Grant,' said the Inspector gravely, dropping without further parley into tones of courtesy, 'is simply your evidence on one very important fact. I am greatly grieved at the misunderstanding by which you have suffered, but I am sure you wish to serve the ends of justice. I believe you came into this bar just after it opened, at half-past five, and were served with a glass of whisky. We are not certain what servant of the hotel, whether the barman or the manager or some subordinate, was in the bar at the time. Will you look round the room, and tell me whether the bar-attendant who served you is present here.'

'Aye, he's present,' said Mr Grant, grimly smiling, having swept the group with a shrewd glance. 'I'd know him anywhere;

and ye'll agree he's big enough to be seen. Do ye have all your inn-servants as grand as yon?'

The Inspector's eye remained hard and steady, and his voice colourless and continuous; the face of Father Brown was a blank; but on many other faces there was a cloud; the barman was not particularly big and not at all grand; and the manager was decidedly small.

'We only want the barman identified,' said the Inspector calmly. 'Of course we know him; but we should like you to verify it independently. You mean...?' And he stopped suddenly.

'Weel, there he is plain enough,' said the Scotchman wearily; and made a gesture, and with that gesture the gigantic Jukes, the prince of commercial travellers, rose like a trumpeting elephant; and in a flash had three policemen fastened on him like hounds on a wild beast.

'Well, all that was simple enough,' said Father Brown to his friend afterwards. 'As I told you, the instant I entered the empty bar-room, my first thought was that, if the barman left the bar unguarded like that, there was nothing in the world to stop you or me or anybody else lifting the flap and walking in, and putting poison in any of the bottles standing waiting for customers. Of course, a practical poisoner would probably do it as Jukes did, by substituting a poisoned bottle for the ordinary bottle; that could be done in a flash. It was easy enough for him, as he travelled in bottles, to carry a flask of cherry brandy prepared and of the same pattern. Of course, it requires one condition; but it's a fairly common condition. It would hardly do to start poisoning the beer or whisky that scores of people drink; it would cause a massacre. But when a man is well known as drinking only one special thing, like cherry brandy, that isn't very widely drunk, it's just like poisoning him in his own home. Only it's a jolly sight safer. For practically the whole suspicion instantly falls on the hotel, or somebody to do with the hotel; and there's no earthly argument to show that it was done by anyone out of a hundred customers that might come into the bar: even if people realized that a customer could do it. It was about as absolutely anonymous and irresponsible a murder as a man could commit.'

'And why exactly did the murderer commit it?' asked his friend.

Father Brown rose and gravely gathered the papers which he had previously scattered in a moment of distraction.

'May I recall your attention,' he said smiling, 'to the materials of the forthcoming *Life and Letters of the Late John Raggley?* Or, for that matter, his own spoken words? He said in this very bar that he was going to expose a scandal about the management of hotels; and the scandal was the pretty common one of a corrupt agreement between hotel proprietors and a salesman who took and gave secret commissions, so that his business had a monopoly of all the drink sold in the place. It wasn't even an open slavery like an ordinary tied house; it was a swindle at the expense of everybody the manager was supposed to serve. It was a legal offence. So the ingenious Jukes, taking the first moment when the bar was empty, as it often was, stepped inside and made the exchange of bottles; unfortunately at that very moment a Scotchman in an Inverness cape came in harshly demanding whisky. Jukes saw his only chance was to pretend to be the barman and serve the customer. He was very much relieved that the customer was a Quick One.'

'I think you're rather a Quick One yourself,' observed Greenwood; 'if you say you smelt something at the start, in the mere air of an empty room. Did you suspect Jukes at all at the start?'

'Well, he sounded rather rich somehow,' answered Father Brown vaguely. 'You know when a man has a rich voice. And I did sort of ask myself why he should have such a disgustingly rich voice, when all those honest fellows were fairly poor. But I think I knew he was a sham when I saw that big shining breast-pin.'

'You mean because it was sham?' asked Greenwood doubtfully.

'Oh, no; because it was genuine,' said Father Brown.

3

THE BLAST OF THE BOOK
(First published in *Liberty* Aug 26, 1933 as "The Five Fugitives")

Professor Openshaw always lost his temper, with a loud bang, if anybody called him a Spiritualist; or a believer in Spiritualism. This, however, did not exhaust his explosive elements; for he also lost his temper if anybody called him a disbeliever in Spiritualism. It was his pride to have given his whole life to investigating Psychic Phenomena; it was also his pride never to have given a hint of whether he thought they were really psychic or merely phenomenal. He enjoyed nothing so much as to sit in a circle of devout Spiritualists and give devastating descriptions of how he had exposed medium after medium and detected fraud after fraud; for indeed he was a man of much detective talent and insight, when once he had fixed his eye on an object, and he always fixed his eye on a medium, as a highly suspicious object. There was a story of his having spotted the same Spiritualist mountebank under three different disguises: dressed as a woman, a white-bearded old man, and a Brahmin of a rich chocolate brown. These recitals made the true believers rather restless, as indeed they were intended to do; but they could hardly complain, for no Spiritualist denies the existence of fraudulent mediums; only the Professor's flowing narrative might well seem to indicate that all mediums were fraudulent.

But woe to the simple-minded and innocent Materialist (and Materialists as a race are rather innocent and simple-minded) who, presuming on this narrative tendency, should advance the thesis that ghosts were against the laws of nature, or that such things were only old superstitions; or that it was all tosh, or, alternatively, bunk. Him would the Professor, suddenly reversing all his scientific batteries, sweep from the field with a cannonade of unquestionable cases and unexplained phenomena, of which the wretched rationalist had never heard in his life, giving all the dates and details, stating all the attempted and abandoned natural explanations; stating everything, indeed, except whether he, John Oliver Openshaw, did or did not believe in Spirits, and that neither Spiritualist nor Materialist could ever boast of finding out.

Professor Openshaw, a lean figure with pale leonine hair and hypnotic blue eyes, stood exchanging a few words with Father Brown, who was a friend of his, on the steps outside the hotel where both had been breakfasting that morning and sleeping the night before. The Professor had come back rather late from one of this grand experiments, in general exasperation, and was still tingling with the fight that he always waged alone and against both sides.

'Oh, I don't mind you,' he said laughing. 'You don't believe in it even if it's true. But all these people are perpetually asking me what I'm trying to prove. They don't seem to understand that I'm a man of science. A man of science isn't trying to prove anything. He's trying to find out what will prove itself.'

'But he hasn't found out yet,' said Father Brown.

'Well, I have some little notions of my own, that are not quite so negative as most people think,' answered the Professor, after an instant of frowning silence; 'anyhow, I've begun to fancy that if there is something to be found, they're looking for it along the wrong line. It's all too theatrical; it's showing off, all their shiny ectoplasm and trumpets and voices and the rest; all on the model of old melodramas and mouldy historical novels about the Family Ghost. If they'd go to history instead of historical novels, I'm beginning to think they'd really find something. But not Apparitions.'

'After all,' said Father Brown, 'Apparitions are only Appearances. I suppose you'd say the Family Ghost is only keeping up appearances.'

The Professor's gaze, which had commonly a fine abstracted character, suddenly fixed and focused itself as it did on a dubious medium. It had rather the air of a man screwing a strong magnifying-glass into his eye. Not that he thought the priest was in the least like a dubious medium; but he was startled into attention by his friend's thought following so closely on his own.

'Appearances!' he muttered, 'crikey, but it's odd you should say that just now. The more I learn, the more I fancy they lose by merely looking for appearances. Now if they'd look a little into Disappearances—'

'Yes,' said Father Brown, 'after all, the real fairy legends weren't so very much about the appearance of famous fairies; calling up Titania or exhibiting Oberon by moonlight. But there were no end of legends about people disappearing, because they were stolen by the fairies. Are you on the track of Kilmeny or Thomas the Rhymer?'

'I'm on the track of ordinary modern people you've read of in the newspapers,' answered Openshaw. 'You may well stare; but that's my game just now; and I've been on it for a long time. Frankly, I think a lot of psychic appearances could be explained away. It's the disappearances I can't explain, unless they're psychic. These people in the newspaper who vanish and are never found—if you knew the details as I do ... and now only this morning I got confirmation; an extraordinary letter from an old missionary, quite a respectable old boy. He's coming to see me at my office this morning. Perhaps you'd lunch with me or something; and I'd tell the results—in confidence.'

'Thanks; I will—unless,' said Father Brown modestly, 'the fairies have stolen me by then.'

With that they parted and Openshaw walked round the corner to a small office he rented in the neighbourhood; chiefly for the publication of a small periodical, of psychical and psychological notes of the driest and most agnostic sort. He had only one clerk, who sat at a desk in the outer office, totting up figures and facts for the purposes of the printed report; and the Professor paused to ask if Mr Pringle had called. The clerk answered mechanically in the negative and went on mechanically adding up figures; and the Professor turned towards the inner room that was his study. 'Oh, by the way, Berridge,' he added, without turning round, 'if Mr Pringle comes, send him straight in to me. You needn't interrupt your work; I rather want those notes finished tonight if possible. You might leave them on my desk tomorrow, if I am late.'

And he went into his private office, still brooding on the problem which the name of Pringle had raised; or rather, perhaps, had ratified and confirmed in his mind. Even the most perfectly balanced of agnostics is partially human; and it is possible that the missionary's letter seemed to have greater weight as promising to support his private and still tentative hypothesis. He sat down in his large and comfortable chair, opposite the engraving of Montaigne; and read once more the short letter from the Rev. Luke Pringle, making the appointment for that morning. No man knew better than Professor Openshaw the marks of the letter of the crank; the crowded details; the spidery handwriting; the unnecessary length and repetition. There were none of these things in this case; but a brief and businesslike typewritten statement that the writer had encountered some curious cases of disappearance, which seemed to fall within the province of the Professor as a student of psychic problems. The Professor was favourably impressed; nor had he any unfavourable impression, in spite of a slight movement of surprise, when he looked up and saw that the Rev. Luke Pringle was already in the room.

'Your clerk told me to come straight in,' said Mr Pringle apologetically, but with a broad and rather agreeable grin. The grin was partly masked by masses of reddish-grey beard and whiskers; a perfect jungle of a beard, such as is sometimes grown by white men living in the jungles; but the eyes above the snub nose had nothing about them in the least wild or outlandish. Openshaw had instantly turned on them that concentrated spotlight or burning-glass of sceptical scrutiny which he turned on many men to see if they were mountebanks or maniacs; and, in this case, he had a rather unusual sense of reassurance. The wild beard might have belonged to a crank, but the eyes completely contradicted the beard; they were full of that quite frank and friendly laughter which is never found in the faces of those who are serious frauds or serious lunatics. He would have expected a man with those eyes to be a Philistine, a jolly sceptic, a man who shouted out shallow but hearty contempt of ghosts and spirits; but anyhow, no professional humbug could afford to look as frivolous as that. The man was buttoned up to the throat in a shabby old cape, and only his broad limp hat suggested the cleric; but missionaries from wild places do not always bother to dress like clerics.

'You probably think all this another hoax. Professor,' said Mr Pringle, with a sort of abstract enjoyment, 'and I hope you will forgive my laughing at your very natural air of disapproval. All the same, I've got to tell my story to somebody who knows, because it's true. And, all joking apart, it's tragic as well as true. Well, to cut it short, I was missionary in Nya-Nya, a station in West Africa, in the thick of the forests, where almost the only other white man was the officer in command of the district,

Captain Wales; and he and I grew rather thick. Not that he liked missions; he was, if I may say so, thick in many ways; one of those square-headed, square-shouldered men of action who hardly need to think, let alone believe.

That's what makes it all the queerer. One day he came back to his tent in the forest, after a short leave, and said he had gone through a jolly rum experience, and didn't know what to do about it. He was holding a rusty old book in a leather binding, and he put it down on a table beside his revolver and an old Arab sword he kept, probably as a curiosity. He said this book had belonged to a man on the boat he had just come off; and the man swore that nobody must open the book, or look inside it; or else they would be carried off by the devil, or disappear, or something. Wales said this was all nonsense, of course; and they had a quarrel; and the upshot seems to have been that this man, taunted with cowardice or superstition, actually did look into the book; and instantly dropped it; walked to the side of the boat—'

'One moment,' said the Professor, who had made one or two notes. 'Before you tell me anything else. Did this man tell Wales where he had got the book, or who it originally belonged to?'

'Yes,' replied Pringle, now entirely grave. 'It seems he said he was bringing it back to Dr Hankey, the Oriental traveller now in England, to whom it originally belonged, and who had warned him of its strange properties. Well, Hankey is an able man and a rather crabbed and sneering sort of man; which makes it queerer still. But the point of Wales's story is much simpler. It is that the man who had looked into the book walked straight over the side of the ship, and was never seen again.'

'Do you believe it yourself?' asked Openshaw after a pause.

'Well, I do,' replied Pringle. 'I believe it for two reasons. First, that Wales was an entirely unimaginative man; and he added one touch that only an imaginative man could have added. He said that the man walked straight over the side on a still and calm day; but there was no splash.'

The Professor looked at his notes for some seconds in silence; and then said: 'And your other reason for believing it?'

'My other reason,' answered the Rev. Luke Pringle, 'is what I saw myself.'

There was another silence; until he continued in the same matter-of-fact way. Whatever he had, he had nothing of the eagerness with which the crank, or even the believer, tried to convince others.

'I told you that Wales put down the book on the table beside the sword. There was only one entrance to the tent; and it happened that I was standing in it, looking out into the forest, with my back to my companion. He was standing by the table grumbling and growling about the whole business; saying it was tomfoolery in the twentieth century to be frightened of opening a book; asking why the devil he shouldn't open it himself. Then some instinct stirred in me and I said he had better not do that, it had better be returned to Dr Hankey. "What harm could it do?" he said restlessly. "What harm did it do?" I answered obstinately. "What happened to your friend on the boat?" He didn't answer, indeed I didn't know what he could answer; but I pressed my logical advantage in mere vanity. "If it comes to that," I said, "what is your version of what really happened on the boat?" Still he didn't answer; and I looked round and saw that he wasn't there.

'The tent was empty. The book was lying on the table; open, but on its face, as if he had turned it downwards. But the sword was lying on the ground near the other side of the tent; and the canvas of the tent showed a great slash, as if somebody had hacked his way out with the sword. The gash in the tent gaped at me; but showed only the dark glimmer of the forest outside. And when I went across and looked through the rent I could not be certain whether the tangle of the tall plants and the undergrowth had been bent or broken; at least not farther than a few feet. I have never seen or heard of Captain Wales from that day.

'I wrapped the book up in brown paper, taking good care not to look at it; and I brought it back to England, intending at first to return it to Dr Hankey. Then I saw some notes in your paper suggesting a hypothesis about such things; and I decided to stop on the way and put the matter before you; as you have a name for being balanced and having an open mind.'

Professor Openshaw laid down his pen and looked steadily at the man on the other side of the table; concentrating in that single stare all his long experience of many entirely different types of humbug, and even some eccentric and extraordinary types of honest men. In the ordinary way, he would have begun with the healthy hypothesis that the story was a pack of lies. On the whole he did incline to assume that it was a pack of lies. And yet he could not fit the man into his story; if it were only that he could not see that sort of liar telling that sort of lie. The man was not trying to look honest on the surface, as most quacks and impostors do; somehow, it seemed all the other way; as if the man was honest, in spite of something else that was merely on the surface. He thought of a good man with one innocent delusion; but again the symptoms were not the same; there was even a sort of virile indifference; as if the man did not care much about his delusion, if it was a delusion.

'Mr Pringle,' he said sharply, like a barrister making a witness jump, 'where is this book of yours now?'

The grin reappeared on the bearded face which had grown grave during the recital. 'I left it outside,' said Mr Pringle. 'I mean in the outer office. It was a risk, perhaps; but the less risk of the two.'

'What do you mean?' demanded the Professor. 'Why didn't you bring it straight in here?'

'Because,' answered the missionary, 'I knew that as soon as you saw it, you'd open it—before you had heard the story. I thought it possible you might think twice about opening it—after you'd heard the story.'

Then after a silence he added: 'There was nobody out there but your clerk; and he looked a stolid steady-going specimen, immersed in business calculations.'

Openshaw laughed unaffectedly. 'Oh, Babbage,' he cried, 'your magic tomes are safe enough with him, I assure you. His name's Berridge—but I often call him Babbage; because he's so exactly like a Calculating Machine. No human being, if you can call him a human being, would be less likely to open other people's brown paper parcels. Well, we may as well go and bring it in now; though I assure you I will consider seriously the course to be taken with it. Indeed, I tell you frankly,' and he stared at the man again, 'that I'm not quite sure whether we ought to open it here and now, or send it to this Dr Hankey.'

The two had passed together out of the inner into the outer office; and even as they did so, Mr Pringle gave a cry and ran forward towards the clerk's desk. For the clerk's desk was there; but not the clerk. On the clerk's desk lay a faded old leather book, torn out of its brown-paper wrappings, and lying closed, but as if it had just been opened. The clerk's desk stood against the wide window that looked out into the street; and the window was shattered with a huge ragged hole in the glass; as if a human body had been shot through it into the world without. There was no other trace of Mr Berridge.

Both the two men left in the office stood as still as statues; and then it was the Professor who slowly came to life. He looked even more judicial than he had ever looked in his life, as he slowly turned and held out his hand to the missionary.

'Mr Pringle,' he said, 'I beg your pardon. I beg your pardon only for thoughts that I have had; and half-thoughts at that. But nobody could call himself a scientific man and not face a fact like this.'

'I suppose,' said Pringle doubtfully, 'that we ought to make some inquiries. Can you ring up his house and find out if he has gone home?'

'I don't know that he's on the telephone,' answered Openshaw, rather absently; 'he lives somewhere up Hampstead way, I think. But I suppose somebody will inquire here, if his friends or family miss him.'

'Could we furnish a description,' asked the other, 'if the police want it?'

'The police!' said the Professor, starting from his reverie. 'A description... Well, he looked awfully like everybody else, I'm afraid, except for goggles. One of those clean shaven chaps. But the police... look here, what are we to do about this mad business?'

'I know what I ought to do,' said the Rev. Mr Pringle firmly, 'I am going to take this book straight to the only original Dr Hankey, and ask him what the devil it's all about. He lives not very far from here, and I'll come straight back and tell you what he says.'

'Oh, very well,' said the Professor at last, as he sat down rather wearily; perhaps relieved for the moment to be rid of the responsibility. But long after the brisk and ringing footsteps of the little missionary had died away down the street, the Professor sat in the same posture, staring into vacancy like a man in a trance.

He was still in the same seat and almost in the same attitude, when the same brisk footsteps were heard on the pavement without and the missionary entered, this time, as a glance assured him, with empty hands.

'Dr Hankey,' said Pringle gravely, 'wants to keep the book for an hour and consider the point. Then he asks us both to call, and he will give us his decision. He specially desired. Professor, that you should accompany me on the second visit.'

Openshaw continued to stare in silence; then he said, suddenly: 'Who the devil is Dr Hankey?'

'You sound rather as if you meant he was the devil,' said Pringle smiling, 'and I fancy some people have thought so. He had quite a reputation in your own line; but he gained it mostly in India, studying local magic and so on, so perhaps he's not so well known here. He is a yellow skinny little devil with a lame leg, and a doubtful temper; but he seems to have set up in an ordinary respectable practice in these parts, and I don't know anything definitely wrong about him—unless it's wrong to be the only person who can possibly know anything about all this crazy affair.'

Professor Openshaw rose heavily and went to the telephone; he rang up Father Brown, changing the luncheon engagement to a dinner, that he might hold himself free for the expedition to the house of the Anglo-Indian doctor; after that he sat down again, lit a cigar and sank once more into his own unfathomable thoughts.

Father Brown went round to the restaurant appointed for dinner, and kicked his heels for some time in a vestibule full of mirrors and palms in pots; he had been informed of Openshaw's afternoon engagement, and, as the evening closed in dark and stormy round the glass and the green plants, guessed that it had produced something unexpected and unduly prolonged. He even wondered for a moment whether the Professor would turn up at all; but when the Professor eventually did, it was clear that his own more general guesses had been justified. For it was a very wild-eyed and even wild-haired Professor who eventually drove back with Mr Pringle from the expedition to the north of London, where suburbs are still fringed with heathy wastes and scraps of common, looking more sombre under the rather thunderstorm sunset. Nevertheless, they had apparently found the house, standing a little apart though within hail of other houses; they had verified the brass-plate duly engraved: 'J. I. Hankey, MD, MRCS.' Only they did not find J. I. Hankey, MD, MRCS. They found only what a nightmare whisper had already subconsciously prepared them to find: a commonplace parlour with the accursed volume lying on the table, as if it had just been read; and beyond, a back door burst open and a faint trail of footsteps that ran a little way up so steep a garden-path that it seemed that no lame man could have run up so lightly. But it was a lame man who had run; for in those few steps there was the misshapen unequal mark of some sort of surgical boot; then two marks of that boot alone (as if the creature had hopped) and then nothing. There was nothing further to be learnt from Dr J. I. Hankey, except that he had made his decision. He had read the oracle and received the doom.

When the two came into the entrance under the palms, Pringle put the book down suddenly on a small table, as if it burned his fingers. The priest glanced at it curiously; there was only some rude lettering on the front with a couplet:

They that looked into this book
Them the Flying Terror took;

and underneath, as he afterwards discovered, similar warnings in Greek, Latin and French. The other two had turned away with a natural impulsion towards drinks, after their exhaustion and bewilderment; and Openshaw had called to the waiter, who brought cocktails on a tray.

'You will dine with us, I hope,' said the Professor to the missionary; but Mr Pringle amiably shook his head.

'If you'll forgive me,' he said, 'I'm going off to wrestle with this book and this business by myself somewhere. I suppose I couldn't use your office for an hour or so?'

'I suppose—I'm afraid it's locked,' said Openshaw in some surprise.

'You forget there's a hole in the window.' The Rev. Luke Pringle gave the very broadest of all broad grins and vanished into the darkness without.

'A rather odd fellow, that, after all,' said the Professor, frowning.

He was rather surprised to find Father Brown talking to the waiter who had brought the cocktails, apparently about the waiter's most private affairs; for there was some mention of a baby who was now out of danger. He commented on the fact with some surprise, wondering how the priest came to know the man; but the former only said, 'Oh, I dine here every two or three months, and I've talked to him now and then.'

The Professor, who himself dined there about five times a week, was conscious that he had never thought of talking to the man; but his thoughts were interrupted by a strident ringing and a summons to the telephone. The voice on the telephone said it was Pringle, it was rather a muffled voice, but it might well be muffled in all those bushes of beard and whisker. Its message was enough to establish identity.

'Professor,' said the voice, 'I can't stand it any longer. I'm going to look for myself. I'm speaking from your office and the book is in front of me. If anything happens to me, this is to say good-bye. No—it's no good trying to stop me. You wouldn't be in time anyhow. I'm opening the book now. I... '

Openshaw thought he heard something like a sort of thrilling or shivering yet almost soundless crash; then he shouted the name of Pringle again and again; but he heard no more. He hung up the receiver, and, restored to a superb academic calm, rather like the calm of despair, went back and quietly took his seat at the dinner-table. Then, as coolly as if he were describing the failure of some small silly trick at a seance, he told the priest every detail of this monstrous mystery.

'Five men have now vanished in this impossible way,' he said. 'Everyone is extraordinary; and yet the one case I simply can't get over is my clerk, Berridge. It's just because he was the quietest creature that he's the queerest case.'

'Yes,' replied Father Brown, 'it was a queer thing for Berridge to do, anyway. He was awfully conscientious. He was also so jolly careful to keep all the office business separate from any fun of his own. Why, hardly anybody knew he was quite a humorist at home and—'

'Berridge!' cried the Professor. 'What on earth are you talking about? Did you know him?'

'Oh no,' said Father Brown carelessly, 'only as you say I know the waiter. I've often had to wait in your office, till you turned up; and of course I passed the time of day with poor Berridge. He was rather a card. I remember he once said he would like to collect valueless things, as collectors did the silly things they thought valuable. You know the old story about the woman who collected valueless things.'

'I'm not sure I know what you're talking about,' said Openshaw. 'But even if my clerk was eccentric (and I never knew a man I should have thought less so), it wouldn't explain what happened to him; and it certainly wouldn't explain the others.'

'What others?' asked the priest.

The Professor stared at him and spoke distinctly, as if to a child: 'My dear Father Brown, five men have disappeared.'

'My dear Professor Openshaw, no men have disappeared.'

Father Brown gazed back at his host with equal steadiness and spoke with equal distinctness. Nevertheless, the Professor required the words repeated, and they were repeated as distinctly. 'I say that no men have disappeared.'

After a moment's silence, he added, 'I suppose the hardest thing is to convince anybody that 0+0+0=0. Men believe the oddest things if they are in a series; that is why Macbeth believed the three words of the three witches; though the first was something he knew himself; and the last something he could only bring about himself. But in your case the middle term is the weakest of all.'

'What do you mean?'

'You saw nobody vanish. You did not see the man vanish from the boat. You did not see the man vanish from the tent. All that rests on the word of Mr Pringle, which I will not discuss just now. But you'll admit this; you would never have taken his word yourself, unless you had seen it confirmed by your clerk's disappearance; just as Macbeth would never have believed he would be king, if he had not been confirmed in believing he would be Cawdor.'

'That may be true,' said the Professor, nodding slowly. 'But when it was confirmed, I knew it was the truth. You say I saw nothing myself. But I did; I saw my own clerk disappear. Berridge did disappear.'

'Berridge did not disappear,' said Father Brown. 'On the contrary.'

'What the devil do you mean by "on the contrary"?'

'I mean,' said Father Brown, 'that he never disappeared. He appeared.'

Openshaw stared across at his friend, but the eyes had already altered in his head, as they did when they concentrated on a new presentation of a problem. The priest went on: 'He appeared in your study, disguised in a bushy red beard and buttoned up in a clumsy cape, and announced himself as the Rev. Luke Pringle. And you had never noticed your own clerk enough to know him again, when he was in so rough-and-ready a disguise.'

'But surely,' began the Professor.

'Could you describe him for the police?' asked Father Brown. 'Not you. You probably knew he was clean-shaven and wore tinted glasses; and merely taking off those glasses was a better disguise than putting on anything else. You had never seen his eyes any more than his soul; jolly laughing eyes. He had planted his absurd book and all the properties; then he calmly smashed the window, put on the beard and cape and walked into your study; knowing that you had never looked at him in your life.'

'But why should he play me such an insane trick?' demanded Openshaw.

'Why, because you had never looked at him in your life,' said Father Brown; and his hand slightly curled and clinched, as if he might have struck the table, if he had been given to gesture. 'You called him the Calculating Machine, because that was all you ever used him for. You never found out even what a stranger strolling into your office could find out, in five minutes' chat: that he was a character; that he was full of antics; that he had all sorts of views on you and your theories and your reputation for "spotting" people. Can't you understand his itching to prove that you couldn't spot your own clerk? He has nonsense notions of all sorts. About collecting useless things, for instance. Don't you know the story of the woman who bought the two most useless things: an old doctor's brass-plate and a wooden leg? With those your ingenious clerk created the character of the remarkable Dr Hankey; as easily as the visionary Captain Wales. Planting them in his own house—'

'Do you mean that place we visited beyond Hampstead was Berridge's own house?' asked Openshaw.

'Did you know his house—or even his address?' retorted the priest. 'Look here, don't think I'm speaking disrespectfully of you or your work. You are a great servant of truth and you know I could never be disrespectful to that. You've seen through a lot of liars, when you put your mind to it. But don't only look at liars. Do, just occasionally, look at honest men—like the waiter.'

'Where is Berridge now?' asked the Professor, after a long silence.

'I haven't the least doubt,' said Father Brown, 'that he is back in your office. In fact, he came back into your office at the exact moment when the Rev. Luke Pringle read the awful volume and faded into the void.'

There was another long silence and then Professor Openshaw laughed; with the laugh of a great man who is great enough to look small. Then he said abruptly:

'I suppose I do deserve it; for not noticing the nearest helpers I have. But you must admit the accumulation of incidents was rather formidable. Did you never feel just a momentary awe of the awful volume?'

'Oh, that,' said Father Brown. 'I opened it as soon as I saw it lying there. It's all blank pages. You see, I am not superstitious.'

4

THE GREEN MAN
(First published in *Ladies Home Journal,* Nov 1930)

A young man in knickerbockers, with an eager sanguine profile, was playing golf against himself on the links that lay parallel to the sand and sea, which were all growing grey with twilight. He was not carelessly knocking a ball about, but rather practising particular strokes with a sort of microscopic fury; like a neat and tidy whirlwind. He had learned many games quickly, but he had a disposition to learn them a little more quickly than they can be learnt. He was rather prone to be a victim of those remarkable invitations by which a man may learn the Violin in Six Lessons—or acquire a perfect French accent by a Correspondence Course. He lived in the breezy atmosphere of such hopeful advertisement and adventure. He was at present the private secretary of Admiral Sir Michael Craven, who owned the big house behind the park abutting on the links. He was ambitious, and had no intention of continuing indefinitely to be private secretary to anybody. But he was also reasonable; and he knew that the best way of ceasing to be a secretary was to be a good secretary. Consequently he was a very good secretary; dealing with the ever-accumulating arrears of the Admiral's correspondence with the same swift centripetal concentration with which he addressed the golf-ball. He had to struggle with the correspondence alone and at his own discretion at present; for the Admiral had been with his ship for the last six months, and, though now returning, was not expected for hours, or possibly days.

With an athletic stride, the young man, whose name was Harold Harker, crested the rise of turf that was the rampart of the links and, looking out across the sands to the sea, saw a strange sight. He did not see it very clearly; for the dusk was darkening every minute under stormy clouds; but it seemed to him, by a sort of momentary illusion, like a dream of days long past or a drama played by ghosts, out of another age in history.

The last of the sunset lay in long bars of copper and gold above the last dark strip of sea that seemed rather black than blue. But blacker still against this gleam in the west, there passed in sharp outline, like figures in a shadow pantomime, two men with three-cornered cocked hats and swords; as if they had just landed from one of the wooden ships of Nelson. It was not at all the sort of hallucination that would have come natural to Mr Harker, had he been prone to hallucinations. He was of the type that is at once sanguine and scientific; and would be more likely to fancy the flying-ships of the future than the fighting ships of the past. He therefore very sensibly came to the conclusion that even a futurist can believe his eyes.

His illusion did not last more than a moment. On the second glance, what he saw was unusual but not incredible. The two men who were striding in single file across the sands, one some fifteen yards behind the other, were ordinary modern naval officers; but naval officers wearing that almost extravagant full-dress uniform which naval officers never do wear if they can possibly help it; only on great ceremonial occasions such as the visits of Royalty. In the man walking in front, who seemed more or less unconscious of the man walking behind, Harker recognized at once the high-bridged nose and spike-shaped beard of his own employer the Admiral. The other man following in his tracks he did not know. But he did know something about the circumstances connected with the ceremonial occasion. He knew that when the Admiral's ship put in at the adjacent port, it was to be formally visited by a Great Personage; which was enough, in that sense, to explain the officers being in full dress. But he did also know the officers; or at any rate the Admiral. And what could have possessed the Admiral to come on shore in that rig-out, when one could swear he would seize five minutes to change into mufti or at least into undress uniform, was more than his secretary could conceive. It seemed somehow to be the very last thing he would do. It was indeed to remain for many weeks one of the chief mysteries of this mysterious business. As it was, the outline of these fantastic court uniforms against the empty scenery, striped with dark sea and sand, had something suggestive of comic opera; and reminded the spectator of Pinafore.

The second figure was much more singular; somewhat singular in appearance, despite his correct lieutenant's uniform, and still more extraordinary in behaviour. He walked in a strangely irregular and uneasy manner; sometimes quickly and sometimes slowly; as if he could not make up his mind whether to overtake the Admiral or not. The Admiral was rather deaf and certainly heard no footsteps behind him on the yielding sand; but the footsteps behind him, if traced in the detective manner, would have given rise to twenty conjectures from a limp to a dance. The man's face was swarthy as well as darkened with shadow, and every now and then the eyes in it shifted and shone, as if to accent his agitation. Once he began to run and then abruptly relapsed into a swaggering slowness and carelessness. Then he did something which Mr Harker could never have conceived any normal naval officer in His

Britannic Majesty's Service doing, even in a lunatic asylum. He drew his sword.

It was at this bursting-point of the prodigy that the two passing figures disappeared behind a headland on the shore. The staring secretary had just time to notice the swarthy stranger, with a resumption of carelessness, knock off a head of sea-holly with his glittering blade. He seemed then to have abandoned all idea of catching the other man up. But Mr Harold Harker's face became very thoughtful indeed; and he stood there ruminating for some time before he gravely took himself inland, towards the road that ran past the gates of the great house and so by a long curve down to the sea.

It was up this curving road from the coast that the Admiral might be expected to come, considering the direction in which he had been walking, and making the natural assumption that he was bound for his own door. The path along the sands, under the links, turned inland just beyond the headland arid solidifying itself into a road, returned towards Craven House. It was down this road, therefore, that the secretary darted, with characteristic impetuosity, to meet his patron returning home. But the parton was apparently not returning home. What was still more peculiar, the secretary was not returning home either; at least until many hours later; a delay quite long enough to arouse alarm and mystification at Craven House.

Behind the pillars and palms of that rather too palatial country house, indeed, there was expectancy gradually changing to uneasiness. Gryce the butler, a big bilious man abnormally silent below as well as above stairs, showed a certain restlessness as he moved about the main front-hall and occasionally looked out of the side windows of the porch, on the white road that swept towards the sea. The Admiral's sister Marion, who kept house for him, had her brother's high nose with a more sniffy expression; she was voluble, rather rambling, not without humour, and capable of sudden emphasis as shrill as a cockatoo. The Admiral's daughter Olive was dark, dreamy, and as a rule abstractedly silent, perhaps melancholy; so that her aunt generally conducted most of the conversation, and that without reluctance. But the girl also had a gift of sudden laughter that was very engaging.

'I can't think why they're not here already,' said the elder lady. 'The postman distinctly told me he'd seen the Admiral coming along the beach; along with that dreadful creature Rook. Why in the world they call him Lieutenant Rook—'

'Perhaps,' suggested the melancholy young lady, with a momentary brightness, 'perhaps they call him Lieutenant because he is a Lieutenant.'

'I can't think why the Admiral keeps him,' snorted her aunt, as if she were talking of a housemaid. She was very proud of her brother and always called him the Admiral; but her notions of a commission in the Senior Service were inexact.

'Well, Roger Rook is sulky and unsociable and all that,' replied Olive, 'but of course that wouldn't prevent him being a capable sailor.'

'Sailor!' cried her aunt with one of her rather startling cockatoo notes, 'he isn't my notion of a sailor. The Lass that Loved a Sailor, as they used to sing when I was young... Just think of it! He's not gay and free and whats-its-name. He doesn't sing chanties or dance a hornpipe.'

'Well,' observed her niece with gravity. 'The Admiral doesn't very often dance a hornpipe.'

'Oh, you know what I mean—he isn't bright or breezy or anything,' replied the old lady. 'Why, that secretary fellow could do better than that.'

Olive's rather tragic face was transfigured by one of her good and rejuvenating waves of laughter.

'I'm sure Mr Harker would dance a hornpipe for you,' she said, 'and say he had learnt it in half an hour from the book of instructions. He's always learning things of that sort.'

She stopped laughing suddenly and looked at her aunt's rather strained face.

'I can't think why Mr Harker doesn't come,' she added.

'I don't care about Mr Harker,' replied the aunt, and rose and looked out of the window.

The evening light had a long turned from yellow to grey and was now turning almost to white under the widening moonlight, over the large flat landscape by the coast; unbroken by any features save a clump of sea-twisted trees round a pool and beyond, rather gaunt and dark against the horizon, the shabby fishermen's tavern on the shore that bore the name of the Green Man. And all that road and landscape was empty of any living thing. Nobody had seen the figure in the cocked hat that had been observed, earlier in the evening, walking by the sea; or the other and stranger figure that had been seen trailing after him. Nobody had even seen the secretary who saw them.

It was after midnight when the secretary at last burst in and aroused the household; and his face, white as a ghost, looked all the paler against the background of the stolid face and figure of a big Inspector of Police. Somehow that red, heavy, indifferent face looked, even more than the white and harassed one, like a mask of doom. The news was broken to the two women with such consideration or concealments as were possible. But the news was that the body of Admiral Craven had been eventually fished out of the foul weeds and scum of the pool under the trees; and that he was drowned and dead.

Anybody acquainted with Mr Harold Harker, secretary, will realize that, whatever his agitation, he was by morning in a mood to be tremendously on the spot. He hustled the Inspector, whom he had met the night before on the road down by the Green Man, into another room for private and practical consultation. He questioned the Inspector rather as the Inspector might have questioned a yokel. But Inspector

Burns was a stolid character; and was either too stupid or too clever to resent such trifles. It soon began to look as if he were by no means so stupid as he looked; for he disposed of Harker's eager questions in a manner that was slow but methodical and rational.

'Well,' said Harker (his head full of many manuals with titles like 'Be a Detective in Ten Days'). 'Well, it's the old triangle, I suppose. Accident, Suicide or Murder.'

'I don't see how it could be accident,' answered the policeman. 'It wasn't even dark yet and the pool's fifty yards from the straight road that he knew like his own doorstep. He'd no more have got into that pond than he'd go and carefully lie down in a puddle in the street. As for suicide, it's rather a responsibility to suggest it, and rather improbable too. The Admiral was a pretty spry and successful man and frightfully rich, nearly a millionaire in fact; though of course that doesn't prove anything. He seemed to be pretty normal and comfortable in his private life too; he's the last man I should suspect of drowning himself.'

'So that we come,' said the secretary, lowering his voice with the thrill, 'I suppose we come to the third possibility.'

'We won't be in too much of a hurry about that,' said the Inspector to the annoyance of Harker, who was in a hurry about everything. 'But naturally there are one or two things one would like to know. One would like to know—about his property, for instance. Do you know who's likely to come in for it? You're his private secretary; do you know anything about his will?'

'I'm not so private a secretary as all that,' answered the young man. 'His solicitors are Messrs Willis, Hardman and Dyke, over in Suttford High Street; and I believe the will is in their custody.'

'Well, I'd better get round and see them pretty soon,' said the Inspector.

'Let's get round and see them at once,' said the impatient secretary.

He took a turn or two restlessly up and down the room and then exploded in a fresh place.

'What have you done about the body, Inspector?' he asked.

'Dr Straker is examining it now at the Police Station. His report ought to be ready in an hour or so.'

'It can't be ready too soon,' said Harker. 'It would save time if we could meet him at the lawyer's.' Then he stopped and his impetuous tone changed abruptly to one of some embarrassment.

'Look here,' he said, 'I want ... we want to consider the young lady, the poor Admiral's daughter, as much as possible just now. She's got a notion that may be all nonsense; but I wouldn't like to disappoint her. There's some friend of hers she wants to consult, staying in the town at present. Man of the name of Brown; priest or parson of some sort—she's given me his address. I don't take much stock in priests or parsons, but—'

The Inspector nodded. 'I don't take any stock in priests or parsons; but I take a lot of stock in Father Brown,' he said. 'I happened to have to do with him in a queer sort of society jewel case. He ought to have been a policeman instead of parson.'

'Oh, all right,' said the breathless secretary as he vanished from the room. 'Let him come to the lawyer's too.'

Thus it happened that, when they hurried across to the neighbouring town to meet Dr Straker at the solicitor's office, they found Father Brown already seated there, with his hands folded on his heavy umbrella, chatting pleasantly to the only available member of the firm. Dr Straker also had arrived, but apparently only at that moment, as he was carefully placing his gloves in his top hat and his top hat on a side-table. And the mild and beaming expression of the priest's moonlike face and spectacles, together with the silent chuckles of the jolly old grizzled lawyer, to whom he was talking, were enough to show that the doctor had not yet opened his mouth to bring the news of death.

'A beautiful morning after all,' Father Brown was saying. 'That storm seems to have passed over us. There were some big black clouds, but I notice that not a drop of rain fell.'

'Not a drop,' agreed the solicitor toying with a pen; he was the third partner, Mr Dyke; 'there's not a cloud in the sky now. It's the sort of day for a holiday.' Then he realized the newcomers and looked up, laying down the pen and rising. 'Ah, Mr Harker, how are you? I hear the Admiral is expected home soon.' Then Harker spoke, and his voice rang hollow in the room.

'I am sorry to say we are the bearers of bad news. Admiral Craven was drowned before reaching home.'

There was a change in the very air of the still office, though not in the attitudes of the motionless figures; both were staring at the speaker as if a joke had been frozen on their lips. Both repeated the word 'drowned' and looked at each other, and then again at their informant. Then there was a small hubbub of questions.

'When did this happen?' asked the priest.

'Where was he found?' asked the lawyer.

'He was found,' said the Inspector, 'in that pool by the coast, not far from the Green Man, and dragged out all covered with green scum and weeds so as to be almost unrecognizable. But Dr Straker here has—What is the matter. Father Brown? Are you ill?'

'The Green Man,' said Father Brown with a shudder. 'I'm so sorry ... I beg your pardon for being upset.'

'Upset by what?' asked the staring officer.

'By his being covered with green scum, I suppose,' said the priest, with a rather shaky laugh. Then he added rather more firmly, 'I thought it might have been seaweed.'

By this time everybody was looking at the priest, with a not unnatural suspicion that he was mad; and yet the next crucial surprise was not to come from him. After a dead silence, it was the doctor who spoke.

Dr Straker was a remarkable man, even to look at. He was very tall and angular, formal and professional in his dress; yet retaining a fashion that has hardly been known since Mid-Victorian times. Though comparatively young, he wore his brown beard, very long and spreading over his waistcoat; in contrast with it, his features, which were both harsh and handsome, looked singularly pale. His good looks were also diminished by something in his deep eyes that was not squinting, but like the shadow of a squint. Everybody noticed these things about him, because the moment he spoke, he gave forth an indescribable air of authority. But all he said was:

'There is one more thing to be said, if you come to details, about Admiral Craven being drowned.' Then he added reflectively, 'Admiral Craven was not drowned.'

The Inspector turned with quite a new promptitude and shot a question at him.

'I have just examined the body,' said Dr Straker, 'the cause of death was a stab through the heart with some pointed blade like a stiletto. It was after death, and even some little time after, that the body was hidden in the pool.'

Father Brown was regarding Dr Straker with a very lively eye, such as he seldom turned upon anybody; and when the group in the office began to break up, he managed to attach himself to the medical man for a little further conversation, as they went back down the street. There had not been very much else to detain them except the rather formal question of the will. The impatience of the young secretary had been somewhat tried by the professional etiquette of the old lawyer. But the latter was ultimately induced, rather by the tact of the priest than the authority of the policeman, to refrain from making a mystery where there was no mystery at all. Mr Dyke admitted, with a smile, that the Admiral's will was a very normal and ordinary document, leaving everything to his only child Olive; and that there really was no particular reason for concealing the fact.

The doctor and the priest walked slowly down the street that struck out of the town in the direction of Craven House. Harker had plunged on ahead of him with all his native eagerness to get somewhere; but the two behind seemed more interested in their discussion than their direction. It was in rather an enigmatic tone that the tall doctor said to the short cleric beside him:

'Well, Father Brown, what do you think of a thing like this?'

Father Brown looked at. him rather intently for an instant, and then said:

'Well, I've begun to think of one or two things; but my chief difficulty is that I only knew the Admiral slightly; though I've seen something of his daughter.'

'The Admiral,' said the doctor with a grim immobility of feature, 'was the sort of man of whom it is said that he had not an enemy in the world.'

'I suppose you mean,' answered the priest, 'that there's something else that will not be said.'

'Oh, it's no affair of mine,' said Straker hastily but rather harshly. 'He had his moods, I suppose. He once threatened me with a legal action about an operation; but I think he thought better of it. I can imagine his being rather rough with a subordinate.'

Father Brown's eyes were fixed on the figure of the secretary striding far ahead; and as he gazed he realized the special cause of his hurry. Some fifty yards farther ahead the Admiral's daughter was dawdling along the road towards the Admiral's house. The secretary soon came abreast of her; and for the remainder of the time Father Brown watched the silent drama of two human backs as they diminished into the distance. The secretary was evidently very much excited about something; but if the priest guessed what it was, he kept it to himself. When he came to the corner leading to the doctor's house, he only said briefly: 'I don't know if you have anything more to tell us.'

'Why should I?' answered the doctor very abruptly; and striding off, left it uncertain whether he was asking why he should have anything to tell, or why he should tell it.

Father Brown went stumping on alone, in the track of the two young people; but when he came to the entrance and avenues of the Admiral's park, he was arrested by the action of the girl, who turned suddenly and came straight towards him; her face unusually pale and her eyes bright with some new and as yet nameless emotion.

'Father Brown,' she said in a low voice, 'I must talk to you as soon as possible. You must listen to me, I can't see any other way out.'

'Why certainly,' he replied, as coolly as if a gutter-boy had asked him the time. 'Where shall we go and talk?'

The girl led him at random to one of the rather tumbledown arbours in the grounds; and they sat down behind a screen of large ragged leaves. She began instantly, as if she must relieve her feelings or faint.

'Harold Harker,' she said, 'has been talking to me about things. Terrible things.'

The priest nodded and the girl went on hastily. 'About Roger Rook. Do you know about Roger?'

'I've been told,' he answered, 'that his fellow-seamen call him The Jolly Roger, because he is never jolly; and looks like the pirate's skull and crossbones.'

'He was not always like that,' said Olive in a low voice. 'Something very queer must have happened to him. I knew him well when we were children; we used to play over there on the sands. He was harum-scarum and always talking about being a pirate; I dare say he was the sort they say might take to crime through reading shockers; but there was something poetical in his way of being piratical. He really was a Jolly Roger then. I suppose he was the last boy who kept up the old legend of really running away to sea; and at last his family had to agree to his joining the Navy. Well... '

'Yes,' said Father Brown patiently.

'Well,' she admitted, caught in one of her rare moments of mirth, 'I suppose poor Roger found it disappointing. Naval officers so seldom carry knives in their teeth or wave bloody cutlasses and black flags. But that doesn't explain the change in him. He just stiffened; grew dull and dumb, like a dead man walking about. He always avoids me; but that doesn't matter. I supposed some great grief that's no business of mine had broken him up. And now—well, if what Harold says is true, the grief is neither more nor less than going mad; or being possessed of a devil.'

'And what does Harold say?' asked the priest.

'It's so awful I can hardly say it,' she answered. 'He swears he saw Roger creeping behind my father that night; hesitating and then drawing his sword... and the doctor says father was stabbed with a steel point ... I can't believe Roger Rook had anything to do with it. His sulks and my father's temper sometimes led to quarrels; but what are quarrels? I can't exactly say I'm standing up for an old friend; because he isn't even friendly. But you can't help feeling sure of some things, even about an old acquaintance. And yet Harold swears that he—'

'Harold seems to swear a great deal,' said Father Brown.

There was a sudden silence; after which she said in a different tone. 'Well, he does swear other things too. Harold Harker proposed to me just now.'

'Am I to congratulate you, or rather him?' inquired her companion.

'I told him he must wait. He isn't good at waiting.' She was caught again in a ripple of her incongruous sense of the comic:

'He said I was his ideal and his ambition and so on. He has lived in the States; but somehow I never remember it when he is talking about dollars; only when he is talking about ideals.'

'And I suppose,' said Father Brown very softy, 'that it is because you have to decide about Harold that you want to know the truth about Roger.'

She stiffened and frowned, and then equally abruptly smiled, saying: 'Oh, you know too much.'

'I know very little, especially in this affair,' said the priest gravely. 'I only know who murdered your father.' She started up and stood staring down at him stricken white. Father Brown made a wry face as he went on: 'I made a fool of myself when I first realized it; when they'd just been asking where he was found, and went on talking about green scum and the Green Man.'

Then he also rose; clutching his clumsy umbrella with a new resolution, he addressed the girl with a new gravity.

'There is something else that I know, which is the key to all these riddles of yours; but I won't tell you yet. I suppose it's bad news; but it's nothing like so bad as the things you have been fancying.' He buttoned up his coat and turned towards the gate. 'I'm going to see this Mr Rook of yours. In a shed by the shore, near where Mr Harker saw him walking. I rather think he lives there.' And he went bustling off in the direction of the beach.

Olive was an imaginative person; perhaps too imaginative to be safely left to brood over such hints as her friend had thrown out; but he was in rather a hurry to find the best relief for her broodings. The mysterious connection between Father Brown's first shock of enlightenment and the chance language about the pool and the inn, hag-rode her fancy in a hundred forms of ugly symbolism. The Green Man became a ghost trailing loathsome weeds and walking the countryside under the moon; the sign of the Green Man became a human figure hanging as from a gibbet; and the tarn itself became a tavern, a dark subaqueous tavern for the dead sailors. And yet he had taken the most rapid method to overthrow all such nightmares, with a burst of blinding daylight which seemed more mysterious than the night.

For before the sun had set, something had come back into her life that turned her whole world topsy-turvy once more; something she had hardly known that she desired until it was abruptly granted; something that was, like a dream, old and familiar, and yet remained incomprehensible and incredible. For Roger Rook had come striding across the sands, and even when he was a dot in the distance, she knew he was transfigured; and as he came nearer and nearer, she saw that his dark face was alive with laughter and exultation. He came straight toward her, as if they had never parted, and seized her shoulders saying: 'Now I can look after you, thank God.'

She hardly knew what she answered; but she heard herself questioning rather wildly why he seemed so changed and so happy.

'Because I am happy,' he answered. 'I have heard the bad news.'

All parties concerned, including some who seemed rather unconcerned, found themselves assembled on the garden-path leading to Craven House, to hear the formality, now truly formal, of the lawyer's reading of the will; and the probable, and more practical sequel of the lawyer's advice upon the crisis. Besides the grey-haired solicitor himself, armed with the testamentary document, there was the Inspector armed with more direct authority touching the crime, and Lieutenant Rook in undisguised attendance on the lady; some were rather mystified on seeing the tall figure of the doctor, some smiled a little on seeing the dumpy figure of the priest. Mr Harker, that Flying Mercury, had shot down to the lodge-gates to meet them, led them back on to the lawn, and then dashed ahead of them again to prepare their reception. He said he would be back in a jiffy; and anyone observing his piston-rod of energy could well believe it; but, for the moment, they were left rather stranded on the lawn outside the house.

'Reminds me of somebody making runs at cricket', said the Lieutenant.

'That young man,' said the lawyer, 'is rather annoyed that the law cannot move quite so quickly as he does. Fortunately Miss Craven understands our professional difficulties and delays. She has kindly assured me that she still has confidence in my slowness.'

'I wish,' said the doctor, suddenly, 'that I had as much confidence in his quickness.'

'Why, what do you mean?' asked Rook, knitting his brows; 'do you mean that Harker is too quick?'

'Too quick and too slow,' said Dr Straker, in his rather cryptic fashion. 'I know one occasion at least when he was not so very quick. Why was he hanging about half the night by the pond and the Green Man, before the Inspector came down and found the body? Why did he meet the Inspector? Why should he expect to meet the Inspector outside the Green Man?'

'I don't understand you,' said Rook. 'Do you mean that Harker wasn't telling the truth?'

Dr Straker was silent. The grizzled lawyer laughed with grim good humour. 'I have nothing more serious to say against the young man,' he said, 'than that he made a prompt and praiseworthy attempt to teach me my own business.'

'For that matter, he made an attempt to teach me mine,' said the Inspector, who had just joined the group in front. 'But that doesn't matter. If Dr Straker means anything by his hints, they do matter. I must ask you to speak plainly, doctor. It may be my duty to question him at once.'

'Well, here he comes,' said Rook, as the alert figure of the secretary appeared once more in the doorway.

At this point Father Brown, who had remained silent and inconspicuous at the tail of the procession, astonished everybody very much; perhaps especially those who knew him. He not only walked rapidly to the front, but turned facing the whole group with an arresting and almost threatening expression, like a sergeant bringing soldiers to the halt.

'Stop!' he said almost sternly. 'I apologize to everybody; but it's absolutely necessary that I should see Mr Harker first. I've got to tell him something I know; and I don't think anybody else knows; something he's got to hear. It may save a very tragic misunderstanding with somebody later on.'

'What on earth do you mean?' asked old Dyke the lawyer.

'I mean the bad news,' said Father Brown.

'Here, I say,' began the Inspector indignantly; and then suddenly caught the priest's eye and remembered strange things he had seen in other days. 'Well, if it were anyone in the world but you I should say of all the infernal cheek—'

But Father Brown was already out of hearing, and a moment afterwards was plunged in talk with Harker in the porch. They walked to and fro together for a few paces and then disappeared into the dark interior. It was about twelve minutes afterwards that Father Brown came out alone.

To their surprise he showed no dispostion to re-enter the house, now that the whole company were at last about to enter it. He threw himself down on the rather rickety seat in the leafy arbour, and as the procession disappeared through the doorway, lit a pipe and proceeded to stare vacantly at the long ragged leaves about his head and to listen to the birds. There was no man who had a more hearty and enduring appetite for doing nothing.

He was, apparently, in a cloud of smoke and a dream of abstraction, when the front doors were once more flung open and two or three figures came out helter-skelter, running towards him, the daughter of the house and her young admirer

Mr Rook being easily winners in the race. Their faces were alight with astonishment; and the face of Inspector Burns, who advanced more heavily behind them, like an elephant shaking the garden, was inflamed with some indignation as well.

'What can all this mean?' cried Olive, as she came panting to a halt. 'He's gone!'

'Bolted!' said the Lieutenant explosively. 'Harker's just managed to pack a suitcase and bolted! Gone clean out of the back door and over the garden-wall to God knows where. What did you say to him?'

'Don't be silly!' said Olive, with a more worried expression. 'Of course you told him you'd found him out, and now he's gone. I never could have believed he was wicked like that!'

'Well!' gasped the Inspector, bursting into their midst. 'What have you done now? What have you let me down like this for?'

'Well,' repeated Father Brown, 'what have I done?'

'You have let a murderer escape,' cried Burns, with a decision that was like a thunderclap in the quiet garden; 'you have helped a murderer to escape. Like a fool I let you warn him; and now he is miles away.'

'I have helped a few murderers in my time, it is true,' said Father Brown; then he added, in careful distinction, 'not, you will understand, helped them to commit the murder.'

'But you knew all the time,' insisted Olive. 'You guessed from the first that it must be he. That's what you meant about being upset by the business of finding the body. That's what the doctor meant by saying my father might be disliked by a subordinate.'

'That's what I complain of,' said the official indignantly. 'You knew even then that he was the—'

'You knew even then,' insisted Olive, 'that the murderer was—'

Father Brown nodded gravely. 'Yes,' he said. 'I knew even then that the murderer was old Dyke.'

'Was who?' repeated the Inspector and stopped amid, a dead silence; punctuated only by the occasional pipe of birds.

'I mean Mr Dyke, the solicitor,' explained Father Brown, like one explaining something elementary to an infant class. 'That gentleman with grey hair who's supposed to be going to read the will.'

They all stood like statues staring at him, as he carefully filled his pipe again and struck a match. At last Burns rallied his vocal powers to break the strangling silence with an effort resembling violence.

'But, in the name of heaven, why?'

'Ah, why?' said the priest and rose thoughtfully, puffing at his pipe. 'As to why he did it ... Well, I suppose the time has come to tell you, or those of you who don't know, the fact that is the key of all this business. It's a great calamity; and it's a great crime; but it's not the murder of Admiral Craven.'

He looked Olive full in the face and said very seriously: 'I tell you the bad news bluntly and in few words; because I think you are brave enough, and perhaps happy enough, to take it well. You have the chance, and I think the power, to be something like a great woman. You are not a great heiress.'

Amid the silence that followed it was he who resumed his explanation.

'Most of your father's money, I am sorry to say, has gone. It went by the financial dexterity of the grey-haired gentleman named Dyke, who is (I grieve to say) a swindler. Admiral Craven was murdered to silence him about the way in which he was swindled. The fact that he was ruined and you were disinherited is the single simple clue, not only to the murder, but to all the other mysteries in this business.' He took a puff or two and then continued.

'I told Mr Rook you were disinherited and he rushed back to help you. Mr Rook is a rather remarkable person.'

'Oh, chuck it,' said Mr Rook with a hostile air.

'Mr Rook is a monster,' said Father Brown with scientific calm. 'He is an anachronism, an atavism, a brute survival of the Stone Age. If there was one barbarous superstition we all supposed to be utterly extinct and dead in these days, it was that notion about honour and independence. But then I get mixed up with so many dead superstitions. Mr Rook is an extinct animal. He is a plesiosaurus. He did not want to live on his wife or have a wife who could call him a fortune-hunter. Therefore he sulked in a grotesque manner and only came to life again when I brought him the good news that you were ruined. He wanted to work for his wife and not be kept by her. Disgusting, isn't it? Let us turn to the brighter topic of Mr Harker.

'I told Mr Harker you were disinherited and he rushed away in a sort of panic. Do not be too hard on Mr Harker. He really had better as well as worse enthusiasms; but he had them all mixed up. There is no harm in having ambitions; but he had ambitions and called them ideals. The old sense of honour taught men to suspect success; to say, "This is a benefit; it may be a bribe." The new nine-times-accursed nonsense about Making Good teaches men to identify being good with making money. That was all that was the matter with him; in every other way he was a thoroughly good fellow, and there are thousands like him. Gazing at the stars and rising in the world were all Uplift. Marrying a good wife and marring a rich wife were all Making Good. But he was not a cynical scoundrel; or he would simply have come back and jilted or cut you as the case might be. He could not face you; while you were there, half of his broken ideal was left.

'I did not tell the Admiral; but somebody did. Word came to him somehow, during the last grand parade on board, that his friend the family lawyer had betrayed him. He was in such a towering passion that he did what he could never have done in his sense; came straight on shore in his cocked hat and gold lace to catch the criminal; he wired to the police station, and that was why the Inspector was wandering round the Green Man. Lieutenant Rook followed him on shore because he suspected some family trouble and had half a hope he might help and put himself right. Hence his hesitating behaviour. As for his drawing his sword when he dropped behind and thought he was alone, well that's a matter of imagination. He was a romantic person who had dreamed of swords and run away to sea; and found himself in a service where he wasn't even allowed to wear a sword except about once in three years. He thought he was quite alone on the sands where he played as a boy. If you don't understand what he did, I can only say, like Stevenson, "you will never be a pirate." Also you will never be a poet; and you have never been a boy.'

'I never have,' answered Olive gravely, 'and yet I think I understand.'

'Almost every man,' continued the priest musing, 'will play with anything shaped like a sword or dagger, even if it is a paper knife. That is why I thought it so odd when the lawyer didn't.'

'What do you mean?' asked Burns, 'didn't what?'

'Why, didn't you notice,' answered Brown, 'at that first meeting in the office, the lawyer played with a pen and not with a paper-knife; though he had a beautiful bright steel paper-knife in the pattern of a stiletto? The pens were dusty and splashed with ink; but the knife had just been cleaned. But he did not play with it. There are limits to the irony of assassins.'

After a silence the Inspector said, like one waking from a dream: 'Look here ... I don't know whether I'm on my head or my heels; I don't know whether you think you've got to the end; but I haven't got to the beginning. Where do you get all this lawyer stuff from? What started you out on that trail?'

Father Brown laughed curtly and without mirth.

'The murderer made a slip at the start,' he said, 'and I can't think why nobody else noticed it. When you brought the first news of the death to the solicitor's office, nobody was supposed to know anything there, except that the Admiral was expected home. When you said he was drowned, I asked when it happened and Mr Dyke asked where the corpse was found.'

He paused a moment to knock out his pipe and resumed reflectively: 'Now when you are simply told of a seaman, returning from the sea, that he had drowned, it is natural to assume that he had been drowned at sea. At any rate, to allow that he may have been drowned at sea. If he had been washed overboard, or gone down with his ship, or had his body "committed to the deep", there would be no reason to expect his body to be found at all. The moment that man asked where it was found, I was sure he knew were it was found. Because he had put it there. Nobody but the murderer need have thought of anything so unlikely as a seaman being drowned in a landlocked pool a few hundred yards from the sea. That is why I suddenly felt sick and turned green, I dare say; as green as the Green Man. I never can get used to finding myself suddenly sitting beside a murderer. So I had to turn it off by talking in parables; but the parable meant something, after all. I said that the body was covered with green scum, but it might just as well have been seaweed.'

It is fortunate that tragedy can never kill comedy and that the two can run side by side; and that while the only acting partner of the business of Messrs Willis, Hardman and Dyke blew his brains out when the Inspector entered the house to arrest him. Olive and Roger were calling to each other across the sands at evening, as they did when they were children together.

5

THE PURSUIT OF MR BLUE
(No record of prior magazine publication found)

Along a seaside parade on a sunny afternoon, a person with the depressing name of Muggleton was moving with suitable gloom. There was a horseshoe of worry in his forehead, and the numerous groups and strings of entertainers stretched along the beach below looked up to him in vain for applause. Pierrots turned up their pale moon faces, like the white bellies of dead fish, without improving his spirits; niggers with faces entirely grey with a sort of grimy soot were equally unsuccessful in filling his fancy with brighter things. He was a sad and disappointed man. His other features, besides the bald brow with its furrow, were retiring and almost sunken; and a certain dingy refinement about them made more incongruous the one aggressive ornament of his face. It was an outstanding and bristling military moustache; and it looked suspiciously like a false moustache. It is possible, indeed, that it was a false moustache. It is possible, on the other hand, that even if it was not false it was forced. He might almost have grown it in a hurry, by a mere act of will; so much was it a part of his job rather than his personality.

For the truth is that Mr Muggleton was a private detective in a small way, and the cloud on his brow was due to a big blunder in his professional career; anyhow it was connected with something darker than the mere possession of such a surname. He might almost, in an obscure sort of way, have been proud of his surname; for he came of poor but decent Nonconformist people who claimed some connection with the founder of the Muggletonians; the only man who had hitherto had the courage to appear with that name in human history.

The more legitimate cause of his annoyance (at least as he himself explained it) was that he had just been present at the bloody murder of a world-famous millionaire, and had failed to prevent it, though he had been engaged at a salary of five pounds a week to do so. Thus we may explain the fact that even the languorous singing of the song entitled, 'Won't You Be My Loodah Doodah Day?' failed to fill him with the joy of life.

For that matter, there were others on the beach, who might have had more sympathy with his murderous theme and Muggletonian tradition. Seaside resorts are the chosen pitches, not only of pierrots appealing to the amorous emotions, but also of preachers who often seem to specialize in a correspondingly sombre and sulphurous style of preaching. There was one aged ranter whom he could hardly help noticing, so piercing were the cries, not to say shrieks of religious prophecy that rang above all the banjos and castanets. This was a long, loose, shambling old man, dressed in something like a fisherman's jersey; but inappropriately equipped with a pair of those very long and drooping whiskers which have never been seen since the disappearance of certain sportive Mid-Victorian dandies. As it was the custom for all mountebanks on the beach to display something, as if they were selling it, the old man displayed a rather rotten-looking fisherman's net, which he generally spread out invitingly on the sands, as if it were a carpet for queens; but occasionally whirled wildly round his head with a gesture almost as terrific as that of the Roman Retiarius, ready to impale people on a trident. Indeed, he might really have impaled people, if he had had a trident. His words were always pointed towards punishment; his hearers heard nothing except threats to the body or the soul; he was so far in the same mood as Mr Muggleton, that he might almost have been a mad hangman addressing a crowd of murderers. The boys called him Old Brimstone; but he had other eccentricities besides the purely theological. One of his eccentricities was to climb up into the nest of iron girders under the pier and trail his net in the water, declaring that he got his living by fishing; though it is doubtful whether anybody had ever seen him catching fish. Worldly trippers, however, would sometimes start at a voice in their ear, threatening judgement as from a thundercloud, but really coming from the perch under the iron roof where the old monomaniac sat glaring, his fantastic whiskers hanging like grey seaweed.

The detective, however, could have put up with Old Brimstone much better than with the other parson he was destined to meet. To explain this second and more momentous meeting, it must be pointed out that Muggleton, after his remarkable experience in the matter of the murder, had very properly put all his cards on the table. He told his story to the police and to the only available representative of Braham Bruce, the dead millionaire; that is, to his very dapper secretary, a Mr Anthony Taylor. The Inspector was more sympathetic than the secretary; but the sequel of his sympathy was the last thing Muggleton would normally have associated with police advice. The Inspector, after some reflection, very much surprised Mr Muggleton by advising him to consult an able amateur whom he knew to be staying in the town. Mr Muggleton had read reports and romances about the Great Criminologist, who sits in his library like an intellectual spider, and throws out theoretical filaments of a web as large as the world. He was prepared to be led to the lonely chateau where the expert wore a purple dressing-gown, to the attic where he lived on opium and acrostics, to the vast laboratory or the lonely tower. To his astonishment he was led to the very edge of the crowded beach by the pier to meet a dumpy little clergyman, with a broad hat and a broad grin, who was at that moment hopping about on the sands with a crowd of poor children; and excitedly waving a very little wooden spade.

When the criminologist clergyman, whose name appeared to be Brown, had at last been detached from the children, though not from the spade, he seemed to Muggleton to grow more and more unsatisfactory. He hung about helplessly among the idiotic side-shows of the seashore, talking about random topics and particularly attaching himself to those rows of automatic machines which are set up in such places; solemnly spending penny after penny in order to play vicarious games of golf, football, cricket, conducted by clockwork figures; and finally contenting himself with the miniature exhibition of a race, in which one metal doll appeared merely to run and jump after the other. And yet all the time he was listening very carefully to the story which the defeated detective poured out to him. Only his way of not letting his right hand know what his left hand was doing, with pennies, got very much on the detective's nerves.

'Can't we go and sit down somewhere,' said Muggleton impatiently. 'I've got a letter you ought to see, if you're to know anything at all of this business.'

Father Brown turned away with a sigh from the jumping dolls, and went and sat down with his companion on an iron seat on the shore; his companion had already unfolded the letter and handed it silently to him.

It was an abrupt and queer sort of letter. Father Brown thought. He knew that millionaires did not always specialize in manners, especially in dealing with dependants like detectives; but there seemed to be something more in the letter than mere brusquerie.

DEAR MUGGLETON,

I never thought I should come down to wanting help of this sort; but I'm about through with things. It's been getting more and more intolerable for the last two years. I guess all you need to know about the story is this. There is a dirty rascal who is a cousin of mine, I'm ashamed to say. He's been a tout, a tramp, a quack doctor, an actor, and all that; even has the brass to act under our name and call himself Bertrand Bruce. I believe he's either got some potty job at the theatre here, or is looking for one. But you may take it from me that the job isn't his real job. His real job is running me down and knocking me out for good, if he can. It's an old story and no business of anybody's; there was a time when we started neck and neck and ran a race of ambition—and what they call love as well. Was it my fault that he was a rotter and I was a man who succeeds in things? But the dirty devil swears he'll succeed yet; shoot me and run off with my—never mind. I suppose he's a sort of madman, but he'll jolly soon try to be some sort of murderer. I'll give you £5 a week if you'll meet me at the lodge at the end of the pier, just after the pier closes tonight—and take on my job. It's the only safe place to meet—if anything is safe by this time.

J. BRAHAM BRUCE

'Dear me,' said Father Brown mildly. 'Dear me. A rather hurried letter.'

Muggleton nodded; and after a pause began his own story; in an oddly refined voice contrasting with his clumsy appearance.

The priest knew well the hobbies of concealed culture hidden in many dingy lower and middle class men; but even he was startled by the excellent choice of words only a shade too pedantic; the man talked like a book.

'I arrived at the little round-house at the end of the pier before there was any sign of my distinguished client. I opened the door and went inside, feeling that he might prefer me, as well as himself, to be as inconspicuous as possible. Not that it mattered very much; for the pier was too long for anybody to have seen us from the beach or the parade, and, on glancing at my watch, I saw by the time that the pier entrance must have already closed. It was flattering, after a fashion, that he should thus ensure that we should be alone together at the rendezvous, as showing that he did really rely on my assistance or protection. Anyhow, it was his idea that we should meet on the pier after closing time, so I fell in with it readily enough. There were two chairs inside the little round pavilion, or whatever you call it; so I simply took one of them and waited. I did not have to wait long. He was famous for his punctuality, and sure enough, as I looked up at the one little round window opposite me I saw him pass slowly, as if making a preliminary circuit of the place.

'I had only seen portraits of him, and that was a long time ago; and naturally he was rather older than the portraits, but there was no mistaking the likeness. The profile that passed the window was of the sort called aquiline, after the beak of the eagle; but he rather suggested a grey and venerable eagle; an eagle in repose; an eagle that has long folded its wings. There was no mistaking, however, that look of authority, or silent pride in the habit of command, that has always marked men who, like him, have organized great systems and been obeyed. He was quietly dressed, what I could see of him; especially as compared with the crowd of seaside trippers which had filled so much of my day; but I fancied his overcoat was of that extra elegant sort that is cut to follow the line of the figure, and it had a strip of astrakhan lining showing on the lapels. All this, of course, I took in at a glance, for I had already got to my feet and gone to the door. I put out my hand and received the first shock of that terrible evening. The door was locked. Somebody had locked me in.

'For a moment I stood stunned, and still staring at the round window, from which, of course, the moving profile had already passed; and then I suddenly saw the explanation. Another profile, pointed like that of a pursuing hound, flashed into the circle of vision, as into a round mirror. The moment I saw it, I knew who it was. It was the Avenger; the murderer or would-be murderer, who had trailed the old millionaire for so long across land and sea, and had now tracked him to this blind-alley of an iron pier that hung between sea and land. And I knew, of course, that it was the murderer who had locked the door.

'The man I saw first had been tall, but his pursuer was even taller; an effect that was only lessened by his carrying his shoulders hunched very high and his neck and head thrust forward like a true beast of the chase. The effect of the combination gave him rather the look of a gigantic hunchback. But something of the blood relationship that connected this ruffian with his famous kinsman showed in the two profiles as they passed across the circle of glass. The pursuer also had a nose rather like the beak of a bird; though his general air of ragged degradation suggested the vulture rather than the eagle. He was unshaven to the point of being bearded, and the humped look of his shoulders was increased by the coils of a coarse woollen scarf. All these are trivialities, and can give no impression of the ugly energy of that outline, or the sense of avenging doom in that stooping and striding figure. Have you ever seen William Blake's design, sometimes called with some levity, "The Ghost of a Flea," but also called, with somewhat greater lucidity, "A Vision of Blood Guilt," or something of that kind? That is just such a nightmare of a stealthy giant, with high shoulders, carrying a knife and bowl. This man carried neither, but as he passed the window the second time, I saw with my own eyes that he loosened a revolver from the folds of the scarf and held it gripped and poised in his hand. The eyes in his head shifted and shone in the moonlight, and that in a very creepy way; they shot forward and back with lightning leaps; almost as if he could shoot them out like luminous horns, as do certain reptiles.

'Three times the pursued and the pursuer passed in succession outside the window, treading their narrow circle, before I fully awoke to the need of some action, however desperate. I shook the door with rattling violence; when next I saw the face of the unconscious victim I beat furiously on the window; then I tried to break the window. But it was a double window of exceptionally thick glass, and so deep was the embrasure that I doubted if I could properly reach the outer window at all. Anyhow, my dignified client took no notice of my noise or signals; and the revolving shadow-pantomime of those two masks of doom continued to turn round and round me, till I felt almost dizzy as well as sick. Then they suddenly ceased to reappear. I waited; and I knew that they would not come again. I knew that the crisis had come.

'I need not tell you more. You can almost imagine the rest, even as I sat there helpless, trying to imagine it; or trying not to imagine it. It is enough to say that in that awful silence, in which all sounds of footsteps had died away, there were only two other noises besides the rumbling undertones of the sea. The first was the loud noise of a shot and the second the duller noise of a splash.

'My client had been murdered within a few yards of me, and I could make no sign. I will not trouble you with what I felt about that. But even if I could recover from the murder, I am still confronted with the mystery.'

'Yes,' said Father Brown very gently, 'which mystery?'

'The mystery of how the murderer got away,' answered the other. 'The instant people were admitted to the pier next morning, I was released from my prison and went racing back to the entrance gates, to inquire who had left the pier since they were opened. Without bothering you with details, I may explain that they were, by a rather unusual arrangement, real full-size iron doors that would keep anybody out (or in) until they were opened. The officials there had seen nobody in the least resembling the assassin returning that way. And he was a rather unmistakable person. Even if he had disguised himself somehow, he could hardly have disguised his extraordinary height or got rid of the family nose. It is extraordinarily unlikely that he tried to swim ashore, for the sea was very rough; and there are certainly no traces of any landing. And, somehow, having seen the face of that fiend even once, let alone about six times, something gives me an overwhelming conviction that he did not simply drown himself in the hour of triumph.'

'I quite understand what you mean by that,' replied Father Brown. 'Besides, it would be very inconsistent with the tone of his original threatening letter, in which he promised himself all sorts of benefits after the crime... there's another point it might be well to verify. What about the structure of the pier underneath? Piers are very often made with a whole network of iron supports, which a man might climb through as a monkey climbs through a forest.'

'Yes, I thought of that,' replied the private investigator; 'but unfortunately this pier is oddly constructed in more ways than one. It's quite unusually long, and there are iron columns with all that tangle of iron girders; only they're very far apart and I can't see any way a man could climb from one to the other.'

'I only mentioned it,' said Father Brown thoughtfully, 'because that queer fish with the long whiskers, the old man who preaches on the sand, often climbs up on to the nearest girder. I believe he sits there fishing when the tide comes up. And he's a very queer fish to go fishing.'

'Why, what do you mean?'

'Well,' said Father Brown very slowly, twiddling with a button and gazing abstractedly out to the great green waters glittering in the last evening light after the sunset. 'Well ... I tried to talk to him in a friendly sort of way—friendly and not too funny, if you understand, about his combining the ancient trades of fishing and preaching; I think I made the obvious reference; the text that refers to fishing for living souls. And he said quite queerly and harshly, as he jumped back on to his iron perch, "Well, at least I fish for dead bodies."'

'Good God!' exclaimed the detective, staring at him.

'Yes,' said the priest. 'It seemed to me an odd remark to make in a chatty way, to a stranger playing with children on the sands.'

After another staring silence his companion eventually ejaculated: 'You don't mean you think he had anything to do with the death.'

'I think,' answered Father Brown, 'that he might throw some light on it.'

'Well, it's beyond me now,' said the detective. 'It's beyond me to believe that anybody can throw any light on it. It's like a welter of wild waters in the pitch dark; the sort of waters that he ... that he fell into. It's simply stark staring unreason; a big man vanishing like a bubble; nobody could possibly ... Look here!' He stopped suddenly, staring at the priest, who had not moved, but was still twiddling with the button and staring at the breakers. 'What do you mean? What are you looking like that for? You don't mean to say that you... that you can make any sense of it?'

'It would be much better if it remained nonsense,' said Father Brown in a low voice. 'Well, if you ask me right out—yes, I think I can make some sense of it.'

There was a long silence, and then the inquiry agent said with a rather singular abruptness: 'oh, here comes the old man's secretary from the hotel. I must be off. I think I'll go and talk to that mad fisherman of yours.'

'Post hoc propter hoc?' asked the priest with a smile.

'Well,' said the other, with jerky candour, 'the secretary don't like me and I don't think I like him. He's been poking around with a lot of questions that didn't seem to me to get us any further, except towards a quarrel. Perhaps he's jealous because the old man called in somebody else, and wasn't content with his elegant secretary's advice. See you later.'

And he turned away, ploughing through the sand to the place where the eccentric preacher had already mounted his marine nest; and looked in the green gloaming rather like some huge polyp or stinging jelly-fish trailing his poisonous filaments in the phosphorescent sea.

Meanwhile the priest was serenely watching the serene approach of the secretary; conspicuous even from afar, in that popular crowd, by the clerical neatness and sobriety of his top hat and tailcoat. Without feeling disposed to take part in any feuds between the secretary and the inquiry agent. Father Brown had a faint feeling of irrational sympathy with the prejudices of the latter. Mr Anthony Taylor, the secretary, was an extremely presentable young man, in countenance, as well as costume; and the countenance was firm and intellectual as well as merely good-looking. He was pale, with dark hair coming down on the sides of his head, as if pointing towards possible whiskers; he kept his lips compressed more tightly than most people. The only thing that Father Brown's fancy could tell itself in justification sounded queerer than it really looked. He had a notion that the man talked with his nostrils. Anyhow, the strong compression of his mouth brought out something abnormally sensitive and flexible in these movements at the sides of his nose, so that he seemed to be communicating and conducting life by snuffling and smelling, with his head up, as does a dog. It somehow fitted in with the other features that, when he did speak, it was with a sudden rattling rapidity like a gatling-gun, which sounded almost ugly from so smooth and polished a figure.

For once he opened the conversation, by saying: 'No bodies washed ashore, I imagine.'

'None have been announced, certainly,' said Father Brown.

'No gigantic body of the murderer with the woollen scarf,' said Mr Taylor.

'No,' said Father Brown.

Mr Taylor's mouth did not move anyone for the moment; but his nostrils spoke for him with such quick and quivering scorn, that they might almost have been called talkative.

When he did speak again, after some polite commonplaces from the priest, it was to say curtly: 'Here comes the Inspector; I suppose they've been scouring England for the scarf.'

Inspector Grinstead, a brown-faced man with a grey pointed beard, addressed Father Brown rather more respectfully than the secretary had done.

'I thought you would like to know, sir,' he said, 'that there is absolutely no trace of the man described as having escaped from the pier.'

'Or rather not described as having escaped from the pier,' said Taylor. 'The pier officials, the only people who could have described him, have never seen anybody to describe.'

'Well,' said the Inspector, 'we've telephoned all the stations and watched all the roads, and it will be almost impossible for him to escape from England. It really seems to me as if he couldn't have got out that way. He doesn't seem to be anywhere.'

'He never was anywhere,' said the secretary, with an abrupt grating voice, that sounded like a gun going off on that lonely shore.

The Inspector looked blank; but a light dawned gradually on the face of the priest, who said at last with almost ostentatious unconcern:

'Do you mean that the man was a myth? Or possibly a lie?'

'Ah,' said the secretary, inhaling through his haughty nostrils, 'you've thought of that at last.'

'I thought of that at first,' said Father Brown. 'It's the first thing anybody would think of, isn't it, hearing an unsupported story from a stranger about a strange murderer on a lonely pier. In plain words, you mean that little Muggleton never heard anybody murdering the millionaire. Possibly you mean that little Muggleton murdered him himself.'

'Well,' said the secretary, 'Muggleton looks a dingy down-and-out sort of cove to me. There's no story but his about what happened on the pier, and his story consists of a giant who vanished; quite a fairy-tale. It isn't a very creditable tale, even as he tells it. By his own account, he bungled his case and let his patron be killed a few yards away. He's a pretty rotten fool and failure, on his own confession.'

'Yes,' said Father Brown. 'I'm rather fond of people who are fools and failures on their own confession.'

'I don't know what you mean,' snapped the other.

'Perhaps,' said Father Brown, wistfully, 'it's because so many people are fools and failures without any confession.'

Then, after a pause, he went on: 'But even if he is a fool and a failure, that doesn't prove he is a liar and a murderer. And you've forgotten that there is one piece of external evidence that does really support history. I mean the letter from the millionaire, telling the whole tale of his cousin and his vendetta. Unless you can prove that the document itself is actually a forgery, you have to admit there was some probability of Bruce being pursued by somebody who had a real motive. Or rather, I should say, the one actually admitted and recorded motive.'

'I'm not quite sure that I understand you,' said the Inspector, 'about the motive.'

'My dear fellow,' said Father Brown, for the first time stung by impatience into familiarity, 'everybody's got a motive in a way. Considering the way that Bruce made his money, considering the way that most millionaires make their money, almost anybody in the world might have done such a perfectly natural thing as throw him into the sea. In many, one might almost fancy, it would be almost automatic. To almost all it must have occurred at some time or other. Mr Taylor might have done it.'

'What's that?' snapped Mr Taylor, and his nostrils swelled visibly.

'I might have done it,' went on Father Brown, 'nisi me constringeret ecclesiae auctoritas. Anybody, but for the one true morality, might be tempted to accept so obvious, so simple a social solution. I might have done it; you might have done it; the Mayor or the muffin-man might have done it. The only person on this earth I can think of, who probably would not have done it, is the private inquiry agent whom Bruce had just engaged at five pounds a week, and who hadn't yet had any of his money.'

The secretary was silent for a moment; then he snorted and said: 'If that's the offer in the letter, we'd certainly better see whether it's a forgery. For really, we don't know that the whole tale isn't as false as a forgery. The fellow admits himself that the disappearance of his hunchbacked giant is utterly incredible and inexplicable.'

'Yes,' said Father Brown; 'that's what I like about Muggleton. He admits things.'

'All the same,' insisted Taylor, his nostrils vibrant with excitement. 'All the same, the long and the short of it is that he can't prove that his tall man in the scarf ever existed or does exist; and every single fact found by the police and the witnesses proves that he does not exist. No, Father Brown. There is only one way in which you can justify this little scallywag you seem to be so fond of. And that is by producing his Imaginary Man. And that is exactly what you can't do.'

'By the way,' said the priest, absent-mindedly, 'I suppose you come from the hotel where Bruce has rooms, Mr Taylor?'

Taylor looked a little taken aback, and seemed almost to stammer. 'Well, he always did have those rooms; and they're practically his. I haven't actually seen him there this time.'

'I suppose you motored down with him,' observed Brown; 'or did you both come by train?'

'I came by train and brought the luggage,' said the secretary impatiently. 'Something kept him, I suppose. I haven't actually seen him since he left Yorkshire on his own a week or two ago.'

'So it seems,' said the priest very softly, 'that if Muggleton wasn't the last to see Bruce by the wild sea waves, you were the last to see him, on the equally wild Yorkshire moors.'

Taylor had turned quite white, but he forced his grating voice to composure: 'I never said Muggleton didn't see Bruce on the pier.'

'No; and why didn't you?' asked Father Brown. 'If he made up one man on the pier, why shouldn't he make up two men on the pier? Of course we do know that Bruce did exist; but we don't seem to know what has happened to him for several weeks. Perhaps he was left behind in Yorkshire.'

The rather strident voice of the secretary rose almost to a scream. All his veneer of society suavity seemed to have vanished.

'You're simply shuffling! You're simply shirking! You're trying to drag in mad insinuations about me, simply because you can't answer my question.'

'Let me see,' said Father Brown reminiscently. 'What was your question?'

'You know well enough what it was; and you know you're damned well stumped by it. Where is the man with the scarf? Who has seen him? Whoever heard of him or spoke of him, except that little liar of yours? If you want to convince us, you must produce him. If he ever existed, he may be hiding in the Hebrides or off to Callao. But you've got to produce him, though I know he doesn't exist. Well then! Where is he?'

'I rather think he is over there,' said Father Brown, peering and blinking towards the nearer waves that washed round the iron pillars of the pier; where the two figures of the agent and the old fisher and preacher were still dark against the green glow of the water. 'I mean in that sort of net thing that's tossing about in the sea.'

With whatever bewilderment, Inspector Grinstead took the upper hand again with a flash, and strode down the beach.

'Do you mean to say,' he cried, 'that the murderer's body is in the old boy's net?'

Father Brown nodded as he followed down the shingly slope; and, even as they moved, little Muggleton the agent turned and began to climb the same shore, his mere dark outline a pantomime of amazement and discovery.

'It's true, for all we said,' he gasped. 'The murderer did try to swim ashore and was drowned, of course, in that weather. Or else he did really commit suicide. Anyhow, he drifted dead into old Brimstone's fishing-net, and that's what the old maniac meant when he said he fished for dead men.'

The Inspector ran down the shore with an agility that outstripped them all, and was heard shouting out orders. In a few moments the fishermen and a few bystanders, assisted by the policemen, had hauled the net into shore, and rolled it with its burden on to the wet sands that still reflected the sunset. The secretary looked at what lay on the sands and the words died on his lips. For what lay on the sands was indeed the body of a gigantic man in rags, with the huge shoulders somewhat humped and bony eagle face; and a great red ragged woollen scarf or comforter, sprawled along the sunset sands like a great stain of blood. But Taylor was staring not at the gory scarf or the fabulous stature, but at the face; and his own face was a conflict of incredulity and suspicion.

The Inspector instantly turned to Muggleton with a new air of civility.

'This certainly confirms your story,' he said. And until he heard the tone of those words, Muggleton had never guessed how almost universally his story had been disbelieved. Nobody had believed him. Nobody but Father Brown.

Therefore, seeing Father Brown edging away from the group, he made a movement to depart in his company; but even then he was brought up rather short by the discovery that the priest was once more being drawn away by the deadly attractions of the funny little automatic machines. He even saw the reverend gentleman fumbling for a penny. He stopped, however, with the penny poised in his finger and thumb, as the secretary spoke for the last time in his loud discordant voice.

'And I suppose we may add,' he said, 'that the monstrous and imbecile charges against me are also at an end.'

'My dear sir,' said the priest, 'I never made any charges against you. I'm not such a fool as to suppose you were likely to murder your master in Yorkshire and then come down here to fool about with his luggage. All I said was that I could make out a better case against you than you were making out so vigorously against poor Mr Muggleton. All the same, if you really want to learn the truth about his business (and I assure you the truth isn't generally grasped yet), I can give you a hint even from your own affairs. It is rather a rum and significant thing that Mr Bruce the millionaire had been unknown to all his usual haunts and habits for weeks before he was really killed. As you seem to be a promising amateur detective, I advise you to work on that line.'

'What do you mean?' asked Taylor sharply.

But he got no answer out of Father Brown, who was once more completely concentrated on jiggling the little handle of the machine, that made one doll jump out and then another doll jump after it.

'Father Brown,' said Muggleton, his old annoyance faintly reviving: 'Will you tell me why you like that fool thing so much?'

'For one reason,' replied the priest, peering closely into the glass puppet-show. 'Because it contains the secret of this tragedy.'

Then he suddenly straightened himself; and looked quite seriously at his companion.

'I knew all along,' he said, 'that you were telling the truth and the opposite of the truth.'

Muggleton could only stare at a return of all the riddles.

'It's quite simple,' added the priest, lowering his voice. 'That corpse with the scarlet scarf over there is the corpse of Braham Bruce the millionaire. There won't be any other.'

'But the two men—' began Muggleton, and his mouth fell open.

'Your description of the two men was quite admirably vivid,' said Father Brown. 'I assure you I'm not at all likely to forget it. If I may say so, you have a literary talent; perhaps journalism would give you more scope than detection. I believe I remember practically each point about each person. Only, you see, queerly enough, each point affected you in one way and me in exactly the opposite way. Let's begin with the first you mentioned. You said that the first man you saw had an indescribable air of authority and dignity. And you said to yourself, "That's the Trust Magnate, the great merchant prince, the ruler of markets." But when I heard about the air of dignity and authority, I said to myself, "That's the actor; everything about this is the actor," You don't get that look by being

President of the Chain Store Amalgamation Company. You get that look by being Hamlet's Father's Ghost, or Julius Caesar, or King Lear, and you never altogether lose it. You couldn't see enough of his clothes to tell whether they were really seedy, but you saw a strip of fur and a sort of faintly fashionable cut; and I said to myself again, "The actor."

'Next, before we go into details about the other man, notice one thing about him evidently absent from the first man. You said the second man was not only ragged but unshaven to the point of being bearded. Now we have all seen shabby actors, dirty actors, drunken actors, utterly disreputable actors. But such a thing as a scrub-bearded actor, in a job or even looking round for a job, has scarcely been seen in this world. On the other hand, shaving is often almost the first thing to go, with a gentleman or a wealthy eccentric who is really letting himself go to pieces. Now we have every reason to believe that your friend the millionaire was letting himself go to pieces. His letter was the letter of a man who had already gone to pieces. But it wasn't only negligence that made him look poor and shabby. Don't you understand that the man was practically in hiding? That was why he didn't go to his hotel; and his own secretary hadn't seen him for weeks. He was a millionaire; but his whole object was to be a completely disguised millionaire. Have you ever read "*The Woman in White*"? Don't you remember that the fashionable and luxurious Count Fosco, fleeing for his life before a secret society, was found stabbed in the blue blouse of a common French workman? Then let us go back for a moment to the demeanour of these men. You saw the first man calm and collected and you said to yourself, "That's the innocent victim"; though the innocent victim's own letter wasn't at all calm and collected. I heard he was calm and collected; and I said to myself, "That's the murderer." Why should he be anything else but calm and collected? He knew what he was going to do. He had made up his mind to do it for a long time; if he had ever had any hesitation or remorse he had hardened himself against them before he came on the scene—in his case, we might say, on the stage. He wasn't likely to have any particular stage-fright. He didn't pull out his pistol and wave it about; why should he? He kept it in his pocket till he wanted it; very likely he fired from his pocket. The other man fidgeted with his pistol because he was nervous as a cat, and very probably had never had a pistol before. He did it for the same reason that he rolled his eyes; and I remember that, even in your own unconscious evidence, it is particularly stated that he rolled them backwards. In fact, he was looking behind him. In fact, he was not the pursuer but the pursued. But because you happened to see the first man first, you couldn't help thinking of the other man as coming up behind him. In mere mathematics and mechanics, each of them was running after the other—just like the others.'

'What others?' inquired the dazed detective.

'Why, these,' cried Father Brown, striking the automatic machine with the little wooden spade, which had incongruously remained in his hand throughout these murderous mysteries. 'These little clockwork dolls that chase each other round and round forever. Let us call them Mr Blue and Mr Red, after the colour of their coats. I happened to start off with Mr Blue, and so the children said that Mr Red was running after him; but it would have looked exactly the contrary if I had started with Mr Red.'

'Yes, I begin to see,' said Muggleton; 'and I suppose all the rest fits in. The family likeness, of course, cuts both ways, and they never saw the murderer leaving the pier—'

'They never looked for the murderer leaving the pier,' said the other. 'Nobody told them to look for a quiet clean-shaven gentleman in an astrakhan coat. All the mystery of his vanishing revolved on your description of a hulking fellow in a red neckcloth. But the simple truth was that the actor in the astrakhan coat murdered the millionaire with the red rag, and there is the poor fellow's body. It's just like the red and blue dolls; only, because you saw one first, you guessed wrong about which was red with vengeance and which was blue with funk.'

At this point two or three children began to straggle across the sands, and the priest waved them to him with the wooden spade, theatrically tapping the automatic machine. Muggleton guessed that it was mainly to prevent their straying towards the horrible heap on the shore.

'One more penny left in the world,' said Father Brown, 'and then we must go home to tea. Do you know, Doris, I rather like those revolving games, that just go round and round like the Mulberry-Bush. After all, God made all the suns and stars to play Mulberry-Bush. But those other games, where one must catch up with another, where runners are rivals and run neck and neck and outstrip each other; well—much nastier things seem to happen. I like to think of Mr Red and Mr Blue always jumping with undiminished spirits; all free and equal; and never hurting each other. "Fond lover, never, never, wilt thou kiss—or kill." Happy, happy Mr Red!

He cannot change; though thou hast not thy bliss,
Forever will thou jump; and he be Blue.'

Reciting this remarkable quotation from Keats, with some emotion, Father Brown tucked the little spade under one arm, and giving a hand to two of the children, stumped solemnly up the beach to tea.

6

THE CRIME OF THE COMMUNIST
(First published in *Collier's Weekly*, Jul 14, 1934)

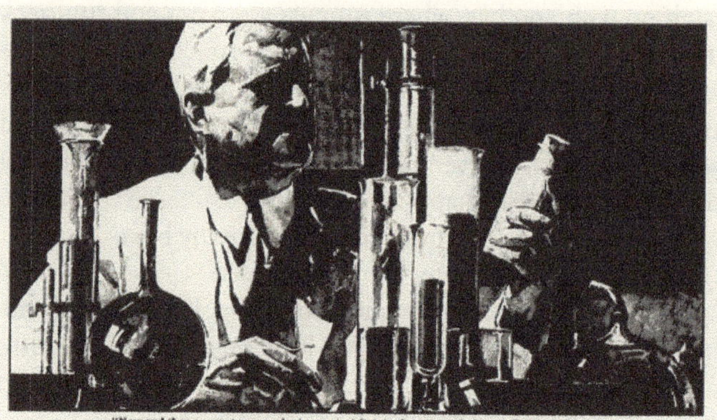

"Now and then you get a man who is a materialist, in the sense of a beast. He is a bad man."

The Crime of the Communist

A mystery story, in which more, far more, than a corpse is found. The law's master-mind is the famous Father Brown, the world's most studious detective

By G. K. Chesterton

ILLUSTRATED BY GEORGE HOWE

Three men came out from under the lowbrowed Tudor arch in the mellow facade of Mandeville College, into the strong evening sunlight of a summer day which seemed as if it would never end; and in that sunlight they saw something that blasted like lightning; well-fitted to be the shock of their lives.

Even before they had realized anything in the way of a catastrophe, they were conscious of a contrast. They themselves, in a curious quiet way, were quite harmonious with their surroundings. Though the Tudor arches that ran like a cloister round the College gardens had been built four hundred years ago, at that moment when the Gothic fell from heaven and bowed, or almost crouched, over the cosier chambers of Humanism and the Revival of Learning—though they themselves were in modern clothes (that is in clothes whose ugliness would have amazed any of the four centuries) yet something in the spirit of the place made them all at one. The gardens had been tended so carefully as to achieve the final triumph of looking careless; the very flowers seemed beautiful by accident, like elegant weeds; and the modern costumes had at least any picturesqueness that can be produced by being untidy. The first of the three, a tall, bald, bearded maypole of a man, was a familiar figure in the Quad in cap and gown; the gown slipped off one of his sloping shoulders. The second was very square-shouldered, short and compact, with a rather jolly grin, commonly clad in a jacket, with his gown over his arm. The third was even shorter and much shabbier, in black clerical clothes. But they all seemed suitable to Mandeville College; and the indescribable atmosphere of the two ancient and unique Universities of England. They fitted into it and they faded into it; which is there regarded as most fitting.

The two men seated on garden chairs by a little table were a sort of brilliant blot on this grey-green landscape. They were clad mostly in black and yet they glittered from head to heel, from their burnished top hats to their perfectly polished boots. It was dimly felt as an outrage that anybody should be so well-dressed in the well-bred freedom of Mandeville College. The only excuse was that they were foreigners. One was an American, a millionaire named Hake, dressed in the spotlessly and sparklingly gentlemanly manner known only to the rich of New York. The other, who added to all these things the outrage of an astrakhan overcoat (to say nothing of a pair of florid whiskers), was a German Count of great wealth, the shortest part of whose name was Von Zimmern. The mystery of this story, however, is not the mystery of why they were there. They were there for the reason that commonly explains the meeting of incongruous things; they proposed to give the College some money. They had come in support of a plan supported by several financiers and magnates of many countries, for founding a new Chair of Economics at Mandeville College. They had inspected the College with that tireless conscientious sightseeing of which no sons of Eve are capable except the American and the German. And now they were resting from their labours and looking solemnly at the College gardens. So far so good.

The three other men, who had already met them, passed with a vague salutation; but one of them stopped; the smallest of the three, in the black clerical clothes.

'I say,' he said, with rather the air of a frightened rabbit, 'I don't like the look of those men.'

'Good God! Who could?' ejaculated the tall man, who happened to be the Master of Mandeville. 'At least we have some rich men who don't go about dressed up like tailors' dummies.'

'Yes,' hissed the little cleric, 'that's what I mean. Like tailors' dummies.'

'Why, what do you mean?' asked the shorter of the other men, sharply.

'I mean they're like horrible waxworks,' said the cleric in a faint voice. 'I mean they don't move. Why don't they move?'

Suddenly starting out of his dim retirement, he darted across the garden and touched the German Baron on the elbow. The German Baron fell over, chair and all, and the trousered legs that stuck up in the air were as stiff as the legs of the chair.

Mr Gideon P. Hake continued to gaze at the College gardens with glassy eyes; but the parallel of a waxwork confirmed the impression that they were like eyes made of glass. Somehow the rich sunlight and the coloured garden increased the creepy impression of a stiffly dressed doll; a marionette on an Italian stage. The small man in black, who was a priest named Brown, tentatively touched the millionaire on the shoulder, and the millionaire fell sideways, but horribly all of a piece, like something carved in wood.

'Rigor mortis,' said Father Brown, 'and so soon. But it does vary a good deal.'

The reason the first three men had joined the other two men so late (not to say too late) will best be understood by noting what had happened just inside the building, behind the Tudor archway, but a short time before they came out. They had all dined together in Hall, at the High Table; but the two foreign philanthropists, slaves of duty in the matter of seeing everything, had solemnly gone back to the chapel, of which one cloister and a staircase remained unexamined; promising to rejoin the rest in the garden, to examine as earnestly the College cigars. The rest, in a more reverent and right-minded spirit, had adjourned as usual to the long narrow oak table, round which the after-dinner wine had circulated, for all anybody knew, ever since the College had been founded in the Middle Ages by Sir John Mandeville, for the encouragement of telling stories. The Master, with the big fair beard and bald brow, took the head of the table, and the squat man in the square jacket sat on his left; for he was the Bursar or business man of the College. Next to him, on that side of the table, sat a queer-looking man with what could only be called a crooked face; for its dark tufts of moustache and eyebrow, slanting at contrary angles, made a sort of zig-zag, as if half his face were puckered or paralysed. His name was Byles; he was the lecturer in Roman History, and his political opinions were founded on those of Coriolanus, not to mention Tarquinius Superbus. This tart Toryism, and rabidly reactionary view of all current problems, was not altogether unknown among the more old-fashioned sort of dons; but in the case of Byles there was a suggestion that it was a result rather than a cause of his acerbity. More than one sharp observer had received the impression that there was something really wrong with Byles; that some secret or some great misfortune had embittered him; as if that half-withered face had really been blasted like a storm-stricken tree. Beyond him again sat Father Brown and at the end of the table a Professor of Chemistry, large and blond and bland, with eyes that were sleepy and perhaps a little sly. It was well known that this natural philosopher regarded the other philosophers, of a more classical tradition, very much as old logics. On the other side of the table, opposite Father Brown, was a very swarthy and silent young man, with a black pointed beard, introduced because somebody had insisted on having a Chair of Persian; opposite the sinister Byles was a very mild-looking little Chaplain, with a head like an egg. Opposite the Bursar and at the right hand of the Master, was an empty chair; and there were many there who were glad to see it empty.

'I don't know whether Craken is coming,' said the Master, not without a nervous glance at the chair, which contrasted with the usual languid freedom of his demeanour. 'I believe in giving people a lot of rope myself; but I confess I've reached the point of being glad when he is here, merely because he isn't anywhere else.'

'Never know what he'll be up to next,' said the Bursar, cheerfully, 'especially when he's instructing the young.'

'A brilliant fellow, but fiery of course,' said the Master, with a rather abrupt relapse into reserve.

"Fireworks are fiery, and also brilliant," growled old Byles, 'but I don't want to be burned in my bed so that Craken can figure as a real Guy Fawkes.'

'Do you really think he would join a physical force revolution, if there were one,' asked the Bursar smiling.

'Well, he thinks he would,' said Byles sharply. 'Told a whole hall full of undergraduates the other day that nothing now could avert the Class War turning into a real war, with killing in the streets of the town; and it didn't matter, so long as it ended in Communism and the victory of the working-class.'

'The Class War,' mused the Master, with a sort of distaste mellowed by distance; for he had known William Morris long ago and been familiar enough with the more artistic and leisurely Socialists. 'I never can understand all this about the Class War. When I was young, Socialism was supposed to mean saying that there are no classes.'

'Nother way of saying that Socialists are no class,' said Byles with sour relish.

'Of course, you'd be more against them than I should,' said the Master thoughtfully, 'but I suppose my Socialism is almost as old-fashioned as your Toryism. Wonder what our young friends really think. What do you think. Baker?' he said abruptly to the Bursar on his left.

'Oh, I don't think, as the vulgar saying is,' said the Bursar laughing. 'You must remember I'm a very vulgar person. I'm not a thinker. I'm only a business man; and as a business man I think it's all bosh. You can't make men equal and it's damned bad business to pay them equal; especially a lot of them not worth paying for at all. Whatever it is, you've got to take the practical way out, because it's the only way out. It's not our fault if nature made everything a scramble.'

'I agree with you there,' said the Professor of Chemistry, speaking with a lisp that seemed childish in so large a man. 'Communism pretends to be oh so modern; but it is not. Throwback to the superstitions of monks and primitive tribes. A scientific government, with a really ethical responsibility to posterity, would be always looking for the line of promise and progress; not levelling and flattening it all back into the mud again. Socialism is sentimentalism; and more dangerous than a pestilence, for in that at least the fittest would survive.'

The Master smiled a little sadly. 'You know you and I will never feel quite the same about differences of opinion. Didn't somebody say up here, about walking with a friend by the river, "Not differing much, except in opinion." Isn't that the motto of a university? To have hundreds of opinions and not be opinionated. If people fall here, it's by what they are, not what they think. Perhaps I'm a relic of the eighteenth century; but I incline to the old sentimental heresy, "For forms of faith let graceless zealots fight; he can't he wrong whose life is in the right." What do you think about that, Father Brown?'

He glanced a little mischievously across at the priest and was mildly startled. For he had always found the priest very cheerful and amiable and easy to get on with; and his round face was mostly solid with good humour. But for some reason the priest's face at this moment was knotted with a frown much more sombre than any the company had ever seen on it; so that for an instant that commonplace countenance actually looked darker and more ominous than the haggard face of Byles. An instant later the cloud seemed lo have passed; but Father Brown still spoke with a certain sobriety and firmness.

'I don't believe in that, anyhow,' he said shortly. 'How can his life be in the right, if his whole view of life is wrong? That's a modern muddle that arose because people didn't know how much views of life can differ. Baptists and Methodists knew they didn't differ very much in morality; but then they didn't differ very much in religion or philosophy. It's quite different when you pass from the Baptists to the Anabaptists; or from the Theosophists to the Thugs. Heresy always does affect morality, if it's heretical enough. I suppose a man may honestly believe that thieving isn't wrong. But what's the good of saying that he honestly believes in dishonesty?'

'Damned good,' said Byles with a ferocious contortion of feature, believed by many to be meant for a friendly smile. 'And that's why I object to having a Chair of Theoretical Thieving in this College.'

'Well, you're all very down on Communism, of course,' said the Master, with a sigh. 'But do you really think there's so much of it to be down on? Are any of your heresies really big enough to be dangerous?'

'I think they have grown so big,' said Father Brown gravely, 'that in some circles they are already taken for granted. They are actually unconscious. That is, without conscience.'

'And the end of it,' said Byles, 'will be the ruin of this country.'

'The end will be something worse,' said Father Brown.

A shadow shot or slid rapidly along the panelled wall opposite, as swiftly followed by the figure that had flung it; a tall but stooping figure with a vague outline like a bird of prey; accentuated by the fact that its sudden appearance and swift passage were like those of a bird startled and flying from a bush. It was only the figure of a long-limbed, high-shouldered man with long drooping moustaches, in fact, familiar enough to them all; but something in the twilight and candlelight and the flying and streaking shadow connected it strangely with the priest's unconscious words of omen; for all the world, as if those words had indeed been an augury, in the old Roman sense; and the sign of it the flight of a bird. Perhaps Mr Byles might have given a lecture on such Roman augury; and especially on that bird of ill-omen.

The tall man shot along the wall like his own shadow until he sank into the empty chair on the Master's right, and looked across at the Bursar and the rest with hollow and cavernous eyes. His hanging hair and moustache were quite fair, but his eyes were so deep-set that they might have been black. Everyone knew, or could guess, who the newcomer was; but an incident instantly followed that sufficiently illuminated the situation. The Professor of Roman History rose stiffly to his feet and stalked out of the room, indicating with little finesse his feelings about sitting at the same table with the Professor of Theoretical Thieving, otherwise the Communist, Mr Craken.

The Master of Mandeville covered the awkward situation with nervous grace. 'I was defending you, or some aspects of you, my dear Craken,' he said smiling, 'though I am sure you would find me quite indefensible. After all, I can't forget that the old Socialist friends of my youth had a very fine ideal of fraternity and comradeship. William Morris put it all in a sentence, "Fellowship is heaven; and lack of fellowship is hell."'

'Dons as Democrats; see headline,' said Mr Craken rather disagreeably. 'And is Hard-Case Hake going to dedicate the new Commercial Chair to the memory of William Morris?'

'Well,' said the Master, still maintaining a desperate geniality, 'I hope we may say, in a sense, that all our Chairs are Chairs of good-fellowship.'

'Yes; that's the academic version of the Morris maxim,' growled Craken. '"A Fellowship is heaven; and lack of a Fellowship is hell."'

'Don't be so cross, Craken,' interposed the Bursar briskly. 'Take some port. Tenby, pass the port to Mr Craken.'

'Oh well, I'll have a glass,' said the Communist Professor a little less ungraciously. 'I really came down here to have a smoke in the garden. Then I looked out of the window and saw your two precious millionaires were actually blooming in the garden; fresh, innocent buds. After all, it might be worth while to give them a bit of my mind.'

The Master had risen under cover of his last conventional cordiality, and was only too glad to leave the Bursar to do his best with the Wild Man. Others had risen, and the groups at the table had begun to break up; and the Bursar and Mr Craken were left more or less alone at the end of the long table. Only Father Brown continued to sit staring into vacancy with a rather cloudy expression.

'Oh, as to that,' said the Bursar. 'I'm pretty tired of them myself, to tell the truth; I've been with them the best part of a day going into facts and figures and all the business of this new Professorship. But look here, Craken,' and he leaned across the table and spoke with a sort of soft emphasis, 'you really needn't cut up so rough about this new Professorship. It doesn't really interfere with your subject. You're the only Professor of Political Economy at Mandeville and, though I don't pretend to agree with your notions, everybody knows you've got a European reputation. This is a special subject they call Applied Economics. Well, even today, as I told you, I've had a hell of a lot of Applied Economics. In other words, I've had to talk business with two business men. Would you particularly want to do that? Would you envy it? Would you stand it? Isn't that evidence enough that there is a separate subject and may well be a separate Chair?'

'Good God,' cried Craken with the intense invocation of the atheist. 'Do you think I don't want to apply Economics? Only, when we apply it, you call it red ruin and anarchy; and when you apply it, I take the liberty of calling it exploitation. If only you fellows would apply Economics, it's just possible that people might get something to eat. We are the practical people; and that's why you're afraid of us. That's why you have to get two greasy Capitalists to start another Lectureship; just because I've let the cat out of the bag.'

'Rather a wild cat, wasn't it?' said the Bursar smiling, 'that you let out of the bag?'

'And rather a gold-bag, wasn't it,' said Craken, 'that you are tying the cat up in again?'

'Well, I don't suppose we shall ever agree about all that,' said the other. 'But those fellows have come out of their chapel into the garden; and if you want to have your smoke there, you'd better come.' He watched with some amusement his companion fumbling in all his pockets till he produced a pipe, and then, gazing at it with an abstracted air, Craken rose to his feet, but even in doing so, seemed to be feeling all over himself again. Mr Baker the Bursar ended the controversy with a happy laugh of reconciliation. 'You are the practical people, and you will blow up the town with dynamite. Only you'll probably forget the dynamite, as I bet you've forgotten the tobacco. Never mind, take a fill of mine. Matches?' He threw a tobacco-pouch and its accessories across the table; to be caught by Mr Craken with that dexterity never forgotten by a cricketer, even when he adopts opinions generally regarded as not cricket. The two men rose together; but Baker could not forbear remarking, 'Are you really the only practical people? Isn't there anything to be said for the Applied economics, that remembers to carry a tobacco-pouch as well as a pipe?'

Craken looked at him with smouldering eyes; and said at last, after slowly draining the last of his wine: 'Let's say there's another sort of practicality. I dare say I do forget details and so on. What I want you to understand is this'—he automatically returned the pouch; but his eyes were far away and jet—burning, almost terrible—'because the inside of our intellect has changed, because we really have a new idea of right, we shall do things you think really wrong. And they will be very practical.'

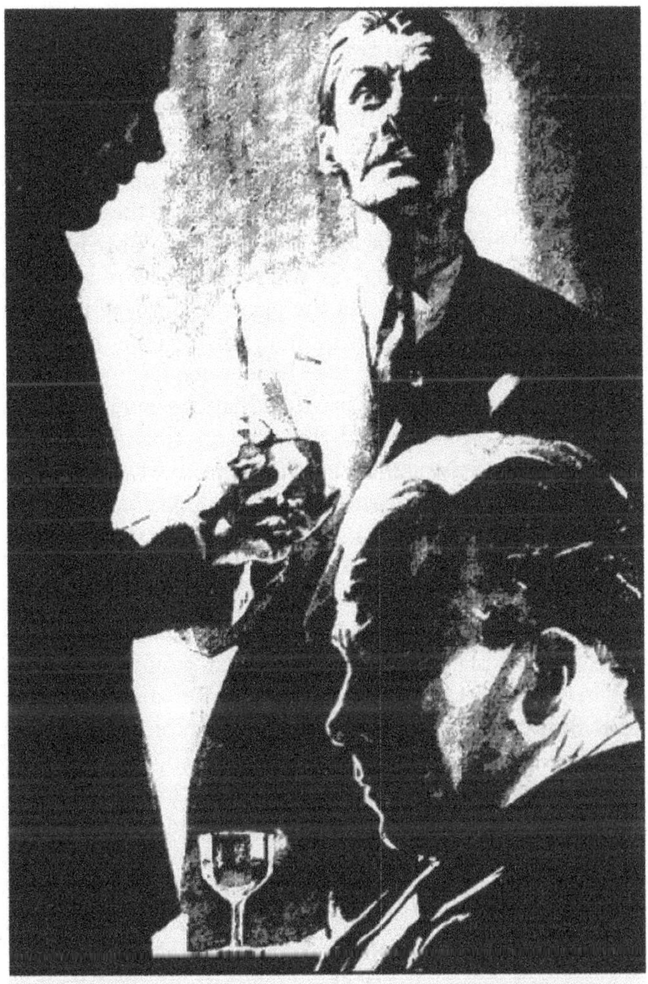

He returned the pouch, his eyes were far away and burning.

'Yes,' said Father Brown, suddenly coming out of his trance. 'That's exactly what I said.'

He looked across at Craken with a glassy and rather ghastly smile, saying: 'Mr Craken and I are in complete agreement.'

'Well,' said Baker, 'Craken is going out to smoke a pipe with the plutocrats; but I doubt whether it will be a pipe of peace.'

He turned rather abruptly and called to an aged attendant in the background. Mandeville was one of the last of the very old-fashioned Colleges; and even Craken was one of the first of the Communists; before the Bolshevism of today. 'That reminds me,' the Bursar was saying, 'as you won't hand round your peace pipe, we must send out the cigars to our distinguished guests. If they're smokers they must be longing for a smoke; for they've been nosing about in the chapel since feeding-time.'

Craken exploded with a savage and jarring laugh. 'Oh, I'll take them their cigars,' he said. 'I'm only a proletarian.'

Baker and Brown and the attendant were all witnesses to the fact that the Communist strode furiously into the garden to confront the millionaires; but nothing more was seen or heard of them until, as is already recorded, Father Brown found them dead in their chairs.

It was agreed that the Master and the priest should remain to guard the scene of tragedy, while the Bursar, younger and more rapid in his movements, ran off to fetch doctors and policemen. Father Brown approached the table on which one of the cigars had burned itself away all but an inch or two; the other had dropped from the hand and been dashed out into dying sparks on the crazy-pavement. The Master of Mandeville sat down rather shakily on a sufficiently distant seat and buried his bald brow in his hands. Then he looked up at first rather wearily; and then he looked very startled indeed and broke the stillness of the garden with a word like a small explosion of horror.

There was a certain quality about Father Brown which might sometimes be called blood-curdling. He always thought about what he was doing and never about whether it was done; he would do the most ugly or horrible or undignified or dirty things as calmly as a surgeon. There was a certain blank, in his simple mind, of all those things commonly associated with being superstitious or sentimental. He sat down on the chair from which the corpse had fallen, picked up the cigar the corpse had partially smoked, carefully detached the ash, examined the butt-end and then stuck it in his mouth and lit it. It looked like some obscene and grotesque antic in derision of the dead; and it seemed to him to be the most ordinary common sense. A cloud floated upwards like the smoke of some savage sacrifice and idolatry; but to Father Brown it appeared a perfectly self-evident fact that the only way to find out what a cigar is like is to smoke it. Nor did it lessen the horror for his old friend, the Master of Mandeville, to have a dim but shrewd guess that Father Brown was, upon the possibilities of the case, risking his own life.

'No; I think that's all right,' said the priest, putting the stump down again. 'Jolly good cigars. Your cigars. not American or German. I don't think there's anything odd about the cigar itself; but they'd better take care of the ashes. These men were poisoned somehow with the sort of stuff that stiffens the body quickly ... By the way, there goes somebody who knows more about it than we do.'

The Master sat up with a curiously uncomfortable jolt; for indeed the large shadow which had fallen across the pathway preceded a figure which, however heavy, was almost as soft-footed as a shadow. Professor Wadham, eminent occupant of the Chair of Chemistry, always moved very quietly in spite of his size, and there was nothing odd about his strolling in the garden; yet there seemed something unnaturally neat in his appearing at the exact moment when chemistry was mentioned.

Professor Wadham prided himself on his quietude; some would say his insensibility. He did not turn a hair on his flattened flaxen head, but stood looking down at the dead men with a shade of something like indifference on his large froglike face. Only when he looked at the cigar-ash, which the priest had preserved, he touched it with one finger; then he seemed to stand even stiller than before; but in the shadow of his face his eyes for an instant seemed to shoot out telescopically like one of his own microscopes. He had certainly realized or recognized something; but he said nothing.

'I don't know where anyone is to begin in this business,' said the Master.

'I should begin,' said Father Brown, 'by asking where these unfortunate men had been most of the time today.'

'They were messing about in my laboratory for a good time,' said Wadham, speaking for the first time. 'Baker often comes up to have a chat, and this time he brought his two patrons to inspect my department. But I think they went everywhere; real tourists. I know they went to the chapel and even into the tunnel under the crypt, where you have to light candles; instead of digesting their food like sane men. Baker seems to have taken them everywhere.'

'Were they interested in anything particular in your department?' asked the priest. 'What were you doing there just then?'

The Professor of Chemistry murmured a chemical formula beginning with 'sulphate', and ending with something that sounded like 'silenium'; unintelligible to both his hearers. He then wandered wearily away and sat on a remote bench in the sun, closing his eyes, but turning up his large face with heavy forbearance.

At his point, by a sharp contrast, the lawns were crossed by a brisk figure travelling as rapidly and as straight as a bullet; and Father Brown recognized the neat black clothes and shrewd doglike face of a police-surgeon whom he had met in the poorer parts of town. He was the first to arrive of the official contingent.

'Look here,' said the Master to the priest, before the doctor was within earshot. 'I must know something. Did you mean what you said about Communism being a real danger and leading to crime?'

'Yes,' said Father Brown smiling rather grimly, 'I have really noticed the spread of some Communist ways and influences; and, in one sense, this is a Communist crime.'

'Thank you,' said the Master. 'Then I must go off and see to something at once. Tell the authorities I'll be back in ten minutes.'

The Master had vanished into one of the Tudor archways at just about the moment when the police-doctor had reached the table and cheerfully recognized Father Brown. On the latter's suggestion that they should sit down at the tragic table, Dr Blake threw one sharp and doubtful glance at the big, bland and seemingly somnolent chemist, who occupied a more remote seat. He was duly informed of the Professor's identity, and what had so far been gathered of the Professor's evidence; and listened to it silently while conducting a preliminary examination of the dead bodies. Naturally, he seemed more concentrated on the actual corpses than on the hearsay evidence, until one detail suddenly distracted him entirely from the science of anatomy.

'What did the Professor say he was working at?' he inquired.

Father Brown patiently repeated the chemical formula he did not understand.

'What?' snapped Dr Blake, like a pistol-shot. 'Gosh! This is pretty frightful!'

'Because it's poison?' inquired Father Brown.

'Because it's piffle,' replied Dr Blake. 'It's simply nonsense. The Professor is quite a famous chemist. Why is a famous chemist deliberately talking nonsense?'

'Well, I think I know that one,' answered Father Brown mildly. 'He is talking nonsense, because he is telling lies. He is concealing something; and he wanted specially to conceal it from these two men and their representatives.'

The doctor lifted his eyes from the two men and looked across at the almost unnaturally immobile figure of the great chemist. He might almost have been asleep; a garden butterfly had settled upon him and seemed to turn his stillness into that of a stone idol. The large folds of his froglike face reminded the doctor of the hanging skins of a rhinoceros.

'Yes,' said Father Brown, in a very low voice. 'He is a wicked man.'

'God damn it all!' cried the doctor, suddenly moved to his very depths. 'Do you mean that a great scientific man like that deals in murder?'

'Fastidious critics would have complained of his dealing in murder,' said the priest dispassionately. 'I don't say I'm very fond of people dealing in murder in that way myself. But what's much more to the point—I'm sure that these poor fellows were among his fastidious critics.'

'You mean they found his secret and he silenced them?' said Blake frowning. 'But what in hell was his secret? How could a man murder on a large scale in a place like this?'

'I have told you his secret,' said the priest. 'It is a secret of the soul. He is a bad man. For heaven's sake don't fancy I say that because he and I are of opposite schools or traditions. I have a crowd of scientific friends; and most of them are heroically disinterested. Even of the most sceptical, I would only say they are rather irrationally disinterested. But now and then you do get a man who is a materialist, in the sense of a beast. I repeat he's a bad man. Much worse than—' And Father Brown seemed to hesitate for a word.

'You mean much worse than the Communist?' suggested the other.

'No; I mean much worse than the murderer,' said Father Brown.

He got to his feet in an abstracted manner; and hardly realized that his companion was staring at him.

'But didn't you mean,' asked Blake at last, 'that this Wadham is the murderer?'

'Oh, no,' said Father Brown more cheerfully. 'The murderer is a much more sympathetic and understandable person. He at least was desperate; and had the excuses of sudden rage and despair.'

'Why,' cried the doctor, 'do you mean it was the Communist after all?'

It was at this very moment, appropriately enough, that the police officials appeared with an announcement that seemed to conclude the case in a most decisive and satisfactory manner. They had been somewhat delayed in reaching the scene of the crime, by the simple fact that they had already captured the criminal. Indeed, they had captured him almost at the gates of their own official residence. They had already had reason to suspect the activities of Craken the Communist during various disorders in the town; when they heard of the outrage they felt it safe to arrest him; and found the arrest thoroughly justified. For, as Inspector Cook radiantly explained to dons and doctors on the lawn of Mandeville garden, no sooner was the notorious Communist searched, than it was found that he was actually carrying a box of poisoned matches.

The moment Father Brown heard the word 'matches', he jumped from his seat as if a match had been lighted under him.

'Ah,' he cried, with a sort of universal radiance, 'and now it's all clear.'

'What do you mean by all clear?' demanded the Master of Mandeville, who had returned in all the pomp of his own officialism to match the pomp of the police officials now occupying the College like a victorious army. 'Do you mean you are convinced now that the case against Craken is clear?'

'I mean that Craken is cleared,' said Father Brown firmly, 'and the case against Craken is cleared away. Do you really believe Craken is the kind of man who would go about poisoning people with matches?'

'That's all very well,' replied the Master, with the troubled expression he had never lost since the first sensation occurred. 'But it was you yourself who said that fanatics with false principles may do wicked things. For that matter, it was you yourself who said that Communism is creeping up everywhere and Communistic habits spreading.'

Father Brown laughed in a rather shamefaced manner.

'As to the last point,' he said, 'I suppose I owe you all an apology. I seem to be always making a mess of things with my silly little jokes.'

'Jokes!' repeated the Master, staring rather indignantly.

'Well,' explained the priest, rubbing his head. 'When I talked about a Communist habit spreading, I only meant a habit I happen to have noticed about two or three times even today. It is a Communist habit by no means confined to Communists. It is the extraordinary habit of so many men, especially Englishmen, of putting other people's matchboxes in their pockets without remembering to return them. Of course, it seems an awfully silly little trifle to talk about. But it does happen to be the way the crime was committed.'

'It sounds to me quite crazy,' said the doctor.

'Well, if almost any man may forget to return matches, you can bet your boots that Craken would forget to return them. So the poisoner who had prepared the matches got rid of them on to Craken, by the simple process of lending them and not getting them back. A really admirable way of shedding responsibility; because Craken himself would be perfectly unable to imagine where he had got them from. But when he used them quite innocently to light the cigars he offered to our two visitors, he was caught in an obvious trap; one of those too obvious traps. He was the bold bad Revolutionist murdering two millionaires.'

'Well, who else would want to murder them?' growled the doctor.

'Ah, who indeed?' replied the priest; and his voice changed to much greater gravity. 'There we come to the other thing I told you; and that, let me tell you, was not a joke. I told you that heresies and false doctrines had become common and conversational; that everybody was used to them; that nobody really noticed them. Did you think I meant Communism when I said that? Why, it was just the other way. You were all as nervous as cats about Communism; and you watched Craken like a wolf. Of course. Communism is a heresy; but it isn't a heresy that you people take for granted. It is Capitalism you take for granted; or rather the vices of Capitalism disguised as a dead Darwinism. Do you recall what you were all saying in the Common Room, about life being only a scramble, and nature demanding the survival of the fittest, and how it doesn't matter whether the poor are paid justly or not? Why, that is the heresy that you have grown accustomed to, my friends; and it's every bit as much a heresy as Communism. That's the anti-Christian morality or immorality that you take quite naturally. And that's the immorality that has made a man a murderer today.'

'What man?' cried the Master, and his voice cracked with a sudden weakness.

'Let me approach it another way,' said the priest placidly. 'You all talk as if Craken ran away; but he didn't. When the two men toppled over, he ran down the street, summoned the doctor merely by shouting through the window, and shortly afterwards was trying to summon the police. That was how he was arrested. But doesn't it strike you, now one comes to think of it, that Mr Baker the Bursar is rather a long time looking for the police?'

'What is he doing then?' asked the Master sharply.

'I fancy he's destroying papers; or perhaps ransacking these men's rooms to see they haven't left us a letter. Or it may have something to do with our friend Wadham. Where does he come in? That is really very simple and a sort of joke too. Mr Wadham is experimenting in poisons for the next war; and has something of which a whiff of flame will stiffen a man dead. Of course, he had nothing to do with killing these men; but he did conceal his chemical secret for a very simple reason. One of them was a Puritan Yankee and the other a cosmopolitan Jew; and those two types are often fanatical Pacifists. They would have called it planning murder and probably refused to help the College. But Baker was a friend of Wadham and it was easy for him to dip matches in the new material.'

Another peculiarity of the little priest was that his mind was all of a piece, and he was unconscious of many incongruities; he would change the note of his talk from something quite public to something quite private, without any particular embarrassment. On this occasion, he made most of the company stare with mystification, by beginning to talk to one person when he had just been talking to ten; quite indifferent to the fact that only the one could have any notion of what he was talking about.

'I'm sorry if I misled you, doctor, by that maundering metaphysical digression on the man of sin,' he said apologetically. 'Of course it had nothing to do with the murder; but the truth is I'd forgotten all about the murder for the moment. I'd forgotten everything, you see, but a sort of vision of that fellow, with his vast unhuman face, squatting among the flowers like some blind monster of the Stone Age. And I was thinking that some men are pretty monstrous, like men of stone; but it was all irrelevant. Being bad inside has very little to do with committing crimes outside. The worst criminals have committed no crimes. The practical point is why did the practical criminal commit this crime. Why did Baker the Bursar want to kill these men? That's all that concerns us now. The answer is the answer to the question I've asked twice.

Where were these men most of the time, apart from nosing in chapels or laboratories? By the Bursar's own account, they were talking business with the Bursar.

'Now, with all respect to the dead, I do not exactly grovel before the intellect of these two financiers. Their views on economics and ethics were heathen and heartless. Their views on Peace were tosh. Their views on Port were even more deplorable. But one thing they did understand; and that was business. And it took them a remarkably short time to discover that the business man in charge of the funds of this College was a swindler. Or shall I say, a true follower of the doctrine of the unlimited struggle for life and the survival of the fittest.'

'You mean they were going to expose him and he killed them before they could speak,' said the doctor frowning. 'There are a lot of details I don't understand.'

'There are some details I'm not sure of myself,' said the priest frankly. 'I suspect all that business of candles underground had something to do with abstracting the millionaires' own matches, or perhaps making sure they had no matches. But I'm sure of the main gesture, the gay and careless gesture of Baker tossing his matches to the careless Craken. That gesture was the murderous blow.'

'There's one thing I don't understand,' said the Inspector. 'How did Baker know that Craken wouldn't light up himself then and there at the table and become an unwanted corpse?'

The face of Father Brown became almost heavy with reproach; and his voice had a sort of mournful yet generous warmth in it.

'Well, hang it all,' he said, 'he was only an atheist.'

'I'm afraid I don't know what you mean,' said the Inspector, politely.

'He only wanted to abolish God,' explained Father Brown in a temperate and reasonable tone. 'He only wanted to destroy the Ten Commandments and root up all the religion and civilization that had made him, and wash out all the common sense of ownership and honesty; and let his culture and his country be flattened out by savages from the ends of the earth. That's all he wanted. You have no right to accuse him of anything beyond that. Hang it all, everybody draws the line somewhere! And you come here and calmly suggest that a Mandeville Man of the old generation (for Craken was of the old generation, whatever his views) would have begun to smoke, or even strike a match, while he was still drinking the College Port, of the vintage of '08—no, no; men are not so utterly without laws and limits as all that! I was there; I saw him; he had not finished his wine, and you ask me why he did not smoke! No such anarchic question has ever shaken the arches of Mandeville College Funny place, Mandeville College. Funny place, Oxford. Funny place, England.'

'But you haven't anything particular to do with Oxford?' asked the doctor curiously.

'I have to do with England,' said Father Brown. 'I come from there. And the funniest thing of all is that even if you love it and belong to it, you still can't make head or tail of it.'

7

THE POINT OF A PIN
(First published in *The Saturday Evening Post*, Sep 17, 1932)

Father Brown always declared that he solved this problem in his sleep. And this was true, though in rather an odd fashion; because it occurred at a time when his sleep was rather disturbed. It was disturbed very early in the morning by the hammering that began in the huge building, or half-building, that was in process of erection opposite to his rooms; a colossal pile of flats still mostly covered with scaffolding and with boards announcing Messrs Swindon & Sand as the builders and owners. The hammering was renewed at regular intervals and was easily recognizable: because Messrs Swindon & Sand specialized in some new American system of cement flooring which, in spite of its subsequent smoothness, solidity, impenetrability and permanent comfort (as described in the advertisements), had to be clamped down at certain points with heavy tools. Father Brown endeavoured, however, to extract exiguous comfort from it; saying that it always woke him up in time for the very earliest Mass, and was therefore something almost in the nature of a carillon. After all, he said, it was almost as poetic that Christians should be awakened by hammers as by bells. As a fact, however, the building operations were a little on his nerves, for another reason. For there was hanging like a cloud over the half-built skyscraper the possibility of a Labour crisis, which the newspapers doggedly insisted on describing as a Strike. As a matter of fact, if it ever happened, it would be a lockout. But he worried a good deal about whether it would happen. And it might be questioned whether hammering is more of a strain on the attention because it may go on forever, or because it may stop at any minute.

'As a mere matter of taste and fancy,' said Father Brown, staring up at the edifice with his owlish spectacles, 'I rather wish it would stop. I wish all houses would stop while they still have the scaffolding up. It seems almost a pity that houses are ever finished. They look so fresh and hopeful with all that fairy filigree of white wood, all light and bright in the sun; and a man so often only finishes a house by turning it into a tomb.'

As he turned away from the object of his scrutiny, he nearly ran into a man who had just darted across the road towards him. It was a man whom he knew slightly, but sufficiently to regard him (in the circumstances) as something of a bird of ill-omen. Mr Mastyk was a squat man with a square head that looked hardly European, dressed with a heavy dandyism that seemed rather too consciously Europeanized. But Brown had seen him lately talking to young Sand of the building firm; and he did not like it. This man Mastyk was the head of an organization rather new in English industrial politics; produced by extremes at both ends; a definite army of non-Union and largely alien labour hired out in gangs to various firms; and he was obviously hovering about in the hope of hiring it out to this one. In short, he might negotiate some way of out-manoeuvring the Trade Union and flooding the works with blacklegs. Father Brown had been drawn into some of the debates, being in some sense called in on both sides. And as the Capitalists all reported that, to their positive knowledge, he was a Bolshevist; and as the Bolshevists all testified that he was a reactionary rigidly attached to bourgeois ideologies, it may be inferred that he talked a certain amount of sense without any appreciable effect on anybody. The news brought by Mr Mastyk, however, was calculated to jerk everybody out of the ordinary rut of the dispute.

'They want you to go over there at once,' said Mr Mastyk, in awkwardly accented English. 'There is a threat to murder.'

Father Brown followed his guide in silence up several stairways and ladders to a platform of the unfinished building, on which were grouped the more or less familiar figures of the heads of the building business. They included even what had once been the head of it; though the head had been for some time rather a head in the clouds. It was at least a head in a coronet, that hid it from human sight like a cloud. Lord Stanes, in other words, had not only retired from the business but been caught up into the House of Lords and disappeared. His rare reappearances were languid and somewhat dreary; but this one, in conjunction with that of Mastyk, seemed none the less menacing. Lord Stanes was a lean, long-headed, hollow-eyed man with very faint fair hair fading into baldness; and he was the most evasive person the priest had ever met. He was unrivalled in the true Oxford talent of saying, 'No doubt you're right,' so as to sound like, 'No doubt you think you're right,' or of merely remarking, 'You think so?' so as to imply the acid addition, 'You would.' But Father Brown fancied that the man was not merely bored but faintly embittered, though whether at being called down from Olympus to control such trade squabbles, or merely at not being really any longer in control of them, it was difficult to guess.

On the whole, Father Brown rather preferred the more bourgeois group of partners. Sir Hubert Sand and his nephew Henry; though he doubted privately whether they really had very many ideologies. True, Sir Hubert Sand had obtained considerable celebrity in the newspapers; both as a patron of sport and as a patriot in many crises during and after the Great War. He had won notable distinction in France, for a man of his years, and had afterwards been featured as a triumphant captain of industry overcoming difficulties among the munition-workers. He had been called a Strong Man; but that was not his fault. He was in fact a heavy, hearty Englishman; a great swimmer; a good squire; an admirable amateur colonel. Indeed, something that can only be called a military makeup pervaded his appearance. He was growing stout, but he kept his shoulders set back; his curly hair and moustache were still brown while the colours of his face were already somewhat withered and faded. His nephew was a burly youth of the pushing, or rather shouldering, sort with a relatively small head thrust out on a thick neck, as if he went at things with his head down; a gesture somehow rendered rather quaint and boyish by the pince-nez that were balanced on his pugnacious pug-nose.

Father Brown had looked at all these things before; and at that moment everybody was looking at something entirely new. In the centre of the wood-work there was nailed up a large loose flapping piece of paper on which something was scrawled in crude and almost crazy capital letters, as if the writer were either almost illiterate or were affecting or parodying illiteracy. The words actually ran: 'The Council of the Workers warns Hubert Sand that he will lower wages and lock out workmen at his peril. If the notices go out tomorrow, he will be dead by the justice of the people.'

Lord Stanes was just stepping back from his examination of the paper, and, looking across at his partner, he said with rather a curious intonation: 'Well, it's you they want to murder. Evidently I'm not considered worth murdering.'

One of those still electric shocks of fancy that sometimes thrilled Father Brown's mind in an almost meaningless way shot through him at that particular instant. He had a queer notion that the man who was speaking could not now be murdered, because he was already dead. It was, he cheerfully admitted, a perfectly senseless idea. But there was something that always gave him the creeps about the cold disenchanted detachment of the noble senior partner; about his cadaverous colour and inhospitable eyes. 'The fellow,' he thought in the same perverse mood, 'has green eyes and looks as if he had green blood.'

Anyhow, it was certain that Sir Hubert Sand had not got green blood. His blood, which was red enough in every sense, was creeping up into his withered or weather-beaten cheeks with all the warm fullness of life that belongs to the natural and innocent indignation of the good-natured.

'In all my life,' he said, in a strong voice and yet shakily, 'I have never had such a thing said or done about me. I may have differed—'

'We can none of us differ about this,' struck in his nephew impetuously. 'I've tried to get on with them, but this is a bit too thick.'

'You don't really think,' began Father Brown, 'that your workmen—'

'I say we may have differed,' said old Sand, still a little tremulously, 'God knows I never like the idea of threatening English workmen with cheaper labour—'

'We none of us liked it,' said the young man, 'but if I know you, uncle, this has about settled it.'

Then after a pause he added, 'I suppose, as you say, we did disagree about details; but as to real policy—'

'My dear fellow,' said his uncle, comfortably. 'I hoped there would never be any real disagreement.' From which anybody who understands the English nation may rightly infer that there had been very considerable disagreement. Indeed the uncle and nephew differed almost as much as an Englishman and an American. The uncle had the English ideal of getting outside the business, and setting up a sort of an alibi as a country gentleman. The nephew had the American ideal of getting inside the business; of getting inside the very mechanism like a mechanic. And, indeed, he had worked with most of the mechanics and was familiar with most of the processes and tricks of the trade. And he was American again, in the fact that he did this partly as an employer to keep his men up to the mark, but in some vague way also as an equal, or at least with a pride in showing himself also as a worker. For this reason he had often appeared almost as a representative of the workers, on technical points which were a hundred miles away from his uncle's popular eminence in politics or sport. The memory of those many occasions, when young Henry had practically come out of the workshop in his shirt-sleeves, to demand some concession about the conditions of the work, lent a peculiar force and even violence to his present reaction the other way.

'Well, they've damned-well locked themselves out this time,' he cried. 'After a threat like that there's simply nothing left but to defy them. There's nothing left but to sack them all now; instanter; on the spot. Otherwise we'll be the laughing-stock of the world.'

Old Sand frowned with equal indignation, but began slowly: 'I shall be very much criticized—'

'Criticized!' cried the young man shrilly. 'Criticized if you defy a threat of murder! Have you any notion how you'll be criticized if you don't defy it? Won't you enjoy the headlines? "Great Capitalist Terrorized"—"Employer Yields to Murder Threat." '

'Particularly,' said Lord Stanes, with something faintly unpleasant in his tone. 'Particularly when he has been in so many headlines already as "The Strong Man of Steel-Building."'

Sand had gone very red again and his voice came thickly from under his thick moustache. 'Of course you're right there. If these brutes think I'm afraid—'

At this point there was an interruption in the conversation of the group; and a slim young man came towards them swiftly. The first notable thing about him was that he was one of those whom men, and women too, think are just a little too nice-looking to look nice. He had beautiful dark curly hair and a silken moustache and he spoke like a gentleman, but with almost too refined and exactly modulated an accent. Father Brown knew him at once as Rupert Rae, the secretary of Sir Hubert, whom he had often seen pottering about in Sir Hubert's house; but never with such impatience in his movements or such a wrinkle on his brow.

'I'm sorry, sir,' he said to his employer, 'but there's a man been hanging about over there. I've done my best to get rid of him. He's only got a letter, but he swears he must give it to you personally.'

'You mean he went first to my house?' said Sand, glancing swiftly at his secretary. 'I suppose you've been there all the morning.'

'Yes, sir,' said Mr Rupert Rae.

There was a short silence; and then Sir Hubert Sand curtly intimated that the man had better be brought along; and the man duly appeared.

Nobody, not even the least fastidious lady, would have said that the newcomer was too nice-looking. He had very large ears and a face like a frog, and he stared before him with an almost ghastly fixity, which Father Brown attributed to his having a glass eye. In fact, his fancy was tempted to equip the man with two glass eyes; with so glassy a stare did he contemplate the company. But the priest's experience, as distinct from his fancy, was able to suggest several natural causes for that unnatural waxwork glare; one of them being an abuse of the divine gift of fermented liquor. The man was short and shabby and carried a large bowler hat in one hand and a large sealed letter in the other.

Sir Hubert Sand looked at him; and then said quietly enough, but in a voice that somehow seemed curiously small, coming out of the fullness of his bodily presence: 'Oh—it's you.'

He held out his hand for the letter; and then looked around apologetically, with poised finger, before ripping it open and reading it. When he had read it, he stuffed it into his inside pocket and said hastily and a little harshly: 'Well, I suppose all this business is over, as you say. No more negotiations possible now; we couldn't pay the wages they want anyhow. But I shall want to see you again, Henry, about—about winding things up generally.'

'All right,' said Henry, a little sulkily perhaps, as if he would have preferred to wind them up by himself. 'I shall be up in number 188 after lunch; got to know how far they've got up there.'

The man with the glass eye, if it was a glass eye, stumped stiffly away; and the eye of Father Brown (which was by no means a glass eye) followed him thoughtfully as he threaded his way through the ladders and disappeared into the street.

It was on the following morning that Father Brown had the unusual experience of oversleeping himself; or at least of starting from sleep with a subjective conviction that he must be late. This was partly due to his remembering, as a man may remember a dream, the fact of having been half-awakened at a more regular hour and fallen asleep again; a common enough occurrence with most of us, but a very uncommon occurrence with Father Brown. And he was afterwards oddly convinced, with that mystic side of him which was normally turned away from the world, that in that detached dark islet of dreamland, between the two wakings, there lay like buried treasure the truth of this tale.

As it was, he jumped up with great promptitude, plunged into his clothes, seized his big knobby umbrella and bustled out into the street, where the bleak white morning was breaking like splintered ice about the huge black building facing him. He was surprised to find that the streets shone almost empty in the cold crystalline light; the very look of it told him it could hardly be so late as he had feared. Then suddenly the stillness was cloven by the arrowlike swiftness of a long grey car which halted before the big deserted flats. Lord Stanes unfolded himself from within and approached the door, carrying (rather languidly) two large suitcases. At the same moment the door opened, and somebody seemed to step back instead of stepping out into the street. Stanes called twice to the man within, before that person seemed to complete his original gesture by coming out on to the doorstep; then the two held a brief colloquy, ending in the nobleman carrying his suitcases upstairs, and the other coming out into full daylight and revealing the heavy shoulders and peering head of young Henry Sand.

Father Brown made no more of this rather odd meeting, until two days later the young man drove up in his own car, and implored the priest to enter it. 'Something awful has happened,' he said, 'and I'd rather talk to you than Stanes. You know Stanes arrived the other day with some mad idea of camping in one of the flats that's just finished. That's why I had to go there early and open the door to him. But all that will keep. I want you to come up to my uncle's place at once.'

'Is he ill?' inquired the priest quickly.

'I think he's dead,' answered the nephew.

'What do you mean by saying you think he's dead?' asked Father Brown a little briskly. 'Have you got a doctor?'

'No,' answered the other. 'I haven't got a doctor or a patient either... It's no good calling in doctors to examine the body; because the body has run away. But I'm afraid I know where it has run to ... the truth is—we kept it dark for two days; but he's disappeared.'

'Wouldn't it be better,' said Father Brown mildly, 'if you told me what has really happened from the beginning?'

'I know,' answered Henry Sand; 'it's an infernal shame to talk flippantly like this about the poor old boy; but people get like that when they're rattled. I'm not much good at hiding things; the long and the short of it is—well, I won't tell you the long of it now. It's what some people would call rather a long shot; shooting suspicions at random and so on. But the short of it is that my unfortunate uncle has committed suicide.'

They were by this time skimming along in the car through the last fringes of the town and the first fringes of the forest and park beyond it; the lodge gates of Sir Hubert Sand's small estate were about a half mile farther on amid the thickening throng of the beeches. The estate consisted chiefly of a small park and a large ornamental garden, which descended in terraces of a certain classical pomp to the very edge of the chief river of the district. As soon as they arrived at the house, Henry took the priest somewhat hastily through the old Georgian rooms and out upon the other side; where they silently descended the slope, a rather steep slope embanked with flowers, from which they could see the pale river spread out before them almost as flat as in a bird's-eye view. They were just turning the corner of the path under an enormous classical urn crowned with a somewhat incongruous garland of geraniums, when Father Brown saw a movement in the bushes and thin trees just below him, that seemed as swift as a movement of startled birds.

In the tangle of thin trees by the river two figures seemed to divide or scatter; one of them glided swiftly into the shadows and the other came forward to face them; bringing them to a halt and an abrupt and rather unaccountable silence. Then Henry Sand said in his heavy way: 'I think you know Father Brown... Lady Sand.'

Father Brown did know her; but at that moment he might almost have said that he did not know her. The pallor and constriction of her face was like a mask of tragedy; she was much younger than her husband, but at that moment she looked somehow older than everything in that old house and garden. And the priest remembered, with a subconscious thrill, that she was indeed older in type and lineage and was the true possessor of the place. For her own family had owned it as impoverished aristocrats, before she had restored its fortunes by marrying a successful business man. As she stood there, she might have been a family picture, or even a family ghost. Her pale face was of that pointed yet oval type seen in some old pictures of Mary Queen of Scots; and its expression seemed almost to go beyond the natural unnaturalness of a situation, in which her husband had vanished under suspicion of suicide. Father Brown, with the same subconscious movement of the mind, wondered who it was with whom she had been talking among the trees.

'I suppose you know all this dreadful news,' she said, with a comfortless composure. 'Poor Hubert must have broken down under all this revolutionary persecution, and been just maddened into taking his own life. I don't know whether you can do anything; or whether these horrible Bolsheviks can be made responsible for hounding him to death.'

'I am terribly distressed, Lady Sand,' said Father Brown. 'And still, I must own, a little bewildered. You speak of persecution; do you think that anybody could hound him to death merely by pinning up that paper on the wall?'

'I fancy,' answered the lady, with a darkening brow, 'that there were other persecutions besides the paper.'

'It shows what mistakes one may make,' said the priest sadly. 'I never should have thought he would be so illogical as to die in order to avoid death.'

'I know,' she answered, gazing at him gravely. 'I should never have believed it, if it hadn't been written with his own hand.'

'What?' cried Father Brown, with a little jump like a rabbit that has been shot at.

'Yes,' said Lady Sand calmly. 'He left a confession of suicide; so I fear there is no doubt about it.' And she passed on up the slope alone, with all the inviolable isolation of the family ghost.

The spectacles of Father Brown were turned in mute inquiry to the eyeglasses of Mr Henry Sand. And the latter gentleman, after an instant's hesitation, spoke again in his rather blind and plunging fashion: 'Yes, you see, it seems pretty clear now what he did. He was always a great swimmer and used to come down in his dressing-gown every morning for a dip in the river. Well, he came down as usual, and left his dressing-gown on the bank; it's lying there still. But he also left a message saying he was going for his last swim and then death, or something like that.'

'Where did he leave the message?' asked Father Brown.

'He scrawled it on that tree there, overhanging the water, I suppose the last thing he took hold of; just below where the dressing-gown's lying. Come and see for yourself.'

Father Brown ran down the last short slope to the shore and peered under the hanging tree, whose plumes were almost dipping in the stream. Sure enough, he saw on the smooth bark the words scratched conspicuously and unmistakably: 'One more swim and then drowning. Goodbye. Hubert Sand.' Father Brown's gaze travelled slowly up the bank till it rested on a gorgeous rag of raiment, all red and yellow with gilded tassels. It was the dressing-gown and the priest picked it up and began to turn it over. Almost as he did so he was conscious that a figure had flashed across his field of vision; a tall dark figure that slipped from one clump of trees to another, as if following the trail of the vanishing lady. He had little doubt that it was the companion from whom she had lately parted. He had still less doubt that it was the dead man's secretary, Mr Rupert Rae.

'Of course, it might be a final afterthought to leave the message,' said Father Brown, without looking up, his eye riveted on the red and gold garment. 'We've all heard of love-messages written on trees; and I suppose there might be death-messages written on trees too.'

'Well, he wouldn't have anything in the pockets of his dressing-gown, I suppose,' said young Sand. 'And a man might naturally scratch his message on a tree if he had no pens, ink or paper.'

'Sounds like French exercises,' said the priest dismally. 'But I wasn't thinking of that.' Then, after a silence, he said in a rather altered voice:

'To tell the truth, I was thinking whether a man might not naturally scratch his message on a tree, even if he had stacks of pens, and quarts of ink, and reams of paper.'

Henry was looking at him with a rather startled air, his eyeglasses crooked on his pug-nose. 'And what do you mean by that?' he asked sharply.

'Well,' said Father Brown slowly, 'I don't exactly mean that postmen will carry letters in the form of logs, or that you will ever drop a line to a friend by putting a postage stamp on a pinetree. It would have to be a particular sort of position—in fact, it would have to be a particular sort of person, who really preferred this sort of arboreal correspondence. But, given the position and the person, I repeat what I said. He would still write on a tree, as the song says, if all the world were paper and all the sea were ink; if that river flowed with everlasting ink or all these woods were a forest of quills and fountain-pens.'

It was evident that Sand felt something creepy about the priest's fanciful imagery; whether because he found it incomprehensible or because he was beginning to comprehend.

'You see,' said Father Brown, turning the dressing-gown over slowly as he spoke, 'a man isn't expected to write his very best handwriting when he chips it on a tree. And if the man were not the man, if I make myself clear—Hullo!'

He was looking down at the red dressing-gown, and it seemed for the moment as if some of the red had come off on his finger; but both the faces turned towards it were already a shade paler.

'Blood!' said Father Brown; and for the instant there was a deadly stillness save for the melodious noises of the river.

Henry Sand cleared his throat and nose with noises that were by no means melodious. Then he said rather hoarsely: 'Whose blood?'

'Oh, mine,' said Father Brown; but he did not smile.

A moment after he said: 'There was a pin in this thing and I pricked myself. But I don't think you quite appreciate the point... the point of the pin, I do'; and he sucked his finger like a child.

'You see,' he said after another silence, 'the gown was folded up and pinned together; nobody could have unfolded it—at least without scratching himself. In plain words, Hubert Sand never wore this dressing-gown. Any more than Hubert Sand ever wrote on that tree. Or drowned himself in that river.'

The pince-nez tilted on Henry's inquiring nose fell off with a click; but he was otherwise motionless, as if rigid with surprise.

'Which brings us back,' went on Father Brown cheerfully, 'to somebody's taste for writing his private correspondence on trees, like Hiawatha and his picture-writing. Sand had all the time there was, before drowning himself. Why didn't he leave a note for his wife like a sane man? Or, shall we say...

Why didn't the Other Man leave a note for the wife like a sane man? Because he would have had to forge the husband's handwriting; always a tricky thing now that experts are so nosey about it. But nobody can be expected to imitate even his own handwriting, let alone somebody else's when he carves capital letters in the bark of a tree. This is not a suicide, Mr Sand. If it's anything at all, it's a murder.'

The bracken and bushes of the undergrowth snapped and crackled as the big young man rose out of them like a leviathan, and stood lowering, with his thick neck thrust forward.

'I'm no good at hiding things,' he said, 'and I half-suspected something like this—expected it, you might say, for a long time. To tell the truth, I could hardly be civil to the fellow—to either of them, for that matter.'

'What exactly do you mean?' asked the priest, looking him gravely full in the face.

'I mean,' said Henry Sand, 'that you have shown me the murder and I think I could show you the murderers.'

Father Brown was silent and the other went on rather jerkily.

'You said people sometimes wrote love-messages on trees. Well, as a fact, there are some of them on that tree; there are two sort of monograms twisted together up there under the leaves—I suppose you know that Lady Sand was the heiress of this place long before she married; and she knew that damned dandy of a secretary even in those days. I guess they used to meet here and write their vows upon the trysting-tree. They seem to have used the trysting-tree for another purpose later on. Sentiment, no doubt, or economy.'

'They must be very horrible people,' said Father Brown.

'Haven't there been any horrible people in history or the police-news?' demanded Sand with some excitement. 'Haven't there been lovers who made love seem more horrible than hate? Don't you know about Bothwell and all the bloody legends of such lovers?'

'I know the legend of Bothwell,' answered the priest. 'I also know it to be quite legendary. But of course it's true that husbands have been sometimes put away like that. By the way, where was he put away? I mean, where did they hide the body?'

'I suppose they drowned him, or threw him in the water when he was dead,' snorted the young man impatiently.

Father Brown blinked thoughtfully and then said: 'A river is a good place to hide an imaginary body. It's a rotten bad place to hide a real one. I mean, it's easy to say you've thrown it in, because it might be washed away to sea. But if you really did throw it in, it's about a hundred to one it wouldn't; the chances of it going ashore somewhere are enormous. I think they must have had a better scheme for hiding the body than that—or the body would have been found by now. And if there were any marks of violence—'

'Oh, bother hiding the body,' said Henry, with some irritation; 'haven't we witness enough in the writing on their own devilish tree?'

'The body is the chief witness in every murder,' answered the other. 'The hiding of the body, nine times out of ten, is the practical problem to be solved.'

There was a silence; and Father Brown continued to turn over the red dressing-gown and spread it out on the shining grass of the sunny shore; he did not look up. But, for some time past he had been conscious that the whole landscape had been changed for him by the presence of a third party; standing as still as a statue in the garden.

'By the way,' he said, lowering his voice, 'how do you explain that little guy with the glass eye, who brought your poor uncle a letter yesterday? It seemed to me he was entirely altered by reading it; that's why I wasn't surprised at the suicide, when I thought it was a suicide. That chap was a rather lowdown private detective, or I'm much mistaken.'

'Why,' said Henry in a hesitating manner, 'why, he might have been—husbands do sometimes put on detectives in domestic tragedies like this, don't they? I suppose he'd got the proofs of their intrigue; and so they—'

'I shouldn't talk too loud,' said Father Brown, 'because your detective is detecting us at this moment, from about a yard beyond those bushes.'

They looked up, and sure enough the goblin with the glass eye was fixing them with that disagreeable optic, looking all the more grotesque for standing among the white and waxen blooms of the classical garden.

Henry Sand scrambled to his feet again with a rapidity that seemed breathless for one of his bulk, and asked the man very angrily and abruptly what he was doing, at the same time telling him to clear out at once.

'Lord Stanes,' said the goblin of the garden, 'would be much obliged if Father Brown would come up to the house and speak to him.'

Henry Sand turned away furiously; but the priest put down his fury to the dislike that was known to exist between him and the nobleman in question. As they mounted the slope, Father Brown paused a moment as if tracing patterns on the smooth tree-trunk, glanced upwards once at the darker and more hidden hieroglyph said to be a record of romance; and then stared at the wider and more sprawling letters of the confession, or supposed confession of suicide.

'Do those letters remind you of anything?' he asked. And when his sulky companion shook his head, he added: 'They remind me of the writing on that placard that threatened him with the vengeance of the strikers.'

'This is the hardest riddle and the queerest tale I have ever tackled,' said Father Brown, a month later, as he sat opposite Lord Stanes in the recently furnished apartment of No. 188, the end flat which was the last to be finished before the interregnum of the industrial dispute and the transfer of work from the Trade Union. It was comfortably furnished; and Lord Stanes was presiding over grog and cigars, when the priest made his confession with a grimace. Lord Stanes had become rather surprisingly friendly, in a cool and casual way.

'I know that is saying a good deal, with your record,' said Stanes, 'but certainly the detectives, including our seductive friend with the glass eye, don't seem at all able to see the solution.'

Father Brown laid down his cigar and said carefully: 'It isn't that they can't see the solution. It is that they can't see the problem.'

'Indeed,' said the other, 'perhaps I can't see the problem either.'

'The problem is unlike all other problems, for this reason,' said Father Brown. 'It seems as if the criminal deliberately did two different things, either of which might have been successful; but which, when done together, could only defeat each other. I am assuming, what I firmly believe, that the same murderer pinned up the proclamation threatening a sort of Bolshevik murder, and also wrote on the tree confessing to an ordinary suicide. Now you may say it is after all possible that the proclamation was a proletarian proclamation; that some extremist workmen wanted to kill their employer, and killed him. Even if that were true, it would still stick at the mystery of why they left, or why anybody left, a contrary trail of private self-destruction. But it certainly isn't true. None of these workmen, however, bitter, would have done a thing like that. I know them pretty well; I know their leaders quite well. To suppose that people like Tom Bruce or Hogan would assassinate somebody they could go for in the newspapers, and damage in all sorts of different ways, is the sort of psychology that sensible people call lunacy. No; there was somebody, who was not an indignant workman, who first played the part of an indignant workman, and then played the part of a suicidal employer. But, in the name of wonder, why? If he thought he could pass it off smoothly as a suicide, why did he first spoil it all by publishing a threat of murder? You might say it was an afterthought to fix up the suicide story, as less provocative than the murder story. But it wasn't less provocative after the murder story. He must have known he had already turned our thoughts towards murder, when it should have been his whole object to keep our thoughts away from it. If it was an afterthought, it was the afterthought of a very thoughtless person. And I have a notion that this assassin is a very thoughtful person. Can you make anything of it?'

'No; but I see what you mean,' said Stanes, 'by saying that I didn't even see the problem. It isn't merely who killed Sand; it's why anybody should accuse somebody else of killing Sand and then accuse Sand of killing himself.'

Father Brown's face was knotted and the cigar was clenched in his teeth; the end of it plowed and darkened rhythmically like the signal of some burning pulse of the brain. Then he spoke as if to himself:

'We've got to follow very closely and very clearly. It's like separating threads of thought from each other; something like this. Because the murder charge really rather spoilt the suicide charge, he wouldn't normally have made the murder charge. But he did make it; so he had some other reason for making it. It was so strong a reason that perhaps it reconciled him even to weakening his other line of defence; that it was a suicide. In other words, the murder charge wasn't really a murder charge. I mean he wasn't using it as a murder charge; he wasn't doing it so as to shift to somebody else the guilt of murder; he was doing it for some other extraordinary reason of his own. His plan had to contain a proclamation that Sand would be murdered; whether it threw suspicion on other people or not. Somehow or other the mere proclamation itself was necessary. But why?'

He smoked and smouldered away with the same volcanic concentration for five minutes before he spoke again. 'What could a murderous proclamation do, besides suggesting that the strikers were the murderers? What did it do? One thing is obvious; it inevitably did the opposite of what it said. It told Sand not to lock out his men; and it was perhaps the only thing in the world that would really have made him do it. You've got to think of the sort of man and the sort of reputation. When a man has been called a Strong Man in our silly sensational newspapers, when he is fondly regarded as a Sportsman by all the most distinguished asses in England, he simply can't back down because he is threatened with a pistol. It would be like walking about at Ascot with a white feather stuck in his absurd white hat. It would break that inner idol or ideal of oneself, which every man not a downright dastard does really prefer to life. And Sand wasn't a dastard; he was courageous; he was also impulsive. It acted instantly like a charm: his nephew, who had been more or less mixed up with the workmen, cried out instantly that the threat must be absolutely and instantly defied.'

'Yes,' said Lord Stanes, 'I noticed that.' They looked at each other for an instant, and then Stanes added carelessly: 'So you think the thing the criminal wanted was?'

'The lockout!' cried the priest energetically. 'The Strike or whatever you call it; the cessation of work, anyhow. He wanted the work to stop at once; perhaps the blacklegs to come in at once; certainly the Trade Unionists to go out at once. That is what he really wanted; God knows why. And he brought that off, I think, really without bothering much about its other implication of the existence of Bolshevist assassins. But then... then I think something went wrong. I'm only guessing and groping very slowly here; but the only explanation I can think of is that something began to draw attention to the real seat of the trouble; to the reason, whatever it was, of his wanting to bring the building to a halt. And then belatedly, desperately, and rather inconsistently, he tried to lay the other trail that led to the river, simply and solely because it led away from the flats.'

He looked up through his moonlike spectacles, absorbing all the quality of the background and furniture; the restrained luxury of a quiet man of the world; and contrasting it with the two suitcases with which its occupant had arrived so recently in a newly-finished and unfurnished flat. Then he said rather abruptly: 'In short, the murderer was frightened of something or somebody in the flats. By the way, why did you come to live in the flats?... Also by the way, young Henry told me you made an early appointment with him when you moved in. Is that true?'

'Not in the least,' said Stanes. 'I got the key from his uncle the night before. I've no notion why Henry came here that morning.'

'Ah,' said Father Brown, 'then I think I have some notion of why he came... I thought you startled him by coming in just when he was coming out.'

'And yet,' said Stanes, looking across with a glitter in his grey-green eyes, 'you do rather think that I also am a mystery.'

'I think you are two mysteries,' said Father Brown. 'The first is why you originally retired from Sand's business. The second is why you have since come back to live in Sand's buildings.'

Stanes smoked reflectively, knocked out his ash, and rang a bell on the table before him. 'If you'll excuse me,' he said, 'I will summon two more to the council. Jackson, the little detective you know of, will answer the bell; and I've asked Henry Sand to come in a little later.'

Father Brown rose from his seat, walked across the room and looked down frowning into the fire-place.

'Meanwhile,' continued Stanes, 'I don't mind answering both your questions. I left the Sand business because I was sure there was some hanky-panky in it and somebody was pinching all the money. I came back to it, and took this flat, because I wanted to watch for the real truth about old Sand's death—on the spot.'

Father Brown faced round as the detective entered the room; he stood staring at the hearthrug and repeated: 'On the spot.'

'Mr Jackson will tell you,' said Stanes, 'that Sir Hubert commissioned him to find out who was the thief robbing the firm; and he brought a note of his discoveries the day before old Hubert disappeared.'

'Yes,' said Father Brown, 'and I know now where he disappeared to. I know where the body is.'

'Do you mean—?' began his host hastily.

'It is here,' said Father Brown, and stamped on the hearthrug. 'Here, under the elegant Persian rug in this cosy and comfortable room.'

'Where in the world did you find that?'

'I've just remembered,' said Father Brown, 'that I found it in my sleep.'

He closed his eyes as if trying to picture a dream, and went on dreamily:

'This is a murder story turning on the problem of How to Hide the Body; and I found it in my sleep. I was always woken up every morning by hammering from this building. On that morning I half-woke up, went to sleep again and woke once more, expecting to find it late; but it wasn't. Why? Because there had been hammering that morning, though all the usual work had stopped; short, hurried hammering in the small hours before dawn. Automatically a man sleeping stirs at such a familiar sound. But he goes to sleep again, because the usual sound is not at the usual hour. Now why did a certain secret criminal want all the work to cease suddenly; and only new workers come in? Because, if the old workers had come in next day, they would have found a new piece of work done in the night. The old workers would have known where they left off; and they would have found the whole flooring of this room already nailed down. Nailed down by a man who knew how to do it; haying mixed a good deal with the workmen and learned their ways.'

As he spoke, the door was pushed open and a head poked in with a thrusting motion; a small head at the end of a thick neck and a face that blinked at them through glasses.

'Henry Sand said,' observed Father Brown, staring at the ceiling, 'that he was no good at hiding things. But I think he did himself an injustice.'

Henry Sand turned and moved swiftly away down the corridor.

'He not only hid his thefts from the firm quite successfully for years,' went on the priest with an air of abstraction, 'but when his uncle discovered them, he hid his uncle's corpse in an entirely new and original manner.'

At the same instant Stanes again rang a bell, with a long strident steady ringing; and the little man with the glass eye was propelled or shot along the corridor after the fugitive, with something of the rotatory motion of a mechanical figure in a zoetrope. At the same moment, Father Brown looked out of the window, leaning over a small balcony, and saw five or six men start from behind bushes and railings in the street below and spread out equally mechanically like a fan or net; opening out after the fugitive who had shot like a bullet out of the front door. Father Brown saw only the pattern of the story; which had never strayed from that room; where Henry had strangled Hubert and hid his body under impenetrable flooring, stopping the whole work on the building to do it. A pin-prick had started his own suspicions; but only to tell him he had been led down the long loop of a lie. The point of the pin was that it was pointless.

He fancied he understood Stanes at last, and he liked to collect queer people who were difficult to understand. He realized that this tired gentleman, whom he had once accused of having green blood, had indeed a sort of cold green flame of conscientiousness or conventional honour, that had made him first shift out of a shady business, and then feel ashamed of having shifted it on to others; and come back as a bored laborious detective; pitching his camp on the very spot where the corpse had been buried; so that the murderer, finding him sniffing so near the corpse, had wildly staged the alternative drama of the dressing-gown and the drowned man. All that was plain enough, but, before he withdrew his head from the night air and the stars. Father Brown threw one glance upwards at the vast black bulk of the cyclopean building heaved far up into the night, and remembered Egypt and Babylon, and all that is at once eternal and ephemeral in the work of man.

'I was right in what I said first of all,' he said. 'It reminds one of Coppee's poem about the Pharaoh and the Pyramid. This house is supposed to be a hundred houses; and yet the whole mountain of building is only one man's tomb.'

8

THE INSOLUBLE PROBLEM
(No record of prior magazine publication found)

This queer incident, in some ways perhaps the queerest of the many that came his way, happened to Father Brown at the time when his French friend Flambeau had retired from the profession of crime and had entered with great energy and success on the profession of crime investigator. It happened that both as a thief and a thief-taker, Flambeau had rather specialized in the matter of jewel thefts, on which he was admitted to be an expert, both in the matter of identifying jewels and the equally practical matter of identifying jewel-thieves. And it was in connection with his special knowledge of this subject, and a special commission which it had won for him, that he rang up his friend the priest on the particular morning on which this story begins.

Father Brown was delighted to hear the voice of his old friend, even on the telephone; but in a general way, and especially at that particular moment, Father Brown was not very fond of the telephone. He was one who preferred to watch people's faces and feel social atmospheres, and he knew well that without these things, verbal messages are apt to be very misleading, especially from total strangers. And it seemed as if, on that particular morning, a swarm of total strangers had been buzzing in his ear with more or less unenlightening verbal messages; the telephone seemed to be possessed of a demon of triviality. Perhaps the most distinctive voice was one which asked him whether he did not issue regular permits for murder and theft upon the payment of a regular tariff hung up in his church; and as the stranger, on being informed that this was not the case, concluded the colloquy with a hollow laugh, it may be presumed that he remained unconvinced. Then an agitated, rather inconsequent female voice rang up requesting him to come round at once to a certain hotel he had heard of some forty-five miles on the road to a neighbouring cathedral town; the request being immediately followed by a contradiction in the same voice, more agitated and yet more inconsequent, telling him that it did not matter and that he was not wanted after all. Then came an interlude of a Press agency asking him if he had anything to say on what a Film Actress had said about Moustaches for Men; and finally yet a third return of the agitated and inconsequent lady at the hotel, saying that he was wanted, after all. He vaguely supposed that this marked some of the hesitations and panics not unknown among those who are vaguely veering in the direction of instruction, but he confessed to a considerable relief when the voice of Flambeau wound up the series with a hearty threat of immediately turning up for breakfast.

Father Brown very much preferred to talk to a friend sitting comfortably over a pipe, but it soon appeared that his visitor was on the warpath and full of energy, having every intention of carrying off the little priest captive on some important expedition of his own. It was true that there was a special circumstance involved which might be supposed to claim the priest's attention. Flambeau had figured several times of late as successfully thwarting a theft of famous precious stones; he had torn the tiara of the Duchess of Dulwich out of the very hand of the bandit as he bolted through the garden. He laid so ingenious a trap for the criminal who planned to carry off the celebrated Sapphire necklace that the artist in question actually carried off the copy which he had himself planned to leave as a substitute.

Such were doubtless the reasons that had led to his being specially summoned to guard the delivery of a rather different sort of treasure; perhaps even more valuable in its mere materials, but possessing also another sort of value. A world-famous reliquary, supposed to contain a relic of St. Dorothy the martyr, was to be delivered at the Catholic monastery in a cathedral town; and one of the most famous of international jewel-thieves was supposed to have an eye on it; or rather presumably on the gold and rubies of its setting, rather than its purely hagiological importance. Perhaps there was something in this association of ideas which made Flambeau feel that the priest would be a particularly appropriate companion in his adventure; but anyhow, he descended on him, breathing fire and ambition and very voluble about his plans for preventing the theft.

Flambeau indeed bestrode the priest's hearth gigantically and in the old swaggering musketeer attitude, twirling his great moustaches.

'You can't,' he cried, referring to the sixty-mile road to Casterbury. 'You can't allow a profane robbery like that to happen under your very nose.'

The relic was not to reach the monastery till the evening; and there was no need for its defenders to arrive earlier; for indeed a motor-journey would take them the greater part of the day. Moreover, Father Brown casually remarked that there was an inn on the road, at which he would prefer to lunch, as he had been already asked to look in there as soon as was convenient.

As they drove along through a densely wooded but sparsely inhabited landscape, in which inns and all other buildings seemed to grow rarer and rarer, the daylight began to take on the character of a stormy twilight even in the heat of noon; and dark purple clouds gathered over dark grey forests. As is common under the lurid quietude of that kind of light, what colour there was in the landscape gained a sort of secretive glow which is not found in objects under the full sunlight; and ragged red leaves or golden or orange fungi seemed to burn with a dark fire of their own. Under such a half-light they came to a break in the woods like a great rent in a grey wall, and saw beyond, standing above the gap, the tall and rather outlandish-looking inn that bore the name of the Green Dragon.

The two old companions had often arrived together at inns and other human habitations, and found a somewhat singular state of things there; but the signs of singularity had seldom manifested themselves so early. For while their car was still some hundreds of yards from the dark green door, which matched the dark green shutters of the high and narrow building, the door was thrown open with violence and a woman with a wild mop of red hair rushed to meet them, as if she were ready to board the car in full career. Flambeau brought the car to a standstill but almost before he had done so, she thrust her white and tragic face into the window, crying:

'Are you Father Brown?' and then almost in the same breath; 'who is this man?'

'This gentleman's name is Flambeau,' said Father Brown in a tranquil manner, 'and what can I do for you?'

'Come into the inn,' she said, with extraordinary abruptness even under the circumstances. 'There's been a murder done.'

They got out of the car in silence and followed her to the dark green door which opened inwards on a sort of dark green alley, formed of stakes and wooden pillars, wreathed with vine and ivy, showing square leaves of black and red and many sombre colours. This again led through an inner door into a sort of large parlour hung with rusty trophies of Cavalier arms, of which the furniture seemed to be antiquated and also in great confusion, like the inside of a lumber-room. They were quite startled for the moment; for it seemed as if one large piece of lumber rose and moved towards them; so dusty and shabby and ungainly was the man who thus abandoned what seemed like a state of permanent immobility.

Strangely enough, the man seemed to have a certain agility of politeness, when once he did move; even if it suggested the wooden joints of a courtly step-ladder or an obsequious towel-horse. Both Flambeau and Father Brown felt that they had hardly ever clapped eyes on a man who was so difficult to place. He was not what is called a gentleman; yet he had something of the dusty refinement of a scholar; there was something faintly disreputable or declasse about him; and yet the smell of him was rather bookish than Bohemian. He was thin and pale, with a pointed nose and a dark pointed beard; his brow was bald, but his hair behind long and lank and stringy; and the expression of his eyes was almost entirely masked by a pair of blue spectacles. Father Brown felt that he had met something of the sort somewhere, and a long time ago; but he could no longer put a name to it. The lumber he sat among was largely literary lumber; especially bundles of seventeenth-century pamphlets.

'Do I understand the lady to say,' asked Flambeau gravely, 'that there is a murder here?'

The lady nodded her red ragged head rather impatiently; except for those flaming elf-locks she had lost some of her look of wildness; her dark dress was of a certain dignity and neatness; her features were strong and handsome; and there was something about her suggesting that double strength of body and mind which makes women powerful, particularly in contrast with men like the man in blue spectacles. Nevertheless, it was he who gave the only articulate answer, intervening with a certain antic gallantry.

'It is true that my unfortunate sister-in-law,' he explained, 'has almost this moment suffered a most appalling shock which we should all have desired to spare her. I only wish that I myself had made the discovery and suffered only the further distress of bringing the terrible news. Unfortunately it was Mrs Flood herself who found her aged grandfather, long sick and bedridden in this hotel, actually dead in the garden; in circumstances which point only too plainly to violence and assault. Curious circumstances, I may say, very curious circumstances indeed.' And he coughed slightly, as if apologizing for them.

Flambeau bowed to the lady and expressed his sincere sympathies; then he said to the man: 'I think you said, sir, that you are Mrs Flood's brother-in-law.'

'I am Dr Oscar Flood,' replied the other. 'My brother, this lady's husband, is at present away on the Continent on business, and she is running the hotel. Her grandfather was partially paralysed and very far advanced in years. He was never known to leave his bedroom; so that really these extraordinary circumstances...'

'Have you sent for a doctor or the police?' asked Flambeau.

'Yes,' replied Dr Flood, 'we rang up after making the dreadful discovery; but they can hardly be here for some hours. This roadhouse stands so very remote. It is only used by people going to Casterbury or even beyond. So we thought we might ask for your valuable assistance until—'

'If we are to be of any assistance,' said Father Brown, interrupting in too abstracted a manner to seem uncivil, 'I should say we had better go and look at the circumstances at once.'

He stepped almost mechanically towards the door; and almost ran into a man who was shouldering his way in; a big, heavy young man with dark hair unbrushed and untidy, who would nevertheless have been rather handsome save for a slight disfigurement of one eye, which gave him rather a sinister appearance.

'What the devil are you doing?' he blurted out, 'telling every Tom, Dick and Harry—at least you ought to wait for the police.'

'I will be answerable to the police,' said Flambeau with a certain magnificence, and a sudden air of having taken command of everything. He advanced to the doorway, and as he was much bigger than the big young man, and his moustaches were as formidable as the horns of a Spanish bull, the big young man backed before him and had an inconsequent air of being thrown out and left behind, as the group swept out into the garden and up the flagged path towards the mulberry plantation. Only Flambeau heard the little priest say to the doctor: 'He doesn't seem to love us really, does he? By the way, who is he?'

'His name is Dunn,' said the doctor, with a certain restraint of manner. 'My sister-in-law gave him the job of managing the garden, because he lost an eye in the War.'

As they went through the mulberry bushes, the landscape of the garden presented that rich yet ominous effect which is found when the land is actually brighter than the sky. In the broken sunlight from behind, the tree-tops in front of them stood up like pale green flames against a sky steadily blackening with storm, through every shade of purple and violet. The same light struck strips of the lawn and garden beds; and whatever it illuminated seemed more mysteriously sombre and secret for the light. The garden bed was dotted with tulips that looked like drops of dark blood, and some of which one might have sworn were truly black; and the line ended appropriately with a tulip tree; which Father Brown was disposed, if partly by some confused memory, to identify with what is commonly called the Judas tree. What assisted the association was the fact that there was hanging from one of the branches, like a dried fruit, the dry, thin body of an old man, with a long beard that wagged grotesquely in the wind.

There lay on it something more than the horror of darkness, the horror of sunlight; for the fitful sun painted tree and man in gay colours like a stage property; the tree was in flower and the corpse was hung with a faded peacock-green dressing-gown, and wore on its wagging head a scarlet smoking-cap. Also it had red bedroom-slippers, one of which had fallen off and lay on the grass like a blot of blood.

But neither Flambeau or Father Brown was looking at these things as yet. They were both staring at a strange object that seemed to stick out of the middle of the dead man's shrunken figure; and which they gradually perceived to be the black but rather rusty iron hilt of a seventeenth-century sword, which had completely transfixed the body. They both remained almost motionless as they gazed at it; until the restless Dr Flood seemed to grow quite impatient with their stolidity.

'What puzzles me most,' he said, nervously snapping his fingers, 'is the actual state of the body. And yet it has given me an idea already.'

Flambeau had stepped up to the tree and was studying the sword-hilt through an eyeglass. But for some odd reason, it was at that very instant that the priest in sheer perversity spun round like a teetotum, turned his back on the corpse, and looked peeringly in the very opposite direction. He was just in time to see the red head of Mrs Flood at the remote end of the garden, turned towards a dark young man, too dim with distance to be identified, who was at that moment mounting a motor-bicycle; who vanished, leaving behind him only the dying din of that vehicle. Then the woman turned and began to walk towards them across the garden, just as Father Brown turned also and began a careful inspection of the sword-hilt and the hanging corpse.

'I understand you only found him about half an hour ago,' said Flambeau. 'Was there anybody about here just before that?

I mean anybody in his bedroom, or that part of the house, or this part of the garden—say for an hour beforehand?'

'No,' said the doctor with precision. 'That is the very tragic accident. My sister-in-law was in the pantry, which is a sort of out-house on the other side; this man Dunn was in the kitchen-garden, which is also in that direction; and I myself was poking about among the books, in a room just behind the one you found me in. There are two female servants, but one had gone to the post and the other was in the attic.'

'And were any of these people,' asked Flambeau, very quietly, 'I say any of these people, at all on bad terms with the poor old gentleman?'

'He was the object of almost universal affection,' replied the doctor solemnly. 'If there were any misunderstandings, they were mild and of a sort common in modern times. The old man was attached to the old religious habits; and perhaps his daughter and son-in-law had rather wider views. All that can have had nothing to do with a ghastly and fantastic assassination like this.'

'It depends on how wide the modern views were,' said Father Brown, 'or how narrow.'

At this moment they heard Mrs Flood hallooing across the garden as she came, and calling her brother-in-law to her with a certain impatience. He hurried towards her and was soon out of earshot; but as he went he waved his hand apologetically and then pointed with a long finger to the ground.

'You will find the footprints very intriguing,' he said; with the same strange air, as of a funereal showman.

The two amateur detectives looked across at each other. 'I find several other things intriguing,' said Flambeau.

'Oh, yes,' said the priest, staring rather foolishly at the grass.

'I was wondering,' said Flambeau, 'why they should hang a man by the neck till he was dead, and then take the trouble to stick him with a sword.'

'And I was wondering,' said Father Brown, 'why they should kill a man with a sword thrust through his heart, and then take the trouble to hang him by the neck.'

'Oh, you are simply being contrary,' protested his friend. 'I can see at a glance that they didn't stab him alive. The body would have bled more and the wound wouldn't have closed like that.'

'And I could see at a glance,' said Father Brown, peering up very awkwardly, with his short stature and short sight, 'that they didn't hang him alive. If you'll look at the knot in the noose, you will see it's tied so clumsily that a twist of rope holds it away from the neck, so that it couldn't throttle a man at all. He was dead before they put the rope on him; and he was dead before they put the sword in him. And how was he really killed?'

'I think,' remarked the other, 'that we'd better go back to the house and have a look at his bedroom—and other things.'

'So we will,' said Father Brown. 'But among other things perhaps we had better have a look at these footprints. Better begin at the other end, I think, by his window. Well, there are no footprints on the paved path, as there might be; but then again there mightn't be. Well, here is the lawn just under his bedroom window. And here are his footprints plain enough.'

He blinked ominously at the footprints; and then began carefully retracing his path towards the tree, every now and then ducking in an undignified manner to look at something on the ground. Eventually he returned to Flambeau and said in a chatty manner:

'Well, do you know the story that is written there very plainly? Though it's not exactly a plain story.'

'I wouldn't be content to call it plain,' said Flambeau. 'I should call it quite ugly—'

'Well,' said Father Brown, 'the story that is stamped quite plainly on the earth, with exact moulds of the old man's slippers, is this. The aged paralytic leapt from the window and ran down the beds parallel to the path, quite eager for all the fun of being strangled and stabbed; so eager that he hopped on one leg out of sheer lightheartedness; and even occasionally turned cartwheels—'

'Stop!' cried Flambeau, angrily. 'What the hell is all this hellish pantomime?'

Father Brown merely raised his eyebrows and gestured mildly towards the hieroglyphs in the dust. 'About half the way there's only the mark of one slipper; and in some places the mark of a hand planted all by itself.'

'Couldn't he have limped and then fallen?' asked Flambeau.

Father Brown shook his head. 'At least he'd have tried to use his hands and feet, or knees and elbows, in getting up. There are no other marks there of any kind. Of course the flagged path is quite near, and there are no marks on that; though there might be on the soil between the cracks; it's a crazy pavement.'

'By God, it's a crazy pavement; and a crazy garden; and a crazy story!' And Flambeau looked gloomily across the gloomy and storm-stricken garden, across which the crooked patchwork paths did indeed give a queer aptness to the quaint old English adjective.

'And now,' said Father Brown, 'let us go up and look at his room.' They went in by a door not far from the bedroom window; and the priest paused a moment to look at an ordinary garden broomstick, for sweeping up leaves, that was leaning against the wall. 'Do you see that?'

'It's a broomstick,' said Flambeau, with solid irony.

'It's a blunder,' said Father Brown, 'the first blunder that I've seen in this curious plot.'

They mounted the stairs and entered the old man's bedroom; and a glance at it made fairly clear the main facts, both about the foundation and disunion of the family. Father Brown had felt from the first that he was in what was, or had been, a Catholic household; but was, at least partly, inhabited by lapsed or very loose Catholics. The pictures and images in the grandfather's room made it clear that what positive piety remained had been practically confined to him; and that his kindred had, for some reason or other, gone Pagan. But he agreed that this was a hopelessly inadequate explanation even of an ordinary murder; let alone such a very extraordinary murder as this. 'Hang it all,' he muttered, 'the murder is really the least extraordinary part of it.' And even as he used the chance phrase, a slow light began to dawn upon his face.

Flambeau had seated himself on a chair by the little table which stood beside the dead man's bed. He was frowning thoughtfully at three or four white pills or pellets that lay in a small tray beside a bottle of water.

'The murderer or murderess,' said Flambeau, 'had some incomprehensible reason or other for wanting us to think the dead man was strangled or stabbed or both. He was not strangled or stabbed or anything of the kind. Why did they want to suggest it? The most logical explanation is that he died in some particular way which would, in itself, suggest a connection with some particular person. Suppose, for instance, he was poisoned. And suppose somebody is involved who would naturally look more like a poisoner than anybody else.'

'After all,' said Father Brown softly, 'our friend in the blue spectacles is a doctor.'

'I'm going to examine these pills pretty carefully,' went on Flambeau. 'I don't want to lose them, though. They look as if they were soluble in water.'

'It may take you some time to do anything scientific with them,' said the priest, 'and the police doctor may be here before that. So I should certainly advise you not to lose them. That is, if you are going to wait for the police doctor.'

'I am going to stay here till I have solved this problem,' said Flambeau.

'Then you will stay here forever,' said Father Brown, looking calmly out of the window. 'I don't think I shall stay in this room, anyhow.'

'Do you mean that I shan't solve the problem?' asked his friend. 'Why shouldn't I solve the problem?'

'Because it isn't soluble in water. No, nor in blood,' said the priest; and he went down the dark stairs into the darkening garden. There he saw again what he had already seen from the window.

The heat and weight and obscurity of the thunderous sky seemed to be pressing yet more closely on the landscape; the clouds had conquered the sun which, above, in a narrowing clearance, stood up paler than the moon. There was a thrill of thunder in the air, but now no more stirring of wind or breeze; and even the colours of the garden seemed only like richer shades of darkness. But one colour still glowed with a certain dusky vividness; and that was the red hair of the woman of that house, who was standing with a sort of rigidity, staring, with her hands thrust up into her hair. That scene of eclipse, with something deeper in his own doubts about its significance, brought to the surface the memory of haunting and mystical lines; and he found himself murmuring: 'A secret spot, as savage and enchanted as e'er beneath a waning moon was haunted by woman wailing for her demon lover.' His muttering became more agitated. 'Holy Mary, Mother of God, pray for us sinners... that's what it is; that's terribly like what it is; woman wailing for her demon lover.'

He was hesitant and almost shaky as he approached the woman; but he spoke with his common composure. He was gazing at her very steadily, as he told her earnestly that she must not be morbid because of the mere accidental accessories of the tragedy, with all their mad ugliness. 'The pictures in your grandfather's room were truer to him than that ugly picture that we saw,' he said gravely. 'Something tells me he was a good man; and it does not matter what his murderers did with his body.'

'Oh, I am sick of his holy pictures and statues!' she said, turning her head away. 'Why don't they defend themselves, if they are what you say they are? But rioters can knock off the Blessed Virgin's head and nothing happens to them. oh, what's the good? You can't blame us, you daren't blame us, if we've found out that Man is stronger than God.'

'Surely,' said Father Brown very gently, 'it is not generous to make even God's patience with us a point against Him.'

'God may be patient and Man impatient,' she answered, 'and suppose we like the impatience better. You call it sacrilege; but you can't stop it.'

Father Brown gave a curious little jump. 'Sacrilege!' he said; and suddenly turned back to the doorway with a new brisk air of decision. At the same moment Flambeau appeared in the doorway, pale with excitement, with a screw of paper in his hands. Father Brown had already opened his mouth to speak, but his impetuous friend spoke before him.

'I'm on the track at last!' cried Flambeau. 'These pills look the same, but they're really different. And do you know that, at the very moment I spotted them, that one-eyed brute of a gardener thrust his white face into the room; and he was carrying a horse-pistol. I knocked it out of his hand and threw him down the stairs, but I begin to understand everything. If I stay here another hour or two, I shall finish my job.'

'Then you will not finish it,' said the priest, with a ring in his voice very rare in him indeed. 'We shall not stay here another hour. We shall not stay here another minute. We must leave this place at once!'

'What!' cried the astounded Flambeau. 'Just when we are getting near the truth! Why, you can tell that we're getting near the truth because they are afraid of us.'

Father Brown looked at him with a stony and inscrutable face, and said: 'They are not afraid of us when we are here. They will only be afraid of us when we are not here.'

They had both become conscious that the rather fidgety figure of Dr Flood was hovering in the lurid haze; now it precipitated itself forward with the wildest gestures.

'Stop! Listen!' cried the agitated doctor. 'I have discovered the truth!'

'Then you can explain it to your own police,' said Father Brown, briefly. 'They ought to be coming soon. But we must be going.'

The doctor seemed thrown into a whirlpool of emotions, eventually rising to the surface again with a despairing cry. He spread out his arms like a cross, barring their way.

'Be it so!' he cried. 'I will not deceive you now, by saying I have discovered the truth. I will only confess the truth.'

'Then you can confess it to your own priest,' said Father Brown, and strode towards the garden gate, followed by his staring friend. Before he reached the gate, another figure had rushed athwart him like the wind; and Dunn the gardener was shouting at him some unintelligible derision at detectives who were running away from their job. Then the priest ducked just in time to dodge a blow from the horse-pistol, wielded like a club. But Dunn was just not in time to dodge a blow from the fist of Flambeau, which was like the club of Hercules. The two left Mr Dunn spread flat behind them on the path, and, passing out of the gate, went out and got into their car in silence. Flambeau only asked one brief question and Father Brown only answered: 'Casterbury.'

At last, after a long silence, the priest observed: 'I could almost believe the storm belonged only to that garden, and came out of a storm in the soul.'

'My friend,' said Flambeau. 'I have known you a long time, and when you show certain signs of certainty, I follow your lead. But I hope you are not going to tell me that you took me away from that fascinating job, because you did not like the atmosphere.'

'Well, it was certainly a terrible atmosphere,' replied Father Brown, calmly. 'Dreadful and passionate and oppressive. And the most dreadful thing about it was this—that there was no hate in it at all.'

'Somebody,' suggested Flambeau, 'seems to have had a slight dislike of grandpapa.'

'Nobody had any dislike of anybody,' said Father Brown with a groan. 'That was the dreadful thing in that darkness. It was love.'

'Curious way of expressing love—to strangle somebody and stick him with a sword,' observed the other.

'It was love,' repeated the priest, 'and it filled the house with terror.'

'Don't tell me,' protested Flambeau, 'that that beautiful woman is in love with that spider in spectacles.'

'No,' said Father Brown and groaned again. 'She is in love with her husband. It is ghastly.'

'It is a state of things that I have often heard you recommend,' replied Flambeau. 'You cannot call that lawless love.'

'Not lawless in that sense,' answered Father Brown; then he turned sharply on his elbow and spoke with a new warmth: 'Do you think I don't know that the love of a man and a woman was the first command of God and is glorious forever? Are you one of those idiots who think we don't admire love and marriage? Do I need to be told of the Garden of eden or the wine of Cana? It is just because the strength in the thing was the strength of God, that it rages with that awful energy even when it breaks loose from God. When the Garden becomes a jungle, but still a glorious jungle; when the second fermentation turns the wine of Cana into the vinegar of Calvary. Do you think I don't know all that?'

'I'm sure you do,' said Flambeau, 'but I don't yet know much about my problem of the murder.'

'The murder cannot be solved,' said Father Brown.

'And why not?' demanded his friend.

'Because there is no murder to solve,' said Father Brown.

Flambeau was silent with sheer surprise; and it was his friend who resumed in a quiet tone:

'I'll tell you a curious thing. I talked with that woman when she was wild with grief; but she never said anything about the murder. She never mentioned murder, or even alluded to murder. What she did mention repeatedly was sacrilege.' Then, with another jerk of verbal disconnection, he added: 'Have you ever heard of Tiger Tyrone?'

'Haven't I!' cried Flambeau. 'Why, that's the very man who's supposed to be after the reliquary, and whom I've been commissioned specially to circumvent. He's the most violent and daring gangster who ever visited this country; Irish, of course, but the sort that goes quite crazily anti-clerical. Perhaps he's dabbled in a little diabolism in these secret societies; anyhow, he has a macabre taste for playing all sorts of wild tricks that look wickeder than they are. Otherwise he's not the wickedest; he seldom kills, and never for cruelty; but he loves doing anything to shock people, especially his own people; robbing churches or digging up skeletons or what not.'

'Yes,' said Father Brown, 'it all fits in. I ought to have seen it all long before.'

'I don't see how we could have seen anything, after only an hour's investigation,' said the detective defensively.

'I ought to have seen it before there was anything to investigate,' said the priest. 'I ought to have known it before you arrived this morning.'

'What on earth do you mean?'

'It only shows how wrong voices sound on the telephone,' said Father Brown reflectively. 'I heard all three stages of the thing this morning; and I thought they were trifles. First, a woman rang me up and asked me to go to that inn as soon as possible. What did that mean? Of course it meant that the old grandfather was dying. Then she rang up to say that I needn't go, after all. What did that mean? Of course it meant that the old grandfather was dead. He had died quite peaceably in his bed; probably heart failure from sheer old age. And then she rang up a third time and said I was to go, after all. What did that mean? Ah, that is rather more interesting!'

He went on after a moment's pause: 'Tiger Tyrone, whose wife worships him, took hold of one of his mad ideas, and yet it was a crafty idea, too. He had just heard that you were tracking him down, that you knew him and his methods and were coming to save the reliquary; he may have heard that I have sometimes been of some assistance. He wanted to stop us on the road; and his trick for doing it was to stage a murder. It was a pretty horrible thing to do; but it wasn't a murder. Probably he bullied his wife with an air of brutal common sense, saying he could only escape penal servitude by using a dead body that couldn't suffer anything from such use. Anyhow, his wife would do anything for him; but she felt all the unnatural hideousness of that hanging masquerade; and that's why she talked about sacrilege. She was thinking of the desecration of the relic; but also of the desecration of the deathbed. The brother's one of those shoddy "scientific" rebels who tinker with dud bombs; an idealist run to seed. But he's devoted to Tiger; and so is the gardener. Perhaps it's a point in his favour that so many people seem devoted to him.

'There was one little point that set me guessing very early. Among the old books the doctor was turning over, was a bundle of seventeeth-century pamphlets; and I caught one title: True Declaration of the Trial and Execution of My Lord Stafford. Now Stafford was executed in the Popish Plot business, which began with one of history's detective stories;

the death of Sir Edmund Berry Godfrey. Godfrey was found dead in a ditch, and part of the mystery was that he had marks of strangulation, but was also transfixed with his own sword. I thought at once that somebody in the house might have got the idea from here. But he couldn't have wanted it as a way of committing a murder. He can only have wanted it as a way of creating a mystery. Then I saw that this applied to all the other outrageous details. They were devilish enough; but it wasn't mere devilry; there was a rag of excuse; because they had to make the mystery as contradictory and complicated as possible, to make sure that we should be a long time solving it—or rather seeing through it. So they dragged the poor old man off his deathbed and made the corpse hop and turn cartwheels and do everything that it couldn't have done. They had to give us an Insoluble Problem. They swept their own tracks off the path, leaving the broom. Fortunately we did see through it in time.'

'You saw through it in time,' said Flambeau. 'I might have lingered a little longer over the second trail they left, sprinkled with assorted pills.'

'Well, anyhow, we got away,' said Father Brown, comfortably.

'And that, I presume,' said Flambeau, 'is the reason I am driving at this rate along the road to Casterbury.'

That night in the monastery and church at Casterbury there were events calculated to stagger monastic seclusion. The reliquary of St Dorothy, in a casket gorgeous with gold and rubies, was temporarily placed in a side room near the chapel of the monastery, to be brought in with a procession for a special service at the end of Benediction. It was guarded for the moment by one monk, who watched it in a tense and vigilant manner; for he and his brethren knew all about the shadow of peril from the prowling of Tiger Tyrone. Thus it was that the monk was on his feet in a flash, when he saw one of the low-latticed windows beginning to open and a dark object drawling like a black serpent through the crack. Rushing across, he gripped it and found it was the arm and sleeve of a man, terminating with a handsome cuff and a smart dark-grey glove. Laying hold of it, he shouted for help, and even as he did so, a man darted into the room through the door behind his back and snatched the casket he had left behind him on the table. Almost at the same instant, the arm wedged in the window came away in his hand, and he stood holding the stuffed limb of a dummy.

Tiger Tyrone had played that trick before, but to the monk it was a novelty. Fortunately, there was at least one person to whom the Tiger's tricks were not a novelty; and that person appeared with militant moustaches, gigantically framed in the doorway, at the very moment when the Tiger turned to escape by it. Flambeau and Tiger Tyrone looked at each other with steady eyes and exchanged something that was almost like a military salute.

Meanwhile Father Brown had slipped into the chapel, to say a prayer for several persons involved in these unseemly events. But he was rather smiling than otherwise, and, to tell the truth, he was not by any means hopeless about Mr Tyrone and his deplorable family; but rather more hopeful than he was for many more respectable people. Then his thoughts widened with the grander perspectives of the place and the occasion. Against black and green marbles at the end of the rather rococo chapel, the dark-red vestments of the festival of a martyr were in their turn a background for a fierier red; a red like red-hot coals; the rubies of the reliquary; the roses of St Dorothy. And he had again a thought to throw back to the strange events of that day, and the woman who had shuddered at the sacrilege she had helped. After all, he thought, St Dorothy also had a Pagan lover; but he had not dominated her or destroyed her faith. She had died free and for the truth; and then had sent him roses from Paradise.

He raised his eyes and saw through the veil of incense smoke and of twinkling lights that Benediction was drawing to its end while the procession waited. The sense of accumulated riches of time and tradition pressed past him like a crowd moving in rank after rank, through unending centuries; and high above them all, like a garland of unfading flames, like the sun of our mortal midnight, the great monstrance blazed against the darkness of the vaulted shadows, as it blazed against the black enigma of the universe. For some are convinced that this enigma also is an Insoluble Problem. And others have equal certitude that it has but one solution.

9

THE VAMPIRE OF THE VILLAGE
(First published in *The Strand*, Aug 1936; not included in first edition of *The Scandal of Father Brown*)

At the twist of a path in the hills, where two poplars stood up like pyramids dwarfing the tiny village of Potter's Pond, a mere huddle of houses, there once walked a man in a costume of a very conspicuous cut and colour, wearing a vivid magenta coat and a white hat tilted upon black ambrosial curls, which ended with a sort of Byronic flourish of whisker.

The riddle of why he was wearing clothes of such fantastic antiquity, yet wearing them with an air of fashion and even swagger, was but one of the many riddles that were eventually solved in solving the mystery of his fate. The point here is that when he had passed the poplars he seemed to have vanished; as if he had faded into the wan and widening dawn or been blown away upon the wind of morning.

It was only about a week afterwards that his body was found a quarter of a mile away, broken upon the steep rockeries of a terraced garden leading up to a gaunt and shuttered house called The Grange. Just before he had vanished, he had been accidentally overheard apparently quarrelling with some bystanders, and especially abusing their village as 'a wretched little hamlet'; and it was supposed that he had aroused some extreme passions of local patriotism and eventually been their victim. At least the local doctor testified that the skull had suffered a crushing blow that might have caused death, through probably only inflicted with some sort of club or cudgel. This fitted in well enough with the notion of an attack by rather savage yokels. But nobody ever found any means of tracing any particular yokel; and the inquest returned a verdict of murder by some persons unknown.

A year or two afterwards the question was re-opened in a curious way; a series of events which led a certain Dr Mulborough, called by his intimates Mulberry in apt allusion to something rich and fruity about his dark rotundity and rather empurpled visage, travelling by train down to Potter's Pond, with a friend whom he had often consulted upon problems of the kind. In spite of the somewhat port-winy and ponderous exterior of the doctor, he had a shrewd eye and was really a man of very remarkable sense; which he considered that he showed in consulting a little priest named Brown, whose acquaintance he had made over a poisoning case long ago. The little priest was sitting opposite to him, with the air of a patient baby absorbing instruction; and the doctor was explaining at length the real reasons for the journey.

'I cannot agree with the gentleman in the magenta coat that Potter's Pond is only a wretched little hamlet. But it is certainly a very remote and secluded village; so that it seems quite outlandish, like a village of a hundred years ago. The spinsters are really spinsters—damn it, you could almost imagine you saw them spin. The ladies are not just ladies. They are gentlewomen; and their chemist is not a chemist, but an apothecary; pronounced potecary. They do just admit the existence of an ordinary doctor like myself to assist the apothecary. But I am considered rather a juvenile innovation, because I am only fifty-seven years old and have only been in the county for twenty-eight years. The solicitor looks as if he had known it for twenty-eight thousand years. Then there is the old Admiral, who is just like a Dickens illustration; with a house full of cutlasses and cuttlefish and equipped with a telescope.'

'I suppose,' said Father Brown, 'there are always a certain number of Admirals washed up on the shore. But I never understood why they get stranded so far inland.'

'Certainly no dead-alive place in the depths of the country is complete without one of these little creatures,' said the doctor. 'And then, of course, there is the proper sort of clergyman; Tory and High Church in a dusty fashion dating from Archbishop Laud; more of an old woman than any of the old women. He's a white-haired studious old bird, more easily shocked than the spinsters. Indeed, the gentlewomen, though Puritan in their principles, are sometimes pretty plain in their speech; as the real Puritans were. Once or twice I have known old Miss Carstairs-Carew use expressions as lively as anything in the Bible. The dear old clergyman is assiduous in reading the Bible; but I almost fancy he shuts his eyes when he comes to those words. Well, you know I'm not particularly modern. I don't enjoy this jazzing and joyriding of the Bright Young Things—'

'The Bright Young Things don't enjoy it,' said Father Brown. 'That is the real tragedy.'

'But I am naturally rather more in touch with the world than the people in this prehistoric village,' pursued the doctor. 'And I had reached a point when I almost welcomed the Great Scandal.'

'Don't say the Bright Young Things have found Potter's Pond after all,' observed the priest, smiling.

'Oh, even our scandal is on old-established melodramatic lines. Need I say that the clergyman's son promises to be our problem? It would be almost irregular, if the clergyman's son were quite regular. So far as I can see, he is very mildly and almost feebly irregular. He was first seen drinking ale outside the Blue Lion. Only it seems he is a poet, which in those parts is next door to being a poacher.'

'Surely,' said Father Brown, 'even in Potter's Pond that cannot be the Great Scandal.'

'No,' replied the doctor gravely. 'The Great Scandal began thus. In the house called The Grange, situated at the extreme end of The Grove, there lives a lady. A Lonely Lady. She calls herself Mrs Maltravers (that is how we put it); but she only came a year or two ago and nobody knows anything about her. "I can't think why she wants to live here," said Miss Carstairs-Carew; "we do not visit her."'

'Perhaps that's why she wants to live there,' said Father Brown.

'Well, her seclusion is considered suspicious. She annoys them by being good-looking and even what is called good style. And all the young men are warned against her as a vamp.'

'People who lose all their charity generally lose all their logic,' remarked Father Brown. 'It's rather ridiculous to complain that she keeps to herself; and then accuse her of vamping the whole male population.'

'That is true,' said the doctor. 'And yet she is really rather a puzzling person. I saw her and found her intriguing; one of those brown women, long and elegant and beautifully ugly, if you know what I mean. She is rather witty, and though young enough certainly gives me an impression of what they call—well, experience. What the old ladies call a Past.'

'All the old ladies having been born this very minute,' observed Father Brown. 'I think I can assume she is supposed to have vamped the parson's son.'

'Yes, and it seems to be a very awful problem to the poor old parson. She is supposed to be a widow.'

Father Brown's face had a flash and spasm of his rare irritation. 'She is supposed to be a widow, as the parson's son is supposed to be the parson's son, and the solicitor is supposed to be a solicitor and you are supposed to be a doctor. Why in thunder shouldn't she be a widow? Have they one speck of prima facie evidence for doubting that she is what she says she is?' ,

Dr Mulborough abruptly squared his broad shoulders and sat up. 'Of course you're right again,' he said. 'But we haven't come to the scandal yet. Well, the scandal is that she is a widow.'

'Oh,' said Father Brown; and his face altered and he said something soft and faint, that might almost have been 'My God!'

'First of all,' said the doctor, 'they have made one discovery about Mrs Maltravers. She is an actress.'

'I fancied so,' said Father Brown. 'Never mind why. I had another fancy about her, that would seem even more irrelevant.'

'Well, at that instant it was scandal enough that she was an actress. The dear old clergyman of course is heartbroken, to think that his white hairs should be brought in sorrow to the grave by an actress and adventuress. The spinsters shriek in chorus. The Admiral admits he has sometimes been to a theatre in town; but objects to such things in what he calls "our midst". Well, of course I've no particular objections of that kind. This actress is certainly a lady, if a bit of a Dark Lady, in the manner of the Sonnets; the young man is very much in love with her; and I am no doubt a sentimental old fool in having a sneaking sympathy with the misguided youth who is sneaking round the Moated Grange; and I was getting into quite a pastoral frame of mind about this idyll, when suddenly the thunderbolt fell. And I, who am the only person who ever had any sympathy with these people, am sent down to be the messenger of doom.'

'Yes,' said Father Brown, 'and why were you sent down?'

The doctor answered with a sort of groan:

'Mrs Maltravers is not only a widow, but she is the widow of Mr Maltravers.'

'It sounds like a shocking revelation, as you state it,' acknowledged the priest seriously.

'And Mr Maltravers,' continued his medical friend, 'was the man who was apparently murdered in this very village a year or two ago; supposed to have been bashed on the head by one of the simple villagers.'

'I remember you told me,' said Father Brown. 'The doctor, or some doctor, said he had probably died of being clubbed on the head with a cudgel.'

Dr Mulborough was silent for a moment in frowning embarrassment, and then said curtly:

'Dog doesn't eat dog, and doctors don't bite doctors, not even when they are mad doctors. I shouldn't care to cast any reflection on my eminent predecessor in Potter's Pond, if I could avoid it; but I know you are really safe for secrets. And, speaking in confidence, my eminent predecessor at Potter's Pond was a blasted fool; a drunken old humbug and absolutely incompetent. I was asked, originally by the Chief Constable of the County (for I've lived a long time in the county, though only recently in the village), to look into the whole business; the depositions and reports of the inquest and so on. And there simply isn't any question about it. Maltravers may have been hit on the head; he was a strolling actor passing through the place; and Potter's Pond probably thinks it is all in the natural order that such people should be hit on the head. But whoever hit him on the head did not kill him; it is simply impossible for the injury, as described, to do more than knock him out for a few hours. But lately I have managed to turn up some other facts bearing on the matter; and the result of it is pretty grim.'

He sat louring at the landscape as it slid past the window, and then said more curtly: 'I am coming down here, and asking your help, because there's going to be an exhumation. There is very strong suspicion of poison.'

'And here we are at the station,' said Father Brown cheerfully. 'I suppose your idea is that poisoning the poor man would naturally fall among the household duties of his wife.'

'Well, there never seems to have been anyone else here who had any particular connection with him,' replied Mulborough, as they alighted from the train. 'At least there is one queer old crony of his, a broken-down actor, hanging around; but the police and the local solicitor seem convinced he is an unbalanced busybody; with some idée fixe about a quarrel with an actor who was his enemy; but who certainly wasn't Maltravers. A wandering accident, I should say, and certainly nothing to do with the problem of the poison.'

Father Brown had heard the story. But he knew that he never knew a story until he knew the characters in the story. He spent the next two or three days in going the rounds, on one polite excuse or another, to visit the chief actors of the drama. His first interview with the mysterious widow was brief but bright. He brought away from it at least two facts; one that Mrs Maltravers sometimes talked in a way which the Victorian village would call cynical; and, second, that like not a few actresses, she happened to belong to his own religious communion.

He was not so illogical (nor so unorthodox) as to infer from this alone that she was innocent of the alleged crime. He was well aware that his old religious communion could boast of several distinguished poisoners. But he had no difficulty in understanding its connection, in this sort of case, with a certain intellectual liberty which these Puritans would call laxity; and which would certainly seem to this parochial patch of an older England to be almost cosmopolitan. Anyhow, he was sure she could count for a great deal, whether for good or evil. Her brown eyes were brave to the point of battle, and her enigmatic mouth, humorous and rather large, suggested that her purposes touching the parson's poetical son, whatever they might be, were planted pretty deep.

The parson's poetical son himself, interviewed amid vast village scandal on a bench outside the Blue Lion, gave an impression of pure sulks. Hurrel Horner, a son of the Rev. Samuel Horner, was a square-built young man in a pale grey suit with a touch of something arty in a pale green tie, otherwise mainly notable for a mane of auburn hair and a permanent scowl. But Father Brown had a way with him in getting people to explain at considerable length why they refused to say a single word. About the general scandalmongering in the village, the young man began to curse freely. He even added a little scandalmongering of his own. He referred bitterly to alleged past flirtations between the Puritan Miss Carstairs-Carew and Mr Carver the solicitor. He even accused that legal character of having attempted to force himself upon the acquaintance of Mrs Maltravers. But when he came to speak of his own father, whether out of an acid decency or piety, or because his anger was too deep for speech, he snapped out only a few words.

'Well, there it is. He denounces her day and night as a painted adventuress; a sort of barmaid with gilt hair. I tell him she's not; you've met her yourself, and you know she's not. But he won't even meet her. He won't even see her in the street or look at her out of a window. An actress would pollute his house and even his holy presence. If he is called a Puritan he says he's proud to be a Puritan.'

'Your father,' said Father Brown, 'is entitled to have his views respected, whatever they are; they are not views I understand very well myself. But I agree he is not entitled to lay down the law about a lady he has never seen and then refuse even to look at her, to see if he is right. That is illogical.'

'That's his very stiffest point,' replied the youth. 'Not even one momentary meeting. Of course, he thunders against my other theatrical tastes as well.'

Father Brown swiftly followed up the new opening, and learnt much that he wanted to know. The alleged poetry, which was such a blot on the young man's character, was almost entirely dramatic poetry. He had written tragedies in verse which had been admired by good judges. He was no mere stage-struck fool; indeed he was no fool of any kind. He had some really original ideas about acting Shakespeare; it was easy to understand his having been dazzled and delighted by finding the brilliant lady at the Grange. And even the priest's intellectual sympathy so far mellowed the rebel of Potter's Pond that at their parting he actually smiled.

It was that smile which suddenly revealed to Father Brown that the young man was really miserable. So long as he frowned, it might well have been only sulks; but when he smiled it was somehow a more real revelation of sorrow.

Something continued to haunt the priest about that interview with the poet. An inner instinct certified that the sturdy young man was eaten from within, by some grief greater even than the conventional story of conventional parents being obstacles to the course of true love. It was all the more so, because there were not any obvious alternative causes. The boy was already rather a literary and dramatic success; his books might be said to be booming. Nor did he drink or dissipate his well-earned wealth. His notorious revels at the Blue Lion reduced themselves to one glass of light ale; and he seemed to be rather careful with his money. Father Brown thought of another possible complication in connection with Hurrel's large resources and small expenditure; and his brow darkened.

The conversation of Miss Carstairs-Carew, on whom he called next, was certainly calculated to paint the parson's son in the darkest colours. But as it was devoted to blasting him with all the special vices which Father Brown was quite certain the young man did not exhibit, he put it down to a common combination of Puritanism and gossip. The lady, though lofty, was quite gracious, however, and offered the visitor a small glass of port-wine and a slice of seed-cake, in the manner of everybody's most ancient great-aunts, before he managed to escape from a sermon on the general decay of morals and manners.

His next port of call was very much of a contrast; for he disappeared down a dark and dirty alley, where Miss Carstairs-Carew would have refused to follow him even in thought; and then into a narrow tenement made noisier by a high and declamatory voice in an attic... From this he re-emerged, with a rather dazed expression, pursued on to the pavement by a very excited man with a blue chin and a black frock-coat faded to bottle-green, who was shouting argumentatively: 'He did not disappear! Maltravers never disappeared! He appeared: he appeared dead and I've appeared alive. But where's all the rest of the company? Where's that man, that monster, who deliberately stole my lines, crabbed my best scenes and ruined my career? I was the finest Tubal that ever trod the boards. He acted Shylock—he didn't need to act much for that! And so with the greatest opportunity of my whole career. I could show you press-cuttings on my renderings of Fortinbras—'

'I'm quite sure they were splendid and very well-deserved,' gasped the little priest. 'I understood the company had left the village before Maltravers died. But it's all right. It's quite all right.' And he began to hurry down the street again.

'He was to act Polonius,' continued the unquenchable orator behind him. Father Brown suddenly stopped dead.

'Oh,' he said very slowly, 'he was to act Polonius.'

'That villain Hankin!' shrieked the actor. 'Follow his trail. Follow him to the ends of the earth! Of course he'd left the village; trust him for that. Follow him—find him; and may the curses—' But the priest was again hurrying away down the street.

Two much more prosaic and perhaps more practical interviews followed this melodramatic scene. First the priest went into the bank, where he was closeted for ten minutes with the manager; and then paid a very proper call on the aged and amiable clergyman. Here again all seemed very much as described, unaltered and seemingly unalterable; a touch or two of devotion from more austere traditions, in the narrow crucifix on the wall, the big Bible on the bookstand and the old gentleman's opening lament over the increasing disregard of Sunday; but all with a flavour of gentility that was not without its little refinements and faded luxuries.

The clergyman also gave his guest a glass of port; but accompanied by an ancient British biscuit instead of seedcake. The priest had again the weird feeling that everything was almost too perfect, and that he was living a century before his time. Only on one point the amiable old parson refused to melt into any further amiability; he meekly but firmly maintained that his conscience would not allow him to meet a stage player. However, Father Brown put down his glass of port with expressions of appreciation and thanks; and went off to meet his friend the doctor by appointment at the corner of the street; whence they were to go together to the offices of Mr Carver, the solicitor.

'I suppose you've gone the dreary round,' began the doctor, 'and found it a very dull village.'

Father Brown's reply was sharp and almost shrill. 'Don't call your village dull. I assure you it's a very extraordinary village indeed.'

'I've been dealing with the only extraordinary thing that ever happened here, I should think,' observed Dr Mulborough. 'And even that happened to somebody from outside. I may tell you they managed the exhumation quietly last night; and I did the autopsy this morning. In plain words we've been digging up a corpse that's simply stuffed with poison.'

'A corpse stuffed with poison,' repeated Father Brown rather absently. 'Believe me, your village contains something much more extraordinary than that.'

There was abrupt silence, followed by the equally abrupt pulling of the antiquated bell-pull in the porch of the solicitor's house; and they were soon brought into the presence of that legal gentleman, who presented them in turn to a white-haired, yellow-faced gentleman with a scar, who appeared to be the Admiral.

By this time the atmosphere of the village had sunk almost into the subconsciousness of the little priest; but he was conscious that the lawyer was indeed the sort of lawyer to be the adviser of people like Miss Carstairs-Carew. But though he was an archaic old bird, he seemed something more than a fossil. Perhaps it was the uniformity of the background; but the priest had again the curious feeling that he himself was transplanted back into the early nineteenth century, rather than that the solicitor had survived into the early twentieth. His collar and cravat contrived to look almost like a stock as he settled his long chin into them; but they were clean as well as clean-cut; and there was even something about him of a very-dry old dandy. In short, he was what is called well preserved, even if partly by being petrified.

The lawyer and the Admiral, and even the doctor, showed some surprise on finding that Father Brown was rather disposed to defend the parson's son against the local lamentations on behalf of the parson.

'I thought our young friend rather attractive, myself,' he said. 'He's a good talker and I should guess a good poet; and Mrs Maltravers, who is serious about that at least, says he's quite a good actor.'

'Indeed,' said the lawyer. 'Potter's Pond, outside Mrs Maltravers, is rather more inclined to ask if he is a good son.'

'He is a good son,' said Father Brown. 'That's the extraordinary thing.'

'Damn it all,' said the Admiral. 'Do you mean he's really fond of his father?'

The priest hesitated. Then he said, 'I'm not quite so sure about that. That's the other extraordinary thing.'

'What the devil do you mean?' demanded the sailor with nautical profanity.

'I mean,' said Father Brown, 'that the son still speaks of his father in a hard unforgiving way; but he seems after all to have done more than his duty by him. I had a talk with the bank manager, and as we were inquiring in confidence into a serious crime, under authority from the police, he told me the facts. The old clergyman has retired from parish work; indeed, this was never actually his parish. Such of the populace, which is pretty pagan, as goes to church at all, goes to Dutton-Abbot, not a mile away. The old man has no private means, but his son is earning good money; and the old man is well looked after. He gave me some port of absolutely first-class vintage; I saw rows of dusty old bottles of it; and I left him sitting down to a little lunch quite recherche in an old-fashioned style. It must be done on the young man's money.'

'Quite a model son,' said Carver with a slight sneer.

Father Brown nodded, frowning, as if revolving a riddle of his own; and then said: 'A model son. But rather a mechanical model.'

At this moment a clerk brought in an unstamped letter for the lawyer; a letter which the lawyer tore impatiently across after a single glance. As it fell apart, the priest saw a spidery, crazy crowded sort of handwriting and the signature of 'Phoenix Fitzgerald'; and made a guess which the other curtly confirmed.

'It's that melodramatic actor that's always pestering us,' he said. 'He's got some fixed feud with some dead and gone fellow mummer of his, which can't have anything to do with the case. We all refuse to see him, except the doctor, who did see him; and the doctor says he's mad.'

'Yes,' said Father Brown, pursing his lips thoughtfully. 'I should say he's mad. But of course there can't be any doubt that he's right.'

'Right?' cried Carver sharply. 'Right about what?'

'About this being connected with the old theatrical company,' said Father Brown. 'Do you know the first thing that stumped me about this story? It was that notion that Maltravers was killed by villagers because he insulted their village. It's extraordinary what coroners can get jurymen to believe; and journalists, of course, are quite incredibly credulous. They can't know much about English rustics. I'm an English rustic myself; at least I was grown, with other turnips, in Essex. Can you imagine an English agricultural labourer idealizing and personifying his village, like the citizen of an old Greek city state; drawing the sword for its sacred banner, like a man in the tiny medieval republic of an Italian town? Can you hear a jolly old gaffer saying, "Blood alone can wipe out one spot on the escutcheon of Potter's Pond"? By St George and the Dragon, I only wish they would! But, as a matter of fact, I have a more practical argument for the other notion.'

He paused for a moment, as if collecting his thoughts, and then went on: 'They misunderstood the meaning of those few last words poor Maltravers was heard to say. He wasn't telling the villagers that the village was only a hamlet. He was talking to an actor; they were going to put on a performance in which Fitzgerald was to be Fortinbras, the unknown Hankin to be Polonius, and Maltravers, no doubt, the Prince of Denmark. Perhaps somebody else wanted the part or had views on the part; and Maltravers said angrily, "You'd be a miserable little Hamlet"; that's all.'

Dr Mulborough was staring; he seemed to be digesting the suggestion slowly but without difficulty. At last he said, before the others could speak: 'And what do you suggest that we should do now?'

Father Brown arose rather abruptly; but he spoke civilly enough. 'If these gentlemen will excuse us for a moment, I propose that you and I, doctor, should go round at once to the Horners. I know the parson and his son will both be there just now. And what I want to do, doctor, is this. Nobody in the village knows yet, I think, about your autopsy and its result. I want you simply to tell both the clergyman and his son, while they are there together, the exact fact of the case; that Maltravers died by poison and not by a blow.'

Dr Mulborough had reason to reconsider his incredulity when told that it was an extraordinary village. The scene which ensued, when he actually carried out the priest's programme, was certainly of the sort in which a man, as the saying is, can hardly believe his eyes.

The Rev. Samuel Horner was standing in his black cassock, which threw up the silver of his venerable head; his hand rested at the moment on the lectern at which he often stood to study the Scripture, now possibly by accident only; but it gave him a greater look of authority. And opposite to him his mutinous son was sitting asprawl in a chair, smoking a cheap cigarette with an exceptionally heavy scowl; a lively picture of youthful impiety.

The old man courteously waved Father Brown to a seat, which he took and sat there silent, staring blandly at the ceiling. But something made Mulborough feel that he could deliver his important news more impressively standing up.

'I feel,' he said, 'that you ought to be informed, as in some sense the spiritual father of this community, that one terrible tragedy in its record has taken on a new significance; possibly even more terrible. You will recall the sad business of the death of Maltravers; who was adjudged to have been killed with the blow of a stick, probably wielded by some rustic enemy.'

The clergyman made a gesture with a wavering hand. 'God forbid,' he said, 'that I should say anything that might seem to palliate murderous violence in any case. But when an actor brings his wickedness into this innocent village, he is challenging the judgement of God.'

'Perhaps,' said the doctor gravely. 'But anyhow it was not so that the judgement fell. I have just been commissioned to conduct a post-mortem on the body; and I can assure you, first, that the blow on the head could not conceivably have caused the death; and, second, that the body was full of poison, which undoubtedly caused death.'

Young Hurrel Horner sent his cigarette, flying and was on his feet with the lightness and swiftness of a cat. His leap landed him within a yard of the reading-desk.

'Are you certain of this?' he gasped. 'Are you absolutely certain that that blow could not cause death?'

'Absolutely certain,' said the doctor.

'Well,' said Hurrel, 'I almost wish this one could.'

In a flash, before anyone could move a finger, he had struck the parson a stunning crack on the mouth, dashing him backwards like a disjointed black doll against the door.

'What are you doing?' cried Mulborough, shaken from head to foot with the shock and mere sound of the blow. 'Father Brown, what is this madman doing?'

But Father Brown had not stirred; he was still staring serenely at the ceiling.

'I was waiting for him to do that,' said the priest placidly. 'I rather wonder he hasn't done it before.'

'Good God,' cried the doctor. 'I know we thought he was wronged in some ways; but to strike his father; to strike a clergyman and a non-combatant—'

'He has not struck his father; and he has not struck a clergyman,' said Father Brown. 'He has struck a blackmailing blackguard of an actor dressed up as a clergyman, who has lived on him like a leech for years. Now he knows he is free of the blackmail, he lets fly; and I can't say I blame him much. More especially as I have very strong suspicions that the blackmailer is a poisoner as well. I think, Mulborough, you had better ring up the police.'

They passed out of the room uninterrupted by the two others, the one dazed and staggered, the other still blind and snorting and panting with passions of relief and rage. But as they passed, Father Brown once turned his face to the young man; and the young man was one of the very few human beings who have seen that face implacable.

'He was right there,' said Father Brown. 'When an actor brings his wickedness into this innocent village, he challenges the judgement of God.'

'Well,' said Father Brown, as he and the doctor again settled themselves in a railway carriage standing in the station of Potter's Pond. 'As you say, it's a strange story; but I don't think it's any longer a mystery story. Anyhow, the story seems to me to have been roughly this. Maltravers came here, with part of his touring company; some of them went straight to Dutton-Abbot, where they were all presenting some melodrama about the early nineteenth century; he himself happened to be hanging about in his stage dress, the very distinctive dress of a dandy of that time. Another character was an old-fashioned parson, whose dark dress was less distinctive and might pass as being merely old-fashioned. This part was taken by a man who mostly acted old men; had acted Shylock and was afterwards going to act Polonius.

'A third figure in the drama was our dramatic poet, who was also a dramatic performer, and quarrelled with Maltravers about how to present Hamlet, but more about personal things, too. I think it likely that he was in love with Mrs Maltravers even then; I don't believe there was anything wrong with them; and I hope it may now be all right with them. But he may very well have resented Maltravers in his conjugal capacity; for Maltravers was a bully and likely to raise rows. In some such row they fought with sticks, and the poet hit Maltravers very hard on the head, and, in the light of the inquest, had every reason to suppose he had killed him.

'A third person was present or privy to the incident, the man acting the old parson; and he proceeded to blackmail the alleged murderer, forcing from him the cost of his upkeep in some luxury as a retired clergyman. It was the obvious masquerade for such a man in such a place, simply to go on wearing his stage clothes as a retired clergyman. But he had his own reason for being a very retired clergyman. For the true story of Maltravers' death was that he rolled into a deep undergrowth of bracken, gradually recovered, tried to walk towards a house, and was eventually overcome, not by the blow, but by the fact that the benevolent clergyman had given him poison an hour before, probably in a glass of port. I was beginning to think so, when I drank a glass of the parson's port. It made me a little nervous. The police are working on that theory now; but whether they will be able to prove that part of the story, I don't know. They will have to find the exact motive; but it's obvious that this bunch of actors was buzzing with quarrels and Maltravers was very much hated.'

'The police may prove something now they have got the suspicion,' said Dr Mulborough. 'What I don't understand is why you ever began to suspect. Why in the world should you suspect that very blameless black-coated gentleman?'

Father Brown smiled faintly. 'I suppose in one sense,' he said, 'it was a matter of special knowledge; almost a professional matter, but in a peculiar sense. You know our controversialists often complain that there is a great deal of ignorance about what our religion is really like. But it is really more curious than that. It is true, and it is not at all unnatural, that England does not know much about the Church of Rome. But England does not know much about the Church of England. Not even as much as I do. You would be astonished at how little the average public grasps about the Anglican controversies; lots of them don't really know what is meant by a High Churchman or a Low Churchman, even on the particular points of practice, let alone the two theories of history and philosophy behind them. You can see this ignorance in any newspaper; in any merely popular novel or play.

'Now the first thing that struck me was that this venerable cleric had got the whole thing incredibly mixed up. No Anglican parson could be so wrong about every Anglican problem. He was supposed to be an old Tory High Churchman; and then he boasted of being a Puritan. A man like that might personally be rather Puritanical; but he would never call it being a Puritan. He professed a horror of the stage; he didn't know that High Churchmen generally don't have that special horror, though Low Churchmen do. He talked like a Puritan about the Sabbath; and then he had a crucifix in his room. He evidently had no notion of what a very pious parson ought to be, except that he ought to be very solemn and venerable and frown upon the pleasures of the world.

'All this time there was a subconscious notion running in my head; something I couldn't fix in my memory; and then it came to me suddenly. This is a Stage Parson. That is exactly the vague venerable old fool who would be the nearest notion a popular playwright or play-actor of the old school had of anything so odd as a religious man.'

'To say nothing of a physician of the old school,' said Mulborough good-humouredly, 'who does not set up to know much about being a religious man.'

'As a matter of fact,' went on Father Brown, 'there was a plainer and more glaring cause for suspicion. It concerned the Dark Lady of the Grange, who was supposed to be the Vampire of the Village.

I very early formed the impression that this black blot was rather the bright spot of the village. She was treated as a mystery; but there was really nothing mysterious about her.

She had come down here quite recently, quite openly, under her own name, to help the new inquiries to be made about her own husband. He hadn't treated her too well; but she had principles, suggesting that something was due to her married name and to common justice. For the same reason, she went to live in the house outside which her husband had been found dead. The other innocent and straightforward case, besides the Vampire of the Village, was the Scandal of the Village, the parson's profligate son. He also made no disguise of his profession or past connection with the acting world. That's why I didn't suspect him as I did the parson. But you'll already have guessed a real and relevant reason for suspecting the parson.'

'Yes, I think I see,' said the doctor, 'that's why you bring in the name of the actress.'

'Yes, I mean his fanatical fixity about not seeing the actress,' remarked the priest. 'But he didn't really object to seeing her. He objected to her seeing him.'

'Yes, I see that,' assented the other. 'If she had seen the Rev. Samuel Horner, she would instantly have recognized the very unreverend actor Hankin, disguised as a sham parson with a pretty bad character behind the disguise. Well, that is the whole of this simple village idyll, I think. But you will admit I kept my promise; I have shown you something in the village considerably more creepy than a corpse; even a corpse stuffed with poison. The black coat of a parson stuffed with a blackmailer is at least worth noticing and my live man is much deadlier than your dead one.'

'Yes,' said the doctor, settling himself back comfortably in the cushions. 'If it comes to a little cosy company on a railway journey, I should prefer the corpse.'

THE END

Uncollected Stories

THE DONNINGTON AFFAIR

In the october 1914 issue of the British magazine, *The Premier*, Sir Max Pemberton published the first part of this story, inviting a number of writers, including Chesterton, to use their talents to solve the mystery of the murder described. Chesterton's solution followed in the form of a Father Brown story in the November issue.

IT was natural, of course, that we should think of calling in expert opinion on the tragedy; or, at least, something subtler than the passing policeman. But I could think of few people or none whom it would be useful to consult thus privately. I remembered an investigator who had taken some interest in Southby's original trouble; merely because I remembered the curious surname of Shrike; but report told me that he had since grown rich and retired, and was now yachting inaccessibly among the Pacific Islands.

My old friend Brown, the Roman priest at Cobhole, who had often given me good advice in small problems, had wired that he feared he could not come down, even for an hour. He merely added—what, I confess, I thought inconsequent—that the key might be found in the sentence, that "Mester was the cheeriest soul possible."

Superintendent Matthews still carries weight with any considering person who has actually talked to him; but he is naturally in most cases officially reticent, and in some cases officially slow.

Sir Borrow seemed stricken rigid by this final tragedy; a thing pardonable enough in a very old man who, whatever his faults, had never had anything but tragedy upon tragedy out of his own blood and name.

Wellman can be trusted with anything up to the Crown jewels; but not with an idea. Harriet is far too good a woman to be a good detective. So I was left with my unsatisfied appetite for expert advice. I think the others shared it to some extent; I think we wished a man different from all of us would walk into the room, a man of the world outside us, a man of wider experience, a man of experience so wide—if it were possible—that he should know even one case that was like our own. Certainly none of us had the wildest suspicion of who the man would be.

I have explained that when poor Evelyn's body was found it was clad in a dressing-gown, as if she had been suddenly summoned from her room, and the door of the Priest's Room stood open. Acting on I know not what impulse, I had closed it to; and, so far as I know, it was not opened again till it was opened from within. I confess that for me that opening was terrible.

Sir Borrow, Wellman, and I were alone in the chamber of slaughter. At least we were alone till a total stranger strolled into the room, without even pulling the peaked cap off his head. He was a sturdy man, stained with travel, especially as regards his leggings, which were loaded with clay and slime of innumerable ditches. But he was entirely unconcerned, which is more than I was. For, despite his extra dirt and his extra impudence, I recognised him as the fugitive convict, Mester, whose letter I had so foolishly passed on to his fellow convict. He entered the room with his hands in his pockets, and whistling. Then the whistling ceased, and he said:

"You seem to have shut the door again. I suppose you know it's not easy to open again on this side."

Through the broken window which gave upon the garden I could see Superintendent Matthews standing passively among the shrubs, with his broad back to the house. I walked to the window, and also whistled, but in a far more practical spirit. And yet, I know not why I should call it practical, for the superintendent, who must have heard me, did not turn his head, nor so much as shift a shoulder.

"I shouldn't worry poor old Matthews," said the man in the peaked cap in a friendly tone, "he is one of the best men in the service, and he must be awfully tired. I expect I can answer nearly all the questions that he could." And he relighted a cigarette.

"Mr Mester," I replied with some heat, "I was sending for the superintendent to arrest you!"

"Quite so," he answered, throwing his wax match out of the window. "Well, he won't!"

He was gazing at me with a grave stolidity. And yet I fancy that the gravity of his full face had less effect on me than the large, indifferent back of the policeman.

The man called Mester resumed.

"I mean that my position here may not be quite what you suppose. It's true enough I assisted the young fellow to escape; but I don't imagine you know why I did it. It is an old rule in our profession—"

Before he could finish I had uttered a cry.

"Stop!" I cried out. "Who is that behind the door?"

I could see, by the very movement of Mester's mouth, that he was just about to answer, "What door?" But before the lips could move he also was answered. And from behind the sealed door of the secret chamber came the noise of something that was alive, if it were not human, or was moving, if it were not alive.

"What is in the Priest's Room?" I cried, and looked round for something with which to break down the door. I had half lifted the piece of jagged iron bar for the purpose. And then the horrid part it had played in that night overwhelmed me, and I fell against the door and beat on it with feeble hands, only repeating, "What is in the Priest's Room?" It was the awful fact that a voice, obscure but human, answered from behind the closed door, "The Priest!"

The heavy door was opened very slowly, apparently pushed by a hand no stronger than my own. The same voice which had said "The Priest," said in rather simpler tones, "Whom else did you expect?" The door swung out slowly to the full compass of its hinges, and revealed the black silhouette of a stumpy, apologetic person, with a big hat and a bad umbrella. He was in every way a very unromantic and inappropriate person to be in the Priest's Room, save in the accidental detail of being a priest.

He walked straight up to me before I could cry: "You have come, after all!"

He shook my hand, and, before he dropped it, looked at me with a steady and singular expression, sad, and yet rather serious than sad. I can only say it was the face we wear at the funeral of one dear as a friend, not that we wear by the deathbed of any directly dear to us.

"I can at least congratulate you," said Father Brown.

I think I put my hand wildly through my hair. I am sure I answered:

"And what is there in this nightmare on which I can be congratulated?"

He answered me with the same solid face:

"On the innocence of the woman who will be your wife."

"No one," I cried indignantly, "has attempted to connect her with the matter."

He nodded gravely, as if in assent.

"That was the danger, doubtless," he said with a slight sigh, "but she's all right now, thank God. Isn't she?" And as if to give the last touch to the topsyturvydom, he turned to ask his question of the man in the peaked cap.

"Oh, she's safe enough!" said the man called Mester.

I cannot deny that there was suddenly lifted off my heart a load of doubt, which I had never known was there. But I was bound to pursue the problem.

"Do you mean, Father Brown," I asked, "that you know who was the guilty person?"

"In a sense, yes," he answered. "But you must remember that in a murder case the guiltiest person is not always the murderer."

"Well, the guiltiest person, then," I cried impatiently. "How are we to bring the guiltiest person to punishment?"

"The guiltiest person is punished," said Father Brown.

There was a long silence in the twilight turret, and my mind laboured with doubts that were too large for it. At last Mester said gruffly, but not without a kind of good nature:

"I think you two reverend gentlemen had better go and have a talk somewhere. About Hades, say, or hassocks, or whatever you do talk about. I shall have to look into this by myself. My name is Stephen Shrike; you may have heard of me."

Even before such fancies had been swallowed up in my sudden fear at the movements in the secret room, I had faced the startling possibility that this escaped convict was really a detective. But I had not dreamed of his being so famous a one. The man who had been concerned for Southby, and since gained colossal prestige, had some claim in the case; and I followed Brown, who had already strolled down towards the entrance of the garden.

"The distinction between Hades and hassocks " began Father Brown.

"Don't play the fool!" I said, roughly enough.

"Was not without some philosophical value," continued the little priest, with unruffled good temper. "Human troubles are mostly of two kinds. There is an accidental kind, that you can't see because they are so close you fall over as you do over a hassock. And there is the other kind of evil, the real kind. And that a man will go to seek however far off it is—down, down, into the lost abyss." And he unconsciously pointed his stumpy finger downward towards the grass, which was sprinkled with daisies.

"It was good of you to come, after all," I said; "but I wish I could make more sense of the things you say."

"Well," he replied patiently, "have you made sense of the one thing I did say before I came down?"

"Why, you made some wild statement," I replied, "that the key of the story was in Mester's being cheerful, but—why, bless my soul, and so it is the key, in a way!"

"Only the key, so far," said my companion, "but my first guess seems to have been right. It is not very common to find such sparkling gaiety in people undergoing penal servitude, especially when ruined on a false charge. And it seemed to me that Mester's optimism was a little overdone. I also suspected that his aviation, and all the rest of it, true or false, were simply meant to make Southby think the escape feasible. But if Mester was such a demon for escaping, why didn't he escape by himself? Why was he so anxious to lug along a young gentleman who does not seem to have been much use to him? As I was wondering, my eye fell on another sentence in your manuscript."

"What was that?" I asked.

He took out a scrap of paper on which there were some scribbles in pencil, and read out:

"'They then crossed an enclosure in which other prisoners were at work.'"

After another pause, he resumed:

"That, of course, was plain enough. What kind of convict prison is it where prisoners work without any warders overseeing or walking about? What sort of warders are they to allow two convicts to climb two walls and go off as if for a picnic? All that is plain. And the conclusion is plainer from many other sentences. 'It seemed such an impossible thing that he could evade the hue and cry that must attend this flight.' It would have been impossible if there had been any hue and cry. 'Evelyn and Harriet heard me eagerly, and the former, I began to suspect, was already in possession of the story.' How could she be in possession of it so early as that, unless the police cars and telephones helped to send word from Southby? Could the convicts catch a camel or an ostrich? And look at the motorboat. Do motorboats grow on trees? No, that's all simple. Not only was the companion in the escape a police detective, but the whole scheme of the escape was a police scheme, engineered by the highest authorities of the prison."

"But why?" I asked, staring. "And what has Southby to do with it?"

"Southby had nothing to do with it," he answered. "I believe he is now hiding in some ditch or wood in the sincere belief that he is a hunted fugitive. But they won't trouble him anymore. He has done their work for them. He is innocent. It was essential that he should be innocent."

"Oh, I don't understand all this!" I cried impatiently.

"I don't understand half of this," said Father Brown. "There are all sorts of difficulties I will ask you about later. You knew the family. I only say that the sentence about cheerfulness did turn out to be a key sentence, after all. Now, I want you to concentrate your attention on another key sentence. 'We decided that Harriet should go to Bath without loss of time, in case she should be of any assistance there.' Note that this comes soon after your expression of surprise that someone should have communicated with Evelyn so early. Well, I suppose we none of us think the governor of the prison wired to her: 'Have connived at escape of your brother, Convict 99.' The message must have come in Southby's name, at any rate."

I ruminated, looking at the roll of the downs as it rose and repeated itself through every gap in the garden trees; then I said, "Kennington?"

My old friend looked at me for a moment with a look which, this time, I could not analyse.

"Captain Kennigton's part in the business is unique in my experience," he said, "and I think we had better return to him later. It is enough that, by your own account, Southby did not give him his confidence."

I looked again at the glimpses of the downs, and they looked grander but greyer, as my companion went on, like one who can only put things in their proper order.

"I mean the argument here is close, but clear. If she had any secret message from her brother about his escaping, why shouldn't she have a message about where he was escaping to? Why should she send off her sister to Bath, when she might just as well have been told that her brother wasn't going there? Surely a young gentleman might more safely say, in a private letter, that he was going to Bath than that he was escaping from prison? Somebody or something must have influenced Southby to leave his destination uncertain. And who could influence Southby except the companion of his flight?"

"Who was acting for the police, on your theory."

"No. On his confession." After a sort of snorting silence, Brown said, with an emphasis I have never seen in him, throwing himself on a garden-seat: "I tell you this whole business of the two cities of refuge—this whole business of Harriet Donnington going to Bath—was a suggestion that came through Southby, but from Mester, or Shrike, or whatever his name is, and is the key of the police plot." He had settled himself on a seat facing me, clasping his hands over the huge head of his umbrella in a more truculent manner than was typical of him. But an evening moon was brightening above the little plantation under which he sat, and when I saw his plain face again, I saw it was as mild as the moon.

"But why," I asked, "should they want such a plot?"

"To separate the sisters," he said. "That is the key."

I answered quickly: "The sisters could not really be separated."

"Yes, they could," said Father Brown, "quite simply, and that is why—" Here his simplicity failed, and he hesitated.

"That is why?" I insisted.

"That is why I can congratulate you," he said at last.

Silence sank again for a little, and I could not define the irritation with which I answered:

"Oh, I suppose you know all about it?"

"No, no really!" He said, leaning forward as if to deny an accusation of injustice. "I am puzzled about the whole business. Why didn't the warders find it sooner? Why did they find it at all? Was it slipped in the lining? Or is the handwriting so bad as that? I know about the thing being gentlemanly; but surely they took his clothes! How could the message come? It must be the lining."

His face was turned up as honestly as a flat and floating fish, and I could say with corresponding mildness:

"I really do not know what you are talking about, you and your linings. But if you mean how could Southby get his message safely to his sister without the risks of interception, I should say there were no people more likely to do it successfully. The boy and girl were always great friends from childhood, and had, to my knowledge, one of those secret languages that children often have, which may easily have been turned afterwards into some sort of cypher. And now I come to think of it—"

The heavy-knobbed umbrella slipped from the seat and slammed on the gravel, and the priest stood upright.

"What an idiot I am!" he said. "Why, anybody might have thought of a cypher! That was a score for you, my friend. I suppose you know all about it now?"

I am certain he did not realise that he was repeating in sincerity what I had said in irony.

"No," I answered, with real seriousness; "I do not know all about it, but I think it quite possible that you do. Tell me the story."

"It is not a good story," he said, in a rather stony way—"at least, the good thing about it is that it is over. But first let me say what I least like saying—that you knew well. I have thought a good deal about a certain kind of intellectual English lady, especially when she is at once aristocratic and provincial. I think she is judged much too easily. Or, perhaps, I should say, judged much too hardly; since she is supposed to be incapable of mortal passions and temptations. Let her decline champagne at dinner, let her be beautiful and know what is meant by dignity in dress, let her read a great many books and talk about high ideals, and you all assume that she alone of her kind cannot covet or lie; that her ideas are always simple, and her ideals always fulfilled. But, really and truly, my friend, by your account of it, the character was more mixed than that. Evelyn feigned an indisposition very cleverly. Assuming her to be blameless, I cannot see why she needed to feign anything. But, anyhow, it is scarcely one of the powers given to the saints. You 'began to suspect' that Evelyn already knew about the escape. Why didn't she tell you she already knew about it? You were astonished that Superintendent Matthews had called, and she had been silent about it; but you supposed it was difficult to send. Why should it be difficult to send? You seem to have been sent for whenever you were really wanted. No; I will try to speak of this woman as of one for whose soul I will pray, and whose true defence I shall never hear. But while there are living people whose honour is in cruel danger undeservedly, I simply refuse to start with the assumption that Evelyn Donnington could do no wrong."

The noble hills of Sussex looked as dreary as Yorkshire moors as he went on heavily, prodding the earth with his umbrella.

"The first facts in her defence, if she needed one, are that her father is a miser, that he has a violent temper combined with a rather Puritanic sort of family pride; and, above all, that she was afraid of him. Now, suppose she really wanted money, perhaps for a good purpose; or, again, perhaps not. She and her brother, you told me, had always had secret languages and plots; they are common among cowed and terrorised children. I firmly believe myself that she went a step further in some desperate strait, and that she was really and criminally responsible for the false document with which her brother seemed to be seeking financial help. We know there is often a family resemblance in handwritings almost amounting to facsimile. I cannot see, therefore, why there should not be a similar family resemblance in the flaws by which experts detect a forgery. Anyhow, the brother had a bad record, which goes for a great deal more than it ought with the police; and he was sent to gaol. I think you will agree that he has a very good record now."

"You mean," I said, curiously thrilled by the very restraint of his expression, "that Southby suffered all that time rather than speak?"

"Rejoice not against me, Satan, mine enemy," said Father Brown, "for when I fall I shall arise. This part of the story really is good."

After a silence he continued:

"When he was arrested, I am now almost certain, he had on him some letter or message from his sister. I hope and believe that it was some sort of penitent message. But whatever it was, it must have contained two things—some admission or allusion that made her own guilt clear, and some urgent request that her brother should come straight to her as soon as he was free to do so. Most important of all, it was not signed with a Christian name, but only 'Your unhappy sister.'"

"But, my good man," I cried, "you talk as if you had seen the letter!"

"I see it in its consequences," he answered. "The friendship with Mester, the quarrel with Kennington, the sister in Bath and the brother in the Priest's Room, came from that letter, and no other letter."

"The letter, however, was in cypher; and one very hard to follow, having been invented by children. Does that strike you as paradoxical? Don't you know that the hardest signs to read are arbitrary ones? And if two children agree that 'grunk' means bedtime and 'splosh' means Uncle William, it would take an expert much longer to learn this than to expose any system of substituted letters or numbers. Consequently, though the police found the paper, of course, it took them halfway through Southby's term to make head or tail of it. Then they knew that one of Southby's sisters were guilty, that he was innocent; and by this time they had the sense to see that he would never betray the truth. The rest, as I said, was simple and logical. The only other thing they could do was to take advantage of Southby being asked to go straight to his guilty correspondent. He was given every facility for escaping and communicating as quickly as possible, so long as the police could secure the separation of the sisters, by Mester getting the other one to Bath. Given that, the sister Southby went for must be the guilty one. And when, through those awful nights, the police gathered round you thick as wolves and still as ghosts—it was not for Southby they were waiting."

"But why did they wait for anyone?" I asked suddenly, after a silence. "If they were sure, why didn't they arrest?"

He nodded and sighed:

"Perhaps you're right. Perhaps it's best to take the Kennington case here. Well, of course, he knew all about it from the inside.

You yourself noticed that he had privileges in that prison. It will grieve you, as a law-abiding person, to learn that he used his power to intercept what had been decided. A good deal can be done by missing appointments. A good deal more can be done by not missing people—vulgarly known as hitting them. He used every chance, right or wrong, to delay the arrest. One of the thousand small, desperate delays was 'feigning illness.'"

"Why did Southby call him a traitor?" I said suspiciously.

"On exceedingly good grounds," said my friend. "Suppose you had broken prison in all innocence, and your friend sent his car for you and it took you back there? Suppose your friend offered to get you away in his yacht, and it took the wrong course, till overtaken by a motorboat? Suppose Southby was trying to get to Sussex, and Kennington always headed him off towards Cornwall or Ireland or normandy, what would you expect Southby to call him?"

"Well," I said, "what would you call him?"

"Oh," said Father Brown, "I call him a hero."

I peered at his rather featureless face through the moony twilight; and then he suddenly rose and paced the path with the impatience of a schoolboy.

"If I could put pen to paper, I would write the best adventure story ever written about this. Was there ever such a situation? Southby was kicked backwards and forwards, as unconscious as a football, between two very able and vigorous men, one of whom wanted to make the footprints point towards the guilty sister, while the other wanted to twist the feet away at every turn. And Southby thought the friend of his house was his enemy, and the destroyer of his house his friend. The two that knew must fight in silence, for Mester could not speak without warning Southby, and Kennington could not speak without denouncing Evelyn. It is clear from Southby's words, about false friends and the sea, that Kennington eventually kidnapped Southby in a yacht, but lord knows in how many tangled woods, or river islands, or lanes leading nowhere, the same fight was fought; the fugitive and detective trying to keep the trail, the traitor and true lover trying to confuse it. When Mester won, and his men gathered round this house, the captain could do no more than come here and offer his help, but Evelyn would not open the door to him."

"But why not?"

"Because she had the fine side of fear as well as the bad side," said Father Brown. "'Not a little afraid of life,' you said, with great penetration. She was afraid to go to prison; but, to her honour, she was afraid to get married, too. It is a type produced by all this refinement. My friend, I want to tell you and all your modern world a secret. You will never get to the good in people till you have been through the bad in them."

After a moment he added that we ought to be returning to the house, and walked yet more briskly in that direction.

"Of course," he remarked, as he did so, "the packet of banknotes you took through to Southby was only to help him away and spare him Evelyn's arrest. Mester's not a bad fellow for a 'tec. But she realised her danger, and was trying to get into the Priest's Room."

I was still brooding on the queer case of Kennington.

"Was not the glove found?" I asked.

"Was not the window broken?" he asked in return. "A man's glove twisted properly and loaded with nine pounds in gold, and probably a letter as well, will break most windows if it is slung by a man who has been a bowler. Of course, there was a note. And, of course, the note was imprudent. It left money for escape, and left the proofs of what she was escaping from."

"And then what happened to her?" I asked dully.

"Something of what happened to you," he said. "You also found the secret door difficult to open from outside. You also caught up that crooked curtain-rod or window-bar to beat on it.

You also saw the door opening slowly from within. But you did not see what she saw."

"And what did she see?" I said at last.

"She saw the man she had wronged most," said Father Brown.

"Do you mean Southby?"

"No," he said, "Southby has shown heroic virtue, and he is happy. The man she wronged most was a man who had never had, or tried to have, more than one virtue—a kind of acrid justice. And she had made him unjust all his life—made him pamper the wicked woman and ruin the righteous man. You told me in your notes that he often hid in the Priest's Room, to discover who was faithful or unfaithful. This time he came out holding a sword left in that room in the days when men hunted my religion. He found the letter, but, of course, he destroyed it after he had done—what he did. Yes, old friend, I can feel the horror on your face without seeing it. But, indeed, you modern people do not know how many kinds of men there are in the world. I am not talking of approval, but of sympathy—the sort of sympathy I give to Evelyn Donnington. Have you no sympathy with cold, barbaric justice, or with the awful appeasements of such an intellectual appetite? Have you no sympathy with the Brutus who killed his friend? Have you no sympathy with the monarch who killed his son? Have you no sympathy with Virginius, who killed—. But I think we must go in now."

We mounted the stairs in silence, but my surging soul expected some scene surpassing all the scenes of that tower. And in a sense I had it. The room was empty, save for Wellman, who stood behind an empty chair as impassively as if there had been a thousand guests.

"They have sent for Dr Browning, sir," he said in colourless tones.

"What do you mean?" I cried. "There was no question about the death?"

"No, sir," he said, with a slight cough; "Dr Browning required another doctor to be sent from Chichester, and they took Sir Borrow away."

THE MASK OF MIDAS

A man was standing outside a small shop, as rigidly as a wooden Highlander outside an old-fashioned tobacconist's. It was hard to believe that anyone would stand so steadily outside the shop unless he were the shopkeeper; but there was an almost grotesque incongruity between the shopkeeper and the shop. For the shop was one of those delightful dens of rubbish which children and the very wise explore with their eyes like a fairyland; but which many of a tidier and tamer taste are unable to distinguish from a dustbin. In short, it called itself in its prouder moments a curiosity shop; but was more generally called a junk shop; especially by the hard-headed and hustling commercial population of the industrial seaport in one of whose meaner streets it stood. Those who have a taste for such things will not need to have unrolled the tale of its treasures, of which the most precious were difficult to connect with any purpose whatever. Tiny models of fully-rigged ships sealed in bubbles of glass or glue or some queer Oriental gum; crystal balls in which snowstorms descended on very stolid human figures; enormous eggs that might have been laid by prehistoric birds; misshapen gourds that might have been swollen with poison rather than wine; queer weapons; queer musical instruments, and all the rest; and all sinking deeper and deeper in dust and disorder. The guardian standing outside such a shop might well be some decrepit Jew, with something of the dignity and long dress of the Arab; or some gypsy of a brazen and tropical beauty, hung with hoops of gold or brass. But the sentinel was something quite startlingly different. He was a lean, alert young man, in neat clothes of American cut, with the long, rather hard face so often seen in the Irish- American. He had a Stetson cocked over one eye and a stinking Pittsburgh cigar sticking out at a sharp angle from one corner of his mouth. If he had also had an automatic in his hip-pocket, those then gazing at him would not have been very much surprised. The name dimly printed above his shop was "Denis Hara".

Those thus gazing at him happened to be persons of some importance; and even perhaps of some importance to him. But nobody could have guessed it from his flinty features and his angular repose. The most prominent of these was Colonel Grimes, the Chief Constable of that county. A loose-built man with long legs and a long head; trusted by those who knew him well, but not very popular even with his own class, because he showed distinct signs of wanting to be a policeman rather than a country gentleman. In short, the Constable had committed the subtle sin of preferring the Constabulary to the County. This eccentricity had encouraged his natural taciturnity; and he was, even for a capable detective, unusually silent and secretive about his plans and discoveries. His two companions, who knew him well, were all the more surprised when he stopped in front of the man with the cigar and spoke in a loud clear voice, very seldom heard from him in public.

"It is only fair to tell you, Mr Hara, that my men have received information which justifies my obtaining a search-warrant to examine your premises. It may turn out, as I hope, that it will be unnecessary to incommode you further. But I must warn you that a watch is being kept on any movements of departure from this place."

"Are you all out to get one of my nice little toy ships done up in gum?" enquired Mr Hara with calm. "Well, Colonel, I wouldn't like to set any limits to your free and glorious British Constitution; or I would rather doubt whether you can burgle my little grey home like that."

"You will find I am right," replied the Colonel; "in fact I am going straight to two of the magistrates, whose signatures are needed for the search- warrant."

The two men standing behind the Chief Constable exhibited fine though different shades of a faint mystification. Inspector Beltane, a big dark heavy man, reliable in his work if not very rapid in it, looked a little dazed as his superior turned sharply away. The third man was stumpy and sturdy, with a round black clerical hat and a round black clerical figure, as well as a round face which had looked up to that moment a little sleepy; but a sharper gleam shone between his screwed eyelids; and he also was looking at the Chief Constable; but with something a little more than mere bewilderment; rather as if a new notion had suddenly come into his head.

"Look here," said Colonel Grimes, "you fellows will be wanting your lunch; it's a shame to trail you about like this after three o'clock. Fortunately, the first man I want to see is in the bank we are just passing; and there's quite a decent restaurant next door. I'll dash round to the other man who is only in the next street, when I've settled you down to some grub. They are the only two J.P.s in this part of the town; and it's lucky they live so near together. The banker will do what I want straight away; so we'll just go in and settle that first."

An array of doors decorated with glass and gilding led them through a labyrinth of passages in the Casterville and County Bank; and the Chief Constable went straight to the inner sanctum, with which he seemed to be fairly familiar. There he found Sir Archer Anderson, the famous financial writer and organiser, and the head of this and many other highly respectable banking enterprises; a grave and graceful old gentleman with grey curly hair and a grey pointed beard of a rather old-fashioned cut; but dressed otherwise in a sober but exact version of the current fashion. A glance at him would suggest that he was quite at home with the County as well as the Constable; but he seemed to share something of the Constable's preference for work rather than play. He pushed a formidable block of documents on one side; and said a word of welcome, pointing to a chair and suggesting a readiness to do banking business at any moment.

"I'm afraid this isn't banking business," said Grimes, "but anyhow, my business won't interrupt yours for more than a minute or two. You're a magistrate, aren't you; well, the law requires me to have the signatures of two magistrates, for a search-warrant on premises I have reason to believe are very suspicious."

"Indeed," said Sir Archer politely. "What sort of suspicion?"

"Well," said Grimes, "it's rather a queer case, and quite new, I should say, in these parts. Of course we have our own little criminal population, you may say; and, what is quite different and much more natural, the ordinary disposition of down-and-outs to hang together, even a little outside the law. But it looks to me as if that man Hara, who's certainly an American, is also an American gangster. A gangster on a large scale and with a whole machinery of crime practically unknown in this country. To begin with, I don't know whether you know the very latest news of this neighbourhood?"

"Very possibly not," replied the banker, with a rather frosty smile. "I am not very well instructed in the police news; and I only came here recently to look over the affairs of the branch. Till then I was in London."

"A convict escaped yesterday," said the Colonel gravely. "You know there is a large penal settlement on the moors, a mile or two from this town. There are a good many men doing time there; but there is one less than there was the day before yesterday."

"Surely that is not so very unheard of," said the other. "Prisoners do sometimes break prison, don't they?"

"True," assented the Chief Constable. "Perhaps that would not be so extraordinary in itself. What is extraordinary is that he has not only escaped but disappeared. Prisoners break prison; but they almost always go back to prison; or at least we get some notion of how they managed to get away. This man seems to have simply and suddenly vanished, like a ghost or a fairy, a few hundred yards from the prison gates. Now as I have sceptical doubts myself about whether he really is a ghost or a fairy, I must fall back on the only possible natural explanation. And that is that he was spirited away instantly in a car, almost certainly part of a whole organization of cars, to say nothing of spies and conspirators working out a completed plan. Now I take it as certain that his own friends and neighbours, however much they might sympathise, could not possibly organize anything like that. He is quite a poor man, accused of being a poacher; all his friends are poor and probably most of them poachers; and there is no doubt that he killed a game keeper. It's only fair to say that some thought it ought to have been called manslaughter and not murder; indeed they had to commute the sentence to a long imprisonment; and since then, perhaps on a fairer reconsideration, they have reduced it to a comparatively short sentence. But somebody has shortened it very much more than that. And in a way which means money and petrol and practical experience in such raids; he certainly could not have done it for himself and none of his companions in the common way could have done it for him. Now I won't bother you with the details of our discoveries; but I'm quite certain that the headquarters of the organization is in that little junk-shop round the corner; and our best chance is to get a warrant to search it at once. You will understand, Sir

Archer, that this does not commit you to anything beyond the preliminary search; if the man in the shop is innocent, we are all quite free to testify to it; but I'm certain a preliminary search ought to be made, and for that I must have the signatures of two magistrates. That is why I am wasting your time with the police news; when it is so valuable in the financial news. If you feel you can sign such a document, I have it here ready for you; and there will be no excuse for my interrupting your own financial duties any further."

He laid a paper in front of Sir Archer Anderson; and, after reading it rapidly, but with a frown of habitual responsibility, the banker picked up his pen and signed it.

The Chief Constable rose with rapid but warm expressions of obligation, and passed towards the door, merely remarking at random, as a man might talk about the weather, "I don't suppose a business of your standing is affected by slumps or modern complications. But I'm told these are anxious days, sometimes, even for the most solid of the smaller corporations."

Sir Archer Anderson rose at once swiftly and stiffly, with a certain air of indignation at being even momentarily associated with small corporations.

"If you know anything of the Casterville and County Bank," he said, not without a faint touch of fire, "you will know it is not likely to be affected by anything or anybody."

Colonel Grimes shepherded his friends out of the Bank and, with a certain benevolent despotism, deposited them in the restaurant next door; while he himself darted on to complete his task by pouncing on the other local magistrate; an old lawyer who was also an old friend, one Wicks by name, who had sometimes assisted him in details of legal theory. Inspector Beltane and Father Brown were left facing each other somewhat solemnly in the restaurant, to await his return.

"Am I wrong," asked Father Brown with a friendly smile, "if I suspect that you are a little puzzled by something?"

"I wouldn't say puzzled," said the Inspector. "All that business with the banker was simple enough; but when you know a man very well, there is always a funny feeling when he doesn't act quite like himself. Now the Colonel is the most silent and secret worker I've ever known in the police. Often he never tells the colleagues nearest to him what's in his mind at the moment. Why did he stand talking at the top of his voice in a public street to a public enemy: to tell him he was going to raid his shop? Other people, let alone ourselves, were beginning to gather and listen. Why the devil should he tell this godforsaken gunman that he was going to raid his shop? Why didn't he simply raid it?"

"The answer is," said Father Brown, "that he wasn't going to raid his shop."

"Then why did he shout to the whole town that he was going to?"

"Well, I think," said Father Brown, "so that the whole town might talk about his visit to the gangster and not notice his visit to the banker. The only words he really wanted to say were those last few words he said to the banker; watching for the reaction. But if there are any rumours about the bank, the town would have been all up in the air about his going straight to the bank. He had to have a good ordinary reason for going there; and he could hardly have had a better one than asking two ordinary magistrates to sign an ordinary document. Quite a flight of imagination."

Inspector Beltane was gaping at him across the table.

"What on earth do you mean?" he demanded at last.

"I mean," replied the priest, "that perhaps Colonel Grimes was not so far out in talking of the poacher as a fairy. Or shall we say a ghost?"

"You can't possibly mean," said the Inspector incredulously, "that Grimes invented the murdered gamekeeper and the escaped convict out of his own head? Why, he told me about them himself beforehand, as a bit of ordinary police- business."

"I wouldn't go quite so far as that," said Father Brown indifferently. "There may be some such local story; but it's got nothing to do with the story Grimes is after just now. I wish it had."

"Why do you say that?" asked the other.

Father Brown looked him full in the face with grey eyes of unmistakable gravity and candour.

"Because I am out of my depth," he said. "Oh, I know well enough when I'm out of my depth; and I knew I should be, when I found we were hunting a fraudulent financier instead of an ordinary human murderer. You see, I don't quite know how I came to take a hand originally in this sort of detective business; but almost all my experience was with ordinary human murderers. Now murder's almost always human and personal; but modern theft has been allowed to become quite impersonal. It isn't only secret; it's anonymous; almost avowedly anonymous. Even if you die, you may catch a glimpse of the face of the man who stabbed you. But however long you live, you may never get even a glimpse of the name of the man who robbed you. My first case was just a small private affair about a man's head being cut off and another head put on instead; I wish I were back among quiet homely little idylls like that. I wasn't out of my depth with them."

"A very idyllic incident indeed," said the Inspector.

"A very individual incident, anyhow," replied the priest. "Not like all this irresponsible officialism in finance. They can't cut off heads as they cut off hot water, by the decision of a Board or a Committee; but they can cut off dues or dividends in that way. Or again, although two heads could be put on one man, we all know that one man hasn't really got two heads. But one firm can have two heads; or two faces, or half-a hundred faces. No, I wish you could lead me back to my murderous poacher and my murdered gamekeeper. I should understand all about them; but for the unfortunate fact that they possibly never existed."

"Oh this is all nonsense," cried the Inspector, trying to throw off an atmosphere. "I tell you Grimes did talk about it before. I rather fancy the poacher would have been released soon anyhow, though he did kill the other man pretty savagely, bashing him again and again with the butt of his gun. But he'd found the gamekeeper pretty indefensibly occupied on his own premises. In fact, the gamekeeper was poaching this time. He hadn't a good character in the neighbourhood; and there was certainly what's called provocation. Sort of Unwritten Law business."

"That's just what I mean," said Father Brown. "Modern murder still, very often, has some remote and perverted connection with an unwritten law. But modern robbery takes the form of littering the world with paper and parchment, covered merely with written lawlessness."

"Well, I can't make head or tail of all this," said the Inspector. "There is the poacher who is a prisoner, or an escaped prisoner; there is, or was the gamekeeper; and there is, to all mortal appearance, the gangster. What you mean by starting all this wild stuff about the bank next door is more than I can imagine."

"That's what troubles me," said Father Brown in a sobered and humbled tone. "The Bank next door is beyond my imagination."

At this moment, the restaurant door swung open and the Colonel returned with a swing of triumph; trailing behind him a little lively figure with white hair and a face wrinkled with smiles. It was the other magistrate, whose signature was so essential to the required document.

"Mr Wicks," said the Colonel, with an introductory gesture, "is the best modern expert in all matters of financial fraud. It is sheer luck that he happens to be a J.P. in this district."

Inspector Beltane gave a gulp and then gasped. "You don't mean to say Father Brown was right."

"I have known it happen," said Colonel Grimes, with moderation.

"If Father Brown said that Sir Archer Anderson is a colossal swindler, he was most certainly right," said Mr Wicks. "I needn't give you all the steps of the proof here; in fact it will be wiser to give only the earlier stages of it even to the police and the swindler. We must watch him carefully; and see that he takes no advantage of any mistake of ours. But I think we'd better go round and have a rather more candid interview with him than you seem to have had; an interview in which the poacher and the junk-shop will not perhaps be so exclusively prominent. I think I can let him know enough of what we know to wake him up, without running any risk of libel or damages. And there is always the chance he will let something out, in the very attempt to keep it in. Come, we have heard very disquieting rumours about the business, and want this or that explained on the spot. That is our official position at present." And he sprang up, as if with the mere alertness or restlessness of youth.

The second interview with Sir Archer Anderson was certainly very different in its tone, and especially in its termination. They had gone there without any final determination to challenge the great banker; but they soon found that it was he who was already determined to challenge them. His white moustaches were curled like silver sabres; his white pointed beard was thrust forward like a spike of steel. Before any of them had said more than a few sentences, he stood up and struck the table.

"This is the first time that the Casterville and County Bank has been referred to in this fashion; and I promise you it shall be the last. If my own reputation did not already stand too high for such grotesque calumnies, the credit of the institution itself would alone have made them ludicrous. Leave this place, gentlemen, and go away and amuse yourselves with exposing the High Court of Chancery or inventing naughty stories about the Archbishop of Canterbury."

"That is all very well," said Wicks, with his head at an angle of pertinacity and pugnacity like a bulldog, "but I have a few facts here, Sir Archer, which you will be bound sooner or later to explain."

"To say the least of it," said the Colonel in a milder tone, "there are a good many things that we want to know rather more about."

The voice of Father Brown came in like something curiously cool and distant, as if it came from another room, or from the street outside, or at least from a long way off.

"Don't you think, Colonel, that we know now all that we want to know?"

"No," said the Colonel shortly, "I am a policeman. I may think a great deal and think I am right. But I don't know it."

"Oh," said Father Brown, opening his eyes wide for a moment. "I don't mean what you think you know."

"Well, I suppose it's the same as what you think you know," said Grimes rather gruffly.

"I'm awfully sorry," said Father Brown penitently, "but what I know is quite different."

The air of doubt and difference, in which the small group moved off, leaving the haughty financier apparently master of the field after all, led them to drift once more to the restaurant, for an early tea, a smoke and some attempt at an explanation all round.

"I always knew you were an exasperating person," said the policeman to the priest, "but I have generally had some sort of wild guess about what you meant. My impression at this moment is that you have gone mad."

"It's odd you should say that," said Father Brown; "because I've tried to discover my own deficiencies in a good many directions, and the only thing I think I really know about myself is that I am not mad. I pay the penalty, of course, in being dull. But I have never to my knowledge lost touch with reality; and it seems queer to me that men so brilliant as you are can lose it so quickly."

"What do you mean–reality?" demanded Grimes after a bristling silence.

"I mean common sense," said Father Brown, with one of the explosions so rare in him that it sounded like a gun. "I've said already that I'm out of my depth, about all this financial complexity and corruption. But, hang it all, there is a way of testing things by human beings. I don't know anything about finance; but I have known financiers. In a general way, I've known fraudulent financiers. But you must know much more about them than I do. And yet you can swallow an impossibility like that."

"An impossibility like what?" enquired the staring Colonel.

Father Brown had suddenly leaned across the table, with piercing eyes fixed on Wicks, with an intensity he rarely showed.

"Mr Wicks, you ought to know better. I'm only a poor parson, and of course I know no better. After all, our friends the police do not often meet bankers; except when a casual cashier cuts his throat. But you must have been perpetually interviewing bankers; and especially bankrupt bankers. Haven't you been in this precise position twenty times before? Haven't you again and again had the pluck to throw the first suspicions on very solid persons, as you did this afternoon? Haven't you talked to twenty or thirty financiers who were crashing, just about a month or two before they crashed?"

"Well, yes," said Mr Wicks slowly and carefully, "I suppose I have."

"Well," asked Father Brown, "did any single one of the others ever talk like that?"

The little figure of the lawyer gave the faintest imperceptible start; so that one could say no more than that he was sitting up a shade straighter than before.

"Did you ever in your born days," asked the priest with all his new thrusting emphasis, "know a handler of hanky-panky finance who got on the high horse at the first flash of suspicion; and told the police not to dare to meddle with the secrets of his sacred bank? Why, it was like asking the Chief Constable to raid his bank and arrest him on the spot. Well, you know about these things and I don't. But I'd risk a long bet that every single dubious financier you have ever known has done exactly the opposite. Your first queries would have been received not with anger but amusement; if it ever went so far, it would have ended in a bland and complete answer to every one of the nine hundred and ninety-nine questions you had to ask. Explanations! They swim in explanations! Do you suppose a slippery financier has never been asked questions before?"

"But hang it all, you generalise too much," said Grimes. "You seem to be quite captivated with your vision of the perfect swindler. But after all even swindlers are not perfect. It doesn't prove much that one bankrupt banker broke down and lost his nerve."

"Father Brown is right," said Wicks, interceding suddenly after a period of digestive silence. "It's quite true that all that swagger and flamboyant defiance couldn't be the very first line of defence for a swindle. But what else could it be? Respectable bankers don't throw out the banner and blow the trumpet and draw the sword, at a moment's notice, any more than disreputable bankers."

"Besides," said Grimes, "why should he get on the high horse at all? Why should he order us all out of the bank, if he has nothing to hide?"

"Well," said Father Brown very slowly, "I never said he had nothing to hide."

The meeting broke up in a silent, dazed disorder, in which the pertinacious Beltane hooked the priest by the arm for an instant and held him.

"Do you or do you not mean," he asked harshly, "that the banker is not a suspect?"

"No," said Father Brown, "I mean that the suspect is not a banker."

As they filed out of the restaurant, with movements much more vague and groping than were normal to any of them, they were brought up short by a shock and noise in the street outside. It first gave the impression of people breaking windows all along the street; but an instant of nervous recovery enabled them to localise it. It was the gilt glass-doors and windows of the pompous building they had entered that morning; the sacred enclosure of the Casterville and County Bank, that was shaken from within by a din like a dynamite explosion, but proving to be in fact only the direct dynamic destructiveness of man. The Chief Constable and the Inspector darted through the shattered glass-doorways to the dark interior, and returned with faces fixed in astonishment; even more assured and stolid for being astonished.

"There's no doubt about it now," said the Inspector, "he's clubbed the man we left to watch to the ground with a poker; and hurled a cash-box so as to catch in the waistcoat the first man who came in to find out the trouble. He must be a wild beast."

Amid all the grotesque bewilderment, Mr Wicks the lawyer turned with a gesture of apology and compliment and said to Father Brown, "Well, Sir, you have completely convinced me. He is certainly an entirely new rendering of the absconding banker."

"Well, you must send our men in to hold him at once," said the Constable to the Inspector; "or he'll break up the whole town."

"Yes," said Father Brown, "he's a pretty violent fellow; it's his great temptation. Think how he used his gun blindly as a club on the game-keeper, bringing it down again and again; but never having even the sense to fire. Of course, that is the sort of man who mismanages most things, even murders. But he does generally manage to break prison."

His companions gazed on him with faces that seemed to grow rounder and rounder with wonder; but they got no enlightenment out of his own round and commonplace countenance, before he turned away and went slowly down the street.

"And so," said Father Brown, beaming round at the company over a very mild lager in the restaurant, and looking rather like Mr Pickwick in a village club; "and so we come back again to our dear old rustic tale of the poacher and the gamekeeper after all. It does so inexpressibly raise my spirits dealing with a cosy fireside crime instead of all this blank bewildering fog of finance; a fog really full of ghosts and shadows. Well, of course you all know the old, old story. At your mothers' knees you have heard it; but it is so important, my friends, to keep those old stories clear in our minds as they were told to us. This little rural tale has been told often enough. A man is imprisoned for a crime of passion, shows a similar violence in captivity, knocks down a warder and escapes in a mist on the moor. He has a stroke of luck; for he meets a gentleman who is well-dressed and presentable, and he forces him to change clothes."

"Yes, I've heard that story often," said Grimes frowning. "You say it is important to remember the story?"

"It is important to remember the story," said Father Brown, "because it is a very clear and correct account of what did not happen."

"And what did happen?" demanded the Inspector.

"Only the flat contrary," said Father Brown. "A small but neat emendation. It was not the convict who set out looking for a well-dressed gentleman, that he might disguise himself in his clothes. It was the gentleman who set out on the moor looking for a convict; that he might enjoy the ecstasy of wearing a convict's clothes. He knew there was a convict loose on the moor; and he ardently wanted his clothes. He probably knew also that there was a well- organised scheme for picking up the convict and rushing him rapidly off the moor. It is not quite certain what part Denis Hara and his gang played in this business; or whether they were cognisant only of the first plot or of the second. But I think it probable they were working for the poacher's friends, and merely in the interest of the poacher, who had very wide public sympathy among the poorer population. I prefer to think that our friend the well-dressed gentleman effected his own little transformation scene by his own native talents. He was a very well-dressed gentleman, being clad in very fashionable gents' suitings, as the tailors say; also with beautiful white hair and moustaches etc. which he owed rather to the barber than the tailor. He had found this very complete costume useful at many times of his life; and you must remember he had only appeared for a very short time as yet, in this particular town and bank. On hailing at last the figure of the convict whose clothes he coveted, he verified his information that he was a man of much the same general figure as himself; and the rest consisted merely of covering the convict with the hat, the wig, the whiskers, the splendid raiment, until the warder he knocked on the head would hardly have known him. Then our brilliant financier put on the convict's clothes; and felt, for the first time for months and perhaps years, that he had escaped and was free.

"For he had no band of poor sympathisers who would help or hide him if they knew the truth. He had no movement in his favour, among the more decent lawyers and governors, suggesting that he had suffered enough or that his liberation might soon be allowable. He had no friends even in the underworld; for he had always been an ornament of the upper world; the world of our conquerors and our masters, whom we allow so easily to have the upper hand. He was one of the modern magicians; he had a genius for finance; and his thefts were thefts from thousands of the poor. When he did cross a line (a pretty faint line, in modern law), when the world did find him out, then the whole world would be against him. I fancy he did subconsciously look towards the prison as a home. We don't know exactly what his plans were; even if the prison authorities captured him and took the trouble to prove by prints and so on that he was not the escaped convict, it's not easy to see what else they could prove against him, at this stage. But I think it more likely that he knew Hara's organisation would help him, and hurry him out of the country without a moment's delay. He may have had dealings with Hara, neither perhaps telling the whole truth; such compromises are common in America between the big business man and the racketeer; because they are both really in the same business.

"Nor was there much trouble in persuading the convict, I imagine. It would seem to him at sight a scheme very hopeful for himself; perhaps he thought it was part of Hara's scheme. Anyhow, the convict got rid of the clothes of conviction, and stepped in first class clothes into a first class position where he might be socially acceptable and at least consider his next move in peace. But, heavens, what an irony! What a trap; what a trick of inverted doom! A man breaking jail nearly at the end of his sentence, for an obscure half-forgiven crime, delighting to dress himself up like a dandy in the costume of the world's greatest criminal, to be hunted tomorrow by searchlights round the whole earth. Sir Archer Anderson has entrapped a good many people in his time; but he never entrapped a man in such a tragedy as the man he benevolently clothed with his best clothes on the moor."

"Well," said Grimes good-humouredly, "now you have given us the tip, we can probably prove it all right; because the convict anyhow will have had his finger-prints taken."

Father Brown bowed his head with a vague gesture as of awe and reverence. "Of course," he said, "Sir Archer Anderson has never had his prints taken. My dear Sir! A man in that position."

"The truth is," said Wicks, "that nobody seems to know very much about him; prints or anything else. When I started studying his ways, I had to start with a blank map that only afterwards turned into a labyrinth. I do happen to know something about such labyrinths; but this was more labyrinthine than the others."

"It's all a labyrinth to me," said the priest with a sigh. "I said I was out of my depth in all this financial business. The one and only thing I was quite sure of was the sort of man who sat opposite me. And I was certain he was much too jumpy and nervy to be a swindler."

Love Golden Age crime fiction? Have you checked out the full yellowback range?

From Locked door mysteries to blind detectives through first women detectives, the yellowback reissues is one of the largest selections of classic crime fictions, in the original format with a modern clean easy read page layout. A sampling below.

For more details and a full list of titles:
visit https://www.hachetteindia.com/home/yellowbacks

H. Rider Haggard

MR. MEESON'S WILL

Melville Davisson Post

MASTER OF MYSTERIES

THE COMPLETE UNCLE ABNER COLLECTION

Jack London

THE ASSASSINATION BUREAU LTD.

Baroness Orczy

THE SKIN O' MY TOOTH

Earl Derr Biggers

SEVEN KEYS TO BALDPATE

Horace Walpole

THE CASTLE OF OTRANTO

Sexton Blake

THE SEXTON BLAKE COLLECTION

VOLUME 1

Francis Beeding

THE HOUSE OF DR. EDWARDES

A. E. W. Mason

AT THE VILLA ROSE

Fergus Hume

THE MILLIONAIRE MYSTERY

Donald Henderson

A VOICE LIKE VELVET

Richard Hallas

YOU PLAY THE BLACK AND THE RED COMES UP